DIRE BOUND

*For everyone who's turned their pain
into power*

Note

This book contains mature and explicit subject matter that might be difficult for some readers, including explicit on-page violence and adult situations. For a full list of content flags and tropes, please visit the author's website: www.sablesorensen.com

Guides and Additional Material

For a breakdown of the four Bonded packs of Nocturna, a glossary of terms used, and a character list with pronunciations, please see the additional materials at the back of the book. Note that there may be light spoilers!

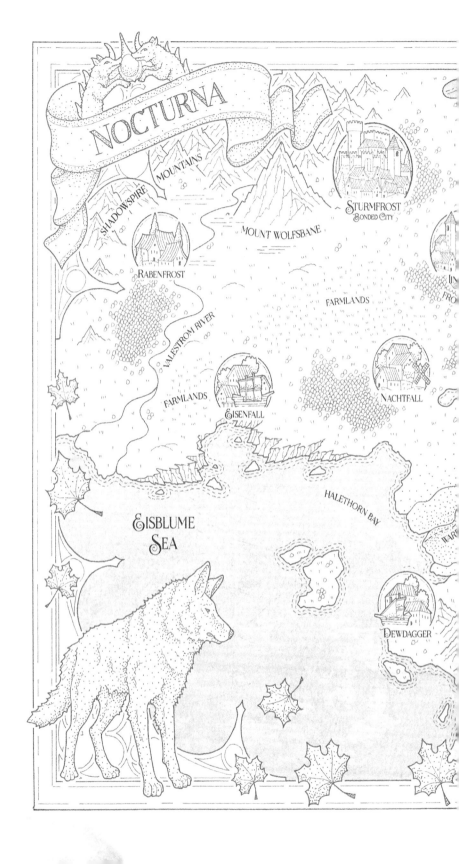

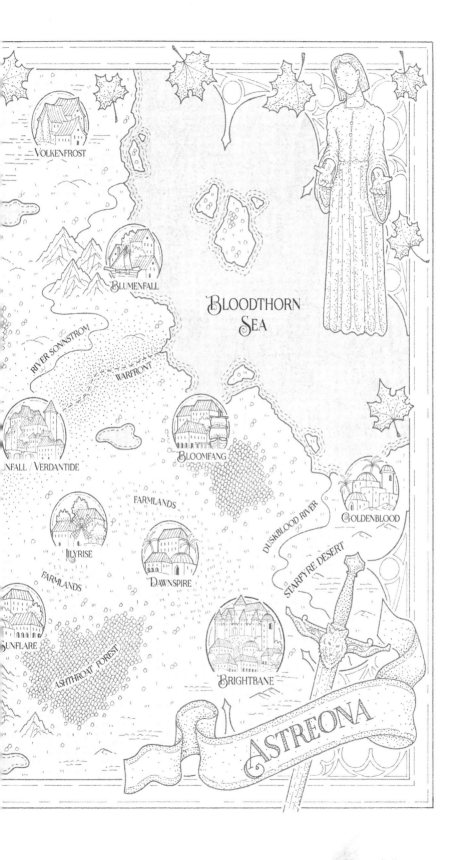

VOLKENFROST

BLUMENFALL

BLOODTHORN
SEA

RIVER SONNSTROM

WARFRONT

NFALL / VERDANTIDE

BLOOMFANG

FARMLANDS

DUSKBLOOD RIVER

GOLDENBLOOD

LILYRISE

FARMLANDS

DAWNSPIRE

STARFYRE DESERT

SUNFLARE

ASHTHROAT FOREST

BRIGHTBANE

ASTREONA

A WOLVES OF RUIN NOVEL

DIRE BOUND

SABLE SORENSEN

CHAPTER ONE

B lood drips into my right eye. Once. Twice. It's blinding and searing at the same time.

I wince, letting out a pained whimper. It fucking burns, blood in the eye.

The pain is real.

The whimper is not.

If there's one thing I've learned in my twenty-three years alive, it's this: women in pain give men confidence. It stirs up something instinctive, deep inside of them, that makes them believe they have the upper hand, even if every logical piece of evidence screams at them they do not.

Confidence makes men sloppy.

And sloppy men are easy targets.

We're in some old emberwine warehouse in the Southern Quarter tonight, the air reeking of rotting fruit. Torches burn around the edges of the ring, illuminating our fight and casting everything else in twisting, dancing shadows. The crowd is hushed in anticipation, but even so, the room seems full.

Good. A bigger crowd means a bigger pot of winnings.

There's a loud *thump, thump, thump* as my opponent slowly

approaches me, his steps heavy. He's a big, meaty man with a good six inches on me, which he undoubtedly thinks makes him powerful. He's not the kind of person who understands how lethal grace can be.

"I'll make you regret ever being born, little girl. You'll need a closed casket."

Goddess, this guy is a bore. But our audience is eating it up, if the frenzied roar is any indication.

More blood drips into my eye. He got me good with a right hook to the forehead, I'll give him that.

I turn my head to the side, feigning weakness, my cheek pressed into the packed dirt floor of the fighting ring. There's a flash of movement in the leering crowd as someone pushes their way toward the edge of the ring.

Lee. He must've just gotten off work.

He folds his muscular arms against his broad chest, his spotless messenger's tunic making him stick out in this seedy place. Then he raises an eyebrow at me in amusement.

I can almost hear his deep voice saying: *Stop toying with him, Meryn, and just end this so we can get on with our night.*

He's right, of course. I'd much rather be in his lap right now than face-down in this stinking pit.

Right, then. Time to finish the show.

My opponent grows closer and I moan again, waiting for him to reach the exact right spot. He doesn't even see the trap I've set for him, even though it's so obvious. Even though I play this move almost every fight.

He doesn't *want* to see it, because I've made him confident. Certain that he will be the man to bring down Meryn Cooper, the infamous Alleycat of the Eastern Quarter.

Idiot.

Finally, he reaches my side, preparing to grab me, or sit on me, or choke me out—something predictable. Another roar kicks up in the crowd, the room full of frothing, drunken gamblers all praying that he'll get me good, that their bet against the woman will pay off.

He leans down toward me, his foul breath hitting my face, and that's when I do it.

I loop my leg around his and drive my heel into the fleshy back of his knee with all the force I can muster. Then I roll to the side, out of his way, and spring up onto my feet.

"Fuck!" He crashes to the ground, hitting it hard, making it shudder beneath me. The air rushes from his lungs in an audible whoosh.

The man pushes up onto his palms, but before he can get any farther, I strike. I kick him in the nose, relishing the sweet crack it makes as it breaks. Ruby red blood gushes down his face, dripping onto the floor. It knocks him backwards onto his ass.

Before he can try to recover again, I jump on him, kneeing him in the groin to keep him down. Then I pin him, peppering his face with more strikes. I'm not going for a kill; I fight dirty, but not like that. But I'll be sure he stays down.

My knuckles burst open under their scars and calluses and blood drips between my curled fingers. For a moment, I let myself relish the adrenaline rush of the pain and the clear-headed focus it gives me.

Then I press a forearm on the man's windpipe until he chokes, "Yield!"

I slap him open-handed. Just for the fun of it, just for the drama of his head snapping to the side. "Louder. With meaning. Let them hear you all the way in the castle."

"I YIELD!"

The crowd erupts into angry mutters as I let go of the man, standing to wipe my blood from my forehead. The host of tonight's shows, a portly man with a thick mustache, steps into the ring, hoists my wrist into the air and declares: "Alleycat wins! Next fight starts in twenty."

Coins change hands, with the bounty going to the few who were wise enough to put money on me.

It always surprises me a little, the sheer number of people who bet for the other man. Even with the history to show them they shouldn't.

3

A towel hits me in the face and I pull it off to see my trainer and neighbor Igor assessing me, his brown, weathered face unreadable. I duck under the sides of the ring and step over to him, my palm held out.

"Always straight to the coin with you, huh?" Igor grumbles.

"Me?" I bat my eyelashes, my voice high and sweet. "A refined lady like me would never think of something so crude as money. All I care about is tea and dresses and gossip."

"Careful, you're going to make that forehead wound bleed again." Igor presses my winnings into my hand. "Good one, kiddo. Went on a little long for my taste, though. You should join a theater guild, with those pained cries of yours."

I shrug, counting the coins and doing quick math. Eight silvers today, which will cover Mother's medicine from the apothecary for the next two weeks. "You know the crowd needs to have hope, Igor. It makes it more fun for all of us if they think they actually have a chance."

"Whatever gets you the win, kid." He hands me a water flask and I gulp it down. "Davey is setting up a fight in two weeks for Colbridge. Remember that slippery motherfucker from last year? Fancy another go?"

I crack my neck, scanning the packed room for Lee. Even at my unusual height, it's hard to see over the heads milling about the crowded floor.

"Sure, as long as you make certain the odds are against me. The apothecary has hiked up their prices. Apparently, some ingredients they need grow close to the front and have gotten hard to acquire. I'd like to see double this amount next time."

Igor's perpetual frown deepens. He's an unhappy-looking person; always has been, for as long as I've known him, which has been my entire life.

He's probably going to offer me help with mother's medicine costs, something I've declined for years. I'm not above accepting help when I need it, but most everyone in the royal city of Sturm-frost, where we live—everyone in this entire goddess-forsaken country, actually—is struggling.

Our money, and our lives, goes to fighting the endless war with the Siphons.

I'm not about to take food off Igor's plate. We'll get by; we always do.

Just then, a warm arm slings around my shoulders and I'm hit by the clean smell of pine soap, a familiar scent that instantly puts me at ease. I lean against Lee's hard body and look up into his face —the sharp lines of his jaw covered in a light scruff, his dazzling sea-blue eyes.

Lee shoots me a wicked grin that makes my thighs tighten and raises up a small clinking bag.

"Nice fight, kitten. Buy your sister something nice from me for her nameday." He slides the bag into my pocket as I lean up, wrapping my arms around his neck and pulling his face down toward mine, desperate for his touch.

Before I can kiss him, a throat clears and I glance up, my lustful brain gone hazy. Igor shifts awkwardly on his feet. Lee and I have been together for over a year now, but Igor still hasn't gotten used to this.

"I'm going to go see Davey about the next fight," Igor says, glancing away from us. "Leave you two at it. Find me before you head out, Meryn."

He turns and walks away quickly, and I can't help the laughter that spills out of me. "Poor Igor. I think we've scandalized him."

Lee grins lazily down at me, his hands gripping my hips and tightening in a way that holds dark promise. He puts his mouth to my ear. "Glad he can't read my thoughts," he whispers, the heat of it sending my pulse into overdrive. "He'd never be able to look at me again."

I move closer, but suddenly, a commotion kicks up. A disheveled man is pushing his way through the crowd.

His yellowed, unfocused eyes glare toward me.

"You cunt!" The man's words slur as he staggers forward. "You fixed the bets, you stupid little bitch. I know you did!"

I laugh. "You kiss your mother with that mouth?"

Lee watches the scene coolly, amusement briefly turning up the edges of his mouth.

The man pulls a knife from his pocket, its dull blade glinting in the dim light. There's always one guy who can't handle me winning, who lets it push him over the edge.

"You lost me my last silvers! You're gonna pay for that."

He brandishes his knife toward me, but before he takes another step, I'm in motion. A sharp kick to his wrist and the knife slips from his grip. I catch it before he can blink, pressing the edge just under his Adam's apple in one swift motion.

"What was the plan here, then? You were going to, what... confront the person who just won a brutal, well-attended fight with this pathetic little dinner knife? Shake me down with it, because I would obviously fear your extremely dangerous weapon that you're so skilled at wielding?"

I press the knife harder into his throat and a thin red line of blood seeps out from under the blade. The man winces. The stench of urine hits me, and I realize he's soiled himself. Pathetic.

"That's what you get for betting against a woman. Get the fuck out of here. If I see your face at one of my fights again, I'll finish the job."

The man shoots me one last wild-eyed look and then turns and scurries back through the crowd. No one bothers giving him a second look. They're too busy getting ready for the next fight in here.

"Fucking idiot," Lee mutters under his breath. Then he grabs my hand in his large one and turns into the crowd, pulling me behind him toward a cluster of tables and chairs at the far end of the warehouse. We settle in and he quickly opens the rucksack he's brought with him, pulling out an antiseptic cream and some bandages.

He pulls me toward him on my chair and then wraps his long fingers firmly around my chin while he dabs the cream onto my forehead, the heat from his touch warring with the sting of the ointment.

"Hold still, kitten," he says, his stern voice brooking no argument. "This one's kind of nasty."

This has been our after-fight ritual, ever since he started coming to these a year ago. I get hurt; he fixes me. I like it more than I'd ever admit, having someone to take care of me.

We met in the market in the Northern Quarter. I'd been coming to pick Saela up from school when a spooked horse broke loose from its merchant. It was heading right for my little sister, and I was too far away to do anything about it. At that moment, I'd been sure that I was going to watch her die in front of my eyes, helpless.

And then Lee jumped in front of it, his hands held up in a calming motion, and the horse just... stopped. He calmed the animal down and saved my sister's life in the process.

I went to thank him, and the moment our eyes met, I knew I would be his. It takes a special man to tame a wild thing.

"Did that worry you? The guy who just attacked me?" I ask. He's been unusually quiet.

Lee's gaze connects with mine, deep and unreadable. "I knew the Alleycat would hold her own. But I wish you'd end your fights faster. Injuries like this aren't necessary. Someday, Meryn... someday, you might come up against someone who has outmaneuvered you. You might not even see it coming."

He strokes a finger down my cheek, and I crawl into his lap, pulling him closer and closer. "Thank you," I whisper against his lips. "For fixing me. For caring if I get hurt."

Lee winds one of his hands into my dark hair, holding me in place as he crashes his lips down on mine. His other hand wraps around my back and he pulls me deeper into his lap, where I sense him hardening underneath me. I groan into his mouth at the feeling, and he pulls back, laying me bare with his look.

"Come back to my place tonight," he says—a demand, not a question.

Lee has a small apartment to himself in the Northern Quarter, though as a castle messenger, he only lives there part time, often grabbing a few hours of sleep in the castle barracks between his duties. I'm there as frequently as I can be, but my mother's condition and Saela's care mean I don't see him nearly as often as either of us would like.

I'm about to assent when a grave voice calls, "Meryn."

I turn around, spotting Igor cutting quickly through the crowd toward us. He approaches, his expression tight, "Word's spreading. Another child's gone missing from Eastern."

My stomach bottoms out as I quickly extract myself from Lee and stand to face Igor. "Description?"

"A girl. Ten or so. They said… they said she has dark hair and hazel eyes."

No.

I shoot Lee a quick look, already thinking about the fastest route home.

"Go," Lee says quickly, standing as well. "You have to." I nod in agreement.

"Meryn," Igor says, "it could be a hundred girls."

But I don't acknowledge him. I'm already shoving my way through the rowdy crowd, my heart pounding a frantic staccato beat. Wood bites into my palms as I shove open the exit to the warehouse, and then the always-frigid night air hits me like a punch. I left so quickly that I forgot to gather my things or put on my threadbare coat, but Igor will grab it, I'm sure.

Who needs a coat, anyway, when panic is setting your blood on fire?

The streets of Southern, the farthest neighborhood from the castle, are eerily dark and as foggy as always. The residents around here don't bother spending their few coins to keep the street torches lit. They can't drive out the darkness of this neighborhood, anyway; this quarter has darkness set deep into its bones.

Southern is the part of the royal city where you go when you want to do something illegal, illicit, or otherwise morally bankrupt. A couple of torches wouldn't stop it.

I do a rapid calculation. A normal route from Southern to Eastern takes at least forty-five minutes if you follow the main path back through the Central Quarter. But I'm fast, a benefit of my long, muscular legs. And I know my way around neighborhoods that no well-bred person should ever know.

I can make it in twenty, maybe fifteen, if I take alleys.

So I take a deep, fortifying breath, and then sprint, heading past the many decrepit warehouses. My legs carry me through the dirty market square in Southern, and then I push into the tenement alleys, the neighborhood that borders both the Central Quarter and Eastern.

The air smells like poverty here, and I try to breathe in through my mouth to avoid the scent of unwashed bodies. Though Southern is the poorest quarter, it's not much better in Eastern; nowhere in Sturmfrost is truly well off.

We do hear rumors about how lavishly the Bonded—the king's elite warriors—live. At the very least, I'm sure they don't have to worry about their children getting kidnapped from their beds in the middle of the night.

Saela.

The thought fuels me, and I pick up my speed, my lungs and legs burning in tandem. As I near the border of Central and Eastern, King Cyril's castle looms over everything, the solid gray stone lurching over the city, and its well-lit walls make the streets brighter.

I duck under clotheslines and hop over broken cobblestones, faster and faster and faster, racing through the edges of Eastern and finally into our quarter's market square. It's cleaner than the one in the Southern Quarter, actually put to use by the people in our neighborhood.

The sound of a mother's wailing carries through the night air. Please, goddess, no.

A crowd huddles together in the fog. I push forward, shoving through the other citizens gathered around until I reach the center.

Not my mother, not my mother, please.

The woman on the ground looks up at me, her eyes wet. It's Mrs. Sawyer, a seamstress who lives several streets away from us. Her husband and older sons surround her. She wails again.

"Leesa," she moans. "Leesa!"

The knot in my chest loosens but doesn't go away.

Leesa Sawyer is one of Saela's good friends from primary school. She always begs me to show her how to throw a punch, but I know her straight-laced parents wouldn't like that. Leesa's bright-eyed and funny and clever. Or she was.

Now, Leesa is just the latest in an ever-growing list of kids that have disappeared.

And the Nabbers never return what they take.

Backing away from the crowd, I try to calm my breathing, still erratic from my run. Then I make my way toward my home. All the dwellings around here are half-timbered and stone, and our home is no exception, although it sits shorter than its neighbors. My father always said he was going to add a second story on it once the baby was born.

Of course, he never returned from the war to build it.

I head down our darkened street, my steps echoing off the stone buildings. The shingles on our roof look worn, I notice—it's time to replace a few of them. Another task for another day.

The interior is dark, except for a single candle burning on our bare wooden mantelpiece in the living area.

Mother paces back and forth, her dark hair unbrushed and wild. She's muttering to herself, yanking at her moth-bitten nightgown, which is inside-out. When she spots me, her eyes alight with an awful, vacant recognition and I wonder which stranger I'm about to get.

She doesn't know me when she's like this. She doesn't know anyone, lost to a world of her mind's own creation. Sometimes, she's sweet in her madness, cooing and loving. And sometimes, she's violent, breaking the few possessions we have and raising her hand to us.

When she gets like this and I'm not here, Saela knows to lock herself in our room from the inside. Only I have the key.

"Lumina!" Mother exclaims now, her voice pained. She races up to me, clutching my arm tightly, almost painfully. "Oh, Lumina. They've been terrors today, the twins. They're trying to find you, but they never listen to me, never, never, never—"

"Mother, hush." I run a hand down her hair, gently, calming.

Lumina and the twins, whoever they may be, are some of her common delusions. "Come to your bed. I'll make the twins go away for you."

I lead her to her room and help her onto the lumpy mattress, then reach for the medicine bottle at her bedside, the one we get from the apothecary. Both he and the medic say it helps with her delusions, and some days it does, but often it's like nothing will bring her back at all. I feed her a thick, pungent spoonful of the sludgy medicine and pull her scratchy, too-thin blanket over her.

Mother takes the dose without protest, her eyes drifting shut almost as soon as her head hits the pillow. I watch over her until her breathing evens out, and then go check on Saela.

As I'd assumed, Saela's locked the door to our room, so I pull out the key and let myself in.

My sister is cozied into her small bed, sleeping soundly, her dark hair spread across her thin pillow. Ten, almost eleven—the same age as Leesa Sawyer.

In her sleep, Saela looks so much like our father, the father she's never known. She has the same stubborn chin, the same aquiline nose. My own memories of him grow fogged as the years pass, but she brings him alive for me.

I sit down next to her on her bed, running the back of my finger down one of her soft cheeks. "I won't let anything happen to you," I whisper, a fierce, protective instinct burning in my chest. "I promise."

This nauseous, terrified churning in my stomach—I'm absolutely fucking sick of it. Of living a life where I just accept that I have no control, that our children can just disappear and no one will do a single thing about it.

Tonight was too close of a call.

And if no one's going to stop this... well, then I will.

CHAPTER TWO

"Do it again," Igor calls during training the next afternoon, unmoved by my heavy breathing, or the patch of sweat soaking through my tunic.

I meet his eyes and groan. He raises his graying eyebrows at me, mouth quirking.

"Again," he repeats. "*Without* telegraphing your next move this time—remember what I showed you."

I straighten up, willing my breath to still. My thighs are screaming already, worn out from the morning's work of endlessly lifting huge buckets of water at the laundry where I work, a job that I inherited from my mom when she stopped showing up eleven years ago.

Someone needed to go in her stead, to make sure that we could keep food on our table and the roof over our heads. I dropped out of school and never looked back.

It doesn't matter that I'm tired. Everyone's tired, and Igor doesn't accept any excuses. Not in the fighting ring, and certainly not here in his yard as he trains me.

He's right. I can't afford to show any weakness.

Not if I want to keep winning. And we need those extra coins.

My foot slams into the practice dummy, and Igor grunts his approval, the closest to a compliment I get during these sessions. I repeat the movement again, two, three more times for good measure, before dancing back on the balls of my feet, grabbing a rag to wipe the sweat off my face.

Igor's side yard is a mess of lopsided practice dummies, rough-hewn weights to build muscle, and a jumble of half-broken furniture that I know his wife Prina wishes he'd spend time fixing rather than sinking more time into training me.

"You okay, Alleycat?" he asks, taking the rag back from me. "Seem a little off today."

I raise an eyebrow at him. Igor is irritatingly perceptive; but then again, he's more of a parent to me than my actual living one.

"I can't stop thinking about Leesa Sawyer," I tell him, the spark of last night's fury still burning inside of me, waiting to catch fire. I've been mulling over it all day, coming closer and closer to a way to take action.

Igor nods as he motions to the practice dummy, instructing me to keep going as we talk. "That's a tough one, the Sawyer girl. Good family. Nice people. Heard her parents were up all night searching for her," he says as I unleash a fast combination of kicks and punches. "But I've yet to hear of a missing kid who's been found."

"Does it seem like it's happening more? The Nabbers, I mean," I say between punches.

They have a silly, childish name, given to them by the very kids who fear them. It's almost hard to take them seriously when you hear it, which is part of the appeal. If you can laugh at it, it doesn't seem true—like the Nabbers are nothing more than a childhood legend.

Unfortunately, their menace is all too real.

Kids have been getting kidnapped for as long as I've been alive; maybe as long as this entire war has been going on. And we all know who the Nabbers actually are.

Siphons, our ancient, monstrous enemy from the neighboring country of Astreona. They steal our kids out of their beds and take them back across the border, turning them into living blood bags, feeding off of them, sucking out their powerful child life force, and eventually draining and killing them.

It makes me sick, thinking how those depraved immortal vampires are going to win this war by slaughtering our innocents.

Igor hums. "Maybe so. Get higher with that kick."

I follow his instructions, my legs continuing to ache. "Isn't it bad enough that our sons and daughters and fathers are being killed by the Siphons at the front? We should be safe in our own homes, shouldn't we? What's the king doing about all this?"

"Don't think the king gives two shits about it, to be honest. Too focused on the war hundreds of leagues away to pay any attention to what's happening in his own city right underneath his nose."

Catching my breath, I glare over at Igor. "I can't stand for that. And I'm going to do something about it."

Igor doesn't question this grand statement, or tell me I'm foolish to think that I can make a change. He knows as well as I do that if you want something done here in Sturmfrost, you have to do it yourself.

Instead, he calmly walks over to one of his debris-strewn tables and opens up a cloth roll. Inside lay a dozen sharply honed, glittering weapons. "You seem angry. Knives?"

A laugh escapes me. "Yes, and yes. Thought you'd never ask."

We don't use knives during the hand-to-hand combat we do in the pits, but Igor's been training me to throw them, anyway. He said you never know when you might need to make someone shit their pants by tossing a dagger at their head.

"What'd you have in mind?" he asks as I head over to the table and select a small and particularly pointy-looking one.

"You taught me to defend myself," I say, turning toward the target he's set up on the far side of the yard. "No Nabbers would've gotten me, not without a fight, once you got me started. Maybe we can teach the kids, too. I could train them to protect themselves."

I throw the knife and it sails through the air, hitting the outer edge of the target. Not good enough.

Igor scoffs, sitting down in his creaky chair and staring up at the cloud cover that threatens snow. "You had the fight in you already.

Not too many kids are gonna throw themselves at danger the way you did."

"The way I still do, you mean," I joke, bravado covering up the painful rush of memory.

When my dad was killed, I was left alone at twelve years old with a pregnant, mentally ill mother. Overnight, everything changed. Saela was born, and she was so perfect and tiny and good. And I was the child put in charge of her.

I was furious at the world, spoiling for a fight.

I used to go out into the alleys and goad older boys twice my size into an altercation just so I could have someone to hit. Just so I could feel something other than the unending, cavernous pain inside of my chest.

Eventually, Igor got tired of watching the little neighbor girl get her ass handed to her. He stomped out into the alley behind our houses, grabbed me by the collar of my shirt, and dragged me hissing and spitting into his kitchen.

He threw me down into a rickety chair and said, "Are you trying to get yourself killed, girl?"

When I didn't deny it, he let out a long-suffering sigh. "Well, if you're going to prowl around acting like an alleycat, then you need to learn to fight like one. Come with me."

Igor led me to this yard and started to train me—that day, and every one that followed. He helped me hone my anger from something feral into something vicious, polished.

Dangerous.

And when the boys in the neighborhood began to look at me in fear, Igor helped me find a healthy new outlet for my rage. I'm still goading men twice my size into fighting me. But now I get paid.

Grabbing my knife from the target, I turn back toward him. "You're right. I'm different. But not everyone needs to be a professional. If these kids just knew a few simple tricks, enough to give them time to make some noise, get some help…"

"Don't think this will get you out of your own training time," Igor warns, and I know he's sold on the idea.

"No, I'd never deny you the pleasure of ordering me around," I tease, and he tosses a knife at me that I dodge easily, laughing.

AFTER I LEAVE Igor's in the late afternoon, I head west to the Central Quarter to pick up Saela from school, weaving through the crowded streets. The sinking sun breaks through the clouds now and again, sending reddish reflections glimmering in the windows as I pass homes and shops—more of the windows in Central are smooth and shiny, unlike our neighborhood where a broken pane gets boarded up more often than not.

Saela used to attend primary school in our neighborhood in Eastern, but she was always top of her class, and last year her teacher recommended her for a more advanced secondary school in Central, which is a wealthier neighborhood.

It's not convenient, and it costs money—not much, but anything is too much for us these days. The sacrifice is worth it for my sister, though. She will not end up like me, dropping out and working herself to the bone just to stay alive.

In a world full of dead ends, I'm going to make sure she has *options*.

Saela's different from me. Bookish, hard working. An optimist. An innocent. She's got a smart mouth on her, which I take credit for, but the rest of it? Must've been from Father, because she just came out that way.

She's standing alone outside the school building when I arrive, dark hair plaited down her back and eyes narrowed in annoyance.

"Late again," Saela says, looking pointedly at me.

"Sorry, kiddo," I say, swinging my arm around her shoulders. "Guess you're just going to have to accept that your big sister is bad with time. How was school today?"

"It was fine," she says in a clipped tone, clearly mulling over something.

"Fine?" I tease. "Well, if we're paying all this money for fine, we can probably switch you back to school in Eastern and—"

"*Meryn*," she whines in annoyance.

I raise my hands. "Sorry! But really, what's going on?"

Saela sighs as we make our way down the cobblestones, heading toward the busier streets that lead into the Central Market. "We were talking about the war with Astreona in history class today."

"Ah," I say. "Siphon stuff?"

She nods, lips pressed together in a tight line. Saela went through a period when she was little where she was having awful nightmares about Siphons. Even though she never met our father, the knowledge of his death has loomed over her childhood, shaped every part of her existence.

"Some kids were talking about how the Siphons feed on regular humans, like suck our blood to stay alive, and it seemed like they thought it was, I don't know, cool or something." Her face flushes with anger. "I don't think it's cool," she adds quietly.

I tighten my arm around her shoulders. "You know, I'm sure you're not the only person in your class who has lost a parent or loved one in the war. There were probably other kids who felt the same way."

She nods. "Half of us have. But the teacher made it seem like…" Saela stops in her tracks and looks up at me, dark brown eyes wide with worry. "Are we losing?"

"I don't really know," I tell her honestly.

The war has been going on for five hundred years, but between our country's Bonded and their direwolves and Astreona's Siphon strength, it's rare for either side to take much ground. And we all know what would happen if Astreona won—the Siphons would hunt down every last human and drain us.

"But here in Sturmfrost, we're as far away from the front as you can get in the entire kingdom of Nocturna. If you're safe anywhere, it's here."

The words are like dust in my mouth. She and I both know it's a lie; one of her friends was kidnapped *last night*.

"Come on," I say, slipping my arm off her shoulders and grabbing her hand to tug her toward the market. "I know just the thing to cheer you up."

While every quarter has their own market square, Central's is the biggest shopping area in the entire city, filled with everything from fishmongers and bakeries to specialty perfume stores. There even used to be a jewelry store here, but that was decades ago, before everyone was encouraged to give extra funds to the war effort in the name of patriotism.

Saela and I like to window shop on our way home, our daily ritual. We daydream about what sweets we would buy if we could.

We head straight to our favorite window display at Diersing's Bakery. Saela sighs, staring into the bakery display and pointing to a glistening pastry topped with deep purple fruit.

"I think I'd take one of those plum cakes."

"Noted," I tell her, thinking again about her approaching name-day. This would be a pleasant surprise, and I have the extra money that Lee gave me after the fight last night. My skin flushes at the thought of him, and how our night got cut short. Thankfully, he's due back from the castle in a couple of days, and I can see him again.

Before I can offer my own fantasy bakery order, there's a commotion behind us. Saela and I turn. A crowd has amassed around the square.

"What's going on?" I ask a man nearby.

"Bonded," he says. "Riding through."

What? Why would the Bonded be coming through *here*?

The Bonded are the king's most elite forces, soldiers who have mental bonds with massive, fearsome direwolves. They ride the wolves into battle and, rumor has it, the riders can even tap into the magic that the direwolves wield.

It's rare that they ever set foot in the commoner side of Sturm-frost, other than coming and going from the front—but even then, they usually skirt around the edges. Their part of the city is on the other side of the castle, bordering the mountain range from which their fearsome direwolves hail.

Saela looks up at me, eyes sparking with excitement. "Can we go watch?"

She's obsessed with the idea of the Bonded. I can't totally blame her—super hot warriors riding mystical beasts and wielding mysterious magic? It's intriguing, if you can set aside the extreme and punishing classism.

I sigh and then grab her hand. I would do literally anything to see this kid smile. "Fine, but stay by my side." Then I tug her behind me through the crowd, elbowing my way to a spot at the front of the square.

The crowd hushes as the Bonded emerge from one of the streets leading into the square. The streets are narrow here, not quite big enough for the direwolves they ride, which only serves to make them look larger.

People idolize the Bonded as much as they revile them. Technically, anyone can become Bonded, and during Bonding Trials, when the direwolves have enough young to bond en masse, all of Nocturna's army recruits have the chance.

But everyone knows that the direwolves almost exclusively choose people who come from Bonded families. Privilege begets more privilege, a never-ending cycle.

There's nothing magical about the riders themselves, but because of generations of natural selection, they just *look* different from the rest of us.

Tall. Beautiful. Honed fighting machines.

Today, there are four of them, all wearing black riding leathers. A stern-faced woman with dark skin on a silver direwolf leads the way, followed by a pale man with a shock of blond hair on a tawny wolf, an older woman with olive skin on a gray wolf.

My eyes barely register the fourth direwolf and its rider—I'm too busy gawking at what they're dragging behind it.

Or... *who.*

Gasps go up in the crowd as people visibly take a step back in horror.

It's a commoner man, hogtied and bumping against on the cobblestones. Blood and bruises cover his face, yet he doesn't fight his shackles. He looks resigned. He's given up.

Rage ignites in my blood. *How dare they?*

The direwolves and their riders edge toward the middle of the square just as the breath leaves my body.

I *know* that man. He was the dumbass who threatened me at the fight last night.

My gaze skirts back to the direwolf dragging him around. Massive is an understatement—the direwolf is easily taller than the most battle-ready horses the commoners ride in the army. His fur is midnight black, and he has a feral, bloodthirsty look in his gaze. He bares his teeth, each sharper than a dagger.

The direwolf's rider matches him in ferocity. He's in his late twenties, I'd wager, with light brown skin and dark, messy hair that has a blood-red streak in it. Like every Bonded I've ever seen, he's undeniably *beautiful*, with deep brown eyes and scruff framing his chiseled jawline. But...

My pulse speeds up as I clock the tattoos completely covering his neck, his hands. Not much makes me afraid, but this? *Run*, a self-preserving, animalistic part of me cries. *Danger*.

Even us commoners know what those are. Kill tattoos.

For someone to be so thoroughly cloaked in them...

He's killed hundreds, easily. Maybe more.

Monster. This guy's a fucking psycho killing machine.

My gaze slides up to his face and my stomach flips as I make eye contact with him. The Bonded man practically glowers at me from a distance. His lip rises in a sneer. Maybe my fear of him is written all over my face. I avert my eyes.

Power radiates off of him in waves. Whoever he is, he's someone important in the king's forces. It would be impressive for someone as young as him... if he weren't absolutely terrifying.

The Bonded man hops off of his vicious direwolf with practiced grace. For the man's gigantic size, he moves like water. In two fast steps, he's reached the commoner tied to the back of his wolf.

He grabs the man off the ground with one hand, displaying an inhuman level of strength. Using his direwolf's magic, maybe.

"This man," the rider calls out, his rumbling deep voice echoing over the silenced crowd, "is a deserter from the front. The king takes deep offense to anyone who would dare abandon their comrades in arms. Do you deny the charge?" he asks the man.

"No," the man mumbles between his split lips.

The rider continues, "We have brought him here today to make sure all the citizens of Sturmfrost are aware of what happens to cowards."

He lifts the man higher and I suddenly know what's about to happen. I have no love lost for deserters, and especially not this piece of shit. But my sister cannot bear witness to this.

"Cover your ears," I whisper quickly to Saela, who complies. My hands slide over her eyes, holding her warm, small body tight to mine.

The rider grabs a dagger with his free hand and guts the man from navel to neck. His anguished screams echo, bouncing off the buildings around the square. Then, as the crowd watches in horror, the Bonded man sticks his hand into the deserter's belly and yanks out his entrails. Somehow the man is not dead yet, gurgling in pain, blood bubbling out of his mouth and dripping down his chin.

The Bonded man tosses the deserter forward to his wolf, who snaps him out of mid-air with his powerful jaws. His direwolf spits the deserter onto the ground and then snaps at him again by his neck, shaking him once, twice. The man—the body—has stopped moving.

The direwolf feasts on him, blood coating his muzzle.

I make myself watch for as long as I can, determined to sear the image into my brain, to remember this for the rest of my life.

To remember how absolutely fucking cold-blooded the Bonded are and how unfairly the cards are stacked against the rest of us.

Eventually the sight turns my stomach and I look away, only to make eye contact with the brutal, maniacal Bonded again. He's looking at me assessingly. I wonder if he gets off on making people cower in fear and pain. If this is fun for him.

I lift my chin higher. *I'm not afraid of you, asshole*, I tell him in my mind even as my hands tremor, even as his bold-faced unblinking violence shakes me to my core.

There's no emotion in his dark eyes, none at all.

The Siphons might be our enemy, but I'm certain that this man is the true face of evil.

CHAPTER THREE

Igor and I were able to round up a dozen of Saela's friends and our neighbors for training, which is a start. Within a few days, we've got them on a schedule, meeting after school as soon as I bring Saela home.

Now, I wince with sympathy as I watch a kid a few years younger than Saela fall face-first into the dirt. Falls like that hurt, but of course it's nothing to his youthful body. He springs up like a hare, grinning, eager to go again.

And it's not just hard knocks from training that they're springing back from, not after last night.

"Which one was it?" Igor asks me, coming up beside me so he can keep his voice low.

"There—Timun, that gangly one," I gesture. Timun is twelve and has just started another big growth spurt. He looks like he's not sure where his body starts or ends.

Last night, a Nabber tried to get him, but Timun fought him off. He used a small carving knife he's been keeping next to his mattress, along with some tricks to get away that we've taught him.

His mother rushed him over to my house this morning so he

could tell me in person. I'm not sure I've ever been more elated than I was when looking at the sheer gratitude written on Mrs. Sulvan's face. Knowing that I'm the one who helped save her kid.

"You should be proud of yourself," Igor murmurs, and I flush.

"He didn't get a look at the asshole's face, though," I say regretfully. "Apparently it was dark, and their face was covered…"

"Hmm," Igor says, and we both fall into silence, watching Timun. He's rolling happily in the dirt with two other boys, practicing their escapes, the trauma of last night seemingly forgotten.

"You're pretty good at this, kid," Igor grunts finally. I struggle for a retort, momentarily thrown off by the rare compliment. "You could think about charging for this, you know."

"What, these kids? Their parents barely have the money to pay for new clothes when the old ones are pinching."

Igor laughs. "No, I was thinking more like in the Northern Quarter, where the parents have a few coins to rub together." He pauses, thoughtful. "Even in those nicer parts of town, things have been getting rougher. I bet the parents would be interested in helping their kids learn some self-defense skills."

He pushes off from the fence and stretches. I can hear the cracks in his back and neck as he moves them.

"Anyway. Something to think about. It'd maybe get you out of the heat and steam of the laundry."

It's an idea. I nod and then turn away, calling in the kids.

"Okay, good job, everyone," I say when they've gathered around me in a circle. Their little faces look up at me attentively. "I can see you've been practicing what we learned last time."

I pause, looking over the dozen children that are gathered in the school's sorry excuse for an exercise yard. Most of them are a little too thin, like they could use an extra meal or three. Signs of their parents' care are abundant, though; little touches sewn into their clothing, like the heart-shaped patch that six-year-old Sami sports on the left knee of her trousers.

Waving Saela up to the front, I announce to everyone, "We're going to show you a demonstration for some new moves you can use if an attacker grabs you from behind."

Saela steps proudly forward, her shoulders back. I grin at her confidence.

"Ready to show what we practiced?" I murmur, voice pitched low so only she can hear.

"I was born ready," Saela scoffs, rolling her eyes at me.

"Everyone, watch this closely," I say.

Saela and I take a few steps further back to make sure everyone can see us. I move behind her and then dart forward quickly, grabbing her and wrapping my long arms around her slim torso. Her arms are effectively pinned to her side. She hesitates for just a moment, but then she's running through the moves that we've practiced at home over the last few days.

She goes slack in my hands, becoming deadweight against my chest. Saela slips downward and I have to adjust my grip to keep her trapped, which gives her valuable seconds to maneuver.

Then, she slams the heel of her boot into my toes—a little harder than she really needs to for the demonstration. My yowl of pain is very convincing.

As soon as she can tell that I'm distracted by the pain, she shoves her arms away from her sides, loosening my grip once more, and slips out and under the circle of my arms, pretending to run away from me as the kids cheer.

"That was great, Sae," I say, and duck down to rub my toes through my boot. "Maybe even a little more impressive than it needed to be?"

Saela giggles.

"So, right. Did everyone see how she used her size against me?" Heads nod, most seeming to grasp the basic principles at play here. "Sometimes it can be helpful to be small. Your attacker might expect you to be weak, to not fight back. Or you can fake at being weak, too."

"Like you do in the ring!" one of the younger teenage boys shouts eagerly.

I give him a mock-stern look. "Not that you'd know anything about that, right?"

More giggles start up among the children. The fighting rings aren't any place for kids, but that doesn't stop some of the rougher dads from bringing their sons along from what is, in my opinion, too early an age.

"Your turn!" I count them into groups of three, making sure they're paired with different kids from last time around. I have them practice until the sun dips toward the horizon. If I hold them here much later, they'll miss dinner at home, and none of them can afford to do that.

Afterwards, I sling an arm around Saela's shoulders as we walk toward home together. She's chattering about her day, something about a mouse that got into her math class. I have trouble focusing on her words, though, Igor's idea still bouncing around in my head.

Could he be right? Could my fighting skills lead to more than just a nasty nighttime habit that leaves me bruised and bloody—might they be my ticket out of this run-down quarter?

LATER THAT WEEK, I race home from training to get the house ready for Lee's visit. He started coming over every two weeks a few months back, when it seemed like Mother's health was taking a turn and I was no longer comfortable leaving Saela alone overnight.

Now, our biweekly dinner dates—with my family in attendance —are some of the few times we see each other outside of my fights.

Before I can make it back to the house, though, I spot Lee turning the corner of our row of houses, and I get a moment to just… stare at him.

He's a few years older than me and taller, which I appreciate as a tall woman, and muscular in a lean way. Tonight, he's out of his messenger's uniform and wearing a blue button-down shirt under his coat that brings out the depth of his blue eyes. His face catches the torchlight from the sconce on the corner and I shamelessly admire the sharp cut of his jawline and cheekbones.

Lee spots me watching him and smirks, the twist of his full mouth setting my insides ablaze. He's so *handsome*.

"I brought that bread your mother liked last time," he says by way of greeting, passing me the packet when he nears. It's still warm.

"Thank you," I say, touched by the small but thoughtful gesture. "I wanted to say, about my mother…"

Her visit to the medic this week was the roughest one yet. My description of how she's been acting lately clearly troubled the medic; plus, my mother was pretty out of it for the entire visit, rambling and vacant. But there was nothing he could do—he said we're already giving her the maximum dosage of her medicine.

And that I need to prepare myself for a future where she's always like this.

Lee is looking at me patiently, waiting for me to go on.

"She's just been pretty bad lately," I finish feebly, not wanting to get into all the details about her latest delusions.

"I'm so sorry, Meryn." Lee's voice is soft. "I know how hard it is to see her that way."

I wrap my arms around him, closing my eyes and resting my forehead on his shoulder, taking comfort from his solid warmth. He brings a hand up to brush my hair aside, his breath hot on my neck.

His teeth nip my skin lightly and I shudder and push closer, heat coiling in my belly.

"If you do that much longer, we will not make it to dinner," I say, my voice rough.

He sighs theatrically and pulls away, his hand coming up to tuck my hair behind an ear. "Have it your way." He gestures toward my door. "After you."

When we push the door open, I startle for a moment, unused to the sight before me: my mother is cooking. Something she hasn't done in… I'm not sure how long.

I raise my eyebrows at Saela, who sits at our kitchen table, working on a row of figures on her chalkboard—prepping for a test tomorrow, I remember.

Saela smiles and shrugs.

"Mother!" I lean in and give her a kiss on the cheek, and she smiles at me.

"What was that for, honey?"

"Nothing." I swallow. "Just... dinner smells good, Mother."

The realization slams into me: it's so rare to see her lucid these days that it's almost weird, wrong. My chest tightens and I turn to Lee, distracting myself. "Hand me that loaf," I say gruffly. "Let's get it sliced up. It'll go perfectly with..."

I turn back to Mom, inquiring with my eyes.

"Your father's favorite—that fish stew he always asked for." Mother continues stirring the fragrant pot calmly, seeming not to notice the silence that descends on the room for a moment as Saela and I savor the rare mention of our father.

Lee looks between the two of us, then moves toward the counter, grabbing a knife from the block and taking the fresh loaf from its bag. "Meryn, go sit."

I collapse into the chair next to Saela, my feet throbbing. I've barely been off them all day. Closing my eyes, I savor the smells of cooking, the warmth from the cookstove and the fireplace at the far end of the room.

Saela bonks me on the forehead with her piece of chalk. "Wake up, sis." I laugh and turn to her, grabbing her chalkboard to see what she's working on. We chat about her school day, but I'm only half listening, my other ear trained on Mom and Lee, who are working side-by-side.

It's too normal.

I try to ignore the thought that it can't last and just enjoy the comfort.

As we take our seats at the table, Saela's asking Lee questions about the Bonded City—the neighborhood on the far side of the castle that only Bonded and their families inhabit. Saela's been interested ever since we glimpsed the Bonded marching through the streets this week.

She's spreading butter across the bread Lee brought, but her eyes are glued on him. "So you've seen it? The Bonded City?"

"Yes, from afar, but you can see a lot of it from the upper floors in the castle," he affirms, smiling at her wondering expression.

"What's it like?" She sets her chin on her hands, rapt.

Lee hums. "Well, it's obvious that it's made for the Bonded and

28

their wolves, for one. All the streets are broader, so that it's easier for the direwolves to pass each other without getting their fur ruffled." He reaches over and ruffles Saela's hair to illustrate.

"Can you see the wolves from the castle?" she asks breathlessly, too enthralled to get annoyed at how he's babying her.

"Sometimes," Lee nods. "And one time I actually saw a direwolf pup, if you can believe it. Even their little ones are huge! They usually keep them out of the main city because they're playful at that age, and don't realize the damage they can do. Think of a baby animal nearly the size of a horse."

Saela gasps. "I bet the pups are *so* cute!"

Lee rolls his eyes at me, and I laugh. "I think she's missing the point about the dangerous wolf monsters with fangs as long as this spoon," he stage-whispers, holding up his cutlery to demonstrate.

Mom is setting down the bowls of stew in front of each of us when I see the change start to come over her. Something shifts in her eyes—she gets that glazed expression that I hate so much. The bowl still in her hands wobbles, splashing broth and chunks of vegetable onto the floor. To my horror, she's staring at Lee when she begins to babble.

I grab the bowl out of her hands before more spills, setting it down on the table.

"Nocturn curses you, traitor," she hisses, and the venom in her voice makes my skin prickle. "He curses you!" Mom has raised a hand to point straight at Lee. He's seen her delusional before, but never aimed at him.

"Mother," I say, trying to draw her attention back to me, to calm her down. It only sets her off more.

"And *you*," she says, turning on me, wild-eyed. "You are not where you are meant to be."

She raises her hand and attempts to strike me, but I catch her wrist in mid-air, holding it tightly. The silver engagement bracelet my father gave her, the one she's never taken off, slips up her thin arm. Mother squirms against my grip as I move to restrain her entirely.

"Sorry," I mumble to Lee. "I'll be back soon."

Then I half-lead, half-carry my mother out of the room.

"Curses upon you! You hear me?" My mother is still ranting as I pull her away.

Behind me, I hear Saela rise to grab a rag for the floor. I'm scared to turn and look at Lee's expression. He's always been kind about my mother's health, but he's never seen her at this level before.

I guide my mother through the short hallway to her bed, and thankfully she gets into bed without a fight, slipping between the sheets, her face expressionless.

"Mother," I start, but then I don't know what to say next that might make a difference. "Here, let's get you your medicine," I say finally, grabbing the vial from the stool next to her bed that serves as a bedside table.

The viscous syrup smells vile, bitter and sharp. I can't imagine what it must taste like, but my mother takes the spoon from me obediently, rolling to face the wall once she's swallowed it down, still murmuring names and curses under her breath.

I sit softly on the mattress next to her, wincing at the lumps—we should have replaced the mattress a long time ago, but we haven't had the money for it.

Carefully, I lift my hand, smoothing it down my mother's arm, repeating the action until her tension eases, her breathing stabilizes.

As I do, I try to calm my own breathing, repeating to myself over and over that she cannot help it, she did not choose to be this way. Some days, I need the reminder—and now is most definitely one of those moments.

More than anything, there's a sting in my chest—the painful knowledge that I was foolish, hoping for a "normal" evening.

This is our normal now.

I douse the lantern and tiptoe out, not wanting to rouse her, hoping she'll stay asleep and leave us in peace for the rest of the evening. I hate myself in that moment, for wishing my mother away, but I shove the feeling aside.

Hesitantly poking my head back into our house's main room, I see that Saela and Lee have left their stew abandoned on the table, half-eaten. They've pulled two chairs together and Lee is reading to her from a legend about lovelorn gods. She's snuggled underneath his comforting arm, engrossed in the story.

I stand there watching for a few moments, leaning into the doorframe. Lee's eyes flick up to mine, and his steady gaze says everything—he's not running away from us, not even after that display.

The tension in my chest eases, and I walk across the room to take a seat on the floor at their feet.

"Meryn does the best voice for the goddess," Saela says proudly. "Meryn, you read this next part!"

"Alright, but just one more chapter and then you need to finish your studying and go to bed," I say, laughing at Saela's groan.

"The goddess was locked in the tower, and nobody knew she was there," I begin, the words of Saela's favorite story familiar in my mouth. "She knew that if she was going to escape, she'd have to find a way to do it herself..."

AFTER SAELA'S IN BED, I lead Lee outside to say goodnight and he turns to me, his face serious. Snowflakes drop on his creased brow. "Meryn, how often does that happen?"

I sigh, leaning my head against his chest. His hands trail up and down my arms. "The delusions? Every day."

Lee's hands tighten around my biceps, and I look up into his eyes. "I'm not talking about the delusions and you know it."

Swallowing hard, I avert my gaze. The woman in there—the one who tried to hit me—wasn't my mother. I've been transparent with Lee about her struggles and he's seen them first-hand many times, but I've never told him about how she gets violent. Putting it into words has felt like a betrayal of the mother I knew.

Maybe it's time to accept that the mother I knew is gone.

And then there's the other thing I've been hiding from him, the part that tortures me in my dreams. How my grandmother had this madness too, and her mother before that. How the madness runs in my blood, lurking in the shadows, waiting to drag me down into its depths.

"I have it under control, as you saw," I mumble.

"I'm not worried about you. *Obviously*, you can hold your own. But what about Saela? It's not safe for her here. What if something happens and you're not around?"

Frustration sparks in my veins. I look back up at him, trying very hard to fight down the tears that are pricking at the back of my eyes. I know he's right but…

"What am I meant to do, Lee? Leave my mother to fend for herself? Take Saela to live elsewhere? How can I pay for two places at once? And who will watch after my mother if I'm not here?"

"Come live with me," he says. "I'll take care of you two. Your mom can stay here and we'll check in on her regularly."

I huff out a surprised laugh. "How could we even manage that? Your apartment is tiny. There's no room for the three of us there."

"Then we'll move, find a bigger place. Or we'll put your mother there and you, Saela and I will live here. We'll figure it out, kitten. But I'm going to protect you, and I'm going to protect your sister. Let me."

The tears are falling now, hot streaks down my cheeks in the cold winter air. My chest tightens and suddenly it's as if I can't breathe. How long has it been since someone genuinely wanted to help us? Since someone saw my situation and offered me a way out?

No, it's more than that—offered, and then insisted I accept.

Where did this man come from, who has the power to melt my heart so thoroughly? I'd trade sun and sky and light itself to know I'd never have to lose him.

I wrap my arms around Lee's neck and pull him toward me, desperate for his mouth on mine. He moves me backward, around the corner, into the alley that runs perpendicular to our street. There are no street lanterns here, so we can fade into the shadows. The closest we get to a private spot.

I stumble breathlessly back into the wall behind me, pulling Lee with me until he's flush against my body, his heat and hard muscle pressing me back into the hard stone.

When our lips connect again, it isn't soft this time, but demanding. I lose myself in the needy tangle of our kiss, circling my hands around his waist, dipping a few fingers into his waistband until my chilly fingers meet his hot skin.

Lee growls into my mouth, pressing me roughly into the wall, and his arousal is hard and insistent against me. I move my hips into him, relishing the sounds he makes. He yanks the edge of my tunic from where it's tucked into my pants, anchoring one hand to my hip as the other slides up over smooth skin to cup my breast, only thin layers of cloth between his hand and my nipple.

Heat surges through me, and I break our kiss to look at him. Both of us look like we're daring the other to take things further.

"We're not done talking about that," he says.

"No," I agree. "Later."

His mouth slams back onto mine, drawing my bottom lip into his mouth, sucking on it until I moan.

My wandering fingers find what they were looking for, Lee's arousal heavy and thick in my hand through his pants. I stroke him, and our mouths part, Lee's forehead resting against mine as he breathes heavily.

"Come back to mine?" His tone is half-question, half-order, and *goddess*, I wish I could. I've taken my monthly contraceptive drought that I pick up alongside mother's medicines at the apothecary. But...

I haven't wanted to leave Saela alone overnight, not since Leesa was kidnapped just a few short blocks from here.

Even the thought now is dousing the flames inside of me.

His face is still flushed from our kissing, hair mussed, and a stab of regret goes through me, but I know I won't be able to think of anything else until I check on Saela, reassure myself that all is well.

"Another night. Look, you should head out, but I'll start thinking about your proposal and... we'll figure out a way to make it work."

"Good," he says, giving me a last parting kiss.

I let myself back into my house, latching the lock firmly behind me, and move swiftly toward Saela's and my room. Opening the door to our room, I shiver in the cool breeze.

That's strange—there shouldn't be a breeze.

My eyes dart to the window, which is shoved open, letting in the icy air. Heart pounding, I run over to Saela's bed.

There's nobody in it.

Saela is gone.

CHAPTER FOUR

This can't be happening.

I stare blankly at the empty bed, mind turning in circles as my body floods with ice.

Saela. *Saela.*

I squeeze my eyes shut, counting to ten, and then open them again, but the empty bed remains, along with the cold draft coming from the open window.

There must be an explanation. How could they have come in here with me just outside on the street? How could I have missed someone entering?

And Saela. She would have defended herself, just like I taught her. She wouldn't have gone quietly.

Not my sister. My *Saela.*

Maybe she's in my mother's room. My frozen muscles jerk to life, and I race out of the room, down the short hallway to my mother's room. Yanking open the door, I scan the dark room frantically, but there's no sign of her.

My mother sits up sleepily, blinking at me, but I can't speak the words, can't explain.

I search the bathroom.

The living space and kitchen.

She's not here. Her coat and boots are, though, neatly tucked next to the front door. I stare at them numbly, then turn back toward our bedroom.

My breath comes in little gasps as I stick my head out the window. Tiny swirls of snow have started, and my breath puffs white in the frigid air. I look back and forth, scanning every inch of the view, willing my eyes to find a clue out in the cold darkness, but there's no sign of what happened, nothing moving in the alleyway beside our house.

Something else catches my eye that I didn't see before, though, as I pull myself back inside the room. In the corner of the window frame, snagged on a long, jagged splinter of wood: a tiny piece of white cloth.

A perfect match for Saela's nightgown.

Sinking down to the floor, I hear a keening sound, and register after a few moments that it's coming from my lips. I shudder and knock my head back against the wall, relishing the jarring pain.

Either Saela snuck out into the snow in her nightgown in the middle of the night... or someone took her.

While I was out in the snow, making plans for a better future with Lee, my sister was stolen in the night.

Even as my mind rejects the words, my body is reacting. I slam the window shut, then tug on boots and throw on a coat as I race out into the darkness.

Lee has to be nearby still, he just departed. I turn left toward his path to the Northern Quarter and *run*. Within a few minutes, I spot his large frame walking purposefully down the quiet street.

"Lee!" I scream. He turns, his face alighting with a smile at the sight of me, which quickly drops at my obvious panic.

He jogs toward me, worry creasing his brow, and grabs me by the arm. "Meryn, what's—"

"Saela," I pant, my breathing ragged from the run. It hurts to say her name. "She was missing when I went back inside." My mind spirals again. *No, no, no, no...*

Lee's hand tightens on my forearm, grounding me, bringing me back into the present. "We'll search for her," he tells me, radiating calm and authority. I sag against him. "Let's get back to your neighborhood and start there. We'll wake your neighbors. We'll find her, Mer. She can't have gone far."

He doesn't put a voice to my fears. To the only logical conclusion: she's been kidnapped.

Time seems to yawn and jump, skipping ahead in starts.

I snap back to focus in front of Igor's door and pound my fist against it. "Igor!" my voice comes out halfway as a sob. I shout his name again and again, slamming my hands into the wood. Lee's hand on my shoulder quells me.

Doors crack to either side of us, cautious faces looking out to see what's causing the commotion. One of my sister's former teachers recognizes me, comes out the door wearing nothing but her nightclothes, a thick shawl, and boots. "Meryn? Is that you?"

Igor's door swings open and he and his wife Prina stand in the doorway, worry etched on their faces. A pit opens up in my belly, and my insides churn, as if caught in a storm.

"It's Saela," I manage. "She's gone. She's—they took her."

"We need to look for her," Lee interjects. "Can you come help us? If you take the northern end of the neighborhood, we can head west, then check Central Market."

Igor's taken two big steps forward, and I start when he wraps his big arms around me. "Meryn," he says, and there's a whole paragraph in those two short syllables. "Of course we'll help you." But I hear in his voice the words he doesn't say.

I break away. "No! *No.* She's not gone. We can't give up on her—"

Igor's already grabbed his coat, pulled on his boots. Saela's teacher joins us, having hastily pulled on some trousers over her nightclothes. "We aren't giving up, Meryn. We're here with you."

The back of my throat burns, and I gaze around me wildly, my mind blank. "We should…"

"Meryn and I will take the blocks west of here," Lee repeats when I drift off. "Can you two start checking north?" He takes me by the arm, tugs.

The icy kiss of snowflakes against my cheeks brings me back into focus. It's coming down harder now, I think absently.

Lee and I are jogging, then running, peeling down each street and alley, shouting Saela's name. The streets are deserted at this hour, apart from a few ragged-looking rats, and one miserable street hound that watches us pass from his modest shelter under a stoop. Broken glass and icy drifts crunch under my boots, the sound muffled by the falling of the surrounding snow. The drifts of white make the streets appear ghostly and barren.

We stop to catch our breath after maybe an hour of searching.

"Maybe we should—"

"Split up?" Lee says. He steps closer, hands coming up to frame my face. "We'd cover more ground that way. But Meryn... are you..."

The concern in his eyes makes me wild, and I spin away out of reach. "I'm fine. Just go. You should head toward Central. She might have gone there... Meet me back at my house in the morning to tell me if you've found anything?" I don't look back to see if he follows my instructions before taking off again down the next alley.

I push faster and faster, zigzagging down each street, eyes darting to every corner, every shadow, every place that she could be. Inside, I block out the voice telling me that the children are never found. That there's nothing anyone can do.

I refuse to do nothing. I refuse.

Hours later, day breaks cold and wet, the snowflakes turning to slush, gray under my boots. The sooty mix drips from gutters, and puddles in street-side ditches. Early morning workers emerge from their homes, giving me a wide berth, averting their eyes.

The world is a blur, my mind numb with exhaustion. I don't know what hour it is when I finally admit defeat, turning toward home.

Igor and Lee are there already, sitting outside my front door. I can tell without either of them saying a word that there's not been any sign of her.

Lee tries to stop me as I go into the house. I just pull away, out of his grip. He's saying something, but all the sounds of the world around me have been replaced by a dull buzzing. I retreat to my room, shut the door in his face.

This is all my fault.

TIME DRIFTS.

I lay mindless in Saela's bed, wrapped in the sheets and blanket that still smell faintly of her.

Mother has checked on me a few times, lucid enough to know what's wrong, to realize what's happened. At the misery in her expression, I turn my face to the wall.

Women from the neighborhood drop by in shifts—workers from the laundry, mothers of Saela's school friends, old friends of my mothers that I haven't seen in years. They bring food, bread, cautiously pushing into my room and leaving plates on the floor when I refuse to speak.

Afterward I hear them chatting in hushed tones with my mother, if she's awake. More times than not, they leave silently, receiving no welcome from either of us.

I can't bring myself to care. The plates of food sit on the floor, untouched.

"She hasn't eaten a bite," comes my mother's voice, hours or days later. I don't know how long it's been.

Mother sounds lucid, sane. As if losing her daughter has shored up what reserves her mind has left.

"It's just like what happened with her father, after his first year at the front. He didn't speak for five days after he got back. Wasted half his leave that way." Mother's voice cracks, and guilt blooms inside me, hot and red.

Father. He was supposed to protect us. And then he left us, left and never came back.

I was supposed to protect Saela. I promised her.

My fingers twitch toward the dagger I keep near my bed. When my father died, that worked, sometimes—giving myself pain to focus on, something to feel other than this. The sharp slice would chase away the darkness from my brain, removing all sensation other than the dagger meeting my arm or thigh.

But I can't find the energy to stir, not even for this. I stare at the ceiling, watching the shadows move strangely across the room as the day comes and goes.

The room is dark again when Igor appears in the doorway, stooping to step through the low frame. "Enough, Meryn." His voice cuts through the room like a knife.

Unlike the others, there's no pity in his tone, no sympathy.

"This isn't you. Get up."

My body is like stone in the bed. I wait, shame and anger roiling in me, squeezing my eyes shut, refusing to look at him. He stands in the doorway for what seems like hours, but eventually, he leaves.

Some time later, Lee quietly lets himself in. I don't turn to look, but I know it's him right away. I can tell by the smell of pine, by the confident tread of his step.

He says nothing, just climbs into the bed with me, fitting his chest against my back, his knees into the crook of mine. At the press of warmth, my eyes prickle, and then I'm sobbing, crying for the first time since Saela was taken.

I cry endlessly, and Lee holds me. When I finally stop, neither of us says anything. Lee just clasps my hand in his, his thumb sweeping across the back of my hand, back and forth, back and forth.

I must fall asleep, because when I open my eyes again, it's bright in the room, the light from the window falling harshly across my face.

Lee has left, but my arms are wrapped tightly around something —Saela's pillow. As my vision comes into focus, I notice a small strand of her hair still on the fabric, the color brown a shade deeper than my own. The single strand shimmers in the square of sunlight.

I sit up.

Something has broken and resettled in my chest. I promised her. Promised Saela that nothing would hurt her.

I fucking keep my promises.

THE ARMY RECRUITMENT center in the Eastern Quarter is next to a butcher's shop. Appropriate, I think grimly as I wait for the recruiter to find my family name on his sheet.

Every quarter has one of these centers, and you can tell the castle cares a bit more about them than anything else—the fire in the hearth is stacked with wood that burns merrily, giving off a dry, seasoned smell unlike the damp peaty aroma of our stove at home. The walls are lined in paper, an indulgence you don't see anywhere else in Eastern. And the furniture is scuffed and worn, but still obviously a higher quality than most.

My eyes skate across the recruiter's uniform, the piles of paper on his desk, jumbles of forms and rosters. An oil lamp flickers, making shadows dance across his hands as he shuffles through the papers. It's like they're reaching for me.

"Ah, here," he says finally. "Cooper. But—" he squints up at me doubtfully. "You weren't summoned to serve. It says you have a caretaker exception."

Everyone gets summoned at some point, unless they're caring for an underage or elderly family member or have a health issue. I've had an exception next to my name since before I was even old enough to serve.

I swallow the lump in my throat. Father would hate it if he knew that I was following in his footsteps, heading to the brutal war front that haunted his dreams.

Father isn't here.

"I know," I say, steel in my voice. "I don't care. I'm volunteering."

It's the only way. If the Nabbers are taking the kids across the borders to the Siphons, this is my only opportunity to get to Saela.

The recruiter and I stare at each other, and he grunts his assent, scribbling something on the sheet in front of him. "Well, in that case—"

"How quickly can you send me to the front?"

The recruiter cocks his head to the side, considering. "We ask new recruits to report for training every six months, which typically gives them enough time to get their affairs in order. We have a boot camp starting up tomorrow, but I would recommend waiting until—"

"I'll be there," I tell him swiftly. "Give me my orders."

The man stares at me for a beat, trying to gauge how serious I am. Something in my face must convince him, because he just shakes his head like he disagrees with me, then stamps something on the paper.

"Done. Welcome to the King's Royal Forces, Recruit Cooper."

CHAPTER FIVE

After I leave the recruitment center, I head straight to find Lee, my breath puffing into the frosty air. I pull my threadbare coat tighter against myself, wishing I had a scarf—but I stormed out of the house with such certainty this morning that I didn't even think of it.

Lee's only at his small apartment a handful of days each week and otherwise stays up at the castle's servant dormitories, but I know his schedule, and he should be home today. My mind is circling, and I set my jaw and study the scenery of Northern as I walk, determinedly putting tomorrow from my mind.

There will be time to panic later. But right now, I need to explain myself to Lee.

The Northern Quarter, the neighborhood closest to the imposing castle, isn't as alien as the Bonded's streets, but it's still very different from Eastern.

The buildings are taller. The roads are more spacious. There are no stray dogs scrounging for scraps. Most obviously, there's no smell. The air isn't clean, but it doesn't reek like too many people crammed into too little space.

The fresher air does nothing to calm my nerves, though. I've been spiraling out ever since I signed the recruitment forms.

I want him to understand. Need him to, really. Lee is my anchor, keeping me in place when the wild tides of my own emotion threaten to pull me into deeper water. If he looks at me like I'm insane when I give him the news, it's going to be difficult not to second-guess myself.

And there's no room for second-guessing now.

Lee's building is half-timbered like mine, but wide and four stories tall, all divided up into small units and mostly inhabited by other royal servants. He lives here alone, in his own tidy space, though he grew up in Northern as well.

Like Lee, his father works in the palace, but their relationship is strained and difficult. His father sounds like, well, an asshole. And his mother passed away when Lee was a child. When he got his messenger job as a teenager, he immediately moved out of his father's place and into his own space.

Reaching his stoop, I push through the front entry and up the stairs to find him, my stomach twisting and turning. The idea of disappointing him makes me want to shed my own skin.

I knock on his door. There's a thud from one of the neighboring apartments. I can hear shouting from the floor above me. My heart is pounding in my chest. My fingers are still cold from the wintry air, so I breathe on them to give myself something to do.

There's a click before the door swings open. And...

I don't know. Seeing him, suddenly everything is alright. I can't remember why I was anxious. That's how it is, with Lee. I take one look at his tall figure silhouetted in the doorway—his broad shoulders, his untucked shirt, his slightly messy dark blond hair, like he just woke from a nap—and I feel safe.

His hand lingers on the door. I watch his grip tighten when he realizes it's me. Lee's eyes are such a beautiful crystalline blue, like the sky on a surprisingly cold winter's day, even in this darkened hall.

"Kitten," he rasps, warmth lacing his voice. "You're back."

I know instantly what he means—*I'm* back. I've banished that part of me capable of falling apart entirely, the part who wept while he held her. She's still here, deep inside, but I refuse to let her control me for another moment.

"I'm back," I agree. *And wait until you hear what I've done...*

His strong arm closes around my waist and he yanks me into the apartment, the heat of his hard body flush against me. Lee tucks a lock of my dark hair behind my ear, kicks the door shut, and says, "Good. I missed you."

Then that gaze of his drops lower, raking over my body, and I'm suddenly not thinking of anything other than this moment. The heat in his gaze flips a switch in my brain, and my whole body reacts with the need to curl against him and surrender to it. My skin tingles. My damn toes curl in my boots.

But as he lifts his head and I catch that hungry gaze again, it all comes crashing back.

This isn't why I came here.

"I need to tell you something," I blurt, pressing a hand to his chest.

His eyes dart between mine briefly, like he's trying to figure out how serious I am. Then he nods, taking me by the hand and leading me into his kitchen, his only seating area other than his bed. He pulls out a wooden chair for me and gestures to it.

"Talk to me," he says as he sits in the chair beside mine. His gaze is steady, his posture relaxed.

Like pulling a splinter, I tell myself. "I enlisted so that I can go to the front and find Saela."

For a moment, he doesn't react at all. He's completely unmoving, still staring at me steadily. I start to wonder if this is worse than if he'd immediately pointed out my recklessness. The not knowing is punishing.

And then he shuts his eyes and sighs deeply. His hand lifts to pinch the bridge of his nose, and despair radiates from him in waves. And no, this is definitely worse than the silence.

"Oh, kitten. What have you done?" He opens his eyes again and levels me with a look filled with both love and heartbreak.

My vulnerability turns me into an asshole. I bristle instantly. "I had to, Lee." My voice is as sharp as a knife. "No one is *doing* anything. Someone has to be down there who cares about the missing kids, who will look for them." My hand clenches into a fist. I hate this. "It's *Saela*. How can you not understand that?"

The question sounds like an accusation, but Lee doesn't lower himself to my level. The injured fondness in his eyes doesn't waver, even as I try to bite his head off.

"I do understand," he tells me. And just like that, I'm not angry any longer. Because the way he said it, I know he meant it.

Lee takes another deep breath and leans back, letting his arm rest on the table beside us. His long fingers scratch absently at the wood grain. Then his face pinches slightly. It looks like pain. Or guilt, maybe. Frustration. Some mix of foul feelings.

"If I could, I would go in your place to find her," he says finally. Quietly.

The royals hire their servants from the children of servants, generation after generation. They make better salaries than most, but once they enter the king's service, they're expected to serve for life, no exceptions.

"I would do anything for you, Meryn. But this…"

I wince. "You think I'm crazy?"

His expression tightens. "I don't," he growls. The ferocity of his reply sounds like a threat against anyone who'd dare question me. "The timing is just… fucking awful."

"The timing?"

He reaches up and pushes his fingers through his thick hair, then lets his hand drop to his knee. "There are about to be Bonding Trials."

His words are like a punch to the gut.

Bonding Trials… a chance to become one of the King's precious Bonded forces, and to form an unbreakable connection with a massive, vicious direwolf.

If that's true, it means I might never even make it to the front. The Bonding Trials are just as dangerous as the war, from what I've heard.

A ragged rush of air chokes up my lungs. "How do you... know that?"

There's no way he could, right? Bonding Trials happen sporadically, and are kept a closely guarded secret so as not to deter soldiers from enlisting. When one is about to happen, every newly enlisted recruit is required to attempt to bond, without exception.

"I overheard whispers in the castle. They've already sent out missives for the instructors," Lee says. His brow is tight. He isn't looking at me. And I know why.

I've just told him that I'm going to throw myself into the most dangerous place possible, and he knows me too well to try to talk me out of it. There's nothing he can do, and Lee hates that. He's always hated not being able to act, maybe as much as I do.

"I'm still going," I tell him. "I have to."

"I know," he says. "Look, they're going to make you do the first Trial. From what I've heard, it's a perilous mountain climb, and the direwolves are at the top. But you don't need to try to bond with one. All you need to do is survive. As long as you do that and avoid bonding, you'll be sent along to the front with the rest of the commoner soldiers afterwards."

I take a deep, shaky breath. That doesn't sound terrifying at all. "Okay."

His eyes find mine again, and they burn with an intensity that makes me feel powerful. "If anyone can survive it, it will be you," he tells me firmly. Courage catches like a bonfire in my chest. "Fight, Meryn. Win. Find Saela and come back to me."

"I will. I—I love you, Lee."

"I love you, too," he says, reaching out to cup my cheek gently.

We've said the words to each other before, but today they sound different.

Today, *I love you* sounds an awful lot like *goodbye*.

I need to banish the sound of it from my mind, and there's one surefire way to quiet all my thoughts. Lee catches my change in mood, stroking my cheek with his thumb, then scratching his nails lightly down my neck and across my shoulder. In a heartbeat, my desperation to have him on top of me, inside of me, gets so searing that my skin grows hot with it.

I reach for Lee and yank him to me by his shirt.

He is over me instantly, on his feet and kissing me with a scorching heat as one of his hands closes around the back of my chair and the other around my neck. And just like that, I'm no longer in control.

My grip on his shirt goes limp as his tongue meets mine, the slick heat of his kiss sinking bliss through my muscles. A needy sound escapes me as I pull weakly at his shirt, and his returning chuckle goes straight to my core.

Neither of us utters a word as our eyes meet again, the intensity in his gaze making me gasp. His big hands slide down my back to my ass, and then in one quick move he's lifted me up and laid me out right there against the kitchen floor, bending me back, following to claim me in a kiss.

I fall backward, arms dropping from his neck to brace myself. The icy cool of the kitchen floor presses into my arms, my rear, my lower back, even as Lee's heat warms me, making me shiver in pleasure.

Lee's mouth licks a trail of fire from my earlobe down to the hollow of my neck, where he suckles, teasing his teeth over my sensitive skin. My head falls back, knocking against the floor.

His mouth disappears, and I prop myself up on an elbow, only for my arm to go weak as he yanks my trousers down past my hips, tearing through my underwear in a single motion. I stare at him, my breathing heavy. His lips curve in a possessive smile, and my body floods with heat.

Slowly, he rises up to his knees and undoes the laces at the front of his own trousers, and I moan as I watch his cock spring free, already achingly hard. He rubs the heel of his hand over the head, once, twice, as I squirm in front of him.

Every part of me wants to grab him and wrap my legs around him, take him inside me immediately, but I know from past experience that right now, he's in charge, not me.

Lee leans forward and drags my tunic up to my neck, pulling off the breast bindings I wear in two short tugs, exposing my breasts. My already-hard nipples tingle in the cool air, and I almost leap off the floor when his fingers tweak my left nipple, hard.

He palms my other breast, then alternates between stroking and pinching my breasts until I'm a mess of moans. Finally, *finally* he drags a hand down my belly, arousal curling through me as he presses me into the ground, then bends down and pushes his hands against my inner thighs, spreading me wide.

I'm already dripping with need, my sensitive flesh clenching at the hot air of his breath against me. Every part of me feels empty, waiting for him to fill me, make me whole.

The first brush of his tongue is so sinful that I almost come on the spot.

Lee pulls away instantly, as if he knows how close I am already. I raise my head to catch his sharp look. He doesn't need to speak for me to understand: we both know this could be our last chance to be together like this for... for a long while.

He's not going to let it be over so quickly.

Slowly, achingly slowly, his mouth returns, tongue dipping inside me and then coming up to circle my clit, working me up before disappearing as soon as I approach the edge. I'm talking now, pleading with him, saying words but not knowing what or which.

My thighs are drenched when he pulls away, kneeling and looking over me, eyes dark.

"Reach your hands over your head," he orders, "and grab hold of that table leg behind you."

Shaking, I do as he says, his eyes never once leaving mine.

"Hold on," he says, gaze sparking. "Don't let go, no matter how badly you want to touch yourself."

Gone is the soft, gentle touching from before. When he finally pushes inside me, I hear myself shout his name, half-nonsensical. I wrap my legs around him, urging him deeper, and he doesn't resist, pushing himself deep before pulling out and slamming back in.

I grip the rough-hewn table leg the entire time, so hard that it digs in my palms. My fingers ache fiercely; the sensation of him pounding between my legs coupled with the helplessness of not being able to seek out my own pleasure has me crying out, begging, grabbing onto the wood like I'll fall off of the edge of the world without it.

He fucks me exactly how I wanted him to, with deep, punishingly fast thrusts that send pulses of pleasure roaring through my body. I can't stop myself from trying to push back into him, pull him deep with my legs, open myself up even wider to give him all of me.

He never takes his eyes off of me—those perfect, crystal-clear blue eyes.

And when the merciless rhythm of his hips starts to stutter, I beg. "Please. Please. F-Fuck. Please. Lee!" I scream.

He smiles at me as he fucks me, as if he likes watching me come undone as much as I like shattering under his touch, pulled apart by the pleasure. He groans and finally moves a hand from my hip to circle his thumb over my clit, and I explode instantly, having been riding the edge far too long to resist that touch.

Blinding pleasure whites out my vision, and I shudder as my muscles clench around him. Ripples of pleasure work their way through me as he continues to thrust, fast and hard as my orgasm goes on and on, my body working him until he also lets go, coming with a shout and a final violent thrust inside of me.

Eventually, my breath starts to even out. I crack my eyes open, vision swimming slightly.

The sound of Lee's satisfied chuckle as he withdraws has me clenching again around nothing, whimpering as he strokes over my hypersensitive nerves once more, tweaking my clit with his thumb.

He stands up gracefully, extending a hand to me and pulling me up beside him. "Alright, kitten?"

I take stock of my body. There's an ache in my skull. I think I probably threw my head back against the floor when I came. And I'm a little raw and exhausted, in the best way possible. Devoured, really.

"More than alright," I breathe. I shut my eyes briefly before attempting to walk.

He loops my arms around his neck and I allow him to half-carry me toward the bedroom. He walks me backward until we hit his washroom, and he puts me down with a laugh, turning back toward his bed while I wash up with trembling hands.

After I'm clean, I collapse on the bed beside him, molding my body to his side. His arm comes down to wrap around my shoulder, other hand pressing my hips back against him until every part of us is touching.

Lee bites my neck a few times playfully, and then whispers to me. "You don't have to go, you know. You could stay. Here. Like this."

My entire chest aches. I refuse to cry, so I ignore the sting in my eyes. "I can't do nothing, Lee."

"I know," he says, then sits up and offers me his hand. "Come on. We should go."

I take his hand and let him pull me to my feet. He collects my clothes from where they're strewn around the kitchen, handing them to me. "Get dressed."

"Where are we going?" I ask.

"Shopping. If you're going to survive the first Bonding Trial they put all the soldiers through, you need some better equipment."

SHOPPING WITH LEE is nearly as torturous as telling him my news. I don't like taking money from anyone, not when I can help it. He insisted he had coin to spare, though, and that he'd blame himself if something happened to me at the Bonding Trials because I didn't have the right gear.

He takes me to a leather shop he likes, right off the main market square in Central. The shop is full of beautiful things, nicer than anywhere I've ever shopped before. Lee greets the shopkeeper as if he's been in here a hundred times, and I study him, surprised. Then again, I suppose he's on his fancy castle servant salary—and he doesn't have a family to feed, like I do.

Together, the two of them select a whole host of items I'll need, ignoring me every time I protest that something isn't necessary.

A new rucksack, with pockets and dividers and straps to secure everything.

A new waterskin, lightweight yet large and durable.

A new pair of boots, specially soaked and stretched and oiled so that the leather is supple enough not to give me blisters from a hard day's walk.

A new jacket, padded and lined with leather, longer and thicker than the one I've had for years now, with pockets lined in fur to keep my hands warm.

A sleek pair of gloves, tight yet flexible enough to allow me full range of motion while wearing them.

I watch helplessly as Lee piles coin after coin on the counter afterward, an impossible amount, more than I've ever spent in one month, never mind one day.

But it doesn't end there. The Trial will be icy, Lee explains. I have to be ready for inclement weather. He takes me down a side street I never noticed before, and we duck into a basement-level shop that's packed to the gills with hunting, trapping, and fishing gear.

Along one wall is mountain gear, like snowshoes and crampons. The shopkeeper carefully fits a pair of crampons to my new boots. We both look over the poles that some hunters use in the winter to keep themselves steady when walking an icy path, but ultimately decide I'll want my hands free, ready to grab for a weapon... just in case.

When we leave, I'm in a daze, loaded up with more expensive things than I've ever owned. Lee offers to walk me home, even though I know it'll make him late for his shift at the castle. I refuse, crack a dumb joke, and he pretends to laugh.

We try not to make a big deal out of our parting.

It's only goodbye for now, he assures me. We'll see each other soon, he insists.

I try to walk away like it's any other day, like I'll see him tomorrow. I wait until I'm sure he can't see me before letting the tears fall.

On my way back into the Eastern Quarter, I duck into the laundry where I work to share my news. Mae doesn't give me a hard time about leaving, but I can see that behind her eyes she's calculating how many more hours per week she'll need from the rest of the women to cover my work. Their soft questions and sympathy make me uncomfortable, so I escape quickly, heading toward Igor's.

Might as well rip off the bandage all at once. Tomorrow will be here swiftly.

He's in his yard, tinkering with a broken table, shaving down a new piece of wood to match the three legs that are still intact. The smell of oil lanterns and leather and wood shavings and dusty earth assaults my nose, and I grit my teeth, determined to hold back the rush of emotion that threatens to swamp me.

"Came by to see you and your mother said you'd headed off to join the army, like a total idiot," he says, voice gruff.

"Hi to you too," I say sarcastically, draping myself across an ugly chair he's been working on back here for weeks. "Is this chair even uglier than it was a week ago?"

"Careful with that smart mouth once you're in the army," Igor warns. "Commanders don't love it when their soldiers talk back."

I laugh, glad that Igor and I are on the same page—better to joke and poke fun at each other than to admit to feeling anything more right now.

"The women at the laundry said they'd watch my mother, make sure she's well, that she's eating and taking her medicine..." I drift off, but Igor catches my meaning, anyway.

"I'll keep an eye on things too," he confirms. "You don't need to worry about that. We'll make sure she has what she needs."

We both fall silent, and I watch the shadows grow as the sun sinks behind the surrounding buildings.

"You know," Igor starts, "I've met a lot of strong people in my day, between the fighting circuits and the army. But I've never known a stronger-willed brat than you."

"Thanks?" I grin at him. "I think?"

"Oh, it's not entirely a good thing," he retorts, leaning down to root around in his tool box until he finds the coarse piece of sandpaper that he's looking for. He resumes his work on the table leg, but his eyes meet mine over the coarse piece of furniture. "But if anyone's fool enough to take the fight to the Nabbers, and strong enough to stop them and bring home our kids, well, it's you."

I'M STILL TURNING his words over in my head as I pack later that evening. The recruitment center gave me a duffel bag, scuffed and stained with goddess-knows-what, but now I have the beautiful new rucksack that Lee bought me, so I fill that up instead.

The rucksack is open on my bed, and I'm sorting through my meager belongings in Saela and my shared chest of drawers, trying to decide whether to take anything sentimental or to just stick with the essentials, when I hear the door to my bedroom creak open.

Mother stands in the doorframe holding something that sparkles in the lamplight. I start to rise but she gestures for me to stay, and instead of crouching back over my bag I sink all the way down to the floor, wrapping my arms around my knees.

Mother comes over and sinks down beside me. Her eyes are clearer than I've seen them in a long time.

"I have something for you," she says, and tips her hand over mine so that the shining object pours into my open palm.

It's an ancient-looking necklace, with a teardrop-shaped opal pendant set in gold, and a delicate gold chain that's been burnished by age. I've never seen it before, which is odd. I thought I knew every inch of our house, especially everything that might be valuable enough to sell should times demand it.

Carefully picking the pendant up between two fingers, I hold it to the light. It's as if a rainbow has been frozen into ice and then polished and chiseled into a precious stone.

"Where did you get this?" I turn the piece over in my hands, looking for some clue to its origins.

"It's for protection," she says. "It's been in our family for generations, passed down from woman to woman for I don't know how many years."

"Mother." I turn to her. "You need this more than I do. You

should keep it. It'll only get broken, where I'm going. A war is no place for an heirloom."

She looks like she's going to argue so I press the necklace firmly back into her hands, wrapping her fingers closed around it, then lean over to kiss her cheek.

"I'll feel better knowing it's keeping you safe, Mother. You can give it to me when I get back."

Mother nods, and her shoulders slump, the fight going out of her. She stares straight ahead, across the room—across at Saela's empty bed.

My head throbs. "I'm going to find her. I promise."

She makes a small noise, like a trapped bird, but whether she's assenting or contradicting my claim, I can't tell.

I can't believe I'm abandoning her here. Alone. But what else am I supposed to do? I can't just give up on Saela.

It's awful to even admit to myself, but there's some dark part of me that made that impossible calculus. Weighed my mother's needs against Saela's; made myself choose between them.

Saela... she's my sister, but I practically raised her.

She's *mine*. My responsibility.

And she's supposed to have a long life of happiness ahead of her, not whatever misery awaits her in Astreona among the Siphons.

A large part of me wonders whether these might be some of my last moments with my mother, with her illness so bad. Even if I make it back...

No, I can't think that way. There can't be any "if."

"I'll bring her back," I say loudly, not sure which of us I'm trying to reassure more.

CHAPTER SIX

Reporting to the army recruitment base is the closest I've ever been to going inside the castle.

The base is set up right inside the castle's outer walls, taking up half of a massive courtyard within. I step carefully over icy flagstones, all of them smooth and flat from centuries of feet and hooves and paws.

The permanent army building, which probably houses offices or barracks for officers or something, is a squat, single story wooden structure, flush against the inner courtyard wall. In every direction, huge tents have been erected to create more space to process recruits, each of which sports heavy canvas walls that barely move in the frigid dawn breeze. Each is painted with the royal coat of arms —a snarling direwolf on a shield, a sword crossed with a spear behind it.

The sun is barely peeking over the horizon but the courtyard is already swarmed with other recruits, most looking just as lost as I feel, if not more so.

My ears perk up at the mix of accents around me—familiar drawls from here, the royal city of Sturmfrost, but also spiky, harsh accents from the seven other fiefdoms throughout our country of Nocturna, many that I can't quite identify.

I've never left Sturmfrost, but we studied the geography of Nocturna back when I was in school and the part of me that craves adventure put the names of all the other fiefdoms in a bank and locked them away in my mind. The closest two, the other winter-dwelling fiefdoms, are Rabenfrost and Volkenfrost. And the most famous of all is Grunfall, all the way in the south, nestled into the River Sonnstrom. That's where many of the battles have taken place over the years.

I pass a young man and woman who look so alike I wonder if they're siblings; they're both gaping, open-mouthed, at the inner walls of the castle and the turrets beyond.

Most carry the standard army-issue bag, and I shift uncomfortably, very conscious of the fancy rucksack slung over my shoulder. Some look very worn, and are decorated with patches and pins, perhaps passed down from parents or siblings who also served.

A pang goes through my heart thinking of my father's military kit. Mother gave it all back to the army to reuse. Said she couldn't stand the sight of it. I wish I had something of his to carry now.

I find the check-in line and join the end of it, behind a boy who looks like he can't be more than a few years older than Saela, scrawnier even than the kids from Eastern and Southern. His boots are so thin and worn, I can't imagine them lasting more than one day's march.

He senses my eyes on him and turns to scowl at me. I snap my gaze away.

The line inches forward. We finally pass out of the cold air and into one of the long tents, its flaps holding in just enough body heat and cast-off warmth from the smoky outdoor fire pits that a few recruits start shucking off their coats.

I keep mine on. No point getting comfortable, not knowing where we're going, what's waiting for us.

The officer at the desk barely looks at me when I finally reach the front of the line. "Name," he says, tone bored.

"Meryn Cooper."

He runs a finger down the list in the leather-bound book in front of him, then scrawls something next to my name. "Got you. Back into the courtyard, be ready for more instructions soon."

The woman behind me catches my eye at this, looking frightened. I just shrug and move along.

Back outside, snow has started softly falling again, and recruits who must be southerners look increasingly uncomfortable in their thinner jackets. While it's perpetual winter here in Sturmfrost, the fiefdoms closer to the border are perpetual autumn.

I pull my coat tighter around myself, begrudgingly grateful for all the coin Lee spent on my equipment. Without him, I probably would have used the same ancient coat I've been wearing for years, a hand-me-down from my neighbors. I'd be in the same worn-out boots I wear every day, too. The new gear is strange, fancier than I'm used to, but it's also warm, and I have a feeling that'll be all I care about soon.

Stepping to the side of the growing group, I scan my surroundings. Imposing walls loom over the barracks and tents, thick as some of the alleyways back in Eastern. Guards pace back and forth at regular intervals, some staring outward, but others clearly directing their attention inward, at us.

An icy chill that has nothing to do with the weather slides down my spine. They're not just keeping other things out—the walls are keeping us in.

But then, what would I do if I found out only now what we were headed for?

The recruits around me start to quiet, an anticipatory hush, and I turn my attention back to the group. Beyond the milling crowd of young people, I see one of the officers from the tent climbing a wooden platform, waving his arms. He holds a cone-shaped voice amplifier.

When everyone is silent, he puts the amplifier to his mouth and his voice booms out. "Congratulations, recruits! You've been chosen to be part of the Bonding Trials."

A few people near me gasp, and a younger kid to my left mutters, "Bonding? But... that's not..."

The announcer's voice cuts him off. "In ten minutes, we'll begin our hike to Mount Wolfsbane. You'll be setting up camp there tonight, your first introduction to the army. You'll each be given a standard issue tent and kit, and a cadet will accompany each group to show you how to set them up."

Around me, people have covered their faces in their hands; one girl is openly crying.

Guess the rumors about the deaths during the Bonding Trials have reached even the farthest-flung fiefdoms.

"Tomorrow morning at dawn, the Ascent begins, the first of the Trials. You will each be given the greatest privilege our country can give you: the chance to bond with a direwolf. If you do not succeed in bonding..." he pauses, and I hear the words he doesn't say: If you do not succeed in bonding, and also manage not to die. "The rest of you will be brought back here after the Ascent, to board transport to the front lines, where your training will be conducted."

A horn blasts, the sound strange and reverberant in the swirling snow. "Head to the tent along the southern wall to grab your gear, and more supplies if you need them," the officer concludes. "Good luck."

One woman turns to me, wide eyed and terrified. "I hear that a lot of people die during this, that's not what I signed up for." Her voice wavers. "I want to go fight, help at the front—not die on my first day."

I nod my agreement, although at least this isn't the first time I'm hearing the news. But being put forward as a Bonded companion to a direwolf? *Definitely* not what I signed up for.

"Looks like the gear tent is over that way," I gesture. "Should we go before all the best stuff is taken?"

She falls in step with me. "I'm Alessandra," she shares, and I give her my name. "Don't you think they should at least give us training first before... before the Ascent?"

Our conversation is cut off when we reach the flaps of the tent and a team of guards and officers is directing us into different lines.

Those who obviously wear clothes designed to keep them warm are directed into a line to grab their tents and gear packs right away.

Others, the ones with threadbare clothing, worn-out shoes—they go into another line, where I glimpse a picked-over table stacked with some outer garments and shoes.

I'm directed toward the line for tents, and I grab my gear in silence—a tent bag that seems impossibly small to contain something that'll truly protect me from the elements; a pack of rations that looks as hard as rock; a case that rattles, presumably containing my army pot and spoon and firestarter.

The waterskins stink of mildew, and I pass over them, preferring to stick with the one I brought.

Back out in the open air, recruits are being directed out a side gate that was locked earlier. I fall in line, and we skirt around the western edge of the castle. The castle looks different from this side; I realize I've only seen it from one angle before. From my quarter, most of what we can see is the massive outer wall and two huge guard towers with meager windows and crenelated walls.

From this angle, we can see beyond those fortifications; more graceful turrets pierce the sky, some with walkways between them or massive stone buildings connecting them. The biggest towers in the center end in pointed roofs, each flying a flag bearing the royal coat of arms. The castle is made from the same gray stone that most of our city is built from, but each wall looks like it's multiple feet thick.

I smile grimly when I realize what I'm about to see, for the first time:

The famous Bonded City of Sturmfrost.

As we come around the side of the castle, murmurs start as others make the same realization that I have.

In some ways, the area doesn't look all that different from the city I know so well. The same gray and black stone forms the walls and streets and bridges, the same snow swirls down from the gray sky above.

The snow, though... it's as if it disappears before it reaches the ground. Nothing's sticking, no ice, no dirty brown sludge like back home. As if the ground is heated from below, somehow.

And the buildings themselves look strange to me, until I realize —they're clean, all of them, instead of stained with the soot and dirt that surrounds us in our city. The walls all gleam with countless windows, too; glass so smooth and clear it sparkles like crystal in the early morning sunlight.

Our path doesn't take us through the Bonded City, just around the side, but I keep my eyes fixed on the place, drinking in the details as I see them; sculpted stone balconies on buildings, some with fancy ironwork rails, some enclosed entirely in glass like giant lanterns.

Statues casually gracing the facades of buildings—the faces of snarling wolves, of impassive men and women, the twisting bodies of other beasts of the forest.

Buildings that look as big as my entire block, but seem to have only one main door—is it possible they house just a single family?

As I stare, a Bonded family comes out the door, wrapped in plush-looking furs. A man is holding a small daughter, who wiggles and laughs, a clear sound like a bell that I can hear from my spot several streets away. Her curtain of brown hair reminds me of Saela and for a moment I stop, transfixed.

The father tosses the daughter into the air, and she screams with delight. Then they both notice us, and soon the daughter is riding on her father's shoulders as they approach the path we're on, just on the other side of the low fence dividing the Bonded City from the wilderness. They come toward us until they're only a block away.

I stare unblinking at the girl. Her face is round, flushed. She watches us with bright curiosity.

She looks like she's never had to go without a meal, nor fear being snatched by Nabbers.

What makes these people so special, that they get access to all this? Fuck them.

"Move along!" comes a barked order, and I'm shocked into movement again, down the trail as it leads away from the Bonded City and into a dense wall of trees.

THE HOURS PASS SLOWLY. I'm at least familiar with the sensation of being on my feet all day, although it's usually not in the frigid wilderness. But some of the recruits are clearly suffering, either out of shape for a forced march like this one or wearing shoes or clothes that aren't doing them any favors.

At each gap in the trees, we all squint toward Mount Wolfsbane, but it never seems to be getting much closer.

While we were shopping, Lee mentioned multiple times that it was important to have allies for the Ascent. It was one of the pieces of his advice that I figured I'd ignore. I do just fine on my own, most of the time.

Yet now as I watch Alessandra shiver and stumble, I can't help but want to help her. I pull a spare sweater from my bag, and encourage her to layer it under her coat.

"Thanks," she whispers, and smiles at me.

"We have to help each other," I say, hoping that someone will return the same sort of kindness to me should I need it.

By the time we reach the base of the mountain, my feet are aching from my new boots— which, despite their high quality, still need to be properly worn in. At least they're warm and dry, which is a big step up from what many of the other recruits are working with. I sling my packs off my shoulders, rubbing my neck with stiff hands.

It takes me a minute to realize that we weren't the first to arrive.

A group of recruits is already here, tents built. They all seem to know each other, and many are wearing furs just like the ones I saw on the family hours ago, back in the Bonded City.

They're the children of the Bonded, I realize. The ones who want a Bonding Trial to come, so that they can try for their so-called "birthright," test their luck against the mountain and the direwolves atop it.

They didn't have to report to the army recruitment base like the commoners, I guess. Their privileges started before we even arrived.

I make my hands busy with my tent bag, pulling out poles and canvas, but I can't keep my eyes off the Bonded recruits.

They're taller than the rest of us, for the most part—I normally tower over most other women but they all have at least an inch or two on me. Their clothes are more colorful than ours, many dyed in jewel tones deeper than I've seen on any fabric in the city.

Two of the women look like mirror images of each other—they must be twins. They have luminous golden brown skin and large, dark eyes. Their only difference is their glossy black hair—one wears hers in a plait down her back, while the other sports a chic bob. I watch as they flash hand signals back and forth between them, faces expressive. They're communicating entirely with their hands, I realize.

A few others gather around one of the fires, joking and jostling each other, and I realize someone is cooking for them—they've brought *servants* with them.

One of the men at the fire turns to look at us, and catches sight of me watching. His expression turns ugly, leering. It isn't hard to guess what he thinks of us, the common-born recruits.

A big part of me wants to walk over there, pick a fight. But I know I'll need all my energy for the task tomorrow.

I force myself to look away.

Alessandra calls my name. "This spot looks good, don't you think?"

It's flat enough, at least, and partially sheltered from the snow by a thick cover of branches above.

"See how the ground is a little higher here?" Alessandra points. "It should help keep us dry—or drier, at any rate. If the snow turns to rain, it should run off, instead of pooling around our tents."

"Good thinking," I agree, and we struggle to put our tents up, starting with hers.

Once it's up, Alessandra holds a hand out toward me when I grab for mine. "Wait," she says sharply, and then walks around to the side of the tent, cocking her head.

"I think… it looks like both of us could fit in mine."

I quirk an eyebrow at her, amused.

"Not like that!" Alessandra's face turns a deep red, but she keeps talking. "I just mean, it's already so cold, and the sun is only just going down. It's going to be freezing tonight. Both our bodies together will produce more body heat for the tent to trap inside. I just think we might be better off," she finishes weakly.

"No, you're right," I say. Alessandra isn't strong like me, but she's smart, I'm realizing.

As good an ally as any.

After checking each of the tent pegs one last time to make sure everything is secure, Alessandra and I toss our sleeping bundles inside, then head toward a cookfire that a few of the other common-born recruits have built.

When they see us they wave for us to join them, and Alessandra sits eagerly, but I stay standing another moment, studying their faces.

A lean, younger man—boy, really, there's barely a hint of beard around his jaw. A strong-looking woman with a head full of braids. As I turn my gaze to the third, he stands as well, then crosses to my side of the fire, extending a hand.

"I'm Henrey." He's in his mid-twenties with close-cropped light brown hair and serious blue eyes, and he seems thickly muscular underneath his winter clothes. His voice and stance exude confidence.

"Meryn," I say, shaking his hand, "and this is Alessandra. How are you all feeling about this?"

"Excited," Henrey quickly responds, his eyes bright, bouncing on the balls of his feet.

Alessandra and I exchange perplexed glances as she takes a seat.

"Did I hear you wrong?" I ask, glancing around at the others huddled around the fire—do they also think this guy sounds unhinged? "Or are you legitimately thrilled to be gambling your life on a climb up a steep and nearly unsurvivable mountain?"

"I've been training for this since I was a kid," he says seriously. "I'm going to become one of the Bonded."

"This guy is crazy," I say to Alessandra, dropping down beside her. I almost moan, it feels so good to get off my feet.

"Tell her what you said to us, Henrey," says the woman with the braids. "About the paths."

"The recruits from Bonded families will be headed straight up the mountain, racing each other to the top. Killing each other off, even. There are a limited number of wolves and plenty of would-be riders who want to bond. The wolves choose their riders from the group that makes it up first."

His eyes flash back to me.

"But there's a way to survive this," he says, clearly comfortable with an audience. "A longer route, but a safer way up. Once upon a time, everyone used to take it, but with direwolf numbers dwindling, the recruits from Bonded families started to find quicker—and more dangerous—routes. If you don't want to bond, you can take the slow path to the top."

Alessandra leans forward eagerly. "And you know the way?"

"I do," he acknowledges. "But I won't be taking it."

Pitching my voice to carry to the rest of the circle, I jerk my head toward Henrey. "There's a safe route, but he prefers danger, risking his life for some dumb wolf ritual that only the recruits from Bonded families can survive?"

"Who wouldn't, for the chance to change your family's fortune for generations?" Henrey's expression loses its showmanship and I see the real hunger there, just beneath the surface. He glances across the clearing toward the area where the Bonded recruits have gathered, keeping entirely to themselves. "Look at them. Don't you want your siblings, your parents, your children to be able to live like that?"

I press my lips together. Henrey has a point. What kinds of medicines might they have that we don't have access to? Things that could maybe help my mother?

My sister, though—I need to get to the front, to find her. She won't be helped by me rolling around in some fancy furs, playing at being an elite soldier.

And she certainly won't be helped if I die trying to make it through the Ascent tomorrow.

"What if we do get to the top, but none of the direwolves wants to bond with us?" Alessandra looks pensive, then horrified. "Do they… eat us?"

"The wolves only choose riders who want to be chosen," I pipe in, repeating information that Lee gave me when he was prepping me on how to survive this. If I get up there and there are still unbonded wolves, all I need to do is repeat mentally that I don't want to bond and they'll let me go. Or so he says, anyway.

Everyone looks over at me, clearly surprised by my intel.

"I know a royal messenger," I say, offering some of the truth. Seems useless to have some information and hoard it to myself when I have the potential to save other people's lives. "He prepped me on what might happen. The wolves *won't* eat us. If we're not picked, they'll let us go."

"Well, they won't be picking me," says the woman with the braids. "So I'd like to hear about that longer way up, if you don't mind."

We all settle into our makeshift seats, holding our hands and feet closer to the fire to thaw them out, gnawing on our rock hard rations as best we can as we listen to Henrey.

I look around the fire again as he talks, studying each face, taking in the ramshackle hiking gear they're wearing, the exhaustion painting their faces.

Please, let some of these people survive tomorrow's test. I know I'll make it through, but this many lives given in sacrifice to some dumb Trial—it's such a waste.

Far off, somewhere in the mountains, a direwolf howls.

The sound echoes in my ears like a warning.

CHAPTER SEVEN

I t isn't hard to wake before dawn the next morning. I've been lying awake for at least an hour before I start to hear others rustling in their tents.

Alessandra wasn't wrong, I'm sure the warmth of us both together was better than apart, but it was still damn cold, and no matter how many times I shifted around, I couldn't get away from the rocks and roots that stuck into my back at jagged angles.

So much for the tough Alleycat. Defeated by a tree root and some cold air.

I kick off my bedroll and gently shake Alessandra's shoulder. Somehow, she managed to fall into a deeper sleep at some point in the night, evident in the high-pitched snore she's been making ever since.

Her eyes snap open right away, and I can tell by the way they dart back and forth that she's having trouble remembering where we are, what's coming next.

"It's time to get ready for the Ascent," I say. "Rise and shine."

Outside, everyone is stirring. Henrey breaks down his tent with cool efficiency. He catches my eye and gives me a nod.

Our packs on our backs, we struggle over to the center of the clearing, where a huge group of recruits is massing. It's hard to tell because I can't see the full group, but between the commoners and the recruits from Bonded families, it seems like there are hundreds of us, maybe as many as a thousand.

Everyone is shivering as the pale dawn light seeps through the fir needles to light up exhausted faces, but it's hard to miss how the Bonded recruits are just so obviously better prepared.

Those twin sisters I noticed are pink-cheeked from the cold, but they're talking fast back and forth with their hands, one laughing at the other's communication, much more alert and cheerful than anyone near me.

"I'd be laughing too if I had some of those thick furs to keep me warm," Alessandra says in a low tone that only I can hear.

I grimace back at her. "Or if I'd been training for this?"

The rich recruits all sport shiny-looking crampons on their boots and carry well-oiled coils of rope over a shoulder. Many of them sling deadly looking pickaxes back and forth, the tools clearly familiar in their hands, warming up their muscles for the climb ahead.

Thankfully, Lee knew enough to get me well kitted out. The equipment we found in Sturmfrost isn't quite as nice as this stuff, but it seems significantly more sturdy than what the army is providing for everyone else.

There are a few clusters of crooked camp tables set up around the front of our gathering with some dingy-looking climbing gear for anyone who hasn't brought the equipment they need. Everyone's hanging back, though, so they must have been instructed not to grab anything yet.

I stoop to pull my own crampons out of my bag, tightening them on my boots one at a time before slinging my pack back over my shoulders. If the Bonded recruits have theirs on already, it must make sense to put them on now.

Watching around me out of the corner of my eye, I make a few adjustments to the straps of my bags, making sure the weight is distributed evenly.

Groups of recruits are hovering as close as they can get to the tables of equipment, trying to identify what to grab when the moment comes. Others squat to adjust their own gear, reshuffling things in their packs and chattering anxiously.

A loud horn sounds and everyone goes silent, looking around for the source—but it's plain to see. At the base of the mountain are two Bonded riders astride their massive direwolves, towering above the crowd. One is a woman, and the other is…

The officer I saw back in the Central Market, the one who was dragging that deserter behind him. The dead-eyed psychotic killing machine.

He's holding one of those cone-shaped voice amplifiers and is absolutely glowering down at the rest of us from astride his hulking black direwolf.

I'm able to get a better look at him, now that I'm not distracted by the way his direwolf is tearing a human being apart.

He's somehow taller than I remembered and broad shouldered, with light brown skin and dark hair that is still surprisingly messy for someone so obviously controlled. He's wearing riding leathers and fur, but even from a distance I can see the bulky muscles of his arms, strong enough that he could undoubtedly kill a man with his bare hands.

Probably has, too.

At that thought, my gaze is drawn again to the kill tattoos littering his hands and neck.

Yep, definitely a murderous monster.

His face is viciously beautiful, with thick eyebrows and full lips that are pulled into a sneer as he looks over the crowd. It's unfair how all the Bonded are so… hot. Even assholes like this guy. He raises the amplifier to his mouth.

"Good morning. For those of you who don't know me—" At this, his gaze trails over the ragged commoner side of the crowd. The disdain in his voice makes it clear what he thinks of anyone who doesn't automatically know him. "I am Stark Therion, Alpha of the Daemos pack and one of the instructors during this year's Bonding Trials."

It's clear that we're supposed to have an impressed reaction to that, based on the excited titters that pass through the Bonded part of the crowd.

Good for you, I want to snark back at him, bristling at his imperious tone. *And I'm the Queen of Shit Mountain*.

He shifts on his wolf as he talks, his movements sharp, precise. "Being Bonded requires great sacrifice. The direwolves have lived in this range since before our history started. They've always been our allies, but before they choose to bond, they need proof that the human they've chosen is... *worthy*."

His eyes sweep over the crowd. I get the sense that he himself is weighing our value and finding us distinctly unworthy.

"As is tradition, of course, any army recruit gets the chance to bond." His tone nakedly betrays his disbelief that anyone but the Bonded progeny will be found worthy. "There are usually about a hundred wolves ready to bond and there are at least a thousand of you. And the wolves will choose from the first who make it to the peak. So. Don't dawdle."

He grins cruelly, exposing his teeth, looking as wolfish as the beast he sits astride.

"Do what you need to do to get to the top first."

Someone from the Bonded family side of the clearing whoops, and a few guys around him snicker. Alessandra and I exchange a loaded look. This man is basically telling us to throw each other off the mountain on our way up.

Good thing she and I both plan to take the long way up, hopefully staying well out of the way of any conflict.

The crowd has begun murmuring, other common-born recruits clearly coming to the same conclusions Alessandra and I have. The man silences us with a shrill whistle, magnified tenfold by his amplifier.

"*Everyone* must attempt the Ascent, as requested by the direwolves. Beta Egith," he gestures to the woman on the wolf next to him, "and I will be here to ensure that you go up that mountain. Our wolves have been away from the front for days and are bored. It would be entertaining for them, and for us, to chase you. You do not want us to do that. You especially don't want us to catch you."

The threat is bone-chilling. We go up the mountain on our own or this living villain and his hell hound will hunt us down and probably kill us.

"Remember! The direwolves are not dumb beasts. They are dangerous, sentient beings and they deserve your utmost respect."

He hands the amplifier to the woman he referred to as Beta Egith and she raises a hand.

"Move out, recruits! Let the Ascent begin."

Immediately, chaos erupts. The group from the Bonded City takes off like a shot. Meanwhile, dozens of common-born recruits have descended on the gear tables. Some grab the piece or two they've been eyeing and then clear out, but others attempt to sort through the gear, and fights erupt over the tables as two or three people try to grab the same item.

Somewhere by one of the tables, a pained scream rings out, then is suddenly muffled.

I take a steadying breath as the bleak truth of this day is brought into sharp relief: people are going to die.

Alessandra looks at me in panic and then starts to move, trying to push her way through the crowd. I grab her arm.

"Stop, Alessandra," I say. "Think for a minute. We should stick together, look out for each other." Her skin is already frosty below her flimsy coat.

"Absolutely not," she says with a sharp edge. I fall back at the tone. Her voice is full of fear and something darker, something like despair. "I can't put my life in anyone's hands, not even yours."

She's gone before I can say anything else. I stare at the spot where she disappeared in shock. Bodies swarm after her, others seeking that slower path up that Henrey told us about.

"Goddess keep you," I mutter, then turn away, looking to find the best path forward for myself, away from the melee of bodies.

Skirting around the edges of the clearing, I watch as the flow of recruits noticeably splits in two, with the tall and handsomely outfitted headed straight for a rocky incline that tips sharply up and up, and many others headed for what looks like a path of to the left.

I press back against a tree, waiting for the way to clear a bit more. I'm not trying to race, I don't care about getting to the top fast.

I *do* care about staying out of the way of some idiot who's so afraid of what's coming that they accidentally swing an ice pick into my face.

Or maybe not so accidentally. To my left, a sharp wail catches my attention, followed by a choked sound.

It's a sound I've heard a few times before, in the fighting ring—that sound when someone gives up hope after an especially brutal hit. And it sounded like a woman.

Shit.

Against my better judgment, I leave the safety of my cover and turn back, checking to find the source.

My eyes dart between the running bodies, searching for a breath or two before I see them. It's the beautiful girl from last night, one of the twins from a Bonded family, the one with the longer hair. She's down on the ground, and there's a dark-haired man atop her, also one of the wealthy Bonded.

He's holding her down by her throat.

I see white, and I'm running toward her without thinking, my body instinctively preparing to fight, muscles tensing.

"I'm going to enjoy this, you little bitch," the man's voice says as I near, though his back is still turned to me. The woman is wheezing below him as he holds her down with one hand, strangling her with the other. "You think you're too good for me? That'll be the last thing you think."

The last word is barely out of his mouth when my foot slams into his face.

I forgot about the metal crampons on my boot—they tear into the meat of his cheek viciously, gouging a hole and ripping the top of his ear. The impact jolts him to the side and he falls to the ground, freeing the woman.

"What the *fuck*," he snarls, turning to face me as he rises. His gorgeous face is wrecked, his cheek like pulped meat. I'd say that I feel bad about it, but I really, really don't.

He reaches under his furs for what I can only assume is his knife.

Before he can grab it, my other foot is already flying around, and the toe of my boot connects with his groin.

His strangled wheeze is the most satisfying thing I've heard all year.

Letting my momentum carry me forward, I slam him down to the ground, holding him firmly down with both knees and tucking my own small dagger, always at the ready in my sleeve, neatly against his neck.

"When you get up, you better fucking run." My voice is calm, almost pleasant. "Or I'll gut you."

I hop off of him and back up, eager to check on the woman to be sure she's not seriously injured, but keeping an eye on him in case he still wants to try something.

He's gotten the message, though. He scrambles away, blood dripping out the wound in his cheek, dotting the neck of his furs in a thick, viscous crimson.

"You cunts better hope you fucking die during the Ascent. Because if you make it out, I'll be waiting, and my wolf will tear you to pieces."

Big words, from someone who was just in the dirt. I wait to be sure he's actually gone before turning around to the woman behind me.

She's pulled herself up and is brushing the dirt and slush off her clothing, breathing heavily.

Our eyes meet. "Thank you," she breathes. At that moment, her sister appears by her side.

"*Izabel.*"

The women clasp each other in a brief hug before breaking apart so that their hands have space to move rapidly in a pattern of communication I can't hope to follow. My eyes bounce back and forth between them, dizzied by the speed of their communication.

Cutting herself off mid-gesture, the second woman turns to me. Up close, she's the mirror image of her twin—same golden skin, same dark eyes—and the only difference is her chin-length hair.

"I'm sorry, you don't have a clue what we're saying. And you saved her. My sister." She gulps a breath. "I'm sorry. I'm Venna.

73

That's Izabel," she waves toward her sister. "I'm hard of hearing so it's easier sometimes to sign."

Izabel smiles at me, gratitude in her eyes.

"It was no problem," I assure them. "I have zero tolerance for people who fight dirty, and can sense a rat from a league away. I'm glad you're okay."

Izabel has started to stalk back and forth, staring off at where the man disappeared into the rush of bodies. Her eyes are ablaze with fury. "*That* rat's name is Jonah. He's been after me ever since I turned him down a fortnight ago. Of course he'd try to attack me here, not even properly on the mountain. That fucker."

Her hands flash again toward her sister, and Venna signs back at her as she says aloud, "I know, I thought you were right behind me." Izabel winces.

I uncork my waterskin and take a quick drink, swishing it around in my mouth while I decide what to do next. The crowd is thinning, so it might be my cue to head to that slower path, perhaps keeping to the rear where I can stay out of the path of assholes—or help anyone else who has fallen behind. I check the straps of my packs, re-sheath my dagger, and then turn to say goodbye to the two women.

Izabel and Venna have been conversing again, and as I open my mouth to speak, Izabel spins toward me and says, "Right then. You'll join us on the Ascent."

Huh.

"That's really not—"

Venna and Izabel exchange a loaded look "You saved Izabel's life," Venna says simply. "So now we'll save yours."

"I'll be fine," I protest. "I'm going to take the slow path. I'm not interested in Bonding."

Izabel shakes her head sharply. "It's not any safer, not really. Especially if you're alone. People are terrified and cold and hungry, they lash out at each other. It's a bloodbath. Plus there are the pricks like Jonah who pick off a few recruits here and there just to see if they have any good gear to grab."

I purse my lips, looking toward the ever-thinning crowds.

Venna clasps her hand around my forearm before I can continue to protest. "There's safety in numbers for this climb, trust us. I know you can protect yourself, I saw how fucking amazing you were just now when Jonah jumped Izabel. But you need someone watching your back."

Izabel nods emphatically.

I shift back and forth, my boots gripping the ground awkwardly with the metal crampons. It's possible they're right.

After all, I wanted to follow Lee's advice to go up the mountain with an ally, and I can tell they'd be good ones. Their packs of gear look new and sleek, and they're both my height or maybe even a touch taller, with broad shoulders and strong-looking legs. The way they move betrays years of training, like dancers... or pit fighters.

Fuck, Izabel was on the ground under her wannabe murderer just moments ago, and she's already back in a fighting stance, ready to get moving.

But following them would go against my entire plan. The wind picks up in a harsh whistle, whipping across my face, and I turn my head to brace myself against it. I notice the two Bonded riders are still waiting at the base of the mountain, watching and waiting as the recruits clear out.

With a jolt, I realize that Stark Therion is staring me down, his gaze nothing short of malevolent. His feral black direwolf bares its teeth, and while I can't hear it from this distance, I can tell that it's growling at me.

A thought hits me with absolute certainty: if I take the slow path, that wicked man and his wicked wolf are going to hunt me down. The only way to survive is to go where they can't follow.

I cock my head at the twins. "Well. After you, then."

WE'VE BARELY BEGUN and we're already scrambling over gigantic slabs of rock, using tree trunks and branches to leverage our way over massive boulders covered with sheets of ice and snow. The path, if it can be called a path, doesn't wind back and forth the way any sane person would make their way up a mountain.

Instead, it seems to go straight up.

We're already behind; signs of boots and crampons and poles and picks mark the way. Big chunks are ripped out of a tree trunk at one of our resting points, and we all gaze at the scars on the wood, silent.

In less than half an hour, any semblance of a path disappears, replaced by a wall of mottled gray stone speckled in ice.

Venna and Izabel are mirror images of each other as they both drop their packs on the ground and begin removing gear—harnesses, ropes, and a pair of small pickaxes each.

"Well, fuck," I say, watching. "I brought some rope, but I didn't expect to need a harness or ice picks…" Lee probably didn't even think of it, since there was no reason I'd be going up the mountain the hard way.

Venna's mouth quirks in a smile. She roots around in her pack, then unearths another harness, holding it out. "No problem."

"We brought an extra," Izabel explains. "We've heard that, well… sometimes the fastest way to beat someone up the mountain is to mess with their gear."

I accept the harness cautiously. "But the picks?"

"We'll trade off," Izabel assures me. "Venna can start without. She's like a spider when she climbs. Her free climbing is insane. You'll see."

Venna removes a pair of supple leather gloves from her pack, pulling them on like a second skin.

"If you're sure…" I grab the axes from Izabel's outstretched hands, tie them to my pack where I can reach them if need be, then look dubiously up at the slabs of rock and jagged boulders above, punctuated by patches of slick black ice. "I just don't see how anyone could climb that, equipment be damned."

Venna laughs, the sound surprising in the bleak landscape. "It's honestly not even the hardest part of this. The hardest part is going to be—"

Something large falls from above, dangerously close to us, and we all flinch to the left. I hear a gruesome wet thud.

A body.

The broken remains of a person are less than three feet away from us. There's something warm and damp on my face, and I realize that in the impact, blood from the person's wounds splattered up in a grisly fountain, landing on me and Venna's furs, and painting Izabel in lines of red.

We all stare.

The corpse looks almost fake, the angles of its body twisted and unnatural, like a statue of a person made by a being that's never seen one of us before. Blood oozes from a massive wound in his chest, and seeps out from his head and mouth, which is still open in a final scream.

I recognize him, I realize. He's the boy from the fire last night, the one who was too young to even grow in his beard.

"That's the hard part," Izabel finishes Venna's sentence finally. "The bodies. Watching out for the bodies."

CHAPTER EIGHT

F ar above us, we hear a scream, then yelling and the sounds of something crashing down further to our right.

I've seen violence. I've *dealt* violence. For sport, for money, sometimes for my own satisfaction.

But this is unlike anything I've ever experienced. This—*this*—is the noble tradition that our Bonded warriors ceremonially endure?

This is what those entitled Bonded families willingly send their loved ones to do each time there's a Bonding Trial?

Another scream echoes off the rock and ice. Then another. And another.

I grit my teeth and begin to climb.

Izabel forges our path, to start. "We'll trade off who's scouting and who brings up the rear," she explains casually as we get going. "Both have their challenges. Although to be frank," she says, slowly and steadily moving up the rock face, "Venna is definitely the better climber of the two of us. I mean, look at her."

We both glance down at Venna. Her special climbing gloves allow her to find handholds in the smallest indents in the rock. Clambering up after us, she looks almost inhuman in her grace.

"She'll lead when we get to the trickier parts."

Trickier parts? I think, already breathing heavily from the exertion of the climb. *Great.*

"But for a climb like this," continues Izabel, "it's important for the leader to stay fresh, focused. So it's good to switch off. So that we can take turns scouting the terrain and also, um, listening for hazards." Another scream echoes off the mountain, far to our left, as if to punctuate her words.

We climb on in grim silence.

The falling bodies slow as the morning wears on, presumably as groups spread out and focus on surviving their own climb. Still, every so often another echoing scream comes, and we all press ourselves as tight as we can against the craggy, icy rock.

A couple times I feel them passing near us, their fall creating an eerie wind. One time, the guy was still alive, falling close enough to touch, and his hand knocked into me briefly as he fell, too fast for me to think to do anything.

I wouldn't have made it even this far without Venna's tips as she climbs, shouted up from below.

"Grab that left handhold, watch for the ice on the right." Every time she calls up an instruction, I follow it carefully, not wanting to take any chances. Venna seems to have a preternatural sense for the smoothest path upward. My respect for her grows.

After the second time that Izabel pauses to survey the route above her, starting again only to lead us at a different angle than before, I call up to her.

"How do you know the way up? It all looks the same to me."

She pauses in her ascent, wedging an arm against the rock ledge she's currently climbing. Her feet are balanced on a small outcropping, barely wide enough to provide a place to rest. With her other hand, she grabs for her waterskin, taking a few swift gulps.

"They teach us all," she says. "The ones from Bonded families, I mean. Our families want us to make it to the top. We've been training for this a long time, hearing stories and directions and advice…"

Her voice sounds exhausted. Below us, Venna's also paused to survey the area.

"We also have our own tricks, each family," Izabel continues. "Tips on which routes to try. Landmarks to look out for. Sharing information with anyone outside of the family is... not encouraged."

"Well, I'm lucky then, to have you two as guides," I say lightly, hauling myself up to where she is so that our faces are level. I carefully balance my feet and let myself rest for a few blessed moments.

The longer I stay motionless, the more my own sweat cools against my skin, making my clothes cling to me like ice.

"Shall we?" I joke, as if we are taking a nice evening stroll. Izabel laughs, and shifts her weight—and the ledge her feet were resting on gives way, tumbling down toward Venna.

I shout a warning, though Venna's a step ahead. She's secured herself against the rock, one arm over her head to prevent any head injury.

Shards of rock rain down on Venna's arm and back, but she has a thick coat on, and none of the pieces are that large. She should be fine.

Izabel needs my help though, and fast. She's hanging on by the left arm she had wedged into a space between the rocks and is using her right hand to reach for the next handhold, something to get her to a more secure position, but all she's grabbing is air.

"Hang on, just hang on," I say and spring into motion.

There's a larger resting spot just above us, and I quickly calculate the least dangerous route up, and then haul myself up to it as fast as my muscles will take me.

"Rope, above you," I call, looping one end around a stubborn tree that has somehow managed to survive up here, then tossing the other down to Izabel.

It's lucky that she insisted we all put harnesses on from the start, even before we get to the ice climbing where it'll be really necessary. Izabel's face is white and her hands are shaking, but that doesn't stop her from quickly and efficiently pushing the rope through the loops of her harness.

Bracing my feet against the tree trunk and an outcropping of the rock, I haul Izabel toward me far enough that she eventually finds another grip and can climb up to me on her own.

There's barely room for the two of us on the ledge, and the wind is howling stronger, slicing through every small opening in my clothing, but as Izabel and I pant and grin at each other, I find I've never loved a slab of rock more.

Moments later, Venna's head pops up over the ledge.

"Should we move on, give Venna a chance to rest on this beautiful, beautiful rock?" My words come out labored as I struggle to regain my breath.

Izabel nods, and I watch as she visibly shakes off the near-fatal experience. She unwraps the rope still securing her to the tree and holds it back out to me. I tie it back at the top of my pack, in easy arm's reach, as she begins to make her way further up.

Only moments later, though, she stops again, sooner than I expect based on the pace she's been setting.

I pull myself up next to her. "What is it?"

Izabel's brow is furrowed as she takes in the dangerous mix of ice and gravel and sheer rock face above us. "This route should have avoided terrain like this. It must have shifted since the last time our family brought information back." She stares at the treacherous path above her.

I scan the ridge, looking for other options.

"Maybe——" she starts, looking to the left, her body poised for movement but then Venna, just below us, calls out:

"Wait, not that way."

Izabel pales.

"What is it?"

"Venna saw something I didn't at first," Izabel says. "See the way the light is hitting that patch of ice? It's not thick enough there ——wouldn't take much for it to all come loose."

Venna scrambles up past us and carves a route to the right, putting her superior climbing skills and instincts to use, taking the lead for a while. We follow after, carefully using the same hand and footholds that she did as we go.

Lee was right. I never would have made it half this far without allies, I think as I finally pull myself up to a larger shelf in the mountain's face. Thank the goddess for that beautiful man and his advice.

When I behold the sheer icy wall in front of me, I shudder.

I'm not sure how much farther I'll make it, period.

We all take a short rest, doing our best to ignore the mangled body of a climber that came before us toward the other edge of the frozen platform. I shove some of the hard-packed army ration in my mouth, and gratefully accept when Venna offers me something from her pack that looks like a meat jerky.

"Thanks," I say, heartfelt.

She nods, efficient, then stands and holds out a hand. "Ice pick?"

"She's going to show you how to use the picks," Izabel clarifies for me. "And also good technique for this next section, now that we're going to be climbing mostly ice."

They spend easily twenty minutes showing me how to best use my crampons to lock a foot in before removing my ice pick; how to test the ice's stability before giving it my weight. We bring out our rope and the twins show me what knots to use on my harness.

Sure hope they're right about the knots. I can too easily imagine the harness giving way, the fast slip through icy air...

Acid fills the back of my mouth.

Ten minutes into our slow crawl up the face of the icy wall, and it happens.

I'm removing my right pick from the ice when my feet slip, and my stomach does a sickening flip as the world falls out from under me.

I'm in the air, out of reach of anything solid, for forever and no time at all, when my harness catches me, and my momentum swings the rope I'm on like a pendulum and slams me against the ice.

It takes all of my training from Igor to keep my cool and not let go of the precious ice picks.

My left shoulder screams from the impact and I lick my lips and taste blood—my nose must have smashed against the ice wall too.

I'm still attached, though. Still alive.

It takes me a few more breaths to tune into the advice Izabel is yelling down to me, properly reattach my crampons to the ice, leverage my picks, get back into the rhythm of climbing at least for a few feet to reduce the pull on Izabel and Venna's harnesses—and the danger that the ice they're clinging to for dear life might simply crumble from the pressure.

We shake off the panic and start to climb once more.

After the adrenaline leaves my body, exhaustion replaces it. I'm used to hard labor, used to being on my feet constantly, straining my muscles at work and training all day just to use them all night.

But even though it gets frigid down in the city, it's nothing like the temperatures here. The ice wall bounces the wind back onto us, so that it lashes into us from all directions. My entire body is compressed by the tension of trying to retain heat, maintain control of what I'm doing, not let a shiver or a moment of tiredness turn into the fall that actually kills me this time.

Thinking about Saela helps me keep focus. Lee, too. *Find my sister, return to him.* It repeats over and over in my head like a religious chant.

I'm not sure how much time has passed when we finally crest the seemingly endless sheet of ice, pulling ourselves up onto a rock ledge that's blessedly big enough to sit down on, even lie down on, without fear of tumbling off.

"Thank you," I say, wincing at the helplessness I feel at the words. They should be so much bigger.

Izabel squints at me. "You saved me, too, remember? So we're even."

I bark a laugh. "Fair enough!"

Venna smirks. "You know, you're heavier than you look," she says and snorts.

"It's all the muscle," I say boastfully.

"Yeah, that and the humility," Izabel retorts.

It's surprisingly nice to laugh. Weird, too, to be laughing with women my own age. I stopped spending much time with other girls when I dropped out of school at twelve. In the years since, all the friends I once had have grown into soldiers, or mothers.

In a different life, I could've had friends like Izabel and Venna. It's a bittersweet thought. I'll likely never see them again once they bond.

Venna and Izabel are taking turns vigorously rubbing heat back into each other's hands through their climbing gloves when I hear the sound of voices.

"Heads up," I say sharply to them, and they both pivot, staring at me.

I gesture toward the other side of the ledge, where another group of climbers is just cresting. "We have company."

The three of us are all thinking about the bodies that lie shattered at the base of the mountain, or broken and bloodied on the rocks on the way down. I don't have to look the sisters in the eyes to know that. Our positions grow subtly defensive, but I at least try to keep a casual stance.

No sense inviting trouble if these people don't want to cause any.

"Hey there," calls the woman who seems to be their leader.

She lets out some slack in the rope attaching their harnesses together, and edges over toward us—there's a part in the middle where the ledge gets thin, enough to make anyone nervous, before it widens out again.

"Good to see some others have made it this far. Pretty brutal down there." Her tone is friendly, but it has a little edge to it that I don't like. I can tell instantly that she's commoner-born, too. Her clothes and gear are worn.

"How have things been going for you all?" Izabel asks, her casual tone belied by subtle movement as her hand slowly inches toward one of her ice picks, where it's been re-strapped to her pack.

"Nice-looking picks you guys are carrying," the woman says, and all of our hands go toward weapons as she reaches around to her own back for a pick. She holds it out in front of her with both hands like an offering, and the tension comes back down a notch. "Problem on our side is, we didn't pack any extra. And as you can see, this one's not worth the weight at this point."

The pick has snapped in two, so that the handle is being held on just by a few leather straps.

She tosses it down at her feet. "You guys seem to have more than enough... care to share?"

"Not happening," I say simply. I follow the track of the woman's gaze down toward Izabel's pack—she was still tightening straps, readjusting weight—so I'm ready to intercept when the woman lunges in suddenly, grabbing for Izabel's equipment.

Her two companions, both lanky men who look like they haven't eaten enough in years, were waiting for her movement as well. In moments they're also on our side of the ledge, and then it's too tight of quarters to see what everyone else is doing.

My brain flips through every tip Igor has ever given me about fighting in dangerous terrain, in small spaces, anything. I dodge in front of the woman and get a few punches in, only to realize she's been letting me hit her.

It's a distraction, so I don't see that she's reached for the knife strapped to her leg.

I dodge to the side—into the mountain, not toward the drop—and narrowly miss being stabbed in the side. She's fast. She feints like she's about to stand, and then instead brings her knee up into my nose.

Dammit, that just stopped bleeding from the hit against the ice wall. I meet her knife with my own, pushing her back, back.

I don't know what the endgame is here, because as much as I hate the idea of letting these idiots get away with taking anything from us, I don't want them dead. The woman ducks down and shoots forward, and I brace for impact, knowing I don't have room to get out of her way.

But the impact never comes.

Her progress is suddenly halted, like she's a child's toy on a string, snapped back. And then I see what's happened.

One of her friends has slipped backwards, off the ledge entirely. The other is hanging on with just his pick to the edge of the cliff of ice.

The slack rope tightens, pulled down, down by the weight of her friend.

It yanks the woman backward, back into the man hanging on to the ledge for dear life.

He yowls once with surprise.

And then they're gone, all three slipped over the side.

Izabel, Venna, and I look on in silence for a minute.

Eventually, I walk over to the edge and unhook the man's ice pick from where he left it, jolted from his grip by the weight of the woman slamming into him.

"At least now we don't have to switch off," I say darkly, and tuck the pick into my belt.

But even as I try to sound confident, I can't hide the way my hands are shaking.

Three people are dead, just like that—and it could've just as easily been me.

CHAPTER NINE

The rest of the climb up the ice wall is sheer torture.

My face throbs from the multiple beatings it's taken today.

My muscles are screaming at me; Venna explained before we got going again that I was probably depending too much on my strong upper body muscles, when experienced climbers draw strength from their legs and their core.

How helpful of her to share that tidbit now.

It's probably a few more hours by the time we finally reach another resting place, but it feels like it's been days. We've reached the ridgeline of the mountain, though not the true peak—that I can still see rising above us, shrouded in cloud.

The ridge is made of more than just ice, though, thankfully—a few scattered trees offer some slight shelter from the relentless wind, and we crouch next to one, inhaling pieces of hardtack ration and a few more strips of jerky from Izabel's pack. We all carefully gauge how much water is still in our skins, then drink just a bit.

Venna and Izabel confer for a few minutes, defaulting to signing with their hands, while I let my eyes close, trying to take a few minutes of rest. When I open them, Izabel is biting her lip, and Venna's staring down at the ground.

I crook an eyebrow at Izabel and she sighs. "It's one thing to know that this was going to be difficult. That we would have to watch people fall to their deaths, to know just *how many* people would be sacrificed on this climb. It's... it's different, knowing the numbers, and..."

I clear my throat. "Actually seeing people die?" She's put into words exactly what I've been feeling.

Izabel nods and swallows, and we both stare into the distance.

I wonder how much more death Izabel and Venna will have to see—have to *deal*—during their quest to become Bonded.

If I weren't so cold, and tired, and desperate for this to be done, I would probably find the view beautiful. We're high enough that we can see the Bonded City's spires, the castle rising up above the sprawl of roofs around it. The forest we trekked through yesterday looks like a long black smudge on the landscape; beyond the castle, more smears of black must be trees and fallow soil, broken up occasionally by the thin lines that I realize are the king's roads south and west and east, to other fiefdoms.

The mountain we're climbing is by far the tallest in the range, but there are other mountains stretching out to either side of us, each draped in sparkling snow and ice, starkly beautiful against the clouds.

Izabel's hands are dancing again, responding to something Venna tells her. "She's right of course," Izabel says, halfway to herself.

"Like usual," Venna retorts. I raise my eyebrows in inquiry.

"This is what it means to become Bonded," Izabel continues. "We have to harden ourselves, have to be strong. Only the strongest deserve the Bond."

"You guys are a special kind of crazy, you know that, right?" I shake my head, unable to fathom how someone would walk into this hellscape with eyes wide open. "I meant what I told you, I don't want to bond. I just want to save my sister."

The words slip out of my mouth in my exhaustion. I hadn't

shared anything with them yet about why I'm actually here. Hadn't wanted to open the wound.

"Your sister?" Venna asks, hesitant.

I lean back into the tree, reassured by the press of the rough pine bark through my coat. "Saela." The shape of her name scrapes against my throat and I realize I haven't said it aloud since I left the commoner side of the city—only two days ago, though it seems like a lifetime. "She was taken. The Nabbers. That's why I'm here, so I can save her."

Venna and Izabel are frowning in confusion. "Nabbers?"

I huff out a laugh, my breath swirling up in ribbons of steam. "Of course you wouldn't have the Nabbers in the Bonded City. Of course."

As I tell the two of them about the disappearances in Eastern and all around Sturmfrost, about the horror of finding my sister gone in the night, snatched right under my nose, their faces grow grave.

"That's horrible, Meryn," Izabel says. "I'm sorry it's happening. And that we didn't know about it. I can't imagine what I'd do if my sister was taken. We do everything together. Always have, ever since the day we came out of the womb, and—"

Izabel is cut off by a punch in the shoulder from Venna, and she rolls her eyes.

"Sorry. Everyone says I over share."

"Everyone is right," Venna says, laughing quietly.

Movement catches my eye to the right of us, and I spot another group cresting the ridge, heading away from us—looks like they plan to dip down into the valley between us and the peak and then climb straight up.

I recognize one of them. Henrey, the commoner who was determined to forge a bond. He pauses to help someone from his group get down a tricky drop.

It's nice to see he's made it this far. I find myself rooting for him to get to the end.

Venna stands to stretch, and then clearly sees something she doesn't like in the sky. She turns to us, face troubled. "Storm's coming," she says flatly. "Coming fast. We need to get moving. Now."

Instead of following Henrey's group down into the valley, we move along the ridgeline, which eventually curves back toward the climb to the peak ahead of us. A less direct route, but for at least a little while we're on our feet instead of hanging off a sheet of ice, so I'm not complaining.

We go faster than caution would dictate, but there's panic underlying Venna's swift movements, and I've already grown to respect her instincts enough that I know whatever is coming is an even worse danger.

Snow and ice and gravel crunch underfoot, our crampons still helping us not to slip but also kicking up clods of dirty ice as we half-walk, half-run through the rocks and trees.

Inevitably, the trail turns upward again, at first just a rocky barren slope that we scramble up using our hands, and then the patches of sheer ice become more and more frequent, until we once more take out our ropes and fumble to tie ourselves together.

On this next climb, the storm hits us.

It's brutal in its speed, the air turning thick and white with snow in mere moments. Izabel taught me signals that she and her sister use when climbing in adverse conditions—tugs on the safety rope, different numbers to signify different messages, for when the snow is too thick for us to hear each other.

We advance slowly, our pace at a crawl.

Several times I wonder if I should speed up, try to catch Izabel, who's leading once more, and convince her to move more quickly— this slow pace is hell on my body, and I'm honestly not sure how much longer I can keep it up.

Each time I get close to attempting it, though, another scream of a falling climber filters through the storm, coming from nowhere and everywhere, the sounds scattered and distorted by the swirl of the blizzard.

I don't know if it's Izabel's knowledge of the route to take or just sheer luck that saves us the same fate. And I don't want to push it.

Time crawls.

Ice crystals blur my eyes, and I blink over and over to clear them, and to keep my eyelashes from freezing together.

Every so often—three tugs on the rope from above. Izabel is still okay. I give three to confirm that I'm here, I'm alive, I'm still climbing. Venna does the same.

We climb.

My whole body is pain. Every single muscle aches. I ignore it.

I know it's dangerous to lose focus, but my mind keeps slipping out of this place and into memory.

Training with Igor. Reading to Saela. Cooking dinner for my mother, mixing her medicine in with her food on the days she refuses to take it straight. Kissing Lee. Lee's strong, bare body pressed against mine. Warmth. Anything but icy pain.

Then, finally, four tugs: Izabel can see the top.

The line goes slack from above a few minutes later—Izabel has reached a summit and tied off her part of the rope, which now gathers more slack as I continue my climb. I heave myself up, scramble back from the edge, and Venna follows close behind me.

I can't tell if we're at the top—the fall of the snow is too thick to see much at all. So when a shape comes toward me through the snow, at first I think it's one of the twins.

A huge, meaty hand grabs me by the throat, and then another pair of arms comes from behind to wrap around my front, trapping me in place.

It's Jonah, I realize as I fight for air. That bastard from this morning. The one who wanted to kill Izabel.

That asshole was probably waiting up here, hoping and praying he'd have a chance to get his revenge.

"Gutter slut," Jonah growls, his hand tightening on my throat, and I see spots of white. "You're just a nasty common whore."

My vision starts to dim around the edges. Use it, Igor's voice says in my head, and I slump against the man behind me, faking defeat. Just like in the ring.

Jonah's not so easily fooled. His hand is still a vise on my throat, but the man behind me loosens his grip, just enough to give me room to move again. I slam an elbow back into his gut, and his grunt of pain distracts Jonah enough that I can rip myself from his grasp, slamming my head backward, hearing the satisfying crunch of a nose breaking.

The only time today it's not *my* nose breaking, I think wryly, already moving again, sinking into one of Igor's combinations, one he designed specially for the fights where I take on two opponents at once.

My limbs are a blur of movement, reserves of energy coming from somewhere I didn't know I had. I revel in the satisfying crunch of the metal spikes on my feet into someone's leg, dancing back.

A slash of pain—I wasn't far back enough. Of course, because it's not just street knives I'm facing here—someone's wielding their ice pick as a weapon against me.

The pain makes me see red, and after that, the fight moves fast. My second attacker takes off after being on the receiving end of my fist a few more times, and I let him go.

Jonah comes at me with the ice pick again but I'm ready for him this time, dancing back and to his left, sweeping his feet out from under him and stomping on his hand, forcing him to drop the pick. He swivels around and looks like he's about to come at me again, and I deliver one of my favorite training combinations, feinting twice and then spinning to land a brutal roundhouse kick.

He stumbles backwards just as the storm picks up again, and the snow swallows him.

My blood pounds in my ears as I stare at the place where he disappeared. Is he gone? Did he run?

Did he fall?

Did I kill him?

I don't know if I should be ashamed that I hope the answer is yes.

Breathing hard, I struggle to hold on to the adrenaline rush that was keeping me moving. Keeping me alive.

Izabel stumbles out of the fog and snow, Venna just behind her. Venna's coat is ripped at the shoulder, and a wound there is weeping blood. She leans on Izabel.

She doesn't look good.

"Are we close?" I say under my breath to Izabel, and we both look at each other silently, understanding. Venna's not going to be able to climb much longer, not with one arm basically out of commission.

"We'd better be," Izabel says grimly, and leads the way into the swirl of gray. "Come on."

We've made it this far. I may not want to bond, but I'm not about to let Izabel and Venna fail now.

CHAPTER TEN

Venna almost doesn't make it up the last stretch. It's a black sheet of slick ice, at times so steep that it's concave. My feet dangle in total open air as I reach for the next grip. I'm convinced that every inch I gain will be my last.

Venna climbs for a while on her wounded shoulder, but she's falling behind us, favoring the unwounded arm more and more. I barely need the yank on my tether rope as a signal from Izabel; we both sense that she's flagging and pause on our climb, clinging to the sheer wall, waiting painful minutes for Venna to reach us.

Adjusting the lengths of our rope and re-knotting them around our harnesses, Izabel and I tether ourselves to Venna's with equal slack between us, so that we can climb in tandem, pulling her up with us as she uses her feet and a single pick to brace herself.

We haul her up the final stretch by sheer strength of will.

When we reach the actual summit, I'm so exhausted that I briefly consider laying down and letting the direwolves eat me as a snack.

At least it would be fast.

We all stumble forward, putting distance between ourselves and the nightmarish drop behind us. Venna and Izabel fall to their knees, arms around each other, faces creased with exhaustion and relief.

The temperature is dropping, and as high up as we are, I doubt it gets above freezing even at the sun's peak. Even when it's not a blizzard. My skin hurts from the cold, even beneath my thick clothes.

I should probably keep moving my body in order to keep myself warm, but it's hard to make myself care, I'm so tired.

The summit stretches out before us, a long, barren plateau stretching across the highest ridge of the mountain. After a while, the snow eases enough that we can see dips and hollows and stubborn scrubby plants that somehow hang on in this desolate place.

As the storm calms down, we see something else, too: other climbers.

Lots of them.

We're very far from the first to arrive.

A flash of worry hits me, and I look over to Izabel and Venna, wondering if they're thinking the same thing, that we may have arrived too late for them to bond. Will the direwolves think that she and her sister are too weak, that they arrived after all these others?

Or will their persistence be rewarded?

Then the shadows and tricks of the stormy light start to materialize around us, and thought becomes impossible.

Direwolves—dozens of them. They're massive. My head doesn't even reach up to their shoulders. Even having seen direwolves and their Bonded before, I'm unprepared for their size and majesty, the way they dominate this desolate, eerie landscape.

I hang back, observing, as Izabel and Venna both rise, their faces set with pain and purpose.

"Don't forget," Izabel murmurs to me. "You don't approach them directly. Don't look any of them in the eye, or reach for them, or do anything else to indicate your interest. They choose you, not the other way around."

She steps forward before I have a chance to remind her that I'm not here for that. That I've already achieved my goal—*I've survived.*

And I've gotten these two women up with me, to achieve the goal they've been planning for since they were children.

I'm happy for them. Even though I think their goal is nuts.

The twins walk forward, into the mass of bodies, human and wolf. Venna stops and cocks her head—as if she is listening to someone speak, although I haven't heard a sound. Moments later, a towering gray direwolf pads up to her, staring down at her for a frightening moment before dipping its head.

Relief floods through me, and then I squint, the stormy afternoon light doing something strange to my vision. It almost looks like—

It's not a trick of the light. The man directly in front of me bonds, then, too, and his hair changes as I watch, a streak of silver threading through his tangled locks. A perfect match for the wolf that towers over him.

I search the area for Izabel, hoping she's also found a wolf who's willing to bond. My chest warms when I catch sight of Henrey in the distance, also standing next to a brown wolf, his hand tangled in its fur. He made it. He's alive.

I take a few more paces, trying to get out of the crush, avoid being noticed. A few times a wolf approaches me, and there's a strange sensation, almost like a press on my mind, but I block it out.

No, not me, I think, focusing all my attention on the words. *Not me, I'm not here to bond.*

Whatever I'm doing, it seems to work. Any wolf that looks my way soon moves off toward another potential match.

When I look back at Izabel, Venna's rejoined her side, a massive wolf of her own padding after her. Their wolves look different, I realize; Venna's is dark gray, while Izabel's is a light silver. They also have new streaks of color in their hair—silver for Izabel, deep blue for Venna. Does that mean...

Four different packs, Lee said. My eyes dart back and forth as I notice the newly Bonded pairs coming together into clusters, like with like. Venna and Izabel must have joined two different packs.

Ice gives way under my foot as I take another step backward, away from the Bonding, and I stumble and catch myself awkwardly, ankle almost turning as I fall through the top layer. My foot crunches down into snow and shards of ice.

I'm distracted, freeing my foot from the tangle of vicious ice, so I almost miss the moment that Jonah crests the mountain and pulls himself up, walking purposefully toward the direwolves despite his many clear injuries.

My mouth twists as a coal black wolf approaches him almost immediately. The wolf looks vicious, nasty. A perfect pair. Jonah shouts in triumph, and his wolf snarls. Jonah's dark hair gains a blood-red streak, the same color that Stark Therion has in his hair. So Jonah must have joined Daemos.

And at the same time, the angry wound on Jonah's face stitches itself closed. Healing magic from the direwolves, I realize with a jolt. I'd heard rumors of such a thing but always assumed it was an exaggeration.

Everyone around them takes a step or two backward. Disgusted, I look away.

That's when I see her for the first time: a direwolf who stands apart, her silver fur gleaming in the dim light.

Unlike the other wolves, who prowl around in search for the right rider, or stand watchfully by their new human match, she doesn't move. Something about the set of her stance, the slant of her golden-yellow eyes, communicates her disinterest—and her authority.

She looks simultaneously older and more powerful than any of the others. I take a step toward her before I realize what I'm doing, then stand stock still as she turns her head toward me, studying me with ancient eyes.

Not me, I think. *I'm not here to bond.*

My feet feel frozen to the ground as she rises, padding slowly toward me, her massive feet striking the snow silently in her grace.

From the corner of my eye, I see the wolves and their riders still, as each of them notice her movement toward me.

"It's Anassa," whispers one of the men near me, his gaze as focused on the massive silver wolf as everyone else's. "She never bonds. They say she's been here for hundreds of years…"

She draws closer, steadily and confidently, and I can't look away from her eyes. They shine like golden stars in the sky on the coldest evening of the year. Her gaze sears into me, and then suddenly my head seems like it's being crushed, squeezed.

Not me, I don't want to bond, I repeat in my mind.

Pain spikes and I yowl, falling to my knees, but never taking my eyes from Anassa.

The pressure in my head builds and my vision whites out. But in my mind, images swirl. Anassa, running in the moonlight, racing down the mountainside, faster than wind. A sun rising, rays blinding and beautiful. A crown, its metal glinting, then drenched in blood.

I cry out.

My senses undulate, as if my spirit has suddenly broken free of the confines of my body. I'm in the rock, sensing the vibrations of the thousands of creatures and plants that cling to my surface. I'm stretching upward, a pine tree, centuries old, reaching for the stars. I'm inside Anassa, my sense of smell almost painful in its keenness, the world a rich feast for my senses, its secrets laid open to me.

Sharp heat stabs behind my eyes, and then gradually fades, leaving behind a steady pulse of dull pain, surging in time with the beat of my heart.

The wound on my chest from the ice pick warms—and *heals*.

The direwolf's breath is hot on my face, her massive presence above me. Unthinking, I fling out a hand, as if I can somehow stop her coming, stop this.

My hand hits silver fur, and like they have a mind of their own, my fingers close, grasping thick strands, pulling me up to stand.

The pain in my head slowly eases, and I blink, unsteady, clinging to the wolf's fur as a lifeline.

What the fuck just happened?

CHAPTER ELEVEN

There's still a disorienting ringing in my ears. The ground's gone unsteady beneath my feet, my body numb from the biting wind and *whatever* that was. My mind starts to cling to miniscule details.

The way the direwolf's coarse fur beneath my fingers turns soft deeper down. The intermittent sting of snow slicing my cheeks. The heavy, rhythmic sound of Anassa's breathing.

A lock of my hair, tugged loose from my ties, whips past my gaze. It re-centers my focus.

Silver. All my dark hair has turned a luminous silver-white, the same color as Anassa.

My eyes slice back to Anassa and I untangle my hands from her fur as quickly as if she'd burned me. I know what the changed hair color means.

Bonded.

Muted horror floods my veins and I glance around at the other recruits in a panic. The younger woman nearest me has dark hair. Even in the insistent tug of the wind, I can see a silver streak in it. The rest of her hair is still black.

Heart rate escalating again, my eyes jump around to the other recruits. I blink rapidly, trying to focus my mind.

Regulate my breathing, first. That's what Igor always taught me. In and out. Slow, to trick my body into believing nothing's wrong.

Izabel is close, staring at me with wide eyes, a silver streak in her hair. Beyond her, across the mess of crushed snow and lingering recruits, is Venna, with her blue-black streak. The others... Henrey, a tawny color. That asshole Jonah, a sickening bloody red.

All of them have only a streak in their hair to mark their packs. I yank my hair out of my tie and pull it in front of me to confirm—and yes, it's all changed, every fucking strand. I'm an anomaly.

I glance back to the massive, silver-white direwolf at my side. She's stock still, assessing me.

"This was a mistake," I hiss at Anassa. "Take it back. I don't want to be Bonded. I *said* I didn't. You're not supposed to bond with the unwilling."

Her eerie yellow eyes narrow at me, and I remember Izabel's warning from before, to not look any of them in the eye. What, is she going to bite me? Now that she's forced a bond on me?

Anassa starts to pull back her lips in a growl, revealing terrifyingly sharp teeth. But before she can fully react, there's a shift in the air.

Every recruit falls utterly silent. Even the direwolves quiet. The only remaining sounds are the howling of the wind and the occasional crunches of paws and feet in the snow. Anassa huffs beside me, making me flinch, but I can't take my eyes off...

Him. Them.

The deathlike shadow of Stark Therion's direwolf looms over us all from atop a snow-covered boulder. He looks even more massive than when I saw him at the base of the mountain, with his pitch black fur and dagger-like claws.

Flashes of the brutality he's capable of—they're both capable of—return to me. Blood, viscera, unfeeling eyes.

I wonder if they made good on their threat to chase the unwilling up the mountain. How much blood might be coating that direwolf's muzzle, unseen in his black fur?

The wolf bares his teeth as Stark steps forward, smaller than his mount but no less imposing. There's a reason every single person here fell silent the moment he crested the slope of the mountain.

His presence is commanding just the way a thunderhead swallows up the sky. Unstoppable, flashing with danger, a low, rumbling warning striking fear through us.

A thought emerges from the chaos of my mind. Stupid, really, but it's there all the same.

He must be strong to ride that beast.

Stark glides his hand along his wolf's coat, leaving it there as his dark gaze sweeps over us. When it passes over me, some instinct deep within me forces me to lift my chin and draw my shoulders back.

I've seen men like him before. The quiet ones. The dangerous ones. The men who don't shout threats because they simply *don't need to.*

When I look at Stark, I see a calm, wicked confidence sharp as a knife, honed from endless fights and very few losses.

The power of his towering body, the ferocity in his gaze, the scars and dark tattoos peeking out of his gear, and the ironlike set to his shadowed jaw are there for all to see.

He's as feral and dangerous as his direwolf.

My hair whips in front of my eyes again, a bolt of light against the endless shadow of him. An energy buzzes in my muscles, electric and hot, flooding me with strength. Something in me sees all that power and wants to *move.* Throw a punch or take it all in my hands and twist it up.

His direwolf takes a heavy step forward and lets out a low, menacing growl from deep in his belly.

The recruits around me jostle backwards at the sound, even those with enormous wolves standing over them for protection.

Stark's lips twitch like he finds it amusing. When he lifts an amplifier and speaks, it's like the wind itself quiets to listen, the deep, gravely sound of his voice carrying clearly across the blood-stained snow.

"If you were not lucky enough to become one of the Bonded,

you can now make your way back down the mountain via the path to report for military duty as a soldier. If you've Bonded, congratulations," he says, the boredom in his voice making it clear that he's unimpressed. "Your training starts right now with the first test of your bond."

My mind whirs into motion again. *Testing* our bonds? I drag my attention from Stark's imposing figure and dare to glance at Anassa.

She stands still, not looking at me, lithe muscles locked as her silvery white fur ripples in the breeze.

"You and your wolf must make it back to the training center in the castle before nightfall. From that point forward, you will be officially considered a Rawbond, a trainee. If you do not make it in time, do not bother trying to enter the castle. Because if you fail..." Stark goes on, leaning against his direwolf's leg and crossing his arms, "your connection with your wolf will sever and you will die. Good luck."

You will die.

There's still blood smeared across my face from the people who've already lost their lives during the Ascent, and he stands up there and speaks of death with such complete indifference.

I hate him. I fucking *hate* him.

Stark is callous and bloodthirsty and *dangerous*. Men like that have no true loyalty to anyone but themselves. They don't care about anyone else, not about the lives at risk or the people lost in the cracks of the world.

He lithely mounts his wolf, muscles pulling him up with a practiced grace only possible from performing the same motion thousands of times.

I clench my jaw so hard that my teeth ache as I watch Stark and his direwolf disappear into the snow, barreling down the mountain.

The mountaintop has turned into chaos. Many of the recruits are grabbing at their direwolves' coats, scrambling to try to mount. Some of the wolves swipe at their would-be riders, snarling and stumbling away from them. Other, more patient recruits gaze up at their beasts, clearly trying to attempt to reason with them.

My head is still spinning from the absolute *wrongness* of this. But

I did not spend all day breaking my body—watching other people fall to gruesome deaths—in order to just quit now.

If I want to survive, if I want to save my sister, I need to at least *try*.

Anassa won't look at me, gaze locked somewhere in the distance, silver coat gleaming. She's larger than the other wolves around us. More imposing. Regal and terrifying and clearly stubborn.

Clearing my mind, I try to tap back into that swimming, dizzying stream of energy I felt when she first approached me, but I get... nothing. Utter silence.

Maybe I'm doing this wrong. After all, most of the people on this mountaintop grew up watching their families communicate with wolves. Likely, they were taught how to do it.

My best guess is that I should think words at her, feel intent, open myself up to her mind. I reach out toward the place in my consciousness where I felt her power earlier.

BAM.

My mind impacts against an iron wall, steely and impassable between us. It's as cold as her icy eyes, towering as her hulking body, and sharp as her glinting claws.

Something's not right. The others are starting to mount properly now. Some are even bounding off down the mountain, direwolf after direwolf disappearing into the snow. This must be working for them.

Am I doing it wrong? Is this because I don't want to be Bonded?

But then why the fuck did she *do* this?!

My fractured mind latches onto Izabel in the mess of bodies before me. She's climbing onto her silver direwolf's back, taking fist-fuls of fur as her mount watches her every move closely. I don't see Venna anywhere—she must have already started back down the mountain.

I glance nervously at Anassa and then turn to sprint towards Izabel. "Hey!"

Izabel turns and looks down at me as she settles atop her direwolf, sitting back. Her eyes widen when she sees me, and her brow pinches up. "Meryn."

"Was he serious?" I choke out. I don't know why I say it. Stark was obviously serious, not a lighthearted bone in his massive body.

"Yes," she says so quietly it's almost lost in the wind. "People who don't make it back in time die."

"I didn't even want this," I breathe, looking back at Anassa who still hasn't budged. She's staring at me now, though, cold gaze steady.

"I know, but you can do it," Izabel says. Her direwolf shifts beneath her, massive muscles stretching, tail swishing. She pats its shoulder. "I have to go. It's—"

"She's not talking," I blurt, hating the vulnerability in my voice.

Izabel looks briefly horrified before she deftly conceals it. "Not talking?"

"I'm not getting anything from my wolf, I don't know what I'm supposed to be doing."

Izabel winces. "Just... try harder, Meryn. Some people die along the way because they're not communicating well with their wolves. The packs think that it's not worth the time to train pairs who can't communicate."

"So, what?" I ask. "This is some sort of twisted way of weeding people out?"

Izabel's nonresponse is confirmation.

Because this isn't a test, in the end. It's an execution.

Why am I surprised? People like me die every day. In the streets and alleys. On the front lines. Scrambling up a freezing, icy mountain.

Abducted by Nabbers in the night.

No. I can't think like that. The hope that Saela is alive is the only thing keeping me moving.

"Anassa chose you," Izabel says, her dark eyes sympathetic, even as she looks at me like I'm a doomed cause. Well, fuck that. "That has to count for something, Meryn."

Her direwolf starts to shift its weight, rumbling out an impatient growl.

Izabel breathes deeply and nods, jaw set. "I wish you all the best. I truly do. And I hope to see you down there."

With that, her mount turns and races away, and she's gone with the rest.

There are almost none of us left atop the mountain now. Those still remaining are struggling to mount. That, or they're mounted and their direwolves aren't moving or are trying to buck and roll them off.

There's a massive tawny direwolf sitting in the snow across the bloody snowfield, gnawing on a severed arm, staring at me.

My stomach turns as I march back to Anassa, hands in fists. Even though my wound has healed, my muscles still ache, hot and insistent. They're locking up and screaming at me for overworking them. My hands are basically blocks of ice. My head still pounds from the bonding.

But that's life. It's always *been* my life. Pain and persistence.

There's only one way forward, and I'm not dying on a lonely, icy mountain. I refuse to die until I know Saela is safe in her bed again. I lean into the pain, into the indignant fury at the injustice of what's happening. It fuels me.

Anassa watches my approach, expression unchanging, body utterly still. I stare back at her and take a deep breath, trying to ensure my voice is soothing despite the churning chaos in my mind.

Slowly, I hold out my hand to her and speak, "Okay girl, it's just us, then."

Her huge paws dig into the snow and her bushy tail lifts slightly, and I have the distinct sense that those two things in combination are a warning. Her eyes slice into me, and ice creeps through my veins.

"I'm *trying* here," I growl, then clear my voice to calm myself, "but maybe I'm not good at this because it's not in my blood. All I know is that we need to get down there. And quickly, for both our sakes."

She still doesn't move, but her muscles are taut and her flanks are twitching restlessly.

Stepping closer, I smooth my voice out, speaking in gentle tones. "Can I get on your back? Can I ride you, girl?"

Her teeth snap. A loud, menacing *click* strikes at my heart like a hammer. I recoil as her fangs flash, massive canines dripping with saliva. A barking growling rips from her throat, and a paw drags a huge canyon through the snow.

My heart slams in my chest. I nearly just lost a hand. Or an entire arm.

"What the fuck?" I shout up at her, furious.

She snarls at me, tail flicking restlessly. The scream gathers behind my ribs, unbearable pressure pushing outward. I swallow around the angry, terrified lump in my throat.

"Why?" I shout at her. Why did she do this? If she hates me so much, *why* did she force a bond on me? Why did she doom us both?

Anassa huffs at me, a gust of hot air impacting my face. She stomps one foot, then turns and runs.

I stand there staring after her, my entire body going slowly numb again. I watch as her silvery white coat disappears into the snow, blending in seamlessly until she's utterly gone. I still have that uncomfortable pulsing ache in my head, but it hardly matters now. She abandoned me here.

And you know what?

Fuck her.

She doesn't realize just what a stubborn bitch I am.

I'll get down the mountain with or without her useless furry ass.

"Fine!" I shout. Then I can't hold it in any longer. I double over and scream, fingers twisting in my silver-white hair. Awful, piercing sound scrapes from my throat, and I keep going until I run out of air.

When it's done, I straighten and get to work.

I've been on my own before, and I haven't let it kill me yet. I'm not going to start today.

Striding to the edge of the compacted snow, I find a clean patch and gather it up in my hands, bringing it to my mouth and letting it melt against my tongue. I swallow the water down, letting it soothe my raw throat and wake my mind up.

Then I slip my pack from my shoulder and dig into it, retrieving the dried meat Izabel gave me, tearing at it with my teeth and chewing without tasting. After, I don't bother picking my pack back up. It's too heavy, and I can't have anything weighing me down.

Because I need to *run*. I need to run like I've never run before, if I'm going to reach the castle in time.

Maybe it's useless. Maybe I'll die halfway down the mountain in an avalanche or perish the moment Anassa's bond fractures and snaps to pieces. But I'll never stop fighting.

Not when Saela's waiting for me.

Taking one last deep breath, I fill my lungs with freezing air and then start the descent. The safe path winds around the side of the mountain in a zigzag to create a smoother slope, but I don't have time for the comfortable route.

I bolt past the trail of unbonded recruits making their way slowly down the mountain. Some of them jump or shout at me as I sprint past them, but my heart is pounding too hard to care.

Slipping through a gap in the trail of soldiers, I take the plunge. My body slides over a snowdrift as I launch myself headlong over the edge of the path and down into the wildness between the path's comfortable winding curves.

Here, it's deep snow, sudden rocky drops, massive trees with jutting branches, and death.

My clothes are soaked through immediately as I wade and fall and sprint, feet pounding over stony flats. I whip pine needles out of my face and duck under branches. I leap over logs and slide on my side at truly dangerous speeds over long stretches of icy rock, knees and elbows and feet slamming against bits of stone that jut out.

My feet impact the path again, and I sprint right through it. There are hardly any unbonded recruits this far down the mountain, so the way is clear.

Someone shouts at me as I hurtle back into the terrifying descent again. My lungs are frozen over, excruciating pain coursing through me with each icy heave of breath. My legs are shaking as I run, barely keeping me upright.

It's just a matter of time before they give out and I'm more falling than running down the mountain.

But it doesn't matter. The world is narrowed down to my survival. To my purpose. To Saela, alone and afraid, her survival dependent upon me reaching the bottom of this stupid fucking mountain. To my mother waiting for me to bring her home.

To Lee, and the life we can build together when this is all over.

Soon, it's like I'm flying. Trees and rocks rush past me. I stumble and fall, spinning through the snow until I right myself, new pain erupting in my shoulder that I don't have time to address.

There's a body on the next stretch of path I pass through. It's a gory spread. A woman lies on her back, staring sightlessly up at the sky. Her blood is smeared across the snow in a long line, as if she impacted the ice and slid several feet before finding her final resting place.

I stand there only for a moment, catching my breath, entire body trembling as my eyes rest on the cavernous hole where her stomach should have been.

She's been ripped open. Claws, I think. Shredded right through her coat. Through the sweater beneath it. *My* sweater, I realize.

Alessandra.

She's mutilated, eyes still as wide with fear as they were in life.

I wonder if a direwolf got her on the way down or if this was the work of that piece of shit Stark.

It's a shame. She was a good person, I think. But it's too cold out here. The frigid air has seeped right into my chest, ice coating my heart.

I can't mourn her. I don't have the time.

Turning away from her, I keep running. My lungs have never been this cold, never stung like this before even after hours and hours of training with Igor. The exposed parts of my skin burn like they're on fire. My joints ache from the endless impact of my boots on rock and ice. I think I must be bleeding from falls and from the stinging whip of the tree branches.

My feet are beginning to crack and bleed in my boots.

And there's no direwolf magic healing me this time—either I'm too far from Anassa or she's choosing to withhold her help. I'm not quite sure how it works.

It hurts. *Fuck*, it hurts. But that's another thing Anassa doesn't know about me.

I've always used pain to fuel my anger, to keep myself going. It washes over me, burning and biting, and I swallow it down. It ignites something in me.

Something merciless. Determined. Unstoppable.

Saela, Saela, Saela. Her name is in the pounding of my heart. In the thudding of my boots. In the rush of wind and the haunting echo of howls along the mountainside.

Shapes shift in my peripheral vision. Trees rushing past, maybe. Snow falling. Ghosts against the endless white oblivion.

There are more bodies as I run. I see them in bizarre sharpness despite the painful blur of the world around me. The first is a man lying in a snowdrift. A wolf stands over him, black as night against the snow. I veer left to avoid them. The image of blood on shining white teeth and the terrifying red gash where the recruit's throat should have been flashes over and over behind my eyes as I run.

The wolf glares at me as I run past it and I try to blink the image away, snow whipping at my cheeks. But I blink and blink and it won't leave. It gets worse, and I start to see Anassa's eyes instead, yellow and furious and unforgiving.

The next body is a woman lying face-down at the bottom of a chasm. I skid to a stop, gripping a tree branch with a numb hand and barely managing to use it to slow my momentum before I skid over the same sudden, sheer drop that killed her.

Her corpse is utterly still against the dark rock below me, white bones jutting up through her skin at her elbow and her thigh. Her skull is caved in, blood splattered over the snow and stone. Her wolf is beside her, massive and unmoving.

It's dead too, I realize, its massive muzzle slack and its eyes unseeing. Died on impact, probably. Its fur still rustles in the breeze.

Doesn't matter. I turn and sprint around the edge of the drop, descending over a smoother bit of snow and ice. And I keep going.

I run and run until I'm not even present in my body, until my mind starts to dissociate back to a warm bed, a little nose buried in a book, a story about a goddess who saves herself. I don't even notice when I hit the base of the mountain. The forest we hiked through yesterday passes in a blur. I see none of it.

The light's changed by the time my legs give out and I tumble to a slow, painful stop. I'm breathless and dizzy. Delirious, really. The sky is darkening. It will be night soon, and I'll be too late.

I let out another strangled, hoarse scream as I fight to my feet. It sounds more like a cry, like a desperate sob. But I'm almost there.

As I pull myself to my feet, entire body one riotous frisson of agony, I realize I've almost made it. There are tracks in the snow. Massive paw prints leading onward. I stoke the anger in my chest and summon the energy for one final push.

Speeding past the Bonded City, I follow the tracks towards the castle. The leisurely walk past these neighborhoods feels ages away. There's no time to stop and gawk at the disgusting wealth. There's not even any room in my brain to hate the castle for what it is and all it represents any longer.

I only look at its hulking stone mass and think *get there. Get to Saela. Survive.*

The sky changes color, deepening to a lazy gray. The sun is low in the sky, dipping down to touch the dark horizon.

I reach the gate with barely any light left, every inch of my body screaming at me.

There's a woman with dark skin and a glaringly obvious silver streak in her close-cropped dark hair. She's one of the high-ranking Bonded that was leading the Ascent. Beta Egith, I think Stark said.

She turns when she hears me crunching closer, gait uneven because I'm limping badly. Her eyes narrow when she sees me.

I try to summon words. *I'm here. I made it. Please.* But nothing will come.

It hardly matters, though. She takes one look at me and says, "No direwolf, no entry."

The scream gathers in my chest again. There's a sudden, vicious urge to take hold of this woman's head and plunge my thumbs into her eye sockets. I take a step closer, hands clenching into fists, endless expletives about to pour out of me.

But then a growl rumbles from behind me.

I tense and whirl around, eyes wide.

She's there. She's just *right there*. The fucking *bitch*.

Anassa stalks towards me, heavy paws crunching on snow, puffs of vapor huffing from her nose. She walks with her head low beneath her shoulders, her ears forward, her gaze steady on me. Coat silvery white against the snow… A ghost.

She was following me. She was right there the entire time, watching me descend.

Fury pummels my heart as the woman manning the gate perks up.

"Well, then," the woman says, voice brighter and gaze keener. "Welcome to training, Strategos Rawbond."

CHAPTER TWELVE

T he gate behind the woman, I realize now, is an elaborate
wrought iron depiction of two direwolves howling. The
woman turns to push it and the direwolves part and swing
away.

I stare at it so that I don't have to venture a look at Anassa, who
I already know will be intentionally avoiding my gaze. I can
somehow *feel* the tension in her massive muscles.

And worse, there's still that unyielding iron wall between our
minds.

Even so, there's a warmth in my boots; I think she's healed my
cracked, aching skin.

"Go on, then. Find your pack in the courtyard," the woman
says, jutting a hand out.

I hesitate only briefly. Something about the towering stone castle
walls makes me claustrophobic. But I don't really have a choice, at
least not tonight. I need time to figure out how to get out of this
bond.

"You know where to go," the woman says, craning her neck to
meet Anassa's gaze. The direwolf huffs dismissively and pads past
me, galloping off beyond the castle's walls.

I can sense the woman's impatience, so I sigh and step forward, too, heading in the same direction Anassa disappeared. But when I round the corner, she's nowhere to be seen.

Instead, a large courtyard reveals itself to me. The same mighty walls surround the enclosed space, but here, the supporting pillars are adorned with carved wolves sitting regally atop every column. They sit high above us, staring down with their muzzles tucked close to their chests, eternally glowering.

In the center of the courtyard is a similar statue with two wolves perched atop an artistically carved rock. Along the interior colonnade, there are several arched doors made of heavy, marred wood. At the corners of the courtyard, there are four oriel windows jutting out of the walls, implying a second traversable floor along the wall walks above.

At the edges of the courtyard, separate groups of recruits—no, *Rawbonds*—gather up, clearly separated by the differently colored marks in their hair.

The rest of the silver-marked Rawbonds are in the center of the courtyard, mostly huddled around the large statue. The snow beneath their feet has been crushed beneath many boots, revealing some dead grass and more of the same ice-slick cobblestone I trod across now, boots thudding heavily.

The massive interior space makes me leery. The courtyard has clearly been carved large enough to give the direwolves room to maneuver freely, but I'm used to narrow alleys and tiny houses. I'm used to having a wall at my back at all times.

Standing here, an attack could come from any direction and I'd have very little to use to my advantage beyond my own strength. Which is nothing to scoff at, of course.

But being able to hurl a chair at someone or yank down a dangling laundry line to blind them would make me feel safer.

Some of my energy returns when I pick Izabel out of the crowd of silver streaked-heads. I trudge towards her and grunt out her name. She tenses and turns, but her eyes light up when she sees me.

"Meryn! You made it in one piece!"

"Sort of. I left my dignity up on that mountain."

Izabel laughs. "Well, you've got all your body parts, still. So that's something. Anassa's warmed up to you?"

"If the warmth you're referring to is fiery rage, then *yes*. Very much so." I suck in a trembling breath, still weak and aching from my tumble down the mountain, and look around at the rest of the recruits. "Wow."

"I know. There are a lot of us," Izabel replies.

But that wasn't at all what I was commenting on. It's devastatingly clear that nearly all of them are from the Bonded City. I can tell just looking at them. The colorfully dyed coats, heavy furs, draping scarves. The healthy build to their muscles. Their towering height.

Goddess, even their skin looks healthier than people's did back in Eastern.

My eyes catch on a particularly boisterous pale-skinned Rawbond. He's one of the older ones, tall and handsome with vibrant red hair that stands out against the gray stone and pale snow. He's all smiles and laughter, with a small group of admirers gazing at him and tumbling into laughter alongside him as if we didn't just watch leagues of people die.

It's that unwavering confidence that unnerves me, like they all own the world.

Even the quieter ones exude it. A wiry girl with that same silver streak in her brown, curly hair stands apart from the rest of our group. Tears are streaking silently down her face—she's distraught about something, and even so, her eyes burn like she thinks she could cut any one of our throats without consequence.

"You must feel a little lost," Izabel says, interrupting my stewing thoughts.

"Understatement. But it's like I told you. I'm not supposed to be here," I reply.

"And yet, you are. It could be worse. We're both in the Strategos Pack," Izabel says proudly, beaming at me. That's the same word I heard the woman at the gate use. "The leaders."

I raise a brow. "Leaders?"

"Mmm-hmm. My parents are both in Strategos, too, but I'm not surprised that Venna joined Kryptos." She points at the smattering of Rawbonds in the eastern corner of the courtyard. The ones with the deep bluish streaks in their hair. "They're the spies," Izabel explains. "Venna's always been hard to pin down…" she smiles, a memory alight in her eyes.

"Then over there," Izabel resumes, pointing to the western corner, where a group of particularly brutish-looking people have gathered. "Daemos. The warriors."

The warriors with the bloody red streaks. I frown.

Every single one of them looks like they're just waiting to tear someone's throat out with their teeth. They're even larger than the rest, buzzing with an energy that I'd assume was nervousness if their eyes weren't so keen. I'm pretty sure they're just restless to fight something.

Unsurprisingly, Jonah's in that group, glaring out at everyone.

"Lastly, there's the Phylax, or the guardians," Izabel goes on, gesturing to the calmer looking group where Henrey stands with his hands resting passively on his hips.

So leaders, spies, warriors, and guardians. "Roles in combat?"

"Sort of. But it also has to do with pack dynamics, culture, and even the wolves' demeanors," she says. "Each of us has our purpose, and we work together. In theory."

I'd been starting to lean into the intrigue of it all. The inner workings of this privileged, exclusive part of society that always loomed over those of us toiling below. But that one word, *purpose*, jars me from my curiosity.

Saela is my purpose, not leading a bunch of pompous, overly cocky Rawbonds.

I have more important questions to ask. Like, *how the fuck do I get out of this and reach the front lines?*

But before I can start interrogating Izabel about how difficult it may or may not be to wriggle out of this particular sort of enlist-ment—specifically, how possible it might be to break my bond without dying—the metal gate we all entered through clangs loudly, the sound echoing over stone.

We all fall silent as the woman who admitted us strides forward, frowning slightly. "That's it, then!" she announces, voice carrying. "Sundown. Let's get you to your quarters."

One look at the darkening sky and I realize that she's right. The day's over. Anyone still beyond those gates is probably dead.

I give myself only a moment to think of the lost, then the high-ranking Bonded woman sweeps past us, speaking loudly and quickly as she walks. "I am Egith Hartsfeld, Beta of the Strategos pack," she says without looking at any of us.

The group of Rawbonds startles and stumbles after her, trailing after her authority without needing to be told. I try to work through the term she just used.

Beta, she said. But apart from knowing the Alphas are in charge, I don't know anything about Bonded terminology, and it passes right over my head.

I take it that she's someone important, though.

We head to the eastern part of the courtyard where the Kryptos pack waits, all funneling through the colonnade and into the interior of the castle. The wide wooden door creaks open before Egith as she approaches it, and I realize belatedly that there are two men standing on the other side, pulling it open for her.

But how long were they standing there? Is that all they do? Are they just paid to *stand* there and wait to open the door for the all-important Bonded?

Egith talks while she walks, not bothering to look back to see if she's being followed. "This half of the castle was constructed for Rawbond training. We train here, in close proximity to the king, so that he is able to keep an eye on the progress."

An entire half of the castle is dedicated to training? I had no idea. And it *all* looks like this? Goddess.

When I step inside, a wave of welcoming warmth envelops me. There must be a hundred hearths crackling within these walls to keep the cold out so efficiently. Everything is polished and gleaming, even the exposed stone of the walls. The floor gleams beneath our messy boots.

More imposing statues flank the walls of the entryway, faces of what I presume are renowned Bonded staring down as if they're assessing us.

Izabel looks unbothered, eyes glued to Egith as we delve deeper into the castle, but this is all *too much.*

Disbelief simmers in my gut.

There's no need for any of this opulence. The deeper rooms of the castle's interior warm further, walls covered in paneled, rich wood. Tapestries hang on every surface, woven with gold and silver threads, each depicting direwolves, elaborate crowns, or swirling designs that look like snowdrifts and stormy clouds.

The hostile, cold stone turns to marble and high, vaulted ceilings with carved wooden support beams. Everything is just as wide open as the courtyard, with massive arched doorways and floor-to-ceiling windows with intricate latticework. The halls are lit with flickering oil lamps, warm light pooling over shining marble and the excited faces of the other Rawbonds.

"You *do not* leave this half of the castle," Egith says, her voice echoing through the halls alongside the blunted sound of our many footsteps. "The other half is for the royal family and you are forbidden from stepping foot in it except on special occasions."

It seems impossible to me that there's a part of the world that possesses this much obvious wealth. The hallway we're walking through is wider than the streets back home.

"As you can see, our half of the castle was built for wolves to be able to navigate it," Egith says, gesturing to a tall doorway as we pass it by.

"Where *are* our wolves?" Henrey pipes up from nearby.

People around him snicker or smirk like his question was stupid. It makes sense to me, though. Anassa disappeared. I thought it was just because she wanted to get away from me, but I haven't seen a single direwolf since arriving.

"Ah, there's always one," Egith says as we pass through a set of massive iron-studded doors and turn down another equally elaborate hallway. Some servants scuttle past us, eyeing us with blatant apprehension. "Learn quickly, Rawbond. The wolves prefer to be outdoors. While in training, the wolves stay in pack terraces carved into the mountainside across from the outdoor training grounds. You will get a full tour of the facility tomorrow."

To his credit, Henrey nods sternly, focused, and ignores the assholes muttering about him under their breaths. His cheeks are ruddy, though.

We reach the end of the hallway and approach yet another pointed stone archway. This one has lush red velvet curtains draped over the bend of its arch, dripping down to the shiny floor in gentle folds.

Egith bats a curtain aside carelessly as she steps through. We all follow her like a gaggle of ducklings imprinted on the only authority figure in sight.

The circular room we enter is massive. It's clearly some sort of common space, if you could call a place like this *common*.

It's well-lit with flickering oil lamps covered in warm-colored shades. One half of the room has dozens of long, polished dining tables set with delicate, spindly chairs. The other half has huge, plump couches and chaises set around several enormous fireplaces. One of the gargantuan fireplaces is being stoked by a servant in castle livery, who doesn't look up when the crowd of us enters.

The walls are lined with stacked bookshelves, tapestries, or massive portraiture and landscapes. The walls themselves are made of a rougher stone, scenes of hunting wolves carved in bas-relief throughout the entire room.

It's immaculate, of course, as the rest of the castle is. Every detail is in place, down to the perfectly pruned flowers in the vases. How they managed to get this many flowers from the outer fiefdoms, I have no idea; they don't grow outdoors in Sturmfrost. We see them occasionally in the markets, but they're exotic, priced high.

I guess that's one of the unnecessary things rich people like to spend their money on.

As the rest of the crowd files inside, my eyes catch on the large adjoining doors set around the room. Four of them, spaced out evenly. They're very clearly labeled with the pack names Izabel shared earlier.

Strategos, Kryptos, Daemos, Phylax.

Below each gilded inscription, there's a unique symbol crafted from some sort of runes. I'm just starting to examine them when Egith's voice rings through the room again.

"This is the Rawbond common lounge, where you will receive your meals," she announces, finally stopping to turn and look at us. "Behind your respective pack doors are your pack dormitories. Each pack has its own common space, bunk room, bathing areas, and private rooms for the instructors. You'll eat within your pack dorms tonight, but starting tomorrow, all packs eat in this shared lounge."

Silence settles over the room, punctuated only by the shuffling of feet and a loud pop from the fire. Seconds pass before Egith rolls her eyes and juts her hand towards the labeled doors.

"*What* are you waiting for? Go!"

Immediately, the Rawbonds flood towards their pack quarters. I clench my jaw as Izabel waves to her sister, smiling and signing a few words. Then she turns to me and touches my elbow gently. I fall into step with her as we head towards the Strategos quarters.

"Home sweet home," Izabel says as we step inside.

I sway slightly on my feet at the sight of it. It's equal parts sickening and thrilling, seeing all this luxury.

We've stepped into a massive antechamber crammed with comfort. There's seating everywhere, including plush-looking nooks by the windows. More bookshelves line the walls. Mountains of pillows heap on the various chairs and couches. Soft, ornate rugs blanket the floor. A chandelier hangs low, flickering with gentle light.

There's another massive fireplace, big enough to fit my entire body standing upright within. The walls are covered in shimmering wallpaper, a deep mauve color with silver damask patterns reflecting the roaring fire's light. The windows have stained glass patterns on them—silver wolves in various states of elegant motion. Above the mantel is a massive carving of the military crest.

Goddess, it even *smells* rich in here, like someone's burning incense somewhere. Cloves, maybe?

"What the fuck?" I mumble under my breath, gaze catching on

the crystalline tea set sitting on the low table near the fire. Who needs that? Aren't we meant to be fighting a war?

Around the anteroom are four closed doors and one that's open.

"Welcome to the Strategos dormitory," Egith says as she moves toward one of the closed doors. I'd wager that all of those doors lead to the private rooms for the instructors. "For those of you who need clothes to change into," her eyes linger on me at this, "there's a store closet in the bunk room that has everything you'll need in a variety of sizes. Sleep well."

I stare back at the servants that start to pour into the room as Izabel drags me through the open door. This is clearly the sleeping quarters. There are thirteen bunk beds lining the walls, all identical and separated by matching dressers. There's another hearth burning at the end of the long room, with a stack of wood next to it and a grate with a howling wolf sparing the lavish rug from rogue sparks.

At the end, an ajar door reveals a lavatory and washroom, likely just as large, luxurious, and gleamingly clean as the rest of this place.

As Izabel and I wander among the other Rawbonds, looking for a spot, I drag my hand over the linens on one of the beds. Soft. *So* soft. Nicer than anything I ever washed back home, let alone owned.

My mind spins. This is what Bonded *trainees* get?! We're not even proper soldiers yet!

The contrast is ridiculous. The recruitment center I visited was run-down and barebones in comparison. What are the soldiers on the front lines getting? Probably a cold bed roll and gruel for breakfast.

We constantly hear about how we need to tighten our belts for the war effort, to make sacrifices so that soldiers could get what they needed to protect us.

But all the food we couldn't have ended up here, in Bonded bellies. The fuel for our fires ended up in these hearths. The taxes and the lowered wages, too, all so that the Bonded could hire servants to open their doors for them and sleep on silky sheets.

We're *all* putting our lives on the line in the war against the Siphons. Why should the Bonded get this luxury when soldiers on the frontline are struggling, when commoners are starving to death and living in fear?

What, because they have big scary direwolves?

I'm in a bit of a trance as Izabel picks a bed for us to share. She thuds her pack down, and I stand there a little numbly, remembering that I don't have a pack any longer. I had to leave all my things up on top of the mountain, right next to my dignity.

Rest in peace.

I spot the store closet Egith mentioned and note to myself to grab some things to wear.

"We should eat," Izabel says. "And clean up. But food first."

"Yeah," I say, nodding absently.

By the time we make it back into the anteroom, the tables are laden with a feast. It smells amazing, like fresh bread and herbed meat and the gentle sting of wine.

I sit beside Izabel and load a plate, inhaling the food without a care for manners. It's probably the best thing I've ever tasted, and it's not just because I'm half-starved. I wouldn't be able to afford a meal as nice as this with a week's wages back home. People in Eastern don't even make food like this, because no one would be able to buy it.

But it's *so* good. Rich and buttery. Spicy. Fatty. It's bliss on a plate.

"Hungry?" Izabel teases as I chew.

I swallow and nod. "Fattening myself up for when Anassa decides to eat me. Want to make the experience nice for her."

Izabel laughs. We eat in silence for a few more minutes and I consider refilling my plate, but my stomach already aches from the rich meal and the sheer amount of it that I've already downed.

"Ready to turn in?" Izabel asks.

"Fuck yes," I reply, pushing my chair out and standing.

Back in the bunkroom, many of the Bonded are unloading bags and stocking their dressers, draping blankets over their beds, hanging curtains along their bunks for privacy.

I frown. "Did they have all that stuff in their packs?"

Izabel shakes her head. "No one would climb with a spare

pillow in their bag. Our families deliver our things to the castle when we head to the Ascent."

I scoff. "Presumptuous."

A muscle in her jaw twitches as she drags a bag out from beneath our bed. "For a Bonded family, there's no such thing as failure. If you fail to bond in your Trials, you're out. You're dead to them. Not one of them any longer."

Bitterness seeps into my blood. None of this makes sense. None of this is just. This system grinds people up and spits us out.

I glance around, cursing under my breath. It's going to be even more obvious that I don't fit in here, what with my bare bunk and regulated clothing. As if my shiny silver hair and asshole of a direwolf weren't bad enough already.

Not that I want to fit in here. My goal is Saela. I just need to live long enough to find a way out of here.

But that's tomorrow's problem.

I grab some old—but still soft and expensive—pajamas from the store closet, as well as new packs of underwear and a uniform for tomorrow. Then, I head to the lavatories, changing quickly so the next girl can use my stall. The connected washroom is tempting, but I'm so exhausted that I can't think of anything other than falling face-first into a pillow.

Back in the bunk room, I start to climb up to my top bunk, but Izabel stops me, her eyes filled with concern.

"Don't let your guard down," she says quietly. "Everyone's wiped out tonight, but training has started and everyone is going to want to prove themselves as the strongest recruit in the pack."

I nod. "I'm going to keep my head down. Don't worry."

Izabel looks decidedly worried, but nods and reclines in her bunk. I wince as my muscles strain on the way up to the second level of the bed, but even once I'm there, the tension doesn't leave me. Izabel's words were hardly comforting.

It's like I thought, like Lee said.

The Bonding Trials are vicious and cutthroat. The Ascent may be over, but the Trials are still just getting started. I have to watch my back.

My mind is rifling through possibilities as I close my eyes. Would someone try to attack me in my sleep here? Will my faulty bond with Anassa end up killing me first? I'm convinced I'll never fall asleep up until the very moment my mind starts to away, exhaustion getting the better of me.

The sleep that takes me is deep and unbearably heavy. Dark, even.

And in that darkness, a voice that turns my blood cold, chanting like the beat of a heart.

"*Lumina, Lumina, LUMINA.*"

CHAPTER THIRTEEN

I 'm jolted awake.

At first, my scattered brain thinks the ceiling is caving in. The sound that rattles through my skull is so loud and deep that it's borderline apocalyptic. But as I bolt upright, mouth dry and hair a mess, I realize it's a horn meant to wake us. The resonating note of it lingers in my ears even as the brutal sound fades, and alongside the low note, a high-pitched hiss.

Lumina.

I swallow, trying to combat the dryness of my mouth. My head is pounding. My muscles are horribly sore. It's barely brightening outside, yet the room is a flurry of activity all around me. From my perch atop my bunk, I can see that all the other Rawbonds are already dressed and done up, their bunks tidied, their hair wet from their baths.

They move with a practiced efficiency. I watch blearily as the beautiful blonde woman in the next bunk over cinches the leather straps across her uniform with ease, like her hands have been repeating that complicated maneuver her entire life. In moments, the uniform leathers are snug, buckled tight as if they were made for her body.

Then again, maybe they were. They've been readying themselves for this their entire lives, I recall suddenly. They knew that
horn blast was coming. They all know precisely how to wear their
uniforms and how much time they'd have this morning to prepare
for the day.

"Meryn," Izabel says, smacking the side of our bed. "Hurry up.
Come on."

I scramble into motion, tearing my blanket away and stiffly
descending the slats of the bed.

"What is all this?" I ask, hurrying to my dresser to grab my
things.

"We're already supposed to be assembling in the common
lounge for breakfast. You need to get ready." Her eyes move over
me. "Tidy your hair, maybe. Looks matter around here."

Looks matter, whatever that means. I tug my hair out of its ties,
nearly scaring myself shitless when the silver-white of it flashes
across my eyes.

Right. That.

Apparently, I don't have time to bathe because Izabel half-drags
me out of the room the moment I return in uniform. I'm still struggling with the stiff leather jacket and the various straps and buckles
when we pass through the Strategos antechamber and enter the
common lounge.

Most of the Rawbonds have made it here before us, including
Venna, so we snag the only remaining spot big enough for the two
of us to sit side-by-side.

Izabel grumbles under her breath as we approach. "Just ignore
him," she warns.

"Well, well, well." It's the redhead I noticed chattering loudly in
the courtyard before. There are eyes on him always, like people are
looking to him as an example. "How are you two this fine
morning?"

Izabel slides in beside him. "Fine," she grunts out and pats the
seat beside her. I sit, studying the man she seems to have no patience
for. He's stereotypically handsome, slightly older than the other

Rawbonds, with pale eyelashes and a few freckles on the tip of his nose. "This is Tomison."

He leans around Izabel to smile at me. It's a smile that screams, *I'm likeable, and you're meant to like me.* I'm pretty sure it usually works on people.

"I'm Tomison Thorne. Future Alpha of the Strategos Pa—"

"His ego is compensating for something," Izabel interrupts, making me snort.

Tomison just chuckles good heartedly. "Eat up, Izabel. We've probably only got a few minutes before we're heading out."

The atmosphere between them is unexpectedly easy, and I realize that they already know each other. They're both from Bonded families. They likely grew up together or at the very least crossed paths.

The list of ways I don't fit in here is growing long enough that I'm going to start tripping on it soon.

It doesn't matter. I won't be here much longer, anyway.

Shoving my worries aside, I turn my attention to the food before me. It's just as extravagant as it was last night, so this is just how they always eat here—at a table covered in enough food to feed a family of four for a week.

I try to sample different foods. A flaky pastry with chocolate in the center. A flat cake dusted in powdered sugar. Succulent sausage links. Actual fucking fresh strawberries. *Coffee*, for goddess's sake. There are even some delicate boiled eggs with blue shells, right next to the platter of greasy bacon and a bowl with some sort of crisp fried bread I've never seen before.

I'm halfway through eating when my stomach begins to churn. This much rich food is actually starting to make me nauseous. How do they eat this every day?

"Okay?" Izabel asks, apparently noticing my discomfort.

I sip my coffee and nod. "Fine."

She slides a small cup over to me; there's one for every Rawbond. "Don't forget this."

"What is it?" I say, eying the viscous green liquid inside.

"Contraceptive draught. Everyone takes it. You don't want to ruin your chances of passing the Trials by, you know… getting in the family way."

The draught looks identical to the one I take from the apothecary at home, I realize. I knock it back without arguments. I won't be here long enough to let anyone touch me like that, but I'm not about to raise eyebrows by refusing.

The door to Strategos quarters swings open. In strides Egith Hartsfeld, looking fresh and well-rested. "It's orientation day! The one and only!" she booms, wasting zero time.

The other Rawbonds are already standing, chairs screeching and silverware clattering. I'm really just longing for a stupid bath.

"Strategos Rawbonds, follow me," Egith says. I noticed that instructors have emerged from the other pack quarters and are rounding up the other Rawbonds accordingly. "You'll be touring the facilities today. Don't ask me stupid questions."

Touring the facilities. Thank the goddess. I might be able to come up with a potential exit strategy if the straightforward method doesn't work for me.

Egith doesn't say anything else before turning on her heel and striding back out of the room.

"Woman of few words," I remark as Izabel and I head for the door with the rest of the Rawbonds.

"If only some people could be just like her when they grow up," Izabel replies, glancing at Tomison who's already chattering away with his group of followers.

As we trail Egith through the castle, she talks about the various wings we're passing through and their purposes. Something about kitchens and larders, medrooms, guardrooms, a tunnel to an undercroft.

But my eyes are carefully scanning for routes and noting landmarks so that I might navigate my ass out of here at the drop of a hat.

There are a few obvious servant passages that I could use. They're marked by narrow, short doorways too small for even an unbonded to pass through without bending over. A direwolf wouldn't fit one paw through, so there's no way they're used by anyone the Bonded consider consequential.

Our group steps into a wide hall with blazing braziers lining the walls. High above us, there's a mural on the ceiling depicting two stylized wolves, one white and one black, spinning around each other in an impressively lifelike dance.

I'm staring at it, neck craned, when one of the Rawbonds next to me whispers. Footsteps slow. A hush moves over them.

They're staring down the hall towards a set of wide open double doors four times taller than I am. Beyond those doors, there's an expansive space with a floor of packed dirt. It looks like daylight out there, but there's no frigid rush of air, so it's likely a large enclosed space with glass ceilings. I can make out a line where the smooth edges of carved architecture meet the jagged stone of the natural rock of the mountain.

"As many of you have obviously already noticed, *yes*. Down that way is the arena where your remaining Trials will take place." Remaining Trials, plural?! "Moving on."

What the fuck? How many more times do we trainees have to face death and dismemberment?

We're hurtling down the halls again, passing by various training areas dedicated to each pack. They're labeled just as the quarters were. I only catch brief glimpses as we pass by.

The Kryptos training yard is basically just an obstacle course with high guard towers. Daemos has several practice dummies lined up and weapons lining the walls, the dirt gouged with claw marks and what looks like the charred remnants of vicious magic. Phylax is equipped with a massive, odd device that looks like a series of swinging pendulums, as well as some more dummies and sets of heavy weights.

Strategos is by far the most boring looking, filled with tactical gear like harnesses and hooks, as well as several strategy tables and maybe two dozen maps covering the walls. Exciting stuff, peering at maps all day.

We linger briefly at the entrance to the Strategos training area as Egith explains that we're going to be spending a fair amount of our time here. My eyes wander beyond the dismal space. There are two tall doors on either side of a wall of floor-to-ceiling windows, beyond which snow slowly drifts.

I squint through the snow and realize suddenly what I'm seeing.

The mountainside looms tall. Embedded in the rocky cliff face, there are massive caves and outcroppings of stone. Lounging above are our wolves, staring down at us or minding their own business.

The wolf terraces, I realize, where they stay while we're in training.

I spot Anassa almost immediately. She's a shimmering silver-white that stands out against the darker stone, and she's reclined as far from the other direwolves as physically possible. Anassa's eyes meet mine briefly, and she immediately looks away from me, tail flicking in agitation. I curl my fingers into tight fists, hissing a breath through my nose.

Fine. Fuck her. I don't need her. She can disappear back to the mountain, for all I care. She forced me into this bond against my will, and then abandoned me.

As soon as I get the chance, I'm going to talk to Egith and get myself out of this screwed up situation, whatever it takes.

Our happy little tour ends in what looks like an auditorium. It's set up so that a semicircle of maybe a hundred seats funnels down towards a central raised dais. Like the rest of the castle, the walls are intricately carved wood and the ceilings are vaulted, with circular skylights between the supporting beams. The acoustics make our footsteps echo as we're all herded inside.

The other packs are here, too, joining from different doors across the rows of seats.

"Sit," Egith orders, and then strides down the rows to join the other people standing in center-stage.

We were the last to arrive, so we file into the back rows. I absently follow Izabel, studying the people waiting for us to find our seats so they can start talking.

There are five of them total, including Egith. Four of them are younger and one of them is a very obviously ancient relic, seventies at the youngest.

Stark is the tallest of them, standing with his arms crossed over his chest and several feet apart from the others. He's scowling again, his jaw ticking like he doesn't want to be on that stage and hates all of us for having the audacity to take more than thirty seconds to sit down.

In the more generous lighting, I can make out the dark ink of his tattoos more clearly, especially now that he's in a short-sleeved shirt. They twist around his arms and up to his neck in intricate designs. On his arms, they look runic, naturally inspired—geometric shapes hidden between chaotically elegant lines that make me think of fir forests and heavy antlers. They climb up the side of his neck and disappear beneath the curl of his dark hair behind his ear. Up higher, they almost start to look like claw marks around his throat, a collar of pain.

He's just too… *careful*. Honed. Attuned.

His eyes track movement like a predator does prey. His body remains tense enough for instantaneous response to threats.

Being in his presence is like standing with a knife at my throat, and I find myself settling very slowly into my seat so that I don't risk his attention slicing my skin open.

They're to be our instructors, I assume. One from each pack, maybe? Egith takes her place beside them, and the shuffling of the Strategos Rawbonds falls quiet just in time for me to hear the tail end of a hushed conversation from the row in front of me.

"—still can't believe they spared the *Alpha* of Daemos for this," one woman is saying. "He's the Sovereign Alpha's son, too, you know."

"Look at his tattoos," the other whispers back. "He's killed so many. And he's not even thirty yet. I heard he Bonded at eighteen and was the Daemos Alpha by the time he was twenty-one."

"*Fuck*, Stark is so hot," the first woman chokes out, slumping in her seat.

I raise a brow and study Stark again. I… guess?

Or, *yes*.

It's obvious. It's really obvious. He's probably six and a half feet of bulky, toned muscle with a perfect jawline, and eyelashes prettier than mine. His lips are full and his perpetually messy dark hair is actually artfully tousled and thick, the kind of hair that you'd want to pull when you're—

No, not going there.

And there's that way he holds himself. Not condescending like the other Bonded. More... challenging. Like he's daring the world to test his strength because he knows he'll come out on top.

The idea of all that strength and precision homed in on you, on your needs and wants and desires—

No! I shake my head. None of that matters. He may as well have "murderous psycho" carved into his forehead. He actually *does* have that tattooed across his hands, arms and neck.

The brief spark of interest I felt studying him—I'm only *human* —extinguishes instantly when I remember the things he's done and said.

You don't let someone that dangerous close to you. Not even just for sex.

"I would do criminal things to get that man between my legs," the second woman whispers.

Huh. Guess I'm alone in that opinion.

"Good morning, Rawbonds!" the older man says, stepping forward. He's wearing casual robes, a far cry from the tight-fitting, leather uniforms we wear.

"I am the former Alpha of Strategos, Aldrich Gnosis. You can refer to me as Leader Aldrich. I am to be the head of Rawbond training this season," he says, stroking his beard. "I want to welcome you to this process. The turnout this year is wonderful, and it has been a promising start to your four months here."

Four *months?*

I glance at Izabel beside me in shock, but she sits facing forward, inadequately alarmed.

Four fucking months. There's no way Saela can wait that long. Riding this nonsense out to reach the front isn't an option, then.

"These following months will prove whether you are fit to be in a pack and call yourselves Bonded. Many will survive the process, but make no mistake, many will not," he tells us. "Your training begins with the Forging, a two-month process with your own pack's Rawbonds. This period is intended for you to get to know your future packmates and ensure you are able to work together. Does anyone know what Trials occur during the Forging period?"

Izabel's hand shoots up instantaneously into the air, and she's practically vibrating on the edge of her seat. Ah, she's that kind of student, then. I'm not surprised, and it honestly endears her to me more—Saela's like this, too.

"Yes, in the back," says Leader Aldrich.

"In a month, we'll have the Voice Trial," Izabel recites as if from a book, "where we prove that we can communicate well with our direwolves."

Good thing I'm getting out of here; I'd never pass something like that.

"Indeed. And at the end of Forging?"

"The Purge Trial," Izabel says confidently. "Where the packs have a chance to cull their own numbers and remove any riders and direwolves that are not fit to join them."

My stomach freefalls from beneath me. The packs are going to *kill* their own?! No one else seems to so much as blink at this.

"Followed by the Forging Ball, of course," Izabel adds on quickly.

Sure, because who wouldn't follow a brutal massacre with a fancy ball?

"Precisely. Then we move onto Proving period, where—"

Izabel's hand shoots back up into the air, and Leader Aldrich chuckles.

"Yes, Miss...?"

"Izabel Brooks, sir."

"Oh, I know your father, Conrad Brooks! Great warrior. There was a moment in the Battle of Grunfall ten years ago, when he—ah, look at me, getting carried away with reminiscing." Leader Aldrich beams out at the crowd of Rawbonds. "Before you know it, you'll all be retired soldiers, too, thinking back on the thrilling days of war."

Thrilling. Definitely. If we don't die a vicious, painful death in training first.

"Anyway, carry on, Rawbond Brooks. Tell us what happens in the Proving period."

Izabel straightens in her seat. "The Proving is a two-month period where packs learn to work together in coordination. There are no additional Trials during the period, but it culminates in the Unity Trial, a mock-battle between all the packs, and then graduation."

Aldrich nods, clearly impressed. "Thank you, yes. The Unity Trial is the final culling to weed out the weak."

My eyes catch on Stark again only to find him already staring at me. *Right* at me. I tense in my seat, heart rate picking up speed. The back of my neck tingles and my hair rises. I resist the stupid instinct to turn and see if there's someone behind me who he might be staring at. I'm in the back row.

Which means that glower is for me, then, with that slight curl of his upper lip and those narrowed eyes.

Disdain. That's what it looks like. The words just spoken echo around the room's perfect acoustics.

Culling. He doesn't think I'll survive.

But I have no intention of suffering through their meaningless Trials. This place isn't for me, so he can sheathe his glower or point it at someone else more deserving. He's wasting it on me, honestly.

Leader Aldrich goes on to introduce the rest of the instructors. "Alpha Stark Therion of Daemos was spared from the front to train you all to be the best fighters you can possibly be. Respect his wisdom and learn everything you can from him."

He turns.

"Beta Egith Hartsfeld of Strategos is here to teach you battle strategy." I can't help but notice that her introduction was significantly shorter and without flair.

Guess Stark's ass is the only one he's interested in kissing.

He gestures to a pale man with a shock of blonde hair in his thirties. "Samson Whyte, Gamma of Kryptos, will teach you communication and concealment." Finally, he nods to a middle-aged woman with olive skin and dark hair. "And Elinoor Gardner, Gamma of Phylax, will instruct you in history and pack dynamics."

Aldrich continues his speech. "Now, as you all already know," I've learned that this means I should expect him to say something absolutely insane, "this will be bloody." Yep. "And though many of you will die in training exercises and in healthy competition, we do not condone violence in the pack quarters."

So I won't be murdered in my bunk at night. In theory.

"Believe it or not, you are *valuable* to us and to the king. Our goal is for as many of you to survive this process as is possible. So behave yourselves outside of class. Violations will be harshly penalized."

There's a swell of murmurs in response to Aldrich's admonishment.

Not killing each other every chance we get? The horror!

It all quickly hushes, though, when Stark steps forward, powerful arms dropping to his sides. He doesn't have to say a word for Aldrich to step aside and bow his head, a show of unusual deference. I thought Aldrich was in charge?

My skin prickles with terror and awareness as Stark's night-black direwolf pads into the room from a wide door behind him. He doesn't turn as the beast joins him on the stage, his wolf coming to stand behind him like his shadow.

The two of them swallow up the space. Stark's presence is palpable, the entire auditorium growing heavier as his eyes move over the crowd and his wolf's ears twitch forward.

"Your training has already started. It began the moment you touched that mountain. Your mistakes and your... *weaknesses*... have already been noted," he says.

There he goes again, staring directly at me. He must have seen me struggle with Anassa. Or maybe he considers my messed-up hair a mark of failure. I checked again at breakfast—no one else has a full head of hair in their pack's color. That dubious honor falls only to me.

I try to separate myself from his glare, but it's like trying to read a book while sitting under a guillotine.

"Those of you not fit to run with a pack will die. Without question. Without mercy."

I suppress my wince. Izabel's hand smooths over my wrist in my lap. She's not looking at me, but she's clearly also noticed how obviously he's glowering at me. Her touch does basically nothing to shield me from his hatred.

"But you know that. You've been practicing your entire lives for this… haven't you?" he says, quirking a dark brow at me. I clench my jaw tightly. "You understand that these halls demand respect. Generations of your ancestors have walked the same path as Rawbonds, have fought the same battles, have practiced the same drills. They understood, every step they took to becoming *true* Bonded, that this is survival of the fittest."

He strides forward on the stage. "You've bonded with a direwolf now, and there is no going back. Hesitation and fear are out of the question. Cowardice will get you killed."

Is there anything in this place that *won't* get us killed?

"We dress you in thick leather, but make no mistake—if a wolf decides to tear you open, it'll do nothing to stop their claws. If you want to keep your intestines where they belong, if you're sentimentally attached to your limbs, *step up*. Fight to the top, because those struggling on the bottom end up in direwolf bellies."

He makes a show of looking at the rest of the Rawbonds, but his eyes keep snapping back to me. His comments about survival of the fittest and generations of ancestors didn't escape my notice.

He thinks I'm weak for my common blood, then.

It fills me with the sort of spitting, hissing fury that could get me killed if I don't manage to wrangle it and direct it towards something useful rather than the classist, cruel man in front of me.

Still, something rises up in me at the sight of him and at those harsh words.

Rebellion. That's what it is. A need to prove him wrong. A need to break his will before he can break mine. It's that air of competition he projects. I breathe it in and my muscles buzz with the need to show the world that it can't break me.

"You will have two months to prove pack loyalty, then two more months of combat training, and you will be watched every step of the way. Do everything in your power to prepare yourselves and your wolves for the Trials ahead." He straightens. "Dismissed."

The room erupts into motion. Rawbonds flood from their seats, fires lit under their asses by all the talk of disembowelment, no doubt. The instructors disband, too, heading out through different doors.

I grab Izabel's arm. "I'll catch up with you."

"What? You're leaving? We're not going to talk about the Alpha of Daemos staring at you like——"

"We're not talking about it. My plan is to crush it down and repress the memory for the rest of time. Later," I say, releasing her and shoving my way through the stream of Rawbonds.

Egith disappears through the lower door on the right side of the room, the same one Stark's wolf came through. I make sure not to glance back towards the stage where I'm sure he's still standing, probably glaring at me. I swear I can sense his piercing eyes on me even as I flee after Hartsfeld.

In the Strategos quarters, I finally catch up to her. Egith ducks into one of the four side rooms off of the pack common area. We beat all the other Rawbonds back here, the path Egith took turning out to be a shortcut. I push past the knot of fizzling anxiety in my stomach and knock on the open door.

Egith turns and stares at me. This room is hers, I realize.

It's sparsely furnished, with only a bed, a side table, a dresser just like the ones we have, and a small table and chairs. Despite that, there are hidden luxuries everywhere. A heavenly-looking throw blanket draped over one of the chairs. Exorbitantly expensive-looking weapons hanging on the walls. Oil lamps instead of candles. Even a few stacks of personal books on her windowsill.

She doesn't say anything. Just keeps staring at me, a brow lifting and the corners of her mouth dragging downward. The look screams, *what the fuck are you doing here?*

"I don't belong here," I blurt.

"Excuse me?"

"I need to get out of here. My sister was taken by Nabbers and I have to get to the front to find her."

Egith crosses her arms. "What are you talking about? Nabbers?"

I shift my weight. "You know? Nabbers?"

"I *don't* know, actually," she says dryly. Which lights the same rage I felt earlier again.

The spark of it catches and spreads, and my cheeks heat. *Of course*, she doesn't know. I just thought... she's important, right? Everyone's always known that the king doesn't give a shit about the commoners, but even such a high-ranking Bonded doesn't know? Doesn't *care* to know?

"The Siphons have been kidnapping kids from the commoner side of Sturmfrost," I tell her, unable to keep acid out of my voice. Egith's eyes widen. "For generations, actually. That's why I enlisted, to find Saela."

Egith stares at me again. She does that a lot. When she speaks, there's no pity in her voice. "There's no leaving."

"Why?" I ask her point-blank.

Egith's eyes narrow. "It's not done, Rawbond."

My blood pressure rises at that complete and total non-answer. "But I can't even communicate with my wolf! *She* doesn't want me, so why do you?! Just let me go!"

Egith is suddenly right in front of me, moving so fast my eyes hardly catch it. "*Shut up*," she hisses, glancing over my shoulder. "You need to keep that to yourself."

"Wha—"

"You're already drawing attention, what with," she gestures to my hair, "all that. That's fucking strange enough. If anyone else finds out that your wolf isn't communicating with you at this stage, they'd take you out immediately."

"But they can't," I reply weakly. "Not in the quarters."

"They'll find a way," she says gravely. "Survival here is binary. You live or you die, and I can tell you right now which it's going to be if you keep this shit attitude going forward. The only way out is through, and the packs do *not* tolerate weakness amongst their ranks. If you want any chance of finding your sister, you need to keep your head down and fight for it."

So Egith is not going to help me leave, and if I draw any more attention to myself, someone will gut me before long.

Shit.

Shit.

Egith takes a step back. "I'll look into this Nabbers issue. It's…" Her brows pinch. I think she's upset this was the first she'd heard of it. "I'll find out more."

"Why do you even care?" I ask.

"Excuse me?" she growls out.

"You could just let me be… *culled*, or whatever it is you do here," I say.

"Whatever it is *we* do, Rawbond. And the answer is simple," she says, hands on her hips. *I care about you*, I muse cynically. *Not.* "We have a bet going."

I nearly snort. "A bet."

"There's a betting pool amongst the instructors on which pack will lose the fewest recruits. I really don't want to lose to that fucking asshole Stark, so stay alive. Please." She moves to her table and sits. "I have money riding on it."

Yeah. Seems about right.

She gives me a look that clearly says, *you're excused*, so I take a deep, deep breath through my nose and then turn on my heel, a plan already percolating in my mind.

If she's not going to help me, I'm going to find my own way out of this mess.

CHAPTER FOURTEEN

My drive mounts with every step I take back through the anteroom and toward the dorms. I'm not staying here a day longer. An hour, even. I'm only in this position because it was forced unwillingly on me, but I've got places to be. A sister to save. The love of my life to return to.

I know what it's like to have to do everything myself, to be on my own. It's been that way my entire life, really, and I've never let it stop me before.

When I reach my bunk, I catch a lucky break; nobody is here. They must all be making their way back from orientation still.

Without wasting any time, I race to the store closet and grab a spare bag, then hastily start packing, shoving necessities into it—a water skin, a clean set of clothes. I wish I'd had time to pocket some food from breakfast. When I have everything, I glance around briefly and then sling the bag over my shoulder. I slip from the dorms silently, a plan already forming in my head.

The servant passages I noticed during our convenient tour of the castle grounds will work. They're way too small for wolves, so it's unlikely the Bonded ever use them. Even without their wolves, they're probably too worried about getting cobwebs on their fancy uniforms.

I pause briefly at the door to the Rawbond common lounge. Some people have started to trickle in here. Most are clustered in groups of three or four, chatting or sitting on each other's laps flirtatiously or else perched at a table, playing a spirited game that seems to involve stones and dice.

Nobody is paying much attention to the exit. I eventually slip into the room, keeping my pace casual and concealing my bag with my body as best as I can. No one stops me.

Out in the halls, I do my best to silence my footsteps, putting most of my weight on my toes. Getting caught isn't an option, so I pause at corners to listen for anyone coming from the other direction. As I move strategically, I call up the landmarks I noted on our tour and picture the path I need to take to get out of this mazelike castle, where that entrance to the servant's corridors began and what direction to go from there.

The service passages are exactly as I imagined them—narrow, dusty, and clearly not used by anyone important. Everywhere in this place that a Bonded could touch has been polished and elaborately decorated. But the servants' tunnels are dark and sparse, practically empty.

Every once in a while a servant bustles past, carrying a tray or a bundle of laundry or a broom. We nod at each other in the gloomy light, but nobody stops me. I'm not sure if they mistake me for one of them, or if they prefer not to question a Rawbond's movements, no matter how strange.

I don't stick around to find out.

I check off the list of landmarks that I should be passing by as I move, occasionally ducking out into a main corridor to check my progress and make sure I know where I am. The training yards. A kitchen storage area. A drafty corridor with a cracked stone wall, the fissures messily filled with a mortar patchwork that's already struggling under the weight of the ceiling, pointed out as a back way to get to some of the classrooms.

The farther I get from the heart of the Bonded castle, the

steadier I become. I'm doing something. I'm acting when no one else will. I can almost picture my sister standing at the end of the dimly lit hallway, reaching for me.

Eventually, I no longer bother to quiet my steps because I'm close enough to the castle walls now that I haven't seen any servants for ages.

I finally find the courtyard I entered through, the gate where Egith waved me inside and I walked right in like an idiot. The cold air cools my sweaty skin. I reach for the heavy metal gate, briefly terrified that it's going to be locked. But it opens with a screech, the wolves carved into the metal parting before me.

My surprised exhale drifts into the air, and I step through. The moment I do, a heady mixture of relief and elation surges through me.

I made it. No one stopped me. No one could. No one even knows I'm gone.

But three steps past the gate, pain slices through my skull.

I try to ignore it and push onward. At first, it's nothing but a splitting headache. I can handle pain. I know how to endure it, if only because I never had any other choice. Maybe I didn't eat enough, or maybe it's just the stress of the past few days finally getting to me.

Too quickly, the pain escalates. My bones are turning to ice. Radiating outward, shards of blade-like agony rupture forth, cutting my insides, pushing outward towards my skin until my entire body is freezing over, ready to crack. My limbs go stiff, nausea spills through me, and I stagger.

What is this? Some sort of dark wolf-sorcery they've cast on the gates? Gritting my teeth, I push forward.

I barely make it ten more paces before my legs give way and I collapse face-first into the snow. I don't even realize I've fallen, at first. One second, I'm on my feet and walking clumsily, using the castle walls for support.

The next, I'm staring at snowflakes gathered two inches from my nose, pain ravaging my nerves and muscles seizing slightly.

I don't know how long I lie there.

A hand lands on my shoulder, and I'm still able to feel it through the cold. The world spins around me, but through it all, I can make out two familiar faces.

Izabel and Venna hover over me. Venna is closer. Hers is the hand on my shoulder, her tight grip and the twisting of her features expressing both frustration and concern. Izabel's expression is one of pure sympathy. Her eyes are glassy, like she's on the verge of tears solely because someone she barely knows is shivering pathetically in the snow.

Venna says something I can't quite make out, then the two of them take my arms and haul me upright. I grunt and clench my chattering teeth. I hate this. I hate the twins seeing me like this, as if I'm some trembling weakling.

They know I was trying to leave, and my failure to do so is embarrassing. Humiliating, really.

Trying to maintain some pride, I attempt to walk on my own, but my legs won't listen to me. I end up wriggling in their grip like a drunkard until we draw closer to the castle and the pain begins to abate.

Venna's right hand clamps even harder on my arm as I begin to stand straighter. "What were you thinking?"

I want to spit something venomous back at them, but my mouth doesn't want to listen to my brain quite yet. I might immediately vomit if I try it.

Izabel chimes in. "She's right. You could've died."

Scoffing, I finally get my feet under me. I shove the twins off and stagger towards the closest wall because I'm not entirely certain I'll be able to remain upright otherwise. Yet the agony is very quickly leaving me. It's shocking how normal I feel so soon after being wracked by the sensation of my insides shattering.

When I turn to look at them, Venna's hands are on her hips and Izabel is hugging herself. "What *were* you doing?" Izabel asks.

"Leaving," I rasp out.

She rolls her eyes. "I know that, but——"

"I have to get to my sister," I snap. No one in this entire fucking castle seems to give a shit, but I do. "I can't stay here. I have to reach her. I don't know what just happened, but it can't keep me from going after her. I can't be stuck here for *four months*, while Saela…" I can't even finish the thought.

Venna's eyes are downcast, face pale. Izabel's face crumples. "I get it, but—"

"You don't," I growl and slide down the wall. I rest my elbows on my knees and sink my hands into my silver hair. "You don't," I murmur under my breath.

Venna steps closer and sits beside me with her back against the wall. She holds out a hand, which Izabel takes as she, too, settles in front of me.

"Look," Venna says slowly, "you need to understand that the bond between wolf and rider is fragile at first. I think yours might be especially fragile. Distance creates physical strain, which I'm guessing you felt? And that strain can snap it entirely, killing both wolf and rider."

The enormity of that statement doesn't entirely sink in, at first.

Izabel picks up where her sister left off. "It isn't just something you can overcome through sheer determination. Only time and trust can strengthen the bond enough to allow distance. So unless you can convince your direwolf to take off to the front with you…"

Her voice trails off, and I realize the reality of the situation. It hits me like a hammer over the head. That pain…

I'm not going anywhere. I'm trapped. Truly, utterly fucking trapped.

If I try to go, it'll just happen again the same way, and maybe next time, I won't have Izabel and Venna there to drag my limp body from the snow.

Something akin to horror boils in my chest. I try everything I can to hold it together. These two women have just seen me struggling to stay alive in the snow, drunk on pain, helpless. I don't need to let them see my despair, too.

But it's just too much. The soaring hope of stepping out of the castle followed by that crippling pain. And now this. This claustrophobic, wretched truth that makes my skin crawl.

The sob rips from me. All the emotion I've been holding back since my arrival in this awful place, since the Ascent started, really, pushes to the surface. My eyes burn as I double over and start to shiver. My fingers dig into my knees as I try to pull myself from this spiral of grief, but I can't stop it. Anger and fear and shame swirl in my mind, but the twins don't react the way I expected.

I figured they would find my crying pathetic. I'd be weak, right? A common Rawbond unworthy of the bond she forged, already fracturing under the pressure.

But they don't mock me. They don't leave me there to fall apart. Venna reaches out and slides a warm hand down my back. Izabel reaches into her pocket and pulls out a silk handkerchief, holding it out to me. I stare at it for a moment, nearly shocked out of my tears.

Hesitantly, I take it and press it to my cheeks. The pain won't stop, but it's easing slightly with the constant gentle strokes of Venna's hand on my back and the understanding glint in Izabel's eyes.

"Why are you being so nice to me?" I ask and quickly wipe at another tear before it falls.

Venna and Izabel sign to each other quickly, and I internally vow to learn this language fast, so that they can't leave me out. "We're confused," Venna finally says aloud.

I sniff and clutch the silk in my hand, crumpling it. "I'm obviously a weak link. I'm a commoner, and I don't even want to be here. What are you getting out of this?"

Izabel scoffs and shakes her head. She settles back on one hand, propping herself up. "It's not like that."

"Then what?"

She watches me for a long moment. I think she's deciding whether to be honest with me. Her eyes dart to her sister and back to me. Then finally, she takes a deep breath and says, "No one believed the two of us could survive a Bonding Trial."

"What?" I blurt. "Why?"

Venna sighs. "Because of my disability. My hearing... I've been hard of hearing since childhood. I'm usually okay in one-on-one or small groups, but when groups get bigger and noisier..."

"And because of my commitment to her," Izabel adds. "I'd never leave her behind, and everyone thought…" She shakes her head. "They thought Venna would drag us down. When that's the opposite of the truth, obviously."

Venna grins and scoots her foot out to nudge Izabel's leg with her boot. Izabel rests her hand on Venna's ankle and looks at me. "Our parents were our only champions. They taught us that we had to be twice as good as anyone else in order to survive and prove the rest of them wrong."

My mind flashes to Igor, his faith in me. The way he helped me survive against the odds, despite having lost my father and essentially lost my mother, too.

I guess I know a little of what they mean.

"We became fighters because we had to. And like recognizes like, I guess," Venna says with a gesture towards me. My lips part, and I stare at her. She looks amused by my surprise. "Meryn, why do you think we fought through the Ascent with you? You have that strength, too—the same drive to prove everyone else wrong. Maybe you're a commoner. Maybe you're stuck. But who cares? Fight harder."

My breath is uneven. For the first time since arriving at the castle, something in my chest wants to reach out and take hold of the world around me. Venna nudges my elbow gently. She's smiling at me.

"Plus, if anyone took Ven from me, or me from her…" Izabel adds. Her expression darkens. Venna immediately shuffles closer to her and leans against her side. Izabel sighs and meets my gaze. "We get it, Meryn."

I lift my chin and wipe my cheeks with my fist. And I look at the two of them and think that maybe they do get it.

It tastes almost bitter, realizing these Bonded-born women and I are so alike. I already respected them, of course, their strength in the face of the horrors of the Ascent, the way they worked together —worked with *me*—to make it through that hellish climb.

But even so, it's a strange, new feeling, knowing that I have something in common with them. That I... maybe can understand them.

"For Saela's sake, I could do anything," I say, and my voice doesn't shake. "Even if that means making this damned bond work, somehow winning over that bitch Anassa so that she carries me to Saela herself." Something whispers against the bond in my head, as if Anassa's heard me, but I ignore it.

Venna signs something to Izabel, and Izabel laughs. "Good," she says. "Then first things first, Venna and I agree that you need to take a bath because you stink. Tonight is Presentation."

Venna makes a show of pinching her nose and smirking at me. I snort, amused until I register what Izabel just said.

What the fuck is Presentation? Another Trial? And why do I need to smell nice for it?

We make it back to the dorms in much less time than my bid for freedom took, since we don't have to avoid main hallways or being seen. Venna splits off when we reach the common room, heading toward the Kryptos quarters.

By the time we reach the Strategos bunk room again, the other Rawbonds are all inside, a flurry of motion and clothing. I squint at them as I stride past beds to reach mine and Izabel's. But I stop dead when I see one of the other Rawbonds wearing a *cravat* around his neck. And a suit jacket. And shiny shoes.

Wait, they're *all* dressing up, unpacking fancy clothing and meticulously arranging their hair.

"Hurry up," Izabel hisses, gesturing toward the washroom door. "You need to go take a bath, right now, and then get ready."

"So I've been told," I grumble.

"No, you don't understand. You have to look nice. It's like I told you earlier. Appearances matter here. You'll be expected to look like a Rawbond, not just be one," she says urgently.

She tries to shove me towards the washrooms, but I resist. "Izabel, what the fuck is going on?"

"Presentation, I told you," she replies, agitated. Then she double takes and her eyes widen. "*Right.* You don't know what that is. It's where we're all put in front of the royals to show off the new class of recruits. Nobles from across the seven fiefdoms come to see it, too."

"And we dress up?"

"You know how it is…" *Actually, I don't.* "We have to worry about the rankings, but that's not all of it. The royals, the nobles… well, we're the pride of Nocturna, the best of the best. Not just at fighting. We're, well, on display." For the first time, Izabel looks a little uncomfortable about what she's saying, but then she brightens. "You're naturally pretty, you'll do fine. But we need to get you cleaned up."

"Wait—" I'm not ready to let this go. "Rankings?! Like we'll be assigned numbers or something based on how fuckable we look tonight?"

Izabel laughs but shakes her head. "Each pack has its own rankings. Obviously, each pack is led by an alpha, then the beta and a couple of gammas. None of us Rawbonds have titles like that yet, but the wolves are always watching what we do and there's a hierarchy amongst them. The packs will try to pick off the people who fall to the bottom of the ranks."

But Izabel said we'd be on *display.* It's not just about the wolves. We're entertainment for the nobles and the king.

Everyone is judging us.

Right now, I'm significantly more worried about the wolves, who apparently might just decide to murder one of us if we stand with our shoulders slumped or look a little soft around the middle.

"They might even do that tonight, if one of us fails to impress," Izabel adds contemplatively.

Panic strikes me like a hammer to the head. I grip the bunk for balance and gesture to myself. "Failing to impress, Izabel? And how exactly do you think I'll measure up?"

Izabel tenses up. "Right. Shit." Her eyes move over me, and her jaw tightens. "Okay, I have an idea."

CHAPTER FIFTEEN

My footsteps echo faintly against the gleaming white marble of the Strategos washroom as I slink toward one of the enormous tubs sunk into the floor. There are half a dozen of them spaced around the room. They're big enough to fit several people at once and already full of steaming, crystal-clear water.

Shit, even the *baths* here are extravagant.

Back home we have a dented metal tub barely big enough to hold me, and the pump that feeds it produces ice-cold water tinted orange with rust. I didn't even know baths like this could exist, didn't dare to dream of something so luxurious.

The room is cavernous—high ceilings, tall frosted glass windows, golden taps and sinks. Even the grates on the drains set into the floors are gold.

Egith's voice rings out in my memory. *"You're already drawing attention to yourself."* I try to temper my slack-jawed wonder of it, to look *less* like the impoverished commoner I am, as I quickly undress.

At least there's no one else here. But it doesn't escape me that this is a communal space. There aren't any privacy screens, and there's no lock on the door, either. The men and women of the Bonded bathe... together.

My face heats at the thought. No one's ever accused me of being a prude, but something about the idea is almost lewd.

There's a row of shelves set into one wall. Perfectly folded white towels and washcloths, pristine and fluffy. Bottles of perfumed soaps, lotions, and who knows what else.

I grab a bottle and sniff. I don't recognize the scents, but it's divine—fresh flowers and a hint of something deep. Expensive and oddly sensual.

Fuck, I can't use this. Like putting jewelry on a pig.

Wait, did I just call myself a pig?

I clench my teeth. This place is already getting to me, making me feel... inferior. But I'm not. Being born into money and privilege doesn't make these people better than me.

At that moment, I catch sight of myself in the enormous gilded mirror hanging above the sinks. It gives me a start. The woman looking back at me is almost a stranger, her silver hair gleaming in the late afternoon light, her mouth set in a serious line.

I look away quickly, overwhelmed by a rush of jumbled emotions. Familiar rage and pain—and something else. A wobbly confusion that sets my teeth on edge.

This whole ordeal has already changed me in ways I can't begin to understand.

And now I have to primp and pose to entertain a bunch of pompous nobles, like I'm a nice cut of meat on display at the butcher? *It's for Sae,* I tell myself, stiffening my spine. *Remember, this is all for her.*

Survival is all that matters, by any means necessary.

I take the bottle and hurry to the nearest tub, stripping the rest of my clothes off quickly. Hot water envelops me as I climb in.

It's a shock at first—almost scalding. I suck in a breath, gripping the bottle of soap so hard I'm surprised it doesn't shatter in my hand. And then...

Relief.

Heat seeps into every pore, every aching muscle, straight to my bones. All the little pains drift away, replaced by melting pleasure. My eyes roll back in my head and I almost let out a moan.

I had no idea that baths could be like this, like anything other than a chilly race to get myself slightly clean. If I'm going to be stuck here—fighting for my life, captive to an unwanted bond—well then, I'm going to take one of these every fucking night.

Pouring some soap into my hands, I lather it into my hair, trying not to look at the thick silver stands slipping over my shoulder. I'm not sure why it unsettles me so much except… it isn't *right*.

The hair is just another reason I don't belong here. Another sign that screams *outsider*. I can't even bond right.

Whatever. I'm glad I'm an outsider. This world of the Bonded is totally fucked. Except, of course, for these goddess-sent baths.

I duck my head to wash the soap out of my hair and surface again to find a pair of Strategos Rawbonds has joined me in the washroom. One of them is the tall, beautiful blonde woman who sleeps in the bunk next to mine—Perielle, I think her name is. Her skin is luminous and her hair is already glossy and clean. In my part of the city, it would be seen as a waste of water to bathe in her condition.

Even though I haven't spent much time around women my own age, I know how social hierarchies work, and based on what I've observed in the past day, Perielle most definitely sits atop the food chain. While Tomison attracts a crowd of admirers wherever he goes, Perielle seems to have lackeys and those who fear her in an awe-ridden way.

The two young women cast me identical looks of scorn and cross to the tub farthest away, a reminder that I am at the bottom of that chain. They proceed to chat in low tones, ignoring me completely. That's just fine with me.

Except they're not the last to join us. More of my fellow Strategos come trickling steadily in, men and women alike. They all go about undressing and washing like it's totally normal.

Meanwhile, I'm shrinking in the water, brutally aware of my nakedness.

How can they all be so blasé? The two people I've ever seen

completely naked are my little sister—before she was old enough to bathe herself—and Lee, after we'd been seeing each other for months and could finally get some time alone at his apartment. But these people seem totally at ease with their nudity, regardless of gender.

Before long, the steam-slick walls of the washroom echo with voices and laughter. The tubs are full of people—three and four in each. Others wash in the spray of the taps that line the wall behind the tubs, while yet more primp and pose before the big mirror, excitedly talking about dresses and hairstyles for the Presentation.

I finish washing, trying not to stare at all those lean, naked bodies; the smooth skin and gleaming muscles that speak of good nutrition and copious training.

Finally, as I gather my courage to get out of the water, Izabel comes breezing in. She spots me immediately and makes a beeline in my direction.

"Look at this!" she exclaims, shrugging out of her robe. "A whole tub to ourselves!"

I grimace and cross my arms over my breasts as she clambers into the water.

"Careful, you'll catch my commoner disease," I quip. It comes out a lot more bitter than I meant it to.

Izabel laughs. "Ignore those idiots, they're probably just intimidated by you." Then she notices my posture. "Wait, are you *shy?*"

I glare at her.

She laughs again. "You'll get used to it. After all, when you might die tomorrow, why waste time on shame? Plus, we're supposed to be a pack, you know? Gotta get used to sharing everything."

I'm not sharing squat with these bastards, I think. But I wish I could share their ease, even so. All I can do is think about the years of scrubbing other people's clothes in cold wash buckets. Poverty teaches you a whole different set of lessons about modesty.

"You better get out before you start getting pruny," Izabel says, nabbing my bottle of soap. "I'll meet you back in the bunk room shortly."

I nod and force myself to clamber out, careful not to rush. The last thing I need is to slip on the marble and fall on my face in front of everyone. Naked.

Thankfully, no one seems to look at me as I scurry to wrap myself in one of the big fluffy towels. It's so *soft*—far softer than anything I've ever put on my body before.

Once again, it's such an extravagant waste. Why do the Bonded *trainees* get fluffy towels like this, when we're supposed to be in austerity mode as a nation, saving money to send to our troops? Is this just a lie that the king feeds to the commoners, so he can keep his chosen ones in comfort?

But the place in my chest that used to hold my churning anger has been hollowed out. I don't have the mental capacity for the fury at the Bonded anymore. All I can think about is my own survival.

Back at the bunks, Venna is waiting. She smiles when she sees me and gestures to a pile of stuff beside her on Izabel's mattress. There's a dress, fancy boots, jewelry, little tins of makeup, and other things I can't even name.

Well, shit, I think, steeling myself once again. *Here we go.*

An hour later, Izabel and Venna have done their worst. They've been fussing over me like I'm their personal doll, having a lot more fun with it than strictly necessary, in my opinion. I'm adorned in a dozen expensive things the sisters nicked off other trainees they know in all the packs, all the way down to a set of elaborate silken undergarments that make me blush every time I think about them.

I'm a little terrified to see the final look.

I've never considered myself feminine, much less pretty—though Lee made some progress convincing me otherwise. My shoulders are too broad, my calves too thick, my face too round. The only thing I ever really liked about myself was my thick, dark hair.

Of course, this place has taken that from me.

Right now, I'm sure I look absolutely ridiculous. Every bit like a pig in jewelry—plus a fancy dress and makeup, with my hair pinned and curled and gelled into place.

At least the boots fit, and they're gorgeous, too. Sleek and elegant, made of shining, butter-soft leather. They hug my legs like a second skin all the way to the knee. I could do without the heels, but at least they aren't very high.

The dress, on the other hand, I'm not so sure about. It's made of some silky material I can't name and dyed deep, plummy purple. It has a faint shimmer to it, like oil on water, and it's quite revealing, with high slits on either side. It's so light and clingy that I feel close to naked wearing it.

"There," Izabel says, straightening away from me with a little tin of lip dye in one hand. "That's the final touch." She looks at Venna, who grins and nods.

"You look amazing," Venna adds, clearly proud of her handiwork. "Thanks to your talented new friends."

I roll my eyes. "Sure. As long as I don't look out of place at the Presentation."

"Out of place?" Izabel says. "No. But you'll certainly stand out with that *hair*."

Izabel and Venna exchange quick, worried glances. "What?" I ask sharply.

There's a huff from my left and I turn to see a brown-skinned woman with curly hair staring at me in assessment. She was the person crying silently in the courtyard last night. "You wouldn't want to stand out *too* much."

"I know, I know," I say. "I need to fit into the pack."

The woman shakes her head. "It's not about that." She raises her eyebrows at Venna and Izabel, who give her matching winces in return.

"Why are you all being so cryptic?" I ask.

The woman eyes me up and down and says, "I think you'll be fine. The hair is attention-grabbing, but you're not clearly trying to win his eye. Some of the other women here are more obviously vying for that." She gestures behind her, where two women are laced into gowns with such little fabric that they're practically naked, their toned and beautiful bodies on display.

"Nevah," Venna hisses at the woman.

I level Izabel with a look. "*What* is going on? And remember that I know nothing!"

Izabel sighs, shifting uncomfortably. "I told you, we're on display during Presentation for the king and the nobles. This is their opportunity to… choose among us, if they're interested."

The implication slams into me with the force of an unexpected hit from the ring. Choose among them. Among *us*. For… sex.

"That's disgusting," I spit out, my stomach twisting. Sure, the Bonded are granted an opulent lifestyle if they survive this training, but at what cost?

Izabel shrugs. "It benefits everyone," she says, speaking quickly, her cheeks flushing at my judgmental tone. "We get the opportunity to mix with the nobles of the kingdom. I've heard that every once in a while, a Rawbond actually makes a match with a noble. And we're not required to do anything if we don't want to."

I wonder if she believes this load of wolf dung. If she's truly okay with it, or if she too can sense how messed up this is.

Nevah scoffs. "Unless, of course, the king chooses you. That one's not optional. Every time there are Bonding Trials, King Cyril picks a Rawbond to be his companion, for the duration of the four months."

My skin crawls. "And that's why I need to be worried about standing out too much? In case the king of Nocturna decides to turn me into an unwilling sex partner?"

"Don't worry," Nevah says, patting me on the arm. "There are too many obviously willing candidates for him to go for you."

I look again at the women in the flimsy dresses, who are now sending each other icy glares, clearly each put out by the other's lurid appearance. "Why would anyone *want* that?"

"It's an honor for our families," Nevah says, her voice barely masking her own disgust. "You're supposed to be proud to be one of his chosen." I notice that Nevah is wearing a dress that fits in with everyone else's, deep green and cut low at the chest, but not particularly scandalous.

Guess she's not trying to win the king's attention, either.

"Go check yourself out in the mirror," says Venna. "Izabel and I still need to get ready."

With a sigh of dread, I head for the dorm lavatory. As I step in, I look up, meeting my own gaze in the mirror above the lavatory sinks —and freeze in shock.

The woman looking back at me is more alien than ever before. And she's… gorgeous.

Luminous olive skin. Wide hazel eyes shadowed with shimmering purple. Long, thick lashes. Full, wine-red lips. The purple dress hugs every line of my body with sensual grace, turning sturdy to elegant. Athletic to erotic.

Gone is the rugged street fighter from the slums. In her place is a powerful, elegant woman who looks like she can seduce a man as easily as beat him down.

And somehow, the jewel in the crown of this impossibly feminine vision is all that silver-white hair. The twins have pinned some of it up in an effortless chignon, but the rest cascades around my shoulders like curls of living ice, framing my face in a way that softens the features I've always thought were coarse.

I've become a stranger to myself.

The lavatory door bangs open and jolts me out of my dazed self-contemplation. Izabel and Venna enter, dressed in matching slinky, low-cut navy blue gowns. They smile at me and begin making themselves up in the mirror.

Something inside me instantly shrinks when I see our reflections side-by-side.

Despite the transformation, it's clear that we're not the same. Their refined, willowy frames tower over me, practically *screaming* elegance and sophistication. Their faces are twin visions of delicate beauty, utterly antithetical to my own.

And they're not the only ones. Every woman among the Bonded has that same air of elegance. That same graceful, willowy perfection. Even made up like this, I look coarse beside them—my frame much denser, my hips and shoulders wider, my muscles heavier.

The sense of not belonging returns in full force.

Beside these children of the Bonded, I look like exactly what I am.

Defective.

And if it will keep me protected tonight, well that's just fine with me.

BY THE TIME we arrive at the courtyard outside the arena, it's near sunset and the air has a biting chill.

It's a struggle not to gape at the enormous, impossible structure carved into the side of the mountain above us. Its vast, domed ceiling is supported by countless stone pillars and guarded by huge, elaborate carvings that stare down at us with unnerving intensity: direwolves and their riders poised for battle.

I'm relieved to see that the looming building is fully enclosed. At least it'll be warm.

My fellow Rawbonds seem unmoved by the imposing architecture. Each pack is here with their leaders, standing in separate groups along the path leading up to the arena, waiting for the signal to enter. They look like a flock of young royals ready for a gala.

Even Stark is dressed up in a shining black suit. I try not to let my gaze linger on the way it clings to his powerful arms.

There's a lot of hushed chatter and last-minute fussing with clothes and hair. The air is thick with anticipation.

Meanwhile, I feel even more like a walking mistake than I did before. Everyone keeps *looking* at me. Sidelong glances, blatant shock, consternation. Even anger, as though my appearance is some kind of affront.

It's like I'm more naked in this stupid dress than I was in the baths when they were all ignoring me.

Suddenly, a familiar commanding voice rises from somewhere at the front of the path.

"Alright, everyone line up, two by two! It's almost time!" I see Egith's arm wave above the crowd as everyone moves to obey. "Hurry up, now! Nice and orderly!"

The packs begin to melt together as we fall in line. Izabel and Venna pair up behind me. Two more women pair up in front. In a moment, we're all neatly in line—and of course, I'm the only one standing alone.

Egith paces by, checking us over. She pauses when she sees me and her lips compress, but she says nothing. Seconds later, she's back at the arena entrance calling, "Best behavior, Rawbonds! The king will be watching!"

That sentence has new meaning, I think, as the hair rises along my arms.

My heart is in my throat as the big doors creak open and a rush of warm, heavily scented air washes over us. It brings the sounds of hundreds of high-born people waiting in the stands—a low, oddly decorous buzzing of many voices.

Nothing like the wild roar of the onlookers at my fights back home, despite the much larger crowd.

A small portion of the stands is visible through the doorway as the line moves forward. Rows upon rows of nobles in suits and glittering dresses, dressed notably more modestly than us Rawbonds. The sick twisting in my stomach is back at the obvious class distinctions. We're here for their amusement.

The point is driven home when I see the flash of fire on glass and metal and realize the nobles are holding gilded binoculars to their eyes, peering down at us eagerly. Huge golden lanterns dangle from the high glass ceiling, casting the scene in a warm glow.

Izabel nudges me in the back as we file through into the arena. "Head high," she whispers. "You're a Bonded, remember? Make them believe it."

I glance back. Beside her, Venna flashes me an encouraging grin.

Right. I take a deep breath and tell myself this is just like entering a fight. The only difference is posturing—a veneer of gentility and affluence. Potential violence lurks everywhere, and my opponents will leap on any sign of weakness.

Whatever happens in there, I have to project confidence.

The cobbled path underfoot changes to hard-packed dirt as I cross the arena threshold. I catch a distinct, familiar scent under the waft of burning lamp oil and countless perfumes.

Death.

A chill creeps down my spine. I can actually taste that thick iron tang. As the air around me shifts, that smell hits the back of my throat with such strength it threatens to gag me, recalling countless warehouses in the slums. Countless fights.

Only it's magnified a thousand times over.

How many people have died here? I wonder. *Hundreds? Thousands?*

I look down at the dirt crunching faintly under my boots as we move to the center of the field. It's smooth but mottled. Darkened with splatters of old blood that soaked deep into the earth, layer upon layer. Battle upon battle.

Death upon death.

And there's something else. Narrow divots dug into the ground like a web that covers the entire field.

What the hell?

A sudden pulse fills my head. An aching pressure gathers behind my eyes, insistent and strong.

Over the hum of the crowd and the crunch of our footsteps, I start to hear other sounds. Low, hissing voices.

Is that… *whispering?*

No. My fellow Rawbonds are absolutely silent as we approach the center of the field. It must be the crowd. Or maybe just the blood pumping in my ears.

Or maybe you're going mad like your mother.

Hastily, I shove the thought away.

Finally, we reach arena's center. Egith gestures for us to stop, and then turn. On the far edge of the amphitheater, there's another enormous, arched doorway.

A loud *thunk* echoes across the field and the towering doors swing arduously open, pushed by a pair of servants dressed in the king's livery. Beyond lies only shadows.

At once, the crowd falls silent.

The pulsing in my head gets stronger. Now, in the strange thrumming quiet, I *do* hear whispers. But I'm not listening anymore. All my senses are trained on that gaping maw of darkness.

Something is in there. Two pinpricks of greenish light that grow into bright orbs. They flash with an unmistakable night glow. With raw, wild awareness.

Eyes.

More orbs appear, bobbing slowly as they drift towards us.

A huge, black-furred face emerges from the shadows, followed by wide rippling shoulders. Then comes another face, this one silver and white. And another, rust and cream.

Our wolves.

An invisible crackle of wild energy fills the air. Cheers rise from the stands as the massive animals stream onto the field. I watch, heart pounding, as each one approaches its chosen.

The Rawbonds step forward, fanning out to meet their wolves. To stand side-by-side in proud rows, dwarfed by the hulking predators. Many wolves greet their riders, muzzle to hand, reaffirming their bonds through physical contact.

An odd twinge of jealousy hits me. Anassa would never greet me like that.

Wait, where *is* Anassa? All the other wolves are here.

The crowd falls silent once more, their eyes on me like a physical weight. I'm the only Rawbond standing alone. For a moment, I start to panic.

What the fuck am I going to do if that damned direwolf doesn't show?

Then I see it—a final pair of night glow orbs bobbing in the darkness of the doorway.

She appears like a great silver-white ghost, even larger than the rest, trailing into the light with her head lowered in silent aggression. Her upper lip twitches over her teeth, on the edge of a snarl. The light from the lamps above glints gold on her pale fur.

The air grows still. The cheers have died down. The entire arena watches with bated breath as Anassa slowly stalks towards me.

I do not step forward to meet her like the others. Somehow, I know that's the wrong thing to do. Instead, I just stand there, back straight, jaw set, reading the threat of primal violence in every line of her body.

I reach out to her with my thoughts, though. I don't mean to. It just happens—like a reflex.

I'm met with a familiar iron wall of rejection. Her glowing yellow eyes meet mine. There's blatant contempt in them.

Yeah well, fuck you, too, I think, furious.

Is she *trying* to make me look bad? I'd quite like to stay alive.

Her gaze flickers then—some emotion I can't identify. I'm struck again by the ancient intelligence in those eyes. Goosebumps rise along my arms and lift the hair at my nape in primal recognition.

As she nears, the other Rawbond pairs fan out even further to make room for her, their anxiety rippling in the air. Even the other wolves seem to fear her.

At last, Anassa takes her place beside me, standing well out of arm's reach, radiating icy indifference.

I glance up at the crowd, shifting anxiously on my toes. They must be able to see how much she hates me. This is definitely not going to help my chances with... whatever the fuck this is. Or with the inter-pack rankings that Izabel mentioned.

The sinking dread returns. Looks like I'm on my own once again.

There's a stirring in the crowd. Excited murmurs, heads turning. I follow their looks to the enormous balcony above the wolves' entrance.

The rows of seats there are filled with Bonded—our instructors have made their way up there, along with a few other Bonded that I don't recognize who must be high-ranking. A richly carpeted staircase behind them rises to another set of doors. These are elaborately carved with the royal coat of arms.

A herald appears with a voice amplifier in his hand. "Presenting His Royal Highness Cyril Valtiere, King of Nocturna!"

The crowd hushes.

A procession emerges through the gilded doors, led by gold-armored guards and more liveried servants. Behind them comes a regal figure draped in a sumptuous, fur-lined cloak, gold glittering over his brow.

The king.

I've lived my whole life just outside his castle, but I've never seen him before.

His face is pale and narrow, his gray hair neatly arranged. He's trim for a man in his fifties, but he seems small and almost frail amongst the battle-hardened Bonded.

In fact, he's pretty unremarkable—all the pageantry notwithstanding. Only his eyes indicate there's more to him than his appearance suggests. Even at such a distance, I can see the keenness and cunning in his pale blue gaze.

Still, just a man, I think, faintly disgusted. I don't know what I was expecting.

King Cyril mounts a raised platform and crosses to the big jeweled throne at the center of the balcony. He sits and lifts a golden sword across his knee. I can't see the weapon clearly, but I know the stories.

It's the *Diren Blæd*. The fabled weapon that supposedly gives him power over all direwolves, Bonded and unbonded alike. They say the pommel is shaped like a glowering direwolf's head.

It was a gift bestowed upon his ancestors hundreds of years ago by the Faceless Goddess, or so the story goes. She offered it as a means to right the balance between humans and direwolves back when the wolves still hunted us like cattle.

King Cyril's gaze sweeps down to the field, taking us in. For a moment, it settles on Anassa, then shifts to me, narrowing sharply.

With a start, I realize the other Rawbonds are bowing. Even the wolves have lowered their heads—all except Anassa, who stares up at the king with unblinking intensity.

Shit. I bow hurriedly.

Then the herald speaks again. "Presenting His Royal Highness Killian Valtiere, Crown Prince of Nocturna!"

Everyone straightens as one and a ripple of excited whispers starts up around me. The king's heir, Prince Killian, is rarely seen in public. The little that I know about him, I've gleaned from rumors over the years: he's in his late twenties, rumored to be extremely handsome, and is unwed.

"Here he comes," breathes a woman to my left. Clearly, the Rawbonds around me are hoping that the prince will also pick a companion from among them.

"Whoa," Izabel hisses behind me. "He's actually here!"

"He's gorgeous!" says yet another.

Irritated by their fawning admiration, I lift my gaze again to the royal procession. Another pair of guards. More servants. And finally, the prince, a tall masculine figure dressed simply in gold and white.

Wait.

I blink. Shake my head. Look again.

No.

A strange ringing fills my ears, deafening me to all but the raw thud of my heartbeat.

That handsome face, with its sharp jawline and knowing blue eyes. The sleek blonde hair. The broad shoulders.

My thoughts shudder and tumble, shattering into meaningless shards that cut me to the bone.

It *can't* be him.

But it is.

I would know that man at any distance, in any dress.

We shared promises. Secrets. Dreams I never believed I would get to live.

Crown Prince Killian descends to the balcony while I stand there frozen, my whole world crumbling around me. And then, seated at his father's side, he lifts his head and looks right at me, dark blue eyes filled with regret.

My heart cracks.

Lee.

CHAPTER SIXTEEN

The arena tilts and spirals around me until I have to look away from the prince. Have to shut my eyes and focus on forcing my lungs to take even one damned breath. I'm sick, my heart pounding too fast.

Thoughts stream by, rapid-fire.

It's not real, it's not real.

I'm crazy like my mother. I'm hallucinating.

Lee would never do this to me.

But it's no use. I know this isn't madness. It's no hallucination.

I know because I'm *enraged*. It rises up from my guts like slow fire, searing everything in its path. Honing my senses with cutting clarity.

I open my eyes. He's still there. Crown Prince Killian. Lee.

My beloved.

He said he loved me. He made me promise to come back to him. The thought of returning to him, to our lives together, to the future we were going to build—it's been one of the things getting me through these confusing, brutal days.

He fucking *lied*.

Our gazes meet again. I know he can read the betrayal in my

eyes, but he doesn't look away. The pain in *his* eyes makes me want to retch, acid rising in the back of my throat.

Then the king turns to look at him. Lee—Prince Killian—turns his head to whisper something to his father.

The king's voice echoes across the still arena. "What an excellent idea, Killian. Let us go down and closely inspect our new chosen."

My fellow Rawbonds stiffen around me. Anxiety surges over them like a storm cloud. Even the wolves are on edge as the king descends from his balcony with an entourage of guards and servants.

This is bad. I struggle to make myself breathe evenly. I can't lose control. I can't let on that I know Prince Killian. If I do... I don't know what will happen. But I can't imagine it will be good.

It won't end with me and Saela safe at home, that's for sure.

The king is on the field now, emerging from a narrow staircase beside the big balcony. I close my eyes again, wrestling the rage back down.

Breathe, Meryn. Stay calm.

"Here we are," comes the King's deep voice, rich with amusement and condescension. "Hmm. Yes, very nice. So fresh and fit."

Ugh. Bile rises in my throat.

He's walking rows of Rawbonds, pausing now and then to circle someone closely, appraising us like fucking *cattle*.

"Oh, look here, Killian," he purrs, circling a young woman from the Kryptos pack. "This one is quite lovely, don't you think?" He reaches out to knock her ass with one jewel-crusted hand. "So firm."

The woman smiles and blushes as if she's just been paid an enormous compliment. Maybe, for her, she has; maybe she's vying to become the Rawbond he'll choose as his companion.

I see Killian nod out of the corner of my eye, but I can't bring myself to look. Was he planning to pick a companion too?

"A fine young warrior in the making," the prince murmurs.

Fucker.

They move on, row by row until finally, much to my dread, the king draws near.

"Ah, the Strategos," he says in that horrible tone of predatory amusement. "Such elegance and cunning."

He pauses by the girl in front of me, lifting the hem of her dress to peer at her bare legs. I keep my eyes down so he won't see my rage and disgust.

Sick fuck. He better not touch me. I'll fucking gut him, king or not.

At the same time, I'm brutally aware of Prince Killian standing beside him, his gaze heavy on me. It takes every ounce of my self-control not to look back. Not to search those familiar eyes for any sign of—

No. You're supposed to be furious, Meryn. Don't look for anything from him.

The prince crosses toward me, trailing after his father, who's moved on to inspecting the girl immediately to my left.

Something brushes my hand as Killian passes. My heart lurches.

I want to spit at him, to howl in his face, to shove him to the ground.

But it's done. Killian walks away, leaving a small piece of paper pressed into my palm. Heart hammering, I tuck it quickly into the sleeve of my dress.

What the fuck was he thinking? Did anyone see?

I glance around, feeling eyes on me.

It's Stark, standing a few yards away. He's staring right at me, his black gaze murderous, lips curling on the edge of a snarl. Adrenaline flashes through me, cold and then hot.

I tear my gaze away. Did he catch Killian doing that? Or does he just hate me?

I don't have time to think about it. Suddenly the king is at my elbow. There's a pause as he looks me over. Then he hooks his finger around a lock of my hair and lifts it briefly.

"Hmm. Unusual."

I stare at his chest, but I can see his eyes narrow, his lips part to speak—

"My king," Stark interrupts, "shall we show you what our recruits can do? They haven't begun their training yet. No time like the present to test their resolve."

Test our resolve? What is he talking about?

The king's head turns. His lips curl in a wicked smile. "What an excellent idea, Alpha Stark! I do believe I'd enjoy that." He reaches under his cloak, drawing the *Diren Blæd* in a singing hiss of metal against metal.

Then he slams the tip of the sword into the ground with a resounding crack.

"Rawbonds!" King Cyril bellows. "Find and kill the weakest recruit!"

Wait, what?!

At once, the arena bursts into chaos. The crowd howls with delight as the king and his entourage scurry back to their balcony. Rawbonds scramble to mount their wolves. Less than half are successful.

I turn to Anassa, but she's already facing off with another wolf, snarling and snapping. Both animals seem maddened, their eyes glowing with bloodlust.

What the——?

All the wolves seem maddened. They're circling each other like sharks, unheeding the rider's commands. Snapping at each other with slavering violence. The Rawbonds on foot are forced to scatter lest they get caught in the crossfire.

The wolves are gripped by some command from the *Diren Blæd*, I realize. The Rawbonds seem to take it in stride.

Did they hear something I didn't? Feel something I didn't?

As I scan the arena in bewilderment, another pair of wolves thunders past, nearly knocking me down. One of them turns to snap at me as I scramble out of the way, its enormous teeth clacking shut mere inches from my face before it turns on another wolf.

Fuck. I can't survive this on my own. It doesn't take a genius to know that those who failed to mount their wolves are the ones most vulnerable to attack. It's only a matter of time before one of us is marked as the weakest.

Anassa!

I reach out to her desperately in my mind, but she ignores me— the iron wall still separates us.

All I can do is try to stay out of everyone's way.

I pull out the blade that I always have hidden at my thigh and prepare myself for violence.

I'm amazed no one has come after me yet. I thought at least a few of them would decide *I'm* the weakest recruit. But whatever spell the king cast has made the direwolves impossible to control. There's no order, no strategy. The wolves are still circling, lunging, sizing each other up.

And then something changes.

A young man falls from his wolf, landing hard enough to shatter bones. I recognize him from the Ascent, though I don't know his name. He's a Kryptos recruit. Smaller than average and slender. Fine brown hair and freckles. One of the youngest, surely—eighteen at most, a boy more than a man. He was one of the last to be chosen.

His cry of pain echoes loud enough to draw the attention of every predator on the field.

The energy of violence and chaos shifts instantly.

Weakness.

The wolves have scented it. The other Rawbonds, too. They turn almost as one to converge on the wounded guy.

"*No!*"

The word is out of my mouth before I can stop it. It's barely loud enough to compete with the raging of the crowd, much less the deafening snarls of the wolves, but a few of them still hear me.

Instinct crackles up my back as half a dozen maddened lupine faces turn in my direction.

Oh…fuck.

One of them is Jonah's big black monstrosity. Jonah sits astride him, grinning maliciously. Holding my gaze, he throws his head back and lets loose a horrible, bone-chilling battle-cry.

Everyone turns to look.

Weakness.

Just like that, the wounded Kryptos boy is forgotten. Every predator on the field—wolf and human alike—is now focused on me.

Of course, I think, everything inside of me shrinking with panic. *I'm the weakest link. The outsider. The mistake.*

Heart hammering, I take a fighting stance as the wolves fan out around me, but I know it's useless. They're closing in. Everything inside me is sinking, falling. The knife in my hand is about as useful as a toothpick.

There's no way I survive this.

Tears of rage and failure burn my eyes.

At that moment, Anassa breaks away from the rest, bounding toward me ahead of the others, her yellow eyes wild with aggression.

I almost laugh. *Of course.* She's hated me from the start. And now she's going to lead the killing attack.

Something in me hardens at the thought. Fear and defeat compress into cold, cutting fury.

That's how it is, huh? I think, my teeth bared as I hold Anassa's gaze. *Fine! Come taste my knife, you bitch.*

Anassa growls so low it rumbles in my chest. Jonah and his wolf are right behind her, poised to attack. Jonah laughs like a fucking madman and screams, *"Now!"*

His wolf lunges forward. At the same moment, I dive for Anassa's throat—

And *miss.*

I hit the hard-packed earth on my hands and knees, dazed, and turn to see Anassa slamming Jonah's wolf to the ground. With a yelp, Jonah flies off, skidding across the hard-packed dirt.

The fuck?

Before I know it, Anassa is up again, lunging at another wolf. Her snarl is deafening.

Confused, I scramble to my feet.

Is Anassa *protecting* me?

I watch in astonishment as she body slams another wolf and then lunges for a third. The rest shrink back in the face of her ferocity, but they're whining, pacing, still gripped by bloodlust.

Anassa stands over me, head lowered and hackles raised, growling loud enough to shake the fucking earth.

Mine! the growl practically says. *My kill! My prey!*

There's a moment of heart-stopping stillness as Anassa stands her ground. I can actually *sense* the other wolves judging her, sizing her up. Trying to decide if it's worth it to challenge the oldest and most powerful among them.

My heart and breath are loud in my ears—even louder than the raving crowd. They know the other wolves can take Anassa if they come at her together. I know it. The other Rawbonds know it.

But for some reason, they don't. All at once, the tension shifts and the wolves just… back away.

Relief floods my limbs, turning my muscles to water. Anassa turns to glare at me, jaws open and streaming with saliva.

The iron wall is still there between us, but I understand the threat in her gaze perfectly. She could kill me in an instant. And maybe she will.

But not today.

She turns and stalks after the others, leaving me shaken and bewildered.

My relief is short-lived.

A scream echoes through the arena. "Jagir! Help me!"

The Kryptos boy. He's on his feet now, one arm dangling uselessly at his side. Calling desperately for his wolf.

I lose sight of him almost immediately in the wild surge of bodies as the wolves and Rawbonds converge on their target.

Horror fills me as more screams rend the air—the boy's wails of pain and terror.

The roar of sound in the arena is deafening. The snarling of the wolves is so loud it makes my ears ring. Under that is a horrible tearing—cloth and flesh being rent.

The mass of bodies breaks apart for a moment and I see him— the Kryptos boy—on his knees and covered in blood. His wolf stands over him, snarling desperately, dark fur glittering with crimson wetness.

I watch in horror as the other wolves circle the pair. There's no chaos now. They're of one mind, united in their hunt.

Like a dance, they take turns darting in to attack, drawing the

Kryptos wolf away from his chosen so another wolf can attack the bleeding boy. The other Rawbonds stand outside the circle, watching. Cheering. As bloodthirsty as their beasts.

And the crowd—

I glance up as their roaring reaches a fever pitch. We're their fucked up entertainment. Their faces are lit with glee, mouths open, *howling*. The king is on his throne, grinning with self-satisfaction. Beside him, Prince Killian looks stone-faced, impossible to read and unable to intervene, even if he wanted to.

I'd like to think he would; that somewhere inside of that *stranger* is the man I loved, who would calmly and authoritatively put an end to any injustice he saw.

What he may or may not want doesn't matter, though. Like me, all he can do is watch.

There's a flash of silver-white fur at the edge of the fight. Anassa, her coat splattered red, muzzle crimson. She launches at the Kryptos wolf and clamps her enormous jaws around his throat.

The Kryptos wolf goes down squealing.

And that's it. The beginning of the end.

I watch in unblinking horror as the other wolves rush in, knowing there's nothing I can do. If I try to intervene, I'll be next.

The first wolf to reach the boy takes hold of his shattered arm. The boy screams—a terrible, childlike sound.

Another wolf lunges for his left leg.

"*No!*" he cries in a high, broken voice. "Please—Mama!"

In an instant, they have him off the ground, strung tight between their jaws. Then there's another wolf on his left shoulder, and yet another takes hold of his right thigh.

They start to shake him. To toss their heads with sickening violence, tearing flesh from bone.

The boy's screams make me want to cover my ears and crumple to the ground, but I'm utterly frozen, unable to look away.

With a loud, echoing *rip* his right arm tears free at the shoulder. His screams are so loud they almost drown out the crowd.

Mercifully, they don't last long.

Another wolf darts in, dark jaws snapping closed on the boy's head.

With a lurch of bone-deep horror, I realize it's *his* wolf. Anassa let him go and he attacked his own rider.

There's a terrible wet crunch as the animal bites down. The screams abruptly cease.

But not the horror.

The wolves are fighting over his corpse now. Tearing it to shreds. The boy's wolf drops down next to him, their severed bond killing him as well, and the other wolves tear him apart next.

The crowd roars as the wolves and their riders start to disperse, leaving what remains of the Kryptos boy in shattered crimson pieces. The Rawbonds are celebrating, lifting their arms and cheering back at the crowd, their faces and skimpy clothes spattered with gore.

Blood and torn flesh paint the ground at their feet, flowing into those little divots. Dazed, I look down.

Realization hits me with overwhelming repulsion.

They're *drains*. To carry the blood away from the battlefield so it doesn't turn the dirt to mud.

This place is a theater of death.

My stomach lurches and I stumble away, desperate to put a little space between myself and that nightmare scene. There are other Rawbonds doing the same. Not *all* of them are celebrating. Many look as dazed and shaken as I am. One girl has tears in her shock-glazed eyes. Another falls to his knees and vomits on the ground.

Meanwhile, the wolves continue to circle. Their gazes lift to the king as though awaiting further command. Will there be another cull? Is the killing done, or has it just started?

I follow their looks. The king's smile brings a renewed wave of nausea. It reminds of Jonah's sadistic grin. He nods regally, lips curling in satisfaction, the keen eyes glinting with something disgustingly close to arousal.

Stark sits a few feet away at the foot of the dais—a place of honor, acknowledging his high rank as a leader of a pack. I'm not even surprised anymore to find he's staring right at me.

He's not smiling, and there's a malicious glitter in his dark eyes. A silent message, as clear as the one I read in Anassa's when she protected me moments ago.

He wants me dead.

I know it with bone-deep certainty. He called for this display because he knew the wolves would choose me. *I* was supposed to be the cull today—the one torn apart for all to see.

But there will be plenty of other chances to see me die an ignominious death. And the look on his face says he's looking forward to it.

This is just the beginning.

Behind him, the king lifts his sword once more. The blade thunks against the dais. At once, the aura of bloodlust and impending violence abates. The wolves are calmed.

The Presentation is done.

THE TRUDGE back to the dorm is made in exhausted silence. Even the Rawbonds who reveled in the kill are quiet. Venna and Izabel walk ahead of me, their twin dresses speckled with blood.

I didn't see them in the fray, but they must have been close at the end. I don't even have the energy to wonder if they enjoyed it. My mind is on Lee's—ugh, *Killian's*—note. It's scratching inside my sleeve, burning against my skin.

As soon as we enter the dorms, I head for the lavatory and lock myself in one of the private stalls. My fingers tremble as I unfold the small square of paper.

East garden at midnight. Please, kitten.

I stare at the words, numb.

I shouldn't go. What can he possibly say to make this canyon-wide lie between us okay? I've spent a year of my life, of my love, with a... *stranger.* The horror I felt when I first saw him standing there still lingers, twisting my insides, the bile rising at the back of my throat.

And the stupidest part is, I've missed him so much over the past couple of days. It felt like my heart was being carved from my chest with his absence. Little did I know that he was holding the knife the whole time.

But I can't pretend that my mind isn't heavy with questions that I'd like to get answered, primarily: why? Why me? Why lie? *Why?*

Shoving the paper back into my sleeve, I exit the stall in a haze. I don't even see the other Rawbonds passing around me, washing away the blood and sweat as they ready themselves for bed.

My reflection in the mirror is pale and horrible. There's blood on my face and in my hair. The crimson lipstick is smudged, my eyes deeply shadowed.

I can see the weakness there. The loneliness. The loss.

Ironically, I wish Lee was here—the one person I could always count on to help me, to take care of me. In another life, I could go to my friends, but I couldn't possibly expose myself to these people I barely know, not when my life hangs on the line. Not even to Izabel and Venna, whom I'm starting to trust.

I stare at myself in the mirror, wishing it could talk back to me. What should I do?

Blindly, I reach out for the connection to Anassa in my head, hoping that she'll choose this moment to lower the wall, to offer me counsel. But there's nothing except my own echoing, spiraling thoughts.

I'm well and truly alone.

CHAPTER SEVENTEEN

Eventually I get back into the baths, scrubbing the blood off my skin for so long and so hard that it begins to hurt, a comfortable sort of pain that I let flood my senses. It gives me something to focus on other than the cavernous hole in my chest where my heart used to be.

After a while, the bathroom quiets and I realize I'm the only one left. I get out and dry myself in those ludicrously fluffy towels, and then pull on undergarments and a clean set of nightclothes: a starchy white button-down nightshirt and some unbelievably soft white nightpants that cling to my body like a second layer.

When I get back into the bunk room, though, I realize it's quiet, nearly empty. That's fine by me; right now, I'm operating through a fog, and I can't make niceties with the people who celebrated that gory scene in the arena so passionately.

I keep seeing flashes of the Kryptos boy behind my eyes. Hearing his horrible screams. His death hangs over me like a cloud, leaving a bitter, metallic taste in my mouth.

And when I'm not thinking about him, my mind is on the prince wearing my lover's face. I still haven't decided what I'm going to do, his note now tucked into the pocket of my nightpants, frayed from the amount of times I've opened and closed it.

But I still want to check on Izabel and Venna and say goodnight to them. They, too, seemed shaken by the boy's death, even if they're used to this world and knew that tonight held the possibility of violence.

Following the sounds of voices, I head to the Strategos anteroom but that's empty too. Then I push open the door to the Rawbond common lounge.

And my mouth drops open in disgust.

Rawbonds from all the packs are here and they're... partying. Commoner servants circle the rooms with trays of deep red emberwine, so close to the color of blood that I just washed from my skin. Platters of meats and cheeses are set out on the dining tables and people are draped sensually over the couches, the chairs, and each other.

The mood in the lounge is heady, as if everyone has taken their pent-up aggression from tonight and they're channeling it into something hedonic. Many people are plainly drunk already—talking loudly, laughing, shooting sultry glances across the room.

Rawbonds have coupled off, too. In more than one corner, I spot tall, beautiful people locked in erotic embraces. One couple is making out in plain sight on a chair in the central area; the woman is straddling the man's lap, grinding against him while he tongues her neck, his hand up her shirt and obviously massaging her breast.

My face flushes hot at the sight. I'm no prude, but I can't believe people are behaving that way out in the open, and after everything we've gone through tonight.

Finally, I spot Izabel and Venna seated on a couch with several other Rawbonds I don't recognize.

"Hey, you made it!" Izabel exclaims when I reach them, her eyes bright. "D'you want a drink?" She holds up her glass of emberwine, the ruby liquid sloshing over the rim.

"Can I talk to you for a second?" I hiss.

She follows me to the edge of the room, and I gesture at the scene before me. "What the fuck is going on here?"

"Hmm?" Izabel looks around the room, dazed, wavering slightly where she stands. Great, she's just as drunk as the rest of them. "Oh, it's a celebration. We survived Presentation. Hooray!" She lifts her glass again, more liquid spilling out of it and onto the floor.

I scoff. "And watching a man get torn apart puts people in the mood?" I ask, looking pointedly at the couple on the chair. The man has now pushed the woman's shirt over her chest and her high, pert breasts are exposed to the whole room as he laves her nipples with his tongue.

Izabel shrugs, the color high on her cheeks. "It's as good of a stress reliever as any. Plus, you might help your wolf find their mate."

I blink. "Mate?"

"Yeah, direwolves have mates. Or they do sometimes. Well, not that often, actually," Izabel babbles. "But it's a thing that used to be more common, wolves would have a mate bond with another wolf, and it would give them extra powers, like they could talk to each other even if they weren't in the same pack, and the riders would feel their heightened emotions. I'm not sure how it works, really, but when riders have sex, it can help their wolves figure out if they're mated or not. So of *course* everyone uses the Trials to try to find their direwolf's mate. Cool, right?"

"Cool," I deadpan, turning away from the party and heading back toward the Strategos quarters, my mind reeling.

"Where are you going?" Izabel shouts after me.

"Bed," I say, not bothering to turn back around.

I cannot *believe* how these people act. I know they are inured to death, raised to find it acceptable and to glorify these Trials.

Being comfortable with bloodshed is one thing.

Celebrating it by fucking as many people as you can is another.

I know I need to be here, to fix my bond with Anassa and survive the next four months. I need this, if I'm ever going to find Saela and bring her home.

But goddess-be-damned, I refuse to behave like one of them.

Back in the Strategos anteroom, I spot a figure in a high-backed chair by the fire; I must've missed her on my way out. It's Nevah, the woman who told me about the king earlier tonight.

She's staring blankly into the fire as the flames throw flickering shadows against her brown skin. She looks ethereal, and deeply sad.

"Not interested in joining the orgy outside?" I quip.

Her gaze drags slowly up to me. She stares at me for a moment, unseeing, and then blinks into focus and tersely shakes her head. "There's only one person I would want to see out there, and he died on the Ascent."

She goes back to gazing into the fire, my presence entirely forgotten. How horrible, to have gone into this process with a partner and lost them during the first trial.

My indignation towards the Rawbonds in the lounge starts to soften. How many other people out there lost friends, family members, or loved ones?

Maybe we all just cope in different ways.

I'm still thinking about that as I lay in my bunk, the evening growing late. People have been trickling back into the bunk room for the past several hours, and now it's grown quiet.

I lost someone during this process, too—Lee. The Bonding Trials have ripped him away from me for good, even though I now know he was never really mine. I'm not sure if I should be mourning him or grateful that I now know the truth.

Certainty drops into my stomach like a cold stone. I'll never be able to sleep again unless I talk to him, confront him.

And maybe sucker punch him in his beautiful face. That might help *me* cope.

At nearly midnight, I slip out of bed, putting my fighting skills to use as I creep out of the Rawbond quarters, unheard and unseen. The corridor outside is dim, the air still. I used to enjoy being awake late at night when everyone else was sleeping. I've always found it peaceful.

But the castle isn't peaceful at all. The quiet is… heavy. And the shadows move strangely, as though alive.

I get lost twice on the way to the east garden, though I passed it on my ill-advised escape attempt earlier. Egith pointed out the entrance to the gardens during our orientation tour.

When I finally find the door and push it open, I forget all about being sneaky.

My gasp echoes in the warm air.

The garden is a sprawling, moonlit wonder—it's not just a garden, it's a greenhouse. A glass ceiling arches above me and the whole room is heated. It's a sumptuous extravagance. Rosebushes line the path and cling to the high stone walls. Everywhere I look I see huge crimson blossoms made velvety black by the moonlight.

Their scent is everywhere, sweet and fresh. I've never smelled or seen anything so beautiful.

I wander for a while, almost forgetting why I'm here, then pause to look at the graceful marble figure poised at the center of a huge fountain.

She's twice the height of a human woman and a hundred times more beautiful. Voluptuous and powerful, her elegantly muscled arms upraised as though in dance.

"Kitten."

The strong, familiar voice sends my heart surging into my throat. I spin around and there he is, standing a few yards away in the shadow of a vine-choked arbor.

Lee.

My heart squeezes.

No. Not Lee. His Royal Highness, Crown Prince Killian Valtiere.

His blond hair is darker in the moonlight, his eyes deep pools. He looks like a stranger in his royal clothing, all white and velvet and bright, braided gold. But when he moves toward me, the confidence in his step is utterly familiar. I used to love to watch him striding toward me, knowing I was his to touch. To kiss.

To love.

It hurts so much I can hardly breathe.

As he nears, I take a step back without thinking. He stops, pursing his lips.

"Thank you for coming," he says. "I'm sure this has been... a shock."

Anguish swells through me at his words, and I cross my arms, looking tough but actually needing to hold myself together in front of him.

This person I know intimately and also not at all.

"Why did you do it?" I ask, trying to sound strong. Putting steel in my voice so he can't see the way he's shattered me. "Why did you hide who you were? Why did you get involved with me in the first place... *your highness?*" The words taste acidic on my tongue.

When I was lying on my bunk, imagining this moment with him, I thought I'd be a terrifying sight to behold—the Alleycat of the fighting pits in all her glory, spitting mad. But face-to-face with him, I can't ignore the grief throbbing behind my breastbone.

"Mer," he says, stepping toward me again slowly, hands held out in a quelling motion. I'm reminded of the day we met and the way he calmed the wild horse. "I never wanted to hurt you. The moment I first set eyes on you, rushing up to me and your sister that day in the market—I knew instantly, Meryn. You had this alleycat fierceness, this spark to you, that was unlike anything I'd ever seen before. You were the blinding beauty of the sun personified."

He's close enough now to reach out and touch me, and a traitorous part of me aches for that, for the arms I know so well to fold around me once more, comforting me.

I squash it. Fuck that feeling. Instead, I shoot him a glare that stops him in his tracks.

"I would've done anything to spend time with you, kitten," he says quietly. "Anything to have the honor of holding you in my arms."

Straightening to my full height, I say, "So you chose to lie."

Lee—Killian—runs a hand through his thick hair in frustration. "What should I have done instead? My title has always defined me, but I didn't choose this life. I hid the truth about my identity so you could get to know me, the real me, without the unbearable weight of the crown bearing down on us from the start. Aside from my job and the details about my parents, everything I've ever told you about myself has been true. But if you'd known I was the crown prince, you never would've given us a chance."

Heat burns behind my eyes and I realize that, mortifyingly, I might be on the verge of tears. He's right, we never would've been together if I'd known he was the prince. That perfect year together, feeling like I finally found a match, an equal—it would've never existed.

But maybe that's the way things should've been. "You took my ability to make that decision away from me," I say, my voice cold. "And it changes nothing, in the end. You're still my future king and I'm still commoner scum, even now that I'm Bonded."

His gazes grows stormy at that. "You're not *scum*."

I laugh bitterly. "If that was true, you would've been honest with me. The fact that you didn't even tell me after I'd enlisted, when you were telling me all about the Bonded Trials—"

"Would that have made things better for you?" he says, cutting me off, the volume of his voice rising. "You had just lost your sister. You had made a life-altering decision. Should I have piled onto your misery by exposing myself, right as you were putting your life on the line? Goddess, Meryn, I never in a million years expected you to *bond*. I didn't think you'd be coming to the castle. I assumed I had plenty of time to tell you the truth when you'd come back from the front with Saela."

Hearing him say her name breaks the dam holding back my tears. They come fast down my face, their heat burning my cheeks.

"And speaking of that," I say, tasting salt. "Why the fuck have you not done *anything* about the Nabbers? You knew! You were staying in the commoner quarters regularly, you knew exactly what has been happening to our kids!"

The rage has finally reached a breaking point inside of me, and I close the gap between us with two quick steps, pounding my fists on his chest hard enough to bruise.

"Why haven't you fucking stopped them? My sister is *gone*!"

Lee wraps his arms around me, pulling me closer to him, even as

I continue to rain my fists on him. He yanks me into a tight embrace, my tears running down the front of his shirt, his chin tucked over the top of my head.

Pine, he still smells like pine, I think stupidly. Every part of my body wants to press itself against him, lighting up at this familiar scent.

"Kitten," he says, his breath warm on my hair. "Of course I've been trying to stop them. I've had my guards hunting them since the very first time you mentioned them."

He pulls back and I look up at him. His eyes are pained.

"I'm responsible for Saela's disappearance," he says. "I didn't do enough. And I'm going to continue putting any resources I can into finding her until the day we bring her home."

Lee reaches up, brushing the tears off of my cheeks, and the motion only makes me weep harder. My stomach is a twisting, writhing mess. I both need him and loathe him in the same breath, and it *hurts*.

"There's no we anymore," I spit at him. Then I press my hands against his chest and *push*. He stumbles backwards on the dirt path, and when I meet his gaze again, he lifts his chin.

"Don't you realize?" he says ferociously. "My love for you is as unwavering and steady as the winds from Mount Wolfsbane. I'd give it all up if you told me to. I'd abdicate tomorrow."

I scoff, folding my arms over my chest again, trying not to flush at his words. Because truthfully, I love him too, even as I hate him. The warring emotions threaten to crater me where I stand.

"You're the most powerful woman in Nocturna, Meryn." The certainty in his deep tone heats my blood, makes me look him straight in his glittering eyes. "You can bring this kingdom to its knees with just a word."

My stomach bottoms out and I look away from him again. I'm not sure what might come out of my mouth if I look him dead-on. "I'm here for Saela and Saela only," I say, reminding him and myself at the same time. "That's all that matters to me."

"I know," he says, his voice filled with regret. "And I'll do everything I can to protect you and help you find her while you're here." I hear his heel turn on the dirt and he starts to walk away, but then stops. "I don't expect your forgiveness. But I hope to earn your understanding."

With that, he leaves me to chew on my regrets and the fragments of our hopes, our promises. The fragrance of the roses has turned cloyingly sweet, choking. A thin veneer of beauty covering up an unending cavern of misery.

I WAIT a few minutes after Killian leaves, wanting to put as much space between us as possible—and also because I need some time to pull myself together. Then I make my way back through the darkened halls toward the Rawbond quarters.

In the corridor right outside the dorms, the attack comes.

I'm not ready for it—more fool me. My thoughts are still tangled up with Killian, and Saela, and the exhausting day I've had. I don't even hear my attacker coming until his fist is in my hair, yanking me backward with brutal force.

I don't scream as he starts to drag me away. Plenty of people were not happy I survived the Presentation. I'll be damned if I'm going to alert the whole fucking compound to my predicament so they can come and help finish the job.

Instead, I twist silently in my attacker's grip, ignoring the searing pain in my scalp as I try to get my feet back under me. I need leverage—and to see my target so I can kick his fucking balls into next week.

He's *strong*. Much stronger than me. Fast, too. He senses me twisting and gives my head another brutal yank. It feels like my hair is about to rip clean off my scalp. But I'm thinking fast even as my feet scrabble and drag against the polished floor.

The violence is clear. Intentional. This guy is going to kill me, rules be damned.

The knowledge pushes me over the edge of an emotional cliff I've been dangling from since I realized I couldn't leave this place.

Shadows move over my vision and enter me, expanding in my

chest. A darkness overtakes my mind as one thought crystalizes, the only thing that matters: *this is not where I die.*

As if possessed by something I don't totally understand, I pull my knife from its hidden sheath and slash at my own hair. The silver strands split instantly. The man, unprepared, loses his balance and tumbles forward.

I'm on him before he hits the ground, one knee on the back of his neck while I bring the knife down hard on the hand still clutching my severed hair.

It's like my common sense has blacked out and my body has been taken over by rage personified.

When my dad was still alive, he used to take me hunting. He taught me the proper way to dismember an animal. The key is working your knife into the joint just right, and then all it takes is a practiced twist—

A hoarse masculine scream echoes through the corridor as my attacker's hand separates from his wrist. Hot blood sprays my face. I taste salt and copper and boiling fury.

His eyes are wide in the dim light, mouth gaping around a wheezing gasp as I lean down to show him his detached extremity. Distantly, I recognize him as one of the Daemos boys that hangs around with Jonah.

"You fucked with the wrong woman," a voice growls—mine, I realize belatedly—as I tear his jaw open and slam his own severed hand into it.

He chokes and gags, eyes widening as I push it deeper down his throat. Cartilage crunches under the pressure. His body starts bucking underneath me, a desperate ploy to shake me off, to free me, to save himself.

I've held men down enough times in my life to know how to do it right.

The iron wall in my mind swings open. On the other side is Anassa, her feelings bare to me for the first time.

There are no words. Just a rush of cold, bloodthirsty approval.

Snarling in disgust, I slam the wall down again.

I don't need your fucking approval.

Beneath me, my attacker gurgles loudly, choking to death on his own blood and fingers.

I've never killed a man before. I never dreamed myself capable of this type of violence; I thought I'd skate through these Trials by avoiding being killed, not by becoming a killer.

But something has unlocked inside of me, a monster I didn't know existed. I'm not sure if it's been formed out of the seething, quiet wrath that's been building in me all day, or if this is some side effect of bonding with a bloodthirsty beast.

Instead of disgust at my own actions, all I feel is... calm. Horrible, stony calm.

That's not right, is it? I shouldn't feel calm. I should feel... *anything.*

What kind of horror is this place making me into?

When I finally find my sister again, will she even be able to recognize me?

CHAPTER EIGHTEEN

There should be a manual for Rawbonds, printed fresh every Bonding Trials, each new edition including better tips and tricks acquired over the course of the training period.

My contribution?

The morning after gruesomely murdering another Rawbond, *don't* get the eggs for breakfast.

I stare at them on my plate, shifting them around with my fork and thinking about brain matter and stringy intestines. Remembering the warm spray of blood and the strangled scream that I cut short.

The back of my neck is cold where my hair used to be. Last night, after I got back into the dorms, I went to the bathroom to wash his blood off me. While the tap warmed up, I stared at the woman in the mirror, once again filled with unreality caused by my own appearance. My hair is shorter than it's been in my entire memory, the silver-white strands cut to a choppy bob, strands ending around the middle of my neck.

I shiver, still staring at my eggs as they grow cold on my plate.

If I'm being honest, it's not just the violence that's getting to me. It's this feeling like I'm suddenly not myself any longer. Something strange happened last night, like someone else took over my body the moment I started to fight back.

Or maybe it was even earlier than that. Maybe the person I thought I was is still lying in my bed at home, borderline catatonic, and the person who managed to get up and drag her ass to the recruitment center is who's really here right now.

Vicious and dangerous. Desperate.

I can't shake the shiver of satisfaction I felt from Anassa. She liked what I did. I know she did. My head pounds from the constant effort of reinforcing the wall of iron between us.

Not to mention that I haven't had a single moment to really think through the whole Lee—ugh, the *Killian* of it all. My heart still aches, thinking of him.

I close my eyes and see death at my fingertips right alongside the bittersweet image of him standing there in his finery.

"*Meryn.*"

My head jerks up. Izabel is staring at me. Venna looks even more concerned. "We've been trying to get your attention," Venna says.

"Sorry," I reply.

"Interesting haircut you have this morning," Izabel says cautiously. Venna offers me a questioning smile.

"Oh, uh." I look around the common room. Rawbonds from every pack lounge on the chaises and chairs, some of them clearly already close enough to drape over each other. "What, you don't like it?" I ask to deflect.

Venna shrugs. "No, I like it. It's actually a good idea. Shorter hair means less to grab." She swishes her own short bob, as if to demonstrate.

Painful flashes of last night return to me. I keep my face still, unwilling to show distress.

"But we're worried," Izabel adds. "Yesterday was a lot. And now this sudden change. Are you okay?"

A lot. That's the understatement of the century.

I open my mouth, scrambling to think of some way to wriggle out of this conversation, but I'm spared excuses by the door to the common area blasting open with enough force that it slams against the wall, rattling the crystal goblets scattered about.

Stark storms into the room, boots thudding heavily, dark brows twisting with fury.

My hackles rise instantly at the sight of him, alarms blaring in my head.

His voice is a menacing boom. "WHO WAS IT? Who here thought they knew better than Leader Aldrich and went against *specific* instructions not to kill any other Rawbonds outside of training?"

Fuck. Not spared at all. Just fresh torture.

Shocked whispers spread through the room. Slowly, eyes start to turn towards me, clocking my shorn hair. The sudden cut is apparently more of a giveaway than I thought. There's no chance even the cleverest of lies will get me out of this.

So I do what I always do when faced with a man seething with fury. I lift my chin and meet his furious glare.

"It was me. Self-defense," I say plainly. Miraculously, my voice doesn't shake despite the pounding of my heart.

Stark steps towards me, his huge form casting an even larger shadow. A few Rawbonds scatter away from him, repelled by a primal fear that has their eyes flashing and their limbs jerky. All I feel is responding fury.

"You think you're above the rules, *princess*?" he growls out.

Calling me princess? Acting like the rules don't matter? Ironic, considering who he serves. My lip twitches with resentment before I can stop it.

"Like I said, it was *self-defense*."

His hands flex into fists and release, the dark lines of his tattoos dancing along them. "It was self-defense to choke someone to death with their own severed hand?" he snarls.

There's another round of shocked whispers. A few of the Rawbonds closest to me push their plates away. Others turn away from me. Izabel and Venna are utterly silent.

But I refuse to avert my eyes in shame or let Stark break something in me. I did what I had to do to protect my own life, and now they'll *all* know better than to fuck with me.

I'd do it again, for Saela.

Stark's challenging gaze burns through me for a long moment, the room suspended in silence. They're all watching us, like they're waiting for us to tear each other apart.

Then he straightens, the tattoos and numerous scars on the backs of his hands flexing around his knuckles as his hands clench again.

"Front of the room," he says, voice low.

Every word is specially crafted for me, perfectly enunciated, quiet but dangerously clear. There will be no argument.

I slowly stand and move towards the front where everyone can see me.

As I do, he addresses the others with a significantly more level voice. "Looks like lessons are starting early this morning," he says, watching me walk.

I turn and stand before him, perching my hands on my hips and standing tall. He still looms over me as he approaches.

"Most of you should know the meaning of Bonded tattoos, but for those of you who don't—" He pointedly shoots a dagger-like glare my way. "—the tattoos on our arms and torsos count Siphon kills. The ones on our necks memorialize our Bonded comrades that we've killed in training. Why do we do the tattoos?"

Because you psychos like war trophies.

There's a long moment of silence before a young man musters the courage to lift his hand. Phylax, judging by the tawny streak in his hair. I don't know his name. Stark bows his head in his direction.

"Because unlike the Siphons, the Bonded cherish life. We get tattoos to remember the steep cost of war."

Bullshit, if I've ever heard it. Did the person who attacked me last night *value life*? Did the rest of them in that arena, as they watched a man be torn apart?

If they valued life, this entire process wouldn't be so brutal and bloody.

Stark nods and turns to me, reaching into his pocket. He produces a small device that looks like a pen, a sharp tip glinting in the light streaming in from the window above us. Alongside it, a bottle of ink.

"Congratulations, princess. You get the first tattoo of these Bonding Trials."

With that, his free hand closes around my shoulder and shoves me down into the chair behind me. I sputter in indignation.

But for some reason, when Stark bends over me, suddenly closer than I've ever seen him before, I can't tear my gaze away from his eyelashes.

It stuns me, briefly. Seeing him up close is different. All that menacing fury still hovers above me like an executioner's ax, but his breath is on my cheek and I can see the precise details of the tattoos on his neck.

Training kills, then, just like mine.

Stark grips my jaw firmly with his calloused fingers, the heat of them sending sparks across my skin. I give him what I hope is a defiant look. I refuse to cower in fear for someone who would so clearly relish it.

He clicks his tongue in irritation and forces my head up at an uncomfortable angle.

The bite of the needle on my neck is sudden and jarring. I refuse to make a sound of pain, clenching my jaw and glaring up at him as the needle tears into me. His hand tightens on my chin like he thinks I'm going to bolt, but I'd rather die than run from him.

My dignity wouldn't survive it, and I'm not sure I would, either, if I turned my back on him.

Still, my breath puffs from me as the needle sends shivers of pain-induced cold through my neck and shoulder. I try to conceal it, but he clearly notices.

A muscle in his jaw feathers, his dark gaze shifting away from the needle for an instant to bore into me, impossible lashes framing his dark eyes.

As the needle goes on, some part of me yawns wide. Hungry. Full of rage.

If this goes on like this for much longer, I might snap and grab the needle out of his hands and plunge it somewhere vulnerable. It's taking all my focus not to give in to my fighter's instincts and do something about the pain I'm in. It's like he's digging his teeth into my fucking throat, and I'm just sitting here baring my neck for him.

Finally, it relents. He tucks the device away again, hand still firmly on my jaw. Then, without warning, he forces my head to the side. He leans down, his breath now hot against my neck.

And his *tongue* streaks over my skin.

I can't repress the sound this time, small and almost angry, like the very beginnings of a growl at the base of my throat. I think he hears it because his hand tightens on my jaw. It's even more shocking than the pain was. My vision sinks into the distance as the slick heat of his mouth contacts my overly sensitive skin.

I want to be angry. I want to shove him off of me and beat the shit out of him. But I can't move.

The wet touch of it soothes the angry stinging in a way that is shockingly intimate even as it's violating. My hands dig into the armrests.

It feels like it takes forever, but a starving part of me wants it to keep going. I hate it, and still my thighs tingle and my nipples harden beneath my jacket. I squeeze my thighs together as a bloom of heat spreads through my stomach and lower.

For a moment, all my mind can focus on is the warmth of his mouth and breath, the tickle of his hair on my cheek, the musky smell of him, the firmness of his hand on my throat.

And a scar. It's hidden, slashed right across the very edge of his jaw, up towards the base of his ear. For some reason, that more than anything compresses my lungs and sends my heart thudding against my ribs like a striking fist.

It's like a secret he didn't mean to share.

Then it's over and he shoves my face away roughly, scowling down at me with cold eyes. The anger floods back to me, even louder and more violent for how lost I just was to my body's whims.

My fingertips bleach against the armrests as he turns without a word and leaves me there.

There are whispers all around me as I stand, refusing to let my legs shake. My face is definitely flushed as I return to my table. Izabel and Venna are staring.

I swallow. "What was that?" I breathe, voice raw.

"A tattoo for your kill," Izabel replies.

"No, why did he *lick* me?" I demand, hands in fists.

Venna's lips purse. "Oh, we lick each other's tattoos when we're done. It's an instinct to help heal the surface of the skin."

I pinch the bridge of my nose, ignoring the tingling at my throat. The world of the Bonded is never going to make sense to me.

THE STINGING at my throat remains painful for the rest of the day. I'm resisting my urge to rub at it as we stride out into the Strategos training grounds that afternoon as a pack. Beta Egith awaits us, dressed in black riding leather and eying us all impatiently. I notice that her sharp gaze lingers on my neck.

Our direwolves await us, some gathered together and socializing—rubbing their sides together, flicking their tails at each other, even playfully biting and snapping.

Anassa, however, stands entirely still apart from the rest, massive and uncaring. Not one of the others approaches her.

Seeing her again reminds me of last night and the vicious approval she felt. I press my palm to my tattoo, wincing when the contact causes the stinging to worsen.

"Good afternoon, Strategos Rawbonds," Egith announces. "Today, we begin your formal training as Rawbonds with your first lesson in riding your wolves. If you're here, you successfully rode your wolf down Mount Wolfsbane, but there's much more to it than just sitting astride your mount."

Well, *some* of us rode our wolves down the mountain.

"Mastering proper form for riding and fighting is also your first step in learning how to communicate well with your wolf. As a reminder, we are on an official countdown to the Voice Trial in one month."

Fuck, right. The Trial that tests how well you can communicate with your wolf. I wasn't worried about it when they told us about it in orientation, because I thought I was going to make an escape.

I prod against the iron wall in my head. Solid as ever. Anassa shows no interest in bringing it down again.

Great. I'm cooked.

"The Voice Trial consists of a complex obstacle course," Egith continues, "so it's important that you are both adept at moving with your direwolf, and that you communicate well with each other."

I can barely even get Anassa to acknowledge my existence—beyond scathing contempt, of course—much less get her to work with me to run an obstacle course. An obstacle course that is probably specifically designed to test whether she's listening to me.

"For today, we're starting easy. It should be a breeze for most of you," Egith explains. "One lap of the arena as fast as you can manage. Then over the hurdles. Crawl under the beams, then a final jump through that hoop. *Do not* fall off. There is risk of trampling as well as frustration from your direwolves. Remember what will happen if they find you wanting."

It's a disaster from the start.

The others' wolves join them quickly, padding across the training grounds. Many of them mount just as easily as they did on the mountain. Izabel thuds my back as she strides forward towards her towering wolf, shooting me a sympathetic glance. Tomison is already up on his wolf's back, sending a wink our way.

When I step towards Anassa, she doesn't snarl at me. That's progress, I guess. But she does sidestep away from me, the tips of her teeth bared briefly.

As it is, I have no choice. The others are already taking off down the course, starting one by one so that the obstacles aren't over-crowded. Izabel is about to take her turn.

Fuck it.

I step forward and reach out, plunging my hand into her fur.

She doesn't move. And she doesn't bite my arm off. Maybe the forceful approach is the way to go.

Don't ask permission; just like how she didn't get my permission to bond.

Just *do it*.

I grip her fur and heft myself up, boots thudding against her leg to give myself a boost, like I've seen the others do it.

Anassa bats her paw right as I try to climb her and I thud back to the ground, landing on my feet. Others turn to watch me and I ignore them, trying again immediately.

This time, I fist her fur with both hands and jump up, not bothering with my feet until I'm already at her shoulder, relying on the muscles of my upper body that I've honed from years in the ring.

They serve me well now. I make it up onto Anassa's back without much trouble.

Fuck, the ground is so far away.

Trampling risk, Egith said. I hate this.

It only gets worse as I try to direct Anassa towards the course. We're among the last to go. I try to lower my mental walls, the very ones I spent time building up last night, but Anassa's barriers hold firm.

Whatever goodwill I earned by committing bloody murder has vanished in this morning's mist.

If I kill someone right now, will she jump through a hoop for me? Doubt it.

Eventually, she seems to get annoyed with me, or maybe just bored, and pads over to the course, facing it and readying herself.

It isn't agreement. It isn't teamwork or cohesion. I don't hear her voice. It's complete and utter rejection.

I don't have two seconds to prepare myself before she hurtles forward at terrifying speed.

Clutching her fur tightly, I fight not to fall. Sprinting around the outside of the course is relatively smooth, but then she starts to leap over the hurdles. I nearly fall on the first one, yanking her fur to keep my balance atop her back. The pull of my weight upsets her own balance, and one of her feet tangles on the hurdle.

She barely catches herself, snarling, clacking her teeth angrily. Then onto the next hurdle, and it's the same thing all over again.

I nearly slide right off trying to duck under the boards. When she leaps through the hoop, her tail whips against the rim and I end up fully dismounted from her back, clinging to the fur of her shoulder blade as my legs dangle and I try to scramble my way back up.

There's no way I'm going to fall, though. I won't let the other Rawbonds see my ass in the dirt.

I hold on to her. I'd rip all her fur out in my grip if it meant making it through this, and I think she knows it.

"Again!" Egith shouts, and I reconsider murder, if it means Anassa'll at least *try* to help me stay mounted.

The other bonded pairs are flowing through the course. That's the worst part. Some are faster than others, but not one of them is struggling like we are.

Even the clumsier ones struggle simply because their direwolves aren't as tall or strong, not because their riders are struggling to stay mounted. I watch as one of the wolves even shifts its center of gravity to support its rider as she's about to fall, tipping her back into her proper spot.

It's grueling the entire way through.

My ass is entirely numb, my arms are limp and useless from clinging and pulling myself back up, and my head is pounding from the scraping, cruel pounding of the wall between my mind and Anassa's.

I'm finally given a reprieve when class draws to a close. The other Rawbonds part lovingly with their wolves. When I slip from Anassa's back, landing painfully on the flats of my feet, she turns tail. Almost instantly, she bounds away, disappearing.

No drawn-out goodbye for us, then.

If I wasn't so exhausted from the complete and utter mayhem of that lesson, I'd be frustrated.

I'm here. I'm committed. I want to make this work, since I have literally no other options—even though, as I remind myself for the thousandth time, this bond was forced on me unwillingly. What else does Anassa want from me?

The other trainees start to head inside but Egith strides toward me before I can follow them.

"Meryn, I need to speak with you. Come with me," she says sternly.

I ignore the curious gazes of the other Rawbonds as I follow Egith from the training yard without another word, heart sinking as I wonder just what it is I've done wrong this time.

At least she isn't shoving a needle into my neck in front of everyone.

Or maybe she has news about the Nabbers? The thought only amplifies the churning anxiety in my gut.

We step into the Strategos quarters. My tattoo tingles as Egith stops in front of one of the private rooms just before the entrance to the bunkroom.

"It's yours now," she says, thudding her hand briefly on the door.

I stare at the door then meet her eyes. "Mine?"

She unlocks the door and swings it open, revealing a generous amount of space with a full bed and a pile of pillows, a tall double-doored wardrobe, an empty bookshelf, a flowering plant in the corner, and a generous window that looks out over a shivering tree.

It's a bigger bedroom than I've ever had. And private, too.

"Since there was an attack on you last night, it has been determined that you are possibly being targeted. So you will now have a private room," she says rigidly. She hands the key to me, dropping it into my palm.

I shake my head and try to hand the key back to her. "No. I don't want this. It puts an even bigger target on my back."

"That it does," she agrees, her expression cheerless. "But this order comes from above my head. There's nothing I can do about it."

She watches as I tentatively step inside. Goddess, there's even a private washroom.

Egith turns to go but pauses briefly. "I'd say enjoy the privacy while you have it. Once you're in the king's forces at the front, you'll never have it again," she says, then shuts the door in my face.

I stare at the door again, a little lost. I can't tell if what she just said implies she has faith I'll survive all of this, or whether she was deliberately trying to break my will by reminding me that I'm *stuck* with all of this.

Stepping further into the room, I shuck my jacket and toss it onto the bed. I open the wardrobe and find plenty of empty hangers for all of my clothes. When I shut it and turn, my eyes catch on my reflection. I step closer to the mirror hanging on the wall, partially shrouded in veil-like translucent curtains.

I guide them aside and tilt my head.

I haven't seen my tattoo since I got it this morning. And it's… oddly beautiful.

It wraps around the side of my neck, mid-way up, about at the same level I had to shear my hair. It's in the same runic style as the others I've seen, but with decorative elements that swirl like dark fire, moving fluidly around a central circle empty of saturation.

It doesn't even really hurt any longer, I realize. I wonder if that's because he… because of his mouth.

His tongue.

I'm briefly taken aback by the artfulness of it. I hadn't thought Stark's brutal hands were capable of creating something like this. Except then I realize what it really is.

The start of a collar.

I clench my jaw and touch it with the very tips of my fingers. How many more of these will I get before training ends?

Maybe enough to wrap around my throat and choke me silent.

CHAPTER NINETEEN

I don't have much in the Strategos bunkroom, but I've filled the dresser by my bed with clothes from the store closet, so I should probably move those. I slink through the busy anteroom unnoticed and when I enter the bunkroom, it's blessedly empty.

Everyone is either training, studying, or lounging in the common room, most likely. It gives me plenty of space to pack my meager belongings without worrying about someone peering over my shoulder and asking questions I'm not ready to answer.

Like, *where the fuck are you taking your things, commoner?*

Swiping a rebellious lock of silver-white hair from my eyes, I throw my things into a bag and then sling it over my shoulder. As I flee back to my new room, anxiety expanding like a balloon in my chest, I spot Izabel across the Strategos common area.

She's straddling the lap of one of our other Rawbonds, perched atop him like an eagle with her prey. Izabel smooths her hands over his broad shoulders and I squint. I can't remember his name. Roddert something?

He looks way more interested than she does. But he's handsome, mumbling words of praise to her as if he's entirely unaware of her talons in his flesh. It's damn admirable, actually, how tightly she seems to have him wound around her finger.

Even more so because she looks bored with him, like this came easily to her.

I'm moving before I can think it through. Seeing Izabel bending the desperate man to her will, I can't help but think, *she knows what she's doing.* And fuck, I'm so tired of feeling clueless.

"—eyes sparkle like gems," Roddert is saying. Robert? No, Roddert.

"Izabel," I interrupt.

She looks up at me. Her eyes remain glazed over with disinterest until they land on me, jump to my bag, then ignite with curiosity.

I dip my head. "Can I talk to you for a minute?"

"Absolutely," she says, sounding sort of relieved. Poor guy.

She leaps from his lap like she's taking flight. His hands follow her briefly before dropping limply to his knees.

I glance over my shoulder at him as we walk away. He's definitely staring at her ass. But he stares at mine, too, so he's clearly not that heartbroken.

Izabel leans close. "I thought I'd give him a try—I mean, *look* at those shoulders! But wow. Rocks for brains. How did he end up in Strategos? He belongs in Phylax with the other pretty bricks."

"I think you're selling him short. Your eyes really *are* like gemstones," I tease.

She rolls them so far back in her head, I'm sure she catches a glimpse of her brain. "Shut *up*," she groans with a smile as she follows me across the anteroom. "What did you want to—"

Izabel cuts off when we stop in front of my new door, her dark eyebrows shooting toward her hairline as I turn the handle.

"Meryn, these rooms are private," she hisses, glancing over her shoulder.

"I know," I tell her, pushing open the door and leading her into the room. "This one is now private to *me*."

Before I can explain, a low whistle rings out from behind us. I turn to see Tomison leaning in the doorway.

His gaze darts around my quarters appreciatively. "Damn, Meryn. This is—"

I snatch his wrist and yank him inside, slamming the door shut behind him. Everywhere Tomison goes, he draws attention, and I don't need *more* people ogling my new room and starting to hate me for it.

I can't hide this forever, but I'd rather control how the news gets out rather than let Tomison's inexplicable popularity spread it for me.

Then again, that popularity might work for me somehow. Tomison steps deeper into the space. He pauses next to the luxurious chair by the foot of my new bed and runs his fingers over the velvet. His red hair burns even in the dim light of the single oil lamp on the bedside table.

"How did you score this setup?" he asks. "I thought only instructors got private rooms."

Izabel scoffs. I'm not sure why. I think it's just a knee-jerk reaction of hers that triggers whenever she hears Tomison speak. I can sense her eyes drilling holes in him from clear across the room, though Tomison seems oblivious.

I take a deep breath and attempt to explain that "safety concerns" after the attack have elevated me and that Egith did not give me a choice about taking the room. I'm stuck here, whether or not I want to be.

Story of my life, apparently.

Izabel frowns at me thoughtfully at the conclusion of my explanation. "This is what you wanted to chat about?"

"Yes." I gesture to the room. "Obviously."

Tomison snorts and looks at Izabel, but she's deep in thought. She pinches her chin and presses her lips together. Then she says, "Who could have ordered this? I wonder if you caught the king's eye at Presentation. I mean, we all know he's creepy, but…"

She and Tomison exchange a look, and I'm sure they're thinking about how the king likes to pick a companion from the Rawbonds. I've heard rumors that he's had his eye on a Phylax Rawbond named Audelie, but maybe he's still searching for his target.

My skin crawls. The mere *thought* of the king's too-blue eyes moving over me like that, lingering in all the places I'd die to protect... I'm legitimately sick for a moment and lean back against the door for support.

Actually, his son is more likely to be responsible. It's the most obvious conclusion, but I keep Killian's name out of my mouth. I'm not ready to open that wound; especially not when I'm already in such a fragile position with the other Rawbonds.

Can't imagine it would help things if I told everyone I've been fucking the crown prince for a year.

"How do I keep this room assignment from making everything worse for me?" I say instead, hoping that these two might be able to give me some reasonable advice.

My gaze darts between them. Izabel looks sympathetic. Tomison looks amused. He shrugs at me. *Shrugs.* "You don't."

"I don't," I repeat, a little annoyed.

"Own it!" he says with a stupidly charming grin. "You can clearly handle yourself. Don't tuck your tail." He claps his hands together. "*Now*, if you'll excuse me, there are some lovely Daemos ladies awaiting my charming presence."

Izabel scowls as he leaves. There's too much venom there. I raise a brow. "Why do your gemstones look so murderous?" I ask.

She clears her throat and mutters, "When he breathes, it annoys me."

I really don't think he's all that bad, though. He gave me an honest answer, didn't he? Not a useful one, but he tried. "How do I get out of this, Izabel?"

She sighs. "I'd rather gouge my eyes out than admit Tomison is right about anything. So I won't. *But.*"

She leaves it at that, because clearly, she can't bring herself to say the words aloud. Tomison is right. And I have to face it head-on.

It's not long before the opportunity presents itself. The next morning, I'm planted beside Izabel in the busy Rawbond common lounge, picking at a plate of fruit. We have a long day of classes and training ahead of us.

My fragile peace shatters when a shadow falls across my half-empty plate. I look up slowly because there's something ominous in the air. The people eating around me have gone silent.

Perielle, the Strategos beauty queen, is standing over me. Towering, really, and she sneers like the best of them. My eyes jump over her perfect eye makeup—soft and warm—which does *nothing* to blunt the edge of her razor-sharp, murderous gaze.

"Everyone's heard about your room, commoner," she says. "Out with it. Who are you fucking?"

Damn. *Right* in the middle of breakfast, too.

I hide a flinch at how close to the truth Perielle's guess hits. I won't let the rest of the pack see weakness in me.

This is a challenge. I know it is because Anassa's irritation crackles like a growl, the walls between us temporarily thinner. She's offended by Perielle's attack, as if a pup just nipped at her heel.

I've been silent too long. I can only hope that it projects confidence rather than cowardice.

"Why are you asking?" Izabel cuts in. "Are you worried there's someone here you *haven't* banged yet?"

I'm sure she's not proud of that one, but I am. I want to take Perielle's regal, pretty façade and fracture it in my bare hands with a sickly crunch, like bone breaking. I want to feel it happen, and Anassa does, too.

"Actually, Venna," Perielle says, deliberately mixing up the twins' names, "I've already found my wolf's mate."

She waves her hand in a halfhearted gesture towards the other half of the common room, and my eyes follow it to Jonah. The cruel Daemos Rawbond waves back with a predatory grin. His eyes glow like he's imagining fucking Perielle in a pool of our blood.

Whispers ignite around the lounge. Based on what Izabel drunkenly told me the other night, mated direwolves are very rare. This has got to be giving Perielle some serious confirmation bias.

In other words: she's certain she's special, and this only proves it.

Before I can process how viscerally disturbing this match is, Perielle sweeps my plate off the table. It tilts at the edge briefly before crashing to the ground, sending chunks of fruit and bits of egg and toast exploding across the floor. The ceramic shatters with a deafening crash that silences whatever conversations were still going.

Every single person in the room is looking at us now.

It's the pettiest playground bullying I've ever seen, and all from a woman who thinks herself a queen. I look around the room, sure that everyone will see right through it.

But it's Perielle. A pretty face like hers brainwashes people into mindless worship. They're glaring at *me*, like they're offended that I've dirtied her boots with the breakfast I'm now not going to get to eat.

"Oops," she says sweetly. Izabel's hand tightens on her fork.

Perielle is worshipped. Breaking her perfect face in front of everyone would hardly help my popularity. It would be like ripping out Tomison's shiny red hair. I can't do that, so I bend down and start to pick up the pieces of my broken plate.

Except the moment I do, the high road I've taken puts me right in the line of fire.

Perielle's boot snaps towards my face. Kicking me like a dog, then?

No.

Instinct slams through me, and I dodge her blow easily. She's slow. Or maybe she thought I'd just roll over and take it like the commoner I am. But she doesn't know how hard people like me have had to fight every fucking day of our lives.

I've never just laid down and taken anything, and I'm not starting today.

It takes a concentrated effort not to slide the broken piece of plate between her ribs. But I manage to release it and rise slowly. There's a pressure in my chest like the beginnings of a growl. Perielle doesn't retreat, but she doesn't try to strike me again, either.

I speak slowly and clearly so that every single person in this room can hear it. "I'm sure that you're used to these other Bonded bowing to you and tearing themselves apart for your approval, but as you're so clearly aware, I am *not one of them*. Try kicking me again, and I'll cut your foot off at the ankle and feed it to my wolf."

Anassa's dark amusement flares in the following silence. She's satisfied, like my fury has filled her belly.

Maybe this is truly what she wants from me, then—more violence.

Perielle steps closer, and I ready myself for anything. I've decided. I *will* break her nose if she pushes me.

"Lock your door tonight, cunt," she hisses before turning on her heel, flicking her hair, and stalking away.

Conversation picks back up around us. No doubt, I'm the subject of most of it. I sigh internally and settle back in my seat. Izabel touches my shoulder briefly before I set about cleaning up after the queen's tantrum.

So. Pack bonding is going great.

The tension from breakfast follows me for the rest of the day. I keep catching glimpses from people around me. Not all of them are scornful—some are more curious—but the constant hum of attention is as annoying as the winter winds banging against a window late at night.

Our first wolf communication class with the Kryptos instructor, Gamma Samson Whyte, helps to divert some of the attention. We all pour into a room together. His voice is clear as he projects across the auditorium.

"Rawbonds always ask how exactly the connection works, because even if you've seen your friends and family communicating with their wolves, you don't truly understand it until you experience it for yourselves the first time. So let me ask you, is your wolf in your head at all times, seeing through your eyes?"

Izabel's hand shoots up first, as usual. "No, sir," she says. "The connection works by linking together our thoughts and our emotions. The direwolves are not actually in our minds or our bodies, it only feels that way because they hear it all."

"Correct," says Samson. "Well, mostly correct. The most powerful direwolves can see through their riders' eyes, but that is very rare and requires an enormously strong bond. For the rest of us, it's just an unending exchange of thoughts and emotions."

Unending. Great.

"It must seem right now that you and your wolves have an open channel of communication that can't be turned off. It's constant, yes?" he asks, pacing around the front of the room, his white-blond hair a shock against the blackboard behind him.

Based on the head nods and the knowing noises, yes, the majority are in agreement.

Well, *shit*. An open channel? Is that what everyone else experiences? No ice-cold, merciless wall to smack up against every time they try to reach for their wolves?

Just me, then?

"Your thoughts and your direwolf's thoughts, right now, are likely passing back and forth regularly. However, that's not the true way of it," he explains. "It only feels that way, as your bond is weak and you're seeking to strengthen it. But both wolves and riders can control their level of mental connection."

He turns to the blackboard and draws crude figures of a person and a wolf, with two horizontal lines connecting them. Then, he draws a thick vertical line intersecting the connections.

"Your wolves don't want to know what you had for breakfast any more than you want to be bombarded with their every passing thought," Samson goes on. "The strongest bonds are selective." With this, he circles the dividing line.

Selective. Well, Anassa is about as selective as they come. Namely, she's *selected* never to speak to me.

The class becomes a guided meditation. Samson instructs us to close our eyes in our seats and *think* towards our wolves. Clear everything out but our connection. Seek out the path between us and follow it to its conclusion, then begin to manipulate and navigate it.

Build up walls. Drop them. Shape the connection like guiding a river.

It's mercilessly pointless.

"By now, you should sense a wall in your mind," Samson calls out.

Now, always, what's the difference?

"You can use that to control what you do or do not let your wolves experience. Imagine lifting the wall, and then bringing it back down. If you can't lift it, think a way through it—imagine you're creating a hole in it."

Anassa is impenetrable, and I'm not making any progress. Whatever dent I might manage to make floods again with cold disregard an instant after I open it up. Before long, my head is starting to ache with the effort.

By the end of class, I'm drenched in sweat and exhausted. It's not just a mental effort. I feel like I've been physically banging my entire body against a metal wall for two hours.

My mind is raw. My thoughts sting like scraped skin exposed to the air.

And I *hate* this eternal sense of rejection.

But I have to master this connection with my direwolf, whether Anassa likes it or not. It's the only way I'll be able to find Saela.

"*Anassa*," I think toward her, unsure of what she's receiving on her end, if she can even hear me. "*If this is some sort of test, fine. You should know that I never give up. I'm going to keep slamming against this wall until you eventually let me in, you stubborn wench.*"

CHAPTER TWENTY

A week passes in a painful, mind-numbing blur.

I wake in pain. I lay myself down to rest in pain. I can't move freely without favoring some part of my body.

Every day: combat training, riding practice, class to go over battle strategy or types of magic or history. Every day, I continue to reach out to Anassa with very little progress.

And every night, when I lock myself in my private room, I try very hard not to think about the man who gave this room to me, or the words he spoke in the garden. I don't have the mental space to nurture a broken heart right now.

I'm still enduring the permanent headache I seem to have lately as I trudge to strategy class this morning. But before I can reach the classroom, a voice calls my name. I stop short and lift my head, confused.

Henrey is standing there with his hands in his pockets. Leader Aldrich is next to him, stroking his beard.

The older man smiles at me, and it's… surprisingly gentle. It's the first truly gentle smile I think I've seen from an instructor. It deepens the age lines around his eyes just so. And it reminds me of my dad, suddenly and jarringly. My shoulders fall.

"Would you join us in my office?" Aldrich asks.

I approach them. "For… what?"

"Class," he says, turning and striding down the echoing halls.

I eye Henrey, brow raised. "The fuck? Just us?" I whisper.

"Just you," Aldrich says over his shoulder, apparently not going deaf in his advanced age. "And please refrain from coarse language."

I snort and cross my arms, following obediently. Not like I wanted to attend another of Egith's strategy lectures, anyway.

Aldrich stops in front of an inlaid silver door with a tall pearlescent bar for a handle. There is a wolf engraved on it—what else—its body bent at impossible angles to emphasize the beauty of its flowing fur. Its eye is a massive ruby lodged right in the elegant silver.

I briefly consider trying to pry the rock out and get it to my mother somehow before Aldrich swings the door open and ushers us inside.

The room is smaller than most in the castle, but it's tall. Every wall is covered in bookshelves, laden with dusty tomes and diamond-shaped cubbies crammed with crinkled scrolls. And the walls go up two, three floors. At each level, there's a small balcony circling the room, accessible by ladders that seem to be mounted on tracks to slide across the shelves.

In the center of the room, there's a round table covered in books and papers, as well as a few jars with what look like dried flowers or herbs in them. There are no candles in here, only enclosed oil lamps. Maybe to protect the paper.

Aldrich grunts as he wheels a chalkboard towards the table, gesturing for us to sit. Henrey doesn't even hesitate, so I swallow my questions and pull out a chair.

I glance at Henrey again, who's looking a bit uncomfortable. He watches as the instructor picks up a piece of chalk and starts writing on the dusty board. I haven't spoken to Henrey much since the Ascent, but he seems like a decent Rawbond.

He rides well. He wields the sword and bow well. He's determined and dedicated.

If this is the remedial class, I have no idea why he's here.

Henrey seems to be wondering that, too, because he pipes up. "Leader Aldrich, if I may ask—"

"You are here because there are lessons you haven't learned. Lessons everyone else learned at their mothers' knees."

Oh. Right.

Bonded family lore, that kind of stuff. Whereas the lessons I was getting at my mother's knee mostly involved insane ravings about "the twins."

Henrey slumps in his chair, his face flushing. He doesn't look at me, but I know what he's thinking.

Us versus them.

This is just another way we aren't like the rest.

"So what… lessons, exactly, will we be learning?" Henrey asks.

"Everything you need to succeed here. The history of the dire-wolves. Pack dynamics. I want to give you the tools you need to see yourselves as truly Bonded," he replies.

Truly Bonded, huh? Not in a thousand lifetimes. I've accepted my situation, but I'll never see myself as one of them. I'd have to erase everything I am to get there, and I'd go down fighting first.

Still, I can't exactly stand up and shout in his face, storming out in a fit of fury. I'm pretty sure they'd send Stark after me.

Just the thought makes me shiver as I settle into my seat for what is no doubt going to be a long, cripplingly boring lesson.

And it is. But at least Aldrich's voice is soft and flowing, not grating like Egith's or fierce and cold like Stark's.

Aldrich discusses general pack structure first. I'd picked up on most of this from Izabel and just generally soaking things in, but he fills in the gaps.

There are the four distinct packs, which he scrawls out on the board with a series of gentle taps and drags of chalk. Each serves a crucial role in defending the kingdom and the humans within it against the aggressor Siphons who would drain us all with their heinous blood magic.

"Daemos are known for their brutality and battle prowess. Their

Bonded tend to be large and temperamental. Their wolves, even more so," Aldrich says.

"Are all of their wolves as brutal as Cratos?" Henrey asks.

Cratos. Stark's direwolf.

"Mm. No," Aldrich says. "Cratos is… dominant. An alpha pair."

"That's a relief," Henrey grumbles. "Still not looking forward to inter-pack training."

"Ah, but you *should*," Aldrich chimes in. "You are of Phylax. The guardians. You learn how to blend in alongside all the other packs, support them and protect them."

His gaze shifts to me.

"And Meryn, Strategos," he says, pointing to the name on the board. "The tacticians and leaders. Masters of strategy. You more than any of the other packs must learn to cooperate with the rest."

Cooperate. I try to picture it. Riding out into the field with the other packs at our side.

Fucking Daemos, with that piece-of-shit Jonah. I'd let Anassa weed out the weak there. I'd rather choke on a luxurious poached egg at breakfast than cooperate with him.

"Then, of course, there's Kryptos, the shadow walkers. They specialize in stealth and intelligence gathering," Aldrich continues. "Above all of us," he goes on, circling a name he's written above the pack names. *Siegrid Therion*. "The Sovereign Alpha, currently a fearsome woman named Siegrid who can communicate with all wolves across all packs. A feat of immense strength and control. She is the head of the Bonded, and she serves as the king's second in command."

A memory hits me from orientation. The two women who were lusting after Stark mentioned that his mother was the Sovereign Alpha. Of fucking course she is. Stark moves with the violent confidence of someone who knows he'll never get in trouble. Nepotism at its finest.

"How is the Sovereign Alpha chosen?" Henrey asks, putting a voice to something I'm wondering too.

"Family line," Aldrich tells him. "The Therions have been the crown's sworn protectors for as long as anyone can remember."

Which means that after his mom, Stark will become the Sovereign Alpha and will be in charge of all of us. Great.

I lean forward. A question wriggles in my mind, one I've wondered for a while.

"If the king isn't actually bonded to a wolf, why does he maintain ultimate control over the wolves and the Bonded?"

Aldrich looks pleased that I'm engaging. "A good question! It has been this way since time immemorial. The king's role is to ensure that the commoners he reigns over always have an equal balance of power with the Bonded and the direwolves. So while Siegrid is the highest in power for the Bonded, we ultimately all answer to the king."

It makes sense, in theory.

But in practice? What are we meant to do when the man appointed to protect the common people's interests starts to ignore us? When he'd rather watch his wolves parade dead men through the streets or sleep with unwilling Rawbonds half his age than look into, or even notice, the abductions of children in his cities?

"Now, *details*," Aldrich goes on. "I'm sure you are both well acquainted with telepathic communication at this point—" *Yikes.* "—but you should know that wolves can telepathically communicate within their own packs but can't typically speak across pack lines unless through the Sovereign Alpha."

"How does *that* work?" Henrey asks.

"She is essentially a conduit. Think of her like a translator, relaying a foreign language to you in words you can understand," he replies. "Within their own packs, wolves can communicate freely. Then, of course, you with your wolves."

"It's the same for every pack?" Henrey asks.

"Yes. The hierarchy is the same, too. One alpha leading each pack, followed by their betas who handle day-to-day operations, then the gammas who handle any other leadership tasks. It's very rare for Rawbonds to have such high-ranking instructors. This year's Trials will churn out incredibly talented Bonded, I can tell."

"Alpha Stark," I blurt. They both stare at me. My cheeks heat and I deftly ignore it. "Why is he here, and not on the frontline?"

Aldrich scratches his beard. "I can't entirely speak to the reasons, other than to say that the Sovereign Alpha makes these choices," he replies. That could mean he doesn't know or it could mean he just doesn't want to or can't tell us. "But it may have something to do with pack influence. Daemos and Strategos often vie for dominance."

A power play of some sort? Some attempt to route Daemos to rise in ranks? Wouldn't put it past him.

Or maybe the Sovereign Alpha just needed a break from her brute of a son.

"You'll find that Kryptos operates more independently and Phylax maintains careful neutrality, in most matters," Aldrich explains.

And he goes on. And *on*.

I start to zone out, my mind drifting to that vision of Lee again. Killian. Standing there in the dim light of the garden, eyes seeking me out.

Stop, I tell myself. *Do not waste brainpower on him.*

Aldrich jumps up from his chair, rushing to the board to answer a question Henrey must've asked.

"Like this," he exclaims, drawing a long squiggly line with his chalk. He claps his dusty hands together. "A flowing bond. A connection like a river. Unstoppable. Constant. Ever-changing."

"Huh?" I grumble, chin resting in my palm.

"The bond you feel," he replies, tapping his temple. "Your energy. Your souls. Your spirits. Wolves choose their Bonded based on compatibility of that unnamable, many-named part of us that defies all true classification. They *know*, instinctively, who we are. Every part of us. And that initial recognition, like calling to like, deepens over time, like a river carving a winding path through the hardest of stone. Shared experiences, emotions. Trust. You will only become closer to your direwolf."

Trust me, Leader Aldrich. It can only go up from here.

What exactly does that say about me? A truly feral, vicious beast took one look at me and thought, "*That one. I'll take that one.*"

Then again, she hates me, so maybe she fucked up.

"I have a question," I interrupt.

Aldrich's enthusiasm doesn't wane. He clearly loves discussing direwolf bonds. "Of course."

"Have wolves ever rejected their chosen riders, after the fact? What happens then?"

He very clearly hesitates. It's the sort of hesitation that means he's carefully considering how to respond because the way he answers matters here. "It's virtually unheard of."

"Virtually?"

"You've seen the wolves in training, Meryn," Henrey says. "When a Bonded isn't good enough for them, they know it. The Bonded dies."

"It's hardly a choice, on the wolf's part. More of an instinct to eliminate weakness and protect the pack at large, even if it means their own death," Aldrich adds. "As you may have learned by now, the wolf/human bond cannot be severed once it is formed—and if it is, it results in death for both beings. Sometimes, wolves reject their chosen during the Ascent, but the bond hasn't solidified at that point and the wolf survives."

"I meant the spirit stuff," I say. "What happens when a wolf changes its mind about that part?"

Aldrich stares at me. "That… No, a wolf recognizes all of us from the beginning. It's not a decision they make lightly. It's intimate. It runs deeper than whim and passing moods. Just like…" He pauses and turns to the board. "Oh, you'll find this part interesting. You've heard of mate bonds?"

Henrey sits upright immediately. "A bond connection between wolves."

"Precisely, recognized in moments of intimacy," he says. "The key of what you just said is *between wolves*. The direwolves, once mated, mate for life. Their riders do not need to be together romantically, although it makes things easier, because the mate bonds have unique properties."

I hate to admit it, but my interest piques.

"These rare connections between wolves allow their riders to communicate telepathically even across pack lines, without the aid of the Sovereign Alpha. Mated direwolves are cherished because they can protect each other—and in turn, their Bonded riders and their packs—even better during battle. Also because mated direwolves often result in direwolf pups, thereby continuing the Bonded line. However," he slumps into the chair again, "mated wolves have become more and more rare over the past several hundred years."

Maybe because you creeps keep letting all the direwolves die in training. Thought about that?

Aldrich takes a deep breath and wipes a hand over his face. "If there's one thing you should take away from this lesson, it's that the Bonded line is to be respected. You simply *cannot* think of your wolves as mere mounts to ride into battle and abandon in the stables when the day's won. They are ancient, intelligent beings with their own culture and traditions. We shape our training around and seek to emulate their way of being. We learn from them. We try to see the world through their eyes. That is how you must move forward, if you want to survive."

Henrey and I leave the lesson with those words still resonating in the musty, papery air. We step into the hallway and start towards the Rawbond quarters, walking in silence for a while before I can't take it any longer.

"I'm glad you made it through the Ascent," I tell him. "I know how much becoming Bonded meant to you."

The halls are empty. I think everyone else is still in class. He stops walking in front of one of the towering windows in the long hall that joins the academic wing with the common room. Beyond it, afternoon sun glints on the snow-covered lawns.

Henrey looks at me warily, then leans against the wall. "What about you? I thought you didn't want this life."

A sharp sting of grief pierces my chest. The cold, heavy weight of it rolls over me like a boulder.

"I don't," I say, before correcting to, "I didn't. Anassa chose me anyway, and I thought I could get out of this, but I've realized that you can't… quit being Bonded. So I have to survive the Trials. My little sister was taken by Nabbers. That's why I enlisted, to try to find her."

Henrey stares at me blankly.

"What?" I ask.

"What's a Nabber?"

My blood goes cold. Dread settles over me like a thick layer of snow. "You don't… have Nabbers in Blumenfall?" Maybe it's a terminology difference, maybe they call them something else. "Siphons who are stealing the children? Kids get kidnapped out of their beds at night."

His brow pinches, and he shakes his head. "I've never heard of—"

The deafening horn calling us to our next class sounds through the halls. I wince, clenching my jaw as the sound worsens my headache. I follow after Henrey quickly, slightly dizzy.

No Nabbers in Blumenfall. I don't understand.

Blumenfall is *much* closer to the front than Sturmfrost. Why would the Siphons bypass closer, easier targets to snatch children from here?

Henrey heads off to whatever class the Phylax pack has, and I go out to the training grounds for combat training.

My own personal torture sessions.

Stark is already striding around the grounds with Cratos. As I join the others, I watch him out of the corner of my eye. He circles us like a predator looking for the weak link in the herd.

Stark's head turns, and his wolf's swivels, too. Cratos moves, and Stark's body follows. His own sturdy form shifts fluidly atop Cratos's back as the wolf's shoulder blades shift beneath him.

I hate seeing it. I'll never be there, never know that total sense of understanding and connection. Rider and wolf moving as one deadly unit, muscle and fur and leather and steel in perfect harmony.

I avert my eyes from him, staring at the messy spot of blood in the sand. Much more likely I end up like *that*.

Yesterday, a Kryptos recruit named Alix lost control during a basic defensive maneuver.

People were talking about it in the common room this morning. It apparently happened fast. Her wolf turned on her suddenly, ripping out her throat before anyone could intervene. She died right there in the sand.

All I can do is fight.

"Focus today, hey?" Tomison says, smacking my arm.

I scowl, annoyed because he's implying I've been lacking in focus until now. "Tell Anassa that," I say, scowling at her as she and the rest of the direwolves enter the training grounds.

He snorts. "I choose life," he says, heading toward his wolf.

"Today we're starting on swords," Stark bellows from astride Cratos. "Get your weapon and get on your wolves. Now!"

This should go great for me, considering I've never touched a sword before.

I grab one of the wooden practice swords laid out near the wall, then mount Anassa. She tolerates that much, at least, and it's becoming easier. But we haven't gotten any better at the rest of it.

She's too hot headed, too independent. Every time I touch her, I slam up against that blockade. She'd rather gnaw off her own tail than let me guide her movements.

Practice goes predictably. Hit. Fall. Hit. Fall. Hit. Fall.

Every time I hit the ground, I find Stark's eyes on me. He's not smiling—I doubt the man is capable of such a frivolous expression —but I can his amusement pierces through his glare all the same. He's absolutely *delighted* that I'm eating dirt.

The ground rushes up to meet me for the fourth time this training session.

I grunt, landing badly on my arm and my hip but lessening the impact with a bit of a roll. Sand kicks into my eyes and mouth, and I spit, blinking rapidly.

"*Up*, princess!" Stark growls at me. "Or are you too delicate for combat?"

I hiss under my breath and dig my fingers into the sand, curling my other hand tight around the practice sword. Anassa stands beside me, staring as always, making absolutely no move to help me.

Shutting my eyes briefly, I focus on the pain in my body, wrestling it under my control, hissing breaths through my nose.

Use it. That's what Igor always preached. That's what my life has taught me.

In pain, there's power.

Although I'd feel pretty powerful if my hateful direwolf ever used any of her healing magic on me. Anassa has continued to deprive me of that, deigning to patch up my injuries only when she wants to—which has been, like the rest of her, totally unpredictable.

I get up. The practice sword is impossibly heavy in my hand, but I lift it all the same. The scream in my shoulder only makes me more determined. My arms are trembling from the exertion.

Blood trickles from my split lip, the thick iron taste mingling with the gritty sensation of sand on my tongue.

The drill should be simple. Ride in a circle while deflecting incoming strikes from other mounted riders. But without Anassa's cooperation—more like *with* her downright rebellion—every movement is a battle.

She keeps deliberately shifting at the wrong moments, throwing off my balance.

I keep falling, yes. But I'm also being whacked over and over with heavy practice swords. It feels like my entire body is one massive bruise.

Back and mounted again, I sense Anassa's emotions again for the first time in a while. It's a sickening trickle of dark, borderline feral amusement. She knows she has me trapped between her teeth, and she's having fun tasting my fear before swallowing me down.

We gallop together. She shifts suddenly. I'm focused on trying to stay mounted. Cold wind whips at me. The weight of the sword and my own body drags at me. The thundering pounding of paws riots in my ears.

Yet still, I hear him. Too late.

"Guard up!" Stark shouts, voice cracking like a whip.

Perielle thrusts toward me and her practice sword impacts my ribs with a vicious smack, sending a white-hot fissure of pain through my already brutally bruised torso.

I choke and double over, eyes tearing up, clinging weakly to Anassa's fur. The sword tumbles from my hand as I clutch my side, squeezing my eyes shut and focusing on not passing out.

Heavy paws thud over the sand beside Anassa.

I force my eyes open, baring my teeth.

"I told you to put your fucking guard up," Stark says, his voice dangerously low. His dark hair curls down into his eyes in a way that would look charming on any other man, but does nothing to soften the murderous look he's giving me.

Before I can even open my mouth to defend myself, he's slid down Cratos, fisted his huge hand around my arm, and yanked me off Anassa. I come tumbling down inelegantly, his hand still tight on my bicep.

Anassa watches all of this with what I can only think of as a smirk.

Then he reaches down with his other hand to the exposed hem of my shirt, and in the blink of an eye, grabs it and yanks it up to just before the bottom of my breasts. The cold winter air is stinging on my skin.

My face flushes hot and I try to wriggle away from him, yanking my arm, but he's an immovable force. "Get your hands off of me," I grit out.

The rest of the pack has gone quiet, watching this spectacle with held breath. Perielle's eyes twinkle with delight. Obviously none of them are going to intervene, and I don't blame them. I wouldn't want to be on the receiving end of this man's wrath either; unfortunately, I seem to have been destined for it.

Stark ignores my demand, moving the hem of my shirt over to the hand that's holding my arm. Then he prods my aching ribs.

I hiss and look down. The area that Perielle hit is a deep red, already purpling. Definitely bruised, possibly even broken. But it's just one of many bruises mottling my torso. I have a veritable collection, built up day after day.

He pokes the bruise again, pain lancing through me. Fuck this guy.

I pull my head back and spit in his face.

Stark's black eyes slowly drag up from my injuries and lock onto my own. I can see his thoughts as clearly as if he's said them aloud.

He's going to make me pay.

But instead of doing anything immediately, he wipes the spit off his cheek and turns to Anassa, pointing at my ribs. "You want to do anything about that?" he asks her, his voice calmer and more deferential than I've ever heard it.

She doesn't move, doesn't even blink her eerie golden-yellow eyes, but he seems to understand her all the same.

No, she does not.

Stark finally lets go of my bicep, which now feels as bruised as my ribs, and I hurriedly yank my shirt back down, buckling the front of my leather jacket up so he can't try that shit again. When I'm done, I look back up, and no surprise, Stark's still glaring at me.

"Pathetic. You are weak," he says cruelly, his voice carrying to everyone else. "And you are going to continue to be weak."

I straighten my spine at the challenge in his voice. He doesn't know me. I've never let difficult things break me and I'm not going to start *now*.

"You pose a threat to all the packs like this," he continues. "And they're going to figure that out real soon unless you do *better*. Get back on your direwolf." He turns around, scowling at how everyone has stopped still, watching us. "Everyone, again!"

Asshole.

"Again!" Stark orders, turning back to me. "Until you get it right or join Alix in the sand."

Jerkily, I scramble for my sword in the dirt. When I do, Cratos snaps at me and I stumble. I push through the fear, the anger, the pain. I mount Anassa again.

I'll keep fighting forever, if I have to.

The other Rawbonds circle us. I have the sense that none of them really want to land another blow against me after the way I've just been publicly humiliated, but they know that they have to obey.

None of them want to let my weakness drag them down, lest the target on my back jump to theirs.

Lifting the sword again, my mind narrows down.

I see red, fury coursing through my blood. It rises to the surface of me through my messy bruises, pouring out into the surrounding air. Something sharp and biting pierces through the iron wall in my mind. Anassa's consciousness, honed into something darker.

Eager. It's almost *anticipation*, disappearing again behind the wall just as quickly as it sparked.

By the end of the session, I'm ruined. My body's a map of fresh injuries. My face. My ribs. My legs. My arms got the worst of it, sore from carrying and swinging the blade as well as from the blows they took when I couldn't deflect properly. There are vicious blisters on my hands, bleeding in places.

I feel torn wide open.

And still that bitch won't heal me.

But it's Stark's parting barb that cuts deeper than the wounds. "At this rate, princess, you won't survive long enough to earn your first real kill mark." A cold glare, a tilting up of his chin. "Pity. That neck tattoo looks lonely."

His words reverberate in my aching head. I touch my fingertips to my tattoo, remembering the bite of the needle, the intensity of his stare.

The lewd heat of his tongue.

I limp my way to my private room, bypassing the now-familiar sounds of mingling bodies emanating from the common areas. I can't spare my eyes entirely, though, catching glimpses of people tangled together on the floor, the beds, against the walls.

In the past week, I've accidentally walked in on people fucking more times than I can count. Every night, the emberwine comes out and people throw themselves at each other. In the down hours between training or meals, they throw themselves at each other. First thing in the morning, they throw themselves at each other.

They take this search for their direwolves' mates *extremely* seriously, I guess.

Izabel has been trying to get me to join in at night, to flirt with people in other packs or play drinking games with them, but I have at most a glass of wine before I lock myself in my room. The Bonded's casual attitude towards sex will never fail to embarrass me.

I hate that it still makes a hot flush move through me. I can't believe my body even has the energy to feel this way after the session I just suffered through.

I yank my door open and step inside, shutting it and thudding back against it in exhaustion.

Then it's just blessed, beautiful silence, free from lectures and assholes shouting at me and people I barely know moaning at the top of their—

"Mer," he says quietly.

Lee. No, *Killian*. Killian.

Alone, in my room, waiting for me.

CHAPTER TWENTY-ONE

t's jarring, seeing him standing there, blond hair golden in the afternoon light. His large silhouette is bold against the pale wall. His deep blue eyes are wide, though I haven't said a word yet. For a moment, it's like I've fallen back through time.

It's like I'm finding Lee waiting for me after a tough fight, and my chest, even now, tightens with a familiar longing.

Then reality comes crashing back in.

"Get *out*," I snap.

Killian sighs and holds up a brown leather bag. I already know what's inside. Medical supplies. "Can I at least tend to you first?"

I hate how I feel when his eyes dart to my bruises. Weak, like Stark said. And worse, lonely.

"Killian—" The name still tastes wrong in my mouth.

"Please."

"I don't—"

"You're hurt," he says plainly. There's no room for argument; I'm hurt, and he'll fix me, like we've always done.

Begrudgingly, without a word, I sit down on the bed. I tell myself that I'm only doing this because I'm injured. I'm already struggling. Training will be even harder if I'm slowed down by stiffness and pain.

If Anassa weren't refusing to help me, these cuts and scrapes wouldn't matter. My injuries *should* already be healed. Every little sting is a reminder of what I'm up against. Anassa's hatred, her disdain, her viciousness. It's eating away at my sanity.

One day soon, I'll either die in training or snap and try to blind her with a practice sword. And probably die.

Killian settles beside me on the bed. I immediately wish I'd chosen a less intimate place to sit, but it's not like my room provides a wealth of options for two people.

He reaches for me to help me ease my jacket from my body, but I shoot him a glare and he immediately backs off. I refuse to show any hint of pain as I pull the leather from my shoulders and toss it aside. I refuse to even speak as he opens his bag and rifles through it.

"How did you know I'd need this?" I finally ask. Has he been spying on me?

"It was just a coincidence," he says, voice weary. He's tired of this, I can tell, of my hardened defenses against him. "I heard from my servants that your wolf was refusing to heal you, and I was just going to drop this in your room. I had no idea you were coming back in right now."

I sit still as he starts to disinfect my wounds. The familiar smell of antiseptic fills my nose, sharp and bitter. Lingering. It messes with my head. Tricks me into thinking I'm an alleycat again, curling up in the lap of the only person who ever bothered to tend to me.

My pride is a snarling thing, though. Some part of me growls that this isn't right. That I can't lay my head down and rest in a place like this. That Killian is the last person I should let see me falter.

Fight, my blood thrums, even louder where it pushes against my skin in the mottled shape of dark bruises.

But it's so, so familiar. Achingly. Reassuringly. Killian's pine-clean smell. The careful movements of his nimble hands. The concentration in his eyes as the entirety of his attention goes to making my life even a touch easier.

I *can't.*

"Killian," I say, shattering the silence.

He doesn't react poorly when I use his full name. Maybe I'm the only one struggling not to slip into the past. Into *Lee* and little smiles and a love I thought could never waver.

His voice is quiet, deep as the sea in his eyes. "What is it?"

I gesture to our surroundings. To my surprise quarters, issued by someone above *Egith's head*. "Are you responsible for this?"

Killian looks up from his work. His eyes meet mine, unblinking and defiant in a way that is so familiar. The look that has always said, "*I'm going to take care of you whether you like it or not.*"

I don't hate it. I never hated it. There were days that I *needed* it. Someone to take me into their arms and promise me safety. Someone strong enough that I could trust that they could keep that promise.

My blood thrums at his dominance, at the way he's daring me to challenge him. Driven by instinct, my thighs tighten. He's just…

Fuck, he's so gorgeous. All his lies, and that truth still remains. Stubborn. Devastating. Damned addicting. He stares up at me and arousal heats my blood instantly. Memories of my legs around him, of his hands on my skin, of the solidity of his abs flash through my mind like lightning strikes.

And that look in his eyes. Unflinching. Angry, almost, but not at me. At the men I fought in the ring, for bruising my body. At the war, for taking my childhood from me. At the touch of the wintery air, for daring to chill my skin.

It wordlessly tells me he's definitely responsible for my private quarters. Of course he is.

I pinch the bridge of my nose. The hand that's been lingering tenderly on my arm smooths over my skin, but I push him away and stand.

I need distance. I need to be able to process things without the incessant thought swirling around my head that if I just leaned forward, I could taste him again.

Taking a stabilizing breath, I turn to look at him. "You painted a target on my back by separating me from my pack," I say coldly. "Do you understand what you've done? The position you've put me in?"

His jaw tightens. "I'm trying to keep you safe, Meryn. You have no idea what you're up against with these people."

Anger spikes through me again, outweighing my confusing affection for him. "What are you even—"

"*I* do. I know them," he snaps. Then he makes a considerable effort to gentle his voice and unfurl his fist. "My father is in direct command of them, and someday, I will be as well. The Bonded are not your friends, not even the ones in your pack. For them, everyone here is disposable, or a bargaining chip. Your life is at risk with them."

I scoff. "That's rich, coming from you. Knowing who your father is and how he treats other people's lives."

Killian's upper lip twitches with frustration. He stands, passion blazing in his gaze. "When I'm king, *everything* will change. I swear it. And if you would give me a chance, I'd tell you more about it."

I stare in silence. Apparently unable to endure it, he approaches me. I tense, but he doesn't try to touch me. His gaze is even more intimate than a touch, though, and I want to curl up. Maybe in his arms, maybe just to die.

"I wanted to tell you. Everything, Meryn. I want…" he swallows. There's something barely restrained in the way he's holding his body. Taut. Hurting. "I want to be with you."

I grit my teeth. "Like how the nobles are with the Bonded during the Trials?" I say, and the tension in him heightens, muscles bunching. Maybe it's cruel, but a part of me relishes wringing that reaction out of him. "You want to fuck me and then discard me when I've grown tiresome?" I say just to make it hurt.

Killian snaps. The strain in him wasn't anger. It wasn't pain. It was *need*. I can see it. It's in the way he pushes me back against the wall, his hand closing around my wrist like he's washing out to sea in a storm and I'm the anchor that can save him.

His blue eyes are lit with that same fire I've always seen in them when something hurts me, like he's going to burn the world down for my sake, until all that's left is him and me, standing in the ashes.

"Don't *ever* talk about yourself that way, Meryn," he says. The growl of his voice thrums in my body where we're pressed together. His hand slides down the wall beside me, the other still grasped firm but gentle around my wrist. And I realize that the burning danger in his eyes *is* directed at me.

Not for resisting him but for belittling my place in his life.

"You are more precious to me than you could ever imagine," he tells me in a quieter tone. And his thumb rubs up and down on my wrist. I resist the responding shiver that prickles over my skin, but I have to curl my fingers into a fist so I won't touch him.

I can't deny the pull to do so. But I also can't let go. So I stand, silent, as he stares at me.

He's imploring. Clearly in pain. His eyes dart between mine, searching for a hint, a hope.

I don't shake him off of me, but I don't pull him in, either. He steps back, eventually. He drops my arm and gives me space, and the cool air between us is an aching relief.

He hangs one hand from the back of his neck and points to the wardrobe with the other. "There's a hidden panel at the back of it. Leads to a servant's passageway. If you take it and stay on the path that goes straight, you'll find your way to my rooms."

I don't know what to say to that. What to think.

Killian shakes his head. "You're welcome to come. Any time, if you want. But if you need more space, I understand."

I swallow. This, I have an answer for. "Thank you."

Because the entirety of this strange new life has felt hostile, pressing in on me from every direction. He's no different, except in his willingness to back off. Training will never end. I can't escape Anassa's bond. The war rages on.

But Killian is willing to give me space. He understands.

He nods. "Even if we never…" His mouth works, testing out the shapes of his words before he says them. "My investigation of your sister's disappearance is not dependent on anything. Same with me taking care of your mom in your absence. I'm actively going to continue to pursue answers, and I'll let you know as soon as I have an update."

I say nothing until he disappears into the wardrobe and leaves me there, staring at the wall and trying to parse out who I am in this place.

I tear myself from the trance and collapse onto the bed. He left the bag of medicine behind. Looking at it upsets me, so I shove it under my bed and roll over to face the wall.

Frustration creeps along the walls of my heart like thorned vines. His sudden presence and even more sudden absence are jarring. I'm left with this cavernous pit in my chest—the space he just occupied, full of sadness and confusion and longing.

I miss him. I can't lie about that. Right now, having *Lee* around to talk through all the shit that's happened to me would be incredible.

And ultimately, he came here to help me. To tend to my wounds. To warn me about the Bonded.

I know he's probably right about them. I'm definitely an outsider. I know I've been marked as one by many of the other Rawbonds, and I've seen firsthand how competitive they all are. Eager to one-up each other. Desperate to snuff me out, like pruning a struggling leaf.

But it doesn't matter how right Killian is. I'm not ready to forgive him for a lie this big.

And I have other things to worry about, anyway. Like figuring out how to get better at this whole Bonded thing. Getting my throat torn out in training would quickly resolve my confused pining, but being dead would be a bit of an obstacle to reaching Saela.

It's deeply infuriating to be so fucking awful at this. A naïve part of me thought, at the start of all this, that I might actually make a decent rider if I just swung hard enough and held on tight.

Even when I was green and needed training before the pits, I was a good fighter. I knew how to move. My mind was quick. I caught on fast. It all came instinctively to me. It felt less like training and more like slowly waking up, as if fighting was in my muscles and my blood from birth and I just needed to find it.

Fuck, it would be amazing to feel that way again. To really hit something. I used to shatter the dummies in training, and even with aching muscles and split knuckles, something in me always felt sated.

I sit up suddenly in bed. Maybe that's a solution to both of my problems.

I'm on my feet and moving before I can second-guess myself. Izabel and Venna are predictably together, settled in the Strategos anteroom and playing a round of the card game Wolves and Siphons. I march right up to their little table and cross my arms over my chest.

"I'm failing, and I need help," I say.

They both look up, questioning.

I take in a deep breath. "Can you train me? With swords, preferably?"

There's a scoff to my left. I turn my head to see Nevah draped over an armchair, holding a book in one hand. She doesn't take her eyes off of it as she says, "It's about time you asked for help. You really suck."

"Thanks for the support," I deadpan. "Want to come train with us?"

Eyes still on her book, she waves her free hand dismissively. "Good luck, though."

"*Ugh,*" Izabel groans. She throws her chin into her palm. "Unfortunately, I know just the person to ask."

Twenty minutes later, Venna and Izabel are standing off at the edge of the training yard and Tomison and I are facing each other, practice swords in hand. His hair is a messy burst of color, and that permanent grin he always sports is predictably on his face.

He agreed so quickly to this, I was sure he'd misheard my request and thought we were marching off to a mildly incestuous four-way.

A regrettably good teacher, Izabel called him. And she was right.

Tomison is straightforward and clear. He's patient. And best of all, he isn't overly mushy. He doesn't shower me in praise when I do something easy correctly. When his eyes flash with approval, I know it's because I earned it. When I stumble over footwork or miss a parry, he just resets and says, "Again."

We practice several forms. Stances meant to ease mounted combat. Tomison positions my body for me, exercising a clinical touch to reposition my limbs into shapes they've never needed to take until now.

"This will all be different on a wolf," he tells me with an easy smile.

"It's fucking awkward right now," I grunt. My arm is raised almost up to my shoulder, the blade arced forward. Apparently, I've been holding it too low. Unready, he called it.

"Well, you've been making things more difficult for yourself," he tells me as he steps away. His eyes assess my posture. I can tell he's testing how long I'm capable of holding it. "Like this, training should be a little easier for you."

I grunt. There's sweat on my brow. "Easy. Yeah. This is the easiest thing I've ever done," I say, purposely adding some strain to my voice.

Izabel snickers from the wall, and I hear the distinct sound of Venna whapping her arm. Tomison glances their way. His gaze catches, then flicks back to me.

"Okay. Parry practice," he says, tapping his blade to the ground.

He swings at me. And keeps swinging. And I'm focusing on my feet. On my arms. On moving my body in ways I've never told it to move before. Muscles I don't normally use are cramping and knot-ting. Sweat soaks my back and beneath my breasts.

When I manage a pretty perfect parry, Tomison lets out a whoop.

Venna claps. Izabel lets out a long, appreciative whistle. Then quickly adds, "That wasn't for you, Tomison!"

"*Sure*, it wasn't!" he calls back.

But when I glance her way, Izabel is smiling, and her eyes are definitely not on me.

Unfortunately, that mild distraction earns me a vicious smack to my left arm.

I jolt and grimace, rubbing the spot. "*Easy*, prick."

"Prick? I'm saving your ass," he protests.

"Don't talk about my ass," I grumble, earning a crackle of laughter before we launch back into it.

At the end of the sparring session, Tomison doesn't hold back. He gives me a list of the muscles I need to strengthen, my apparent weaknesses having become clear to him throughout our practice.

"Side abdominals, too," he says, patting his side. "But most importantly, thighs and glutes. It doesn't matter how well you can hold your sword if you're going to be thrown off of your wolf three seconds into the fight."

Izabel joins in, then, to offer up her own training regimen in combination with Tomison's. Venna joins in, demonstrating a few exercises for me. Things like certain stretches that will make sitting on Anassa's back easier or working out my hands to increase my grip strength and decrease the likelihood of a fall. She even agrees to teach me some sign language.

It's clear that I need to be strength training every day, if I'm going to stand a chance here. Hours of my life are going to be swallowed up by weights and stretches and buckets of sweat. But it suddenly doesn't seem impossible.

It seems like a path I can follow, with clear steps and a destination.

And I'm not walking alone. Sparring in the training yard, stretching in the morning, complaining about soreness and bruises with the others... I can picture it already, and something deep in my gut is suddenly heavier in a not altogether unpleasant way.

I look around at the three of them, stare into our inevitably shared future, and I wonder. I watch them smile and laugh, and I wonder. I know in my tired bones and sore muscles that they've helped me today, maybe *saved my ass*, and I wonder.

Is Killian's warning fair? Is it possible that people like this might actually stab me in the back?

CHAPTER TWENTY-TWO

Time passes strangely. It somehow manages to fly by while also grinding along slowly, kneading salt into my wounded soul as it goes. Everything's a blur of sitting through boring classes and trying to stay awake, desperately clinging to life in training sessions, and trying not to think about Killian.

In the moments between, I'm training on my own. Izabel and Venna have not stopped trying to get me to join their nightly activities, but I've been too busy with the strength routine Tomison gave me. When I've improved my ability with the sword, I also ask for help with a bow and arrow.

Stark hasn't lashed out at me again in the same deeply humiliating way, which I've taken to mean that I'm actually improving. He also hasn't repaid me for the spit in the face, so I continue to keep my guard up around him.

Finally, it's the night before the Voice Trial, the first major test we have to pass. I went to my room early to try to get a good night's sleep, but I've been tossing and turning for hours.

When I eventually doze off, I plummet into a nightmare.

I'm at the medic's office with my mom, except the medic is treating *me*. He stands in front of me, raising his hands to my face, tightening his fingers into my hair until my head is locked in his grip.

"The delusions will start soon," he says calmly, staring straight into my eyes. "Are you ready?"

Suddenly he's gone, and I'm looking at my mother. She looks lucid, nothing like the fuzzy, clouded version of the past decade. She's wearing her nicest clothing, and standing in a dark, viscous pool of blood. On her head is a twisting crown, and it's bloody too. Streaks of blood run down from its peaks and into her fine, wavy hair.

"Meryn," she calls. "Meryn! It's time for you to join me."

I take an unwilling step toward her, unable to look away.

The light changes until mother is shrouded in darkness, and the whites of her eyes turn a deep black. When she next opens her mouth, the voice that comes out is nothing like my mother's.

It's deep and otherworldly, resonant in a way that sets my teeth on edge, makes my bones ache.

"MERYN. Come, now. Nocturn commands it!"

I'm walking closer and closer. I can't control my own body, as if I'm paralyzed inside my skull, watching someone else move my limbs. I draw closer and closer, my eyes locked on hers until I'm drowning in the dark pools of her irises.

With a gasp, I wake up, sitting straight up in bed. My layered blankets fall off my chest, letting in the cold air, soothing against my flushed and sweaty limbs. I breathe heavily, trying to center myself.

Just a dream.

But I can't fall back asleep the rest of the night.

In the morning, I stride into the arena, heart pounding so hard that it pulses in my fingertips and trying to not feel bleary-eyed after last night. The other Rawbonds look just as tense as we move together deeper into the arena.

Leader Aldrich gave us some menacing statistics to prepare us for what's coming during the Voice Trial. Apparently, this first test is specifically designed to challenge our communication skills, and it's estimated that an eighth of us won't survive this.

I'm not optimistic about my chances. My communication with Anassa hasn't improved. We keep shoving each other out of the way.

I can ride her without falling off. Generally. But *not falling off* isn't really good enough when there's an elaborate, terrifying obstacle course laid out before you complete with fiery braziers strategically arranged to force precise navigation.

It's… *a lot*. The arena's been transformed overnight into this nightmarish maze.

And as with the Presentation, the stands are filled with nobles who have come in to watch us succeed—or die. The king sits on his dais, cold amusement clear on his face. Once again, our misery is their entertainment.

Killian is at his side and I ignore the way my stomach flips when I catch sight of him. I need to stay fully focused on Anassa if I'm going to make it through.

Standing next to her, I study the course before us, trying to figure out which part of it my corpse is going to end up draped over.

The series of ascending platforms at the start? Probably not. If I hold on tight enough, I should be able to stay mounted as Anassa leaps across them.

That narrow bridge suspended over a sea of flames, though? Yeah, that one's not looking so promising.

For a sickening moment, I can already smell my flesh and hair cooking.

My eyes catch on a flash of dark. Stark is standing near the other instructors by the king's dais, his huge arms crossed over his wide chest. I catch his malevolent gaze and I swear I almost see a malicious smile flicker across his stupid lips.

This is it, then. The payback for the spit.

I know the obstacle course is meant to be a general test of coordination between the rider and their wolf, but it feels like a deliberate attack against me. Like Stark snuck into the arena in the night, laughing to himself as he set up the targets, probably imagining my crispy corpse just like I am right now.

At least the targets are set up somewhat close to the obstacles. We were allowed to choose our weapons for this portion, and I picked daggers, confident in my aim from my training with Igor. It shouldn't be too hard to hit the targets, assuming they don't spontaneously shrink or one of the braziers doesn't flash brightly in my eyes right as I ready my throw.

The sickly twisting in my gut worsens when the other pairs start to traverse the course before me. It's like I can see the mental connection shimmering between their bodies as they move fluidly through the course.

The wolves leap up over platforms, twisting mid-air to allow their riders clean shots. The riders demonstrate intense focus.

I can tell that they're ready for every twitch in their wolves' flanks, every drop and jump and turn.

Of course, there are failures, too. Spectacular, *messy* failures, just like Aldrich warned.

One wolf miscalculates a jump. I don't know whether it was the wolf's fault or whether its rider guided it incorrectly over the challenge before them, but the result is that the two of them tumble together through the air.

They fall, writhing for handholds that aren't there.

The rider's scream is piercing but cut short by his impact against the ground. His wolf lands on top of him, killing him instantly. It howls in pain, maybe because its rider has died or maybe because it's injured itself in the fall.

Another pair visibly argues as they cross the narrow bridge above the flames. The rider shouts something aloud, and her wolf turns around and snaps at her mid-stride. The wolf's ferocity—or maybe just its stubbornness—causes it to crash headlong into a fire pit, some of its fur catching fire and its rider shrieking with fear.

Izabel navigates the course easily, not that it's surprising. Henrey makes it through, too, though he's significantly slower than some of the other riders. Tomison's time is particularly impressive.

I'm sure I'll be hearing about it later. If I'm still alive.

Stark probably traversed this obstacle course in less than three seconds in his Trials, I think bitterly. *The bastard.*

My turn comes too soon. My name is barked out from the dark, and I step towards Anassa, bracing for the usual stab of pain from the wall between us. But it doesn't come.

I look up at her as I approach and find her already staring at me, silver fur shimmering and gaze steady. She doesn't look away. When I tentatively reach out mentally, I don't sense the vicious scrape of claws or the icy cold of her disdain.

The wall has thinned, turned slightly glassy. It's still cold and unforgiving, but I can almost make out flashes through the barrier. Like a wall of ice, strange distortions of impressions and instincts flickering through in a dance of light over my mind.

I mount her as smoothly as I can, very aware that every eye in the arena is on me right now.

Anassa strides forward, stalking towards the beginning of the course. The first challenge is simpler than the rest, composed of three ascending platforms, each smaller than the previous. It requires careful, precise jumps.

Not a single pair has failed this part yet, and I hope we're not going to be the first.

I tighten my grip on Anassa's fur, winding a bit of it around my hand to ensure that even if my body flies off of her back, I'll still be able to hold on and scramble back up. I prepare myself for the chaos, expecting Anassa to do whatever she wants here, screw the rider she carries on her back.

Then I sense a flash. It's brief, so quick I'm not sure it wasn't just a panic-induced hallucination. But as Anassa's muscles tighten and ready, I know it was real.

It felt like a vision of the future, almost. She's shown me the exact path she means to take to climb the platforms—where she's going to land, the rhythm of her jumps, the speed at which she'll move through it all.

I'm ready for it when she moves, my mind seizing the information she's given me and calculating how I need to hold myself to keep steady. I change my angle, grinding my foot into place to support my weight. When she starts to move, I lean into it.

One jump, shift my weight to the left. The second, the turn-around for this one is fast. I tense my core and grit my teeth, leaning forward to counter the lurch of motion from her ascent.

The last jump, I know she's going to land hard. I tighten my legs and push back with my hands to counter the impact.

Anassa doesn't stop. She hurtles on to the next obstacle, and I can sense her intention. She wants to win, to prove herself the strongest of the pack, to crush anyone who would challenge her.

For the first time since we met, our feelings align.

I want to succeed. I don't give a shit about being Bonded, or rising through the ranks. But I want to prove myself.

No, even more than that: I want to embarrass the people who've dismissed me from the start. I want my victory to sting them as fiercely as my injuries do every night when Anassa refuses to heal them.

I want the power I know I have to carry me through.

The second challenge is the bridge. It's barely wide enough for a wolf's paws, but Anassa's calm, predator's mind is undaunted. She advances without hesitation, feet pounding, huffing breaths into the cold air.

Fire briefly blinds my eyes, but her mind inspires me to lean into the sting of the smoke. My ambition materializes and runs alongside her, just as vicious and determined.

This is where those predisposed to failure faltered. Their communication gave out under the pressure—the bright flames, the targets popping up at dizzying speed, the narrowness of the bridge.

The rider has to focus on the targets or risk missing, while the direwolf has to focus on their feet or risk falling. That split is what I watched tear rider and wolf apart over and over.

But Anassa barely pays attention to the bridge, so surefooted that her speed is almost too much as the targets fly closer. They're unpredictable for each run, so I'm not sure where to aim initially.

Fucking *moving* targets!

A sharp sting of warning impacts my mind, and I turn to the

left. Anassa's predatory instinct flags the sudden movement of one of the targets, and my fighter's instincts respond to her warning and snap into motion as if a fist is flying towards me.

I spin on her back, tossing a dagger that thuds precisely into the target.

Again, the target flashes. Again, her warning just in time. Anassa's movements are suddenly predictable and deliberate.

Her pride won't let her fail in front of the other wolves, and I'm benefitting from it. With her moving steadily beneath me, it's suddenly so much easier to focus. I lead my daggers like I used to lead my punches in the pits, aiming where the target will be—accounting for Anassa's startling speed—rather than where it is.

Six targets. Six hits. Unflinching, unafraid, unstoppable.

Then the course narrows into a spiral descent. I know this is the hardest part. Anassa senses my brief faltering and snarls, her confidence overtaking my fear and strangling it silent.

Other wolves have tried to race through the spiral to hasten their times, but it cost them dearly.

Too fast, and they ended up swinging wide on their turns and crashing or tumbling right over the edge of the platforms. Anassa's cold calculation is ready for the challenge, though.

We take each turn at precisely the same angle, her speed controlled and her movements sharp as a blade. I lean as far as I can into each turn until I'm held to her body by centrifugal force alone, yet I'm ready when she levels out and I need to pull myself back up and reassert my grip.

None of it is beautiful. Of course, it isn't. Both of us are still too independently angry.

There's no *true* communication. I get brief flashes of warning before Anassa hurtles through every turn, and I have to rely on my own strength to respond to her decisions and follow through.

We're two predators who've agreed to hunt together for the sake of the kill, but she doesn't trust me any more than I do her.

We close in on the leap of faith. It's the last obstacle standing between me and survival. Once we've passed this, the wall will go right back up, I expect.

The platform is going to drop out beneath Anassa's feet, and we're expected to twist in mid-air, hit three successive targets during the fall, and land on a small marked area.

Most pairs must rely on their direwolves' instincts for this part, their keen canine eyes indicating and communicating when precisely to release their weapons during the fall. Anassa shreds that idea apart in her teeth as we land on the platform, her chest heaving.

Instead, she gives me another glimpse of her mind. I know the precise jump she's going to take. The moment I have the information, I start anticipating the targets, the speed of the fall, the angle of my throws.

I know how bodies move through space. I know how much force I'll need to reach the targets, with the help of Anassa's momentum. I know how far my body can twist and just how long I'll be able to hold on to her—I've had plenty of practice crossing that line, so I know precisely when my legs are going to give out.

And most importantly, I know when to hit. I know because in the pit, you have to know.

Hit too early, and you're leaving yourself wide open. Hit too late, and you're back against the wall, struggling to fend off an onslaught on the back foot.

Anassa jumps. We fall. Daggers fly. Targets shatter.

We land hard, my jaw clacking and my bones rattling. But we land in the right spot, thanks to Anassa's strength. Her claws leave deep gouges in the designated circle. My eyes are fixated on those gouges as my breaths rip from my throat and my muscles tremble.

We just… *did* that?

"Third!" someone shouts coldly.

Third? As in, third *fastest* time?

I clutch Anassa's fur as she pads away from the course, her sides still heaving from the exertion. I guess that's what you get when you put two stubborn assholes up against a challenge and tell them to prove themselves.

Anassa's disdain still leaks through the barrier between us. She doesn't like that she had to cooperate with me for this. She also doesn't think third is good enough, most likely.

But there's something else there, too. Something like recognition. A brief shimmer of acknowledgement. It's a little like she's recognized that I'm not a spindly piece of human meat only good for eating. Like she saw and *felt* my strength, just now, and she's begrudgingly admitting that I may actually have something to offer her.

It sparks in me, too. Respect bubbles up through the sea of resentment. She ran that course *fast*. She didn't even blink at the obstacles other wolves couldn't best.

If she'd just *listen* to me, we might actually—

The iron slams down between us. Hard. Harder than it ever has. It's like she's slammed a cleaver over my neck.

I choke, doubling over, disoriented.

We did it. We *did*. Third, and I even get to live to see morning. That's a victory.

But right now, it feels like I've lost something, too.

I'm tired of losing. It's depressing as fuck, and it's also just not who I am. Or at least not who I thought I was. I'm a fighter. Someone who holds on tight.

Heart still beating fast, I let myself look back up at the stands, where Killian is watching me intently, his eyes piercing even from this far away, his long fingers steepled under his sharp chin.

Have I really lost him, too? Or, unlike with Anassa, is it me who's shutting him out, when I don't have to be? Could I find a way to trust him again?

CHAPTER TWENTY-THREE

I've grown used to the wild scene in the common lounge every night, but tonight, after surviving the Voice Trial, the other Rawbonds really let loose.

A celebration is in full swing, and all four packs are in attendance. Gone is the tension each of us carried into the arena earlier tonight. The other Strategos throw themselves into the party, drinking and laughing with abandon.

I still find this ghoulish, the way they party after so much death. Eight Rawbonds in total lost their lives, including two from Strategos that I didn't know well. But I'd been so certain that I'd be one of them that I'm having some sort of adrenaline crash, and I can't deny that I'd like to take the edge off too.

Following Izabel and Tomison to one of the couches at the outer edge of the room, I watch the party as they talk and laugh. Servants weave through the crowd with decanters of emberwine and trays of food.

Izabel puts a glass in my hand. It's no sleeping draught, but maybe it'll stave off the nightmares. The warmed, spiced alcohol steams slightly in the cool air, its rich scent driving off the lingering tang of blood and death.

It tastes fantastic—potent, too. A pleasant warmth spreads through my belly at the very first sip. After the third, a faint buzz of relaxation travels the length of my body.

Suddenly, the party doesn't seem so ghoulish anymore.

Izabel and Tomison are flirting playfully. Venna joins us, hugging her sister and grinning with unmistakable pride; Venna ranked second today. One of Tomison's friends from our pack, Kristof, comes to join us too, congratulating Venna warmly, and eyeing her with interest. Everyone seems to be here tonight—except for Nevah, who I saw slink back to the Strategos quarters after the Trial.

Over by the big fireplace, the pack instructors sit together, Egith among them, looking characteristically stern. She catches me eying her and her lips press into an even tighter line. Thought she'd be excited about my third place finish.

Guess not.

Samson, the Kryptos Gamma, says something that makes Egith throw her head back and laugh, the silver streak in her hair catching firelight as she toasts with him. Even the Phylax Gamma Elinor seems to have relaxed her usual rigid posture.

Only Stark maintains his distance, lounging in a shadowed corner like a predator waiting to strike. But he's shed the stiff formal jacket he wore to the arena. His shirt underneath is unbuttoned at the top, offering a glimpse of his muscular, golden brown chest and the tattoos that flow down his neck.

A pretty young Rawbond approaches him, cocking her hip in blatant invitation. He dismisses her with a scathing glance.

As she retreats into the crowd, another woman approaches. Then another, and another. Each one is rebuffed with that same cold look of disinterest.

"He's pretty sexy when he's not bellowing orders at us, huh?" says Izabel, using her hands to sign it as well, since the noise of the party is making it hard for Venna to catch all our words.

I turn to her with a jolt, embarrassed to be caught staring.

Beside her, Tomison grins, his arm draped over the back of the couch behind her. Venna gives me a conspiratorial look, brows bobbing.

"Sure," I grumble, "if you find murderous psychos sexy."

"Do you not?" Kristof quips.

Izabel laughs.

"No," I grate, face heating. "I definitely do not."

Kristof shrugs. "I would ride that man from here to Astreona."

Izabel laughs and interprets for Venna, who laughs too, a deep, throaty chuckle.

"He seems more like the type who prefers to do all the riding," Tomison drawls.

Izabel sighs wistfully. "He does, doesn't he?"

More laughter. I'm happy they're enjoying themselves, but I turn away as the conversation veers hard towards sex. I should probably make a break for the exit. It won't be long before people start pairing off, and I really don't want to see if all the instructors are going to join in.

At that thought, my gaze unwillingly returns to Stark—only to find him staring right at me.

Shit.

It's the same look he gave me at the arena. The same one he always gives me—dark eyes burning a hole through me, full lips practically pulled back in a sneer. I've seen that look enough times from men in the ring; it's full of the promise of future violence.

I glare back for a moment, then look away, draining my glass as an excuse to break the contact.

A servant appears immediately to refill it.

While I'm avoiding Stark's gaze and trying to plan my escape from the party, Kristof gets up to join another group. Tomison, too, wanders away on the hunt for his nightly fuck-buddy.

My head starts swimming pleasantly as I drain my second glass, still sitting between Izabel and Venna. The memory of today's anxiety begins to blur at the edges, replaced with a warm glow of good humor.

Raised voices draw my attention back to Tomison, now across

the room and gleefully demonstrating a complex sword maneuver to a group of Phylax Rawbonds. Beside me, Izabel watches intently.

"What's up with that?" I ask, smirking broadly. "You got a thing for Tomison now?"

Izabel stiffens. "What, that idiot? Never!"

I glance smugly at Venna, who smothers a smile and then signs something rapid at Izabel.

"She says 'You're one to talk,'" Izabel interprets. "'Everyone here has been enjoying the mate search but you, Meryn. What's up with *that*?'"

Tongue loosened by the emberwine, I thoughtlessly let slip the truth. "I'm too busy nursing a broken heart."

The sisters exchange a look, rolling their eyes.

"What, some commoner you left behind?" Izabel asks. "Come on, you're not going back to that world. *This* is your world now. And what if your direwolf has a mate? It's crazy not to try to help her!"

"No, you don't get it," I say, leaning in conspiratorially, and making sure to speak clearly so Venna catches my words above the clamor. "The guy who stomped on my heart is here. In the castle."

Their identical expressions of shock turn quickly to gleeful interest.

"Who is he?" Izabel demands. "Is he a Rawbond? Which pack is he from?"

Before I can gather the words to respond, I realize my glass is empty.

Well, that just won't do.

"Hold on," I say, "I need more wine."

I look around for one of those servants with the decanters. They all seem to be busy elsewhere, but there's a serving table on the other end of the room.

I excuse myself to a chorus of protests from Izabel and Venna, promising to tell them everything later. The room tilts a bit when I rise, and Stark's eyes follow me as I make my way to the table.

To my unpleasant surprise, he appears beside me just as I reach for the decanter of wine.

"Better pace yourself, princess," he says darkly, standing much too close for comfort. His deep voice thrums against my ear. "Wouldn't want you stumbling off somewhere dangerous where accidents could happen. Especially after your miraculous survival today."

Fuck, why does he smell so damn good? Like wood and amber and some kind of musk, maybe.

I fill my glass with a calm I don't feel, then turn to glare at him with emberwine throbbing in my veins.

"Your concern for me is just *so* touching," I drawl. "But I don't get into accidents—I *cause* them."

I see in his eyes that he knows what I mean. The memory of that Daemos Rawbond I strangled with his own severed hand passes between us.

Stark's expression hardens dangerously, but I turn away before he can speak, leaving him there at the table.

Weaving through the crowd, I toss back the wine, ditch my glass, and head for the exit. My happy buzz is gone, burned away by the veiled threat in Stark's words. I'm shaky and out of place again amidst all this celebration.

Izabel and Venna will have to wait. I need to get the fuck out of here.

THE WINE WAS A MISTAKE. Emberwine is always a mistake. I'm sure Last Night Meryn felt it was a great idea, but right now, I'm staring down into my plate of oats and imagining various bloody ways to murder her.

My head *pounds*. My eyeballs feel like they're going to explode. I've managed a few slow bites, but nausea roils in my stomach. Even the smell of the bread is starting to get to me.

But the worst part of it is that despite the fogginess of most of last night's memories, fucking *Stark* threatening my life is still crystal clear. So is my genius response.

Really great move, honestly, deciding to threaten him back like that. As if he doesn't already want to kill me badly enough.

Someone at the next table drops their spoon into their empty bowl, and the clang of metal on porcelain is like someone shoving a dagger into my eye socket. I wince and hiss through the pain, rubbing my temple.

At least I'm not the only one regretting last night. Several of the other Rawbonds look like shit scraped off a horseshoe, which is a big deal for a bunch of people who generally care so much about appearances.

I can't be marked as the weak one in the litter who can't hold her emberwine if *everyone* looks a little green.

"Mer," Izabel groans, flopping into the seat on my left. "Help," she croaks. Tomison sits down on the other side.

I grin. "You're hungover and you still find the energy to braid your hair like that?" I jut my fork at the elaborately coiffed black coils.

"I'd find a way even if I didn't have hands," she replies instantly, shoving my shoulder gently before turning to her food.

We eat in silence for about three seconds before Tomison says, "Anyone else really feel like barfing right now?"

"Always, when I look at you," Izabel replies instantly.

I shake my head. "*Don't* talk about barf right now. I feel like wet paper."

"So," Izabel says, leaning in. She speaks quietly, but not quietly enough. "About this mysterious castle-dwelling heartbreaker you mentioned last night…"

I nearly choke on my tea, setting the cup down too quickly to avoid a punishing clink that penetrates my eardrums and stabs my brain.

"Not here," I hiss at her. Tomison is oblivious, but anyone could be listening.

Even a mild rumor could ruin everything. I can't have other Rawbonds knowing. Honestly, I don't even want Izabel and Venna to know. It was a mistake. A drunken, *stupid* slip.

I lean closer to whisper to Izabel. "Forget about it. I was just drunk and talking nonsense."

Judging by the exaggerated raising of a single brow, Izabel very obviously does not believe me and will not let it go for long. But for now, she very graciously gives me space to finish my breakfast. Maybe the hangover has just robbed her of all the energy she would use for nosiness.

Or maybe she realizes she needs what energy reserves she still possesses to torment Tomison, because she turns away from me and immediately starts bickering with him.

I'm thankful that she's willing to drop the topic for now, but my own mind isn't as merciful. My thoughts immediately wander back to Killian.

The genuine concern on his face last night was almost too much to bear. I could've died without ever resolving—well, all of *this* between us. The thought makes me a little sick.

My saliva turns to paste. My throat closes up as a swell of nausea takes me. Sweat prickles over the back of my neck.

Oh, no…

I bolt up from my seat and hurry across the room, hand over my mouth. I stumble out into the next hall and fumble with the window latch, barely getting it open before bending over and spilling everything I just ate right back up.

I pant, wiping my mouth, bizarrely thinking, *I just suffered through breakfast for nothing.* And then, harsher, *Get it together, Meryn.*

"Cooper," barks a familiar voice.

Ugh.

Wiping my mouth, I turn to face Beta Egith, who's staring me down with a stern, unreadable look.

"My office. Now."

STIFF AND ACHING from yesterday's Voice Trial—not to mention blindingly hungover—I stand at attention in Egith's office.

I've seen her private quarters but haven't actually been into her office before. It's just as large as Leader Aldrich's, but instead of three stories of books, Egith has maps. Everywhere. It's like a cartographer's private storehouse exploded in here.

Most of the maps seem to be of the border between Nocturna and Astreona, where the front is situated. There's one huge one behind her, though, that's a detailed atlas of Nocturna itself. It catalogs every feature of the country, from the mountains here in the north to the river that slices down through the south of our country, and all the fiefdoms in between. I find myself wanting to get close, to study all of these places in our country that I've never been to or even dreamed about.

Egith sits at a small, scuffed table across from an empty chair, not looking at me as she pours herself tea from a delicate ceramic pot. She hasn't said two words to me since cornering me in the hallway, and I cannot read her body language for the life of me.

I'm surprised when Egith pours me a cup. She hasn't given me permission to sit, though, so I don't dare touch it.

Finally, she sets down the pot and looks me in the eye.

"You fucked up."

And there it is.

"I shouldn't have puked out of the window," I say quickly. "Sorry..."

Egith sighs deeply. "This is not about your... illness, Cooper. Do you want to survive this? Do you want to become one of the Bonded?"

Do I have a choice? I think bitterly.

I grit my teeth. "Yes." It's not a lie, exactly—I do want to survive and become officially Bonded so I can get to the front already.

Egith stares me down for so long that I have the urge to fidget like a nervous child.

"I don't believe you," she grates. "And neither would anyone who saw your performance yesterday."

That gives me a start. "But I thought—"

"What?" she snaps, eyes flashing. "You thought because you completed the exercises your performance was a success?"

"I did everything that was asked of me," I say, bewildered.

Egith groans. "I didn't take you for stupid, Cooper. Arrogant, maybe. Bull-headed. But not stupid. The *purpose* of the Trial was to test your ability to communicate with your wolf. To prove your growing bond—your ability to act as one in battle!"

"Didn't we… do that?"

"*No!*" she shouts. "All you did was cooperate—and not even well! You looked like enemies who grudgingly chose to work together to survive. Every single moment betrayed your mental and emotional disconnection. Every instance of failed communication was obvious!"

She pauses and takes a sip of tea like she's waiting for me to speak.

"We got third place, though," I venture weakly. "Isn't that—"

"You *survived*," she says in a voice that could strip paint. "By the skin of your teeth! You think that's enough?" She sets down her teacup with a clatter that makes me flinch. "Anassa chose, for whatever reason, to *let* you survive. To *let* you finish third! That's not success—that's barely avoiding death. Your lack of communication with your direwolf is a failure, Cooper."

Frustration boils inside me. "I'm doing my best. I'm *trying* to—"

"You are *not* trying," she interrupts, waving her hand to cut me off. "In fact, I don't believe you've fully accepted any of this yet. I know your driving force for being here is to find your sister, but *this* is your life now. If you want to make it to the front lines, you need to accept it. You are Bonded. This isn't temporary. You can't escape it. You are bound to Anassa for the rest of your life," her expression turns dour, "however long that may be."

I'm speechless for a beat.

For the rest of your life echoes in my head.

I already knew there was no way out, but part of me refuses to believe it, even now.

"I know this is a hard adjustment for you," Egith says, her voice softening.

"Oh, yeah?" I snap. "What do you know about it?"

"My father was born a commoner," she says, and the confession shocks me to my core. I never would've expected an exacting, perfect Bonded like Egith to have commoner blood, especially given how rare it is for commoners to succeed in the Trials. "He had to fight his way to survive in this world, and he never let me forget how tough it was."

I'm genuinely speechless at that.

"You seem married to this idea that you're an outsider," Egith continues, a little calmer, "and you're using it as an excuse to hold yourself apart from the other Rawbonds. But it's time to face facts, girl. You are *not* an outsider."

She stares me down again like she's trying to drive the truth into me by sheer force of will.

"You're one of them, Meryn. One of *us*. You've survived this long by being clever and tough, but you will continue to fail—and eventually *die*—if you don't accept that this is your life now."

I shake my head. "But most of them *treat* me like an outsider. They have from the very start."

"They treat you like an outsider because you *act* like one," she says with a huff. "They sense that you see yourself as one, and they behave accordingly—just as Anassa does. Why she's chosen to cooperate with you when you keep rejecting her, I don't know."

Me, rejecting *her*?

When Anassa forced me into this bond in the first place and has soundly refused to cooperate with me ever since?

"But you're damn lucky she does, or you'd already be dead. I saw the way you lunged at her during the Presentation when she came to protect you. You don't trust her at all, so how can you expect her to trust *you*?"

I open my mouth to protest, but Egith holds up one hand in a sharp gesture of refusal.

"Listen to me, Meryn Cooper. I won't give you this advice again. Accept Anassa. Accept this life—or you won't make it through the next challenge."

Egith's warning is still heavy in my gut like a stone when I arrive at our joint History of War lecture an hour later. And it's not just her. I recounted the conversation to Izabel after I left Egith's quarters. She agreed with the Strategos Beta wholeheartedly.

"Look, I know this is hard for you," Izabel told me gently, "but she has a point. You treat almost everyone but me and Venna like enemies, including Anassa. Half our training is about learning how to be part of a pack. You need to loosen up, hang out with the pack more. Show everyone that you *want* to be here."

I promised Izabel I would make an effort to connect with the rest of the pack. I just don't know *how*.

While I grapple with that, the Phylax Gamma instructor, Elinor Gardiner, starts class with a question that snaps me right out of my thoughts.

"Alright, everyone," Gamma Elinor says loudly, drawing attention to the front of the room. She's older than most of the other instructors, maybe in her early fifties, with long dark hair and olive-toned skin. "What do we know about our enemy, the Siphons?"

A Kryptos Rawbond raises his hand. "They're blood-sucking vampires who steal life force and energy to extend their own lives and make themselves more powerful."

The professor nods indulgently. "Well, yes. A little dramatic, but basically correct."

A brief discussion ensues as other students volunteer basic information about Siphons.

"In the Siphons' country, there are no humans left—they drained them all for power. That's why they invade our lands. To find more prey."

"Correct," says Gamma Elinor. "There have been no humans living in Astreona for centuries. Anything else?"

One of my fellow Strategos raises her hand. "Siphons subsist on the spoils of war. They feed on our captured soldiers."

Like my father, I think, clenching my hand. Drained and consumed like an animal.

Everyone in Sturmfrost knows that this is the whole reason the Nabbers have been taking children from our city. Children have the strongest life force energy and therefore give the Siphons the most fuel.

"Very good," Elinor says, "but they don't just feed on our soldiers, do they? Siphons use the blood of their captives to wield powerful blood magic. Can anyone tell me why?"

I lean forward, senses heightened. I knew that the Siphons wielded some sort of blood magic, but the details of what that actually entails have always been fuzzy.

"They use blood magic to control our minds and weave illusions!" somebody calls from the back. "They don't have their own Bonded creatures, so that's the only way they can fight us. They use their magic to turn drained humans into more Siphons as well."

"Excellent," says Elinor. "This is why the war has gone on so long. Through their blood magic, Siphons have achieved functional immortality and the ability to manipulate human perception. This is how they infiltrate our borders and defend against our Bonded attacks. And the older a Siphon is, the more powerful their abilities become. We don't even know half of what they're truly capable of, as we interact primarily with their youngest soldiers—the more senior Siphons are rarely part of their forward guard."

I wonder if they use blood magic when they're capturing our children. If they somehow trick them into coming with them willingly.

"The Bonded are the ultimate protectors of the humans," Elinor continues, "and we are all that stands between the commoners and the Siphons. Without the direwolves and our bonds, humans would be extinct by now. Or bred like cattle in a world overrun by Siphons."

"But the war has been at a stalemate for as long as anyone can remember," somebody interjects. "So how can we win?"

Elinor lifts her chin, her eyes alight. "Only by finding a way to fully invade Astreona and eliminate every last Siphon in existence." The way she said it makes me think that she fully believes we're capable of this.

Oh, I think faintly, head spinning. *Is that all?*

As Elinor speaks of invasion and victory, my whirling thoughts crystalize around a single gut-wrenching truth.

Crossing into Astreona is my only hope of finding Saela. And the only way I'm going to get there—the only way I can survive invading Siphon territory is…

Anassa.

Egith and Izabel are right. I need to do anything within my power to get Anassa to accept me. Even grovel, if it comes to that.

DUSK SETTLES over the castle as I approach the wide terrace that opens from the back of the Strategos common room, a bundle of dried mountain sage clutched in my hand. I overheard some of the other Rawbonds talking about bringing the herbs to their wolves as a treat. Apparently, it's like catnip for Direwolves. They crave it.

The fragrant leaves crackle faintly in my anxious grip as I scan for Anassa. The time has come for a real conversation with my wolf.

Whether either of us wants it or not.

The terraces rise before me like giant steps carved into the mountainside, each one occupied by several lounging Direwolves. In the dying light, I can make out the shapes of sleeping wolves on the lower levels, too.

Anassa is nowhere in sight. I crane my head to look up at the terraces above, wondering if she's in the caves. But then I spot her, identifiable only as a distant silver-white blob at the edge of the uppermost terrace.

Of course, you're way the fuck up there, I think dryly.

It takes me almost half an hour to climb the narrow staircases connecting each terrace in a zig-zagging path.

The climb feels symbolic. Each step carries me further and further from the world I know and deeper into the one I hate and resent. It's like I'm leaving something vital behind—some part of myself I'll never get back.

But it's worth it, I think, steeling myself. *As long as I get Saela back.*

Cold wind whips my short hair around my face as I reach Anassa's terrace. It appears empty at first, the stone worn smooth by the scrape of countless wolf claws over countless centuries.

Anassa has moved from the terrace edge into the deep shadows at its back, as though she sensed my approach and wants to avoid me.

Not a good sign, but definitely not a surprise.

I settle cross-legged near the edge, careful to respect the distance she's placed between us.

Without a word, I place the bundle of sage on the floor before me—a peace offering that seems trite and painfully inadequate.

Then, I reach out to her through our bond. The iron wall is there, immovable as ever. But I don't press. Instead, I give it a gentle mental stroke, like coaxing a feral cat.

Instantly, Anassa's energy shifts, prickling with interest—or perhaps hunger. Her body is a dim gray shape in the shadows, but I see it move. Yellow eyes turn to me, gleaming faintly.

"Hi," I murmur.

Her gaze sharpens, catching the fading light as a flash of silvery night glow.

Slowly, she rises, emerging soundlessly from the darkness, each measured step a reminder of her lethal power. In the twilight, her fur looks like liquid silver, so similar to my transformed hair.

My heart pounds in my chest as her shaggy head comes into view.

A trickle of feeling travels through our bond. Anassa's lips pull back from her fangs in what might be a snarl—or a chilling lupine smile.

There's no welcome in her eyes. Not that I expected any. But there is something…

The iron wall cracks open. Not much—just enough that there's a stirring of direct communication.

No words. Just a tangle of conflicting impulses.

Interest. Disdain. Ancient wisdom warring with primal fury.

Cold sweat gathers along my spine as she stalks slowly toward me. It's a struggle not to cringe away when her head sinks down to my level, lips curling back over teeth the size of daggers.

As her hot breath gusts against my face, I get a clear pulse of feeling from her:

I rejected her over and over, and *now* I want to make friends?

CHAPTER TWENTY-FOUR

The evening shadows stretch into night as Anassa lowers her head to scent the bundle of mountain sage I brought for her. Moonlight spills across the terrace, gilding her fur in an otherworldly blue-white glow.

I hold my breath, heart thundering inside my ribs, caught between fear and desperate hope.

Through the bond comes another shift. The impenetrable iron wall seems to thin, becoming permeable, like silk rippling in the wind.

Her voice fills my head with startling clarity, deep and rich as aged wine, carrying the weight of centuries.

"You finally wish to be here."

Each word rolls thunderously through my consciousness, stealing my breath with its raw power and beauty.

Over the past month, I've imagined many scenarios where Anassa and I finally talked, communicated, connected. But I never actually put a voice to her words. Hearing her speak in my mind for the first time is like seeing the sun rise across a field of ice.

It paints the world in colors I didn't even know existed.

An incredible sense of rightness unravels inside my chest. This whole time, our fractured bond was chafing against me in a way that I didn't even realize or sense until now, when it's finally disappeared. It's like sitting down after a long day at the laundry and realizing I'd been ignoring my entire body's aches.

It's relief—stunning, world-shattering relief.

Eventually, I'm able to take a breath, and I realize what she's said—a statement, not a question. A protest rises up inside of me, and I start to claim that I've wished to be here the whole time.

A ripple of amusement—*her* amusement—washes my denial away.

"*Do not pretend. Before, you fought against what you are. Against what we could be. But you've decided not to fight any longer.*"

The words sting with truth. And more.

Through our connection, I feel Anassa's assessment of me—a surprisingly gentle dressing down that pinpoints every time I've pushed her away. Every time I've doubted her, fought her, rejected her.

Every time I've insulted our bond by thinking of it as temporary.

And every time I've impressed her with my fighting spirit, too.

That's the only reason she didn't give up on me, I realize. The only reason she protected me during the Presentation. The only reason she cooperated to get me through the Voice Trial.

She *wants* this bond—or at least, she wants to try.

And she's pleased that I'm finally accepting it, even if she doesn't trust me yet. Even if part of her still wants to tear me apart for all the disrespect I've given her.

Goddess, my head is spinning. Her mind, her *feelings*—they're so overwhelming. It's hard to get to my own thoughts in my head, buried underneath the wave after wave I'm receiving from her. Part of me wonders if she's been protecting me from this, too, by keeping the wall up between us. She knew I wasn't strong enough yet to receive her in full.

My eyes sting and burn with inexplicable tears.

"*I'm sorry,*" I think, too overwhelmed to speak the words aloud. "*I didn't know—I didn't understand.*"

Another wave of feelings washes over me. There's satisfaction in it. Annoyance, too. Hope and distrust.

"*I will work with you,*" Anassa declares finally, her mental voice carrying both promise and warning. "*But know this—I chose you for a reason. Do not make me regret it.*"

Before I can summon the ability to ask why she chose me, the connection closes. It's not like before—there's no slamming of that iron wall—but it's clear the conversation is over.

As Anassa retreats once more into the shadows, I'm left with a sense of immense emptiness I don't quite understand.

Like I've lost something I didn't even know I was missing until now. It was the same feeling I had after the Voice Trial, when she let me see glimpses of a potential connection, but amplified by an unbelievable magnitude.

I make my way back down to my room in a cloud of unanswered questions, the echo of Anassa's regal voice still loud in my head.

WHEN ANASSA MEETS me on the training field the next morning, I know today is going to be different. She doesn't speak to me again, but the barrier between our minds is little more than a porous membrane. Through it, I can sense her feelings, her focus, her every intention.

She looks me in the eye when Stark commands us to mount up. Her mistrust flares again as she waits for me to push the connection away.

I don't. I just put my hand on her broad, furry neck and nod.

"*I'll do my best,*" I think toward her. "*I'm willing to try.*"

She blinks slowly in wordless acknowledgment and turns her head away, waiting for me to climb on her back. As we begin our mounted warm-ups, I brace reflexively for her resistance, unconsciously expecting her to try bucking me off again.

Only she doesn't. She glances back at me with irritation, though.

I send her a wordless apology and force my limbs to relax. A subtle tension I didn't even notice before leaves Anassa, too. The muscles in her back go lax.

Today's warm-ups start with a few laps around the training field, then agility drills with the enormous weave poles and hurdles on one end of the arena.

The instinct to direct Anassa is hard to resist. It's terrifying to sit astride such an enormous animal and know you're not in control. But Anassa can sense my anxiety. The fur between her shoulders ripples with responding ire.

Trust, I tell myself sternly, leaning into the enormous wolf. *You have to trust her, Meryn. Otherwise, this will never work.*

Again, Anassa responds, though I didn't mean for her to hear my thoughts. I'll have to start finally using some of the communication strategies we've gotten in Samson's class, I realize. The bristling fur subsides. Her running gait grows longer, more confident.

I'm still nervous as I focus on matching Anassa's rhythm, moving with her instead of trying to direct her.

Listen. Hear.

The command comes as a wordless thought—a vague intuition—but my mind translates it easily. I turn all my senses to the wolf. To the beat of her paws against the ground. The way her weight shifts with each stride. The way her ears angle and her head turns just before she changes direction.

By the time we reach the hurdle jumps at the end of the agility course, I'm aware of every muscle in her body coiling and uncoiling, all the way down to the flex of her toes as her claws dig into the earth.

Somehow, I know just how far to lean over her neck at the start of every leap. And how to hold my weight off her back when she lands so the impact doesn't disrupt her stride.

She doesn't tell me any of this in words or images—or even feelings.

I just... *know.*

The practice scenario Stark gives us today is focused on defensive maneuvers. Several Rawbond pairs are chosen to play "injured" pack mates while others are "attackers." The rest, including Anassa and me, are instructed to protect the injured pack mates.

I can tell the moment my fighting instincts align with Anassa's battle experience, clicking together like gears in a machine. I don't need to direct her like I tried to before; all I have to do is adjust my swordwork to fit her natural hunting patterns.

It's almost like a dance.

When she lunges into an attack, my sword is there to strike in the opening she leaves behind. When she leaps away again, I swing to defend her exposed flank.

Trust builds slowly between us with each maneuver, and an unexpected giddiness bubbles in my chest. Gone is the awkward cooperation, the sense of grudging teamwork. We move together with lethal precision—if not with the fluid unity of Stark and his wolf.

Their coordination carries a predatory oneness, like two killers who share a single mind, a single goal:

Hunt. Kill. Triumph.

The thought that Anassa and I might actually one day achieve that kind of unity fills me with unexpected eagerness. It feels *good* to work together instead of being so at odds with each other.

It feels *powerful.*

With Anassa's help, I might actually have a chance of finding my sister.

But that's a ways off. We're still finding our rhythm.

Through it all, Stark circles on his massive black wolf, watching like a hawk. I try to ignore him, but I catch sight of his face again and again. Each time, his expression is darker and more vicious than before.

His bellowed orders drive our "attackers" into a killing frenzy. In a flurry of movement and clanging metal, Anassa and I successfully defend against three simultaneous assaults.

"Again!" he barks. "Harder this time!"

Suddenly we're surrounded. Three attackers on one side, two on the other.

What the hell? Nobody else is getting this treatment! Why is he always singling us out?

What a sadistic asshole.

But I grit my teeth and focus in, trusting that Anassa knows what to do.

She darts and leaps with incredible speed, attacking and defending at turns. I don't even know how I manage to stay on her back, but I do. It almost feels like I'm fused directly to her spine. My sword arm flies without thought, following her lead with choreographed precision.

Miraculously, the session ends with both of us breathless and spattered in blood, but undefeated.

I'm actually a bit disappointed it's over, much to my surprise. I look up at Anassa as I dismount and smile without thinking.

"*That felt good*," I direct at her.

Anassa doesn't return my sentiment—she just turns and walks away, as usual. But I catch the waft of her satisfaction.

And for once, the bruises on my body warm and heal. She's finally using her healing powers on me again.

Then I notice the strange quiet that's fallen over the training field. The other Rawbond pairs are staring at us like they've never seen us before. A few of them whisper to each other in tones of astonishment.

Huh. I guess we impressed them.

Sensing his gaze, I glance over at Stark as everyone starts leaving the training field. I want to see some sign of approval in his stormy eyes, as much as I hate to admit it.

What the fuck is wrong with me that I'd seek praise from someone who very recently threatened to make an "accident" happen to me?

As usual, his vindictive scowl could darken the skies in sunny Astreona. I wonder if that's his secret weapon on the battlefield: snarling at all the Siphons like the feral creature he is.

I lift my chin at him, challenging. We both know my success today means I'm a lot less likely to get murdered by one of the other Rawbonds.

I hope.

When I get back to my room this evening, I notice a note sitting on my small table. The room was locked, which means that this can only be from one person.

Killian.

I approach the note warily and Anassa's curiosity perks up at the back of my mind.

"*From the man I used to... see,*" I tell her.

"*I've gathered,*" she responds tersely. She's probably annoyed that I've spent so much mental energy on Killian when I'm meant to be training and strengthening our bond.

She agrees.

Sighing, I unfold the note. I'm not sure what I want from him. After seeing him at the Voice Trial, all I wanted was to seek him out, mend what was broken between us, and find a way to move forward. But can I truly trust him again?

The note stills all my thoughts of trust.

"Come to my quarters when you receive this. I have an update on the Nabbers. Straight through the servant's tunnel, ignore all turns. It ends at my rooms. —K."

If he's found something out about the Nabbers, about Saela, I need to go to him. I grab my oil lamp and open the wardrobe, pushing my clothes to the side. Then I feel for the panel and eventually my finger snags on a button.

I push it and the wooden panel swings open to reveal a darkened stone tunnel. Take the straight path, Killian said. Easy enough.

But as the stone walls twist deeper and deeper into the heart of the castle, my hair starts to raise on the back of my neck, like something is wrong.

Just like in the halls that night after Presentation, the shadows seem to move with a will of their own. Faint whispers echo off the walls, coming from nowhere and everywhere at once. They're too faint to make out words, but they carry an unnerving thrum of energy that settles behind my eyes and leaves me dizzy.

Head swimming, I pause in the dim glow of the oil lamp, bracing my hand against the wall to steady myself.

What the fuck is this?

The voices grow stronger.

Pressing my palm against the cool stone to steady myself, horror spirals down into my gut. *This is just like one of Mother's episodes.*

I shake my head, whether to refute the thought or to dislodge the voices, I don't even know.

A vision hits me of my mother sitting at the kitchen table in a daze, staring at nothing. Speaking to ghosts.

Is this what it was like for her? Am I descending into madness now, too?

I lurch forward, determined not to give in to whatever this is. If I can just get to Killian's rooms, maybe the voices will stop. Reality will reassert itself and I'll feel normal again.

The path continues winding deeper into the bowels of the castle, but I reach what looks like a fork. I'm turned around and I suddenly can't tell which path I'm supposed to take next. Pressing onward, I realize minutes later that I've started to descend instead of ascend to rooms. The air is stiff down here, musty with damp and age.

I stumble in the dark and my shoulder catches on something soft.

Heavy, dusty fabric collapses over me—a tapestry, ancient and faded. The whispers peak in a wild crescendo as the fabric slithers off me onto the floor.

My gasp echoes eerily against the cold stone walls.

Where the tapestry hung is a huge, intricate image carved directly into the stones—a woman astride a massive wolf, her face serene. Her head is adorned in an intricate crown composed of two direwolves leaping toward each other.

Vaguely, I recognize the style of the art is ancient. Very different from the other carvings and statues around the castle. It's rougher, bearing subtle marks from the carver's tools, yet no less elegant for it.

My vision swims strangely as I trace the woman's face with my fingers. With a start, I realize it's the bond—Anassa comes to life at the other end of it, her attention shifting to me, full of curiosity.

Why would this carving be hidden in the castle? And *here* of all places?

I touch the carving again as though to confirm its existence. I'm not imagining this, am I? Like the whispers?

As though in response to my thoughts, the whispers surge again. My hand trembles against the woman's crown and the voices press against my skull like a physical weight.

My breath hitches. My vision darkens. As if from somewhere far away, my legs start to buckle.

The last thought I have before consciousness fades is that Killian will be waiting, wondering what's become of me.

CHAPTER TWENTY-FIVE

Consciousness returns in bits and pieces. Sensations float around me, disconnected from each other. Warm silk against my skin. The scent of burning oils. A face hovering over me, painted with warm lamplight.

I blink slowly, struggling to focus on those familiar sharp features, drawn tight with worry.

Killian.

With a gasp, I snap back into full awareness.

"Thank goodness you're awake," Killian says as I struggle to sit upright. "No, don't move. You're safe, everything is fine."

Reluctantly, I settle back against the velvet pillows and look around. We're in Killian's quarters, I think.

His bedchamber is a study in royal luxury. Silk and satin and velvet everywhere. Crystal lamps and elaborate tapestries. Enormous paintings with gilded frames. It makes the Bonded areas seem modest by comparison.

But I'm not interested in cataloging the details right now.

"What happened?" I rasp, trying to shake off the disorientation. My head is still swimming.

"I was about to ask you that," Killian says, reaching for a bowl of water on the bedside table. He presses a cool damp cloth to my forehead. "You never showed up, so I went searching for you. You were unconscious when I found you in the passage."

It all comes back to me in a rush.

The passage. The carving on the wall...

The whispers.

"Kitten?" Killian says softly, concern evident in every line of his face.

I shift away from his touch, smarting at the familiarity of it even as I crave it.

I can't tell him about the whispers—the growing fear that I've inherited my mother's madness. As much as I'd love to unburden myself, I still can't trust him that way.

"I don't know," I say, forcing a dismissive laugh. "I guess I passed out from exhaustion. The training has been intense the last few days." I look around for a clock. "What time is it?"

"Late," he says. "You've been asleep for hours."

That gives me a chill.

Shit. This can't be good.

"When you found me in the passage..."

His brows rise when I trail off. "What?

Dammit. This might be a bad idea—but I have to know.

"Did you see a carving on the wall?" I ask. "A woman riding a direwolf, wearing a crown made of leaping wolves?"

He gives me a blank look and my stomach sinks.

"No. It's an old servant's passage," he says. "There are no carvings in the servants' passages."

To my surprise, Anassa stirs at this—her low growl fills my head.

"What the hell does that mean?" I demand of her.

No answer from the wolf, of course. Did she see the carving, too? Was it real, or can Anassa see my delusions?

Meanwhile, Killian is gazing at me expectantly, fresh worry knitting his brow.

"Oh," I say faintly, hoping he can't sense my rising panic. "I… must have dreamed it, then."

Killian sighs. "I asked you to come here for a reason, Meryn, but I'm thinking we should save it for when you're feeling better."

"Just tell me," I say. "If it has anything to do with my sister, I want to know."

He levels me with a deep stare and then, finally, says, "We caught one. A Nabber."

My heart lurches. "*What?!*"

The carving, the whispers, my impending madness—they're instantly forgotten. I'm up and out of the bed, ignoring Killian's protests.

"Wait, Mer, you need to rest—"

"*Where's the Nabber?*" I demand. "Are they here in the castle?"

"Meryn," he says, trying to herd me back toward the bed, "your health—"

I cut him off with ferocious intensity. "Take me there—*now!*"

THE CASTLE DUNGEONS are a shock after the opulence of Killian's royal chambers. The place smells of piss, shit, old blood, and unwashed bodies—not unlike parts of the city. I feel a twinge of self-disgust, wanting to withdraw from the squalor.

In reality, the dark stone walls and straw-strewn floors are cleaner than some of the streets I grew up on.

Have I already become so accustomed to luxury?

Two royal guards stand at attention as Killian and I pass by. I glance at them nervously, though Killian already reassured me they're loyal to him and won't tell anyone we were here. I hope he's right.

Most of the cells are empty, their heavy iron bars black in the dim light. We pass a large communal cell with a pair of sleeping drunks inside, stinking of potent liquor; then a series of smaller cells. Finally, we reach the end of the row. The smell of fresh blood fills my nose.

A pale-skinned man sits slumped in a rough wooden chair, his arms and legs bound with heavy rope. He's been badly beaten. His face is swollen and bloody, the features unrecognizable. There's a little wooden table just outside the cell door. On it lies an assortment of bloodied implements. Pliers, knives, something that looks like a corkscrew.

The man lifts his head, eyes nothing but a black gleam in his ruined face.

Killian nods to me.

"Are you a Siphon?" I demand through the bars.

There's a pause as the man looks at me with exhausted wariness.

"No."

I step closer to the bars, anger crackling through my veins. "Who are you?"

"Nobody," he rasps. "Just a man from the slums in the Southern Quarter."

His ratty clothing and rough speech confirm it.

"Who hired you?"

"I already told the guards," he grates. "You gonna finish me off or what?"

Killian steps closer, his large presence both calming and dominating. "Answer her," he commands coolly.

The man grunts. "I don't know. Whoever it was wore a mask and paid in gold. I didn't ask questions."

Fucking monster.

"What happens to the children that are taken?" I ask, anger boiling into rage. This man has been snatching children from their families. He could even be the one who took Saela.

"I don't know," the man says, gaze sliding away.

The rage flares higher inside me. I slam my hand against the bars hard enough to make him flinch. "You're fucking lying!"

His jaw tightens. "Look, I don't hurt 'em, alright? They're still alive when I hand 'em over to the buyer."

I turn to Killian in silent appeal. I don't know what to do.

The prince's gaze is flinty, his mouth pressed into a firm, furious line. Without a word, he produces a key and unlocks the cell. Then, he takes the pliers from the table and steps inside.

The fear in the Nabber's eyes fills me with dark satisfaction. Killian lifts the pliers and applies them carefully to the nail of the prisoner's left index finger.

Killian's voice is low and dangerous. "What happens to the children?"

The Nabber starts to shake, swollen lips trembling. "I d-don't know!"

His scream echoes off the walls as Killian wrenches the finger-nail nail from its bed of flesh.

Fuck.

I've never seen Killian like this before. I had no idea he could be so... brutal.

He leans threateningly over the prisoner and an unexpected spark lights in my veins at the sight of this refined man resorting to untamed violence on my behalf.

"Let's try this again," Killian says softly, placing the pliers against another fingertip. "What. Happens. To. The. *Children?*"

"P-please... I d-don't—"

Another scream rends the air, raising the hair at my nape and making my heart pound. Killian lifts the pliers, holding the prisoner's pain-glazed eyes as he lets the bloodied nail drop to the floor.

"Eight left," the prince drawls. "Then we start on the toes."

"They'll kill me!" the man cries.

Killian tips his head to one side, dark blond hair falling into his steely blue eyes. He looks like a vengeful god. "You think I won't?"

The man starts to cry, tears making clean tracks over his bloodied cheeks. "Alright! We t-take the kids to an abandoned warehouse in the Southern Quarter!"

"And then what?" Killian demands.

"The masked person takes them from there and moves them out of the city. Th-that's all I know, I swear!"

I push into the cell, coming to stand next to Killian. "Which warehouse is it?" I cut in. "On what street?"

He gives us the address through hitching sobs.

"How many Nabbers are there?" I ask. "Where can we find them?"

The man shakes his head. "I'm the only one."

Without a word, Killian bends down and rips off another fingernail.

The man's howl of pain makes my blood pound in my ears.

"My brother!" the man cries. "He's the one who brought me in. Some of our friends, too." His head hangs as more sobs fill the room. "I'm sorry! I'm sorry! The money—we n-needed the money!"

"You disgusting vermin," Killian growls. "They were *children!* You deserve to die for what you've done."

"Give us their names," I say. "Your brother and the other Nabbers."

The man does, through more of that pathetic weeping. Then Killian looks at me in silent question.

Are we done here?

I shake my head. I have one more question.

Bending down to look the prisoner in the eye, I say, "A little over a month ago, one of you took a girl from a house in the Eastern Quarter. Saela. Long dark hair, hazel eyes. Eleven years old. What happened to her? Is she at the warehouse?"

"I don't know!" the man whimpers. "I didn't take no girl!"

A fourth fingernail joins the others on the floor as the man's screams vibrate in my ears. Dark satisfaction floods my veins, feeding the rage still burning in my gut.

"*I said I don't know!*" the man wails. "There's been too many kids! I don't remember their faces no more!" He sobs so hard he starts to choke. "Please, I swear, I don't know no Saela!"

Killian turns to gesture for the guards to come to us while I stare at the shuddering prisoner in sadistic gratification.

"Get as many guards around that location as possible," Killian says to one of the guards. "Find the other Nabbers and imprison them. We are shutting down their operation."

The guard nods and hustles away as Killian turns to the second. "Kill him."

Something inside me snaps at that. Dark shadows swarm around my vision, just like that night in the corridor when I killed the Daemos Rawbond. A primal feeling surges, bringing Anassa with it.

Bringing raw, feral *fury*.

"No," I snap, violence rising in me like an unstoppable tide. "This scum is *mine*."

I don't even look at the others as I advance on the Nabber, my dagger suddenly in my hand. From somewhere far away, I hear his pathetic pleas, his sobs of terror. His eyes roll as he struggles against his bonds.

None of it touches. Nothing can penetrate the shroud of dark bloodlust that's overtaken me.

"*Mercy!*" he wails. "*Please!*"

I hear myself speak in a voice like metal grinding on stone. "Did those kids get any mercy? Did my *sister* get any mercy?"

I don't wait for an answer.

My blade plunges home, splitting flesh and muscle, scraping against bone. A spray of hot blood wets my hand and face.

I don't know how many times my blade rises. How many times it splits the Nabber's skin. I don't even notice when the screaming stops. All I know is killing rage, driven by the scent of blood and Anassa's vicious approval.

Finally, I hear Killian shouting my name. Feel his hands pulling me back.

"He's dead, Meryn. He's gone."

I turn to him in a daze, blinking away blood, then peer at the prisoner again. His upper body is a mass of gleaming crimson. His beaten face is pale and lax, head hanging against the back of the chair. Blood trickles down his legs and pools on the stones under his feet. My face and hands are sticky with it.

Killian is looking at me with unguarded worry. We're alone. The second guard is long gone. But he must have seen... must have heard the screams.

I lift the red-slick knife in my hand and wait to be disgusted at what I've done.

But I don't. I can't. I'd do it again and again to protect my sister and all the other commoner children.

Anassa's voice fills my head, thick with wrath.

"*Some people deserve to die.*"

CHAPTER TWENTY-SIX

I don't remember most of the trek back to Killian's chamber. A miserable sort of numbness falls over me, thinking of Sae. Wondering if the man I just killed really was the one who took her away.

Not for the first time, I think of how terrified she must have been. How alone she must have felt.

The numbness melts away, replaced by that dark, shadowed wave of violence once more. It makes me want to kill that piece of shit all over again. And his brother and all their friends, too.

Scum of the fucking kingdom.

I start to come back to myself when Killian guides me into the bathing chamber connected to his bedroom. This place puts the Bonded washroom to shame. Elaborate mosaics cover the walls, dotted with precious stones that catch the lamplight like stars. There's a deep tub set into the floor, large enough that it could hold ten people comfortably, steam already rising from water that smells of richly fragrant oils.

"You should clean up," Killian says, his gaze scouring me without judgment. "I'll give you some privacy."

I'm sure I look awful right now, given how sticky my face and hands are. But he's not flinching from the sight. He never has. Killian has always, *always* taken me as I am. Accepted my wild side and helped me resist my more self-destructive instincts.

He turns to go and I catch his wrist, the part of me that has been fighting him finally turned silent. I think back to how he tortured the prisoner so calmly.

How calculated and brutal he was. How much I liked seeing him that way.

I'm exhausted and disappointed that we didn't find out anything about Saela, and more than anything, I'm done.

Done fighting this, done pretending that I don't ache to be in his arms, having him take care of me.

"Stay," I say plainly.

His sapphire eyes snap to mine and he takes a step closer. "You're sure?" he asks.

"Positive," I say. "I've missed you."

He reaches out, calmly taking one of my hands into his larger ones and turning it over. "I've missed you too, kitten. You didn't cut yourself?" The blood on them is dried and cracking now. It starts to flake away under his unflinching touch.

"I don't think so," I murmur.

"Good," he says. "Let's get you bathed."

He unbuttons my blood-soaked shirt and peels it away, stepping closer to me, the heat of his body already warming me. Killian leans down and kisses my filthy cheek, my shoulder, my breastbone, working my breast binding off with his agile fingers. His hands slide down to my hips and he helps me wriggle out of my pants and underthings.

Then he steps back and stares hungrily at my naked, bloodied form. My cheeks flush.

"I'm sure I look frightful," I say.

"You're the most beautiful you've ever been."

My heart swells and suddenly I can sense Anassa's presence growing stronger in my mind. Mortified and acting on instinct, I slam down the iron wall between us.

"*Not this*," I think desperately at her, hoping it reaches her behind the barrier. "*You are not welcome to my intimate moments.*"

There's only silence on her end.

"Mer?" Killian says, looking quizzically at me.

"Sorry," I say, then grab at his shirt, eager to have him undressed. To see the hard lines of his body, feel his hands on me.

I can finally admit I've been craving this, wanting him despite my anger and hurt. That night after night, I've watched the other Rawbonds find their satisfaction with each other, and in my mind it was only him—*Killian*.

Killian undresses quickly. His familiar form is as beautiful as ever, lean and hard with muscles. My gaze skirts his chiseled abdominals and dips down to the hardening length between his legs. My thighs clench at the sight. Guess he's been frustrated, too.

He guides me down the steps into the steaming water. We settle on a tiled bench built into the side of the pool.

"Here," Killian murmurs, snagging a bottle from the shelf set into the wall. "Let me."

I nod and duck my head under the tap to wet my hair. Then I turn to lean back against his chest. The sensation of his hands in my hair—his fingers gliding tenderly against my scalp—is so soothing and full of affection that tears threaten. I've been starved for his love and tenderness.

When he's done with my hair, he moves on to my body. And the comforting touch soon turns to something else.

The slick of the soap is sinful even as it washes away the last traces of my violent sins. His hands reach around me, one sliding down the length of my throat, the other cupping my breast, then skimming down my side.

Killian's touch doesn't change—he still carefully soaps every inch of me, his fingers gentle and purposeful. My eyes drop to watch them trace their path down my body, and my face flushes at the erotic sight.

His hands drift to the tops of my thighs, then back up, massaging soap into both breasts, and the gentle tug of his palms rubbing over my nipples lights me on fire. I lean my head back against his shoulder, unable to hold back a moan.

Killian's breath huffs out against my skin, and I can picture the exact amused yet aroused look that's on his face.

His hands know my body so well. His every touch stokes my arousal, and I'm getting wetter and wetter between my legs somehow, despite the sudsy water I'm immersed in.

Without warning, his mouth comes to my neck, teeth grazing and then nipping, and I yelp, my back arching involuntarily.

Finally his touch grows harder, possessive. One hand splays against my stomach, fingers pressing into my lean abdomen, clamping me tight against his chest and stomach, his erection insistent against the curve of my ass. I grind back against him, the slip and slide of the soapy water insanely erotic between his cock and my curves.

He stiffens behind me, his teeth sinking harder into my neck. "Killian," I gasp, and he groans, then.

"Say my name again," he rasps, lips against my ear.

"*Killian.*"

Still pressing me firm against him with one hand, his other sinks lower, lower to the needy place between my thighs. The slide of his fingers against me in the warm water is electric. I squirm and keen as he touches me just how he knows I like it, speeding up then slowing down.

My breathing hitches as my orgasm comes at me fast. "Oh goddess—yes—" and then in one swift motion he pulls his hand away, grabbing my hips and repositioning us so that when I sink back down, it's onto his cock, his hot length filling me tighter and tighter. After weeks without him, he's almost too much for me; I'm panting as he pulls me the last inch downward, sheathing himself completely inside of me.

He pulls one of my own hands over to the apex of my thighs, his fingers interweaving with mine as together, we find my clit again, every touch like fire with the added feeling of him deep inside me, somehow getting even harder as I clench around him.

Then his hands are back on my hips and he's lifting me, pulling me down, fucking me as I find my own pleasure, desperately touching myself as I start to shatter around him.

"Come for me, kitten," he growls, and that's all it takes to put me over the edge—I cry out as I come, pushing my hips hard against him, wanting to feel every inch, and then he's coming too, sharp thrusts that drive him even deeper as I pant, the waves of my orgasm still crashing over me.

Finally, we both stop moving, and I relish the feeling of him still inside me, still filling me as both of us fight to catch our breath.

"That was…" I'm not sure I have words to describe it. The pleasure, the comfort of his hands, the warm water, the sting of his teeth.

Exhaustion hits me, and I sink back against him more fully. His arms wrap around me, possessive.

"I'm sorry," he murmurs against my hair. "Sorry we didn't learn anything about Saela."

Heart swelling with love and grief, I turn in his arms, wrapping my legs around his waist and pressing my mouth to his.

"Don't be sorry," I whisper. "Because of you, the Nabbers will be shut down. No more kids will go missing from Sturmfrost. It's a victory, even if we didn't find out anything about Saela. It's more than I ever expected. Thank you."

He smiles, but there's pain in his eyes. "We'll find her. I promise. I won't give up until we do."

The tears that threatened earlier return. With them comes a steely certainty that settles deep into my bones.

He's right. One way or another—whether through Killian's power, my bond with Anassa, or with the strength of my own blood-soaked hands—I'm *going* to bring my sister home.

CHAPTER TWENTY-SEVEN

The next morning, Egith meets us at the Strategos training field. She waits until we've all lined up beside our wolves. Anassa pads over to me, her silver-white fur shining in the winter sunlight, but she doesn't spare a look at me.

"*Good morning to you, too,*" I direct at her. Nothing.

"Congratulations, Rawbonds," Egith announces. "You have reached a crucial new phase of your training."

There's a murmur from the others and Izabel shoots me an excited glance. Not sure why she's so happy,

A new phase means tougher challenges. More opportunities to fail.

"Now that you've passed the Voice Trial, we must begin training to access the deeper abilities unique to each pack," Egith continues. "As you well know, every pack has its own powers. Among the Strategos, our wolves can share their enhanced strategic abilities, which are heightened by pack unity."

Here Egith pauses, her sharp gaze swinging over us to ensure we're all paying attention.

"In battle," she says, "these skills are absolutely indispensable. They manifest in several key ways. One: an almost prescient understanding of troop movements. Two: the ability to spot weaknesses in enemy formations. Three: to calculate odds and outcomes with supernatural precision. However," she turns to look directly at me, raising one eyebrow, "accessing this power requires complete synchronization between wolf and rider."

I sigh. *Great, thanks for the vote of confidence, Egith.*

"When I say your connection with your wolf must be complete, I mean it," Egith adds, pacing down the first row of Rawbonds, passing Perielle, who stands haughtily next to her wolf. They probably have a perfect connection.

"You must think as one mind, share the same purpose. Only when you can all achieve that kind of unity with your wolves will you be able to link mentally as a pack—a skill that heightens your powers in times of great need. So trust your wolves and let them guide you into the pack unity. They know what to do."

Again, Egith glances at me.

"Make no mistake, Rawbonds—this will not be easy. Some of you will fail. And if you can't overcome that failure, it will end in your elimination from the pack."

Really loving the pep talk.

With that, she gives the 'go ahead' gesture and waits for us to… I don't know what.

I look around at the other Rawbonds to find them all closing their eyes and breathing deeply as though in meditation. A few of them gasp, jolting visibly as something passes between them and their wolves.

Oh. Right. Guess we're doing the thing.

To my left, Izabel releases a long, shuddering breath. "I see… a battlefield."

"Me, too," says another Rawbond near the front of the group. "It's so clear—like I'm watching it happen with my own eyes!"

"Good," says Egith. "Focus in. Let the visions unfold. What are your wolves trying to show you?"

I glance at Anassa while the others begin describing their visions of battles and the strategies that won—or lost—them.

"So… *should we try it?*" I ask her.

No answer. She doesn't even look at me. When I reach out to her through the bond, my heart drops.

The iron wall is back, just as impenetrable as before.

"Dammit, I thought we were past this crap!" I think at her, knowing she can sense my feelings even if she won't hear my words.

No response.

Fuck.

I have no choice but to stand there and pretend to meditate so Egith's watchful gaze doesn't clock my failure. At least I'm not the only one who doesn't seem to receive any visions.

One of a few, anyway.

Eventually, Egith calls the exercise to a close, ending our lesson with a bone-chilling announcement.

"Practice deepening your bonds with your wolves as much as possible in the following weeks, Rawbonds," she says gravely. "The Purge Trial will be here before you know it, which is the end of the Forging period. After that point, the Rawbonds that remain will move into the Proving period, where you learn to work together as packs."

The Rawbonds that remain. I can't believe we're facing death again so soon. And if I remember correctly, this is a chance for the packs to cull any members they think are too weak to survive.

This process is ridiculous.

"Hold on," I say, unable to hold back my frustration. "I don't understand the whole purging thing. Why kill each other? Why thin our own ranks when we need every warrior we can get to fight the Siphons?"

Egith just frowns at me in baffled disappointment.

I glance around at the others. Perielle smirks like I've just loudly announced that I'm the village idiot.

"Seriously, somebody explain it to me," I say. "Why are we culling Bonded pairs when they're already so rare? Why does the king require this? Why does everyone just *accept* it?"

The silence that follows is deafening. Beside me, Anassa bristles with silent scorn. Even Izabel winces in embarrassment when I look her way.

Egith's voice rings out again, carrying the strain of barely controlled temper. "It has *nothing* to do with the king."

I meet her frustrated gaze. "Alright, so why, then?"

"Direwolves are pack creatures," she grates, "in case that was not abundantly clear to you. These Trials are created *by* and *for* them."

Wait… *what?*

"You're saying the direwolves created this training?" I demand. "They want us to cull each other?"

"Yes," Egith growls. "In war, the weakest link endangers everyone. We can only succeed against our enemy if we work together. And if there are any direwolves or Bonded riders who might endanger the pack's safety, it is in everyone's best interest to cull them now—before we are at war and *all* our lives are at risk."

My ears start to ring in the silence that follows.

Oh.

Oh… shit.

Realization dawns with cold, sinking dread.

Good job, Meryn. You just painted another fucking target on your back.

Through my tenuous bond with Anassa, I sense the wolf's agreement with Egith's words. And something else—a warning. Or perhaps a challenge.

If I fuck this up, she'll be happy to cull me herself.

AFTER CLASS, I head straight for the terraces to find Anassa. She's on the uppermost terrace again, and the mental wall between us is bigger and more impenetrable than ever. My frustration builds with each failed attempt to connect through our bond.

Why the fuck is she doing this? I thought we had an understanding.

This goddess-damned wolf is going to get me killed.

A twinge of shame follows me as I climb, however. I know I screwed up today by questioning the process. If I don't get Anassa back on my side, the Purge Trial is going to be just like the Presentation—only it'll end with me splattered all over the floor. For real this time.

Anassa could have told me that these Trials were designed by the direwolves, I think, temper rising with each step I climb. *She could make this whole business so much easier if she fucking helped me out once in a while.*

She's the one who chose me, after all. So why do I often think she wants me to fail?

By the time I reach the upper terrace, I'm practically seething. Anassa lies at the back where the rock wall of the mountain shields her from the cold, whipping wind.

"What is your problem?" I demand, both aloud and through our bond. "How am I supposed to access your power if you keep shutting me out?"

Anassa doesn't move, but I hear her voice in my head, rich and thunderous as before.

And thick with disdain.

"What right do you have to access my power?" she growls. *"You place your own walls between us and then dare to demand that I lay myself bare to you?"*

The accusation catches me off guard. What the hell is she talking about?

Then I remember—last night. Killian.

"You're mad because I won't let you observe intimate moments?" I say. *"Seriously?"*

At last, Anassa lifts her head, turning to pin me with furious yellow eyes. *"You ignorant child. You still do not understand what this bond means, do you?"*

"Fuck the bond!" I snarl. "I deserve to have a little privacy now and then—especially when all you want to do is judge me!"

Anassa's mental voice grows icy and dangerous. *"My ability to sense your emotions at all times, and for you to sense mine, is what keeps us both safe."*

"What exactly are you keeping me safe from, huh? You shut me out for weeks after you chose me," I scoff. "My own pack members —my friends—would tear me apart if they sense their direwolves demand it. As far as I can tell, Killian is the *only* person in this whole fucking castle that I can trust not to kill me, including you."

Anassa's eyes narrow, her voice sharp with warning. *"If I were trying to kill you, you'd already be dead."*

I turn away from her in boiling frustration, pacing along the edge of the terrace. Cold wind tosses my hair into my eyes, but I don't care.

"Fine, you're not trying to kill me. But you're not exactly trying to keep me alive, either, are you?" I demand, turning back to her. "And now you're shutting me out because I'm having sex without you peeping? *Seriously?* Is it because he's not one of the Bonded? You don't want me hooking up with him because it won't help you find your mate?"

At once, my head is filled with booming, derisive laughter.

"Why the fuck is that funny?" I practically scream. "That's why all the Rawbonds fuck each other's brains out every night, isn't it? So everyone can find their direwolves' mates?"

Anassa's rich voice is thick with condescension. *"The constant coupling amongst the Rawbonds is little more than entertainment—for your benefit more than ours. We let you humans have your fun simply because it is the part of the training you most enjoy."*

"Right," I grate. "I'm supposed to believe you don't care about finding your mate?"

"Stupid girl," the wolf growls with razor-sharp amusement. *"Do you truly think I need your help to find my mate? I have known him for years."*

The words hit me like a sucker punch and send me reeling. I freeze, my shock reverberating along our bond. If Anassa knows who her mate is, that means...

"Who?" I hear myself rasp. "Who is it?"

It could be someone at the castle, or an older direwolf down at the front. It could be *anyone*, from any pack, one of the thousands of direwolves out there...

Her condescension hits me again, colored with Anassa's amusement—and an unmistakable challenge.

"I will tell you who he is when you can prove to me that you are worthy of the knowledge."

My head knocks back in affront. "Are you fucking kidding me?"

Her cold stare and a wave of icy disdain are the only answers I get.

I stand there for a long moment, grappling with anger and a growing sense of inevitability. *This is my life now,* I remind myself. There's no escape. I made peace with that already.

And there's no use fighting with Anassa, as much as I hate to admit it.

"Well, worthy or not, you're stuck with me," I grumble. "And I'm stuck with you."

"For now," she drawls.

I sigh heavily. "Right. I get it. You could rip my throat out at any moment—if one of the others doesn't do me in first. But you know damn well I won't give up—not while there's any chance of finding Saela. I will fight to the fucking death to save her, Anassa. I'll jump through all the fucking hoops, alright? I don't give a fuck about mates or anything else."

Anassa is silent, apparently unmoved. But she's listening. Assessing.

The last of the anger drains out of me, replaced by something like resignation. "I will try to let you sense my emotions when I'm with Killian, but I need some privacy and I also need you to be okay with that. Promise me we'll be okay for the Purge Trial," I say quietly. "Please."

Another lengthy silence ensues. Anassa stares me down, her yellow gaze weighing me carefully.

Finally, in a tone of both warning and promise, her words echo in my mind. *"We'll be okay."*

THAT NIGHT, terror follows me into my dreams.

I'm in the castle, lost in its maze-like corridors. The shadows dance like living things and the walls change every time I look away.

I can hear my mother's voice calling me. It echoes strangely, coming from every direction. There's something wrong about it. A distortion that chills me to my bones.

"Meryn... Meryn! I'm here!"

It feels like I'm following her voice for hours, getting more and more lost. More and more afraid.

Until I find myself standing before a wide, familiar archway. Towering doors open into a massive arena, the web of gutters in the dirt floor flowing with blood.

My mother stands at the arena's center, her back turned. She's dressed in a crimson gown, her head adorned in a twisting crown slick with blood.

"Mom..." My voice comes out weak and childlike. But it reaches her.

She turns.

Icy terror surges in my veins.

Her eyes are black as pitch—no whites, no pupils. Just pure, demonic black.

I stumble back as she opens her mouth to speak.

No words come. Black blood pours from her lips and streams from her unseeing eyes.

An echoing, disembodied voice thunders through the arena, filling me with terror unlike any I've known before.

"Nocturn is calling. Are you listening?"

I JOLT awake with those awful words still booming in my ears.

Fresh terror awaits. My vision is blurred, my senses spinning. Something presses my face so hard I can barely take in a breath. I taste blood and dirt and the acrid tang of my own fear.

I realize I'm lying on the ground, my face in the dirt. I lift my head, overwhelmed by the familiar scent of death.

The dark arena looms above me, the stands encased in shadow. Moonlight filters down from the glass ceilings in the dome. Just enough that I can see my hands on the ground as I lift myself onto my knees.

My fingers meet with gritty dirt and cold metal.

A drain, I realize, still dazed.

Slowly, my vision adjusts to the darkness. Moonlight plucks details from the shadows, tracing the web of gutters in the floor. Highlighting the angles where they meet. The metal grates set into those junctures make dark dimples in the earth.

With slow-darning horror, I realize I'm lying at the convergence of all those gutters. The place where the blood and gore are drained away after every battle.

The exact place my mother stood in my nightmare.

CHAPTER TWENTY-EIGHT

My hands tremble wildly as I rise from the blood-strained arena floor.

I've never once sleepwalked in my whole damn life —yet here I stand wearing nothing but my nightclothes, the chill night air raising goosebumps all over my body.

My feet are bare and icy, covered in dirt. The whole front of my nightshirt is dusty with it, too. Heart pounding with anxiety and confusion, I try to wipe the bloody grit from my face, wondering how I must look.

I need to get back to my room without anyone seeing me.

As I turn toward the exit, Anassa's awareness trickles through the bond. My instinct is to shut her out—I don't want anyone to know about this—but I don't. I can't afford to piss her off again.

"Are you well?" she asks.

The genuine concern in her voice takes me by surprise.

"I'm fine," I answer, hoping she can't read the truth in my feelings. *"I just had a nightmare."*

The lie tastes bitter on my tongue. I can tell Anassa doesn't totally buy it, but she doesn't argue.

"Well, go back to sleep," she says. *"You're keeping me up."*

So much for her concern.

I approach the arena exit and peer outside. The castle is dark. Thank the goddess. No one is around to witness my shame.

Mom had episodes just like this. She would wander at night, muttering about voices only she could hear. I'd find her outside sometimes, standing in the neighbor's yard or crouching in a nearby alley. Once she climbed up on the roof.

That was the day I finally took her to the healer, and we started giving her sedatives.

I find myself fighting tears of panic as I slink back to my room. The walk seems endless and the shadows have that unnerving *aliveness*. Every little sound in the castle recalls the whispers, my mother's eerie voice.

Her open mouth, pouring blood.

Fuck. I can't pretend this isn't happening forever. Eventually, someone is going to notice. The madness is going to interfere with my ability to fight. Anassa will reject me. Killian, too.

And Saela…

How the fuck can I save her if I can't trust my own mind?

And how long do I have before I can't function on my own anymore? Months? Years?

I don't know, but the clock is ticking. I feel it in my bones.

My time is running out.

I'M off my game the next day, exhausted after barely sleeping. We have training with Egith and Stark as we work on our pack unity while practicing combat maneuvers.

My whole world is the rush of fur, the thud of paws, the flash of fangs. Snarls and chuffs fill the air alongside Stark's precise instructions as his voice echoes over the training yard. He has us executing a complicated formation composed of three concentric circles, each ring of wolves moving in the opposite direction to the one before it, covering all sightlines.

According to Stark, this precise formation would be used in

battlefield conditions, when we might need to coordinate smoothly while surrounded by chaos.

The tightly knit outer circle protects against exterior attacks, the frontline of our defense. The central circle, safer from danger, has more room to assess the battlefield at large and relay information to the second circle, who can be deployed at notice to reinforce the outer circle should they waver.

For now, though, we're barely managing to move in tidy circles.

The balance is delicate. Every single one of us has to move at the same pace, aware of those in front of us, behind us, to either side. It's difficult, even without a Siphon attack to worry about.

Anassa moves smoothly today, keeping pace with the wolf in front of us. I've gotten much better at remaining mounted, but I still feel clumsy when I look at the other riders all around me and see effortless grace. Cooperation.

Stark's constant violation of my eardrums isn't helping. Neither is the sun beating down over us, catching on swords and causing light to glare in my eyes. The wintery air is cool, but icy sweat trickles down my back as I push my body to perform.

Energy hums in the air around us. I'm not sure whether it's the sheer power of so many wolves gathered and working together to form this mesmerizing pattern or if it's something more.

Something deeper.

We're at it for about an hour when something shivers through the pack. I'm suddenly more aware.

That river I've barely managed to brush my fingertips through crackles with energy. It's suddenly not liquid but electric, like a forked bolt of lightning carving across the sky or the waking of a neuron.

"Give into it!" Egith orders, apparently having sensed the shift in us. "Let the connection happen!"

I grip my sword tighter and try to focus, tuning into Anassa's bond and reaching out towards that crackling bolt of awareness. The moment I brush closer, my blood wakes. My heartbeat speeds up and my senses heighten.

I start to become aware in a way I've never been before.

The circles continue to rotate in perfect synchronization. My breath moves in time with Anassa's steps. My heartbeat pounds with the heavy footsteps around me. Flashes of recognition cut through the churning circle of fur and muscle.

Through the bond, I sense the spiraling brush of other minds. The other wolves, I realize, each with their own emotion, intent, awareness. There's a physical sensation, like the pressure expanding inside my skull, pushing outward in a surge of thought.

Instinct fizzles over the stream of connection, and along that path, *understanding*.

In a brilliant burst, I can suddenly sense every node of the inter-connected web. I'm aware of each pair of wolf and rider, sensing their movements before they happen and the careful hum of their concentration.

When Izabel and her wolf pass on my left, her mind sparks on mine wordlessly. Her focus feels like a knife's edge, perfectly balanced and attuned to her mount's motion.

Then on my left, Tomison. He rides perfectly. The confidence radiating from his mind makes me feel like I've downed a draft of emberwine, heady and intoxicating.

My mind breaks wide open as I give into the pull.

This is it, I realize.

This is true pack unity—an extension of myself beyond every-thing I've ever known. A new way of being joined with the spirit of my packmates.

Submerged in it, I feel more than human.

It's powerful and vibrant and explosively intricate.

Anassa's emotions shift over the bond, flickering away from annoyed boredom and towards tickles of curious attention. I clutch her fur and lean into it further, drowning out the sound of Stark's voice and the movement of bodies until I feel like I'm made up of twenty-three wolves and twenty-two other riders, all operating on a single impulse.

But I lean too far. Darkness creeps at the edge of my vision.

Flickers of shapes that shouldn't be there amongst the spiral of bodies, glimpses between the wolves' legs. Whispers hiss from beneath the sound of paws on packed earth and breaths in lungs, growing louder with each terrified heartbeat.

I try to ignore them and push through to that crackling flow of energy, but the whispers become more insistent until they start to drown out all other sound.

Voices I don't recognize. Words I can't make out.

But *deafening.*

Then the worst of it. I gasp and look up, trying to keep my balance as blood starts to seep down over the walls around us and into the training yard, bright red against the cold sky, moving in a thick, tar-like dribble towards me.

A strangled sound breaks from my chest. I barely manage to prevent it from ripping through my throat as a panicked scream. My concentration shatters totally as the blood seeps towards me.

It's all I can see and all I can think about. I can't hear anything.

I can't *breathe.*

How many people, I can't stop thinking. *How many would have to die to spill this much blood?*

Vertigo starts to dislodge me from Anassa's back. The riders around me tense and turn. Anassa growls and side steps, alarm spiking through her as she moves to counter my compromised balance and keep me mounted.

But in doing so, we both stumble and falter out of formation.

Perielle stops short behind me, her wolf snapping. The middle circle halts, and a cascading chaos takes the pack.

There's still scarlet lingering in my peripheral vision, but I growl and pull myself up. I fight through the dizziness and urge Anassa onward. My head is throbbing, but I manage to set us both back into the proper rhythm, the rest falling back into line once I've recovered.

But as I make another turn around the circle, I look up and see him.

Stark, standing with his arms crossed, staring at me. He watches me from his position across the yard with his dark eyes narrowed, calculating. He cracks his neck, and the tattoos that cover every inch of skin are a visible threat.

Fuck up again, and this psycho will take me out himself, adding me to the trophies on his skin.

He saw me falter, and he won't forget it.

I struggle for the rest of the session to reach that borderline euphoric connection I almost grasped. By the time it's over and the direwolves are wandering back to the terraces, I'm exhausted and acutely frustrated with myself. I want to slip away and hide from the annoyed glances I keep getting from my packmates, but Egith's voice cuts through the yard.

"Rawbond Cooper. A moment."

Great. I turn and watch Anassa's silver coat disappearing towards the terraces. I'm on my own, then. The rest of the Rawbonds file out of the training yard. My footsteps sound loud as I approach Egith, my boots leaving distinct impressions in the churned earth.

The beta's expression is unreadable, as always.

The instant I reach her, she jumps right into it. "Your bond with Anassa has improved," she says kindly, "but it isn't enough."

I bristle instantly. *Nothing* is ever enough in this place. I'm half-convinced she thinks I'm not even trying, at this point. "I—"

Egith raises her hand, cutting me off. "I watched you today. I saw it happen."

"What?" I breathe.

"You touched it just for a moment. What we're striving for here," she says. Her voice hushes slightly, as if in reverence. "And you felt it, didn't you? The unity of the pack?"

I shiver at the memory and nod.

Egith sighs. "Then you also felt how easily you shattered it. One moment of weakness from you disrupted the *entire* formation." She steps closer, voice dropping. "The pack needs to function as one entity. One mind. One purpose. If you can't maintain that connection… They'll all take note of that. And the Purge Trial is only a week away."

Her meaning is clear. If I can't maintain the connection, I'm going to get culled.

"I bet you'd hate to lose that bet," I say bitterly, remembering how she told me that all the instructors were betting on which pack would have the most Rawbonds left at the end of the Trials.

Egith laughs, surprised. "Actually, Cooper, you've kind of grown on me. I'd hate to lose *you*."

The words mean more than I'd care to admit and I look away, my eyes burning. "I'm trying," I tell her. She says nothing, so I glance back. Her expression is unchanged, and I wonder if she really does think I don't care. "I *am*," I insist. "I'm—"

"Try harder," she says sharply. "I mean this as advice, Cooper, not a lecture. Unity is survival. Division will mean death. You cannot break formation like that again with the Purge coming up."

Because if I do, I'll die. The Pack won't forgive me a second time. Not when it counts. If I am a danger to them, I'll be extinguished.

The needs of the many.

Walking away, Egith's words echo in my head, exacerbating the headache that began with that horrible vision. I know Egith is right.

When I first wavered, barely still holding onto pack unity, I felt the confusion and frustration from the rest of them. Anger burned in some of them when they saw the formation endangered because of one person's failure. Even Izabel shot me an exasperated look.

The worst of it is that for a single instant, I *did* feel it. The perfection of that unity haunts me now, like I stared at a beautiful light too long and the afterimage is burned painfully into my eyes, following me everywhere I look.

For a few meager breaths, I truly felt like I *belonged*.

I felt like I was a part of a bigger whole, like I had purpose, like I was connected and grounded.

I never felt that way growing up in Eastern, fighting alone.

But then the voices came, dragging me back into isolation and fear.

As I step inside the castle and start towards our quarters, the fear won't leave me. I think the episodes are getting worse. More frequent. I have no idea how I'm supposed to maintain the intricate mental connection required for the Trials when I can't even trust my own mind.

It's not my *fault* that the world turned to blood and terror.

"*Anassa*," I whisper over the bond, hugging myself as I walk.

There's a sensation like rolling over in my mind, and her attention's on me.

"*Did you sense what happened back there?*" I ask.

"*Be specific,*" she orders.

"*I saw things. Heard things,*" I tell her. She responds with silence. "*I know you're only supposed to get my thoughts and feelings through the bond but… can you sense what I sense when I'm experiencing it?*"

A shiver of confirmation reaches me. A yes. Strangely, it makes me feel less alone.

"*Then can you stop it?*" I ask.

"*No. I cannot,*" she replies. My heart falls instantly as I shuffle towards my room. "*And moreover, I would not.*"

I let her sense my shock.

"*Visions like the ones you are experiencing are powerful. They may mean something,*" she tells me.

"Yeah, it means I'm losing my mind!" I snap aloud, fractures of anger cracking through the bond. "*And my inability to stop it might get us both killed,*" I add venomously.

Anassa is unimpressed with my display of emotion. "*Will you listen to me?*"

I pause, surprised by the calmness in her voice. It wasn't an accusatory question. It was honest. My muscles unwind, and I nod.

"*We have more power over our minds than we realize. You need to focus on our connection when you're on my back. Do not let your mind wander. Breathe deeply and open your mind to the power that runs through you.*"

Her words resonate through my consciousness, but I still feel lost. Avoiding my mind's wandering is harder than it sounds.

I keep feeling it slip through my grip and disappear into that terrifying, distant place my mother inhabits.

But I know she's trying to guide me. Genuinely trying. More power over my mind than I realize, she said. I can't just ignore her wisdom. She's centuries older than me and lives in this strange world of telepathic connection and shared consciousnesses.

If Anassa thinks I can take control, I have to try. Try harder.

CHAPTER TWENTY-NINE

I mproving my connection to pack unity over the weeks leading up to the Purge Trial is like being told to carry a weight in one of my hands and to never let it drop. Sometimes, I can forget about it. Other times, I have to adjust how I do something to make room for it.

And always, it's exhausting.

Every training exercise we run, every time I need to prove my ability to hold the connection, I end up with a blistering headache.

But then training stops, and I can breathe again, and in those moments between: there's Killian.

At night, I make my excuses to my friends, and I seek him out—in his quarters, or in mine. I've gotten used to the path to his rooms; I've never strayed off of it again, or found that strange carving, and I try to ignore the possibility that I hallucinated it entirely.

Time slips right through my fingers, and then somehow, the Purge is upon us.

The night before the Trial, the common lounge may as well be hosting a wake. All the Rawbonds, myself included, sense tomorrow's Purge like a threatening blizzard on the horizon.

We can look away from it, but that won't stop it coming. Tomorrow, some of us will die.

No one is drinking. No one would, too worried that a hangover might compromise their performance. A drink to take the edge off tonight isn't worth risking your life tomorrow.

The sobriety in the air after so many jovial nights here is, frankly, depressing. Instead of drinking, people are trying to distract themselves in other ways—card games, or reading. Small groups gather and chat, Tomison at the center of one of the most boisterous circles.

He's cracking incessant jokes, as is his signature, but he's even louder than usual. I'm sitting with Venna and Izabel on a couch, all of us with books open in our laps. Izabel keeps looking up from hers and sighing loudly, shooting Tomison irritated looks. He doesn't notice, or if he does, he doesn't care.

Venna slams her book shut. "I can't read with you so tightly wound next to me," she huffs at Izabel.

"Well, I can't read with all the *noise* in here," Izabel snaps, glowering at Tomison again. She turns to me. "Distract me, Meryn. What are you going to do with your mother on your day off?"

The day after the Purge Trial, the Rawbonds have the day off and everyone will be going home to visit their families in the Bonded City… so of course, I'll head home, too.

"Assuming I'm still here," I mutter.

Venna didn't catch that and Izabel interprets for her. Her eyes widen and she smacks me in the arm. "Positive attitude!"

I shoot her a guilty grin. She's right. Normally, my problem is *over*-confidence and stubbornness. But there are so many unknowns about tomorrow that even I'm finding myself shaken to the core. And I keep glancing around at all the other Strategos Rawbonds, weighing their strengths against my own.

And wondering if it will be enough.

"It will be enough," Anassa growls in my head.

Of course she'd think that; she doesn't want to die, either.

I ignore my direwolf and finally respond to Izabel. "We probably will just stay at home and catch up. I have a little farther to go than you all, so I won't have a ton of time. When do we have to be back at the castle, again?"

"Sundown," Izabel says.

Our day off is followed that evening by the Forging Ball, a big celebration to mark the halfway point of the Trials. The king and nobles from all the other fiefdoms will be in attendance.

My gaze drifts across the room again, wondering who will be missing from our pack that evening, if not me.

Nevah's sitting alone, as usual, obsessively sharpening her blade with slow, grinding shrieks of metal on whetstone. She won't take her eyes off of it. She's a possibility; she's continued to resist making friends in the pack, still clearly in mourning.

Perielle is subdued, curled up next to Jonah and watching Nevah's repetitive motions. Probably not her; she's divisive, but she inspires fear and the pack members may be too afraid to go against her.

Neither Jonah nor Perielle has their usual outgoing viciousness about them tonight. They've retreated into each other, hiding like the rest of us. Preparing.

Her eyes meet mine, and I tense instinctively. I'm too on edge. The other Rawbonds are assessing me the same way I am them. Unspoken questions hiss in the air.

Who's stronger? Who's faster? Who's smarter? Who will be dead this time tomorrow?

Roddert's cards slip from his grip and scatter in a messy flutter to the floor, and three different Rawbonds instantly reach for their weapons; everyone is so tense. He awkwardly bends to gather them up again.

It hits me. Hard. I could die tomorrow without having told Killian that I love him again, that my heart's found a way back.

Weeks have passed, and I haven't summoned the courage. The words just get stuck in my throat. I'm afraid, I think.

But right now, the fear of death is even louder, thundering in my ears like a direwolf's howl.

What's a little emotional honesty next to blood in the sand?

"I need to breathe," I tell the twins, thudding my book shut, standing, and tossing it into my seat behind me.

Izabel doesn't say anything. She settles for a muffled grunt of affirmation. Venna's fingertips brush against my wrist as I leave them there, a gentle indication of concern and reassurance.

The entire walk to his quarters, I try to figure out how to go about this.

Hey, Killian, I'm maybe probably going to die tomorrow, so…

"*I need privacy now,*" I tell Anassa. We've gotten better at this part. She's stopped shutting me out in anger and I've started communicating when I'm going to alter our connection.

She huffs. She's still not thrilled that I'm partitioning off part of my mind from her, but she accepts it—for now. I won't have to worry about her going incommunicado on me during the Purge Trial tomorrow, or actively trying to get me killed.

I can tell that she thinks I'll get used to her over time, that I'll stop being so modest. We'll see about that.

Reaching for the mental barrier, I pull down the wall but leave it porous. Some feelings will reach her. If I'm in danger, she'll know. But my immediate thoughts and subtler emotions will stay with me.

From inside the tunnel, I push the door open without knocking. Killian is at his desk, reviewing documents.

He's silhouetted by moonlight streaming through the tall window behind him. It makes his hair look silver-gold. When he hears the door, his head snaps up in surprise. But when he sees me, his muscles relax instantly, and he melts back into his chair.

Killian says nothing as I stride towards his desk. I round it and reach for him. The floorboards creak slightly beneath my feet. The legs of his chair scrape over the rug as he makes room for me.

He welcomes me close wordlessly. I fold myself into his arms, straddling his lap, wedged between his warm body and the edge of his desk.

We watch each other for a long moment. His hand strokes up and down my back. I lean a little closer. His fingers snag on my shirt, and his touch finds its way under the hem on its next pass. I shiver at the slide of skin on skin, and he clearly notices.

Killian's pupils widen in the moonlight. His lips press together, and his eyes ease from mine and down to my mouth.

"I love you," I tell him. The words crackle through the silence like ice straining under heavy weight.

No explanation. Nothing else. We don't need it.

"I know," he says softly. He pulls me closer until my hips are pressed close, until his heat spread between my legs. "I love you, too. Even if you'd never come back to me, I would have kept on loving you."

I shut my eyes briefly, tilting forward to press my forehead against his. The smell of pine fills my nose. His breath is on my cheek. His heart beats steady beneath my palm.

This, right now, feels inevitable. I can sense the waiting clash already gathering speed, sinking low.

"I'd tell everyone tomorrow, if you'd let me," he says seriously, his deep blue eyes locking onto mine.

I stroke my fingers over his cheek and the slight rasp of his evening stubble. "The king doesn't have some noble bride picked out for you already?"

Killian's hands close around my thighs. Hard.

"You're mine," he growls. "I don't need anyone's permission for that other than yours." His teeth nip at my jaw and heat thrums through me, making my nipples tighten.

I pull back, though. "Seriously," I say, needing to know where this is going. "What would he say? What would the court think?"

His eyes soften. "He already knows I'm seeing a Rawbond and that it's serious. He has no objections. I alone choose who I love."

Killian's hands slip up to my hips, squeezing almost rhythmically. It's tricking my body into painfully vivid awareness. I can feel the muscle of his thighs beneath me. I can sense each fingertip digging into my flesh.

My hips rock without my telling them to, seeking friction, and he lets out a low, brief groan before he can master it.

"Kitten," he murmurs, "give me permission to claim you in front of the whole world, and I will."

I'm awash in it, swept out to sea. His eyes find mine again, and

I'm drowning in blue. The enormity of what he's offering is over-whelming.

But I can't deal with it right now. I just need to breathe. I need him to carry me away from here. Death is on the horizon, and it's a patient hunter.

I don't say yes. I don't say no.

Instead, I say, "If I die tomorrow, find Saela for me. Get her to safety."

Killian's grip on me tightens like his touch alone can keep me safe, but he says, "I swear it, Meryn."

Gratitude and desperation and fear and love swirl together and drag me under. He pulls me to him right as I lean in.

It's a rough, almost painful kiss, both of us grabbing at each in desperation. I nip his lip and he bites right back and I moan, pushing myself closer to him, grabbing at his clothes.

I need this, need him.

He lowers his head and starts kissing my neck, slowing us down. He weaves his fingers into my short hair and pulls my head back, making room for worship. My breath shudders. I grip his shoulders tightly as pleasure drips from his lips and down to my depths.

The sudden change in pace calms me. I sink into it, forgetting the desperation and turning toward something more. Something that'll last.

Something that defies the dawn.

Killian leans back in his chair. His hair is mussed. His lips are swollen. His hands close around my ass as his glassy eyes move over me.

"Strip," he orders.

I swallow, and my throat clicks. My tongue darts over my lips, which still throb from the rough attention.

He sees it and his gaze ignites. "*Now*, kitten."

I scramble from his lap. Killian leans forward and slowly rolls his shirt up to his elbows as he watches me drag my jacket from my shoulders. While I unbutton my shirt, he rests his elbows on his knees, his forearms flexing as he clenches his hands into fists.

My gaze darts quickly lower. He's already clearly hard beneath his clothes. I wonder if he's barely holding himself back. When I'm bare from the waist up, I don't have to wonder any longer.

Killian lets out another rumbling sound and grinds his hand over himself through his pants. The sight of it pools between my legs. When I guide my underthings from my hips, they're already embarrassingly wet.

Killian reaches out and sweeps his hand across his desk, crumpling papers and scattering objects. A few clatter to the ground or thud against the rug.

"Sit," he orders.

Stepping out of the pile of my clothes, I glide towards him. Slowly. Daintily. I love this feeling. When he looks at me like this, I'm delicate. I get to be delicate. To be breakable without risking a fracture.

The desk is cool against my skin when I ease myself up. It's going to be a mess when I'm done with it.

I wait patiently, but Killian doesn't move. He sits in his chair like it's a throne, eyes moving over me. Torture, really, when there's already a deep throb between my legs in anticipation.

I bite my lip and spread my legs further. His eyes snap down. When my fingers dust over my need, he lets out a muffled groan and wipes his hand over his mouth.

"Touch yourself," he growls, nodding.

And I do. And it's profoundly unsatisfying. I like the feeling of his eyes on me. I like that he looks like he's about to snap into pieces. I *hate* that he isn't taking me.

I want to forget what tomorrow brings. I want him to overwhelm me. Help me forget.

Still, I start to tremble soon enough. Sweat prickles at my forehead. Killian rakes his fingers through his hair, breathing heavily through his nose.

The beginnings of a gentle orgasm trickles through me. My thighs tingle and clench slightly, and I let out a low moan. That's what finally does him in.

Killian snaps forward, suddenly on his feet, hands gripping my thighs and spreading them to aching. The moan I let out is even louder this time. His clothed hips grind against me, replacing the stroke of my fingers, and my back arches.

Killian tilts me forcefully until I thud back against his desk. I look up at him, lingering on the edge as he looms over me. Then his hand cups me, a couple fingers slipping into my wetness. I cry out and try to pull him closer with my legs.

"Close your eyes, kitten," he says.

I whimper and shake my head. The sight of his eyes glazed over by lust is too precious to surrender. But he removes his hand to punish me.

"Now, Meryn. You want to. I know you do."

I bite my lip. My hips ease forward, but he pins them to his desk to stop my searching grind. "I…"

Killian slowly smiles. "Shut your eyes, kitten. I'm going to take care of you."

Surrender, I realize. That's right. I exhale shakily and let my eyes flutter closed. The moment I do, his praise showers over me like kisses. I shiver and groan as his hands streak over my thighs. He leans over me, I can hear it in the creak of the floorboards.

"Good girl," he whispers against my skin. And his mouth closes over my nipple.

I whimper and clutch his hair, holding him to me as his tongue circles around me. His hips fall between mine again. The delicious scrape of his rough clothes over the insides of my thighs starts to sink deep into my flesh.

It does something to me, knowing he's fully dressed while I'm naked and spread open on his desk, eyes closed and at his mercy.

"Keep them closed no matter what, Meryn," Killian warns.

"Y-Yeah," I rasp, struck by wave after wave of shivers.

His hands streak down over my sides. Then, with a rush of cold air, he's gone. I whimper in protest, reaching for him in the dark. I can't open my eyes. Right now, there's only darkness and his touch.

"Killian," I beg.

A low chuckle strikes me at my core. I clench at the sound of it. One of my hands moves to my chest, massaging my breast, pinching my own nipple between my fingers. The absence of him, the bonfire of need, obliterates what was left of my fear. The rest of the world drops away.

All that remains is anticipation.

Where will he touch me when he comes back?

Right where I need him, is the answer. He must've kneeled before the desk, because his hot tongue streaks suddenly between my legs.

I immediately cry out, the sound of my pleasure mingling with the groan he lets out when he tastes me. Sensation pulses through me with the thrust of his tongue.

One of his hands moves over the inside of my thigh. The other is a ghost, lost in the dark, until I feel two fingers join his tongue. He skims them along the outside of my lips.

The quiet orgasm I felt gathering earlier changes into something else altogether.

His tongue dips deep, then finds my clit. He sucks, and a scream gathers in my throat. Then those two fingers slip into me and curl, starting to fuck me, striking me from inside, and the scream rips free.

I come apart right there on his desk, eyes obediently closed. There's nothing but pleasure. Nothing but him and the promise in his touch radiating through me.

He falls still while my muscles remain tight and torturous for a devastatingly long period. Then when I start to ease back down, his fingers make a filthy noise inside me and his tongue strokes slowly, drawing it out.

I moan and streak my fingers through his hair affectionately. But he slips from my grasp again. I hear the sound of his pants unbuttoning and before I can even say his name, he sinks inside of me, his cock thick and hot as it fills me.

My eyes snap open. The breath rushes from me. My shaky hands reach for him, finding purchase on his wrists where he's gripping my hips.

He grins. *"Meryn,"* he growls. Almost like a taunt.

I choke and something like crazed laughter bursts from my

chest. My orgasm is still pulsing through me, tingling over my skin, making everything more intense.

Killian doesn't wait. He starts to thrust fast and deep, the stretch of accommodating him dizzying me. Fuck, the sight of him moving in me, leaned over me and reaching for pleasure, is pushing me higher.

I moan again and pull at him. He grunts and removes one hand from my hip, taking hold of my arm and yanking me upright and against his chest.

The shift in position makes him brush up against my clit with every thrust, and my lingering orgasm starts ramping up again. The pleasure never really stopped. It just quieted for a moment. But a new wave is about to crash over the first as it retreats.

"Fuck. F-fuck!" I choke out.

The desk scrapes over the floor from the force of it, sending more objects clattering. I'm raw and full. Climax is closing in on me, even faster than the first.

"I'll claim you right now, Meryn," he rasps, the words interrupted by the curling of his muscles as he buries himself inside of me. "You're all mine," he hisses as his hips maintain their merciless pace.

"I love you," I whimper, nodding. My body rolls against his, meeting every thrust of his hips with my own. Trying to pull him deeper. Trying to reach that screamingly silent place again, where there's nothing but Killian's body tangled with mine.

"I want you to come around me, kitten," he says. I nod weakly, too distracted by the sight of our bodies moving. But he lets out a discontent sound and closes his hand around my throat, placing gentle pressure on the sides and forcing me to look into his eyes. "Let go. *Now.*"

It happens instantly. Everything inside of me tightens. My mouth falls open, but the scream is silent this time. I don't have the breath for it.

Satisfaction floods Killian's gaze as I start to feather around him and contort, clenching into a vise-like grip. He shudders in response.

The snap of his hips as he takes advantage of my tightness feels like praise. He's wild inside of me for a few more thrusts. Unleashed.

And then comes the rush of hot warmth, the spill of him. His muscles tighten beneath his clothes as he sinks as deep as he can.

Claim me, he said. I cling to his shoulders because if I don't, I'll dissolve into sweat and satisfaction.

We fall still save for the heaving of our chests. There's an ache in my body from the roughness of it. I love it. My hands smooth over his shoulders and up to his neck, into his hair.

"Killian," I breathe. There's a dumb smile on my face when he lifts his head.

He soon mirrors it. "Fuck," he rasps, and I laugh.

But when the levity fades, his smile falls. "I..." His brow knits. "Meryn, tomorrow you—"

I press my thumb over his lips. "It's okay," I whisper.

He doesn't believe me. Can't. But he still gingerly picks me up off of his desk. I wrap my legs around his hips and let him carry me to his bed. "I'm not done with you yet. I can't be," he whispers against my bare shoulder.

I kiss his neck and nod. "Okay."

"Once more, and I'll let you sleep," he promises.

I guide his face up and kiss him slowly. "Once more," I agree.

"Well," he smiles quietly, "maybe two, for you."

I grin as he tosses me onto his bed. Afterward, I fall asleep quickly, listening to his heartbeat beneath my ear. It's a dreamless sleep that takes me, quieted by the weight of his arm across me and the exhaustion from such good sex.

A scream echoes in my ears, jolting me awake.

I think, at first, that it isn't real.

Maybe it's my failure coming back to haunt me, the shriek that I didn't hear that night when I should've been there to protect Saela.

Glancing around the dark room in terror, my heart slams through my body. My surroundings return to me as sleep falls away.

There's a push against the barrier in my mind; Anassa's been woken by my fear. I push back, letting her know I'm safe.

Killian is dead asleep, breathing slowly. "Hey," I beg, jostling him.

He grunts and peels his eyes open. His hair is wild and his lids are heavy. "What? Meryn?"

"Did you hear that?" I demand. It echoed through the halls. It sounded too real, too close.

Killian blinks slowly at me. "Hear what?" he asks, sleep crackling in his voice.

"There was a—"

Another scream shrieks through my bones. I flinch, and goosebumps streak over my bare skin.

Horrifyingly, Killian doesn't even slightly react. He sits up, concern pulling him towards wakefulness. But his attention is entirely on me, not towards the door where the sound came from.

"Meryn? Talk to me."

I'm shivering as his hands close around my shoulders. The realization hits me like icy water. It wasn't real. He didn't hear it. None of it was real. Not the voices my mother hears. Not the blood I saw during training. Not this.

"I thought I heard something," I explain weakly.

Killian's shoulders relax. He misunderstands my fear. "If someone finds you here, I'll protect you. I'll keep it from getting out, if you still want that."

I swallow and let myself fall back against the plush pillows. He settles in beside me. "Thank you," I whisper. I don't tell him that I don't think he'll be able to protect me. Not from this.

"Sleep. You need your strength," he breathes, already giving himself back over to his dreams.

I curl closer to him. Close enough that I can almost convince myself that the horror of tomorrow won't reach me. That the horror of the rest of my life won't, either.

Because there's a terrible truth reverberating in my skull alongside the phantom screams.

Even if I survive the Purge, that won't keep me from following my mother into madness.

CHAPTER THIRTY

I spent the rest of the night in and out of sleep, never able to return to the deep rest I'd been enjoying. When I wasn't mulling over the phantom screams, my mind returned to the Trial ahead of me—back and forth, a vicious cycle. Finally, I dragged myself back to my own room around dawn and fell back into another few hours of dreamless yet fitful slumber.

We arrive at the arena in the late afternoon. The other Strategos are cheerless and quiet as we reach the center of the field—twenty-three wolves and riders arranged in a perfect circle.

The arena looms massive in the slanted sunlight, its tiered rows already packed with chattering spectators. There are more people here now than there were for the Voice Trial. I wonder if the promise of certain bloodshed has drawn them in. Nobles in their finery crowd the upper levels while the other packs fill the lower seats.

Since the Purge is done pack by pack, the three others wait in the stands during each Purging. Of course we drew the short straw.

Strategos is going first.

The king's elevated platform dominates the western wall, draped in lush fabrics of royal purple and gold. King Cyril sits with deceptive nonchalance on his ornate throne, that infamous wolf-pommeled sword at his hip.

Audelie, a Phylax Rawbond, is perched on the older man's lap. She's the… companion… he's chosen for the Trials. It's no wonder why; she's stunningly beautiful with long, dark hair and glittering emerald eyes. He gropes her chest over her clothes while she smiles widely and placidly, and my stomach twists in disgust.

She's a visceral reminder that, to the king, we're merely objects for his entertainment and pleasure.

But even Audelie is dressed in her fighting leathers today. She might be the king's chosen one, but she's still part of a pack, and will still have to participate in the Purge when it's her turn.

Killian stands at his father's right hand. My eyes are drawn to him despite myself. His presence is both a comfort and a worry. I don't want him to see me die today, but if things go wrong, at least the last thing I get to see will be his face.

Stark is also on the king's balcony in his place of honor, dressed in unbroken black, his dark hair slicked neatly back. Our eyes meet, as usual, and the malicious smugness in his gaze says it all.

Today is the day you die, princess.

An avalanche of violence unleashes inside me, the shadows around the arena growing long and strange. For once, I'm almost glad the bastard is here. I needed that extra bit of motivation to prove the fucker wrong.

Hopefully.

I grit my teeth and stiffen my spine. If I die today, I'm sure as shit not going to go down without a fight.

I turn to Anassa, feeling her predatory focus grow sharper.

She meets my gaze when I put my hand on her shoulder.

"Stay on my back, no matter what."

I don't have time to answer.

All at once, the wolves look up toward the king, responding to some silent signal. He has the *Diren Blæd* sword in his hands, and like he did at Presentation, King Cyril thrusts it into the platform floor at his feet.

With that, the test begins.

In a flash, I'm on Anassa's back, opening myself wide to our connection. I catch a flash of something pass between her and the other wolves. Not words, exactly, but intentions, judgments. They're not letting any of the riders tap into the pack unity today; the time to impress them with our abilities has passed.

With a start, I realize they're deciding who's a target—who among us needs to die for the pack to grow stronger.

If any consensus is reached, I'm not privy to it.

The wolves begin to move, circling and passing each other in a bizarre dance that makes no sense to human eyes. But there's a terrible purpose to it, written in the savage lines of their muscled haunches.

A flash of movement catches my eye just before the chaos starts —a massive silver wolf lunging for Anassa's flank. It's Pietr, one of Perielle's friends.

Anassa spins, faster than I knew she could, and I throw all my focus into staying on her back, tuning every sense to our connection.

Our minds snap together with an odd, psychic click, and suddenly we're moving as one.

We turn in perfect synchrony to face our attacker, and I catch sight of the king leaning forward in his seat, that strange sword gleaming in the dying light.

Then my awareness narrows with Anassa's. There's no more king, no more crowd.

There is nothing now but the Purge.

Pietr's wolf lunges with impossible speed, darting in and out as the other wolves circle around us. We've been chosen—marked again for *my* weakness.

Our determination hardens into killing resolve. Through our bond flows pure instinct—when to duck, when to weave, how to use our massive bulk to throw off the timing of Pietr's silver wolf. We're one body, one mind, moving together like we've trained for years instead of weeks.

Killing resolve is joined by a wild electricity I recognize distantly as joy. The joy of the hunt—of a predator going in for the kill.

In a blur of vicious excitement, Anassa's teeth find Pietr's wolf's flank. The scent of hot blood fills her nose, rich with a thousand primal messages. I can taste it on her tongue, feel the droplets peppering her fur.

The silver wolf falls back, shaking off the pain, her rider still in place. Our fight is just beginning, but the first blood has been drawn.

The hunt is on.

All around us, the arena erupts in violence. We turn in unison as two more Bonded pairs approach, falling in with Pietr to form a coordinated team bent on taking Anassa down.

One of them is Perielle and her direwolf. The woman sits tall and proud on her mount, Jonah's love bites visible on her neck.

Our focus spirals into a razor's edge.

Perielle radiates confidence—*arrogance*.

Weakness.

We can smell it on her. See it in the feverish glow of cruelty in her eyes.

And so can the others.

There is no room for her kind of posturing in a pack. Packs demand unity, and Perielle's cliquey, cruel instincts will always end up dividing us. It matters not that her direwolf has a mate. It's a sacrifice that must be made for Strategos's protection.

I can hear Anassa's instruction to the other wolves, and in synchronicity, the word comes out of my mouth. *"Her."*

Her decision is my decision, too. Shadows are edging into my vision now, making me hunger for Perielle's death.

She doesn't sense the moment the wolves' focus shifts, crystalizing into fatal judgment—but her wolf does.

In a single practiced movement, Perielle's wolf bucks her off. She lands in the dirt with a bone-jarring impact—right at the feet of the other three wolves.

Anassa lunges forward, her massive jaws closing around Perielle's throat. I get a flash of the woman's shocked expression just before Anassa's fangs tear through flesh and ligaments. Blood arcs through the air as the other wolves move in to finish Perielle off.

With a jolt of horror, my mind pulls away from Anassa, realizing this was all planned by the wolves, coordinated from the very start. Our fight with Pietr was a distraction—bait to draw out Perielle's arrogance. To prove her weakness.

She was marked for death before we ever entered the arena.

"Stay focused!" Anassa snarls in my mind, furious at my withdrawal.

Survival instinct snaps me back into our connection. I cannot risk putting myself at odds with my wolf—or I might end up like Perielle, who lies broken on the ground, her blood soaking into the drains in the dirt.

Perielle's wolf lays down in the dirt next to her, their severed bond killing them both.

The other two wolves disperse as one, moving to join the others in their deadly dance.

Anassa's satisfaction radiates through my body. There's no cruelty in it—at least, not precisely. But there is pleasure. Gratification for an important task efficiently completed.

The pack will be stronger now.

There's no time to process it further. The direwolves draw inward again as the ritual dance continues. Wolves and riders measure each other with cold eyes, trying to identify who will be next.

It doesn't take long.

In a matter of seconds, the wolves zero in on their target and start circling someone again. With a flash of horror, I realize it's Nevah, perched on her dark silver wolf. Her deep brown curls bounce as she turns her head frantically, eyes wide, searching for help.

Izabel and Tomison are closer to her and their wolves bolt over, defending her from the closing pack.

Nevah might be standoffish, but she isn't weak—she doesn't deserve to die.

To my surprise, Anassa's agreement flows along the bond. She's actually listening to me on this. She leaps into the fray, knocking two attackers aside.

I see Nevah's surprise and relief when she realizes we've come to help. Then her face goes hard with resolve.

That's right, you are not *going to die today.*

Four against eighteen isn't great as far as odds go, but to my surprise, the others back off almost immediately. Nevah and her direwolf take the lead and she defends herself against two or three would-be attackers. Izabel, Tomison and I stay behind her as additional defense if she needs it.

Again, I catch snatches of communication between Anassa and the other wolves—just enough to understand that they aren't willing to go against all four of us if we believe Nevah is worthy.

For a moment, I think that might be the end of it, but the wolves prove me wrong. Before the test is done, another two pairs fall, each death seemingly predetermined among the direwolves.

When the bellow of a horn announces the end of the Strategos purge, the arena floor is once again painted with blood and gore.

Twenty Bonded pairs remain standing. But the fighting isn't done yet; three packs left to go.

As the crowd cheers and servants drag away the bodies, Anassa's mind prods at mine, offering what feels almost like… comfort.

"We survived," I say to her in relief. *"But that still sucked."* Every time I blink, I see Perielle's quick look of shock before her throat was torn out. It happened so quickly she almost couldn't process it.

And her blood is on my hands.

"I don't regret any of it," Anassa tells me, *"and you shouldn't either. But you chose well in coming to Nevah's aid."*

"Nevah would've done just fine without our help," I say, eying the woman as she bids her large wolf goodbye. Nevah has an unbelievable strength to her. I only hope that she'll start to open up to the rest of us more, now. That she'll realize that friendship can be a strength, too.

Anassa nods to me and then leaves with the rest of the Strategos direwolves, back through the large door that will take them to their pack terraces. I fall in with Izabel and Tomison as we head toward the stands to watch the remainder of the gruesome Trial unfold.

As we near the seats, my gaze drifts upward, toward the beacon of Killian in the stands.

I can't help it; I smile at him, and his handsome face splits into a responding grin. He shoots me a quick thumbs up that I'm positive no one clocked.

I made it. I survived. We have more time together. I have more time to save Saela.

But when I sit down in my uncomfortable wooden seat, the hair raises at the back of my neck.

Stark's eyes are narrowed on me, his arms crossed over his chest, the dark kill tattoos on his hands visible from even this distance.

He saw us.

CHAPTER THIRTY-ONE

The Strategos anteroom is heavy with shared grief as we return from the Purge Trial. There isn't a lot of talking, but everyone clusters together. Even those who usually stand apart, like Nevah, seek the comfort of the group. I find myself drawn in as well.

All twenty of us sit around the roaring fireplace, soaking in its glow. Low conversation ensues—discussions of how we each might spend our day off, which family members we'll visit, what news we'll share. But the excitement is muted.

Overshadowed by the choice we made as a pack to execute three of our fellow Rawbonds. At the moment, caught up in the Trial, it felt like the right decision, despite its brutality. But now...

Eventually, people start to drift toward the bunkroom. No parties tonight, it seems. I'm grateful for that.

I retreat to my own room with a bone-weary sense of relief, thinking of my bed. Something tells me I won't be finding sleep quickly, though. The blood on the arena floor stains my mind every time I close my eyes.

It was hard dealing the death, but it was just as hard watching the other packs engage in it. Daemos culled *five* of their own; Jonah was on a tear after watching his direwolf's mate die. What got Perielle killed in Strategos—arrogance and cruelty—is apparently an asset for Daemos. I'm going to need to watch my back more than ever around him.

I've just finished changing into a clean shirt and pants when there's a sharp knock at the door.

Dammit, what now?

I open the door impatiently.

Stark stands on the other side.

Fear darts up my spine in a hot rush and I instinctively let out a small gasp. Why is he here at this hour? Did he finally come to make good on all his threats?

Does he want to confront me about the moment he saw between Killian and me in the arena?

"Princess," he says by way of greeting, his voice more frigid than the snowstorm outside.

Before I can speak, he forces his way inside, crowding me back from the doorway.

I stiffen as he invades my personal space, my heart thumping. He slams the door behind him, then looks at me, his expression is unreadable in the dim lamplight. There's something different about his posture than usual. I can't quite put my finger on it.

Every instinct tells me to back away, get out, but I hold my ground. The room is suffocatingly small with his huge frame in it. He towers over me, all chest and shoulders and unforgiving muscle.

The scent of amber and musk tickles my nose, faint, but rich.

"Why are you—" I start.

At the same moment, he pulls something out of his pocket. A familiar needle and a small pot of ink.

Oh.

Perielle's blonde hair, matted in blood. The command to kill her coming out of my own mouth as shadows urged me toward murder.

The one death from today that is definitely on my hands more than anyone else's.

Stark seems to read the memory on my face. His expression turns somber, and he gestures to the chair beside my little desk.

Right.

I pull the chair into the center of the room and sit, unbuttoning the top of my shirt to give him access to my neck.

This feels... Fuck, I don't even know. I've never been alone with him before. I've never seen him so gloomy, either. There's no aura of impending violence around him—none of the usual malice in his eyes.

He looks almost... mournful.

It sets everything inside me on edge and the discomfort bubbles up into words.

"This must thrill you. I didn't die today but you still get a chance to hurt me," I say, my voice biting. His eyes flash dangerously, confirming my suspicion. "Do I alone get the good fortune of a tattoo?"

The faint tremble in my voice belies the flippant tone but his jaw ticks at my antagonization.

"Everyone who made the final call on a death, whose direwolf killed one of their pack members, is receiving their marks," he says tersely. He steps closer beside me, needle in hand, one knee brushing my leg. "You're my fourth visit tonight."

"You really know how to make a girl feel special," I joke as he grabs my jaw with rough fingers, pushing my head to one side.

"You're *special*, all right," he mutters darkly. For some reason, his responding joke makes the faint tremble inside me grow stronger, radiating outwards.

As the needle bites into my skin, I realize what that feeling is.

I survived. *I survived.*

I might make it through this. I might save my sister.

But at what cost? Her life matters to me. It's *all* that matters to me. Yet is it worth so many other lives in exchange? This is the second person I've killed since I've been here—third, actually, counting the Nabber.

Three deaths on my hands. Who am I to say that she matters more?

My own eyes blur slowly with tears and I try to sink into the sweet sting of the pain, with no success.

"This doesn't seem like an achievement," I hear myself whisper.

The needle pauses against my throat. "Achievement?" Stark's laugh is harsh, devoid of humor. "Is that what you think these are?"

Confused, I turn my head to look up at him. "They're not?"

His expression darkens, one hand rising to the intricate patterns that decorate his own neck. "These aren't trophies, princess," he says, "they're reminders."

Stark's eyes are pitch black in the dim chamber, but they gleam with emotion, reflecting the lamplight like banked coals.

"We cannot afford to forget the sacrifices we must make," he says, voice dropping to a rumble that prickles along my skin. "Every life we've had to take to maintain the pack's strength. Every person who didn't make it. Every loss is recorded in our flesh so we never forget the price of survival."

His fingers fall away from the marks on his neck, and for the first time, I really look at them.

Not trophies, I muse, a little ashamed that I ever made such an assumption. *Reminders.*

Stark's voice drops lower as I silently count the losses ingrained on his skin like claw marks.

"No one wants these tattoos, princess," he murmurs. "There is no place for pride in war."

My throat tightens as he bends over me once more. The needle returns to my skin. The pain is a distant burn now, dulled by grim revelation. It's a balm, in a way, knowing that the tattoos aren't worn as badges of honor—the trophies of heartless killers.

The knowledge casts Stark in a new light. It casts all the Bonded in a new light. Every mark on their bodies represents a day like today. A death like Perielle's.

A cruel necessity made unavoidable by war.

It's right that they—that we—should be marked forever by them. That the inner scars of pain and loss should show outwardly for all to see. For all to remember.

"You should give me a third," I say quietly, and Stark stills above me. His jaw tightens, making that scar alongside it jump underneath his light scruff.

His eyes slide slowly down to mine, his hand still clenched on my chin. "Who?" he says, his voice low and carrying an edge.

"Not—not another Rawbond," I say, my mouth suddenly dry, trying not to cower at the intense look he's giving me. "Just… someone else. But I should remember it."

He stares at me, hard, for another silent moment and then nods, going back to the needle.

Relief rushes through me when he doesn't ask questions. No part of me mourns the man I killed in the dungeon, but I refuse to forget the high cost of finding my sister.

The price of survival.

A strange and unexpected sense of comfort blossoms inside me, though it does little to dispel the grief.

When Stark is done, he leans down to lick the wound clean as custom dictates. His hair brushes my cheek, then the wet heat of his tongue traces the marks he made in blood and ink.

My body responds with a fierce rush of arousal, like before, even as my mind reels in denial. I clench my teeth against it, terrified Stark will read it in my face or posture.

I tell myself it's just exhaustion—a physiological reaction triggered by vulnerability in the aftermath of today's violence and loss.

It feels like a lie, though.

I can sense Anassa listening. I almost expect her to call me out—to challenge the thought—but she doesn't. She's been silent through all of this.

His work done, Stark leaves my room without a word, closing the door quietly behind him.

I rise and go to the little mirror on the wall, peering at the new tattoos. They blend perfectly with the first one, creating a shadowed band with three points that makes me think again of a collar.

When I touch the swollen skin, my fingers come away smeared with blood and saliva.

THE NEXT MORNING, as I prepare for the trip home, I'm vividly aware of the new tattoo. It stings even now, a constant reminder of yesterday's events.

It's strange to think of going back to my neighborhood. My old clothes are gone—disposed of in the aftermath of the Ascent. I'll have to go home dressed in the clothes of a Strategos Rawbond recruit.

The uniform is simple and unadorned, especially compared to what the Bonded wear, but I'm going to stand out in the quarters, even so.

What will everyone back home think, seeing me like this?

I've gotten used to fine fabrics tailored perfectly to my body, I realize. That gives me a spurt of shame, but it's short-lived.

I know now what being Bonded really means.

My hand rises unconsciously to the tattoo, which has already begun to scab over.

I can't be ashamed of what I've become, even if I'm still not sure I like it. Being ashamed would cheapen everything I've been through. Every death I've witnessed.

Every life I've taken.

It's all for Saela, I remind myself. *It's worth it, so long as I get her back.*

In the Rawbond common lounge, yesterday's mournful mood has dispersed. There's an excited energy from all the other Rawbonds who are heading home to see their families. I spot Henrey sitting by himself, picking at a plate of breakfast cakes, and make my way toward him.

"Hey," he says, looking up as I sit down across from him. I notice there's a new reddened tattoo on his own neck this morning. "Congrats on, you know, not dying."

"Yet," I remind him. "Not dying *yet*. But thanks, you too. What are you going to do today?"

Henrey shrugs. He's from Blumenfall, which is a seaside fiefdom leagues away. It would take at least a week for him to journey there normally, though likely he could make it in only a couple days on the back of his wolf.

Still, he won't be going home for a visit. Guess us commoners who aren't from Bonded City weren't really considered when this special treat was devised.

"I might go into the city, to the commoner side," he says. "I don't really have much money to shop, but we have that ball tonight. For Presentation, I borrowed a formal jacket from my packmate Olivier but…"

He doesn't need to finish that sentence. Four wolves tore Olivier to pieces last night. One of them was Henrey's.

Can't borrow clothes from a dead man.

"There's a second-hand clothes shop in the Northern Quarter that carries formal wear," I tell him, explaining where it is. We never could afford anything from there, but I liked to look through the window when I'd take Mother to her medic.

It's silly to have to worry about dressing appropriately when we just witnessed so much bloodshed, but Henrey and I both know that tonight's ball is just another Trial in a beautiful costume.

It's another opportunity for the two of us to blend in… or draw a target.

We chat for a few more minutes about shops I like, supplies Henrey hopes to pick up in the day off, and then I grab a couple of buttered rolls from the breakfast table and retreat back to my room. I don't have much appetite.

A few minutes later, Izabel bursts in without knocking, dressed in a deep purple riding suit that screams of Bonded wealth. Her long hair has been artfully arranged like usual, the silver streak prominently displayed.

"Meryn!" she exclaims, practically bouncing with enthusiasm. "I'm ready to go, what about you? Before we left for the Trials, my parents said they'd throw me and Venna a big luncheon if we made it through to today, with our whole extended family—well, everyone who's not at the front, that is. They're all *dying* to hear about training, I'm sure. Are you going to see anyone other than your mother?"

"Probably not," I mutter, lifting my collar to make sure it covers my fresh tattoo. I don't want to draw attention to it at home. "I'll just check on her. Maybe visit with my neighbor, Igor."

She brightens. "Oh, you mean the one who trained you to fight?"

I nod, thinking of Igor's familiar scowl. Funny how the idea of his sour old face can make me so warm. So that's one good thing about going home, I guess.

The rest of it is going to be just plain weird.

Izabel seems to sense my sober mood. She perches on the end of my bed and tilts her head. "Do you want to talk about it?"

We've spent so much time together over the past two months that she's collected all of my history, in pieces here and there. She knows that my mother is mentally ill, that I had to raise Saela practically on my own.

Izabel must be able to see that I'm dreading this little family visit, even after all the darkness we've been through.

Killian has continued to check in with Mother regularly and says she's doing fine, but I'm terrified of finding her lost to her delusions again, talking to people that aren't there. I don't even have a good update for her about Saela.

I shake my head and Izabel takes that in stride.

"Well, don't forget about tonight," she says. "You need to be back by sundown to get ready for the Forging Ball. It's important! All the nobles will be there. Maybe you'll even meet someone, like I hope I will."

Despite the gross implications—I still can't get over the fact that the nobles treat the Rawbonds like a meat market—my face heats.

I bend down, futzing with the laces of my boots so Izabel can't see that I'm flustered. I still haven't told her about Killian, though I know she suspects I'm seeing my "castle heartbreaker" again, since I haven't been around as much. She's been a good friend in not pressuring me about it.

He'll be there tonight, of course. Will everyone be able to tell by the way that we look at each other?

Would I want that, even?

I think back to his words two nights ago. *"Give me permission to claim you in front of the whole world, and I will."*

"Yeah, yeah," I grumble, finally straightening. "I'll be there. I don't have anything to wear, though."

"Just pick something up from home," Izabel says.

I snort. "Izabel, we don't typically have ball gowns hanging around in the commoner neighborhoods. The closest I had was a nameday dress that got so worn down over the years that we eventually turned it into a pillowcase."

"Oh. Right." She pauses. "Well, that's no problem! Venna and I will bring back something for you, so don't worry about it."

I give her a lopsided smile, hoping it doesn't look pained. I'm grateful to have her help, even if it makes me feel like a charity case. But I'm not looking forward to being the twins' dress-up doll again, particularly since the Bonded try to wear as little clothes as possible for these functions.

"Nothing too skimpy, please?" I ask.

Izabel laughs like I made a joke and bounces up off my bed. "No promises!" she calls as she sails out the door with a wave.

Well, that's ominous.

ANASSA MEETS me at the castle gates for the trip home. We don't talk. There's no room in my brain for conversation while I grapple with the experience of riding her through the quarters.

There was never a question in my mind about whether I'd bring her. Riding her will get me home and back faster, letting me have more time with my mom. But it's more than that. It feels important that my mother meets her, this being who has become a part of me.

We head through the Northern Quarter, then onward to the Central Market, the same place I watched Stark execute that deserter.

Anassa ignores the people we pass, though I can sense her awareness of them—of their fear. They leap out the way when they see us coming, pressing themselves to the walls and yanking their children back as though afraid the wolf will devour them. Even the merchants posted at the sides of the road abandon their carts to shrink away from Anassa's bulk.

Most of them don't even look at me. Not that I mind—it's actually kind of a relief. The fear and awe in the eyes of those that do leaves me queasy with discomfort.

And here I was worried what people would think seeing me in my Rawbond uniform.

We take a turn from Central toward Eastern, finally back to my own quarter.

Anassa's massive paws leave deep prints in the muddy snow that chokes the streets where I played as a child. Where I picked fights with bigger boys after my father died at war. Where I carried loads of other people's laundry to pay for my mother's medicine.

The same streets where my sister walked to school and back.

Everything seems smaller and dirtier than it did before. Surreal after the weeks I've spent in luxury.

Much to my dismay, I feel even more out of place here than I did at the castle.

Shit. The fucking *irony*.

Just two months ago, I was one of these people, cursing under my breath as Bonded riders invaded my streets. Bristling with indignation that we should all be forced to scatter because some uppity Bonded *deigned* to walk by. Back then, it seemed the big wolves were willing to trample anyone who got in their way.

Now, from Anassa's back, I see the truth.

She's aware of every one of them, every movement, every possible point of interaction. She adjusts her stride to avoid collision, to give people the time to move away. Yet she doesn't look directly at any one of them, knowing that even a moment of eye contact could cause a panic.

There's no empathy in her actions, per se. But there is a sort of kindness—under the usual hard-edged lupine pragmatism, that is. These people are innocent, and they're not a threat to her. She has no desire to frighten them.

I'm grateful for that. And a little ashamed again, too, for all the assumptions I made about the Bonded.

Yes, they've led privileged lives. They have all the luxuries they could ever dream of. But in exchange, they live on the constant edge of death.

In exchange, they are treated like entertainment for the king and his nobles—in more ways than one. I shudder again, thinking about the excitement in Izabel's eyes as she talked about *meeting someone* tonight.

And Audelie, perched on the king's lap during the Purge with that vacant smile pasted on her face.

All along, my neighbors and I have resented the Bonded. But they're not the enemy. In the end, they are—*we* are—also just toys for the king to use and then throw away. Toy soldiers, to throw against the Siphons. Toy gladiators, to fight for the rich nobles' amusement.

Toy companions, to sleep with and discard.

The commoners shouldn't resent the Bonded. They should resent the nobles… and the king.

The thought is disloyal. Treasonous, even. I push it out of my mind the moment it occurs, worried that if I prod it for too long, it will expand and blossom in my chest like some sort of carnivorous plant.

Our people can't even win a war; we'd never survive a revolution.

We turn onto the street where I was born and raised. I almost don't want to see it through my new eyes. At the same time, the familiar details draw me in.

The ramshackle houses with their rotting wood and muddy walkways. The gutted storefronts and crumbling walls of homes long abandoned. The children scuttling through the streets dressed in lovingly patched rags.

Fuck. It *hurts* to see this, knowing there's nothing I can do to change it right now.

When this day is over, I'll return to my clean bed and my soft sheets. I'll have all the food I could ever want. All the warmth and comfort these people have never known.

Killian could do something about it, though, when he takes his father's place. We've talked about it, these past weeks. He'd spread out the resources more evenly between the Bonded and the rest of Nocturna's populace. He'd stop hosting lavish parties for the nobles, and force those lords who have never worked a day in their lives to stop plundering from their people.

That treasonous voice is back. *Why wait for the king's natural death, when there's someone more fit to rule the throne?*

"There is," Anassa agrees, hearing my thoughts.

"Stop," I tell her. *"We are not planning a mutiny on our day off."*

By the time we arrive at my mother's house, I'm sick with dread. There it is—that tiny, drab house.

But… the sagging roof is no longer sagging. The walls have been properly patched up for once and finished with new stucco. The crooked front gate has been installed upright. And there aren't any holes in the porch awning anymore.

Killian. He hasn't been just checking in on my mother; he's been putting her world back together, piece by piece, in my absence.

Heat builds behind my eyes and I take a deep breath of the cold air, clearing my throat. I am not going to weep in the streets like a child.

As Anassa halts outside the gate, her bulk casting one long shadow that swallows the whole front of the house, the neighbors stare from their windows.

I don't look as I dismount and head for the door. I don't want to see the awe in their faces—or the resentment. I don't want to see myself reflected as a stranger in their gazes.

My heart thrums in my ears as I approach the door. I pause on the stoop, gripped by a sudden confusion.

Should I knock? Or just walk in? This is my home, but somehow, it doesn't feel like home anymore.

Before I can make up my mind, the knob turns. The door opens.

And I close my eyes, terrified to find out which version of my mother I'm going to get today.

CHAPTER THIRTY-TWO

"Meryn!" Mother cries, and my eyes fly open. She stands in the doorframe with warm firelight glowing behind her. Her dark, graying hair is neatly combed and plaited down her back. There's a healthy glow to her olive-toned skin, her cheeks flushed. She's wearing a dress that looks freshly washed.

And her eyes—they're bright and clear. Gone is the vacant stare.

She throws her arms around my neck and pulls me in as I blink in confusion.

"Blessed Goddess, I can't believe you're here!" she cries. I don't know whether to hug her back or pull away and inspect her, so I pat her on the back. "Lee had told me you'd get a day off, but it's still a wonderful gift to hold you in my arms."

Eventually she pulls away and I notice she has an apron on, smeared with flour. She's been *baking*.

"Mother?" I hear myself say, staring in complete disbelief. "Is that really you?"

She laughs. "Who else would I be?" Her gaze snags behind me and her eyes go wide with wonder.

She's spotted Anassa.

"Oh," Mother breathes, stepping past me, "this must be your direwolf."

"Right, yeah," I turn and say awkwardly, "Mother, this is Anassa. Anassa, this is my mother."

I expect the direwolf to be her usual self: aloof, standoffish, maybe even a touch threatening. To my utter astonishment, Anassa turns to face my mother... and *bows.*

The fuck?

Mother gasps as Anassa goes down on her haunches, lowering her enormous head to rest on her front paws.

"Oh, she's *beautiful*, Meryn!" Mother gushes softly, stepping closer. "That fur... and those eyes!" She lifts a hand as though to touch the wolf and then thinks better of it, shaking her head in quiet awe. "She is special, isn't she? A queen among wolves."

Anassa just blinks her yellow eyes at my mother in silent agreement.

"That's all it takes to win you over, huh?" I drawl through the bond. *"Flattery? You don't even bow for the king."*

Anassa's mind ripples with irritation. *"I give respect where respect is due."*

I roll my eyes.

"Speaking of beautiful," my mother says, turning to me. She lifts one hand to touch my shorn silver-white hair. "This suits you."

"Oh. Thanks," I mumble, touched by the pride in her eyes.

"Come, let's go inside," Mother says, then glances back at my wolf. "Anassa, I'm sorry you can't fit in our little house. I'll bring you a snack later." She glances at me. "Is that alright? Will she eat human food?"

I look over my shoulder at Anassa, who says nothing—though she seems pleased by my mother's fussing.

"Probably not," I say. "She hunts her own food in the mountains outside the castle."

My mother nods. "Ah. Probably doesn't want a slice of sour-dough, then."

As we step into the fire-lit warmth of the cottage, I'm struck by a wave of nostalgia. I haven't seen the house this tidy and bright since before Saela was born.

The floor has been swept, the windows cleaned, every surface dusted. The little fireplace is blazing and the lamps are all lit. The whole place smells like baking bread and Mother's spiced beef stew —the one she used to make on holidays when Dad was still alive.

"I guess Ki—Lee also told you I'd bonded with Anassa," I say, following Mother to the living room. "I wasn't sure you knew I'd become Bonded."

"Oh, yes!" she says, gesturing for me to sit beside her on the couch. "Lee visits me every week. He's been such a dear, bringing me food and firewood and anything else I might need. He also brought some tradesmen to fix up the house, did you see?"

"I did," I say, my throat tightening. "It looks really nice."

"I don't ask for anything, mind you!" she hurries to reassure me. "The last thing I want is to put him out. He really is a good one, that Lee." She leans over to pat my leg, smiling conspiratorially. "Definitely a keeper."

My cheeks heat as I think yet again about his desire to claim me publicly.

Clearly, my mother doesn't know yet that "Lee" is the crown prince. What would she think if she knew the truth? Would she be even more excited? Would she warn me off the relationship, worried to see her daughter involved with a royal?

The urge to confess everything rises inside me with startling strength. Mother hasn't been this lucid for years. I almost forgot how I used to confide in her—how we'd sit by the fire just like this and I'd tell her about my day or whatever else was on my mind.

Suddenly I miss that so much I could cry. I want to lay down with my head in her lap like I did as a child and tell her every-thing—about the castle, the training, Anassa, Killian. I want her to pet my hair and tell me everything will be alright, like she used to.

But I shove it all back down again. I'm not that little girl anymore. Life forced me to grow up and there's no turning back the clock.

I grab her hand. "Mother, I'm really glad Lee is taking care of you. I'm sorry I can't be here."

When she starts to protest, I cut her off.

"No, please listen," I say fiercely. "This isn't for nothing, me being gone. I'm going to fight my way through to the end of the training. Then I'm going to find Saela and bring her home—even if I have to kill every Siphon in Astreona to do it. I swear, I'm *going* to bring her home."

Mother's eyes fill with tears even as her lips curve in a proud, pained smile. She clasps my hand between her own.

"I know you will," she whispers. "I have so much faith in you, Mer. You've been our protector all these years since your father passed. I know you won't let us down now." Her face crumples with grief and regret. "I'm so sorry that I haven't been well—that I couldn't be the mother you deserved."

My breath catches in my chest.

Haven't I wished for that, too? Wasn't I just thinking I missed that mother, the kind of parent every child should have? One who's dialed in enough to meet their kid's basic needs? One who comforts and consoles and cares for their family?

And, yet…

"Don't say that," I whisper, eyes prickling with tears as I battle my internal war. I'm pissed about the card Saela and I were dealt, but I can't be mad at *her* about it. "It isn't your fault you've been ill. I'm just glad you're feeling better." I sniffle and wipe my eyes quickly. "Speaking of that—what's going on? Did you get new medicine, or…?"

"No, not at all." She shakes her head, shrugging helplessly. "It's the strangest thing. I've been better for weeks now. I would have gone back to working at the laundry again, but Lee and Igor insist I stay at home."

"Good," I say. "Home is where you belong. As long as they're taking care of you."

"They are," she says. "I feel a bit guilty, relying on everyone. But they've been so kind. The other neighbors come by to check on me, too."

Before I can respond, there's a knock at the door.

"Get that, will you?" Mother says, rising to go to the kitchen, "I have to take the bread out of the oven."

I nod and cross to the door, already knowing who's waiting on the other side.

Igor looks me over, eyes widening as he takes in my hair—and then yanks me into a bone-crushing hug.

I'm frozen in his grip for a second, stunned by the show of affection, then I throw my arms around him.

"I'm so damn happy you're still alive, kid," he grunts, voice rough with emotion.

I clear my throat awkwardly as he lets me go. "Haven't found Saela yet, though."

He clasps my shoulder, his craggy face grim. "You will."

"At least the Nabbers are under control now, right?" I say, ushering him inside as Mother comes out of the kitchen.

The two of them exchange a confused look.

"Wait. The attacks have stopped," I say, glancing between them, "…right? No more kids are getting taken?"

Igor's face darkens. "No, Meryn. The attacks haven't stopped. In fact, they've increased."

"*What?*"

Mom steps forward, reaching for me with a worried grimace. "Mer—"

"Three more children were taken in the past week alone," says Igor, his face pinched. "What made you think they'd stopped?"

A cold knot of fear and disbelief hardens in my stomach. The Nabber we questioned. The warehouse. It should have stopped their operation.

Did something go wrong? Were Killian's guards not able to find it?

I wear a new kill mark on my throat for that man, and yet the attacks continue. I've failed.

Igor claps me on the shoulder again, snapping me out of my frantic internal spiral.

"Listen, that ain't your problem right now," he says in his gruff way. "You need to focus on surviving your training—*then* you can get back to saving the world."

"Right," I mutter, resolving to talk to Killian about the Nabbers later. Right now, I just want to spend time with my family. I muster a wry smile. "It's not just the training though. Tonight I have to survive a fucking *ball*."

"Language, Meryn!" Mother exclaims as Igor barks a laugh.

"Sorry, Mother."

"A ball, huh?" Igor quips. "Rather fight a damn Siphon, myself."

"Me, too," I grunt as we gather in the living room once more.

"Oh, stop, you two," Mother says, her eyes glimmering with wistful excitement. "A ball at the castle sounds *wonderful*."

"Not when you're a podunk nobody commoner," I mutter. "One of only two, out of all the Rawbonds this year, I might add. All the others come from Bonded families. One of the fancy gowns they wear to things like this could buy us food for a whole year."

Igor chuckles. "Bet you just love getting all dolled up for those blowhards."

Mother swats at him. "You leave her be. Every girl deserves to wear fancy things now and then."

I huff out a breath. "Yeah, sure. Except I don't *have* fancy things."

Mother brightens. "Oh, but you do! Come with me—come, come!"

I cast Igor a bewildered look as I follow mom into her bedroom. He just gives me a lopsided grin.

Everything else aside, it's really good to see him smile. To see both of them smile.

Mother is already lifting the threadbare rug and bending to the loose board where she hides all her most precious possessions. While she digs her treasures out with purposeful intensity, I take in the familiar room.

Like everything else, it seems much smaller and dingier after weeks in the castle. It's clean, though, and the bed is made. Another sign of my mother's improved health.

"Here," she says, straightening with a familiar pendant in her hand. Sunlight catches on the opal as she holds it out to me, little shards of rainbow light glimmering from deep within the stone.

I open my mouth to protest, but something in my mother's eyes stops me. I've never seen her gaze so clear—so insistent. Her hands tremble slightly as she holds the opal out to me.

"Wear it tonight at the ball," she says. "It needs to be seen."

"Needs to be seen?" I repeat, bewildered. "What do you——?"

The words die in my throat as my mother's eyes glaze over. My heart drops—I know that vacant stare all too well. But in another instant, it's gone. Her eyes clear once more.

"Here, let me put it on you."

My gaze is drawn to the pendant as she lifts it. It's light against my skin, despite the stone's size and the intricate gold work into which the opal is set. It's clearly very old, tarnished with age and disuse.

It's beautiful, and far nicer than anything else I own, but I know it will look antiquated next to whatever glittering jewels the other Rawbonds wear tonight.

When Mother places it around my neck and the opal settles over my sternum, I realize the stone is unnaturally warm.

It feels almost…alive.

My mother's hands linger on the clasp, and I catch a rapid series of expressions crossing her face.

Relief, fear, and something that looks almost like triumph.

At the same moment, Anassa's attention focuses on what we're doing. Her sudden interest pulses through the bond.

"What do you care about a necklace?" I ask.

No answer. Just that sense of Anassa listening, watching.

Whatever. I don't have time to question the wolf. The daylight filtering through the window says it's already afternoon. I'll need to return to the castle before long.

I set all other thoughts aside while Mom, Igor, and I sit down to a wonderful meal. It's bittersweet without Saela there, but I tell myself that it's only temporary. Soon enough, we'll all be back together again, safe and sound.

When dusk begins to darken the sky outside, I make my good-byes. Mother gets a little teary. Me, too, if I'm honest. Even Igor's eyes hold a faint gleam of wetness, though he smiles and tells me, "Don't get soft sleepin' on those fancy castle sheets, eh?"

"Eat shit," I say, laughing through my tears.

"Meryn!" my mother scolds.

Igor thumps me on the back and pushes me toward Anassa. "Get lost, kid."

"I love you both," I say with a final wave. "I'll be in touch soon."

I mount Anassa quickly, turning to look back at my childhood home one last time as we go.

Mother stands in the open doorway, one hand raised in parting. A piece of her hair has come out of her neat braid and is whipping around her face in the cold winds.

Nostalgia strikes me again like a slow wave, but it's different now. It comes with a sense of mourning. Of something truly lost. My life has taken an unexpected path—one I never dreamed of, never wanted.

I'm not the person I was the last time I left. I've moved on, whether I like it or not.

And when I graduate, I'll be given housing in the Bonded City, in the Strategos neighborhood. I'll be expected to live there whenever I'm not at the front. It's still unclear to me whether I'll be able to bring my mom—and Saela—to live with me.

Maybe that's why I get the overwhelming feeling that this it—the final goodbye.

This place will never truly be my home again.

CHAPTER THIRTY-THREE

When I return to the castle, the Strategos common area is buzzing with pre-ball excitement. The air is thick with perfume and anticipation. My fellow Rawbonds dart back and forth between rooms in various states of undress, as usual unashamed to show a little skin, helping each other with hair and makeup and complicated clothing.

I'm still dreading the ball, but I find myself warmed by the air of cheerful chaos. It's quite a contrast to yesterday's grief—and to the usual military precision of our daily lives.

"Meryn! There you are!"

Izabel and Venna erupt from the dorm room and corner me with identical conspiratorial grins. The eagerness in their expressions fills me with half affection and half dread.

"Hey," I say cautiously.

"Don't 'hey' us like this is just any old day!" Izabel exclaims, grabbing my arm. "We have a royal *ball* to prepare for! Come see the dress we brought for you!"

Venna takes my other arm and they tug me forcefully into the dorm.

Embarrassment and gratitude keep me silent as they present the dress to me. It has an off-the shoulder silver lace bodice and a black satin skirt with a large slit up the side. The cut of the bodice is low and revealing.

I can't say I'm surprised by the style; after all, the goal of tonight for the Bonded is to look as sexy as possible in front of all the nobles there to ogle them.

"Now, we know it's a bit dated," Izabel says apologetically, as if I have any clue what up-to-date Bonded fashions look like, or would be offended by the relevancy of a dress. "It was the most modest thing we had, though. It's only been worn once—to our cousin's sixteenth nameday celebration a few years ago. You have fantastic legs, so we thought the slit would suit you."

I blink at her. No one has ever told me I have fantastic legs before.

It's amusing that either of them find this dress modest, though.

"What do you think?" Venna asks. "Do you like it?" They both gaze hopefully at me.

"It's beautiful," I say, taking the dress. "Thank you. Really."

Izabel frowns. "You're sure? You seem a little upset."

"No. Shit. I'm sorry," I mutter. "It's not the dress." I pause, thinking about my trip to the city—about Mom and Igor and leaving my home behind. "I just have a lot on my mind."

Izabel nods in understanding. "You're nervous about the ball. I totally understand. But don't worry, okay? Like I told you before Presentation, you don't need to hook up with any nobles if you don't want to, it's not required of us."

I muster a smile and another thank you. I'm not sure I could even explain what I'm feeling—or that they would understand if I could.

"Go try it on!" Venna says. "We'll help you with your hair and makeup after we're done getting ready."

I nod and head for my room, relieved to have a moment alone. I need to get my head screwed on straight. The ball might be a party, but it's not just for fun. This, like everything here, is another Trial. We've survived our individual packs' culling, but now we're going to be thrown into a social competition.

Everyone tonight will be trying to impress King Cyril and the hundreds of nobles visiting from the seven fiefdoms in Nocturna. They'll all be watching, judging. I need to be clear and alert. Ready for anything.

We're all still jockeying for rank within our own packs, too. After my survival in the Purge, the competitive side of me is coming alive again. I'm not just trying to avoid death anymore, I'd like to actually earn the respect of the other Rawbonds.

Anassa growls an agreement.

Hopefully this dress will be enough to help me look the part of the role I'm ready to claim.

I take a steadying breath as I push open my bedroom door—and then freeze on the threshold.

What the…

A dress lies waiting on my bed—a masterpiece of emerald silk and delicate black lace. Not the kind I described to Mom and Igor.

This dress could feed our whole neighborhood for a year.

I approach it slowly, Izabel and Venna's gift forgotten in my arms.

The layered emerald skirts cascade like a waterfall, each tier trimmed with exquisitely beaded black lace that glitters in the light. The fitted bodice boasts more of the same beaded lace, emphasizing the heart-shaped neckline and capping the sleeveless shoulders in delicate, feathery veils.

It's stunning, more akin to the extravagant gowns that the nobles wear to watch us fight than the lewd pieces of tied together fabric that the Bonded like to pretend are dresses.

Beside this miraculous confection lies matching black satin gloves and a pair of elegant heels.

I run a finger along the dress and gasp when I realize it's decorated not in beads, but in actual *jewels*. Tiny sprays of emerald and obsidian in delicate swirls.

Only one person could be responsible for this.

There's no note—no indication whatsoever of who left the dress here for me. But of course, I know. There's only one person in this world who would give me such a gift.

Oh, Killian…

My thoughts drift yet again to his words when we were together the other night. Even if I wasn't ready to call him mine in public, this dress says it all. It lays claim to me in a way that words never could. It will tell every person in attendance tonight that I am someone important, someone to be admired.

I set Izabel and Venna's dress aside, hoping they won't be hurt by it. I'm certain they'd want me to wear this one instead.

Suddenly, I want very much to go to this ball, if only to be seen in this dress, this gesture of love.

I wiggle out of my clothes and then slowly and reverently don the dress, careful not to dislodge any of the delicate jewels. It fits perfectly, like it was made for my body alone. Every detail has been considered, every element chosen with care.

This is what it means to be loved by a prince.

The heels are perfect, too. Just the right height, and much more comfortable than heels ought to be. I pull my mother's opal necklace out from underneath the dress. Even though it looks worn and aged compared to the glittering jewels of the dress, it will compliment the outfit perfectly.

For the first time, I wonder if I might dance. It is a ball, after all.

Igor made me take lessons from a neighbor as part of my fight training.

Fighting is a lot like dancing, he said. *You need to move fluidly, every motion precise and controlled. Learning to dance will help you anticipate your opponent's movements and respond in time.*

I laugh softly to myself. Who would have predicted I'd ever need to do *actual* dancing?

With the dress on, I head for the small mirror in my room. It's not enough to see the whole picture, but I'm floored by the woman looking back at me. I saw a warrior seductress after Izabel and Venna's initial make-over—and that was revelation enough.

But now…

The gown transforms me from a fighter into something… ethereal. I barely recognize the elegant woman my reflection presents.

Between the dress and my mother's opal, I look like one of the Bonded for the first time. Like I truly *belong* in this world.

The feeling is foreign and not entirely unpleasant.

When I emerge into the Strategos anteroom, heart pounding, the excited chatter dies. The twins are seated on the couches by the fireplace, Nevah and Tomison beside them. I'm glad to see Nevah hanging out with everyone tonight. They all look up as the room falls quiet and a dozen other heads turn my way.

Wordless shock vibrates the air for a moment before Izabel's delighted squeal shatters the silence.

"Meryn! What in all of Nocturna!"

The twins rush forward to encircle me. Tomison gives an appreciative whistle. Nevah shakes her head in amazement, lips curving into a rueful smile. Across the room, somebody calls, "Damn, Cooper! Looking good!"

The twins pepper me with questions as they draw me back to the couch and start fixing my hair and makeup. Where did I get the dress? Is this a gift from my secret lover? Who *is* he? He must be one of the Bonded—one of the richest ones, too.

I put them off as best I can. "I don't know for sure who it's from. It just appeared in my room."

Izabel gives me a knowing look. "One of these days you're going to *have* to tell us!"

Thankfully, she leaves it at that.

When my hair and make-up are done, there are more exclamations.

"The contrast between your hair and the emerald is just perfect," Izabel says. "You look more like a goddess than ever."

"Otherworldly," Venna interjects.

"Yes!" Izabel says. "You're a mythical being, Meryn. No one will be able to take their eyes off of you."

"I don't know why you're so happy about it," Nevah drawls. "I'm not keen on the competition, myself." She looks at me, mouth twisting into a wry smile. "Nothing personal, Meryn, but I'll be keeping my distance."

"Er… thanks, I guess?" I say, burning with embarrassment.

Tomison chuckles. "It's kinda cute how the big bad street fighter gets all flustered when people tell her she's pretty."

I shoot him a glare and so does Izabel. He just grins.

"You guys look amazing, too, by the way," I say.

The twins are wearing matching backless gowns, but in different colors—Izabel in silver, Venna in black. They're incredibly skimpy, with plunging necklines and clinging, translucent skirts. Nevah's blood-red gown has a wide v-shaped opening in the front that exposes her long, slender legs clear to the upper thigh, and a neckline that goes so low it exposes her belly button. Tomison's suit is perfectly fitted to accentuate his lean frame, the jacket embroidered heavily with silver.

"We do look amazing, don't we?" he says, gaze lingering on Izabel's naked back as she turns to make a last-minute adjustment to my hair.

"I should head back to Kryptos so I can go with my pack," Venna says.

"Yeah, I believe it's time to get moving," says Nevah, nodding to the exit. The other Strategos are already gathering near the door.

When all of us are ready, we join with the other packs in the lounge and make our way through the castle to the royal wing in a long procession. Most of the other Rawbonds haven't been to this part of the castle before. They *ooh* and *ahhh* over the elaborate tapestries and gilded statues that line the wide corridors.

I haven't seen much of the royal wing outside Killian's chambers, either—and always at night, in the dark—but still, it's not exactly new to me. I have to make an effort to appear surprised by the ostentatiousness of it all.

It gets easier as we near the famous central ballroom where the king holds all his most important parties.

I hear orchestral music first, then the corridors swell into a cavernous entryway bracketed by enormous marble staircases with gilded railings. The ballroom doors at the far end are open, towering golden direwolf statues standing sentry on either side.

There are people everywhere, dressed in outrageous finery, some dancing, some milling around with glasses of champagne, talking and toasting. Yet more sit at the many tables arranged around the room. The nobles around the room are clearly marked by their extravagant outfits, which are more modest and more expensive-looking than what the Bonded wear.

The contrast between their clothes and ours has always been noticeable but I'm so much more aware of it now that they're here in front of us and not up in the stands of the arena. I glance around at the other Rawbonds in their barely there clothing and wonder if any of them have the same queasiness about this.

The Bonded are just beautiful, violent dolls for the actual elites.

The music swells as we reach the door.

My gaze is drawn upward to the glitter of a thousand crystals hanging above—a massive chandelier poised over the center of the sprawling dancefloor. Beyond it, the panels of the domed ceiling are painted with elaborate frescoes depicting ancient battles between humans and Siphons—direwolves and their riders frozen in elegant poses of attack.

We pause at the threshold, lined up to wait for our cue. Each Rawbond pack enters in formation, the herald announcing their individual names one by one.

My gaze sweeps the ballroom, taking in the soaring marble columns and automatically noting the various exits. There are wide glass doors at either side of the room leading to spacious balconies. Tall windows look out onto the moonlit royal courtyards below.

Stark is at the edge of the dance floor, dressed in a suit so black it stands out amongst all the glittering dresses. The suit is perfectly tailored, lending a cutting elegance to his warrior's body, empha-sizing the broad shoulders and narrow hips, hugging his long, muscular legs like a second skin.

No gold or silver embroidery for him. No gaudy jewelry, either. Just that deep black suit sucking up the light in the room—like a deliberate defiance against the glamor and pageantry that surround him.

A beautifully cut suit can't hide the wildness that seeps from him like an aura of aggression. It's in the neck tattoos peeking above his perfectly knotted cravat, the dark symbols covering the large hands that hold a glass of champagne.

The signature predatory intensity with which he watches the party, too.

I have to admit, he looks unnervingly good.

But I'm not here for Stark. My eyes veer away from him, searching the crowd until they find Killian.

He's sitting on the dais with his father near the back of the room, dressed in gold and royal purple—looking every bit the crown prince. The cut of his jacket emphasizes his muscular frame, and his burnished-gold hair shines in the light of the thousands of candles and lanterns in this cavernous space. If Stark is a black hole, Killian is a luminous sun. The whole party tilts toward his warmth. Our eyes meet and my heart stutters.

Then the herald cries, "Strategos Rawbonds!"

The air is thick with excitement and nerves as our names are announced one by one.

"Rawbond Izabel Brooks... Rawbond Tomison Thorne....Rawbond Nevah Rivenson..."

Then finally, "Rawbond Meryn Cooper!"

I step into the ballroom, my heart loud in my ears. The weight of countless nobles' gazes presses down on me—the common-born girl who survived the Trials. The outsider in the emerald dress.

Anassa's presence ripples along our bond, carrying her amusement. She finds this human pageantry silly—but there's something else under that. A thread of warning.

Immediately, I start to question her. Does she expect an attack? This isn't going to turn into another bloodbath like the Presentation, is it? Or is she warning me about the lecherous nobles?

"Watch your back," is all she says.

Helpful.

Perturbed, I join the other Rawbonds at our table where we wait for the rest to make their entrance. Audelie, the king's chosen companion, gets both claps and smirks from the nobles when she enters with the Phylax pack.

That roil of disgust is back; they demand we're on display for them, then dare to ridicule us for it?

Audelie's in a white dress that goes up to her neck, with long sleeves and a skirt that hits her ankles... but it's entirely translucent and she's wearing nothing underneath. I realize with muted horror that her full breasts and nipples, and even the curl of hair between her legs, are exposed to the entire ballroom. She keeps her head high as she slinks over to the king's side and arranges herself artfully on his lap.

Monster.

Finally, a few minutes later, everyone is here. The king shoves Audelie off him and rises, voice booming over the ballroom.

"Welcome, everyone, to the Forging Ball," he says with pomp and grandiosity. "I am so pleased to have you all here to celebrate the successful completion of this year's Purge Trial. Please, eat, dance, and enjoy your evening."

With that, he gestures to the orchestra, and the music strikes up again. I catch Killian's deep blue gaze, aching to go to him—but he's already surrounded by a group of young nobles vying for his attention. An uncomfortable spark pings through me.

Jealousy, I realize. We've never been in a position before where I've had to watch him around other women.

Turns out, I fucking hate it.

Almost everyone at our table gets up to join the party. Izabel and Venna are talking beside me, gossiping about the nobles in attendance, their hands fluidly in motion as the clamor of the ballroom starts to make it hard for Venna to hear. I catch something about an affair and a bastard child, but I'm only half listening and watching, trying not to be too obvious as I track Killian's movement through the crowd.

Eventually I lose him in the sea of suits and dresses, though I find myself fielding a lot of curious looks from the other nobles.

Dammit. Where did he go?

I can't help myself—I need to have him in my sights. Standing, I make my excuses to the twins, and start moving purposefully toward the crowd.

Unfortunately, I don't get far before a short, middle-aged man with a bushy mustache and a leer steps into my path. There's a thin, horse-faced woman at his side—his wife, perhaps. She leers at me, too, her lips pulling back from her gummy teeth in what might be an impression of a smile.

"Look at this one, Dinah," says the man—talking *about* me I realize, and not to me. "What an unusual hair color."

The wife reaches out and pokes me in the upper thigh. "Wider hips than the others, though," she says, as if she's appraising cattle. "A bit shorter, too. Common-born, maybe?"

The whole thing shakes me so much that it's thrown off my instincts. I try to step back, my stomach churning, and the man grabs me by the wrist, yanking me toward him.

"Come now, girl," he says, chastising. "We're all here for fun, right? Dinah and I are curious what's underneath that overly demure dress of yours. A bit ill-mannered of you to cover up so much, no?"

Don't punch the nobles, don't punch the nobles, I chant to myself, even though I really, really want to slam my fist in this man's face.

But thankfully, I don't have to. I feel a presence behind me just before a warm, masculine hand touches my back.

Killian.

The nobleman's face pales a little as he looks up in fear behind me. He bows, and then yanks his wife, confused, also into a bow, before dragging her back toward the crowd.

Turning with a smile, I look up into glowering dark eyes.

The smile withers on my lips.

It's Stark. His glare could raise the shadows from the corners of the room and snuff out all the light.

I edge backwards, away from him, even as his hand is still on my back. He's livid, and I've seen what this man can do when he's pissed. I'd like to put as much distance between me and his bad mood as possible.

"What were you doing?" he growls, loudly enough that a couple of people around us shoot him worried looks.

"Considering homicide," I mutter. He doesn't respond so I say,

"None of your business, actually. Thanks for the save, but it's a ball and you're making a scene, so…"

"You're right. We need to keep talking and we're drawing attention." Stark's hand closes around my wrist like an iron vise. "Dance with me."

My thoughts stutter to a stop. I look at his hand, then back into his eyes.

Surely, I didn't hear that right.

I find my voice. "No, thank y—"

He yanks me onto the crowded dance floor. "Wasn't a request, princess."

I have no choice but to fall in line—the blaze of command in his eyes says he's not going to let me go.

My heart is in my throat as he pulls me into his arms. His broad chest fills my vision and his musky, amber cologne tickles my nose.

We fall into step with disconcerting ease, moving together like we've been dance partners for years. He leads like he teaches—with immense force and precision. Even rusty as I am, I have no trouble following. The press of Stark's hand on my waist guides me unerringly, though it feels more like combat than dancing.

When that hand spreads possessively across my back and pulls me closer, I look up at him in shock.

What the fuck is happening right now?

His gaze is narrowed, and drops to my neck.

"Interesting necklace," he says, voice pitched low, oddly intimate and antagonistic at once. "Something so opulent on a commoner might draw the wrong kind of attention. Where'd you get it?"

I brittle instantly. "I'm not a thief, if that's what you're implying."

Stark's lips pull into a cruel smile as he leans down to put his mouth next to my ear, hot breath gusting against my skin. "Well then, you might want to read up on the history of that kind of opal before you start parading it around."

The fuck does that mean?

Before I can demand an explanation, a low, familiar voice interrupts.

"Pardon me. I'd like to cut in."

I turn in surprise as our dance comes to an abrupt halt.

Killian stands an arm's length away, his face a polite mask. But I know him all too well. When he's angry, it comes out in a terrifying calm like this—just like it did when we were with the Nabber in the dungeon. I can see it in the clench of his fists, the tight pull of his smile, the way his eyes are currently skewering Stark.

He's enraged that Stark is touching me like this.

"The lady is spoken for," Stark says sharply, his hand tightening on my waist.

I'm *what?!*

That's it.

I've been trying all night to act like one of these genteel weirdos. To play by the rules that the nobles and the king have set for us, to bend my manners to my own will like one of the Bonded.

But I'm not a polite woman. I'm hard edges and impulse and self-destruction. I don't care if this world hates me for it; I wouldn't have myself any other way.

"I am," I tell Stark, putting my hands on his hard chest and pushing him away forcefully. He falls back on his heel but doesn't stumble; the man's entirely incapable of being taken off-guard. "I'm claimed by Crown Prince Killian."

The room quiets around the three of us, people turning to stare openly now. I shift toward Killian until he's at my back. He snakes a warm arm around my hips and I breathe in pine, letting it calm me.

Then, loudly so everyone can hear, I say, "I'm his, and his alone."

CHAPTER THIRTY-FOUR

People gasp and whisper at my declaration.

Anassa's attention pulses down our bond, and I slam the iron wall down between us, unable to handle or process what I'm feeling at this moment, let alone how she might react.

I'm used to facing down a bloody beating, or an empty stomach, or my mother's ravings. I'm even getting used to the threat of death and dismemberment, being part of this crazy place, participating in these insane Trials.

But the weight of the whole ballroom's eyes on me is another thing entirely.

If it weren't for Killian's arms around my hips, I might have already bolted. Instead, I lean back into his solid weight for a moment, letting his reassuring presence ground me.

"Shall we?" he purrs into my ear, and the pleasurable shiver that races down my spine does wonders to dispel the anxiety about our audience.

I pivot in his grasp, placing my hands for a waltz. It's only then that I realize even the music has died down in the aftermath of my declaration. Killian must realize the same, because he signals sharply to the musicians on their riser, and they awkwardly launch back into the song they had been playing before.

Curious noble couples make their way to the dance floor around us, using the waltz as an excuse to come closer, examine this Rawbond who dares to touch their prince. I fix my eyes on the elegant lines of Killian's neck, his powerful shoulders. Pretend that nothing beyond him exists in this moment.

"Your training must be going well," Killian whispers to me and my eyes fly up to his. He's smirking. "I'm not sure I've ever danced with a partner who's gripped me quite this hard before."

I laugh and relax a fraction. The whirling of our steps and the floating music and the tension leaving me gives me a curious sensation, as if we're in a dream, or a vision.

That's when it finally sinks in. No more hiding. No more sneaking. I'm his, and he's mine—and now everybody knows it.

No taking that back.

Things are only going to be more complicated for a while. But with Killian's strong arms around me, claiming me, it's suddenly hard to care.

"You are so beautiful," he murmurs, holding me close enough to kiss. His thumb traces little patterns on my waist, silently echoing the desire in his eyes. "You look like a queen in this dress."

"Thank you," I murmur. "For saying that, and for the dress. It's absolutely perfect."

His gaze on mine is steady. "It's perfect for you. And yet, all I can think about is taking it off you," he says.

"While everyone's *watching*?" I whisper, playfully scandalized.

He grins. "Definitely not. All the delicious wonders under that dress are for me and me alone."

Killian doesn't let me go when the song ends. We dance the next one together, and the next, and the next. At some point I try to find my packmates in the crowd—seeking out Izabel's face, in particular—but when I spot her and Tomison, they're chatting at one of the food tables, eyes turned away from the dance floor.

I should probably talk to her, find Venna too and explain myself, but just staying upright feels overwhelming at the moment.

And through it all, there's Stark, a dark presence lurking at the edges of the room, watching us with unwavering focus.

I don't know what his problem is—and right now, I don't give a damn. Even the burn of his predatory gaze can't pierce the bubble of happiness that surrounds me and Killian.

Eventually, he says, "I think it's time you met my father, don't you?"

The glow of romantic delirium abruptly dims, cut by a bolt of raw anxiety.

"Don't worry," Killian whispers with smiling reassurance. "I'll be right there with you. Just smile and try to be deferential."

I nod and allow him to lead me to the dais where the King holds court with a dozen lounging nobles.

Smile and be deferential. Sure. No problem. I can do that. Even though the king is the cause of so much of my and my family's misery. I can pretend, for Killian.

Right?

King Cyril looks up as we approach, but doesn't rise from his ornate, throne-like chair. The wolf-pommel sword lies across his lap, as always, displayed for everyone to see. He's wearing a different crown than usual, something ornate and even more flashy, with dozens of multi-colored gems embedded in the spires of gold.

Audelie sits on his lap again, quiet and exposed in her sheer dress. She doesn't meet my eyes, though her head is held high. I wonder, briefly, what she thinks of this.

While Killian introduces me with princely formality, I meet the King's pale, eerie gaze. It's the first time I've really looked at him up close. I can see where Killian gets his features, though King Cyril's face is harder and lined with age.

As I bow to him, the King's assessing gaze turns almost invasive. Like he's mentally stripping me down to my component parts, weighing each one's ultimate value.

Like I'm not a person so much as a product he's thinking of purchasing.

"Ah, yes," he drawls when Killian's introduction is finished. "The commoner Rawbond. I've heard much about you from my son, though nothing quite as impressive as your ruthless efficiency during the Purge Trial." His gaze sharpens with memory—and a horrible gleam of pleasure.

"I've seldom seen a Rawbond dispatch one of her comrades so unhesitatingly," he purrs. "You were grace and brutality personified, my dear. One could almost imagine you *enjoyed* ordering that woman's death. It's always nice to see a little girl-on-girl action."

The edge of sensuality in his tone makes my stomach lurch with disgust. He speaks of Perielle's death like it was staged specifically for his pleasure.

Bile rises in my throat as I force myself to give the response expected of me.

"Thank you, Your Majesty. I'm… honored that my performance pleased you." The words taste like ash in my mouth.

He nods in regal acknowledgment, apparently satisfied with my gratitude. Then something subtly shifts in his demeanor. The king's eyes flick between me and Killian, that assessing gaze taking on new weight.

"Killian, your choice is acknowledged with due approbation." He gives me a smile of kingly satisfaction. "Be honored, Meryn Cooper."

I blink in confusion as Killian bows beside me, then places a hand on my waist and guides me down from the dais.

When Killian turns to smile at me with triumph glowing in his eyes, I realize what just happened.

The king has formally approved of our relationship.

I know I should be happy, but the words still tug at me. *Due approbation? Why did he say it like that?*

"That was a little weird," I mutter.

"It was," Killian agrees. He leads me off to the side of the ballroom, where he fetches me a glass of sparkling emberwine. I down it in a single gulp, eager to forget the loathsome weight of the king's gaze.

"Steady there, kitten," Killian teases, then his gaze sharpens, the intensity making me flush. "Don't get too drunk. I have plans for you."

I blush, looking around to see if anyone has heard him. The nobles and Rawbonds nearby are pretending to carry on their own conversations, but I can tell they're just disguising their sidelong looks.

"Tell me about these plans," I murmur, stepping closer.

Killian's mouth quirks, one hand tightening around my hip in a way that makes my thighs tighten. "I'd rather show you."

A thrill of arousal pulses through me. "Yes, please."

"Excellent." He pulls me close and whispers, "There's a servant's entrance over by the west balcony. We'll slip out when nobody is looking."

We make our way to the entrance, Killian driving off curious nobles with nothing more than a look.

A few minutes later, we're safely ensconced in his chambers.

Killian guides me into his bedroom and then lights the fireplace himself rather than calling on his servants. It's an intimate gesture that reminds me of our days in the city—back when he was just Lee, a palace messenger stealing romantic moments with a bloodied street fighter.

Damn, so much has changed. He's a prince, I'm bonded to a direwolf, and the king himself just authorized our relationship before the entire court.

Again, I tell myself I should be happy about King Cyril's public approval, but a lingering uneasiness pushes the feeling away.

As the warm firelight casts the room in a rich golden glow, words bubble up inside me.

"Killian… your father…"

Killian straightens from the fireplace and turns to look at me. "Yes?"

"The way he talked about Perielle's death," I begin hesitantly. "He spoke of it as though he *enjoyed* it. I killed Perielle out of necessity. For the good of the pack. But King Cyril made it feel… dirty."

Killian's face darkens. "I know. I'm sorry, Mer. He's…" He sighs, loosening his cravat and tossing it onto a nearby wingback chair. "My father's bloodthirsty nature is precisely why things must change."

Brow furrowing, he crosses to the window and looks out over the world beyond—the kingdom he will someday rule.

Moonlight silvers his handsome profile as he murmurs, "I want to change it. The current system—all the bloodshed, the cruelty. I want to believe there's a way to fix it. With the right ruler at the helm. One who doesn't view death as a form of entertainment."

He turns to look at me and something in his face makes my heart stutter.

"You could be that ruler," I murmur, my mind drifting briefly again to my traitorous thoughts when I was in the city earlier today. That Killian will make a much better king than his father.

He smiles a little, then crosses the room to me, holding my gaze with a gravity that tightens my throat.

Killian takes my chin firmly in his fingers, tilting my face up until our lips nearly touch. His breath is hot against mine, and my lips part, hungry for his touch. But instead of kissing me, he spins me around, hooking his chin down over my shoulder, pressing bruising kisses into my neck.

"I *could* be that ruler," he growls. "And you could be by my side."

My breath catches—we haven't talked about this, not truly, since I found out who he really is. All our conversations about our future from the time we spent together as Meryn and Lee are so distant, now that everything has changed. Now that we have changed.

I want to have this conversation, but my mind goes blank as he takes my earlobe into his mouth, rolling it between his teeth. Sharp sparks of heat gather at my core, and I press back into him eagerly.

He's already rock hard for me. The layered material of my dress doesn't do much to disguise his length, pressed firm against my ass.

In three short steps, Killian walks us forward until we're against the wall, still worrying my skin with his teeth as we move. I lean against the tapestry covering the wall, breath coming fast. The fibers of the weaving tease my already-flushed skin, goosebumps pebbling up and down my arms.

Killian yanks my dress up and over my head, tossing it to the floor behind us. Then, he pins my arms in place and presses himself against me, his cock straining against the material of his dress pants.

With his other hand, he makes short work of my breast bindings, which soon fall to the floor, followed quickly by my underthings. I shiver, arousal pulsing through me.

The sudden cool air against my naked skin, against my folds, makes me gasp. Panting, I twist my neck to look back at him and he smirks. "Naughty girl," he rumbles, his voice making my thighs clench, wet heat already spreading down from my core.

He presses even closer, so that my nipples graze against the tapestry in front of me, the scratchy weave against my sensitive skin making me cry out. Without warning, his hand is suddenly there between my legs, fingers moving in confident strokes up and over my clit, down to my entrance, dipping inside, then pushing harder, stretching me.

"You're mine," he says, mouth hot against my ear. His hand presses my wrists even more firmly into the wall, hard enough to ache, but the sensation only makes me more turned on.

"Say it," he instructs, his fingers playing with my clit lightly, then pulling away to wrestle with the fastens of his pants. "Say you belong to me."

I gasp, desperate for his touch to return. "*Killian.*"

"Who do you belong to?" His voice is rough, and he knees my legs open. He presses against me, into me, the thick head of his cock stretching me even more, but then stopping, teasing me.

"I'm yours," I gasp, bucking my hips, trying to ease him further inside of me. "I'm all yours!"

"And now everyone knows it." His teeth sink into my neck and then in one smooth thrust, he buries himself inside of me.

I cry out, startled by the fullness, seeing stars for a moment.

"You're my good girl. *Mine,*" he purrs, then licks the same spot on my neck his teeth just teased, his voice and words and teeth and tongue sending liquid heat through me until I can barely stand.

My knees weaken and I lean my weight back into him. His cock sinks impossibly deeper at the changed position and I cry out, "Please."

"Please what, kitten?" Killian moves his hips subtly and I stretch even more around him, my core clenching down at the sensation.

His free hand comes up to tangle in my hair, and he grabs at the choppy ends, twisting his fingers and pulling my head back hard until his lips are against my cheek. "Beg."

"Please, *fuck me*," I moan, and he finally does, drawing out of me almost entirely before slamming back in to the hilt.

My body presses into the wall, my cheek pressed against the rough weaving, my breasts and belly flush against the wall. Killian's hand drops from my wrists and he grabs my hips roughly, lifting me up with every stroke, only to slam me down on top of him as he pushes in, deeper than I've ever felt before.

I'm moaning, sobbing almost, incoherent. Then suddenly he's gone, and I pivot to see him moving back toward the bed.

"Get over here," he orders, and I move before I realize what I'm doing, desperate for his hands back on me, his cock back in me. I move to get onto the bed but he catches my hips and drags me backward, bending me over the mattress, my feet on the floor, my face pressed into the plush blankets and furs.

Before I can get my bearings, he's inside me again, driving into me faster and harder with every stroke. I try to twist to look at him and he presses me firmly into the bed with one hand, and I moan against the blanket.

"Fuck!" I cry.

He's breathing hard now, too, his pace picking up until I can hear that hitch in his breath that means he's going to come. I grind myself against the edge of the mattress, my swollen clit throbbing with pleasure as he slams into me again and again.

I'm so close, almost at the edge…

"*Fuck*, Meryn!" Killian shouts, and then he spills his hot seed inside me, filling me even more. Desperately, I try to reach my hand down to touch myself, needing my own release, but he grabs my hand and puts it back above my head.

"Don't move," he orders, and then pulls out, cold air rushing over my back and legs where he was pressing against me just a moment ago.

Then I feel it—his hand cups my folds, catching his come as it spills out of me. His fingers, soft but insistent, circle my clit, dip inside of me, teasing, getting me closer and closer before pulling away.

"Please, Killian, please," I sob into the blankets as he fucks me with his fingers, my core clenching over and over, so close to the edge.

When he finally allows me my release, it rips through me like a shockwave.

Killian flips me over to face him, one hand coming up to play with my nipple lazily, then pinch it hard.

The sensation almost puts me over the edge a second time, and tears come to my eyes, my breath going ragged. Killian sees the tears well. Watches them spill over.

He says nothing—just gathers me up into his arms and pulls me fully onto the bed beside him, pillows me against his chest, holding me while I weep in silent relief.

I fall asleep to the sound of his heartbeat.

CHAPTER THIRTY-FIVE

I t lingers; the small kiss Killian placed on my nape as he finished tying the tiny knot at the crest of my dress's bodice. The way his hands smoothed over my shoulders afterward. The way he kissed me again as I stepped into the passageway between our rooms, as if he needed another taste before he could let me go.

My skin shivers with his touch, memories and warm emotion swirling through my mind and dragging me back into bed with him.

When I reach my room, my heart is still thrumming. I nearly trip over my dress as I step inside. My mind is scattered as I clumsily disentangle myself from my ball gown and slip into uniform. Then I take off my mother's opal necklace and tuck it into a safe place in my closet, wondering when I'll ever have an occasion to wear such a precious thing again.

I pause in the middle of fastening my hair, mind drifting back to Killian's fingers in it, pulling just roughly enough that my entire body trembled with the knowledge that I was his.

Biting the inside of my cheek lightly, I finish readying myself for the day, even though I want to linger in this place. I want to trick myself into believing that his arms are still around me.

As I move to step out into the Strategos anteroom, I finally lower the wall between me and Anassa.

The instant I do, horrible emotion floods my heart and streaks through my veins. My bones are heavy. My blood is on fire. There's a vacancy in my chest like someone's carved out all my organs and left the cavity exposed in a howling winter wind.

The worst part is that I've felt something like this before. When I was younger.

When Dad...

It's grief. From the entire pack, all impacting me at once.

And beyond that, rage. Anassa's anger impacts me like a devouring wildfire, incinerating everything that's left after the grief. I choke and thud against the wall, using it to keep my balance as my vision falters.

Anassa's voice is a savage, spitting sound. *"While your pack suffered, you blocked us out for human pleasure."*

Those last two words cause a sickening lump to form in my throat, like the mere thought makes her want to vomit. I grunt and grip my head. I want to defend myself, but it's difficult to even remember my own name through this storm of emotion.

Blinking rapidly, I straighten just in time to see Egith standing in the center of the room, her expression devastated. All around her, my packmates are in various states of distress. Some look despondent. Some look furious. Some weep quietly.

The warm, safe, happy room I was in last night is very, very far away all of a sudden.

"Where have you been?" Egith asks cooly. I flinch at the edge in her voice. Everyone turns to look at me. *Everyone.*

"I..." I manage to force past the lump in my throat. But whatever pathetic defense I was about to mount, it dies and rots in my throat when I see Izabel's face.

She's crying. Her grief finds me through the pack bond. It's a question, asked over and over. *What now? What now?*

The words are like bone-breaking blows. Anassa's continued fury burns down the garden Killian planted in my heart. Izabel's tears salt the earth.

Egith straightens, her dark eyes tired. "Last night, during a Siphon assault in Grunfall, Strategos Alpha Markos was killed."

My mind reels as the wave of grief rises up in me again, spreading across the bond. Alpha Markos Blackwood—the leader of our whole pack. Egith's direct superior, with whom she's probably very close.

When the leader in charge of our strategy is killed... what happens to the war?

"What?" I say, the word coming out choked. "How?"

At this, Egith's lips purse and she crosses her arms over her chest. "I already gave the pack a full debrief. You missed it. I guess you were too busy... entertaining royals."

The implication makes my face burn. I can see clearly what she's thinking; what everyone here is thinking. That my relationship with Killian is no different from Audelie's with the king. That I'm spreading my legs to improve my standing in the social hierarchy here.

My eyes dart over to Izabel. She looks away. *Fuck*, does she think that, too?

Anassa bites at my consciousness, gnawing at the open wounds.

Around me, the smiles of my packmates who were enjoying the ball just hours ago are gone, replaced by grimaces and narrowed eyes. They're looking at me differently.

They see me as some callous ladder-climber who would shut out her pack for a chance to impress the crown. Status is important here, but the pack comes first, always. And people who can't understand that won't make it through training; I've learned that lesson well.

Grief rolls through the pack bond again, a hurt which now encroaches like a deadly illness, infiltrating every part of me.

My hands start to tremble, and I have to clutch them into fists to hide it.

Egith steps closer to me, so close that I can make out her pupils and feel her body heat. Her voice carries a warning, pitched low so only I can hear her.

"The Sovereign Alpha herself is coming here from the front to discuss the situation with the king while the direwolves select our next leader. While she's here, she's going to expect to see that the Strategos Rawbonds are unified, cohesive. Ready to jump into battle when they graduate training. If she senses that anyone is not fitting into the pack at this juncture…"

She doesn't finish her thought. She doesn't have to.

The threat is astoundingly clear.

If I cannot mend my reputation with the pack, the Sovereign Alpha may take me out herself.

THE NEXT FEW days pass in a haze of confusion and mounting tension. The Sovereign Alpha is coming, and my pack is in mourning.

For me, Alpha Markos was a stranger. Through the pack bond and Anassa, I could sense a connection to him, but he was not an important figure to me personally. For the other Rawbonds, however, things are different. They grew up knowing who he was. Many of their parents are also Strategos who fought alongside him.

He was Kristof's uncle. He was Egith's close friend.

And the wolves are in disarray over the loss of their alpha wolf, Markos's mount. The depth of their sorrow fills our heads at all times. I wish, desperately, that I could block some of it out. But I wouldn't dare piss Anassa off again like that.

She's still barely talking to me. I can't find it in myself to try to diminish the blows she keeps giving me.

That night with Killian was perfect. I wouldn't take it back, and a knot of anxiety that I've been carrying has disappeared, now that everyone knows about us. But the pack is still keeping their distance, and Izabel has been taking Anassa's strategy—she's frozen me out.

Egith maintains order efficiently, but everyone can sense that she's waiting for the Sovereign Alpha to arrive. Today, we're in group combat training with Phylax, overseen by Egith and Stark. We're practicing swordplay on foot, giving the direwolves a rest.

It's been unrelenting. Everyone's trying to get a hit in on me.

And when they're not aiming for me, they're testing Henrey, the only other common-born.

During a much needed break, I greedily gulp freezing water from my flask off to the side. There are a few other Strategos Rawbonds gossiping near me, but at arm's length.

"I think it's going to be Egith," Pietr says quietly as he caps his flask.

Allegra cocks her head, staring at the Beta from across the training field. "You're probably right. Is it always the second-in-command? I can't remember."

Pietr shrugs. "Usually. Unless there are special circumstances. Like, you know—"

"Nepotism," I mutter, looking at Stark. I haven't forgotten that his *mother* is the fearsome Sovereign Alpha coming to terrify us all into good behavior. Pietr and Allegra shoot me irritated looks and stalk off.

"What was that about?" Henrey says, coming to take a break next to me at the wall, sweat beading on his forehead.

"My whole pack hates me, haven't you heard?" I ask, trying to laugh it off. It stings, though.

Henrey reddens. "Well… yeah. I've heard some things, I guess. But ignore them, Meryn. You're strong. That'll win them over, in the end."

I clap him on the back. "Thanks for taking time to chat with a friendship-starved outcast."

He raises his water flask to me, a lopsided grin on his face. "We outcasts have to stick together."

Re-energized, I cork my flask, tossing it down into the dirt in exchange for my sword. I spin it around my right hand and lift my head.

I don't have to ask if Izabel is ready. She's already advancing on me, brandishing her own blade. Her dark brown eyes are narrowed, black hair whipping out of its braid in the cold winter wind.

Sword practice on foot is infinitely easier than mounted practice. Normally, I'd probably be enjoying the methodical movements and the satisfying feeling of pushing my muscles to perform.

But not when my closest friend in this entire castle is trying to gut me in the training yard.

Izabel hits her sword against mine with enough strength that it reverberates through my arm. She has the upper hand, and she draws and parries again. And again.

I can't get my footing quickly enough and she's unrelenting.

She's always been a better swordsperson than I am; she's had a lifetime of training. Usually, though, she takes it kind of easy on me. She'll pause and show me what I'm doing wrong, or let me get a few hits on her.

Not today.

She thwacks me in my right arm so hard that I drop my practice sword, and before I can even grab it, she sticks the tip of the practice sword under my chin.

"Dead," she says, a bitter glint in her eyes.

I grab the dull wooden sword by the hilt and yank it from her hands, tossing it into the ground next to my own.

"What has gotten into you?" I hiss at her.

Izabel's cheeks flush and she throws her hands up into the air. "Seriously? You don't know?!"

"You're upset I wasn't around when Egith broke the news that Alpha Markos had died, just like everyone else. You think I prioritized my relationship over our pack."

Izabel lets out a cry of irritation and grabs her sword out of the dirt, waving it at me again. "No, Meryn! I'm *hurt*. You hurt me! You've been hiding this relationship from me for months. I understand not wanting all the Rawbonds to know, but I'm your friend. Or at least I thought I was, but clearly not if you can't trust me with the truth about who you're seeing."

"Oh," I say, feeling suddenly foolish. Of course she's hurt. That's the most obvious thing in the world, probably. But all of this is new to me—not just this world, but having friends.

Guess I'm not a quick study.

Her eyes get glassy. "That's all you have to say? Oh?"

"No, Izabel," I breathe, chest aching. "I—"

Deafening horns sound over the training yard. They don't sound like they're coming from deep within the castle. The three loud blasts echo over the side of the mountain, from the south.

The castle gates, I realize.

The Sovereign Alpha has arrived.

PRACTICE ENDS QUICKLY AFTER THAT, and we're shuffled back toward Rawbond quarters. Izabel and I didn't have a chance to finish our conversation. She stormed away as soon as she could, obviously very eager to put space between us.

No one knows when we'll hear from the Sovereign Alpha. Presumably she's going to commune with the king first, and then discuss the Strategos leadership with the wolves. The whole pack is antsy, even Egith. After a few minutes of pacing in the anteroom, she locks herself in her private quarters.

I'd like to do the same, frankly. I know I need to finish my conversation with Izabel, though. And she's doing an impressive job of avoiding me. She's not in the Strategos anteroom, nor is she in the bunkroom or the bathing area.

Next, I check the Rawbond common lounge, but she's not one of the many people in there, either. I look around the room help-lessly, and then my gaze lands on the door to the Kryptos quarters.

She'll be in there, likely, hiding out with Venna. The two of them regularly go back and forth between each other's pack quar-ters and no one blinks at it. They're identical twins, after all—it would be strange to expect them to keep their distance.

For everyone else, though… it's not the done thing. You don't just go waltzing into another pack's anteroom. Technically, there are no rules disallowing it, but I've never seen a non-Strategos other than Venna in our space.

Nicely played, Izabel.

Resolve bubbles up in my veins. We're going to finish this fucking conversation, even if it makes a whole other pack hate me too.

In a few quick strides, I make my way through the common

lounge and open the door to the Kryptos quarters. It looks identical to the Strategos anteroom; the same plush couches, the same fireplace. And there, in the center of it, sit Izabel and Venna.

A couple of the Kryptos Rawbonds sputter in indignation as I swiftly walk through their space. I don't care.

"I'm sorry," I say, reaching the twins. I sign it, too, moving my hands in the way that Izabel and Venna showed me, in case Venna missed that. They've been teaching me some phrases in sign language when we have the time.

They're unmoved. Izabel glances over to the tapestry on the wall and Venna crosses her arms, scowling.

I sit down at their feet—clearly, I'm unwelcome on the couch with them—and keep going, quietly but loud enough for Venna's ears, although I can tell everyone in this anteroom right now is trying to eavesdrop.

"I'm an idiot. I'm sorry that I didn't realize that I had hurt your feelings, either of your feelings," I say, looking specifically at Venna this time, because she's clearly mad too. "This friendship thing, this is new to me. I know how to be a sister, a daughter, a lover, a fighter. I didn't realize that being a friend meant something different."

Venna softens first. She reaches a hand down and grasps mine, squeezing it. Izabel's a tougher nut to crack.

"I kept this a secret because I wasn't sure how I felt," I continue. "Killian and I have been seeing each other for over a year."

At this, Izabel's head whips back toward me, eyes widening. The juiciness of this is too tempting to her, I can tell. But she doesn't ask any questions, she waits for me to continue.

"We met in the Central Market. He, apparently, ventures into the commoner part of the city on occasion…"

Over the next thirty minutes, I give them all the lurid details of our relationship. Izabel gasps in the appropriate places, and by the time I'm finished, she's pulled me up on the couch to sit between them.

Anassa softens toward me, too. She still hasn't entirely forgiven me for putting up such a big barrier between us, but something has changed—thanks to my openness with the twins, maybe.

"So it's serious," Izabel says, contemplative. "It's not just a Bonding Trials fling."

"It's serious," I confirm.

Suddenly, there's a stirring on the other end of my bond. *"Prepare yourself,"* Anassa commands.

"For what?" I reply, surprised to hear her voice after the silent treatment she's been serving me.

The door to the Kryptos anteroom bangs open, hitting the wall. A liveried messenger enters and she sighs in relief when she spots me.

"Rawbond Meryn Cooper?" the messenger asks.

"Yes?" I say, looking around in confusion. *"What is this?"* I ask Anassa, but there's no reply.

"You are being summoned to see Sovereign Alpha Siegrid. Immediately."

My mind sinks into a vat of cold, devouring dread. Egith's warning returns to me.

The only reason the Sovereign Alpha could want to see me is if I'm going to be punished—or *killed*—for shutting out my fellow Rawbonds.

Izabel looks worried—a good sign for our friendship, if not for my overall health—when I rise. I bid the twins a quick goodbye, then follow the messenger out of the anteroom and out of the common lounge.

The walk to the audience chamber is endless, winding down echoing halls in complete silence. Questions almost burst from my lips multiple times, but I doubt this messenger will be able to answer them, anyway.

Igor would tell me that I've made my bed and now have to lie in it, but this bed feels like it's all just... *spikes.* Everywhere.

We turn one corner and there's Anassa, waiting regally for me, looking slightly bored.

"What are you doing here?" I ask her.

"We have business to attend to," she replies. Helpful, Anassa, thank you.

Anassa's tail swishes as we delve further into the castle. The halls get more elaborate as we draw closer to the royal side, the curtains woven with golden thread, the wall sconces covered in diamond-like glass shades. There are even long, thick tongues of blood-red carpet here rather than bare, polished stone, a rarity on this side of the castle because the wolves' claws could shred right through them.

Though we haven't crossed into the royal wings, it's clear that the Sovereign Alpha enjoys certain luxuries for her position.

Anassa's tail swishes again, brushing my arm. I look up at her, surprised. She doesn't bother looking back at me, but I swear that brief contact was meant to reassure me.

The messenger stops abruptly in front of a massive wooden door. The door knockers are two iron wolves baring their teeth, each biting a heavy metal ring. The messenger reaches up and takes hold of one of those rings, lifting it and bringing it back against the door twice.

The menacing thuds reverberate in my ears. I blink to keep my eyes from watering.

A moment later, the doors before us groan open, revealing a large, sparsely furnished room. A few Bonded soldiers and their wolves line the walls. The space is well-lit, with oil lamps and a pair of large braziers atop a slightly raised stone dais. Atop that dais, there's a long table with high-backed chairs. At the end of it, a chair even taller than the rest.

Standing before it is a woman whose presence makes me feel like gravity has tripled.

She's incredibly tall and well-built, brown skin covered in scars and kill marks, but her presence takes over the space around her, expanding beyond the boundaries of her body. Her power seeps from her pores and spreads through the room with her every breath.

Anassa steps inside, and I force my legs to follow. As we draw closer, Sovereign Alpha Siegrid Therion straightens from where she was leaning over the table. An instinct thrumming in my blood urges my eyes to follow her every movement, every twitch of her muscles and every analyzing sweep of her eyes demanding my attention.

She's older than I expected, I realize. In her mid-fifties, maybe, with graying brown hair that has a blood-red streak. Her age doesn't diminish her physical prowess. If anything, it sharpens the unspoken threat in her gaze.

If Anassa's taught me anything, it's that age and experience only makes a wolf more dangerous.

Siegrid turns towards us, crossing her arms over her chest. They're as heavily tattooed as her son's. Looking at her, a warning similar to the one I heard the first time I looked at Stark sounds in my mind.

Dangerous, instinct screams at me, louder than it ever has before.

Her wolf sits beside her. Massive and black as night. It makes even Anassa look small. Siegrid reaches up and touches her wolf's leg before stepping forward. She looks right past me and inclines her head.

A bow of respect, I realize, meant for Anassa. I watch as Anassa bows in return, extending one paw and dipping her head low to the ground.

Then Siegrid fixes her piercing gaze on me. I'm run through instantly. No, it's more like she's cut me open and is probing around to study my insides.

She's an apex predator judging whether the cut of meat before her is worthy.

I have the distinct sense that she's assessing me—weighing my value. Probably figuring out how she wants to punish me. I have no idea how I'm meant to behave before the Sovereign Alpha.

Should I treat her like a queen? Throw myself to the floor and grovel for my life?

Awkwardly, I bend forward in a bow. It was apparently the wrong move, judging by the disdainful huff it earns.

"Stand, girl."

Her voice is slightly raspy, but it carries through the room like a freezing wind. My entire body reacts, hair rising, muscles twitching. I stand.

She's still staring. I can barely look at her. It's like trying to force myself to look directly at the sun. I can only manage a few seconds at a time. And I'm... *small*, in this room.

"In all my time as a Bonded soldier, as the Daemos Alpha, and then as Sovereign Alpha," she says, "I have never seen anything like… *this*."

Siegrid's voice has a sharp edge to it. It causes a bizarre impulse in me to check to see if I'm bleeding, as though her cutting words have wounded me physically. The worst part is that I suddenly know why she was looking at me that way—assessing and judging.

The irritation in her voice is clear.

This, said with contempt. My relationship with Killian, she means. A Rawbond dallying with the crown prince.

She steps to the edge of the dais, looking down at me. "This has all been very unusual, girl, and you are drawing unnecessary attention to yourself." Attention? What the hell does that mean? "But what's done is done, I suppose," Siegrid says with a weary sigh.

I feel the sudden, uncontrollable need to explain myself to her. I stumble through words, though my thoughts come out fractured.

"Please, Sovereign Alpha. The prince and I started seeing each other long before I became Bonded. I know I shouldn't have kept it from—"

"What are you rambling about?" Siegrid interrupts, her voice extinguishing mine.

"Um." My brain isn't working. My heart thunders in my ears. All I can see is her intense gaze. "The crown prince and I are together?" I offer hesitantly. "That's what you—"

"I am not here to talk to you about your love life, you *child*," she snaps, mouth twisting with displeasure.

Her voice is calm and measured, but her fury is anything but. It explodes through her, Siegrid's face contorting into an expression of pure rage that makes me want to curl into a ball.

A white-out blizzard is howling around me, blinding me to everything, even what's right in front of my eyes. "I'm sorry, but then why did you call me?"

Siegrid raises her face and pulls her broad shoulders back.

"The Strategos direwolves have convened and chosen their next leader. Anassa. You are the new Strategos Alpha."

CHAPTER THIRTY-SIX

I'd be more composed if someone had brought an actual metal club down over my skull.

The words send a reverberation of emotion through me—fear, confusion, resistance. It shatters through my body, rattling my bones, weakening my muscles, weighing me down like shackles at my ankles and a collar around my throat.

I can't entirely process Siegrid's words, at first.

Strategos Alpha.

And she's looking directly at me, her severe expression unchanging. If she's waiting for me to fight through this mire of shock, she'll be waiting a long, long while.

The room starts to tilt around me. If it keeps on like this, I'll start to slip, to fall. I'm being told I'm meant to lead an *entire* pack? I...

Anassa moves closer to me and I put my hand up on her silver-white fur, using her form to steady myself. Gazing upward, I look into her yellow eyes. Suddenly, it's like another wall has flown open in my consciousness, one that I didn't even know was there. A vast library flows through it—ancient knowledge passed through the direwolves, given only to the leaders of each pack.

My knees start to shake. I can't even *breathe* under the crushing weight of it all.

Anassa's carefully maintained distance has disappeared. Either she's chosen to fully forgive me for the other night... or she has no choice, now that we're an alpha pair.

"There must..." I swallow, trying to pick my own words out of the chaos. "There must be some mistake," I finally manage. The shivering echo of my voice sounds small even to my own ears. Pleading, almost. "I'm just a Rawbond. I don't even come from a Bonded family, and I barely know how to—"

Siegrid's hand cuts through the air like the swipe of a claw. "Enough."

Cold sweat causes my shirt to cling to my back beneath my jacket as I stare at her like a woman awaiting her sentencing.

Siegrid lowers her hand, resting it calmly on the table. "Do you accuse the direwolves of making a *mistake* in choosing their leaders?" The danger in her voice is evident, but the sound of her massive wolf's low, warning growl drives her point home.

There will be no resistance.

"This is not a debate, girl. The wolves have convened, they have chosen, and Anassa will lead Strategos. Which means you, as her rider, will serve as Strategos Alpha." Siegrid's voice is frigid with finality.

I resist the urge to hold myself, to dig my nails painfully into my palms, to turn and *run* all the way back to the Eastern Quarter.

Instead, I reach for Anassa, hoping for comfort. Some wisdom or encouragement, perhaps, considering she's the one who's truly been chosen here. Instead, I'm plunged back into that endless ocean of suffocating knowledge. It presses on my mind like waves against a shore, threatening to drag me out to sea and drown me.

Siegrid continues to stare. I can feel the steady eyes of the other Bonded soldiers on me. Siegrid's wolf lowers its head, gaze violating.

And I stand here, not even entirely certain as to what an alpha is meant to do.

What does this mean for me, truly? I've been so focused on surviving and finding Saela that I've barely had any energy left to understand the nuance of pack politics.

I tighten my hands into fists and square my shoulders. "Why me? Why us?" My voice carries more steadily this time.

Siegrid's expression shifts away from that unfeeling, authoritative intensity. It's replaced by something bordering on pity. "The wolves see things that humans cannot. They know what's coming. And for whatever reason," she says, "they believe you—and Anassa together —are what Strategos needs."

The massive doors behind me burst open with a crack, the knockers rattling against wood. Egith strides past a breathless messenger. She's somewhat scattered herself, but she drops into a formal bow before Siegrid seamlessly.

Or she would have, if she hadn't frozen mid-motion the moment she saw me. Egith's sharp eyes dart between me, Siegrid, and our wolves, analyzing the palpable tension in the space between us.

"Rise, Beta Egith," Siegrid commands. "We have much to discuss."

Watching Siegrid explain the wolves' decision to Egith is like sitting back and letting someone wrap a noose around my throat. I watch her expression tighten with every word, pinches of barely suppressed emotion breaking through her stony front with the words "alpha" and "final."

It's shock, initially. Then disbelief, with an incredulous look thrown in my direction. Then something harder to parse in its nuance. But *despondent* would be a very charitable word for it.

She's heartbroken that she's been passed over for the likes of me.

A Rawbond who begged to be let free at the beginning of the Trials. A pack member who recently shut out her direwolf and packmates during a moment of crisis. A ladder-climber sleeping with a royal.

And a commoner, at that.

"May I speak freely?" Egith says. Her entire body looks like it's made of stone. She's eerily still. *Calm before the storm*, I think to myself.

Siegrid nods, and I prepare myself for a verbal evisceration. And maybe a physical one, right after.

"This is unprecedented," Egith says. She does not raise her voice. She addresses Siegrid directly, gaze unflinching. "The pack is already destabilized by Alpha Markos's death. To put an untrained Rawbond in charge now, when we're so crucial to the war effort—"

"The wolves have chosen," Siegrid interrupts.

Egith doesn't flinch. She only bows her head.

"Though you do raise a valid point about the war," Siegrid continues. "I'm not sure how we're going to have this… neophyte… leading Strategos at the front when she hasn't even passed her Trials and graduated." Her terrifying gaze returns to me, and tension knots up my shoulders. "Well, *Alpha*. What do you propose?"

It's like I've suddenly had a sword shoved in my hand, a blinding light shone in my eyes, and been told to parry the blade coming for my throat.

But Anassa finally grants me a handhold to steady myself. *"Let Egith lead for now."*

I take a deep breath and raise my defenses. She's absolutely right.

"Egith should take command at the front," I tell them both. "She possesses crucial knowledge of the forces there, understands the strategy, and has earned the pack's respect." I meet Egith's gaze and find her eyes wide, her lips parted in surprise. "I may not understand why I'm Alpha, but I'm not stupid. I don't know enough yet to lead our forces in battle. But *you* do."

Something shifts in Egith's expression. When the surprise passes, her punishing distress doesn't return at full force.

After a moment of uncomfortable silence, Siegrid speaks. "A wise choice. You can remain here to finish your training. You will also need to spare time and energy to learn how to lead your pack as Alpha."

I nod; all that I'm really capable of at this moment. Her subtext is clear—I'm not fit to be in my position, not yet. Well, we're agreed on that.

Siegrid crosses her powerful arms. "You cannot remain ignorant of battle strategy for long, and you will need to take over responsibilities as soon as possible. Even with Egith's aid, your pack will be weakened so long as it stands without a proper Alpha."

I bow just the way Egith did when she arrived. "I understand."

"Your position, Egith?" Siegrid says.

"Perhaps one of the Strategos gammas might be recalled to take over my role as instructor," Egith says. "We will need to discuss the current training regimen, however. Revise it for these… setbacks."

"Agreed," Siegrid says, then inclines her head only slightly. "You are dismissed."

I stand there numbly for a moment until I realize she's addressing both of us. Then I turn on my heel quickly, shaky and weak as Anassa and I follow Egith from the room.

When the doors thud shut behind us, I manage a quiet, "What now?"

Egith looks at me and takes a deep, weary breath. "You must tell the other Rawbonds."

Right.

On the way back to the Rawbond quarters, I pause in the halls. "Go on without me," I tell Egith. "Gather everyone in the anteroom, I'll be there in just a minute."

Her lips purse—it's weird for both of us, me giving her orders—but she nods and leaves. Then, I turn to Anassa.

The powerful giant has stilled at my side.

"Congratulations," I tell her, weary. It's been so long since she's had a real conversation with me, and the silence has worn me down. Hopefully this will mark the end of the shut-out. *"Is that what I should be saying? Do I congratulate you for being chosen to lead our pack?"*

She inclines her head to the side, studying me with those ochre eyes. *"It is not just me who was chosen. The other direwolves chose us as a pair. A direwolf's individual ability is meaningful but even the strongest among us is weak without a paired rider to guide our powers."*

A disbelieving laugh escapes me. Anassa huffs in irritation when she hears it, her lips pulled back from her long fangs.

"You were born to lead, girl. Whether or not you believe that is of no consequence anymore. You must, so you will."

Well, that's pretty clear. I still cannot fully fathom that this is happening, but I guess it doesn't matter if I want to accept this. It's done.

I've been in that position so many times in my life, now. My father's death. My mother's illness. My sister's kidnapping. The absolutely delightful surprise of the Bonding Trials.

I must, so I will.

With that, Anassa turns tail and trots off back toward the wolf terraces.

"Hey," I mentally shout at her as she goes. *"I'm sorry. For shutting you out so thoroughly. It won't ever happen again."*

"I know," she calls.

By the time I reach the Strategos common area, I'm resolute. Did I waver and once more consider bolting? Pretending none of this happened? Did I imagine myself a thousand leagues away, holed up in a cabin somewhere with Killian?

Yes, obviously. But I'm here. I've been chosen. I *have* to do this.

My heart beats against my ribs like a fist as I enter the Strategos anteroom.

As promised, Egith has gathered the other nineteen Strategos Rawbonds, and they're packed onto the couches and the floor. The room is quiet and everyone stares at me when I enter—some with clear irritation, still mad at me for my disappearing act.

Tomison raises his eyebrows and Izabel mouths, "Are you okay?"

Am I ever? I shut the door behind me and turn to face them all.

My only frame of reference for how Alphas are meant to carry themselves are Stark and Siegrid, and… well, they just do a lot of glaring, don't they?

I settle for what I hope is an authoritative stare, making eye contact with them all as I look around the room. Then I hold my head high and speak as plainly as I can.

"I have an announcement. The direwolves have decided on a new leader. They've chosen Anassa. I will serve as your Alpha."

There's one moment of crystalized, surprised silence before everything erupts into noise. Voices overlap, emotions crashing through our pack unity like rapids crashing over jagged rock. I can only catch fragments through the tumult.

"A *Rawbond*?!" Pietr shouts.

Nevah starts to laugh hysterically, doubling over so that her dark curls almost hit the floor.

Kristof looks around confused. "But Egith——"

"She's not even from a Bonded family," Allegra whispers loudly, dumbfounded.

Anassa's booming voice slams through the pack connection like a crack of thunder, our minds torn in two just the way lightning cleaves through the sky.

"*SILENCE.*"

I know everyone's heard her. This must be a new alpha power. Typically, the pack unity bond works so that we can sense emotions and touches of thought from everyone else, particularly when we're using our group powers, but we cannot normally hear what each other's wolves are saying.

Anassa's ability to speak into everyone's mind at once leaves no more room for argument.

The room instantly quiets again. Instinct has me reaching for her, looking for guidance. But she need not reach back. Her power speaks for itself, vibrating inside my skull. It gives me strength, knowing I'm bound to someone like her.

I draw myself up to my full height, Anassa's authority crackling in my blood. I imagine it as a haze around me, light as silvery bright as her fur emanating from me like armor. I choose to be utterly, wholly honest.

"I hear your confusion and your doubt. I understand it because I felt the same. I don't understand why I've been chosen. Only the wolves truly know," I say. The Rawbonds stir, and there's a shiver of understanding over the pack unity. "Even if you feel uncertain, they have made their decision. We must follow it. One of the very first lessons I learned here, with you, was that we have to trust the wisdom of the direwolves. You do not question it."

There's another stir. A few nods. A small blooming feeling, like the opening of their minds.

"I am your Alpha," I say, projecting loudly into the room now. "You will treat me as such. Yes, like you, I am still a Rawbond. I will stay here with you to complete my training, and Beta Egith has agreed to lead Strategos at the front until I do."

Allegra pipes up, flipping her strawberry blonde hair over her shoulder. "We might not question the direwolves and their choices, but how can we trust you when you're in a relationship with the crown prince? How can we trust that you'll do what's right for the Bonded and not just what's right for the Crown?"

Of course, that's the first question. I open my mouth to respond, but another voice stops me. A shiver of awareness streaks down my spine at the rich sound of it, coming from behind me.

"What's right for the Crown is always what's right for the Bonded."

My eyes find Stark's. He fills the doorway into our anteroom, leaning against the frame with his tattooed arms strategically displayed across his chest. I sense every eye in the room snap to him, drawn to his presence. Responding with respect and interest, clouding over my pack's unity.

Irritation flickers through me.

Of course he'd believe that what's right for the Crown is right for the Bonded. He's the king's perfect honed weapon. As the ultimate insider, destined to lead the Bonded himself one day, he can't see how horrible the king and the nobles treat the Bonded.

Or maybe he *chooses* not to see it.

"The Alpha's time is too valuable to waste on pointless questions," he says.

Stark's dark gaze fixes on me with the same intensity it always has, like the rest of the room doesn't matter so long as he keeps his prey in sight. He tilts his head slightly to the side, and a lock of his dark hair falls across his brow. It's like a tether has snapped taut between us.

"Report to my office at dawn tomorrow. Your alpha training begins."

Without waiting for a response, he turns and vanishes through the doorway, leaving a charged silence in his wake.

Dawn tomorrow.

Fuck.

CHAPTER THIRTY-SEVEN

The skylights are dark as I stride through the silent halls. It feels almost illicit to be creeping around at this hour, right out in the open. Until this point, all of my creeping has been contained to the tunnel between my quarters and the royal wings.

A sharp ache of longing scrapes through my chest when I think of Killian. If only I were gliding my hand along the familiar stone, anticipating the warmth of his skin under my fingertips.

We've barely seen each other since the night of the ball. He came to my room the day after, when he'd heard about Alpha Markos, to check in on me. We agreed to keep some distance until things had blown over. Last night, though, I went to him, told him everything.

All about how I'm now the Strategos Alpha. He swept me into his arms in pride, but I didn't let things get much further. I'm not ready to try filtering my bond with Anassa again—it's too raw between us still.

And now I'm here, walking through dark hallways while the other Rawbonds sleep, headed to find…

Ugh.

Stark, of all people. It feels like I'm waltzing right over the edge of a very perilous cliff. Hurling my body over the side, really.

Granted, the cliff has ridiculous eyelashes and unfairly broad shoulders.

But it's still a *cliff*.

I stand in front of his office door, trying to decide how I'm going to play this. I can still hear his voice and feel his unwavering gaze. *"My quarters at dawn…"*

Shaking off my shivers, I push the door open without knocking, deciding I'd rather be the one catching him off-guard, for once. But I've failed again.

Stark's office isn't anything like I'd imagined. I was bracing myself for heads on spikes. I was anticipating that I'd need to duck occasionally to avoid the hanging, rusty murder weapons.

Maybe there'd even be some animal bones he and his wolf had been gnawing on together.

Bonding, you know?

But it's a library. *A library*.

Or, not entirely. The center of the room predictably has an open space, obviously set aside for sparring. Behind it, there are some wide stone stairs that lead up to a raised section of the room. There, I can see weapon racks, hanging armor, a dormant hearth, and a few comfortable looking chairs.

But all around the central sparring space, there are shelves lining the walls or standing side-by-side to create orderly aisles. The stacks reach all the way to the ceiling, with a ladder propped against the shelf to my right so that he can reach the tallest shelves—similar to the layout in Leader Aldrich's office.

I stand there, staring, suddenly suffering a series of bizarrely crisp images.

Stark, dressed in casual clothing, climbing up that ladder to reach a book he needs. Or Stark sitting in one of those chairs, feet up, reading in silence. Stark alone in the sparring square, sword in hand, practicing maneuvers.

He's not shirtless in my imagination. At first.

I run my hand over my face to wipe my mind of it all. I

shouldn't be thinking about Stark like he's a person with a soul and normal human needs.

He's a killing machine.

That's obviously why he has a soft-looking blanket draped over the arm of his chair. Because even killing machines get cold... apparently.

"Surprised?"

Stark's voice carries that familiar edge of mockery, like he thinks I'm stupid for believing he lives like a feral animal when he acts like one. He emerges between two of his towering bookshelves and leans against one of them, arms crossed.

He's dressed casually. His pants are fighting leathers, but he's wearing a white short-sleeved shirt on top, his huge arms exposed—as well as the absurd amount of tattoos covering them, from his fingers all the way up, disappearing under the cap sleeves, dark and twisting and runic. I swallow at the visceral reminder of just how many lives he's taken.

My brain immediately starts assessing him. How far is he from me? Where are his eyes looking? It's training from the pits, but it's also just self-preservation, being in the same room as someone like Stark.

Alone, I might add.

I make a show of letting my eyes wander around his office. Most of the books look freshly bound, but there are a few with broken spines and even some that look ancient, those being secured behind glass cases that glint in the lamplight.

When my eyes land on a doorway that leads to an adjoining room—spotting an unmade bed bathed in darkness—I avert them instantly. Does he sleep here? Surely he has a private room off of the Daemos quarters, just like Egith and I do. Or maybe that bed's for something other than sleeping...

Another image I don't need.

"This is a lot of books, hoarder," I say, ignoring the heat in my face. Even Leader Aldrich's library pales in comparison. I've never seen this many in one place before.

The thought comes to me unbidden: *Saela would love this*. It's followed by an immediate ache in my chest.

Stark doesn't move from his spot, but his eyes roam. Over his books, at first. Then over me.

I feel it again. That same thing I always do, looking at him. Being looked at by him.

It's a challenge, like he believes he owns the world but wants to see me try to take it from him. "Did you think being Alpha just meant *fighting* well?"

I grind my teeth briefly. My skin prickles, meeting his dark eyes. The challenge simmering in the air is tempting. I sort of want to tear him apart. But ultimately, I *am* here for a reason. A good one.

"That's why I'm here, isn't it? Because I don't know what being Alpha means," I reply. "Or so I've been told. Repeatedly."

Stark pushes off of the shelf and approaches, arms falling to his sides. To anyone else, it would have looked almost lazy. Relaxed. His muscles are loose and his stride slow. But his eyes are sharper than they were a moment ago.

I don't think Stark is capable of relaxation.

"And you listen to everything you're told, princess?" he says, a dangerous edge in his tone.

"Religiously," I deadpan, lifting my chin to show him that his height doesn't scare me.

"Then block," he says.

I don't even fully process his words before my body snaps into motion. His eyes cut downward, his arm whipping towards my face with impossible speed. The flat of a fist flashes in my vision as muscle memory yanks me out of the way.

He's not like any of the opponents I fought in the pits. He's taller, stronger, faster. But more importantly, he's coldly merciless.

Fearless.

I try to rotate my body, shifting my feet, but I'm too slow.

His second blow cracks against my ribs.

Pain explodes through my left side as I stumble back, shoulder slamming into one of the shelves. I clutch my side, trying to catch my breath.

It was a hard hit. I'm only lucky that he's backing away instead of ripping a book from the shelf and knocking me out with it.

"Wh…" I wheeze, still winded.

"In your defense, you did as you were told," he says, raising a brow. "Initially."

"You *f*—" The expletive turns into an angry, strangled growling sound. It's probably best not to curse him out.

This place looks harmless, but there could still be a cellar under the sparring square where he keeps his collection of eyeballs and teeth. The fucker.

Stark gestures to the books. His usual glower is gone, and there's an unfamiliar spark in his eyes.

"Leadership requires both knowledge and strength," he says. I force myself to straighten, but I swear I can hear my ribs creaking. "But you're weak. You have neither."

My mouth drops open in indignation. It stuns me more than the literal punch he just threw. Just because I don't have a personal library and years of fancy training doesn't mean I'm—

Stark's fist flies towards my face again. This time, I sidestep and smack his wrist with the flat of my hand as it whips past my head. If he were a stupider opponent, that would have created an opening.

Instead, he ducks under my returning blow and does the exact same countermove to me. The spark in his eyes is a bonfire now, lit with intense focus. "You have good instincts."

"Thanks," I grit out.

"It won't help you against a Siphon," he says.

Then there's suddenly cloth in my eyes, a fluttering swath of darkness that has me stumbling backward. I barely have time to process it—Stark threw something—and lift my arms defensively before his blow lands.

He doesn't go for the same attack, directed at my torso. Instead, his foot whips out and the toe of his boot lands squarely on the side of my knee. I shout and thud to the ground, catching myself and rolling away instinctively even though he doesn't press the offensive.

"You can't trust your eyes with a Siphon. You can't trust what you already know."

I hiss out breaths, turning the pain to my advantage, using the anger to fuel my focus. Then I wash it from my face, replacing it with fear. I let my eyes well, let my arm tremble as I reach up.

"Okay," I breathe, nodding. I sniff. "Help me up. I'll try again."

Stark stares at me for a long moment, then his brow pinches slightly. My knee throbs as I kneel there, my hand still outstretched. He steps forward, reaching for me.

And just as he's close enough, I grab the cloth he threw in my face right out from under his foot. His breath rushes from him as his balance is compromised, and I lash towards him like a snake, aiming for every man's greatest weakness.

But instead of trying to reassert his footing, he leans into the fall, lifting the foot I stole from him and spiking his knee towards my face. I pull away at the last second, thudding onto my back.

Before I can move, he lets himself fall on top of me. His heavy, muscled legs wrap around my hips, pinning my pelvis in place so I can't kick him again, and he presses a forearm against my throat—hard, then harder.

Psycho. Fucking. Asshole.

I'll show him.

But then his fingers come up, pressing callouses against my lips.

"Thinking about spitting in my face again, princess?" he says, dark amusement in his eyes.

Oh good, so no one here's forgotten that moment.

Suddenly, I realize what a vulnerable position I'm in. We're alone; everyone else in the castle is still sleeping. This violent butcher who hates me has me pinned and choked. A spasm of fear ricochets through me and Anassa perks up on the other end of the bond, though she doesn't say anything.

He could kill me. He *might* kill me.

Stark tilts his head slightly, as if listening to something—maybe his wolf, demanding he finish me off for good. But then, to my utter surprise, he lessens the pressure on my throat, removes his rough fingers from my lips.

He blinks down at me, a slight frown flickering across his face, then rolls off of me and stands up.

Probably would piss his mother off if he murdered the newly named Alpha.

"Decent attempt," he says.

"Decent," I grumble spitefully, pushing to my feet. "How did you get the upper hand? Did you know?"

"I've seen you take much harder hits than that without whining," he says, gaze steady. "And I am always ready, even when my opponent *plays* at weakness."

Because he's merciless. I cross my arms. "You *just* finished calling me weak."

"There are different kinds of strength. Different kinds of weaknesses," he says. He rubs his palms together, eyes darting over me again. He's assessing me for openings, I realize instantly. He's going to attack me again. "Why do you think the packs are separate from each other?"

"Because we needed somewhere to put all the bloodthirsty killers, Alpha Daemos," I respond lightly, with a sweet smile.

His fist lashes out. I step back, then again when another strike comes for me. I make the mistake of blocking with the flat of my palm, and the force of his blow causes my arm to bend at the elbow and pain to burn up my right side.

"Maybe you shouldn't test the patience of a *bloodthirsty killer*, then," he says. But the cold ferocity of his voice is offset by the same simmering glow in his eyes. By that challenge.

"I'm trembling," I snap sarcastically, as if we aren't both incredibly aware that he just scared the shit out of me on the floor.

Stark takes a deep breath and straightens. "The *real* reason is because every pack has a weakness. Just as every soldier does. Strategos are intelligent. Masterful on the battlefield. But their reaction times are often slowed by the information they must constantly process. Phylax are physically formidable, but they're less maneuverable than Daemos."

"And *your* pack's weakness?"

The question earns me another physical assault. Footwork carries us across the room, between the shelves. I'm sweating by the time he relents.

"Daemos get… carried away," he rasps. The breathlessness in his voice and the way his eyes dart over me makes the hair on the back of my neck lift.

My gaze jumps unwillingly to that dark room off the side, where the unmade bed is. I think about the crack that Tomison made about Stark once—about how he seemed like the type who'd do all the riding.

I curl my fingers into fists, letting my fingernails bite into my palms, letting the pain drag me away from that deeply unwanted line of thought.

"And so we compensate for each other's weaknesses," I say, stepping slightly farther from him to ready myself for his next probing attacks.

"Correct. Just the same, every soldier has weaknesses and strengths," he says.

"And our packmates compensate for those. Our—"

"*No*," he snaps harshly.

Another flurry of attacks. I'm stumbling away from the shelves, panting by the time he explains. The severity of his expression is haunting.

"You are an *Alpha*. You are not permitted the luxury of open weakness."

Fuck, this man is intense. "Everyone. Has. Weaknesses," I hiss.

He steps closer to me, crowding my space. His chest is rising and falling rapidly from the exertion. His musky, amber smell reaches my nose, and I immediately breathe through my mouth because I need to stay sharp.

"You're right," he says. My eyes widen. I thought he'd die before saying those words to me. "But we are *selective* about who we show those truths to. Understand?"

I swallow roughly. He doesn't wait for my response, turning away abruptly and striding away from me. I study the slope of his shoulders for a moment. They're rising and falling as if he's agitated.

For a moment, hidden meaning gathers around us like angry storm clouds. His name forms on my tongue. I can't say why. There was just something so heavy, so charged about the way he turned away from me.

"St—"

He whirls on me. I don't have time to dodge fully, so I try to lessen the impact of his blow by moving my body parallel to his momentum. It hurts, but it doesn't break anything. I dance away quickly, catching my balance near one of the glass cases.

Annoyance fizzes in my blood. I can feel bruises already forming.

"Was that playing at weakness, too?" I growl out.

He strides towards me. *Quickly*. "How many gammas are in each pack?"

"Wh… Two?" I say.

He lashes out again. I grunt and deflect, dodge, then suffer another punishing hit. "Two or three," he says. "What is a rider's biggest vulnerability, when mounted?"

I ready myself, widening my stance. "Uneven terrain."

His assault is brutal. His blows are like battering rams. He's faster than anyone I've ever fought, and he isn't even slightly slowing down. He chases me entirely across the sparring square, backing me up against the shelves.

"Your *legs*. If your legs are compromised, you cannot keep seated, no matter how Anassa compensates."

My chest is heaving. Sweat streaks down my face. And something… *shifts* in the corner of my eye. A strange energy streaks over my spine. A few of the books on his shelf, wedged far back in the shadows, old and faded but…

"—primary… Cooper!" he barks.

"What?" I say, head snapping back towards him.

"What is a Siphon's primary weakness?" he practically snarls.

"It's…" My eyes drift again, pulled back to that shadowy shelf.

Then I sense him moving towards me, and I react as quickly as I can. He launches forward and ducks low under my responding swing, bracing his foot and bringing his fist up towards my chin. I arch my back, yanking my head back just in time, then kick my leg towards his side.

But he literally *catches* my ankle and uses his mass to knock me off balance.

His muscles bunch, his grip tightens, and he swings me into a shelf. My shoulder erupts in pain, but I don't have time to process it before he traps my leg between our bodies and pushes me against the shelf so hard that the wood digs into my spine.

I try to leverage my elbow, but he catches my wrist and pins it to my shoulder, his forearm pressed to my throat again.

Resisting, I try to break free from this hold, but I can't manage anything more than a pathetic, writhing rebellion.

And I'm extremely aware of all the points his body is touching mine. His hand on my ankle, my leg raised between us, his hips grinding against my own. His arm burning against my neck, the clasp of his fingers on my wrist. His scent fogging my mind.

I fall still, chest heaving, jaw clenched.

"You're distracted," he growls, the rumble of his voice passing deep into my body.

I'll fucking say. Clearly, it's been too many nights without Killian. I need to get over this privacy stuff with Anassa and start scratching this itch again—directing my sexual frustration at the right person.

Blood leaks from my split lip as I take a deep breath. His eyes dart down as it reaches my chin. His brows twitch together slightly.

I shake my head. "There's too much to learn. I need a plan."

He releases me. Air rushes from my lungs. I'm suddenly cold. Unmoored. I grip the edge of a shelf to steady myself, disoriented by the way my pulse is throbbing.

"You're finally thinking like an Alpha," he says, a touch of approval in his voice.

He jerks his chin, ordering me to follow without a word as he disappears between a couple of shelves. I wipe the blood from my chin and rub my throat, following him.

Stark stands over a desk that's been tucked away behind the shelves. His gaze follows me as I approach. When I reach his side, he slides a piece of paper towards me across the desk's glossy surface.

"Write down what you need to improve upon. Everything."

I perch my hand on my hip and frown. "You mean I should tell you all my weaknesses?"

He laughs. *Stark*, laughing. He rasps his hand over his stubble, eyes warming slightly, and that deep but barely there sound of amusement emanates from his chest.

"Maybe you do listen to everything you're told."

My muscles feel shaky. "See? I'm a star pupil."

He leans his hip against the desk. "You can choose to hold back, but you'll fail. And you'll die." My hand tightens into a fist. A lesson or a threat? His jaw twitches, and he steps closer to me. "I'm your only way through this."

"I'm meant to trust you, then," I breathe.

When he's done nothing but try to break my will from the moment we met.

"Or you could think of it as using me to grow stronger," he says.

Using me. Annoyingly, my cheeks heat.

I scoff, and Stark studies me for a long moment. Finally, he rakes his fingers through his hair.

"These are the difficult decisions an Alpha must make," he says, pushing the paper towards me. "For the good of her pack."

For the good of my pack.

I dart my tongue over my stinging lip and taste blood. Then I nod and sit at the desk, picking up his quill.

"I'm sure there are things I've never heard of that I need to know, so this is on you," I say. "Tell me your list of what an Alpha needs to be, and I'll write down what I'm missing."

His eyes glow again. He liked that answer. "You should... What are you writing?"

I lift up the page to show him what I've scrawled out as my first priority. "*Work on my glower.*"

His lips press together. "Funny."

I pretend to write another note. "Destroy... my... sense of humor," I mock-record. "What's next, oh wise one?"

"Pack politics. Military strategy," he says.

"Thrilling," I say with false enthusiasm, then turn to the page to start writing.

Over the next hour, we catalog the gaps in my knowledge down to the tiniest detail. Then from there, Stark sets about establishing a shiny new schedule for me. Combat at dawn, strategy lessons until noon, pack politics in the afternoon, independent study in the evenings.

Oh, and don't forget all of my regular pack courses and training sessions on top of that. After all, I'm still a Rawbond.

I want to argue that I need *some* time to sleep—and maybe see Killian—but I've clearly exhausted the three ounces of patience he keeps on reserve for me.

Eventually, I stretch back in my chair, arching my back, and then point to the shelf behind him. "And those?"

He turns, stares at the shelf for a moment, then looks at me again. "Excuse me?"

I stand and approach the shelf, intentionally barring the memory of Stark pushing me up against it from my mind. I sidestep that confusion and reach out to dust my fingertips over the books that drew my attention earlier.

"Are they part of my training? My independent study?" I ask.

Even now, there's that shiver of energy along my spine when I look at them. Old, withered, leather-bound and... almost alive.

"Those are books that have passed through my family line," he tells me, his expression is unreadable. "They are not mine to loan. But if you find yourself drawn to any of them and happen to pick them up while I'm not looking, I won't be able to stop you."

"*Yes*," Anassa's voice comes over the bond. "*Do your own research.*" Thanks for that, Anassa. Could have used your guidance during any other part of today's training, but glad some dusty old books have gotten you excited.

I scoff. "You realize how *cryptic* that answer w—"

Stark's fist slams toward my face and I stagger back.

"I thought we were done with this!" I shout.

"Done?" he says scornfully, and we pick up the brutal rhythm of interrogation and sparring again. But even as I defend myself, that odd pulsing energy lingers in the back of my mind, right at the base of my skull.

I can't shake the feeling that those old books are aware. Waiting.

After my long day of torture, I tumble into bed aching and exhausted, thinking I'll sleep like the dead. But almost the instant I shut my eyes, I fall into a vivid dream. Shadows twist around me, lifting me, pillaging my mind.

The air is suddenly cold, my mattress unyielding.

And then the faint scent of old blood fills my nose.

Beneath my hands, there's hard-packed dirt.

Not again, is all I can think. *No, no, no.*

My heart thuds loudly in my ears as I sit up, opening my eyes.

I'm no longer dreaming, and I'm no longer in my room. This is real.

I'm exactly where I was last time, in the very center of the arena floor. But something is slightly different. The usual disorientation that takes me during these episodes is absent, replaced by unsettling clarity.

The moon casts perfect patches of light through the glass ceiling above my head, but around those patches of clarity, strange shadows creep across the earth. At their very edges, they look like they're… shivering. Trembling like a spider's legs.

I push myself to my hands and knees, focusing on my breaths. But my own shadow doesn't seem to follow my movements precisely. Or so I thought, but when I blink, it's right where it belongs.

Through our bond, Anassa's alertness spikes. She can sense this, too, then.

"Be careful," she warns, voice quieter than usual.

I squint into the surrounding darkness. Below me, I can see the center of the draining system again. But as I slide my foot forward to try to find my feet, the angle of the moonlight shifts just enough that something glints in the dark. I lean forward again, peering below.

There's something metallic. Definitely gold. I press myself to the ground, straining. Beside that glint of metal, there's a shimmering stone. Opalescent.

And is that… the curve of a wolf's head?

I shift my weight and push my fingers carefully through the hole, grunting as I reach for the vague shapes lurking down there. I can't say why.

Generally, I'd avoid sticking my entire arm into strange places. But there's an almost instinctual need thrumming in my mind. A pull, like a hand around my wrist dragging me in.

A sound echoes through the arena. Footsteps, I realize.

I jerk upright instantly, scrambling away from the drain. The rapid approach of someone else so late at night makes me suddenly certain that I'm not supposed to be here. Not supposed to see this. I can't be caught.

Hastily, I head for the other side of the arena and slip into the shadows, which have mercifully fallen still. My mind races with questions.

What was buried beneath the arena floor? Why does it feel like it's drawing me in?

And why, as I flee through the halls, does it seem like death is on my heels?

CHAPTER THIRTY-EIGHT

T raining during the Proving period is both the same as the Forging—repetitive, arduous, dangerous—and very, very different. Most notably, we share training with other packs. Every fucking *day*.

It makes sense, we need to learn to work together efficiently. But it's truly a curse to interact this much with Daemos, considering how many of them I've managed to piss off. Their Alpha, included.

Stark has been training me privately for two weeks now, and he seems to take profound pleasure in constantly pushing me to the breaking point. I end every day with sore ribs and aching muscles, having gotten my ass handed to me over and over.

As brutal as he's been, though, I can tell I'm improving. I'm learning something.

Which is a lot more than I can say for any interactions I have with Daegan Prak, the Strategos Gamma who was recalled from the front to take over Egith's instructor position. He has straw-colored hair and a worried-looking countenance.

Useless is too kind a descriptor for the man. He reminds me of Roddert, one of the other Strategos Rawbonds—rocks for brains. Maybe they're related.

Today, Strategos and Daemos are together in the Daemos training yard for joint exercise where we're meant to be tuning into our pack powers. We've been at it for thirty minutes.

"Strategos Rawbonds, move to the side," Gamma Daegan commands, "and—"

He catches my eye and flinches, stopping his instruction mid-sentence.

This has been our adorable little song and dance for the past two weeks. Every time he needs to do his job and teach us, he defers to me because of my status as his Alpha.

He's okay with the other Rawbonds, but I'm getting nothing. He doesn't give me orders, he's slow to criticize my performance, and when he does, it's almost tentative, like he's worried I'm going to snap at him for dominance. *Resistance* is necessary for strength training.

I need him to be a real instructor, or I'm never going to improve.

"Continue, Daegan," I grit out from atop Anassa.

He shakes himself as if coming out of a daze and looks back toward the other Strategos pack members. "Move to the side to allow for Daemos to demonstrate their pack powers. Then tap into Strategos foresight abilities and dodge their strikes."

Stark pipes in. "Daemos Rawbonds, aim for the ground in case Strategos is too slow to dodge. You are not to strike them directly or to use your powers at full strength. Today's goal is improving each pack's powers, not hurting each other."

This is the first time we've had a chance to see Daemos powers up close.

The eighteen Daemos Rawbonds circle together, and without warning, wave after wave of magic pulses through the training grounds. They're drawing force from the very air around them, creating battering rams of energy that punch through the arena like massive fists. Debris flies everywhere.

It's shit-yourself terrifying.

Allegra shrieks when she almost gets knocked off of her wolf. So much for avoiding direct strikes.

I sense eyes on me and search through the cloud of dust until I spot him.

Jonah.

He's been circling around me all training session, enjoying this more than he should. Each time I catch sight of him through the tumult of wolves and riders and the clouds of dust, he's had a spiteful grin on his face.

It was only a matter of time before he found some way to reach me. He's been skulking around ever since the Purge Trial and Perielle's death, making snide remarks and skewering me with his gaze across the room. I'd say he's grieving, but he doesn't seem the type.

Rather, he's acting like I've broken his favorite toy, so he's going to break my bones in retaliation.

"Daemos," Stark calls out, "strike again in 5... 4...."

Mentally, I tap into the pack bond. Everyone else's consciousness flows through me as we use our powers to create a foresight visualization. In the vision, one of the Daemos riders, a woman with shockingly intimidating shoulders, directs a blow to the left of our line.

"3... 2..."

My mind is focused on maintaining the vision and guiding the pack toward the right when a wolf slams into me from the side.

Anassa snarls and whips her head around to bite at the wolf. Pain spirals up my leg from where we collided, and it's making it difficult to stay mounted properly. I sag to one side and cling to her fur.

"You keep getting in my way!" Jonah snarls over the thunderous sound of the woman's blast.

Getting in his way.

He should be halfway across the training yard right now with the rest of his pack. Instead, he's here, pushing so far into the Strategos side the blast of Daemos power sends dirt scattering over him.

"Get in line, Jonah!" I shout, turning on Anassa to fall back into the flow of my pack. They're rippling with fine-tuned attention, moving seamlessly around us.

Daemos aren't so organized or considerate. They surge forward due to the natural rhythms of this exercise, and we're caught up in the swirling crush of fur and muscle between the two packs.

"You don't get to tell me what to do, *commoner*!" Jonah shouts at me.

Anassa snarls and turns viciously, like she's about to eat him.

A massive Daemos wolf shoves past Jonah, blocking him from my vision for a moment. Just then, foresight prickles over my skin and I sense the blow coming.

Too late, though.

Anassa braces herself, but the strike of Daemos power is punishing.

I fly clear off of Anassa's back and land in the sand, rolling and curling up into a ball to minimize the chance of my limbs being trampled.

Did Jonah just…?

Suddenly, he and his wolf are above me, and it's no longer a question at all. Jonah's eyes burn with rage as the second blow comes. I turn to diminish the force of it, but my entire body already burns with pain.

An electric tingling shrieks through me, screaming, *you're about to get hit.*

I hold up my hands, but it's useless.

One of those terrifying blows crashes over me. My head snaps to the side.

Something cracks, and my entire skull explodes in pain. I wish I could stop the blood-curdling scream that wrenches from my throat, but the pain is too much. It rips from me, and the vacant space it leaves behind floods with rage.

Anassa senses my fury. For a thundering heartbeat, I'm certain she's going to attack Jonah and his wolf.

And then someone else does it for us. Jonah is there one moment and gone the next.

Jonah's body slams against the wall of the training yard. A second after it happens, there's a rush of wind, like death just streaked past me and only narrowly left me breathing.

The *sheer* power I just felt, like a glimpse of something primordial…

Someone is shouting. Gamma Daegan, I think. The wolves from both packs fall back, parting to give me a view of Jonah's crumpled body where he's groaning on the ground. My vision swims slightly as blood pours from my nose.

A dark figure is standing over Jonah, shouting. At first, it's garbled by the ringing in my ears. Then the words come through in a deep, enraged voice.

"—you do *not* touch Alpha Meryn that way!"

Stark's chest is heaving. Cratos isn't beside him, but he doesn't need his wolf's sheer size to threaten Jonah. The menacing way his tattooed hands are clenching and unclenching say it all, like he's imagining them around Jonah's throat.

"She's not *my* Alpha, sir," Jonah says, but his eyes are averted.

"*Your* Alpha gave you an order not to use your magic on Strategos at full strength, and you disobeyed it!" Stark bellows. His entire pack stirs at the echo of his voice. Some of their wolves' ears fold back, their heads lowering submissively below their shoulders.

Stark's voice quiets, but only slightly. It's still loud enough for the whole training yard to hear, laced through with menace.

"You are a powerful Rawbond, but strength is not the only thing we value in Daemos. You'd do well to remember that if you want to make it through the rest of Proving. And in case my implication is not crystal fucking clear: you touch her again and I'll cull you myself."

I shakily sit up and cover my throbbing nose with one hand. It warms as Anassa begins to heal it. A hand closes around my shoulder, and I flinch instinctively.

"It's me," Izabel says, her dark eyebrows laced together in worry. "Alright?"

"Alright," I confirm even though there's hot blood running down my throat. "Should I be embarrassed?"

"No," Izabel replies.

I grunt. "Mortified, then."

She lets out a surprised laugh, then offers me a hand and helps me up. Nevah comes over and claps me on the back.

"You fall like an Alpha," she tells me with a half-smile. Then she waves at my face, at my surely pulverized nose. "That, too. Very... authoritative looking."

Nevah has been making an effort since the Purge Trial and since the pack decided to forgive me. She sits with us at meals instead of seeking out a solitary table. She hangs out in the common lounge in the evening, and has even started sleeping with one of the Kryptos women, or so Venna says.

"Thanks," I tell her. "I can break yours too, if you want to match your Alpha. I'm sure it'll be the new hot look at the front."

"Training's over," Stark calls loudly, stalking away from Jonah. His hands are still in fists. Muscles are straining so tight that he looks like he's about to rip himself in two. As he passes us, he growls, "Alpha, my office," without even looking at me.

The three of us watch him go for a moment, as does every other person in the training yard.

Then I spit some blood into the sand. "If I turn up dead, you know who to hunt in your dramatic quest for revenge," I tell the two women, then mentally say goodbye to Anassa.

I follow Stark silently, awkwardly walking through the path he's cleared through wolves and riders. I hold my head as high as I can while covered in blood and struggling to walk in a straight line. There's no space to overthink how pathetic I likely look to my fellow Rawbonds right now; I'm too busy bracing myself for Stark's scolding.

He's in my head already, telling me that I fucked up by yelling at Jonah, that I should've been worried about my own pack, that I made a fool out of myself. Which criticism will he start with?

Our boots echo once we're inside. Stark's hands are still tight. His shoulders are practically at his ears. There's a wildness to him that could mean the criticism I'm going to get is going to be unnecessarily intense.

He slams his office door shut behind us with a bang and I wince.

I wish I didn't care. I wish I could shrug all of this off and act like nothing could ever hurt me. But when Stark turns to look at me, it's like my stomach is going to drop from my body and smack to the floor at my feet.

He stares at me for a long moment. Glares, really, with his terrifyingly dark eyes.

Then his shoulders fall. His eyes slide shut. I watch him take a deep breath and feel like he just put something fragile in my clumsy hands without any instruction as to how not to break it.

The moment passes quickly, though.

His eyes snap open, and he joins me on my side of the room. "Turn," he orders, and I do.

He takes hold of my shoulder briefly and forces me to step toward the round mirror that's beside me.

I grimace. Anassa might have healed my nose, but it's set at a horrible angle. My entire face looks different, rearranged by Jonah's violence. I resist the instinct to reach up and touch it. I resist the sting of tears prickling the back of my eyes.

It's not just vanity. I mean, it is. It definitely is. But it's also…

I don't know who I am, something deep within me whispers, gazing upon my rearranged face. But I do know, don't I? He called my name only minutes ago. Alpha Meryn. That's who I am now. It's who I have to be.

I steady my emotions and clench my jaw. "Guess that's what I deserve, huh?" I say, voice strong. Dismissive, even. I'm heading off his criticism, taking control of it before it can hurt. "I'm a shit Alpha."

"Yes," Stark says instantly.

Ouch. I mean, I know it's the truth, but hearing it from his lips hurts more than I'd ever admit.

My voice wavers slightly when I reply, "Aren't you meant to be encouraging me, *instructor*?"

The snark falls flat. I can't summon the teasing energy I usually use to downplay how serious this all is. But Stark doesn't seem affected. He just stands behind me and stares into my eyes through the mirror.

"I will never lie to you," he says, voice somber, and the words dig down deep into my bones, carving themselves into my very marrow. Just as I can tell that he often fucking hates me, that it brings him pleasure to break me... this, too, I can tell is true.

A small shiver wracks through me and I turn toward him, deflecting. My shoulder nearly brushes his chest as I do. "Well then. Truth," I say and touch my cheek briefly, "how bad does this look?"

His dark gaze moves over my features. I ignore the hair on the back of my neck prickling. "It's awful," he says simply.

Closing my eyes, I let out a soft laugh. Yep, he's not going to lie to me.

I'd like to pretend that I don't care how I look. That I'm a tough warrior woman who doesn't need to feel pretty sometimes. It would be so great to be above any sense of vanity.

Alas, I'm only human. And, like it or not, looks are important here in this den of vipers.

"Fuck," I say quietly. I open my eyes, and with a jolt realize that Stark is still staring intensely at my face.

There's something indecisive at war in his gaze. Then, he says, "I can fix it, if you want. But it will hurt."

It usually does, where he's involved. And what's the alternative, going around with a cabbage for a nose for the rest of my life?

"Break it again," I hear Anassa say through the bond. *"I'll heal it right after."*

That's that. I square my shoulders. "Hurt me, then, Alpha Stark."

The moment the words are out, he moves closer to me and my body lights up with awareness. His calloused, scarred hands close around my shoulders and push me down into the rickety chair next to us. I let it happen and look up at him, my gaze catching on the tattoos on his neck.

He's a broker of pain.

Stark steps closer. His knee pushes mine open, then he kneels down on the floor, nestled in between my legs so that our faces are at the same height. My hands tighten on the armrests, but not for long—he reaches down and takes my wrists.

He pulls my hands to his chest. I let it happen, too lost in this electric silence to resist or ask or even hesitate. His heartbeat thrums under my palm.

"Hold on to me," he says, voice rumbling. "Tight, if you need to."

My throat clicks when I swallow. I stare at my own hands on his chest. Then, inexplicably, I move them to his shoulders.

A better handhold, I tell myself. It has nothing to do with the twitch of his muscles beneath my palms as he lifts his hands to my face.

I expected him to break me apart without warning. It's what he does in training. Punching my nose straight would not have been out of character. But that doesn't happen. He's being almost... kind.

What the fuck is happening right now?

"Take a deep breath," he says quietly, meeting my eyes. "One, two, *three*."

And he breaks my nose back into place.

Tears immediately burst from my eyes, squeezed out as all of my muscles clench in resistance. My nails sink into his skin hard enough to draw blood, but Stark doesn't even flinch. He lets me rip at him, returning a bit of the pain he just gave me.

Fuck, it hurts. Fuck, fuck, fuck.

Worse, somehow, than when it was first broken, maybe because I have no adrenaline to offset the agony.

But as soon as it happens, it's over. Anassa immediately heals the break, and the pain ebbs.

I sniff and look up. Stark is watching me, his expression as iron-clad as Anassa's wall at her worst. Stupidly, I wish I knew what was going through his head. If he felt like something just shifted between us, too.

Maybe he's just trying to hide how much he enjoyed that.

Stark says nothing until he's on the other side of the office and leagues of distance have been established between us. "You need to be better," he says.

Still pissed, then. I scramble to find the energy to rein in my emotional whiplash. "So you keep *telling* me," I snap.

Stark turns to look at me. His brow is pinched tight. "Being Alpha means that you're in charge now. Daegan is an instructor, but *you* are still in charge. He's your Gamma. He reports to you."

"You think I don't know that?"

"I think you don't understand that good leaders are able to learn from their subordinates," he replies coldly. It shuts me right up. "I know the power dynamics are uncomfortable because you need him to teach you, but you also need to get used to giving him instructions. Tell him what you need and be clear about it. Do not expect him to lead you or the rest of the pack. Not while you're around."

He allows a long stretch of silence during which his words latch around my ankles and drag me down like an anchor. But at least I'm no longer drifting.

"This is an important thing for you to learn as Alpha," he continues. "If you can't master this, your pack is going to fall apart. Can you do it?"

His question demands a serious answer. Back home at the laundry, I basically ran things despite the other workers being older and much more experienced. The place needed someone to take on the burden of keeping things organized, and I had no trouble stepping into that role when necessity required it. All I had to do was strike a balance between snapping out orders and being kind about it.

Surely, the same applies here.

"Yes," I say finally. "I can do that."

Stark straightens. "Good," he says tersely. "You're dismissed."

He starts looking over the messages at his desk. I run my fingertips over my set nose and head for the office door. Something unexpectedly has me pausing and looking back, though. He's leaning over his desk, expression stony, a dark lock of hair hanging over his forehead.

"Thanks," I blurt. "For the advice. And for... the nose."

He doesn't lift his head or look at me, which is a blessing because I'm sure my face is bright red.

I don't know what the fuck that was. I've never *thanked* Stark before. I never thought I'd be grateful for anything he could do to me.

For me, I mean.

Actually, I was pretty sure he had a murder-wall with a hundred drawings of my face on it, eyes all scratched out.

He raises his hand in acknowledgment, the only indication that he's heard me, and I leave, trying to ignore the weird disappointment humming through my veins.

CHAPTER THIRTY-NINE

Alpha training with Stark continues to pass with painstaking slowness. Every day is a battle. He seems to take great satisfaction in sending me home battered and exhausted.

It's not for nothing, though.

As much as I hate to admit it, he knows what he's doing. There's a method to his unrelenting brutality.

Sometimes I hate him. Stark isn't above kicking me when I'm down—literally—in fact, he seems to relish taking every opportunity to do so. But after three weeks of his daily lessons, I'm stronger both mentally and physically. My body is hardened from the hours and hours of fight training, my mind sharpened from the endless tactical study.

I'm actually grateful to him—not that I would ever say so. I'm starting to feel like an Alpha. Or at least like there's some hope I can actually fulfill the role.

Today, I've been holding my own for almost the entire lesson. But Stark is significantly stronger than me, has years of battle experience, and his stamina is insane.

My only physical advantage is speed—and it's not a big one. He's a lot faster than a man his size has any right to be.

My other advantage is the down-and-dirty tricks I learned while fighting in the pits. There haven't been many opportunities to use them, though. Stark's superior skills have kept me almost entirely on the defense.

But today, after an hour of savage hand-to-hand, he starts to flag.

It's subtle—I only see it because I've become so intimately familiar with the way he moves. There's no hesitation in his attacks, but he's not hitting quite as hard and fast as before.

He's sweating, flushed, face screwed into a scowl of intense focus.

For the first time since we started this routine, he's nearing his limit. Which means I have an opportunity that might never appear again.

I mirror his slowed movements, projecting my own exhaustion. Letting him think I'm losing my edge.

And just like that, he gives me an opening.

In an adrenaline-driven flash, I drop to the floor and sweep his legs out from under him, rolling onto his chest as he lands.

His hands clamp onto my knee as I press it against his throat. He could throw me off, but if this were a real fight, I would have already crushed his trachea.

He's down. Beaten.

There's a brief moment of shock—mine *and* his—as I stare into his eyes.

Then his hand tightens around my knee, my body hyper-aware of the contact. He strokes his thumb on my leg and warm sparks explode through my body. I'm starved for physical contact that isn't brutal, I remind myself; Killian and I have continued to keep things chaste until I can figure out how Anassa wants to handle the bond.

While I'm distracted by the sensation, he yanks my knee to the side and I tumble forward, the apex between my thighs skirting dangerously close to his mouth.

I roll to the side as quickly as I can, flopping onto the floor next to him. The air is filled with the twin sounds of our ragged breath.

"I beat you," I pant out, pretending that I didn't get thrown entirely off my game at the end.

"You did," he says, letting me have the win.

Oddly humbled and triumphant at once, I get up and offer him my hand.

Stark's eyes narrow, but there's no anger in them. No pride, either—not that I expected any. There is something, though. A gleam of emotion too complex to make sense of.

He ignores my hand and gets up on his own.

"We're done for today," he says, turning away from me quickly. "You're dismissed."

I leave his office drained and sore but elated. I'm making progress—significant, *meaningful* progress.

For the first time since I entered this world, I'm not totally unsure about my chances of survival. I have a long way to go still, but my prospects are looking much better than before, thanks to Stark.

Too bad he's such an asshole, I muse, wandering back to my room. It would be nice to see him as an ally. We are supposed to be part of one big pack, after all.

But whatever. I don't need to make friends with him to get what I need. I'm not sure Stark is even capable of friendship, anyway. He's basically a walking war machine. And it hasn't escaped me that his malicious attitude toward me has been a big motivating factor in my performance.

If he were nicer, I probably wouldn't have come so far so quickly.

My thoughts of Stark scatter when I step into my room to find it occupied.

"Hi," I say with a smile as Killian rises from his seat at my desk.

His face immediately darkens when he sees my bruises. There's still blood on my lip, even though Anassa has healed me. Concern and anger war on his handsome features as he comes to me and gingerly touches my face.

"That fucking *prick*," he growls. "Does he really need to do this to you every day?"

I grin. "It was worth it. I beat him today for the first time."

Killian sighs, lips curving into a rueful smile. "Congratulations. Though I wish your victory didn't require quite so much blood."

Anassa's healing powers don't do much for my bruises or muscle aches, so Killian still tends to me, rubbing healing tinctures into my hurts. I smile and sit down on the bed while Killian retrieves the familiar medicine kit from my wardrobe. He sits beside me and begins tending to my wounds with practiced care.

This has become our ritual. Stark beats me up, Killian stitches me back together again. It's made the whole process a lot easier, knowing Killian will be here to soothe me after Stark's lessons.

Killian's touch is feather light against my bruised flesh, and despite the aches and pains, heat sparks in my body.

I can't take it anymore. These past couple of weeks have been tortuous.

"Can I please have some privacy?" I ask Anassa. *"I'm dying here. I won't block you out if you think I can't do it correctly, but maybe you can put the wall up from your end in a way that is satisfactory for you?"*

There's a long silence and then finally she says, *"Fine."* There's a slight pressure in my head as she erects the wall, and I try to project gratitude through it.

When Killian leans in to examine the place where my lip had split, I catch his mouth with mine. The kiss flares hot, tasting of copper and desire. As it deepens, my body responds with a searing rush of arousal driven by lingering adrenaline and triumph from my fight with Stark—not to mention that weird spark of desire I'd felt.

Killian leans into the kiss urgently, catching my top lip in his teeth, then plundering my mouth with his tongue.

I'm aware of all the pains in my body as he starts undressing me, but somehow, they only feed the desire. I'm feverish—primal.

Impatient, I pull Killian down on the bed roughly, climbing on top of him, both of us still only half-undressed. Grind myself against him, my underclothes already damp. Catching his eyes, I run my tongue slowly across my bottom lip.

Killian groans at the sight, and then flips us over so that he's on top, pinning my arms down on the mattress. His mouth drops to my breasts, teeth grazing one nipple before biting down over the other, and I see stars.

I buck my hips, looking for friction, *needing* that press of him against me. Killian just presses me down into the mattress, looking at me in amusement. "Need something, kitten?"

Half-heartedly, I squirm against his hold. "What if… you let me take charge tonight," I say, mouth going dry at the look in his eyes.

"I'll take good care of you," Killian growls, moving one of his hands down to my hips and yanking off my remaining clothes, then teasing me with his fingers, first one, and then two, relentlessly pushing into my slick heat.

At the stretch of his touch so deep inside of me, heat unfurls in my abdomen, and I move my hips mindlessly. I lose the power of speech for a moment when he curls his fingers at exactly that spot I like.

"*Goddess*, Killian," I moan, and then yelp as his thumb finds my clit, swirling over the sensitive bundle of nerves as a third finger joins the other two inside of me.

"Good girl," Killian says roughly, lavishing kisses and bites along my collarbone, up the column of my neck.

Using a move from the fighting rings, I hook a knee around Killian and flip us back over, relishing the feeling of power as I reposition us on the bed. He watches in amusement as my hands scramble at the tie of his pants, teasing the hard heat of him with my hands as I pull off the last of his clothing, ready to ride him until I find my satisfaction.

Killian lets me shimmy his trousers down his legs, but then as I climb back up him, he wraps a hand in my hair, yanking my face up until we're looking each other straight in the eye.

I moan at the pull of my hair wrapped firmly in Killian's fingers, his grip just tight enough. One of Killian's signature moves in bed, the familiarity and promise in the feeling of his hand in my hair makes me even wetter until I'm dripping for him.

"Use your mouth, kitten," Killian orders, pulling my face down toward his cock. I sink down eagerly, wrapping a hand around the base as I tease the tip with my tongue, loving the way his hips thrust involuntarily at the soft suction of my mouth.

Slowly, surely, I take as much of him into my mouth as I can. The thick head of his cock hits the back of my throat, and I groan around him at the sensation. Killian answers with a groan of his own, then uses his grip on my hair to move me up and down his shaft, my lips making a lewd popping noise as they stretch around the head and then push back down to take him in deeper.

I tongue the bottom of his cock as I take him deeper and deeper, moaning helplessly, tears pricking my eyes as he thrusts back up into my mouth. Just when I think I can't take it any deeper, Killian yanks my head off him and pulls me up, positioning my hips above his and then yanking me down in one sharp motion.

I cry out, the exquisite fullness so intense that it's almost pain. Killian doesn't give me time to adjust, just uses his grip on my hips to pull me up and then sharply back down again, deeper than I thought possible.

I'm astride him, like I wanted, but the punishing pace is too much for me to match, I can't find the rhythm. I let Killian move me instead, up and down his length until I'm babbling his name, pleading, saying I don't know what, words with no meaning, as he drives me insane.

As I fall apart on top of him, Killian lets go too, that steely control slipping for a moment as he slams up into me a final time, finding his release.

Neither of us says anything afterward, just curling around each other in the bed, letting our breathing and heartbeats slow. I try to let myself relax, knowing that moments with Killian might be rare once I've graduated and need to head to the front. Try to focus on his warm body pressed into mine, and the hard planes of his stomach under my lazy touch.

But like every time I've shut my eyes over the past few weeks, a familiar image rises in my memory: that metal object glinting in the arena drain.

Dammit. What *was* that thing? And why do I keep waking up *there* of all places? Is it just my anxiety around the Trials coming to life in my nightmares?

I know there's a good chance that whatever I'm seeing is another delusion, just like the screams I heard or the carving under the tapestry.

The image won't leave me. I have to find out if it's real.

"Killian?" I venture, trying to keep my tone casual. "Do you know much about the Rawbond arena? Like, what's underneath it?"

He makes a drowsy humming sound, one hand trailing aimless circles across my back. "Underneath? Just the drainage system, I assume. Why?"

I shrug. "I was wondering if there are secret passages and stuff there, too."

He makes another contemplative hum. "Could be. This place is ancient—there's much that I don't know about it, even after living here my whole life. The castle has secrets I'll probably never uncover."

Something in his tone catches at me. I prop myself up on one elbow, studying his face. There's nothing unusual to read there, however. He looks sated and a little sleepy.

The castle has secrets I'll probably never uncover.

Strange. He's the crown prince—shouldn't he have access to every part of the castle? Shouldn't he know all its nooks and crannies?

Maybe his father is keeping things from him. The more I get to know about King Cyril, the less I trust him.

"What's the matter?" Killian asks, lifting one hand to trail his fingers across my cheek.

"Nothing," I say, mustering a smile. "Just tired."

Tired of your father's shit. I know Killian has no love spared for the king, but also—it's his *father*. Family is a blind spot for all of us. If it's possible that the king is hiding something from Killian, would Killian even want to know?

Killian kisses me and gets dressed, heading back to his quarters to handle some of his royal duties. All the while, my mind spins.

He disappears through the wardrobe, and my mind spins.

I get dressed, too, and my mind spins.

The more that I think about it, the more certain I become that the king has secrets. And I know just how to figure them out.

VENNA IS NOWHERE to be found. She's not with Izabel in the Strategos anteroom, or in the Rawbond common lounge. She's not in the Kryptos anteroom—and when I poke my head in there, one of the Kryptos recruits snippily says, "You have to stop coming in here!"

Venna's a ghost. Kryptos Rawbonds are trained to move unseen —and they take to those lessons quickly.

Tracking her through the castle proves challenging, but eventually, I find her in one of the lesser-used greenhouse courtyards. The shadowy space is smaller than most of the others, and a little less cultivated. The ancient stone walls are covered in ivy. The wild tendrils drip from the arbors and trail the edges of the cobbled path.

Venna is perched on a weathered stone bench near the central fountain, talking animatedly with another Kryptos Rawbond. They're signing with their hands occasionally. Venna quickly realized how useful it was as a Kryptos to know a language that can be spoken with your hands rather than your voice, and has been teaching all the other Kryptos Rawbonds some sign language.

Venna says something about training as I approach. Then the other Kryptos spots me coming, signs, "Bye," and hurries off.

That's been happening a lot lately. I'm still not popular among the Rawbonds. Not sure if it's because word spread that I shut my direwolf out the night of the ball, or because I'm sleeping with the crown prince, or just because I'm an Alpha now. Maybe all three.

Venna turns to look at me and I can tell she's cataloging the details of my appearance—the fresh bruises from training, the nervousness in my posture, the slight swelling of my recently split lip.

"I need your help," I tell her. Then I move closer, looking

around to make sure no one else is around, listening. I don't know enough sign language yet to do this with my hands, although I really wish I weren't about to say this aloud. "I think the king is hiding things from Killian. Important things. About the castle, maybe."

Her brows go up in question, then down again as her expression turns calculating. "Be careful. That's a dangerous line of thinking."

"I know," I say, "but I just get the sense that something is wrong here. I need someone who can watch without being seen. Someone who notices everything."

Venna smiles, a bit of pride shining through that I've acknowledged her skills.

"I think you're right," she says, voice pitched low. "I've noticed patterns in the castle shadows. Servants moving at strange hours. Doors that should be open that are locked. Sounds that don't match with any of the castle's normal operations."

I'm relieved to have her confirmation that something is amiss, but the implications send a chill down my spine.

Just as I'm about to ask for more details, there's a scuff of footsteps behind me.

"Alpha Cooper?"

I turn to see one of the castle messengers approaching. He holds out a sealed letter. "Urgent message from the front."

Heart speeding, I open the carefully sealed missive, recognizing the handwriting inside as Egith's.

The message is short. As I read, the paper begins to tremble in my hands.

The final line looms large in my vision.

"We may have located the missing children."

CHAPTER FORTY

B ack in my room, all thoughts of the mysteries under the arena are forgotten. My mind races as I stuff clothing and supplies into my pack, Egith's message burning in my pocket.

There have been possible sightings of children near the Grunfall outpost at the front. Egith gave no further details, but the implications...

Could Saela be among them?

Through our bond, Anassa tries to project calm, but my thoughts spiral with mounting intensity.

I might never get another opportunity like this. And I can't trust anyone else to follow through on Saela's rescue. I know there are great, seasoned soldiers and Bonded at the front—better than me, no doubt. But I don't trust anyone but myself with my sister's safety.

I have to get there—fast.

"Going somewhere?"

Stark's voice drawling from the doorway behind me isn't enough to break me out of my near-frantic preparations. I don't even turn to look at him.

"Egith sent me a message, " I say, cramming the healer's kit into my pack. "I'm heading to Grunfall."

"Grunfall?" he repeats. "The front? By yourself? I think not."

"I'm not asking for permission," I grunt as I fasten the ties on my pack.

Starks voice deepens with anger. "You are an Alpha, Cooper. And one still in training, at that. You can't go charging off without protection."

The dangerous tone makes me bristle. Finally, I turn to face him, temper spiking.

"I don't need any damn protection," I snap. "I've been training with you for weeks. Or did you forget how I put you on your back this morning?"

His face turns thunderous. He steps into my room, filling the small space with his looming presence.

"You took me down once," he growls, "and you think that makes you invincible? Alpha or not, you're still a trainee. The Siphons will smell the green on you a mile away—and they'd love nothing more than to capture an Alpha."

Something inside me hardens as I face him. It's the same feeling I got when I was torturing that Nabber. *Nothing* is going to stop me from saving my sister—not even Stark.

"You're going to have to put me down if you want to stop me," I say in a cold, deadly voice.

Stark's expression shifts, reading my face. His jaw tightens. The deep brown eyes narrow with calculation. Silence stretches between us, thrumming with the threat of violence.

"You're not going alone," he grates. "I'm coming with you."

Shock and fury flash through me. "The hell you are!"

"It's not a request," he says in a tone of steely command. "Talk to your wolf about it. I bet Anassa will agree with me."

I reach for her. *"Don't fuck me like this, Anassa,"* I hiss. *"We can't trust him."*

She growls, and it sounds like laughter. *"Of course we can, he's a fellow Alpha. I've decided already. He and Cratos will come with us, for your safety."*

Anassa sounds very pleased to be going around me with this call. *"Traitor."* Cratos will probably eat me for a snack when he gets hungry.

My gaze snaps back up to Stark and I scowl. "Whatever. Come with us or don't, just don't get in my way."

I can't think of anything but getting to the front as quickly as possible.

Stark summons a servant to gather his travel supplies and meet us at the gates. We're packed and ready to go within the hour.

As we mount our wolves and the castle gate cranks open, I feel a brief twinge of guilt. I left a note in my room for Killian explaining everything and promising I'll be back in a week. He's going to be worried, but there's no time to say goodbye.

No time to argue about what I'm doing.

Despite what I said to Stark, I *know* this is reckless. I know it's dangerous—the most dangerous thing I've ever done, which is really saying something. But I don't have a choice.

If I miss this chance and Saela dies—if I never see her again because I waited too long…

I push the thought away. I'm going to find her. Whatever it takes.

We leave the castle walls behind without a backwards glance, our wolves moving in practiced synchronization, their massive paws eating up the distance with otherworldly speed.

Stark and Cratos take the lead at first, guiding us down a broad dirt road that swerves away from the city and spits us out into mountain wilderness.

This is the path the troops take to get to the front. It's forbidden to commoners, so there's nothing to slow our pace. I lower my head and lean into Anassa's body as her speed increases. Even in my state of desperate focus, the pace is exhilarating. We've never moved this fast before, even during the Trials.

Which is good. On horseback, the journey to the front takes two weeks. At this pace, we can be there in two *days*—if we don't run into any trouble.

I glance to my left. Stark and Cratos keep pace beside us with unnerving ease, moving like one creature with two bodies.

Stark watches me intently. I can't tell what he's thinking, but the ferocity of his stare sets my teeth on edge. Maybe he expects me to peel off at any moment and try to leave him behind. Or maybe he just expects me to fall off my direwolf like the greenhorn I supposedly am.

Either way, tension crackles in the air between us. Anassa bristles, irritated by my resistance to having him here.

"Be grateful," she growls into my mind. *"You do not understand the dangers ahead."*

Maybe she's right, but I'm getting really damn tired of Stark and his malicious condescension. The fact that he doubts me so much he's willing to follow me to the front lines like some kind of nanny makes me burn with resentment.

What the fuck does he care if I die? The man *hates* me.

Maybe he just wants to be there to see it happen, I muse darkly.

Anassa bristles again. She doesn't say anything, but her judgment comes through with crisp clarity. She thinks I'm being childish —and ignorant.

I ignore her, focusing in on the path ahead. This isn't about Stark or anybody else.

It's about Saela.

Within minutes, our lightning pace carries us out of sight of the city. As soon as the castle spires disappear behind the treeline, Stark says, "If you're going to be reckless, at least let me keep you alive."

I look at him with a start. Is that *concern* in his voice?

He meets my gaze with the usual scowling intensity, but there's no malice in it. No condescension. Almost like he guessed what passed between me and Anassa just now and he's trying to... what? *Reassure* me?

What the actual fuck?

Thankfully, I'm saved from having to respond by Anassa kicking up her speed. All at once, the air is whipping past with such violence that talking is impossible.

Thank the goddess.

I put thoughts of Stark aside and focus on the path ahead. It's more difficult than expected. I'm all too aware of his wolf racing along beside us.

Focus on the goal, I tell myself, gaze trained on the winding path through the forest ahead. It takes us down from the mountains, over the foothills, and into the sprawling, tree-choked valley below.

We've been on the road for a few hours when the wind starts to pick up, buffeting us despite Anassa and Cratos' unnatural speeds. I glance over at Stark and see that he's adjusted his seat, sinking even deeper into the fur of Cratos' neck and back until they almost look like one mythical creature. I do the same, burrowing into Anassa, and I feel her spark of approval.

None too soon, because shortly after, thick flakes begin to fall. The wind is whipping them into my face, down the collar of my coat, little piles of snow gathering in the joins of my clothing and melting into icy streams of water that dampen my clothes beneath my leathers.

The flakes turn into sheets of snow, and I stop trying to brush them off—it's useless, at this point. The blizzard is raging so furiously that I can barely see Stark and Cratos through the snow, even though they're just a few paces away.

A little of my doubt and worry passes through the bond, and Anassa comes back with fond annoyance.

Okay—she's not worried. That makes me feel a little better.

I press my face against the fur of Anassa's neck until the flakes can't reach me, folding my arms beneath me and pressing them into her fur until all my most vulnerable parts are hidden from the elements. It's not the most comfortable way to ride, but at least I won't get frostbite.

We near Linsfall just before evening—or at least I think we do, it's hard to tell the time of day through all of this snow. I get a little spurt of relief when I see the lights of the fiefdom through the trees up ahead.

This is the halfway point; directly south of Linsfall's city center, within the bounds of their fiefdom, is an outstation where troops and Bonded can set up camp, rest before making the second half of the journey to the front.

The weather is still raging too hard for us to set up our tents, though. I raise my head to watch Stark, possible again as the snow has let up just slightly. He doesn't look back at me, his focus straight ahead at the city walls we're fast approaching.

Some stupid part of me doesn't want to stop. The urgency I felt when I read Egith's message hasn't abated, and the wolves could probably keep going a few hours more.

My rational brain knows that would be idiotic in this weather, though. My body burns with exhaustion and cold, my thighs aching from their grip on Anassa's back. I've never ridden her for this long before and it's making my muscles scream. My back is tender where the moisture from the snow has seeped in and my damp clothes rub against my leathers.

Linsfall is an ancient city, like Sturmfrost, built in stone and timber. Stark guides us to a gatehouse built into the thick wall that encircles the city, and miraculously there's still a gatekeeper holding watch there, though I don't know who she thought could reach Linsfall through all of this snow.

Watching her converse with Stark, I realize—us. They're probably ready for Bonded to show up no matter what, weather conditions be damned.

Inside the walls, the smells and sounds of the city remind me of home in Sturmfrost, though everything is muted by the heavy blanket of snow. Hardly anyone is out on the streets, wisely choosing to stay inside through the worst of this weather.

Stark leads us through the darkening streets, confidently turning corners and choosing roads without ever needing to stop and consider our path.

Anassa and I follow silently, out of our depth. Traveling today, arriving here, has made me realize just how big this world is, and just how little of it I know.

Just when my muscles are cramping up so badly that I think I'm going to fall off Anassa, Stark turns another corner and then hops down off of Cratos, his boots sinking into the snow halfway up his calf.

He's brought us to an inn, and I dismount with relief, only to have my attention caught by the main square up ahead.

"Give me a second," I say to Stark, and head off without a response.

I wade through the deepening snow, Anassa following, and the block empties out into a large empty space, ground eerily smooth with the unbroken snow.

At the center of the square stands the famous, enormous stone statue. The Faceless Goddess.

Even in the dusk, in the middle of a snowstorm, her form commands attention. The statue is carved from a single shining piece of white stone that blends eerily with the snow, making the whole scene feel surreal.

She looks almost alive, despite the signs of centuries past that mark the alabaster stone. She bends in a pose of maternal caring, her hands held out as if in offering. Though her face is smooth and featureless, worn down and unidentifiable from years of pilgrims touching it, her posture suggests both power and grace.

Anassa, too, seems captivated. She pauses just outside the square, making no protest as I move closer to the statue, trying to see it better.

"We should get to the inn," Stark says behind me.

I ignore him. A strange pull draws me to the statue, carrying my feet across the square almost without my participation. Anassa's approval wafts to me along our bond, as though it's right for me to go and greet the image of the goddess.

Stark calls after me, his voice edged with annoyance. "Don't tell me you believe in this commoner nonsense."

Again, I ignore him. I've never been religious, but somehow that doesn't seem relevant.

As I stand at the foot of the statue gazing up at that featureless face, I wonder who she was. It's always seemed strange to me that anyone would worship a nameless, faceless deity whose story has been lost to time, and yet an air of quiet reverence falls over me.

For most commoners, the king is closer to a deity than the goddess, but she's still invoked in prayer—or as a curse. There are small religious sects around the country devoted to her, their members numbering in the thousands. We have a tiny temple devoted to her in Sturmfrost, but I've never been there.

This statue is known around all of Nocturna, though. I had no idea that seeing it in person would evoke such a strong, potent feeling in me.

Without thinking, I turn to look at Stark over my shoulder. "What do *you* believe?"

He frowns as though the question surprises him, then his lips thin in grim disapproval. "The only thing I believe in with any certainty is death. It comes for us all."

I laugh softly, without humor, turning back to gaze at the goddess once more. "Right. All of us except the Siphons."

"They're not immortal," he says. "They might live for thousands of years, but they can die just like the rest of us. You'll see."

I reach out to touch the Faceless Goddess's extended hands. Weirdly, they're free from the heavy snow, as if there's something inside of them warming them. Objects rest in her hands—offerings left by the residents of Linsfall. Coins, fruit, and dried flowers. Bundles of herbs tied with colored ribbon.

These are the people's prayers, I think, something like sadness welling within me. *Pleas for the goddess to bless them, save them. Protect their loved ones.*

"People think the Faceless Goddess made humans," I muse aloud. "That she's the one who gave us life. They believe if they pray to her hard enough that she'll right the imbalance in our kingdom and make life better for the commoners again."

There's a pause, then Starks says, "And you? Do you pray to her, hoping she'll do that?"

I laugh again—a short, cynical gust of breath. "No," I murmur darkly. "I know better. If the Faceless Goddess was ever real, I suspect she's long since abandoned us. If we want things to improve, we have to make that happen ourselves."

Even so, something about the figure calls to me. I reach for her hand again, gloved fingers sliding against the smooth stone. Part of me recognizes that it's freezing right now, but strangely, I don't feel the cold.

For the first time in my life, I close my eyes and pray, thinking of Saela. Thinking of Mom and the madness. Of the voices and dreams that haunt me.

Of the future, which once seemed so clear to me, and now is shrouded in mist.

Help me find the children. Help me understand what's happening. Tell me how to make things better, and I'll do it myself. I'll do everything I can.

When I open my eyes and turn around, I find Stark studying me with inscrutable intensity.

"Are you ready now?" Stark's words are clipped, but they don't hold the annoyance I expected to hear. I nod, turning to face Anassa. For a moment I think I see something in her eyes, sense something in the bond, but then it's gone, whatever it was.

Back at the doors to the inn, a worker appears to lead our wolves away to the nearest stable. Stark hands him a few coins and says, "Fresh meat for both. Make sure it was killed today."

Inside, the inn is bursting with people driven off the roads by the storm. The main room is large, filled with rows of rough wooden tables and benches where dozens of travelers are seated, eating and drinking. The space is oppressively hot after the frigid outdoors, damp with body heat and smelling of woodsmoke. I shuck off my outer layers, bundling them under one arm.

Stark pushes through the crowd to the innkeeper's counter.

"Two," he says to the craggy-faced man standing behind it.

"Alpha Stark! We weren't expecting you," the man says with a grimace. "I'm sorry, sir, I've only got one room left, and it's... well it's not to the usual standard that... I can see if one of the patrons can find another accommodation, if you just give me a moment—"

"No need," Stark says, turning a glare on me for just a moment. "We don't want to put you out. We'll take the room you have."

Great, I think darkly, everything inside me sinking with dread. *As if things weren't bad enough. Maybe he'll kill me in my sleep and it'll be painless...*

I briefly consider heading back outside to brave the frostbite instead.

But Stark is already pushing money across the counter, then clasping the man's hand. The innkeeper leads him across the crowded room and I trail behind, uncertain, but hopeful that whatever is happening is about to involve food.

"You lot, clear out," the innkeeper shouts gruffly at a group of men huddled together at a booth in a prime spot—near the fireplace, but not so close that smoke or ash might drift our way. They look up, clearly about to protest, and then the words die on their lips.

"It's Alpha Stark," one of them murmurs to another, "leader of the Daemos pack..."

"Of course," the men all mumble, one of them even wiping up some spilled ale from the table before he leaves.

I look at Stark sidelong. Is this how he's treated by commoners everywhere? No wonder he's a complete asshole. They're all scared stiff of him, as if he's some kind of vengeful god.

Our asses have barely touched our seats when a busty barmaid comes around with two tankards of ale and an overflowing basket of bread.

"Alpha Stark!" she says breathlessly, her chest heaving lewdly out of her dress. "We didn't know you'd be coming through today. I'm sorry to say that all we have left in the kitchen is some mutton pie; it's not fancy, but it's hot, or it will be once I heat it up for you and..." Her eyes move to me, and she leans against the table. I think it's not an accident that her position puts her chest on full view for *Alpha Stark*.

"This is the new Strategos Alpha," Stark says tersely as I roll my eyes. The sounds around us hush, and I hear the scraping of chairs as people all around the inn turn to get a look at me.

Awkward.

I keep my head up defiantly, looking straight forward, refusing to give them the pleasure of seeing how embarrassed I am.

"Of... of course," the woman says, and inclines her head to me slightly. "Alpha."

I can tell she wishes Stark weren't traveling with a female, and for some reason, it annoys me.

"That pie sounds good," I interject. "We'll take two big portions. And anything else back there you can rustle up."

The woman hurries away, though I notice she's not in too much of a hurry to swish her backside alluringly as she leaves.

"Bit of a cliche, don't you think?" I say sardonically, turning to Stark. "The barmaid who wants to get in the big bad warrior's pants?"

Stark raises one eyebrow at me. "Alisa? She owns this place, and another inn down the street besides."

A flush rises in my face. You'd think I of all people would know not to underestimate a woman, no matter what she looks like.

I bury my face in my ale. The chatter has started up around me again, so I'm safe enough to glance around, reasonably confident that I'm no longer the center of attention.

A few tables are still watching us, but most have turned back toward a stage in the corner where a musician is getting set up. He tunes his instrument for a few minutes and then launches into a song, his gaze seeming to land on me and Stark more often than not. Curious about the strange new Strategos Alpha, no doubt, like the rest of them.

The song is some kind of classic tale about a Bonded hero that saves the whole city of Linsfall during a surprise Siphon incursion, putting his life and his wolf's life on the line for them and valiantly defeating the threat single-handedly. It must be a traditional tune around here, something learned at their mother's knee, as everyone in the inn seems to know the chorus, singing lustily along every time it comes around, some clapping in time with the beat.

Our food arrives shortly after he starts singing, so I'm quickly distracted by the feast of mutton pie, potatoes, and a few boiled leeks, all with a brown sauce I sop up with the brown bread they brought us. It's basic fare, but I've never tasted better.

Stark eats just as wolfishly as I do, starving after the day of travel. We're both silent as we clean our plates.

"Meet you upstairs, room ten," he says shortly once he's done, standing and draining the rest of his ale before making his way across the room. He stops to say something into Alisa's ear as she leaves, and I see her nod and smile.

If he thinks he's bringing some woman to bed while we share a room, even if she is an impressively successful businesswoman...

I'm jolted from my disgust when Stark swerves away from the stairs and strides over to the stage to have a few words with the musician, who has just wrapped up his epic ballad to cheers and applause and many toasts to the Alpha of old, the hero of the song.

I can't make out what Stark and the bard are saying, but it looks like Stark is... reprimanding the man? I'm almost sure the musician is apologizing for something as Stark stiffly walks away again, toward the staircase that leads to the rooms upstairs. The bard is younger than I thought at first glance, his bearded face anxious as he watches Stark leave.

"Huh," I say softly, wondering what that was about.

Someone slides into the booth across from me, into the seat Stark just vacated. I look up in surprise to see that it's Alisa, the owner of the inn.

"Food to your liking?" she asks, and I nod.

"Exceptional," I admit. "Although I'm not sure I'm the best judge, I think I would have loved anything halfway decent you set in front of me, as long as it was warm and plentiful."

Alisa laughs so hard she snorts, and I grudgingly realize that I like this woman. "Guess you liked the music a bit more than Alpha Stark then, if you're sticking around for another song?"

I glance back over toward the musician, bemused. "Does Stark know that man? Or...?"

"Oh, no, I don't think so," Alisa stands and grabs Stark's empty plate and mug. "Another ale?" I shake my head. "No, he just hates it when they do that."

I'm lost. "When they... sing?"

Alisa squints at me, then laughs again. "Strategos Alpha, you must not have been listening closely. That song he sang? That was about Alpha Stark, when he saved half the city from being murdered, oh, five or six years back. Legend has it he killed a good hundred Siphons on his own. Our streets ran red with the blood he spilled for weeks after."

She saunters off and I stare after her, then survey the room again. All these people, their toasts and cheers, their singing and clapping...

That was for *Stark?*

The whole world has gone mad.

CHAPTER FORTY-ONE

I stand in the inn room's doorway, staring at the single bed while snow swirls outside the window. Inside, Stark has done what he can to make room for us to maneuver, but I understand the innkeeper's apologies now—this room is tiny.

There's barely space to stand without knocking your knees against the bed.

"I'll take the floor," Stark says gruffly, gazing at me from his perch on the side of the bed where he's organizing his pack.

I don't argue. I'm exhausted, cold, and sore—all I want to do is get out of these wet clothes, catch a few hours of sleep, and get back on the road.

Ideally with as much space in between me and the grumpy hero of Linsfall as possible.

I set my own pack down on the floor—or try to. The foot of the bed is so close to the wall and door that there isn't even enough space for my bag, so I just wedge it in as best I can before opening the flaps to rummage through.

Stark's taken the one small table in the room for his own use; a little piece of furniture to the left side of the bed, squeezed tight between the bedframe and the wall.

At least the place is clean, I think as I pull out a fresh, dry shirt to sleep in.

If only it wasn't so damn small. The heat coming off Stark's body practically radiates behind me. There's no space to get away from him. I can smell him, too: musk, amber, wood and a hint of masculine sweat.

I hesitate, starting to remove my clothes, knowing that Stark could turn at any time and see me, can probably see my reflection in the dark of the window either way. But what else will I do, change in the hall? Maneuvering until my back is toward him, I quickly shuck off my leathers, and then my wet clothes, pulling on the dry tunic. I stare fixedly at the corner of the room the entire time, where a small lantern is bolted to the wall, the flame inside flickering.

"Should we get some sleep, then?" I ask once I'm done, clearing my throat and turning back toward him. His gaze drops, fixing sharply on my bare legs.

Shit. I glance down, realizing the hem of my shirt doesn't quite cover the marks on my upper thighs. Lamplight gleams on the silvery scars, making them look all the more vicious.

Suddenly Stark is on me, his face thunderous, backing me into the tiny corner.

"Who did this to you?" he demands ferociously, one calloused hand clamping hotly on my thigh.

Heat flashes through me, starting in my breasts and ending low, between my legs.

What the fuck?

I slap his hand away, ignoring my body's humiliating betrayal.

"What the hell do you care?" I snap with acrid sarcasm. "Are you going to *protect* me?"

Stark's face tightens with rage, but he doesn't back down. He crowds closer, looming over me threateningly.

"I know the marks of torture when I see them," he growls. "Tell me who hurt you. Was it him? Your..." he pauses, sneering the word with poisonous contempt, "*prince?*"

Heart pounding, I stare up at him, determined not to be cowed.

"Don't you dare even talk about him. And no, he fucking didn't. *I* did."

The words come out of my mouth before I can stop them.

He stumbles back, his face flashing with surprise, then a string of emotions that stun me to my core: confusion, then understanding, followed swiftly by horror—or is it pain?

"You did that to yourself?" he repeats tightly.

"Yes," I sneer. "So don't worry, you don't need to go sallying forth like the hero of Linsfall to 'protect' your favorite punching bag. Unless, of course, you'd like to take this opportunity to finally rid yourself of me."

I plop down on the foot of the bed, facing away without waiting for an answer—or maybe just because I can't stand seeing that look on his face.

Why is he suddenly acting like he gives a shit, after three months of torment? It's deeply unnerving.

As I yank back the covers on the bed, Anassa's awareness swells through the bond. She's amused by my discomfort with Stark.

"*Shut up!*" I think at her, my heart hammering in my throat.

I can still feel him standing so close to me, in that narrow space to the left of the bed, watching me climb under the covers.

Thank fuck he doesn't say anything more. After a few seconds, I hear him unpacking his bedroll and trying to wedge it into the narrow strip of floor. When the noises continue, I can't help myself: I sit back up, glaring over at him.

"Problems?"

He turns to look at me, his gaze cold. "Nothing I can't handle."

From my viewpoint sitting up, I can see the issue—it's not just that the space is so narrow. Because of the bedside table, the patch of floor isn't actually quite long enough for Stark's bedroll. Maybe if the asshole weren't so damned tall.

He can sleep standing like a horse, for all I care.

Stark finishes making things fit as best he can, and settles in, halfway turned on his side and with his knees up to fit in the tiny space. He doesn't complain, doesn't utter a word, but it's obvious that the position is extremely uncomfortable.

My head falls back against the headboard.

Fuck.

I don't care if he's comfortable. I *don't*.

It's just that—well, he *is* an impressive warrior, psycho killer instincts included, even if I dislike him. And if we might be battling Siphons tomorrow to save Saela and the other kids, I want him rested and at his best.

For Saela's sake.

My breath huffs out in a sigh. "Okay, don't be an idiot."

"I don't follow," comes his dry response.

"You're not going to get any sleep like that. Come on, the bed is big enough to fit both of us."

The words are like pulling teeth, but even as I say them I know that it's definitely the right thing, no matter how much I hate it. I pointedly push the blanket down, move to the far side of the bed as far as I can go, and then beckon at the other edge of the bed.

He stands smoothly, and then hesitatingly sits on the bed before swinging his feet over.

I almost laugh at the way he makes his tall, muscular body compress as small as possible on the bed across from me, as if I carry some kind of carnal disease that is transferred by touch. Yet there's also a strange pang in my chest at the thought.

Annoyed with him and the situation and also with myself, I roll over and blow out the wall-mounted lamp, leaving us in darkness, my nose just an inch from the wall. Behind my back, I can hear him breathing, rustling the pillow under his head, adjusting the blankets.

Despite my exhaustion, I've suddenly never felt so awake.

My back tingles where I swear his eyes linger on me in the darkness. Unbidden, that time in training comes to my mind, when he yanked up my shirt and pressed his fingers against my belly, my ribs, into each and every bruise. But this time instead of feeling pain at his touch, sparks shoot through me at the thought of every press of his fingers.

I clench my jaw and squeeze my eyes shut tighter. I must be delirious from travel. It's been a long day.

Desperate to take my mind off of the handsome psycho an

arm's reach away—close enough to do dangerous or debauched things to me—I focus my attention on reciting Saela's favorite legends from memory. I think about Killian on the couch in my mother's home, reading Sae the story about the goddess who had to save herself.

Then I think about Killian, how he'll have gotten my note by now, how by the next time I see him I might have my sister back again…

Still, it's a long time before I finally succumb to sleep.

I FIND little rest in my dreams. They're broken, disjointed, and filled with anxiety. Images of the Faceless Goddess haunt me, morphing into my mother, blood pouring from every feature. She speaks to me in an immense, ancient voice both alien and familiar, but I can't understand what she says.

I wake the next morning with gritty eyes and travel-stiff limbs, like I barely slept at all. The sky outside the window is dim and gray. Not quite sunrise. And the snow has stopped. Good.

Stark is already up and dressed for the road, packing his things with practiced efficiency. He glances over when I rise, gaze flicking to my legs, but he doesn't say a word.

On the way out of the inn, he picks up a small cloth-wrapped bundle from Alisa.

"Eat," he says, thrusting it into my hands. "I'll get the wolves."

I'm not hungry, but the command in Stark's voice brooks no argument. If I don't eat it by choice, he might shove it down my throat by force.

When I start to unwrap the bundle, he leaves me on the stoop of the inn and takes off toward the direwolf stables. Inside the waxed cloth, I find a day's rations of bread, cheese, and dried meat.

I eat a few bites while I wait for him to return, thinking of the day ahead. In just a few hours, we'll reach the front. Then Anassa and I will investigate the outpost where Egith said the children have been sighted.

Saela. Hold on. I'll be there soon.

We're on the road again in short order. This time, there's no talk at all. We ride hard, crossing miles and miles of rolling wilderness before we reach the border city where the bulk of the kingdom's forces are camped.

Grunfall. The border fiefdom has changed hands back and forth between the Siphons and the Bonded countless times during centuries of warfare.

The city center is farther away—spires rising off the horizon, though even from a distance there are gaps and gashes in the stonework, as if a giant has taken big bites out of the city, evidence of centuries of constant battles. Grunfall is spread over the banks of the River Sonnstrom. Eons ago, the fiefdom was shared between Nocturna and Astreona, with everything north of the river part of our country, and everything south of the river belonging to the Siphons.

It was the perfect place for war to break out.

We're on the northern edges of the fiefdom, though, in Nocturna's war camp. Astreona has control of the city itself currently. The few remaining buildings up here are ancient—squat, crumbling structures of stone that have been patched together with salvaged wood.

Newer structures have been erected—utilitarian huts made primarily of waxed canvas. Beyond that, the dirt ground is packed with hundreds of military tents. Soldiers bustle everywhere, dressed in dusty uniforms stained from countless battles. The smell of woodsmoke and unwashed bodies chokes the air.

Under that—almost too faint to identify—wafts the sickly sweet smell of rotting flesh.

It's a stark contrast to the castle's opulence: all function, no beauty, every element designed—or repurposed—for war.

A bleakness settles over me as we approach. Stark seems affected, too. His usual predatory grace sharpens into something harder, more focused. There's an odd familiarity in it.

He's at home here—if a place like this can be 'home' to anyone.

This is Stark's world, I realize: the world of war. I'm about to see first-hand how he earned his brutal reputation.

Soldiers snap to attention when they see him, fear and respect mingling in their expressions. Bonded emerge from nearby tents as though sensing our approach, offering Stark crisp salutes, fist to the chest. Direwolves meander through it all, and even they pause to look at us, giving their respects to Cratos and Anassa in their silent lupine way.

Stark's gaze passes over everyone, emotionless. He leads us to an enormous tent near the heart of the camp. Soldiers, Bonded, and messengers stream in and out through multiple exits, tending to their wartime duties.

This is Central Command.

Egith meets us inside at the war table where countless maps and diagrams detail the army's many operations.

The Strategos Beta is haggard, but alert, her silver streak dulled with dust, her uniform bearing fresh bloodstains.

She nods to me, then Stark, when she sees us. "Good, you're here. Made fast time, too." She gestures for me to approach the table, wasting no time in delivering the report I came for.

"Three days ago, Kryptos scouts found this," she says, pointing to a spot on the map not far from where we are now. "That's Siphon territory, but it's close to the border. An old religious temple of some sort that they've converted into an outpost. There have been sightings of children being moved in and out by the guards."

My heart clenches at the word "children." Seeing this camp and the immediate reality of war makes their presence here all the more distressing.

"The last sighting was three days ago?" I demand, uncomfortably aware of Stark standing beside me, watching with penetrating shrewdness. "How many guards were there? How many children?"

"That was the last confirmed sighting, but the scouts haven't been able to get close since—didn't want to risk tipping off the blood-suckers," Egith says. "Three children and two guards were sighted, but at a significant distance. No identifying features."

The hint of apology in her tone says she knows I'm thinking of

Saela—that I want to know if any of those children could be her. Stark's eyes are on me, assessing. I gave him the short version of the story about my sister's kidnapping during our ride this morning, though I had a feeling he might have already known via his own sources. I keep my gaze fixed on Egith, unwilling to show Stark a single sign that my emotions could get in the way of this mission.

I can sense Anassa listening, too. A pulse of cautious optimism travels between us—both hers and mine. Saela could be there. Only one way to find out.

Anassa's concern—and her willingness to go after my sister— gives me a shot of strength. I'm grateful beyond words to have the wolf's support. Without her, I'd have no chance of getting Saela back.

"Do you have intel on the temple?" I ask. "Entrances, exits, guard routes?"

Egith nods and reaches for a leather-bound folder while I study the map and the terrain surrounding the temple.

"Here," she says. "This is all the intelligence gathered by our Kryptos spies."

I flip open the folder, shuffling through reports until I find a sketch of the building. When I lift it from the sheaf, another sketch flutters to the table. My breath catches.

"Is this…?"

"One of the Siphons spotted in the area," Egith confirms. "A general in their army, high-ranking. She's been sighted multiple times nearby in recent weeks."

Goddess above, I think, staring at the unearthly face drawn in charcoal lines. *She's beautiful.*

"You've never seen an image of a Siphon before," Stark says beside me.

I shake my head, unable to tear my gaze from the ephemeral face on the paper. It's almost human, but the eyes are too large, the bone structure too delicate—too perfect to belong to any mere mortal.

Egith plucks another portrait from the sheaf and lays it on top of the one I'm holding. "That's their king."

Lucien Brightbane.

My heart stops. *This* is the architect of all our suffering? *This* face?

It's ageless and angelic, *devastatingly* beautiful, even drawn so roughly. I know from my studies that the Siphon king has been around a long time, but there's not a single line on his face—no hint of the ages he's lived except in the cold, bottomless wisdom of his gaze.

There's something familiar about those eyes. Something I recognize faintly in the otherworldly planes of his countenance—but I can't place it.

"He looks a lot younger than I expected," I mutter. "Like he's in his late twenties, tops."

Stark scoffs. "You know they don't age like we do. That *thing* is centuries old."

Shaking my head, I set the portraits aside and nod to the map of the temple. "Tell me about the layout."

"We've identified three potential entry points," Egith says, pointing. "Here, here, and here. A simultaneous assault on all three entrances is our best bet to overcome their defenses. The timing must be perfect—they're strongest at night, but that's also when they're most likely to be feeding and therefore distracted."

Stark cuts in. "They won't be feeding all at once—they're too smart to leave themselves open like that. There will still be guards on duty, and we don't know how many."

Egith nods. "If we place our scouts here and here before sunset, we should be able to track the guards and sight the rest heading out to feed. Once that happens, we'll have a very short window to take advantage."

As the discussion of strategy continues, I find my gaze drawn back to the portrait of Lucien Brightbane. *Why* do I feel like I've seen him somewhere before?

Stark's hand abruptly slaps down on the image.

"Focus, Cooper," he growls. "We move at sunset."

CHAPTER FORTY-TWO

That evening, from a forested ridge overlooking the temple, I stand with Stark and several other Bonded, poring over a map of the ruin below.

We've gone over the plan a dozen times at Stark's command. Everyone knows their part.

The wolves will circle the temple's outer wall to cut off escape routes while three smaller teams infiltrate through its three vulnerabilities—a crumbling section of wall, an old sewage tunnel, and a partially collapsed bell tower.

This is a time-sensitive covert operation. The strike team—both soldiers and Bonded—were chosen specifically for their superior stealth capabilities. The Bonded on each team will coordinate precisely timed attacks through their pack connection. Stark will lead one team, and two Kryptos Bonded will lead the others.

We've had spies watching the ruins for hours, tracking the Siphon guard rotations and sending reports back to our temporary camp here in the forest. We have the intel we need.

It's almost time to move.

We gather on the ridge, keeping low and strictly to the shadows as dusk settles into night. The temple is a dark scar cut into the hillside below us, its narrow windows lit dimly with lamplight. My heart pounds every time I look at it, wondering if Saela is inside. If she's hurt. Scared. Alone.

Every muscle in my body itches to move—to fight. To kill every last *motherfucker* who dared to take innocent children from my country.

Anassa's anticipation radiates along our bond, too. She's more than eager for our first taste of real battle.

Stark, meanwhile, has coordinated this whole operation.

I find myself mesmerized by him, here in this cold mountain wilderness, closed in on every side by darkness and danger.

He's the consummate Alpha—no trace remains of the man who seemed so worried about the scars on my thighs yesterday. I almost don't believe it happened at all, watching him now.

His aura holds none of the malice and impending violence to which I've become so accustomed. There's no bellowing of commands. No bloodthirsty gleam in his eyes.

He's centered. Calm. Completely focused. Coldly efficient.

The perpetual scowl is gone, too, which is more disconcerting than I'd like to admit. His face is *ridiculously* handsome when he's not scowling. Beautiful, even.

This man isn't Stark the Rawbond combat instructor, my personal tormentor. This is *Alpha Stark of Daemos*, the warrior who earned every one of his kill marks. The commander trusted by every soldier in the king's army.

He turns to me as the soldiers begin making their final preparations. "You and Anassa are with me," he says, voice pitched low. "This is your first time in Siphon territory—you follow my lead, understand? You do *exactly* as I say."

I bristle, insulted to be thrust back into the role of trainee. Haven't I proven myself to him yet? Why does he insist on babysitting me?

"Listen to him," says Anassa. *"He knows what he's doing."*

"Traitor," I grumble at her.

Stark is staring at me, eyes narrowed, waiting for me to protest.

"You haven't fought like this yet," he says with quiet intensity,

"Siphons are faster than humans, Cooper. They're stronger, capable of making you see things that aren't real. One mistake and—" He makes a sharp slashing motion with one hand across his throat.

"I *know*," I grate. "I've been studying them for weeks, Stark."

"And I've been fighting them for a fucking decade," he growls. "*Listen* to me, Cooper. You stay close to me, you *follow orders*, and you don't. Take. Risks. *Do you understand?*"

"Alright!" I hiss, taken aback by his intensity. "I understand!"

Before he can say more, a Kryptos scout melts out of the gathering darkness. Stark turns without surprise and says, "Report."

"Movement in the east wing," the scout says, gaze flicking to me. "They've shifted the guard rotation."

Shit. That throws a wrench in our plans.

But Stark shows no hint of stress. I watch him silently absorb the information, his tactical mind working rapidly through the possibilities. He could have easily been a Strategos rather than a Daemos. In mere seconds, he settles on a solution, adjusting our strategy and redirecting resources with impressive efficiency.

Again, I'm struck by the difference in him. Command sits so naturally on those broad, muscular shoulders. There's something almost regal in the way he carries it. He's truly the Sovereign Alpha's son in this moment. The soldiers and Bonded alike respond to his commands without hesitation—with absolute faith.

While everyone is making their final preparations, I check my own weapons for the dozenth time.

Sword secured. Check. Daggers dipped in poisonous herbs that slow Siphon healing. Check.

My hands tremble slightly as I work, though whether from fear or anticipation, I'm not sure. My blood is pumping, but my mind is calm. Focused.

Despite my irritation with Stark's babying, I know I'm the weakest link on the team. Everyone else has copious battle experience. They've fought Siphons before. They've seen war.

I will *not* fuck this up—the rest of the team is counting on me. If I make a mistake, their lives will be at risk, too, not just mine.

When the sun finally sinks below the horizon and the sky turns black and starless, Stark commands the teams to take position, coordinating with lethal precision using hand signals alone.

He nods to me just before we mount our wolves. "Remember, stay close to me. Egith will never forgive me if I get her new Alpha killed."

Something in his tone makes me look at him sharply, but his expression tells me nothing.

Without another word, Stark leaps onto Cratos's back. I follow suit as the other two teams peel off into the night, taking their positions.

Anassa's anticipation builds as Stark signals for our team to move. I take a deep breath, forcing my hands to steady, then lean hard into our connection. The bond swells, enveloping me in Anassa's heightened senses.

Suddenly I can see into the night far better than I could before. I can hear every rustle in the woods, every crackle of leaves underfoot. The breeze moving up from the valley below us carries the scent of moist earth, woodsmoke, and countless living things.

I'm going to survive this, I tell myself as we follow Stark and Cratos into the night. *I've survived the fighting pits, the Ascent, the training—I've survived everything this brutal world has thrown at me. I'll survive this too—and find Saela.*

Whatever it takes.

Anassa's fierce approval washes over me. We'll survive this *together.*

The descent to the temple takes a handful of minutes, and then we're approaching the southwest entry point, Stark in the lead and me just behind with half a dozen soldiers on foot bringing up the rear. I spot the crumbling section of the wall just as Stark turns to give me the signal.

Everyone is in position. The time is now.

I lift one hand, echoing Stark's signal to the soldiers behind me.

At once, we burst into action. Cratos leaps through the breach, a massive black blur against the night. Anassa swiftly follows, the soldiers spilling into the temple courtyard behind us.

Nothing could have prepared me for what follows.

I catch sight of the first Siphon guard an instant before Stark strikes, moving with his wolf like a force of nature. His blade flashes. The guard's head spins away, separated from his body before he can draw breath to call the alarm.

That's the only way to ensure Siphons die; you need to behead them.

I watch in slow motion as the guard's head tumbles to the ground, his face frozen in shock, fangs bared. The body crumples with unnatural grace, beautiful even in death.

Before it hits the ground, Stark and Cratos are leaping toward the temple steps. Anassa follows like a silver shadow, mirroring every movement with stunning precision. She and Cratos seem to be coordinating effortlessly.

Another Siphon falls at the arched doorway to the temple, shredded in an instant by Cratos's snapping jaws. And then we're racing down the narrow corridors, weaving through twists and turns that make me dizzy. The wolves move with impossible stealth despite their massive size, radiating power through our bonds, heightening our senses further. They smell the enemies ahead long before we burst into an open chamber and fall upon them.

Stark and Cratos lunge first, scattering two Siphons in opposite directions. The creatures move like nothing I've seen before—supernatural speed blurs their attacks even as those angelic faces morph into masks of pure horror, fangs extended.

To my eyes, the brutality that follows plays out in total chaos, but through the bond, every strike is anticipated, every movement almost choreographed. Cratos lunges left, Stark's sword flashing right. Anassa dodges right, my sword swings left. The two Siphons fall—one to Anassa's teeth, one to Stark's sword.

The soldiers flow after us, falling upon the bodies and hacking them to pieces with poison-coated blades.

We move into the circular gathering hall at the heart of the temple. Stark draws Cratos to a stop at the center of the room, his head swiveling as he assesses our position. I get a ripple of awareness from Anassa that something isn't right, and then we're ambushed.

Three, four, five, *six* Siphons pour out of the doorways surrounding us, rushing the team in a coordinated attack.

Stark and Cratos unleash a powerful wave of Daemos magic, throwing the Siphons against the walls. The strength of it is easily ten times what Jonah used that day he broke my nose. It's unbelievable. Stark isn't just strong—he's godlike.

Then, Stark moves faster than should be possible, his blade singing through the air as he dismembers the Siphons, their heads crashing to the ground one after another.

Blood sprays across ancient stone as he tears through their ranks, Cratos ripping the Siphons to pieces even as Stark's blade hacks away. I catch sight of Stark's face as Anassa dances along beside them.

His expression never changes—that cold, deadly focus remains unbroken even as he commits absolute brutality.

The sight makes me feel oddly triumphant. From the first day I saw him, I knew he was a psycho, bloodthirsty monster, and here's my proof. He's so much worse than I'd ever imagined.

And for once, it doesn't disgust me. Because this unhinged killer is on *my* side.

Anassa and I stay glued to Stark and Cratos, positioning ourselves at their back as the remaining Siphons close in around us. My direwolf's focus spirals in, and for a moment, I see the room—the soldiers, the Siphons, the wolves and their riders—in crisp detail, like a moving diagram. Calculations flow through my head, rapid-fire, assessing the Siphons for weakness, noting their formations and tactics with insane speed.

A strategy clicks into place. These creatures know their enemies well. They expect practiced military strikes—coordinated attack and defense.

They're not prepared for a street fighter from the slums.

Anassa's mind ripples with violent delight as we shift from defending Stark and Cratos to an all out attack.

As one, we maneuver into a position of apparent vulnerability, drawing the Siphon in. Anassa lunges, feinting expertly, dodging Siphon fangs as my sword darts in to defend her.

Now!

I swing at the Siphon and miss. Anassa takes the swipe of a dagger to the neck—she yelps, drawing back. The Siphon grins in fanged glee just before it launches at us in a pale, deadly blur.

In the same instant, Anassa drops low to the ground, bringing me level with our attacker. My sword is already swinging up again—with all my strength behind it.

The Siphon dies in a spray of black blood, its head tumbling past on one side, its body on the other.

Anassa lets loose a howl that thunders against the stone walls all around us. At our back, Cratos howls in answer.

The remaining Siphons sense the tide turning against them. I'm not sure how I know they're afraid, but I do. Anassa becomes a silver blur of pure aggression, my blades flashing around her in staccato bursts as we take down another Siphon, and then another.

All at once, the room falls still and silent. Bodies lie everywhere. Eight Siphons and three soldiers have fallen. The smell of blood and terror coats the inside of my nose and fills my mouth with a copper tang.

Stark turns to me, his face decorated in a fine spray of blood, chest heaving from exertion. His gaze scans my body briefly for wounds. Finding none, he nods once and signals the team forward again.

We descend into the bowels of the temple, following dark corridors and picking off a few more Siphons until at last, we find the basement holding cells.

The smell hits me first—fear, excrement, unwashed bodies, and something else. A sickly sweet scent that sparks in my nose like champagne. Through the bond, Anassa bristles. Her hackles rise.

"*Siphon magic,*" she says. That's what the smell is.

What have these monsters been doing to the children?

My heart hammers in my head as we near the cells—something is wrong. It's too quiet. Too still.

Stark dismounts his wolf and glances up at me with a look that sends my heart plummeting into my gut.

The cells are empty. Every last one of them.

The children aren't here.

My boots crunch on the dirty stones as I slip from Anassa's back and peer through the bars beside Stark.

"They were here not long ago," he says quietly.

I nod. There are scraps of children's clothing inside the cells. Food bowls, a battered doll. A single stained blanket.

"They knew we were coming," I hear myself say.

My voice sounds hollow. Dead.

I'm numb.

Stark turns as though to speak, but one of the Daemos soldiers interrupts.

"Sir, we've captured one of the Siphon guards," he says.

The numbness inside me darkens into sharp and savage. There's a flicker of shadows around the edge of my vision, urging me toward further violence.

"Good," I say. "I have questions for them."

CHAPTER FORTY-THREE

Back at our camp at Grunfall, the Siphon prisoner has been transferred to an interrogation room set up in one of the old stone buildings. I wanted to interrogate him at the temple, but Stark insisted that this was protocol—Siphons are too dangerous for in-field interrogations.

We had to bring the bastard here, where he could be safely chained to a metal chair bolted to the stone floor. Where, even if he did get out, he'd be surrounded by soldiers and Bonded with no chance of escape.

I agreed—on one condition: that *I* get to be the one who leads the interrogation.

Stark gave me a look when I said that, half irritation and half respect. But he didn't argue.

Now, as I enter the bare interrogation room, shadows twist again at the edges of my vision, and with them, rage burns bright. Somewhere, deep down inside of me, is dread at the idea of torturing another being.

I push the feeling down further.

My sister isn't here. Saela—if she was with those children in the cells—is gone. And this single Siphon guard is my only lead to finding her.

The Siphon guard sits tall in his chains, beautiful even with a bloodied face. The soldiers that captured him managed to knock him unconscious with a crushing blow to the head. The wound has since healed, but combined with a timely injection of the same poison that coats our blades, they managed to keep the Siphon out long enough to chain him.

This is a rare opportunity. One I can't afford to waste.

Stark enters the room behind me, hanging back beside the table of interrogation tools. His presence is heavy, dark. Like pregnant clouds on a horizon, threatening a deadly blizzard.

Odd that it's also sort of comforting.

I approach the prisoner. The Siphon's gaze touches mine with unnerving weight and inhuman calm. No fear. He's still and beautiful in the guttering torchlight.

"Tell me about the children," I say. "Where were they taken?"

His perfect brow furrows with confusion. "You're looking for children?"

Goddess, even his voice is gorgeous—musical and lilting.

"The children you were keeping in the basement cells," I grate. "The ones you sent your Nabbers for in Sturmfrost."

He blinks. "'Nabbers?'" His gaze flicks to Stark in bewilderment. "What is this idiot talking about?"

"Don't play dumb," I growl, impatience thrumming in my veins. "You've been abducting children from Nocturna for years. You were keeping at least three of them at the temple. Now *tell me where they are*."

The Siphon shakes his head, smirking. "They told me all you northerners were wolf-brained lunatics, but I didn't believe it until now."

I pause, arms crossed over my chest, staring the Siphon down in silent calculation.

"He's trying to distract you," Stark says behind me. "Don't fall for it."

I ignore him.

"One more chance to answer me honestly," I say softly, "then I start breaking bones."

"Cute," the Siphon drawls. "Is this what passes for pillow talk north of the border? If you want to know me carnally, darling, just say the word. Your personality is a little sour, but I bet you taste just fine."

Jaw clenching, I turn and stride to the table, aware of Stark looking down at me as I select a pair of pliers from the tools there.

The Siphon makes no sound when I break his right index finger, but his perfect lips part around a sharp, shuddering breath.

"Where are the children?" I ask with an icy calm I don't feel.

"Fuck you," he replies, eyes ablaze.

Crack! His right middle finger gives easily in the metal clamp of the pliers. At the same moment, I look down and realize the first finger has already healed. As I watch, the second finger heals, too.

So I break it again.

The sensation fills me with horrifying delight, so thick and dark that I almost choke on it, shadows growing longer around the room. For a second the wave of feeling threatens to drown me, and Anassa is in my head, like a low growl, ready to rip this Siphon apart if I don't do it first.

The connection with Anassa brings me back to a cold calm. My voice is almost gentle when I ask for the fourth time, "Where are the children?"

The Siphon curses, spits at me. "There *are* no children!"

Crack! Crack! Crack!

Three fingers at once. The Siphon finally cries out, jerking against his chains. But he doesn't get any more helpful, just stares at me tauntingly, panting as his body heals itself.

I return to the table. Stark leans against the wall just behind it, arms crossed, watching with expressionless focus.

The shadows in the room dance, egging me on.

I pick up a dagger, its poisoned blade polished to a dull sheen.

The Siphon's eyes light with something new when he sees it. Dread, I think. He knows it's poisoned, that it will stop him from healing.

"Now, we cut," I say in that same near-gentle tone.

I don't ask about the children again—at least, not for quite a while. I just cut. First the buttons on the front of his dark uniform, then the pale skin of his chest beneath it.

The knife sizzles as it parts his flesh, little curls of smoke rising from the wounds. Sweat breaks out on the Siphon's brow. All the color drains from his skin, leaving him gray and wan, gasping like a fish out of water.

The cuts twitch and tighten, struggling to draw closed.

"You like this, don't you," the prisoner gasps as I settle the tip of the dagger above his left nipple. "You northerners are sick."

A flick of my wrist separates nipple from chest. The Siphon screams.

I take his other nipple, too. Then I draw the edge of the blade in a long, slow caress from his sternum to the hollow of his throat.

"You dirty wolf lover," the prisoner says, defiant even as he slumps in his chains. "I don't know anything about the children, but I wouldn't tell you even if I did!"

Something inside me finally snaps, the shadows at the edges of my vision pulsing into an insistent thrum.

Saela is gone. Lost. The other children... I won't be able to save them. This *creature* isn't going to tell me anything.

I've failed.

Killing rage turns into something darker, deeper—something too ugly for words. It's like the shadows fill me, consume me then. Blackness in my mind, behind my eyes, a deep pit that stretches through me and makes my muscles clench.

No more questions. No more interrogation.

No more thoughts but *hurt. Punish.*

Kill.

I return to the table and pick up the bone saw—a long, narrow implement with fine serrations sharpened to a razor's edge.

The Siphon's final howl of pain and terror is cut short as I saw through his trachea. But he's still alive, blood spurting from his severed jugular as I work the saw deeper, fighting to decapitate him even as his flesh begins to heal around the blade.

When the saw finally bites through muscle and tendon, striking bone, his eyes are still rolling, mouth agape and pooling with blood.

Some distant part of me is aware that what I'm doing is horrific. There's no purpose to this torture now, no goal but pain and revenge.

No justice but death.

When his head finally separates from his body, the perfect features remain unmarred, his eyes open and accusatory.

His skull thunks to the ground, rolling a few feet, leaving a thick crimson trail on the dirty stones.

I stand over the corpse, breathing hard, painted head-to-toe with Siphon blood.

Anassa's approval envelops me. She's *proud* of my brutality.

All I feel is hollow.

I BARELY REMEMBER the walk to my tent. I collapse into my bunk and fall instantly into sleep, still wearing my bloodied clothes.

Hours later, I wake to dull morning light and a soft clinking sound. My dreams were full of shadows and blood and I'm sweating, my clothes damp. I blink, trying to shake off the nightmares.

Stark sits a few feet away, arranging his needle and several bottles of ink on the little table where I left my weapons the night before.

There's a movement in the corner of the tent and I squint at it —are the shadows shifting again? But as I stare, they settle down, back to normal. Great, just another hallucination.

My body protests as I lever myself up from the narrow cot, eyes bleary. It's early. I've only been asleep a few hours.

"Time for new ink again?" I grunt, raspy with sleep.

"These you can be proud of," he says, gesturing for me to take the chair beside him. "Marks that remind us of what we have to do to defeat our enemy. To keep the bloodsuckers from destroying our world and everything and everyone we love."

It's a struggle to rise. My whole body is stiff, aching from battle and exhaustion.

"Shirt off," he says as I sit. "We start with the upper arms for Siphon kill marks."

A prickle of unease starts somewhere in my gut, but I don't protest. I just peel off the filthy garment. The cloth is stiff and reeks of dried blood, and my stomach turns as the smell hits me again, hard. I swallow hard.

Stark's gaze flicks over my bound chest as he draws his chair closer. At least my undergarments are relatively clean.

He has to sit unnervingly close, big hand warm on my arm as he steadies me for the needle.

I must smell terrible. Like death and battle. But if it bothers him, he shows no sign.

Stark's familiar scent fills my head as the needle bites into my flesh. The pain is a relief after the past twenty-four hours.

The little tent is unnervingly quiet. Most of the camp is still sleeping. The stillness of the dawn and the weight of last night's interrogation lie over us like a blanket, creating an air of raw intimacy that sets my heart thumping.

Stark's touch is clinical as he works, but I know he feels the charge in the air. How could he not?

What I don't know is why the fuck it's there, or what to do to dispel it.

As though hearing my thoughts, Stark breaks the silence.

"I've never seen anyone interrogate with that kind of intensity before," he says. "It's clear this mission was personal for you."

The observation—and the lack of censure in his voice, after what he saw me do—catch me off guard.

Maybe it's the vulnerability of the moment, the hypnotic rhythm of the needle in my skin, or simple exhaustion, but I find myself telling him… everything.

The words come with quiet intensity.

I tell more about him why I joined the army in the first place, my mission to find Saela, how I thought I'd be able to find her if I could just get to the front line and across the border.

Then I pause, filled with sickening defeat.

"She's been gone three months," I rasp, voice breaking just a little. "*Three months*, Stark. She turned eleven two months ago, in captivity. If she's even still alive."

The needle pauses on my skin. Out of the corner of my eye, I see Stark's head lift, his gaze moving to my face. I tell myself not to look—I feel like I've just bared my fucking soul to him, and I'm not sure what I'm going to see in his eyes.

But for some reason, I can't stop my head from turning.

Our gazes lock. His eyes are dark, impenetrable. There's something there, lurking behind that signature stoicism, but I can't read it.

"I really thought this would lead to something," I say. "That we might find her at the temple. Or at least get some hints for where to look next. But instead I tortured that *thing* last night—behaved like a total monster, almost like I'm one of them—and still, nothing."

We're both still staring at each other, and I'm drowning in his eyes, waiting for him to say something, tell me if I'm a villain for what I did. He sighs, his breath hot against my arm.

"Don't let it get to you," he says, his voice tight. "We've all had to do things we aren't proud of. Just remember why you did what you did."

When he finally looks away, I realize my throat is burning. I suck in a breath, feeling like I've been released from some kind of spell.

Stark finishes my tattoos without another word exchanged between us. But I'm still raw. The sense of intimacy lingers, setting my nerves on edge.

Making my blood pulse in my ears.

When he finally leans down to lick the wounds on my arms, I get a rush of arousal so intense my breath catches in my throat.

A sound escapes me, low and unmistakably erotic.

Fuck!

Stark's eyes lock onto mine. The hunger in them steals the breath right out of my lungs—sends adrenaline coursing through my veins.

Holding my gaze, he lowers his head and licks the fresh tattoos again, slow and deliberate.

Without thought, my hand flashes out, fingers fisting in his dark hair. It's not gentle. I'm angry, I realize. Or maybe frightened, I don't know.

It must hurt, but he doesn't resist. He just gazes at me in silent challenge.

For a moment, I'm not sure if I'm going to shove him away or yank him closer. The urge to crash my mouth into his surges through me like wildfire.

I need connection, I realize, reeling internally. Physical contact, closeness, comfort. I'm *aching* for it after the emotional violence of the last few days—even from *him*.

Even in the form of… whatever the fuck this is.

Warning bells are going off in my head. This is Stark. He's a monster, a bully, a brute. I'm very, very publicly in a relationship with Killian, who I *love*.

Logic is no match for animal need. My fingers tighten in Stark's hair. He opens his mouth wider, bares his teeth, and bites at my flesh.

The sound—fuck, the *moan*—escapes me again, my nipples tightening.

Then I hear the crunch of boots right outside an instant before the tent flap opens. I jerk back from him as Egith steps inside.

"Alpha Cooper," she says, gaze flicking between us. "Alpha Stark."

"Report," Stark grunts, showing no hint of what just passed between us.

"No news," she replies briskly. "I was just checking on Cooper. You two should get on the road if you're planning to be home by tomorrow evening."

I nod and rise, hoping I don't look as shaky as I feel.

Egith says something about the wolves being ready. Stark gets up to go.

I don't look at him. Whatever that was, I'm not going to touch the feeling again with a ten-foot pole.

CHAPTER FORTY-FOUR

T wo days later, we approach the outskirts of Sturmfrost in the early afternoon.

Stark has been quiet the whole journey, but it's not the quiet I'm used to. He's less surly than before. He maintains a respectful distance. During our stop at Linsfall on the way back, we had two rooms, on opposite ends of the inn. He's behaving as though nothing has changed between us.

I tell myself nothing has, but it sounds like a lie. Guilt prickles the edge of my mind every time I think of Killian.

But I didn't actually kiss Stark, I remind myself for the dozenth time. It was just a thought—a momentary urge driven by the need for human connection in the aftermath of wartime brutality. I was devastated that we didn't find my sister, and demoralized by the hours of brutal torture, all for nothing. I was in a vulnerable place—and he *licked* me.

I might have felt the urge to kiss just about anyone at that moment. It didn't have to be Stark.

It meant nothing.

I have *nothing* to be guilty about.

Sinking my hands more deeply into Anassa's fur, I let my head fall heavy in front of me, cushioned by the soft warmth of her neck. I press my face into her fur, inhaling deeply. Her familiar scent calms me, the rhythm of her huge paws striking the ground beneath me soothing me, slowing my erratic heartbeat.

I just wish I could stop seeing that look in his eyes when he licked me the second time. And then when I grabbed him by the hair...

And when he bit me...

Did he actually *want* me to kiss him?

No. That's fucking crazy. It was a fluke—a freak occurrence. He probably felt the same kind of post-brutality need for human connection that I did. I take back every thought I've ever had about wanting him to be nicer. I liked him better when he wanted me dead.

Anassa's amusement ripples to me through our bond. I ignore it, shoving all thoughts of Stark away.

We're almost home. Killian will be waiting for me. The thought lifts my spirits considerably.

But he's not the only person I suddenly ache to see.

As we skirt around the edges of the Southern Quarter, I turn to Stark.

"Can we make a quick stop?" I ask. "I want to update my mother about Saela."

I know there isn't any real progress to report, but I want my mother to know I'm still searching. That I'm not giving up.

Stark glances at me, face expressionless. "Fine, just keep it brief. I'm sure I don't need to remind you that the Unity Trial is a week away. All the other Rawbonds will have been training without you these past few days. You need to catch up."

I nod, grateful for the reprieve. I don't feel right, after everything that's happened the last few days. This person who rides a direwolf to the front lines, who tortures Siphons for information—I'm losing track of who I was before.

The thought of seeing my mom, of hugging her...

Shit. Maybe this is less about giving her an update and more about me needing to feel human again. That ache for physical contact is still lurking.

When we reach the Eastern Quarter, however, the sight of my childhood home stops me cold. Every window is dark, shuttered.

I know before my feet hit the ground—before I wrench the front door open and rush inside—that nobody's home.

The place is dark, cold. Utterly still.

Stark peers down at me from Cratos' back when I rush back out of the empty house, his brow furrowed. But I'm already running, peeling away down the street towards Igor's house.

The rough door shudders under my pounding. A moment later, Igor opens it.

His face softens out of its usual gruffness, into something foreign. No, that's not right. Not foreign.

I've seen him make this face before, the night Saela was taken.

Panic sweeps from my head to my toes, hot and dizzying.

"Meryn," he says gently. "I'm so sorry."

"No," I whisper, stepping back as though I can remove myself from the ghastly truth painted across his features. "No, it can't be. *Where is she?*"

Igor draws me into the house, his wrinkled hands gentle on my upper arms. I catch sight of Prina in the living room behind him, her plump figure wrapped in a faded dress, her eyes wide and welling with tears of empathy.

"Your mother had another episode," Igor continues quietly. "A bad one. We didn't know… she was doing so well until then."

No.

My mind spins, scrabbling for purchase. For escape. As though I can avert reality by refusing to hear the words.

"Three days ago, she wandered into the city square and… got into some kind of altercation with the guards," Igor says, his words halting. "They… subdued her. Forcefully."

"Stop!" I rasp, frozen in desperate denial. *"Don't—!"*

Igor's face crumples with grief. "She's dead, Meryn. I'm so sorry. They killed her."

My ears start to ring. Igor keeps talking—something about her body being taken to the morgue. About him and "Lee" handling the preparations for her funeral.

But I can't hear him. Something strange is happening. A horrible pulsing thrum gathers behind my eyes. The shadows crouching all over Igor's house start to pulse in answer.

They deepen and solidify, writhing with inexplicable life.

Igor doesn't seem to notice. His face is tight with concern. He reaches for me and I stumble back—directly into Stark.

I turn in a haze of soul-cracking grief to see the Daemos Alpha towering in the open doorway, his shoulders almost touching the jamb on either side. His aura envelops me like a storm cloud, radiating something fierce and... almost *protective*.

"What's going on here?" he demands.

Igor repeats what he told me. I barely hear him, trying not to panic as the shadows pulse all around us, like something alive.

"I sent word to the castle immediately," Igor says, "but clearly, the message never reached you. Someone sent back word you'd gone to the front."

I shake my head, whether in denial or simply rejection of the moment, I don't know.

I wasn't here. She needed me, and I wasn't here.

I'm distantly aware of Stark demanding details about my mother's death, but I can't focus on the exchange. All I can think about is her.

Did she suffer? Did she know they were killing her? Did she call out for help?

I hear myself make a terrible strangled sound.

If I'd been here... if I'd been closer... Helplessness and rage threaten to drown me.

The storm of grief inside me abruptly spirals into a single point of focus.

Killian.

Igor said he was helping with the funeral arrangements. Killian knows what's happened. And he loves me.

Killian will know what to do.

The world rushes by me in strange fits and bursts as I rush out the door, mount Anassa wordlessly. She doesn't need to communicate with me, just immediately starts back toward the castle. My overwhelming need, my sorrow, must be plain enough that she needs no explanation.

Shadows follow in my wake, dancing behind us.

I squeeze my eyes shut, melting into Anassa as she races through the streets, narrowly dodging residents as she runs. She uses one of the Bonded entrances at the side of the castle, bursting into the wide corridors and bringing me straight to his door.

Killian's in his study. He rises immediately from his desk when I enter.

The way his expression falls when he sees me—I look away, unable to process his grief on top of my own.

"Meryn…" Killian says softly, "I'm so sorry. I received word about your mother yesterday—"

"I wasn't here." The words rip out of me like a sob. "Every time, every *fucking time* my family needs my protection, I'm gone. It's all my fault…"

Killian wraps a firm arm around my shoulders, guiding me to a small couch against the far wall.

"No," he says with intensity. "Meryn, you can't blame yourself. You know I've been visiting regularly, bringing food and supplies. I saw her just last week. She seemed a little disoriented, but not in a bad place. You couldn't have possibly known. *Nobody* could have predicted this."

I lean into the protective circle of his arms, desperate for that warmth.

Desperate to believe him that it isn't all my fault.

That I'm not a complete failure, responsible for the death or abduction of everyone I love most in this world.

I taste salt on my lips and realize that tears are streaming down my face. Killian studies me, eyes sympathetic. With a jolt of irritation, I look away. I don't want his sympathy, or anyone's.

Not when I deserve to experience every bit of this pain.

Killian brings a hand up to my chin, wrenching my face back toward his. "Look at me, Meryn. This isn't your fault. There was no way to predict that she'd have another episode. And from what I heard, it happened fast. There's nothing you could have done about it, even if you were here in Sturmfrost."

His voice is rough with emotion, his eyes bright, piercing into mine.

"Mer... If there had been anything that anyone could have done, you know I would have..." His words falter. The genuine anguish in his eyes stabs at me, cutting right into my heart.

That's when it really hits. The loss. The *reality* of it.

Saela will never see Mother again. She won't be there when I finally bring my sister home. *If* I bring my sister home. My failures pile one atop the other. My whole family... I couldn't protect them.

And now she's gone. Forever.

Killian's presence guides me like a beacon of light through the avalanche of my despair. I fall apart against him, burying myself in his chest. The heat and solidity of his body against me is the only point of stillness, of comfort.

When the storm inside me finally subdues, he hands me a gold-embroidered handkerchief and strokes my hair, running his thumb across my cheek to catch a few tears that I miss.

I can't bring myself to look at him, though I stay tucked against his chest, unwilling to relinquish the comfort of his closeness. His hand moves from my hair to my back, still stroking, his fingers firm, moving in circles down my back. His heartbeat is slow and steady under my ear.

He's the only one besides Igor who's been here for me and Mom. He's done so much to protect and care for both of us.

The shadows are back, climbing slowly up Killian's walls, darkening his room. I shut my eyes to block them out.

Goddess, I almost forgot how devastating grief is. How it leaves you husked and raw, but never numb. The pain is like a gaping wound—one no dressing can cover, no shield can truly protect. The agony of it might lessen, but it never truly leaves.

It's not just one feeling, either. Grief has layers and layers: sadness, bitterness, guilt, regret...

At least this time I'm older than when my dad died. I'm not

some lost little kid, wandering the streets hoping to vent my misery by fighting every shithead boy I encounter.

This time, I have to keep it together. I can't get lost in the misery. I have to keep my guard up, my wits about me.

I'm still here in this bloodthirsty world, fighting for my life.

And Saela is still out there.

Saela.

She's all I have left. I will *not* fail her. I will bring her home.

I rest my head on Killian's sternum, exhausted and tremulous, thinking of the weeks to come.

The Unity Trial looms. The funeral will have to be quick, with all the training I still need to do to make sure I survive this long enough to get to Saela.

Quick and also cheap, I think, heart sinking. Rawbond training doesn't pay, and Mom hasn't been working in years. Surely, there's no money left set aside in our house.

Igor and Killian may have started on the preparations, but it's my burden to bear. She's my mother. It's the least I can do for her, now that she's gone.

And Saela…

Fuck. My sister won't even be there to say goodbye to our mother. When I bring her home, it'll be to an empty house and more grief—on top of whatever horrors she's gone through since she was taken.

Fresh tears well behind my closed eyelids as the weight of both their losses settles over me like a heavy cloak.

"I'm all alone," I whisper, pulling from Killian's embrace to stand. "My whole family. They're gone, all of them. And Saela… if I don't find her…"

Killian stands as well, taking both my hands in his. "Meryn. You aren't alone."

I gaze up at him through blurry eyes. Shadows move behind him, taunting.

"But my family…"

"Let me be your family now," he says softly. Taking a step backward, he slowly lowers himself onto one knee.

The world narrows sharply. Time seems to slow.

"Killian?" I hear myself whisper.

"Let me take care of you, now and forever," he says, the words reaching me slowly and then all at once. "You don't always have to be the strong one. Let me help you. I—" he clears his throat. "I meant to do this after you'd graduated the Trials, Meryn, but you need to know you aren't alone in this world. I talked to your mother about this, you know."

I gasp, tears flooding my eyes anew.

"You aren't *alone,"* Anassa growls across the bond. *"You have me."*

It's not the same thing; surely she knows that?

"She gave me her blessing," Killian continues. "Let me be strong for you, Meryn. Be my wife. Marry me."

I can't speak. The air in my lungs grows thin.

Killian produces a bracelet—a band of brilliant gold that catches the firelight, blazing in his hand like living fire. It's a thousand times more opulent than the simple silver engagement bracelet my mother wore. The band is made of elaborate gold filigree that wraps around dozens of small black diamonds. In the center is an enormous round ruby, red as fresh blood.

My own blood thrums loudly in my ears.

"Be my queen," Killian implores softly. "Rule at my side and help me reshape our world, Meryn. Together we'll make the world safer for people like your mother. We'll get Saela back. We'll make things right."

Before I can draw breath to answer, another ripple of disapproval comes from Anassa.

"Meryn," she hisses. *"You are not in the right place to make this decision."*

But I've never felt more clear-headed. This incredible man kneeling before me is far more than I deserve. Me, a commoner. Me, who has no other family to speak of.

Me, who had traitorous thoughts of another man when Killian was *here*, taking care of my mother, helping Igor with preparations. Always steady, always by my side.

I will spend every day of my life trying to make him happy, if he wants me.

"This is not your choice to make," I tell Anassa firmly.

In this moment, I don't care about the politics, or the things that will come between us, the things we'll need to do to right his father's wrongs.

All I want is him.

"Yes," I breathe.

"Yes?" Killian's voice is tremulous, a rare moment of vulnerability from him. My heart squeezes.

"Yes!" I pull him up into me, grabbing his face. My grief and surprise and elation and exhaustion combine into a single pulsing need—for comfort, for Killian's mouth, for one damn place in this whole world where I can just relax and belong and not feel like a constant failure of a person.

He kisses back with equal desperation, his big hands cupping my face firmly, locking my mouth against his.

"Here," Killian pulls back and reaches for my hand. "I want to see this bracelet on your wrist."

The bracelet is hinged, and he opens it, then slips it onto my arm and closes it again. The gold band settles against my skin, almost as if it's tightening against my wrist. I gently twist my wrist back and forth, admiring the winking way the candlelight catches on the depth of the ruby, the way it glints off of the cavernous black of the diamonds.

I will be Killian's queen, and nothing has ever felt more right.

Finally, finally, the shadows disappear.

CHAPTER FORTY-FIVE

My worries about my mother's funeral turn out to be misplaced. Killian handles it all. We argue about it briefly, but he insists on paying for everything.

"You are the future queen, kitten," he says. "Your mother deserves a proper burial in a place of honor. And *you* deserve to be able to visit her somewhere beautiful and comforting."

Which is why he buys her a place in the Garden of Eternal Rest —a lavishly maintained cemetery in the city's wealthy Northern Quarter, where even the smallest plots cost more than my mother made in a year. It's looked after by a small sect devoted to the Faceless Goddess, and they've brought a priestess here today to bless the ceremony.

My mother wasn't religious, but I think she'd have loved that.

The morning of the funeral dawns crisp and clear, a mere two days after I returned from the front. The Garden is closed down for my mother's ceremony, and Killian has spared no expense.

The plot he chose is on a grassy hill, sheltered by an enormous moonbloom tree dripping with gorgeous deep green needles. The headstone is white marble, simply but elegantly engraved with her name and the words *Beloved Mother, Friend, and Neighbor*. Mother's polished mahogany casket is already perched above the open grave, decorated with an arrangement of fragrant white roses.

Tidy hedges grow all over the garden, providing privacy between the larger family plots. Some of them even have hardy winter-blooming flowers on them. There are several greenhouses on the garden property where flowers grow so that families can stop in and pick fresh ones to lay at their loved ones' graves.

I have to admit, after seeing this place, the thought of burying her in the dreary common burial grounds near our neighborhood is… not great. It's a comfort that she'll spend the rest of her days here, in this lush vista where the air smells clean instead of like smoke and poverty.

Killian's right. She *does* deserve it. And Saela would like to visit her here. My sister always loved flowers.

She'd love this ceremony, too, despite the awkward clash of my two worlds coming together. Everyone we know from the Eastern Quarter is here, dressed in their best. They look shabby and uncomfortable in the midst of all this opulence, but I'm still happy they came.

They huddle together on one side of the grave—the women from the laundry, plus a few neighbors and friends. Igor stands straight-backed at the head of the group, looking unexpectedly dapper in his formal military uniform from his service days. His wife Prina is beside him, wearing a new dress.

On the other side are Izabel, Venna, Tomison and Nevah, dressed in formal Bonded attire. I've barely had a chance to see them since I got back from the front.

Anassa is here, too, waiting outside the Garden gates with the other wolves. She's been quiet with me the past two days; not shutting me out, exactly, but making her displeasure about my engagement known.

Still, she's here for me when it matters, and there's a tender nudging from her across the bond.

Killian remains at my side, dressed in an uncharacteristically simple black suit. He still looks like a prince, of course, but I can tell he chose the outfit carefully, so as not to draw undue attention to himself—a deliberate setting aside of his royal status that says he's here simply to support me.

His thoughtfulness and sensitivity through all of this have touched me so deeply—I can't even put it into words.

Just before the ceremony is about to begin, Anassa pricks up. *"More coming. Wait to start."*

More…?

Then, cresting over the hill, the rest of the Strategos Rawbonds arrive, led by Gamma Daegan. He's panting, face flushed—clearly they've run to get here on time. My eyes widen in disbelief.

"Did we make it?" he asks me as he approaches, out of breath. "Sorry, we didn't know—"

"You didn't know because I didn't tell you," I say, my tone softer than the words. "Why…?"

"You're our Alpha," he says like it's obvious, then bows. "Of course we're going to be here for you. The moment Alpha Stark told us—"

"Wait, Stark?" I ask sharply. Then I see him, trailing behind the last of the Strategos.

Stark stands tall at the top of the hill, his dark presence saturating the clear morning air. His unruly hair whips around him in the breeze, and his eyes find mine, locking me in place. He inclines his head toward me and I stiffen, then nod back, acknowledging him.

I've locked him out of my brain over the past two days. Whatever happened in that tent is of no consequence, especially now that I'm engaged to another man. But still, my chest is tight. It astounds me that he thought to tell them. Touches me, as much as I hate to admit it, that he thought it was important that they be here.

"Thank you," I say to Daegan, and discovering that I mean it. The pack has come to support me, and I vow that as their Alpha, I will look out for them in the same ways.

The ceremony begins with my eulogy: a speech I've been struggling to compose for the last two days. I've been so nervous about it, wanting to do my mother proud. But as I step forward to speak, I'm surprised to find the anxiety gone—washed away by the warmth and support of everyone present.

"My mother had a difficult life," I begin, my voice carrying clear and strong through the cold winter air. "But it never made her hard. She raised two daughters alone after losing her husband to the war. Those of you who knew her well know she also struggled with a debilitating illness—one she fought against every day. Yet even in her darkest moments, she never stopped loving her children."

My eyes connect with Igor's and he nods at me, encouraging. I reach up, playing with the opal at my neck; it felt right to have it on today.

"She never gave up," I continue. "Never stopped trying to be the best version of herself—the best mother she could be. She was kind. Compassionate. Understanding. Even when life was cruel to her, as it so often was. Even when her mind and body turned against her."

I pause, throat tight, seeing the many misty eyes among my friends and neighbors and pack.

"I'm so glad you all came to honor her memory," I say, voice trembling slightly. "She would be happy—and proud—to know how much you care. And I know that I speak for all of us when I say that I hope, in her eternal rest, she will finally find the peace she deserved in life."

There's a swell of sniffles and muted applause as I step back.

Killian smiles and takes my hand when I return to his side, and a woman in pristine white robes approaches the casket.

The priestess of the Faceless Goddess begins religious burial rites with a poetic incantation, calling upon the goddess to escort my mother's soul into the afterlife and protect her eternal rest.

I watch with tear-blurred eyes as the casket is lowered into the ground. The priestess scatters soil and herbs of blessing over the grave, invoking the goddess and our ancestors to watch over my mother's surviving loved ones and soothe our grief.

It's a contrast to my father's funeral—a memory I've rarely revisited. We didn't have a body to bury; his platoon had been attacked by Siphons and he and the other soldiers were ripped to shreds. The only thing that they recovered from him was a finger. He was given a nondescript headstone in the soldier's cemetery, marking an empty grave.

I add my own silent prayer to those of the priestess, wondering if our ancestors hear. If the Faceless Goddess hears.

Please, watch over Saela. Keep her safe. Help me bring her home as Mother wanted.

With that, the ceremony ends. The crowd begins to disperse, but I find myself rooted in place, unable to walk away from the grave.

Beside me, Killian squeezes my hand.

"Let's go to your mother's house," he murmurs. "There are things that need to be sorted through, and you shouldn't do it alone."

BACK IN THE NEIGHBORHOOD, the house seems smaller and emptier than I remember.

And... darker.

Like a lamp without a wick, never to be lit again.

I guess I never realized how much light my mother brought to this place. She was the one who made it a home—the one who filled it with life—even in the depths of her illness.

I stand in her empty bedroom and cry while Killian is outside speaking with the landlord about the outstanding rent.

Now, I have to sort through Mother's belongings. Get them out. I won't be returning to this place again, and neither will Saela. Soon, some other poverty-stricken family will live here. When Saela comes back, we'll have to make a new home somewhere else. After I graduate from the Trials, I'll be given a home in the Bonded City.

But... I might be queen by then, as unreal as that sounds, even in my head. We'll live in the castle, I guess. Saela will have everything she ever needed and more.

That ought to be a dream come true, and yet...

My heart breaks, knowing we have to leave this dingy little hovel behind—and all the memories with it.

We'll make new memories, I tell myself.

But it's not the same. Mother won't be there. Her presence in this place is like an imprint, memories embedded in every floorboard, every piece of furniture, every scrape and scuff.

The castle has its own ghosts—no room for my mother.

At least I have her things. I can take a few little pieces of her with me. Save a few fragments of her memory to share with Saela if —when—I bring my sister home.

I collect my mother's favorite scarf from the closet. It was a gift from our father back when they were courting. It's faded and frayed with age, but the woolen pattern of vines and roses still holds a whiff of her scent.

On a whim, I take a pair of her shoes, too; the carefully polished heels she wore only on very special occasions. They won't fit me, but maybe when Saela's older...

And then I remember the floorboard where mother kept her most prized possessions hidden, including the opal necklace.

Inside, I find a stack of leather-bound journals, their pages worn soft from frequent handling. They're full of writings and drawings done in my mother's elegant hand. I'm surprised.

And, for a moment, thrilled by the discovery.

She must have spent many hours filling these pages, yet I never saw her with the journals. To have such a record of my mother's thoughts and feelings...

But when I look closer at the pages, I realize I'm holding a record of her madness.

The drawings are extraordinarily detailed and unnervingly repetitive. Most depict a crown in intricate detail: two wolves leaping at each other over a delicate circlet laden with jewels.

Between the drawings are scattered notes—references to someone named "Lumina," mentions of "Nocturn," and the word "Astreon" appear as frequently as the crown drawings. Like the names of our two countries, but wrong.

I recognize the names immediately. Mother used to mutter them often during her episodes.

"Lumina," I say aloud, wondering where on earth my mother

heard the name. Are these people just figments of her imagination, or did she know them long ago?

"Hide the journals," Anassa growls suddenly over the bond, her tone urgent and filled with warning. At the same time, I hear the thump of Killian's boots in the hallway outside.

Confused, but galvanized by Anassa's intensity, I shove the journals into my bag with the rest of Mother's things just as Killian enters the room.

"Hey," he says with a gentle smile. "Find anything special you want to keep?"

Something in his tone gives me pause. I'm not sure what it is, but it doesn't quite align with the look on his face. There's a hint of tension around his eyes.

"Just a few things," I say, keeping my voice level while my heart beats inexplicably fast. I reach into the bag, surreptitiously shoving the journals deeper as I show him mother's scarf and shoes. There's a bottle of perfume, too, with a single drop of amber liquid still inside.

"She used to wear it when I was little," I say, drawing his gaze from the open bag. "Back when Father was alive, he'd buy her things like this now and then. Little extravagancies to make her feel special." My throat tightens. "It still smells like her. Like the woman she was before he died, I mean."

Killian's face softens with compassion. "He really loved her."

I nod, clutching the bottle hard in one hand.

"Let me see." He takes the bottle gently from my fingers and lifts it to his nose. "Mm. Smells nice. Good quality. I bet the castle perfumer could replicate this scent."

"Really?" I blurt. "You have a designated *perfumer* at the castle?"

He chuckles. "But of course. The king can hardly be expected to venture out into the city every time he wants to try a new scent, now can he?"

We share a laugh, then Killian's expression turns solemn. "Would you like another bottle of your mother's perfume, Meryn?"

My eyes prickle with tears, the journals and Anassa's warning momentarily forgotten.

"I would," I whisper, rising on my toes to kiss him. "I really would."

THAT AFTERNOON, I part ways with Killian and head straight for Anassa's favorite terrace with the journals in hand. She lifts her head when I crest the terrace steps and slap the journals down on the floor in front of her.

"Alright, talk," I say. "What do you know about my mother's journals and why in the goddess's name did you make me hide them from Killian?"

Anassa lounges regally on her haunches, her massive form silhouetted against the mountain and the darkening sky beyond it.

Through our bond comes her maddeningly cryptic response: *"I've told you all I can."*

"You haven't told me *anything*!" I exclaim.

Anassa just blinks at me in impassive silence.

"Dammit! This is important, Anassa. My mother just *died*. And these are her thoughts—a record of her madness, her delusions—on paper. If you know something about it, *I need you to tell me!*"

"What can I possibly tell you that isn't already written there in your mother's hand?" the wolf replies, unmoved by my distress.

"I don't know!" I cry. "That's why I'm asking!"

When Anassa doesn't respond, I flip one of the journals open and gesture to an image of the wolf crown. "Why did she draw this over and over? Do you know what it is? And the names—Lumina, Nocturn, Astreon—what do you know about them?"

Anassa doesn't even look at the page. *"Perhaps it's time for you to do some searching of your own."*

Grief and frustration send me pacing away from her, thrusting my hands through my hair as I go over the facts in my mind.

"My mother's episodes always centered around these names. She would talk about them—to them, even. Nocturn and Astreon almost make sense. Like the personifications of our Kingdoms,

Nocturna and Astreona. It's a basic delusion. But Lumina—I've never heard that name, except from my mother."

I spin back to her, thoughts racing. "And why did Mother get better suddenly when I became Bonded? She was more lucid the last few months than she has been in *years*. Meanwhile, I started having nightmares and hallucinations. None of this makes any *sense*—"

I break off, blinking at the wolf in sudden realization.

Perhaps it's time you do some searching of your own.

She said something like that to me when I started training with Stark and he showed me his library. She wanted me to do research then, but I didn't listen.

Suddenly galvanized, I return to the journals and gather them up off the ground. Anassa watches with the lupine equivalent of a raised eyebrow.

"Fine," I say to my wolf, my decision rising above my grief. "If you won't give me answers, I know where to find them."

CHAPTER FORTY-SIX

T he castle corridors are dark as I make my way to Stark's office, my senses heightened by my subterfuge. I don't want to be seen slinking into his private space at this time of night—by him or anyone else.

Not because it's forbidden, or even frowned upon, but because some creeping intuition tells me the information I'm searching for is… dangerous.

Luckily, after weeks of traversing this path twice a day for training, I know every creaky floorboard, every shadow, every hidden corner. Each time I hear footsteps or voices coming, I melt out of sight.

My mother's journals, tucked safely under my shirt, are heavy against my skin. Like a terrible, dark secret.

Stark's office appears empty when I push the door open and peek inside. No sound. Only one lamp is lit, casting the outer room —his sparring floor and library—in deep, flickering shadows. He must be at a late training session, or back in his quarters off the Daemos pack area. I probably don't have much time.

I slip inside, grab the lamp from its hook beside the door, and cross straight to the shelves. I'm magnetized to a certain one with unnerving certainty. It's that shelf with the ancient books that drew my eyes so powerfully before.

Lamplight illuminates the dusty spines in a dull orange glow.

My hand rises to one in particular. It's visibly older than the others, its leather binding cracked and worn. My heart pounds as I slide it from its perch. The thick volume feels heavier in my hand than it should. The pages are yellowed deeply with age, their edges starting to crumble.

It has no title. No inscription. Nothing to indicate the nature of its contents.

Yet I know it's the right book, without logic or reason.

Blood rushes in my head as I draw the cover open, fingers gentle on the brittle pages inside. There's no title page, either. No table of contents.

The first chapter is titled simply, "The Sturmfrost Queens."

It's a history of Nocturna, I realize, scanning the first few pages. And it's not even printed like a proper book—it's *handwritten*, every page packed edge to edge in careful, curling script.

My eyes scan the pages rapidly, drinking the information in even as my mind struggles to make sense of it.

The Sturmfrost Queens were the original rulers of Nocturna, the book proclaims. A long matrilineal line of Bonded warriors with incredible powers who ruled the kingdom for centuries. The dates listed are long before King Cyril's line took over.

I shake my head in silent confusion. *Is this for real?*

As far as I know, Nocturna has always been ruled by an unbonded human king. There must have been someone ruling over Nocturna before them, but…

I frown, realizing I don't know the history beyond the last five hundred years. They never taught us that in school. I've never seen it mentioned in any history book.

In fact, we were taught that Nocturna as we know it didn't exist before King Cyril's ancestor took the throne. *He* made the kingdom of Nocturna what it is today. *He* brought the humans and wolves together under one rule.

I always assumed Nocturna was just a collection of human

encampments before that. A scattered civilization fighting to survive in a wild, dangerous world populated by voracious predators—direwolves and Siphons who hunted us like cattle, threatening our very existence.

Then, as the legends say, the Faceless Goddess sought to uplift humans and balance the power between us and our enemies. So, she blessed King Cyril's ancestor with the *Diren Blæd*, giving him the power to control the wolves and us the ability to bond with them.

That gave us the strength to drive the Siphons off our land, thus beginning the centuries-long war between our kingdom and Astreona.

But according to this book, none of that is true. Nocturna is *millennia* older than we've been told. And the direwolves were a central part of the Sturmfrost line's rule. They've always been our allies.

This can't be real, I think, staring at the narrow script. *Everything we've been taught… it can't all be wrong. Can it?*

I flip ahead a few pages, scanning names and stories I've never seen or heard before. Queens who ruled with direwolves at their sides, uniting the humans. Protecting them.

And then I find the drawings.

My breath catches in my throat.

I turn and set the book on the little table beside the shelf, pulling out my mother's journals. I don't need to see the drawings side-by-side to know they're the same, but I lay them out, anyway.

It's the crown my mother drew over and over—the twin wolves leaping at a precious gem set between them. Absolutely identical.

This is the crown of the Strumfrost line, forged thousands of years ago and imbued with powerful magic.

My mind reels. How could my mother know about this? Where could she have possibly seen it?

"Anassa?" I reach out, prodding the bond. She's silent. If she knows anything about this, she's not giving me a fucking hint.

I turn the page, looking for an explanation, anything.

What I find is another drawing.

Adrenaline floods my veins.

466

It's an illustration of the carving I found behind that tapestry in the servant's passage: a queen astride her direwolf, the Sturmfrost crown with the two leaping wolves perched atop her head.

Fuck. I almost forgot. *That's* where I've seen the crown before.

But how? *Why?* The questions flash through my mind in a nonsensical tumble.

This is... impossible.

And yet...

Something tugs at my memory. The carving, the illustration, my mother's drawings... this isn't the only place I've seen the crown.

The realization hits me like a blow to the head.

The arena. That flash of metal in the drain—the shape of it.

It was the crown.

Before I can even begin to process what this means, the sound of heavy footsteps approaching the door snaps me out of my thoughts.

My heart stops.

Stark.

The urge to hide the book surges through me, but something tells me it's pointless. This isn't just any book. He's going to know I touched it. Like the knowledge inside has left some indelible mark on me.

That makes no fucking sense, I think, shoving my mother's journals back under my shirt.

But it doesn't make sense that I knew exactly which book to read, either. That this particular volume is the one that called to me. That the illustrations inside match with my mother's drawings, her visions—and mine.

None of this makes sense.

Behind me, the door creaks open.

With my heart pulsing in my throat, I turn.

Stark's face is unreadable, cast in heavy yellow lamplight. He looks at the weathered tome in my hand. Then, slowly, his eyes drag up to the engagement band clamped around my wrist.

"What is this?" I demand. "Is this fiction? A children's story? Where did it come from?"

His eyes darken, jaw drawing tight. "Congratulations on your engagement," he says instead. "You'll make an incredible queen."

I nearly toss the tome at his head but stop myself in time. "The *book*, Stark," I hiss.

Stark shrugs. *Shrugs!*

"I can't tell you anything about that," he says in a carefully neutral tone.

Rage floods my head. Two words burst from my lips like the crack of a whip. "Why not?"

He doesn't answer me. Just stands there staring at me like he's furious with me. His hand falls from the door knob, but he doesn't step into the room. Almost as if he's afraid to come any closer.

Afraid? I think, bewildered. *Stark?*

"What is going on here?" I demand of Anassa. *"You know, don't you? Is this real?"*

Anassa's caution filters through the bond. There's a pause. I can almost feel her calculating what to say. The silence creeps up my back like a premonition, whispering something I can't quite hear.

Her reply comes in the same tone of careful neutrality Stark used. *"I also cannot tell you anything about that."*

I blink.

Also?

ALSO?

Why is my direwolf colluding with Stark?!

They both know more than they're saying. And for some reason, they're in agreement that I don't get to know whatever it is they're hiding—about *my* mother. *My* visions. This history, whatever it is.

I thought I was losing my mind. And all this time… they knew. They knew about this book, these supposed Sturmfrost queens—the things I saw in hallucinations.

Betrayal burns in my chest.

Anassa is *my* direwolf. She is supposed to be my ally, my protector. How long has she been keeping secrets from me? She, who has always treated me so abominably when she feels like I've shut her out. How much is she—are *they*, both—hiding from me?

My mind balks under the weight of everything I've learned in the last half hour—and everything I still don't understand.

It's too much to process. The dots aren't all connected yet.

But they will be.

I hold up the book, glaring directly into Stark's eyes. My voice comes out rough as sandpaper and caustic.

"I'm taking this."

I expect him to protest—to outright refuse. But I'm willing to fight him for it.

His gaze flicks to the book, then back to my face, reading the threat in my posture. In a tone weighted with layers of inexplicable warning, he says, "I would be careful with it."

The fuck?

My eyes narrow. "If you're so worried what I'm going to do with this book, then *tell me what I need to know!*"

Something flickers across his face, too swift to comprehend. He shakes his head.

"I can't. Just… be careful."

"Fuck you," I snap, sweeping past him in a rage.

As I storm away from Stark's rooms, Anassa's thoughts brush cautiously against my own. The touch of her mind is wordless, almost tentative. As though she senses how close to the edge I am—how near to explosive violence.

"What are you going to do?" she asks.

"Oh, now you want to talk?" I snarl. *"Well, too bad. Should have thought about that before keeping secrets, Anassa."*

With that, I slam the iron wall in place between us.

I can't trust Anassa. That much is abundantly clear. What else might she be keeping from me? She's given me only what she wants me to know the entire four months that we've been bonded. She hasn't even given me a hint about who her mate is, for example. That should have been a warning sign.

Her betrayal stings like frostbite. And Stark…

I flash back on our trip to the front again. The moments he showed concern for me. The desire in his eyes when he licked me.

That bastard has been playing games with my head all along, hasn't he?

Fuck it. Fuck them both.

Whatever is going on here—however it's linked to my mother's visions—I'm *going* to get to the bottom of it.

With or without their help.

CHAPTER FORTY-SEVEN

The Unity Trial is in three days, and I need to be sharp. But instead of training with my packmates to make sure my skills are as honed as possible, I'm sitting in my room pouring over an ancient book about queens and magic and history.

There's a burning in me, like I need to figure this out. It's a pull. An instinct. And if Stark and Anassa are going to continue their streak of uselessness, then it's on me.

Briefly, I considered asking for Killian's help. But what would he think of it, this book that offers a completely dissenting story to the narrative his family pushes? Would he want to look further into it, like I do? Or would he dismiss it out of hand?

Plus, Stark's warning that I need to "be careful" with this book won't leave my brain—even if he's an asshole.

Thinking about him irritates me all over again. I've been blowing off Alpha training with *that asshole* since we argued two days ago.

I'm about to dive back into the book when a knock sounds at my door.

Whipping into panicky action, I shove the book under my blanket. "Yeah?"

"It's me." Izabel.

Pulling the door open, I welcome her in.

She drags her fingers through her dark hair as she enters and watches me shut the door.

"Hey," I say, a little awkwardly. I've barely seen her since I returned from the front, aside from my mother's funeral, and the acquisition of this book hasn't helped things.

Izabel bites her lip, then says, "I just wanted to check on you. See if you've been alright, holed up on your own in here."

It's a jab at my open wounds. When I'm training or thinking about this stupid book, it's easier to pretend like nothing's changed. But when she outright asks me how I've been, I'm back at the Garden of Eternal Rest, watching my mother's body disappear into the ground.

Numbness and grief settle over me, but I tell her the truth. "I'm in pieces. I still can't believe she's gone. Is that weak of me to admit, as your Alpha?"

The mother I knew as a child disappeared years ago, but the recent improvement in her condition had given me a foolish kind of hope. Maybe things would finally get better. Maybe Saela would return to a lucid mother, fully capable of taking care of her.

It's like a bruise that won't heal and I've been doing everything in my power to avoid looking too closely at it.

Izabel shakes her head. "I'd be more worried about you if you weren't. But I just want to make sure you remember that the pack is here for you. We miss you. *I* miss you."

Her eyes dart down to the engagement bracelet glittering on my wrist, and just as quickly, she looks away. I'm sure she's been awfully curious about it over the past couple of days, but I haven't been around for her to question me, and she's mercifully been allowing me my space.

Still, I can't keep this from her any longer. It isn't right.

I hold my wrist out so she can see it properly—the wrought gold band, the shimmering black diamonds, the huge blood-red ruby at the center. "It's an engagement bracelet. Killian proposed before the funeral, and I accepted."

There's a brief moment of shocked silence, then Izabel wrenches me closer and *squeals*. Shrieks like a little girl. It's high and piercing and fucking wonderful. "I *knew* it!"

Then she gasps and stops her happy wiggling, pulling back from me.

"Wait, is it okay to be happy right now?"

"Yeah, Izabel. You can definitely be happy." I *need* her happiness. It's infectious and beautiful.

And she delivers. She starts hopping, seizes my wrist, and ogles the bracelet with cooing sounds of appreciation. "I've *never* seen anything like this, Meryn! This is ten times the bracelet my mother wears. Oh!" Her large eyes widen even more, if possible. "I just realized you're going to be queen!"

Queen.

It sounds different, coming out of my friend's mouth—like there's truth to it, for the first time. The word sends a little shiver down my spine.

My face flushes. "Yeah, I guess so."

"We're going to have a Bonded queen! Wow. This calls for a celebration," Izabel announces.

The thought of "celebrating" with the other Rawbonds is slightly nauseating. With the Unity Trial on the horizon, everyone is acting like it's the end times and the situation in the common lounge has turned from a constant, sex-positive party to downright debauchery.

I'm honestly surprised I can't hear the moaning from here.

Izabel must sense my immediate discomfort, because she doubles back. "Okay, not a *celebration*," she says. "How about a casual hang with a couple of friends?"

I exhale in relief. "That, I can do."

Thirty minutes later, I'm stepping into the pleasant heat of the kitchens. The room is unfamiliar to me. I've heard that Rawbonds sometimes come in here to sneak food outside of mealtimes, but I'd never felt the inclination to visit it myself—it's not like they skimp on food at our meals.

The kitchen is massive, with tall cabinets and counters, stone floors, and an arched hearth big enough to fit all five of us inside. There are metal racks over the heat meant for pots, as well as allotted corners near the flames for bread to rise. The air smells like the bundles of herbs hanging all around us, deliciously stinging spice, and the lingering warmth of the stew we had for dinner. The workspace is covered in neatly arranged ingredients.

The space is surprisingly empty of staff, which seems suspicious until I realize that Tomison is here. The man has the uncanny ability to convince people to do whatever he asks with just a smile. No doubt, he's responsible for our privacy.

Nevah sits on the counter near him. Tomison says something to her, and she immediately reaches up to grab a hanging bundle of herbs and smacks him in the face with it.

"Not the face!" Tomison shouts, shielding himself with his arms. "Everyone *loves* the face!"

"That's what you'd like to think," Izabel quips as we walk up to them.

"Good to see you've emerged from hibernation," Nevah says to me as I lean my hip against the counter she's sitting on.

I raise a brow. "I saw you at training only a few hours ago."

"That's different," Tomison says, clapping a hand on my shoulder.

"Pantry is full, Tomison," Venna announces as she joins us with an armful of goods—eggs, butter, and a mixing bowl. "I didn't find flour, though."

Tomison pushes off of the counter. "I know where it is," he tells us and disappears into the pantry.

Nevah slides down and grins, reaching past me for something. She produces a bottle of emberwine and pops it open using just her thumb. "Let's get drunk," she says, and Venna lets out a *whoop*.

Nevah pours cups for us all as Tomison reemerges, clutching a bag of flour. Izabel takes it from him, then points him to the eggs. "Your next task."

I get the sudden feeling that she invited him tonight solely so she could tell him what to do.

"Since when were you in charge of me?" he protests with a little smirk.

"Since I'm making a cake for our *mutual* good friend," she says and takes hold of his shoulders to shove him towards the counter. "Get cracking."

"Yes, ma'am," he says and picks up the first egg.

"Our father always used to bake this cake when there was good news," Izabel explains, turning to me. "I thought it would be perfect."

It shouldn't surprise me that perfectionist, best-in-class student Izabel also loves the precision of baking. "Thank you," I say, touched by the effort.

"Unless there's a particular cake *your* family always liked?" Venna offers.

Izabel points at her. "What she said. I could do that, instead."

No one back in the Eastern Quarter would've ever had enough extra coin for all the eggs, butter, and sugar required to make a cake. But I don't want to bring the mood down with poverty talk, so I say, "No. I'd love to try whatever's special for your family."

"You won't regret it," Venna says and nudges my arm.

"Wait, what are we celebrating?" Tomison asks, looking over his shoulder at us as he continues to crack eggs.

Izabel groans. "You are denser than the cake we're making."

"Rude," Tomison says. "And how am I supposed to guess at something that no one's told me?"

Nevah grabs my arm, lifting it up and shaking it so that the engagement bracelet catches the light.

"Whoa, Cooper!" Tomison exclaims, setting down the eggs and turning towards us. Then he catches my wrist and examines it. "You're engaged?"

My face heats at the attention. I guess I'm going to have to get used to this, although I really hope the news will spread quickly and quietly. "It appears so," I say.

He laughs and then grabs the cup of emberwine that Nevah had poured for him. "Well, I'll drink to that!"

We all take a sip, but Nevah chugs her drink, then slams the empty cup down. She's starting to refill it when Izabel says, "Not so fast, you need to work. You three—" She points to me, Venna and Nevah. "Go get supplies for frosting."

Nevah and Tomison exchange beleaguered looks and Nevah grumbles, "She's being bossier than Alpha Stark."

Izabel clicks her tongue. "We're on a schedule here, cake goes in the oven in five!"

I follow Nevah and Venna to the pantry but hang to the side while the two of them look for powdered sugar and flavorings. I have no idea what goes into a frosting, let alone where I'd find it.

When we reemerge from the pantry a few minutes later, Tomison and Izabel are playfully arguing.

"Sheesh, just fuck already," Nevah says to me and Venna, slurring slightly. We watch Tomison lean too close to Izabel, who shoves him with a floury hand and a fake-looking frown.

"Ew," Venna grumbles. "He's like an annoying brother."

"Not to her," I tease into my cup.

Venna groans. "I don't want to think about this. Nevah, distract me."

"Thought you'd have plenty of distractions already, as the notorious *Kryptos Killer*," Nevah replies.

Venna immediately blushes. "Don't call me that. It's stupid."

"Killer?" I ask.

"She's been working her way through—" Nevah starts, but then Izabel turns around and waves a whisk at her.

"Venna just likes to have fun! Don't bully her," she says before winking at her twin.

Venna rolls her eyes. "I didn't ask for a nickname."

Izabel sets the whisk down. "Half of the Rawbonds *loooove* her," Izabel teases, signing as she speaks. "More than half."

"What happened to not bullying me?" Venna protests.

"We're related. It's my job." She scowls at the rest of us and jabs a floury finger our way. "Neither of you get to, though. Yes, she's a beautifully impressive slut, but she's also—"

"Hey!" Venna protests. "Besides, you two can hardly talk."

Nevah holds up her hands. "I don't know what you mean. I'm a one woman lady."

"Oh, I am aware," Venna says darkly. "Do you and Zadie get any sleep during your 'sleepovers?' Because I'll tell you, you're keeping the rest of us in Kryptos awake."

Tomison turns quickly with an interested grin. "Tell me more about these sleepovers."

Izabel grabs a handful of flour and throws it into his face. "Don't be disgusting."

He sputters and wipes the flour out of his eyes. "Why am I even here?"

"Because we need someone to fill the pan," Izabel replies, sliding a greased cake pan over to him. Tomison groans but does what he's told, and within a few minutes there's a cake baking away in one of the designated shelves in the big hearth.

Izabel, Venna and Tomison start chatting about a bakery they all like back in the Bonded City, and I nudge Nevah with my hip.

"I'm glad to hear that you're seeing someone. I know things were... hard... after the Ascent."

Nevah nods and takes a huge sip of her emberwine. I don't think she's going to really respond to it, but then she says, quietly, "Collin. His name was Collin, the man I loved. It was naïve of us, I guess, to believe we'd both make it though. We'd been together since we were sixteen. We always planned on Bonding together..."

Her voice trails off and I wrap an arm around her.

"Thank you," she says, looking at me. Her eyes are dewy and she sniffs hard, trying to draw her mask of strength back on. "If you—all of you—hadn't come to my side at the Purge Trial, I'm not sure what I would've done. I might've just let it happen, honestly. But seeing that there were other people who cared if I lived, even if I didn't..."

I bite my lip, trying to hold back tears myself. I know exactly what she means; she's describing the way I felt when Igor pulled me off the streets and started training me.

"No thanks necessary," I say. Before I can say anything maudlin, Tomison clambers up onto the counter, standing on it.

"Alright!" he shouts. The emberwine is working fast because he wobbles slightly before righting himself.

"Don't step in the flour, dumbass!" Izabel scolds.

"A toast!" he announces, lifting his cup. Venna and Nevah immediately lift their cups. Izabel rolls her eyes and follows suit. "To our future queen!"

My cheeks are instantly on fire. I wish it were just the wine, but this is embarrassing. "Please stop," I beg.

"You're right. My bad," he corrects. "A toast to our future queen, should she survive the Unity Trials with her life intact!"

We break into messy laughter and drink. It shouldn't be funny, but it really is. The weight that's been on my shoulders lifts the drunker I get, the more laughter I hear, and the more times one of my friends tosses an arm over my shoulder or whispers to me with a conspiratorial smile.

We're having so much fun that we all forget about the cake in the oven… until the *smell* hits us.

Venna's eyes go wide and Izabel shrieks in despair. "I can't believe I forgot to watch the clock! This is all *your* fault," she says, pointing a finger at Tomison.

He tosses his hands in the air. "How is it my fault?"

"You were distracting me!" she shouts, grabbing kitchen gloves and yanking the cake pan out of its shelf on the hearth. Black smoke curls from the top as Izabel pulls the cake out.

It is a burned mess. Absolutely horrific, really. Its acrid smell floods the whole kitchen, and it causes another round of delirious laughter.

"My beautiful cake!" Izabel cries, wiping away her tears of laughter. "I swear, I'm actually good at this, Venna can attest."

We salvage something edible from the middle of it, eat *piles* of cake rather than slices, and talk until the lateness of the hour starts to drag us toward exhaustion.

By the time we finish, Tomison and Izabel have to practically carry Nevah out of the kitchens, though neither of them is much better off.

"Meryn and I will clean up," Venna offers. "You all go on ahead without us." When they leave, she turns to me. "Good, I've been wanting to get you alone all night."

The tone in her voice sobers me up instantly. "Do you have any news?"

She shakes her head. "Unfortunately not. I've been looking into what you asked for," she tells me, and signs "castle" just in case the others might still be close enough to hear. I swallow and nod. "I haven't found anything concrete yet."

Disappointment pings through me, and I try to keep it off my face; after all, she's doing a favor for me.

"I have a weird feeling, though," Venna continues. "I'm sure there's something I'm missing or that I haven't found yet. Just out of reach."

You have no idea, I want to say. *If this book about the queens is real, there's something very strange happening.*

"Keep looking?" I ask gently. "I need to know if—" I sign "the king." "—is up to something."

Venna nods, and says, "I'm planning on it. I'll keep you posted."

I hope she's able to work quickly. In a few days, the Trials will be over, and we'll be sent to the front—those of us who aren't dead, at least.

Our time is running out.

CHAPTER FORTY-EIGHT

The morning of the Unity Trial, the horn blasts through the castle before dawn, so loud the vase on my nightstand rattles slightly.

I'm already wide awake. I've been awake for hours, lying here in the darkness, staring up at the ceiling. I sit up slowly and rub my itchy eyes, then mechanically set about slipping into uniform and readying myself as best I can for what's about to happen.

Our instructors have prepared us as well as they can for this moment, even Daegan, who greatly improved as an instructor once I told him directly that he did not need to look to me for guidance and that he should assume authority during all classes. Today is the culmination of the Proving period, our ability to show the instructors, the king and the nobles that we're capable of working together across packs.

Of course, like every Trial here, it's also an opportunity for bloodshed. Each pack has been assessing the other during the last two months of joint training. Today's the last chance for any direwolf or rider to cull a pair that they find wanting.

Tomorrow, we'll all be on the same side, facing the same enemy.

When I reach the common lounge, the rest of the Rawbonds are already assembled, eating breakfast in tense silence. It's like there are icicles hanging perilously from the ceiling and we're all just waiting for them to fall, wondering which of us will be hit first. Grabbing a roll, I sit down next to Izabel and Nevah, though I can't bring myself to eat it.

A shadow falls over my plate and I look up into Jonah's hard, dark eyes. He fixes me with a burning glare. Ever since he broke my nose and Stark threatened him, he's kept a wide berth, but I've felt his malignant attention on me whenever we're in the same room. Today is the closest he's come since that day in the yard.

"What?" I say with a scowl.

He smiles, and it contains no warmth. "Good luck today, Cooper. You might have aspirations about your station, but mark my word, you'll die in the gutter like the common-born bitch you are."

I push my plate away from me with a huff. "If you're thinking about challenging an Alpha during the Trial today, Jonah, you are far fucking stupider than I assumed, and believe me, I was not giving you much credit as it was."

His smile widens and still does not reach his soulless eyes. "I would never dare challenge an Alpha," he says sarcastically, his voice rising in volume to draw the attention of all the other Rawbonds. "I'm merely pointing out that today is a very good day to weed out any unsuitable common blood."

With that, he turns and stalks off, but he's made the scene he wanted to make. People are whispering. Fucker. Maybe someone will find it fit to take *him* out today.

Leader Aldrich appears then through the door of the common lounge, his face serious. "Rawbonds, form up to move to the arena."

I'm numb as we file out of the common lounge and into the halls, which I suppose is better than trembling or teetering on the verge of vomiting.

Through gaps in the crowd, I catch glimpses of faces I recognize. Venna's distinctive chic hair marks her amongst the Kryptos ranks. Joining us from the other direction is Henrey with the rest of Phylax.

The morning sun hasn't yet crested the castle walls. The early light paints everything in a wash of gray as we arrive at the arena. Despite the hour, the arena is already packed with the usual crowd of finely dressed nobles, shouting and laughing and drunk with anticipation. It's a spectacle no noble would miss. They stare and point like we're animals on show.

Today, though, they're joined by Bonded who have come from the city, family members who are on leave or retired from the forces already. Both the nobles and Bonded will be attending this final Trial and tomorrow's graduation ceremony.

The wolves are waiting for us already, and Anassa lifts her head high and meets my eyes as I approach her. Moving to her side, I run my hand along her fur, feeling the power of her muscles beneath my fingers.

The iron wall between us thins to almost nothing, turning translucent and soft.

I've been continuing to keep that wall up between us, and now she's forcing it away. I'm not ready to forgive her. Not until she comes clean with me. But if we're going to make it through this, we'll need total connection—no hesitation, no holding back. Unity.

My gaze skirts the dirt floor of the arena, following the drains to where the grate is. To where, perhaps, that crown is. I haven't had a chance to get in here since I found Stark's book and I'm burning with curiosity.

But the grate is covered today. A raised stage has been erected in the middle of the arena, where Leader Aldrich stands with the other four instructors. Stark's arms are folded over his chest, and his glower is on full-blast even at this early hour.

The second horn blares to signal the Unity Trial's beginning. I look up just as King Cyril and Killian enter to sit at their usual dais. Killian catches my eye and nods. I nod back, warmth filling me.

Aldrich raises a voice amplifier to his mouth and begins to speak, the sound carrying clear across the arena. "Today's Trial will simulate a coordinated Siphon assault on the castle. Daemos will play the role of the enemy forces, attacking from multiple positions. Phylax must maintain our defensive lines. Kryptos will relay critical intelligence. And Strategos must process all incoming information and coordinate the forces in real-time response."

It's what we've been training for. The stage on which the instructors stand will serve as the castle. The rest of the arena, the open battlefield. Plenty of space for maneuvering, whatever Daemos decides to do.

"As I'm sure your instructors have warned you, one misstep in your strategy, one break in your pack's unity, and the defenses crumble," Aldrich continues.

Frissons of awareness strike through my consciousness. Anassa is reaching out to the other wolves, making initial contact, readying herself for the stream of information she'll have to control.

We'll be leading this as the Alpha pair. It's a good exercise for me—this is what it will feel like when I join the remainder of the Strategos forces at the front.

Flashes of information begin to flow from other riders, through their wolves, back to my bond. Terrain details, potential troop movements, tactical possibilities. Everyone is humming with nervous energy, though some of the emotions I glimpse lean more towards anticipation. I'd bet money that one of those is Tomison.

It should all be overwhelming, but I've gotten slowly more used to the outward expansion of my mind, reshaping myself to allow for a wider current. More information, less painful force. All of it washes over me faster than the human mind can process.

There is no thinking. Only knowing.

"The Trial ends when either Daemos breaches our final defenses or Strategos successfully coordinates a decisive victory," Aldrich says. "But remember! This tests more than strategy. It tests your ability to think and act as *one entity*. It's also one final chance for the wolves to minimize potential weaknesses—in their packs, or any others."

The underlying meaning is clear. Anyone could die today.

The horn blasts again. And we begin.

The Daemos wolves immediately split into attack formations,

wasting no time. Their movements are precise and threatening, a blade of dark fur slicing across the open arena.

I can't waste time. There *is* no time with how fast they're moving.

Through the pack bond, I can sense my packmates' minds analyzing Daemos maneuvers and churning with possible counter-strategies, all offered up for my approval.

My eyes follow the split of Daemos, groups of wolves spreading out across the arena and then whipping back towards us. Anassa's will delves into me like her fangs are dragging me up a cliff. It's painful at first until I realize she's pulling me in the right direction, and I let her influence guide me.

"*Speak*," Anassa orders, her vicious intent clear. "*Strategos leads, so* you *lead*."

"Phylax, form a defensive line!" I shout over the thundering approach of a Daemos wolf. A wall of dark fur descends on us, and we have to meet it with our own force or it will crush us entirely. My mind is so focused on the battle that Anassa's sudden turn beneath me doesn't even startle me. My body moves with hers. "Kryptos! We need eyes on our flanks!"

The other packs move to comply instantly.

The river of the pack bond stills, like a stormy sea going entirely placid. I can see for miles. The full power of Strategos unity locks into place, and my consciousness expands, connecting me with every member of my pack.

It's as though nineteen bolts of light have flashed across the battlefield, converging in my mind, carrying with them instantaneous knowledge.

Izabel calculates probable attack vectors while Tomison analyzes terrain advantages. Nevah is assessing the movements of Phylax to ensure they're complying quickly enough with my order.

Then comes the impact. Daemos's front line slams into the wall of Phylax in a flurry of fur and teeth. Sound erupts in the arena—shouts and clashing blades, pounding feet and the snarls and barks of the wolves.

From there, the true test begins.

I know where all of my packmates are. I can track Phylax and Kryptos movements as they ebb and flow to rise up against Daemos attacks. I know who is injured, who is starting to overexert themselves. I sense spikes of intent as wolves reposition within our defensive line.

Daemos probes against the eastern defenses, and all the knowledge I need comes to me instantly. "*Seven attackers,*" I project over the bond. "*They're going to rush us, pure force.*"

Through the bond, I sense Tomison calculating the structural weakness in their assault pattern. "*One Daemos wolf is lagging, the farthest south in the line. Their attack will be weak there.*"

"Phylax wolves, rotate your line!" Izabel calls, sensing that the front of the line is already weakening under the Daemos attack.

Instinct snaps through me. I see it happening before anyone else does.

Years of fights in the pit have taught me that though the movements of a person's body are important, you also always have to pay attention to where their eyes are. People look where they're going to strike, even if their muscles are pulling in a different direction.

One of the Daemos riders on the eastern front stares up towards the north even as his contingent of wolves launches their attack. A feint.

"*It's a distraction,*" I project through the bond. "*Their main force is gathering for a strike from the north.*"

My insight moves through the pack like electricity leaping across iron nodes. Attention turns to the north.

Where Jonah is leading another contingent of Daemos wolves.

Unease tears through me as our gazes connect. He grins, and this time it does reach his eyes—the look in them so bone-chillingly malicious that my breath catches in my throat.

Then his direwolf lunges for the Phylax pair in front of him, and I recognize who it is.

Henrey.

"*Rid ourselves of any unsuitable common blood.*"

All this time I was worried about what Jonah would do to me, and I missed it. He couldn't have been more clear. He couldn't get to me, so he'd take out the one other commoner Rawbond. And he's attacking to kill.

"No!" The shout bursts forth from me but can't be heard over the clashing fights escalating around the arena.

Jonah's huge black direwolf claws Henrey's light brown wolf across the face. The tawny wolf yelps in pain and pulls back, but Jonah's not done. He instructs his wolf to attack again, and this time, his wolf takes a huge bite from the other wolf's front leg, tearing flesh. Most of the wolf's leg is suddenly a gaping wound.

Henrey's direwolf falls forward, unable to stand on the leg any longer, and a blood-curdling howl reverberates over the arena. Even in the chaos and noise of the battle, it's clear as day.

The sound cuts through my pack's strategic focus like an ax cracking wood in two. My awareness of the battlefield fractures, disorientation taking me for the first time since the battle began. The Phylax on either side of Henrey are wavering now, too, their riders' attention split between the attacking Daemos and their compromised packmate.

There's a low chorus of responding howls as the direwolves realize what's happening to Henrey's pair. Pain. Confusion. Anger.

Through Nevah's mind, I watch as Henrey's wolf turns its massive head towards his rider, eyes wild with pain and fury. The defensive line begins to buckle immediately.

"*Northern defense compromised,*" Anassa's cold voice hisses. "*Adjust formation—*"

Before she can finish the command, Henrey's wolf lunges for his own rider's throat.

CHAPTER FORTY-NINE

Regaining control feels impossible. The many minds connected to mine react with instinctive horror, and a torrent of thoughts carries me away like a white-water rapid river.

The northern defensive line shatters the moment Henrey's wolf attacks him, the frontline giving way to Daemos pressure. Glimpses of the Phylax's second line of defense surging forward reach me over pack unity, but I can't make out the details perfectly any longer.

"*What's happening?*" I ask Anassa in horror. Henrey's wolf shouldn't be hurting him, not at this very last point of training.

"*Sometimes, extreme pain can sever the rider-direwolf bond,*" she replies.

"*But why isn't Henrey's wolf healing himself?*"

She lets out a mournful growl. "*The bite severed an artery. It was a fatal hit. No wolf can heal something that severe; even our magic has its bounds.*"

Too many of us are focused on the blood. Henrey is on the ground, his wolf's massive jaws clamped around his right arm and chest. He's being shaken like a rag doll.

Blood splatters across the disturbed earth in a gory arc. Too much of it. The perfect cohesion of a Bonded pair turning in on itself, tearing itself apart.

But I have to fight through it. I must, for my sake. For *all* of our sakes. Even for Henrey.

Refocusing on the raging stream of consciousness in my mind, I scrape the ruins back together, pulling the shattered halves of our pack back into cohesion. Anassa helps. Her growling, authoritative influence streaks across everyone's minds.

It's a tactical nightmare. My packmates scramble to salvage our strategy, calculating casualty projections, analyzing how this disastrous breach in our defense will affect the entire defensive structure.

Something slots into place in my mind. A *need* unlike any I've ever felt before, backed up by the emotions of countless packmates.

To close the wound. To reinforce our ranks. To *protect* my pack.

The Daemos forces surge toward the gap Henrey and his packmates were meant to defend. The other Phylax meet them as best they can, wolves butting heads and blades clashing. My pack are successfully processing Kryptos information still, which warns me that the reinforcement in the north is starting to leave the east more vulnerable.

But we have no choice. The moment Henrey went down, Daemos gained too much ground.

The urgency of strategic command burns in my veins, but beneath it all is an icy unease. It creeps over me, acute enough to chill the electric connection of the pack bond. All because of a simple truth.

Henrey is going to die today.

Around the arena, the direwolves are becoming agitated. Howls echo off the stone walls. Frontline clashes become rougher, drawing blood and tearing fur. And I can't... look away from him.

He's still alive, still struggling with his wolf, but going pale, losing too much blood. His face is set in a horrifying grimace, his free arm pushing at his wolf's muzzle as if he might free himself. But his right arm is far beyond the point of recovery.

This was Henrey's dream. His lifelong hope was to make it here, to this arena, to partake in these Trials and become Bonded. He made it to the very last task.

And now his dream is tearing him apart.

Some of the Phylax riders around Henrey are backing up. One desperately attempts to remain mounted while his wolf snaps and nearly entirely rolls to tear at the Daemos wolf in front of it. The heightened emotion and savagery are fueling the Daemos wolves as much as they're compromising the rest of us, as if the combined scent of blood and their own fear is strengthening them.

There's still undue strain on the Strategos pack bond, but we're starting to find clarity again. Through it, I know that the eastern side is sparsely defended now. And I know that the north is about to buckle and give way.

If we don't act immediately, the Trial will end in complete failure.

Through the chaos of fur and fear, Henrey's eyes find mine, the look freezing me in place—pure agony, mixed with desperate pleading.

His lips form a single word, clear even across the field. *Please.*

My heart tears in two, even as Anassa's strategic mind delivers heavy, impossible truths to me.

First: our defensive line cannot be salvaged while Henrey's wolf rampages.

Second: his wolf *cannot* be stopped without killing it, which would also kill Henrey.

And third: a quick death now would be mercy, compared to being torn apart slowly.

Someone has to break formation to do this. Someone has to sacrifice their position in the strategic array to end this.

I make my decision quickly. I'm the Alpha; if anyone should make tough calls and risk themselves, it's me. Anassa is fast, and she is merciless. And I'm...

I'm his friend.

"*Hold strategic formation,*" I project through the unity bond. "*I'm breaking ranks.*"

My pack's collective acknowledgment shivers through me.

They're already recalculating for my absence—who will compensate for the gap my eyes and mind leave behind? I leave it in their hands.

Anassa and I turn to streak across the field, ducking under blades and dodging teeth, and several Kryptos wolves move with me, keeping eyes on me to communicate my movements. My pack-mates flow into the gap I left behind and reshape themselves around my actions.

Anassa moves with deadly purpose, carrying us straight toward Henrey. One of the Kryptos wolves yelps as a Daemos maw surges through the Phylax barrier to snap at it. Anassa doesn't stop.

"Can we approach from the front?" I ask Anassa.

"It wouldn't be safe. The wolf's instincts are unpredictable."

We approach from behind them instead and Anassa skids to a stop, teeth bared, suppressing her growl so that she doesn't alert Henrey's wolf to our presence.

Up close, the scene is even more horrific. Henrey's wolf has him completely pinned, one massive paw on his chest, claws dug into his flesh and slowly pulling him apart. His wolf's teeth are partially sunk into his throat, and occasional pulses of thick blood are spurting from open wounds.

There is conflict in the wolf's eyes, in the trembling of its massive body, in the way its tail is tucked so far between its back legs. It's just holding Henrey there, as if fighting against its own savage instincts.

The Phylax frontline surges closer to us. I can make out flashes of Daemos wolves as the line weakens. A few paws stampede closer as our defenses threaten to dissolve. I don't have time.

I slip from Anassa's back and creep closer, animal instinct raging in me as I willingly put myself within Henrey's direwolf's range. I draw my sword slowly, approaching as Anassa suggested.

Through our bond, Anassa tells me what I already know. *"This will mark you."*

Her words echo strangely in my mind, branding deeper into my soul with each reverberation of sound.

It's another impossible truth. Because it isn't self-defense, or an enemy. I'll be killing a friend. I can't deny any of it. I can't escape it. I *must* do this, even if it will irrevocably change me.

As I inch closer, careful not to alert the wolf towering in front me, Henrey's eyes meet mine again. He's pale as the winter sky, his eyes starting to glaze over.

Blood bubbles from his lips as he speaks. "Do it," he chokes out.

I don't hesitate. The instant I'm close enough, I surge forward beneath the wolf's powerful front legs and slide on my knees. Trusting my body as I always have, I twist my torso and lash my arm out in a blow as fast and deadly as a snake's strike. The wolf doesn't have time to react.

My blade slides home, sinking between Henrey's ribs.

His body goes slack instantly, the lingering light vanishing from his eyes. The wolf above me releases him with a soul-shaking, mournful howl. The sound is like the sundering of a soul, all the grief and pain in the world gathered up into one long, haunting note.

Then the wolf thunders to the ground, collapsing beside me, jaw slack and eyes staring forward lifelessly. Their broken bond dragged it to death alongside Henrey.

I can't stay with him. I pull myself to my feet and flee to Anassa's side, my sword dripping with Henrey's blood. She turns her head, dipping it low to drape herself over my shoulder briefly. Her warmth pulls me back to myself, and my mind snaps back to the battle.

Jonah. Where is that fucker? I'm going to gut him for what he did.

Anassa senses my intention. "*No,*" she says. "*You are above retribution. You're an Alpha and your pack needs you. Return to them. Lead them.*"

I hate it, but she's right. Jonah cannot be my focus right now.

I deftly climb Anassa's side, sliding back into place. Around us, the Trial continues. Daemos forces still attack. Phylax are rebuilding their defensive line. Kryptos dart deftly through the violence to gather intelligence.

My packmates welcome me back into formation seamlessly,

sensing my return and pivoting their wolves and their minds to reassert our initial strategy. A hint of relief finds me even through the pain and the noise. Despite what just happened, our unity is unbroken.

The remaining hours of the Trial pass in a blur of violent moves and countermoves. I throw myself into pack unity with a furious intensity, surrendering myself entirely. Through it all, our shared consciousness transforms the battlefield chaos into perfect order, each pack responding to Strategos' guidance with lethal precision.

If I'm focused on the front lines, I don't have time to look down and see the blood still clinging to my skin.

When the final horn sounds, our victory over Daemos is almost… anticlimactic.

My ears ring. I'm breathing hard, still hearing the clash of blades as Aldrich mounts the dais. His gaze sweeps over us. Anassa's sides heave beneath me. She holds her head high even with her pale fur sullied by dirt and blood.

"The Unity Trials are complete," Aldrich announces loudly through his amplifier.

Wolves shift all around us. My packmates' minds still linger alongside mine, sparks of electric awareness lighting up my consciousness. Nevah is staring at Henrey's body.

"Strategos has demonstrated exceptional strategic coordination, even in crisis. Phylax maintained their defensive integrity despite significant loss. Daemos provided a worthy challenge. And Kryptos proved their intelligence network remains unmatched," Aldrich continues.

He doesn't say anything about Henrey's death. Then, he wouldn't, would he? Wolves die. Riders die. We move on.

"No packs broke their mental unity throughout the entire Trial. Congratulations, Rawbonds. Those who survived will officially become Bonded at tomorrow's graduation ceremony."

Those who survived.

Even with those words hanging above us, the air lightens. Aldrich's announcement sends a ripple of excitement through the Rawbonds all around me. Tomorrow, we join the ranks of all their family members. We made it through. We survived and now we're going to become official members of our packs.

I can't feel the same excitement right now, though, not with the blood on my hands.

Servants weave between the wolves, gathering Henrey's ruined body on a stretcher to carry him away.

I lean forward on Anassa's back, jolted from the heavy emotion dragging me down by an odd sight. The servants aren't taking Henrey's body toward the castle gates, towards the room where fallen Rawbonds' bodies are prepared to be returned to their families. Instead, they're heading towards a strange door on the far side of the arena.

I stare as the other Rawbonds around me start to dismount and give into their exhaustion. "*Anassa*," I probe, wanting to know if she finds this odd, too.

She doesn't respond, but she's staring in the same direction. I slip from her back, stroking my hand over her fur briefly before stepping forward to try to see better. The servants swing a heavy, iron-studded door open. Beyond it, there's a dimly flickering torch. I briefly catch a glimpse of stairs that lead down. *Beneath* the arena?

Like where that crown might be buried.

But *why?*

CHAPTER FIFTY

T he celebration in the Rawbond common lounge tonight is truly unhinged. Today, we survived. Tomorrow, we graduate. I understand it, rationally—and I don't blame them for celebrating. We're alive. That's *worth* celebrating.

But not everyone can say the same, and I swear there's still blood trapped beneath my fingernails.

Every peel of laughter is intrusive. Every smile, out of place.

I'm restless, my mind continually returning to Henrey, so I do the only thing I can. I keep moving forward. Surveying the reveling, drunken crowd, I pick out Venna. She's leaned up against another Kryptos Rawbond—soon to be *Bonded*—nursing a glass of ember-wine and watching the people around her with a subtle smile.

I quickly make my way over to her. Venna's eyes immediately widen, and she shrugs off the Rawbond attached to her. "Can we talk?" I ask, and then sign the same thing over a loud drunken cheer.

Venna nods and hooks her arm with mine. A chorus of whistles go up around us. I roll my eyes. Clearly, they're misreading the situation. But I don't correct them because it's honestly better that they believe Venna and I are hooking up.

I bring her to the Strategos anteroom. No one's in here right now; no one would dare miss the party outside. "Did you see what happened at the Unity Trial?" I ask immediately.

Her gaze flashes, and I know she understands what I mean. "What the fuck is under the arena?" she hisses.

I feel sweet relief. "*Thank you*," I breathe. "We need to find out what's down there."

Venna swells with what can only be pride. "You want me to—?"

"Please," I beg, taking her shoulders in my hands. "Find out where they took Henrey's body. But also..." I hesitate, not sure if I should mention it, and then decide I can trust Venna with anything. "I think there's something buried inside of the drain in the center of the arena."

"Okay..." she says. "Ominous. Can you be more specific?"

Can I? Will she believe me? "I think... I think it might be a crown. I'm not sure what it's doing there. I know it sounds crazy. But there's definitely something metal hidden away inside the drain."

Venna doesn't blink, doesn't ask how I know that. She just says, "I'm on it. I'll head out now to look around. And I'll let you know if I find anything."

I raise a brow. "You're sure your pack won't miss the Kryptos Killer?" I tease.

She frowns at me. "Not you, too."

I laugh and pat her arm before she turns to flee my teasing. The moment she's gone, the air around me is heavier again.

No part of me wants to join in tonight's revelry, so I turn and head for my quarters. When I reach it, I shrug off my jacket and move to retrieve Stark's book. My constant companion.

Thinking about the book reminds me of Anassa, and I realize I can still feel her through our connection. I throw the wall back up, reinforce it. We may have needed to work together today, but I refuse to forgive her fully, not until she starts being honest with me.

Then I kneel on the floor and reach for the book under my bed. I've stared at it so much that I swear its words are imprinted on my eyelids. But maybe I missed something in here that could give me answers about the arena. There's a segment about the castle's history, so—

There's a soft creak, and I startle, whipping my hand away from the bed and jumping to my feet. When I spin around, Killian is stepping out of my wardrobe. Instantly, I breathe a sigh of relief.

"You scared the shit out of me."

Killian smiles, but it doesn't reach his eyes. "I came to check on you," he tells me. "Are you okay after everything that happened today?"

I have to fight the urge to pick at my fingernails again in an attempt to get the lingering blood out. *Am* I okay?

I step forward and practically fall into his arms. A lump forms in my throat as he catches me, his embrace strong and steady. I'm just so fucking relieved that *someone* isn't too busy celebrating life to acknowledge the iron stench of death still thick in the air.

I want to taste his concern for me on my tongue, swallow it down, and let it warm me like sweetened emberwine.

Lifting my head, I look into his achingly blue eyes. His hands rub gently over my back as he watches me back. "You…" My voice trails off.

I want to ask him about where the servants took Henrey, but accusing his father of something without proof feels too dangerous. There's only so much Killian can protect me from.

"Me," Killian says softly. He lifts his hand and dusts his knuckles across my cheek. His thumb tugs my bottom lip, and it's like he casts a spell on me.

I push onto my toes and kiss him. Hard. I pull away to suck in a shaky breath, and for the second kiss, he meets me with an open mouth. I wrap my arms around his neck and pull him down against me, practically devouring him.

At first, he's hesitant. Worried about me, maybe. He kisses me deeply, but he keeps trying to slow it down. I like the taste of all this care, but I need a little pain if I want it to sink beneath my skin and linger like a tattoo.

The hesitation stops abruptly when I let out a needy whine.

"Fuck, the sounds you make," he groans. Then he hauls me

against his body and spins us around, pushing me against the wall and grinding into me.

I gasp and grip his shoulder. The other hand tangles in his hair. He kisses me roughly this time. It's bruising.

"Kitten," he pants. "You—"

"More," I beg. "All of it." I yank his shirt up his body and fumble with his belt. He pulls my leg up over his hip and sinks his hips closer to my warmth. I manage to get his belt unfastened, but then he bends down and starts kissing my neck. I shut my eyes and lean into the sensation.

I hope he can feel the quickness of my pulse beneath his lips.

"Leave a mark," I whisper. And instantly, his teeth dig into my skin. Not too hard, but hard enough that I know it'll last. I moan and start to yank his belt out of its loops.

And the door slams open.

"Meryn, have you seen Venn—AGH!" Izabel shrieks and covers her eyes.

Killian and I scramble to fix our clothes. My entire body is one giant blush.

"Izabel, *knock*!" I shout.

Killian tries to stifle his laughter, even hides it behind his hand, but he can't quite manage it. I scowl and smack him.

"It's not funny," I protest, but that last word breaks apart into a slight giggle. And it makes him laugh harder.

"Sorry," Izabel squeaks, peeking out from between her fingers. "Are your tits tucked away?"

I scoff. "Your eyes are safe."

Izabel lowers her hand and curtsies. "Your princeliness."

Killian laughs again. His hands are shoved in his pockets, likely to help conceal the lingering frenzy I worked him into.

"I didn't mean to ogle your royal abs. It just happened," Izabel announces.

I smack a hand over my face. "Goddess, Iz."

She grins and marches across the room, offering her hand. "Nice to meet you finally. Well, we've met. Sort of. I see you places. Up on your pedestals. I'm Izabel."

I'm briefly concerned Killian might be upset. After all, Izabel did just barge in while we were in the middle of something, and now she's blowing through possible boundaries and assuming he wants to chat with a half-hard cock.

But he removes a hand from his pockets and accepts hers. "Nice to meet you, too. I know you and Meryn are close."

"I'd hold her hair while she barfed," Izabel says like it's a brag. I don't have the heart to tell her that I really don't want my betrothed thinking about me vomiting. "Wow, you're better-looking up close. I always thought you looked a bit… statuesque? But something about catching you with your pants down makes you more approachable."

"They weren't *down*," I scold.

"Practically at my ankles," Killian says with an easy smile. I relax slightly. He's clearly managing this better than I am. Of course he is.

I take a deep breath to steady myself. "To answer your question, I think Venna is hooking up with someone. He had dark hair and bushy eyebrows. Might be best to give her some space," I tell Izabel. It's the description of the man she was cozied up to earlier, so hopefully it'll lend credit to my lie.

Izabel frowns. "Makes sense." But apparently, she's completely oblivious to my subtle *give me some space* request because she turns to Killian and grins.

"Prince Killian, have you ever played Ten Wolves?"

"Huh? No, never heard of it," he replies.

"It's a Bonded drinking game, and they have a good round of it going in the common lounge right now. You should come join us!"

It's then that I realize she's a bit toasted. She's always been good at hiding it—never slurs or starts to tilt over—but she's definitely been partaking tonight.

Killian raises a brow and glances at me. It's a very clear, *is this okay?*

I look at Izabel, a giant ball of sunshiny hope, and just shrug. It's a little weird. Killian in the common lounge, and with everyone drinking…

But then, if he's going to be my husband, the other Bonded will need to get comfortable with him, anyway.

Izabel makes an alarmingly high-pitched sound of joy—the squeals are the real indication of her drunkenness—and drags us both back to the party. Her attention is mostly focused on Killian, though. I'm starting to suspect that she's very intentionally pulling him into the fold, giving my future husband a place alongside the pack.

It makes me love her a little more, despite how badly I currently wish I were alone with him.

There are some whistles and hollers as Killian steps up to the table. The Rawbonds are excited to see their prince. I pause to watch them as Izabel settles him at the table. He sends a playful *"help me"* look back my way, and I just grin back at him, certain he's going to immediately charm everyone.

Before I can join them, a familiar looming presence prickles up my spine. I tense as his glare sizzles over my skin; I don't have to see it to know it's happening.

"I have nothing to say to you," I tell Stark without even turning.

"When's the wedding happening, then? You know you ship out to the front right after the graduation ceremony," he says.

I cross my arms and scratch at my elbow. It helps me focus on something other than how his energy is taking up the whole room and swallowing up the air. Then I force myself to turn and look at him because I don't want him to think I'm a coward.

Alphas face their problems head-on.

"We haven't started planning it yet, and it's actually none of your business."

He's wearing his typical glower. His tattoos look darker in the dim light. So does his hair. "Actually, the crown is very much my business, since my family are their sworn protectors," he tells me.

Fuck. That's a bleak realization. He's probably going to become Sovereign Alpha during Killian's reign. He's basically destined for the role.

Which means I'm going to have to deal with him *constantly*.

I'm never going to live a life without mean stares and dramatic looming.

I realize his words have been left lingering too long when his gaze wanders. It finds my neck, and his brow pinches. *He's looking at the mark Killian left*, I think to myself, and I hold my head higher. I'm not ashamed.

But then he says with undeserved harshness, "You need your tattoo for tonight."

"I don't want you fucking touching me," I snap instantly.

His lip curls. "*Good*. Agreed," he growls. We stare at each other for a long moment, and unrealized energy gathers in my muscles. I'm really thinking about punching him.

Then he turns and says, "Gamma Elinor."

A few Rawbonds look over drunkenly, disturbed by Stark's authoritative voice. But they go back to their business quickly. I drag my eyes from Stark to Elinor, who sweeps her long black hair from her shoulder as she walks over. "Hello, Alpha."

I bow my head respectfully, relieved.

"She needs her tattoo," Stark grunts out.

"Ah," Elinor says with a nod. "Sit, then."

"How many of these have you done?" I ask as I move to sit in the closest chair.

"Too many, in my years," she sighs as she produces the ink and needle. To her credit, she says nothing about the love bite on my neck.

Her years. Elinor has a youthfulness to her, but she's still somewhere in her middle years. Her olive skin is mostly smooth, save from a few very slight hints of aging. I wonder what she's seen at the front in the decades she's been in service. If having been here for the last four months has been a good reprieve for her, or if she misses the action of battle.

My quiet hope that Stark would fuck off flickers out when he continues to intrusively loom over us.

The needle digs into my skin. I force my body to remain relaxed, unwilling to let him see my pain right now. Elinor's needle moves steadily, drawing a horizontal line through the three points of the existing design, bridging the remaining gap.

Collar's complete, I think.

"Finished," Elinor says. She straightens and leans in to drag her tongue over my skin. It's the epitome of unsexy, like getting licked by a lizard. The thought nearly makes me giggle, though my next thought sobers me up.

I guess I can't keep pretending that it's the act alone that heats my blood when Stark does it.

As Elinor stands to go, I refuse to think any more about Stark's stupid tongue. I stand as well, and glare at him. Then I turn on my heel and stalk back to Killian.

When he sees me, his face immediately drops, and he gets up from the table.

"Hey!" someone protests.

"Round's not over yet."

"We're in the middle of a game, man!" Izabel says.

Killian summons a polite smile for them. "I'll be surrendering, I think. If things keep going this way, I'll be out the entirety of the crown's coffers."

There's a chorus of laughter, and Killian turns to me and takes my elbow gently.

"You look upset." His eyes dart over my shoulder. I know Stark's still there, staring at me. I can feel his malice. Killian's eyes darken.

"He's just an enormous asshole," I grumble.

Killian's thumb strokes over my skin. "Let's go, then."

I nod, relieved. "Please. Thanks."

He guides me from the busy room and through the pleasantly quiet Strategos anteroom. Then he pushes my door open and ushers me inside, shutting it with a tap and twisting the lock.

I turn to look at him. He leans against the door, hands back in his pockets, hair slightly messier than usual. His eyes glint in the low light.

"Why did you kiss me like that earlier?" he asks immediately.

I'm briefly disoriented by the sudden question. "Wasn't... it obvious?"

He knows it's not really an answer. His gaze is prying me open. He steps closer slowly, then reaches up. His fingertip strokes over my fresh tattoo, and I wince from the sting of it. Unexpected pleasure follows the hurt, though, and I shiver.

"You didn't answer me before, so I'll ask again." He wraps his hand gently around my throat, covering up my tattoo. "Are you okay?"

Anxiety pulses through me alongside my already-raised heart rate. I can't tell him everything. I'm too confused. Too overwhelmed to sort out which steps are safe and which are pitfalls. But I can tell him part of the truth.

"There's so much in my head. It's... *loud*. I want to scream, but when I open my mouth, no sound will come out. I'm stuck. Something is stuck."

Killian's gaze changes. He tilts his head down, drenching his eyes in shadow, a storm cloud gathering above the ocean blue. His hand remains on my throat as he steps closer. He's suddenly entirely in my space.

"I know what you need," he says. His voice has sunk lower. His fingers rub once, twice over my tattoo, and I wince, but a thousand aching thoughts flood my mind.

"Tell me," I say. The words come out in a rush of air.

"Sit," he orders.

I back away from him slowly, never taking my eyes from his. The backs of my knees meet the edge of my bed, and I sit. He steps closer. His belt buckle clings. I watch, flushed, as he slips his belt slowly from his hips. When it's free, he wraps it around one of his fists.

"Against the headboard."

I ease backward onto the bed until my back knocks against the headboard. He follows me, moving to rest one knee on the bed and leaning over me. I don't move as he reaches for me. I let him take one of my hands and lift it above my head, then the other. He moves slowly, maybe waiting for me to protest.

But I won't. I want this. I want to let everything go.

The leather of the belt slides over my skin. My nipples harden beneath my clothes, and goosebumps shiver over me as he fastens it. Tight. Tighter. So tight that my engagement bracelet digs painfully into my skin, and I grunt.

"Scared, kitten?" he asks.

I shake my head.

"Good." He backs away, and I let out a whine of protest. But he doesn't leave me entirely. He smiles knowingly as he starts to unlace my boots. Everything he does, he does slowly. "You're being quiet."

I realize that he's right. I haven't managed a single word since this started. And maybe I want it that way. Maybe I want him to coax and coerce.

"We'll see how long that lasts," he adds. And he's suddenly above me, warm and heavy. And his mouth is on mine. I sigh and strain against the belt, wishing I could sink my fingers into his soft hair.

Wishing I could pull him closer and pursue that brutal connection between us again.

But Killian is the one in charge right now. "I have this image. In my head," he starts to tell me. His voice is like silk. He speaks close to me so that I can feel every word on my skin as he unbuttons my shirt. "You and I are both in it."

He pushes my shirt open, and my skin prickles from the cold and the sudden sensation of being vulnerably bare. Only for a moment, though, before his warm hands are streaking fire over my ribs. He cups my breasts and squeezes, pressing his thumbs over my nipples. I jolt.

My legs spread instinctively. His eyes are icy fire.

"In this image, I'm sitting on the throne, halfway to making a better world. And you are there with me, perched on my lap."

He pulls my pants down my body, tossing them aside. Then his fingers play at the edges of my underthings, which are already soaked in anticipation.

"There's a crown sparkling in your hair," he tells me, and I nod. "Your pretty silver hair…"

His fingers press into me through the damp fabric, and an unintentional moan escapes me. I quickly stifle it, but his eyes flick to mine and his breath quickens.

"Things change in my imagination. Sometimes you're on your own throne. Sometimes your hair is long, spilling everywhere. Sometimes it's up, exposing this pretty neck of yours." His fingers dance over my tattoo, and I strain against the belt to chase his touch. "But one thing is the same. Every time."

What? I want to scream. My hips push up against his hand.

He grants me a brief rush of pleasure before his fingers curl beneath my underthings and pull, stripping me entirely naked save for my shirt where it's trapped at my shoulders.

"Every single time," he tells me as he pushes my legs farther open. "You're naked."

I moan. Just those two words sent me into a spiral of lust. He sees it and sates it. Killian leans over me and slides a finger through my folds. He sinks deep into me, his long fingers reaching deeper than mine ever could.

Then his thumb, pressing my clit. And I moan again, tears welling in my eyes. Already, my body is swelling with need. The sound of his fingers is so fucking filthy.

"Just like this. Naked and spread on my throne as I touch you. And your moans echo through the throne room," he says right in my ear. "You are my queen, Meryn," he pants. "All mine."

The short time it takes him to rip his shirt from his shoulders has me writhing, trying to pull him in with my legs, doing everything I can not to beg for his fingers back.

He falls over me, pressing his chest to mine. I'm breathless from the slide of his heated skin on mine. I arch against him, pressing my breasts to his chest so that I can feel the tiny spikes of pleasure it causes me.

"Let's hear that voice now," he says, still stroking me towards my climax.

I shake my head and bite at my lip.

"Still being a stubborn little kitten, then," he says. His taunting chuckle makes me wild. He kisses me, and it earns another groan. I'm fully riding his hand now. "You want me?"

I nod. My chest heaves, my insides tightening and tightening. It's good. It's so *fucking* good.

And then it stops. Killian leans away from me and removes his hand entirely. I was about to come, and the sensation slips away and sinks back into my muscles, unsatisfied.

"*Killian*," I beg.

"She speaks," he says with a laugh. Then I watch as he lifts his hand, the one that was inside me, and sucks his fingers into his mouth. Watching it, my climax flutters back to the surface. Shivers pass back and forth over my entire body. And it gets even more torturously perfect.

He leans back on the mattress and frees himself from his pants. My mouth waters as he strokes slowly over his cock, his eyes raking over my body, pausing at my breasts before settling between my legs where I'm still parted and soaked for him.

I clench around nothing and whimper.

"I want to hear you ask for it, Meryn," he tells me. His voice is husky.

I yank my hands. I don't know whether I want my hands to break free so that I can grab him or if I want them to remain trapped. All I know is that I like this delicious push and pull. He's drawing me out. Drawing out the parts of me that I usually keep in the dark.

"Please," I manage. I pull my thighs closer to my body, opening myself up, testing his will.

But he just smiles. "Please what?"

"Killian, *please*."

"Say it, Meryn."

A strangled growl rips from me, and then I break. "*Please, fuck me*," I say. It's a whine. A needy keen. And I don't fucking care. I'm not afraid to throw this desperate part of me into his hands.

"You're mine," he says, drawing closer.

"I'm yours," I repeat submissively. "Yours."

"My queen."

"Your queen," I whimper, nodding.

Killian slams into me to the hilt. I cry out at the sudden feeling of being split apart. Emotion pours from my chest, broken loose from the force of it. Tears streak down my face as his hands close punishingly hard around my thighs and his hips start to slam his cock deep, again and again.

I'm barely strong enough to push back now, but I try. Deep need has me struggling to match his pace, pushing myself forward to receive everything he's giving me.

I grip the belt and lift myself off of the mattress, using my legs to meet his thrusts. Killian growls and bends over me, biting the same spot on my neck as the wild, borderline violent thrashing of his hips drives me against the headboard.

I can't think. All I can focus on is sensation and the release that's hitting me like a drug, way before my climax is even here. My head bumps against the wood behind me. My wrists are screaming in blissful pain. My legs are spread so wide that my muscles are straining and protesting.

And the sight of Killian's body moving over me, muscles rippling and sweat beading on his chest, is the sexiest thing I've ever seen.

That hungry, dominating look in his eyes is mine for the rest of fucking time.

It goes on until my entire body throbs with the rough rhythm of it. Moans are pouring from my throat. He continues to pound into me until the whole world starts to churn and ripple around me, like our bodies are sending reverberations into the air.

I try to warn him that I'm about to tip over the edge, but words won't come.

This is momentary, total obliteration at his hands.

He's right there when I need him, his mouth claiming mine in a dizzying kiss and his fingers pressing down on my clit firmly. I'm helpless against it. Everything tightens.

He groans as I come around him. His fingers don't stop, though, stroking me until it's too much.

And I scream. I scream *loudly*, the sound high and so laden with pleasure and release that I can't believe it came from my own throat.

I'm so lost to it that I struggle to pay attention to Killian's climax. I want to watch it because he's always so beautiful when he unravels. But all I can really focus on is the pulsing throb of his cock and the various little pains around my body that make me feel *had* in an indescribably perfect way.

He groans above me, hips falling still. He doesn't withdraw, though, choosing to remain close as I twitch with little aftershocks. We stay like that for a while, my wrists still bound, his head on my shoulder, our chests heaving.

Eventually, though, he lifts himself up on powerful arms and meets my eyes. "Got the scream out," he says.

I laugh and realize that he's right. I'm so unburdened. So relieved. And maybe it's just the heady post-sex feelings talking, but I don't care right now. He was *right*. It's what I needed.

He grunts as he withdraws from me. "Let me fix this, kitten."

If I were actually an alleycat, I would've started purring right then and there. Because he reaches up and gently unfastens the belt, brings my red and swollen wrists to his mouth, and trails kisses over the agitated skin.

"Thanks," I breathe.

His answer is to take my engagement bracelet between his teeth and bite, his eyes darting up to mine. I grin and turn my hand to pull him in. He lets me, and he lets me kiss him, too, soft and slow.

He leaves my side only to fetch something to clean our bodies, then we lay down together to rest. My head is clear. I feel stronger than I have in days. I curl against his side and sleep, glad that I have someone who understands me the way he does.

I wake late in the night to a gentle knock on my door. I lift my head, instantly alert. Killian sleeps right through the sound, his bare body shining in the moonlight from my window.

I let myself hesitate only long enough to gently stroke my fingers through his hair. Then I leap to my feet and slip quietly into my clothes. I ease the door open slowly, peering around it.

Venna is there, her face worried. Before she speaks, I lift a finger to my lips to silence her and glance behind me meaningfully. I step outside and tap the door shut quietly.

"What is it?" I whisper.

"I found something," she tells me. "You need to come with me. Now."

CHAPTER FIFTY-ONE

I follow Venna without question, without hesitation. The urgency in her eyes is contagious. As we move quickly through the castle halls, nervous energy riots through me. "Venna, where—"

She makes a short hissing sound and presses her pointer finger to her lips to silence me. I nod to tell her I've understood, then do my best to quiet my footsteps. It's difficult, with the echoing hallways and vaulted stone ceilings. Venna moves almost entirely silently— like Kryptos are taught to do—only occasionally causing slight creaks as she pushes a door open or a brief rustle as her clothes shift.

Realizing that we're doing something dangerous, I partially lower the barrier to me and Anassa again. If something goes wrong tonight… she needs to know.

I try to predict the route we're taking through the castle, but it's impossible. We move in random directions, turning right three times before doubling back in the other direction. After a while, I realize what this is. Her urgency. The need for silence. The indecipherable route.

These are the movements of a prey animal, deliberately

complex to evade capture. She's worried we might be followed. Seen. There's danger here.

My suspicions are confirmed when the open hallways of the lower castle turn to servant passageways. I have to duck low under the door frames. The entrances and exits are much too small for the average Bonded's height. My trembling nerves heighten further when we take a sudden left and slip into an even narrower tunnel.

These aren't even servant passageways any longer. They look like they're from another age entirely.

Spiderwebs cling to corners. The walls are exposed stone, unadorned and with a patina that speaks of centuries of no upkeep. There's nothing down here but more tunnels, each just as dark and punishingly narrow as the last. It's suffocating.

I start to sweat despite the rapidly cooling temperature.

Venna pauses at a fork and touches my arm briefly. Her eyes meet mine to ensure I'm watching, then she flickers her hands. I stare, trying to recall the signs I've managed to learn, but her meaning evades me. I huff in frustration and she presses her finger to her lips again.

I nod. I need to be quiet.

Venna's lips turn upward, and she points at me, then two fingers at both her eyes, then at herself. Watch her. I nod, and she takes my wrist, pulling me along into the dark.

I watch her closely, as instructed. Soon, I realize that her movements are intentional. It's her Kryptos training, I suspect, guiding her through the shadows like she was born of them.

Her feet test each step cautiously before she rests her weight. She walks on her toes, mostly, carefully sidestepping anything that could create even the slightest sound. When the ground beneath us starts to show its age further, smooth stone turning to uneven, cracked rock, she follows a very specific path like she can somehow anticipate which rocks are loose.

A few times, she touches my wrist and gestures. Two fingers from each hand, positioned in V, with wrists touching. *Careful*, that means.

I do my best to pay attention to her instructions, but my mind wanders. Maybe it's the instincts Strategos training has taught me, but I can't stop wanting to ask questions. What's buried down here? Who or what is it that demands utter silence of us, for fear of discovery?

We descend past multiple levels of the castle this way, but the claustrophobic feeling never lets up. At one point, we hurry down a narrow hallway with windows cut from the stone. On the other side, I swear I catch a glimpse of the dungeon I saw with Killian when we tortured the Nabber. We're deep, then. But we *keep* descending, creeping down stairs and hurrying down long, anxiety-inducing slopes of earth, or more loose rock.

Eventually, the walls change again. Everything changes.

The air turns freezing and heavy, the cold stinging my lungs and the lack of airflow starving me of oxygen. There's an odd metallic taste on my tongue, growing stronger with every breath. The walls weep moisture through cracks caused by the immense weight of the earth bearing down on these passages.

My breath turns to vapor in front of my eyes, and goosebumps start to shiver over my skin.

All of this is unnerving, but it's Anassa's emotions that truly start to scare me. She's uneasy. If I didn't know her better, I'd think she was afraid.

The thought of Anassa afraid is like imagining a mountain trembling. It just isn't right.

And it's that sense of wrongness that lingers like a thick fog in these tunnels. There's something wrong about the air here—not just the cold and the dark, but a tangible weight that presses in on me from every direction.

I try to convince myself that it's just the claustrophobia of being so far underground, but logic doesn't work. Anassa's projected unease fuels mine, and I'm horribly on edge.

The descent is endless. Venna leads us through a labyrinth. That's the only word for it, like someone's carved a maze to deliberately confuse anyone trying to reach deeper. Venna takes three rights in a row, and my struggling logical mind tells me that should bring us back to the starting point. But instead, we end up even deeper, new twisting passageways revealing themselves.

We pass multiple doors and adjoining tunnels, which Venna ignores. I touch her arm and point to one of the doors, raising a brow. She shakes her head. Then she points down one of the adjoining tunnels and lifts one hand, guiding the other to her palm and stopping abruptly when her fingertips touch skin.

I have to assume she means it's a dead end. It confirms my theory. This is a true maze with twists *meant* to disorient anyone who might accidentally find these passages.

Eventually, once I'm practically crawling out of my skin, we reach what looks like the bottom. At the end of the tunnel, there's a single door with a faint light emanating from behind it. When Venna leads me to it, I can't help it, I gasp. A slight breeze stirs my hair in front of my eyes.

There's airflow on the other side.

She turns to me. "There are guards," she says, so quietly it's almost inaudible. "They're on rotation right now, but we only have a few minutes."

I nod to confirm that I understand, and Venna pushes the door open, revealing a narrow corridor.

The sight disarms me. It's nothing like the rest of the tunnels we've traveled through. For one thing, it's clean and well-kept, lit with steadily burning oil lamps.

But it's also carved from smooth, white marble veined with *gold*. The air is fresh, hinting at some sort of ventilation system. There's a lingering heat here, too, emanating from the stone to stave off the cold of the depths.

Venna and I walk quietly down the long hallway, towards another interior door. More light shines from beyond.

Then, the sound of children's voices.

It stops me short. I freeze up, heart pounding. Venna looks back at me, wearing an expression of understanding. She nods, once. And I know.

Nothing could stop me in that moment. I rush forward, pushing the door open and stepping through.

It's just as bright and warm as the tunnel we just walked through, carved of the same blinding marble. Oil lamps hang from the ceiling, casting warm and steady light. I blink in confusion. For all its elegance, I know what this is.

A prison.

Along both sides of the long room stretch mirrored rows of cells. They're small alcoves in the marble, each containing proper furnishings: real beds with clean linens, shelves filled with books, even small desks. The luxuries might trick the eye into seeing an innocuous, restful space.

If you can overlook the gilded bars holding in children.

Dozens of kids linger behind the bars, all wearing identical gray clothing. They look *haunted*, hollowed out and gaunt, like they've been wasting away down here. I can tell that they've been fed, but they're definitely not healthy. There's a pallor to their sun-starved skin.

Each cell seems carefully controlled, with four to five children each. The kids grouped together look roughly the same age, too, with the youngest no older than five and the oldest maybe ten to twelve.

My eyes immediately snap to the cells towards the end, where the older kids are. I'm not mindful of my thudding footsteps as I rush forward, desperate, shaking.

And then I see her. Part of me can't believe it's real.

Saela.

For a single moment, my lingering fear tells me that this might be another hallucination. It's almost preferable to the thought that Saela might have been trapped down here, right below my feet, the *entire* time I was fighting to reach her.

Then I realize what she's doing. Saela's curled up around a book.

Her dark hair is longer than I remember, falling past her shoulders, and her body is slightly thinner, but she's still Saela. Always with her nose between the pages. The sight of it would have even been comforting, if it weren't *here*, in this awful place.

The familiarity of it all snaps me out of my fears right as Saela seems to sense that she's being watched. She looks up from her book, eyes finding me.

For several long seconds, all we can do is stare. Time stretches thin, the weeks and weeks of fear and pain and hope strangling the breath from my lungs. I cover my mouth with one hand, distantly aware that burning tears are falling.

Then the book drops from her hands with a loud smack. Her eyes flood with tears.

"Meryn?" she squeaks, voice cracking like heartbreak.

It snaps me into motion. I gasp raggedly for air and sprint toward her. The children around me gasp and rush to the bars to watch. Saela scrambles to her feet, sobbing, reaching shakily for the bars.

I slam into them, shoving my arms through because I need to *feel* her. She lets out a small, keening cry as I pull her as close as I can.

"Sae," I choke out, cradling her head. She's warm beneath my hands, unlike in my nightmares.

"M-Meryn," she whimpers. Her hands cling to my jacket like she's afraid I'm going to disappear, her knuckles whiting. "Y-Your hair!"

I choke out a wet laugh and nod. "*Your* hair."

She sobs and clings to me. The desperate, searching nature of her touch wounds me. I can't let her go. I won't.

"I've got you," I breathe, stroking her hair. She leans close, crowding the bars to reach me. "I've got you, Saela. You're okay."

Her breaths slow somewhat, but she won't let go of me. I wish I could tear these fucking bars down. Rip them right out of the floor and hold her properly, pull her all the way into my arms and make her feel safe again.

Dry her tears. Read to her. Tuck her in to sleep.

I shake my head and bend to kiss her hair, tearing my eyes from her briefly. The other children in her cell and those gathered at the other cell doors are watching with something hungry in their eyes.

Aching jealousy, I realize. Loneliness.

I don't know how long they've been down here, but no one's been caring for them the way a child needs care. No one's been here to love them. They must have gone to sleep each night longing for their homes, their families, for the sun.

A deep sadness settles over my heart like glinting frost blanketing the earth.

Anassa's, I realize. I can sense my wolf's gaze moving over these lost children. Seeing these children disturbs Anassa deeply, like the ache of long-lost memory, but the feeling remains immaterial and vague.

Saela pulls back in my arms, just enough to look up at me with teary hazel eyes. "It's not what you think, Meryn. It's so much worse than anyone knows," she whispers. Her eyes dart around like she's afraid there are eyes on her. Her grip on me tightens.

I reach up to sweep her hair from her eyes. "Right now, I only care that you're alright," I breathe.

Saela shakes her head. "Listen. Please."

Jerkily, I nod.

Her voice drops further, like she's hissing secrets, as the other children drift tentatively closer to listen to us. "The Nabbers were just like people said. They came through the window. I tried to fight but there were two of them. A-And—"

"You did well, Sae," I reassure her shakily.

Her smile trembles, then it falls. "They didn't take me away from the city. The buildings got taller instead of smaller. They took me *here*. They gave us to the king's guard. I recognized their armor."

My mouth drops open. I know we're under the castle, I know this explanation makes sense, but a desperate part of me still hoped that there could be some sort of explanation that didn't mean I'd have to fucking *kill* a king for what he's done to my sister.

Wrath flares through me, glowing like a weapon in the forge.

"Did they hurt you?" I growl. To my surprise, Anassa's growl follows mine.

Saela shakes her head. "They tied my hands, but I'm okay."

"You are," I nod. "You're stronger than anyone I know."

Her fingers tangle with mine. "I was brought here quickly. I've been counting the days i-in one of the books. It's been four months here. I think. It's hard to tell, without the sun, but the guards come in a pattern."

Four *months*. She's been here the entire time. The *entire* time.

"The guards aren't cruel. They bring regular meals, clean clothing, books to read. But they don't speak to us directly, never answer questions. They act like we're not here. Or like we're…"

Like they're animals to be tended to and ignored. "I'm so sorry," I whisper, tears threatening to fall again. "I've been looking for you from the start. From the start, Sae."

She smiles. "I've known that. From the start," she whispers back to me. I exhale shakily and nod, leaning forward to kiss her forehead.

"It's why I kept track. To tell you everything, so that you can fight back," she says, a hint of pride in her eyes. "I knew you'd find us here."

"Fight who? The guards?"

Her expression darkens. Fear flashes in her eyes. Fear I wish I could take into my hands and crush for her, like grinding bones to dust. But all I can do is hold her and promise her everything I am, everything I've become.

"Not the guards. The king," she whispers, voice breaking.

That motherfucker. I'm going to end him, and I'm going to enjoy every second of it.

Anassa growls with approval in my mind; she wants to taste his blood.

Saela must see a flash of the promised violence in my gaze because her eyes widen.

"It's okay," I say, wiping her cheek with my thumb. "You know I'll take on anyone. Even a king."

"H-He comes every few weeks. He walks between the cells, studying us. He has the guard take down notes. Then he'll… *choose* one of us. Sometimes two."

"For what?" I ask shakily.

She shakes her head, eyes welling. "We never see them again, but sometimes I think I can hear them screaming somewhere far away. And I've b-been passed over *six* times. I've been here the long-est. He's going to choose me next. I know he is. Meryn!"

She lets out a horrible, pained sob, shaking her head. But when there's a sound from above—maybe a door opening or a piece of furniture moving—her voice silences instantly. She sucks in a breath, muffling her tears and wiping her cheeks.

The children grow quiet, huddling back against the walls. Fear spills sickly into the air, bitter and cold.

Saela grips my hands urgently. "He's going to choose again soon. I can feel it. Please don't let him take me," she whimpers.

I won't. I *won't*. Strategies race through my head. How to break her out of here. How to dismantle the bars. How to avoid the guards. How to get her out of the castle.

But every turn my plans take, I meet impossible odds. We're hundreds of feet below ground. How long do I realistically have before her absence is noticed? And could I really leave *all* these other kids behind?

I don't… I'm not…

A hand touches my shoulder, and I flinch.

But it's Venna, eyes flashing with warning. "We're almost out of time," she says, then backs away to give me this moment with my sister.

I turn to Saela, cradling her sweet face in my hands. The horrible truth spreads like poison in my veins, weakening me, rotting my heart. I can't break her out now.

There are too many kids, too many guards throughout the castle, and too high a risk of everyone getting caught.

But leaving Saela here, knowing she might be taken? Might be hurt? It's that night all over again, taking my eyes off of her for a second and losing her in the space of a single breath.

It's the smart move. The strategic move. But it hurts. So I do what I always do. I turn the pain into strength.

"I'll come back, Saela," I tell her firmly.

Her face crumples. "Meryn," she begs.

"I *will* get you out of here," I insist.

"I'm scared," she whispers.

I crush her to me so that I can hide my tears from her. I need her to know I'll be strong for her. "You trusted me until now, right? Can you keep that going just a little longer?"

She pulls me close but nods silently in my arms.

"I'll return with help, okay?" I suck in a breath and compose myself, pulling away to look down into her eyes. "We're Mother's daughters, right? We're strong. Always."

She clenches her jaw tightly and nods, curling her hands into fists. "Yeah."

"Keep your head down, alright? Don't do anything to draw the king's attention."

"Okay."

Venna taps my shoulder gently again and glances towards the door. I nod to her and then look back at Saela. "I love you," I tell her, backing away. "With everything, Sae."

Her hands fall from mine, but she nods, putting on a brave face. "I love you, too. And I'll… I'll see you soon."

When I turn away from her, I plunge into a blizzard of pain and rage. The door shutting between us is excruciating. I clutch my chest, half-expecting to feel a torrent of steaming hot blood pouring down my front.

Venna touches my wrist gently, tears in her eyes, but I can't find the space to thank her.

I can't free Saela on my own. Not as I am.

Thankfully, I know someone who can. Someone with real authority. Someone who can officially order these dungeons opened, and the children released.

Someone who *loves* me, who would do anything to help Saela. Who always has.

Over our bond, Anassa's mind spikes with an immediate, sharp warning, like a needle jabbing into my brain. "*You cannot get anyone else involved,*" she urges, voice strained.

I push her back, straining against her panicky strength and throwing up the wall between us again, reinforcing it. She's kept *so much* from me. From the moment we bonded, she's never told me the truth.

She hid her voice from me, shoved me away, concealed her mate's identity. She knows more about that book than she will tell me, and she knows how my visions are connected, but she's decided to hide the truth instead of helping me.

I've never been able to shake the acute feeling that she possesses every answer I could ever need but refuses to give me the knowledge. Why, when she forced this bond on me to begin with? I really don't know.

But I'm done pretending I trust her.

There's someone else that I *do* trust, who has always prioritized me. Who looks out for me. Who understands my pain and tends to my wounds. Who tells me everything he knows. Killian was horrified by the Nabbers. He brought one of them to me and helped me torture the man for information. He's voiced his suspicion of his father and his desire to change the kingdom so many times.

I've *seen* the spark in his eyes when he talks about the future, about the world he dreams of building. Together.

He'll be even more furious to learn of his father's actions than I am. Betrayed by his own blood.

Killian will help. He always has and always will.

As I follow Venna back through the passages, I rub my thumb over my bracelet and make a silent vow. The king will pay for this.

CHAPTER FIFTY-TWO

By the time I reach the empty Rawbond common lounge and part with Venna, it's become a powerful need. How many times have I gone to him, wounded and in pain, only for him to take me into his hands and smooth it all away?

Help, my bloodied heart screams. I need his help. I need something to make sense again.

I find him still curled up in my bed, sleeping peacefully. I lock the door to my room behind me, then race to him urgently, shaking him awake.

Killian's dark blue eyes blink open blearily. "Meryn?"

I was right. Just looking at him makes me feel more in control. "I..."

"Are you alright?" he asks, snapping awake and sitting up. "You—"

"I found her," I blurt.

The moment the words are out, my eyes well again. I huff in frustration and angrily wipe my face. "Sh-She's right *here*. Below the castle. The entire time, and I never knew. I was right here, and she was so afraid, Killian. It was my job to keep her safe. To make sure she felt *safe*, and I failed."

He reaches out, taking both of my hands in his. His skin is warm. His grip is firm. He's quiet, but he pulls me closer. "You found her," Killian repeats. "Saela?"

I nod, chin trembling. Killian moves deeper into the bed so that I can sit next to him. Once I'm there, he rests a reassuring hand on my thigh, smoothing his touch back and forth. It slowly starts to calm me. "Take a breath, Meryn."

"I don't have *time*. I need—"

"Look at me," he says. I drag my tear-filled gaze up to his. "That's better," he says, nodding. I breathe out shakily, reaching up with slightly trembling hands to hold his face. "Talk to me. I'll listen."

I take a deep breath. "There's a prison beneath the castle. I went down through some tunnels. It was a maze, but at the end of it, I found her. And dozens of other kids, mostly young. They're all behind bars, Killian. And Saela was there."

Killian's brow tightens, his skin paling. There's a razor-sharp grief in his eyes, like this revelation is taking something precious from him. "Is she alright?"

I shake my head. "They're being kept for something. Taken every few weeks for goddess-knows-what. I think they're dying. They could take her any moment."

Killian sinks back against the walls. He shakes his head, hand covering his mouth. Then he looks up at me. His voice is hoarse. "Who takes them? Did you see them?"

"Your..." I don't want to do this. I don't want to hurt him. But there's no other way. "Your father," I breathe.

His eyes widen and he presses his lips into a thin, pale line.

"Saela said he's the one who picks the children. Takes them away. This is because of him. All of it is him," I say.

Killian looks hollowed out, like I've just extinguished his soul in a single breath. I think this might've been the same look I wore on my face, having to leave Saela. It's loss. Killian and the king have long been at odds, but surely even he wouldn't think his parent capable of such a thing.

"My father?"

"I'm sorry," I whisper.

"My father?" he repeats, blinking slowly. "He... My *father* did this?"

Like the crack of a whip, the horror turns to anger. Tension ripples through his muscles.

"*No,*" he growls, throwing back the covers of the bed. "He *won't.* I won't let him," he mutters, shaking his head. "*Shit,* Mer. I should have *seen* this. There were signs that he was up to something horrible."

I reach out, stroking a hand up his arm. "We know now. We can do something now."

"I was suspicious, but this is entirely different..." He breathes out shakily. "*Children,*" he says, pained.

"I know," I say. Then I take a breath, steeling my resolve. "Killian, look... I made a promise to Saela. And I'm keeping that promise. No matter what I have to do. No matter whose blood I have to shed."

His eyes widen slightly, then they narrow. He grabs my shoulders, pulling me roughly to him, and tucks my head under his chin. "I know."

"He's your father."

"It's *Saela,*" he says. "*He* did this. Now he'll have to face it."

"I'll tear his throat out," I snarl.

Killian pulls back and his eyes are slightly wild. He reaches up and cups my cheek with trembling fingers. It isn't fear. It's rage. "He betrayed the kingdom first. He betrayed *me.* He took your family, Meryn. Whatever it takes, we *will* stop him, free the children, and end this nightmare. I swear it to you."

I breathe out shakily, nodding. When he holds me like this, I feel stronger. The challenge before me is like another Ascent—a cold journey bathed in blood, all the way up to the throne.

"Tomorrow, at the graduation ceremony," he says, leaving no room for questions. "It can't wait."

"It can't," I agree. "But how?"

"All the Rawbonds go to the king to receive his blessing as they become Bonded," he tells me. "That will be your opportunity. You'll have to strike then, and you can't falter or you'll fail."

"Believe me," I say, my voice dangerous. "I won't miss. How much control do you have of the castle guard?"

"I can access information, change orders," he says. "Good thinking, I'll work on the prison security and figure out how to get in and get the kids."

Hope beats erratic in my chest. After everything I've been through to try to get Saela, it's too much to believe that we might actually be there. Still, I ask, "Do you think this will work?"

The resolve in Killian's gaze sets me on fire. "It will work. Tomorrow, you'll get your sister back. Tomorrow, we'll make my father pay. Tomorrow, the throne is ours."

THE ARENA IS DEAFENING the next afternoon, the stands packed once again with nobles and Bonded alike. The nobles look bored—with the bloodshed of the Unity Trials behind us, today's graduation ceremony must seem dull for them. But I suppose it would've been impolite for them to skip it, after relishing our gore so many times.

All of us Rawbonds are in our training uniforms for the last time, complete with ceremonial swords. The afternoon sun casts long shadows across the arena. The air is cool, but sweat trickles down my spine and beads on my upper lip. Anxiety coils around my insides, twisting my mind.

It starts to make the shadows look strange.

I blink rapidly and wipe sweat from my eyes, averting my gaze. My eyes are drawn right to him, though. King Cyril. He sits above us all, resplendent in his royal purple and gold, that infamous wolf-pommel blade resting across his lap.

Even from here, I can see his fingers stroking over the handle repetitively as he stares down at us, eyes dragging over our wolves and bodies like a violating touch.

I know him for what he is now. Beneath that glittering mask of nobility, there's a hideous fucking monster. Whatever he's doing to those kids—whatever he's *already* done—it's going to end. Today.

And I'm going to be the one to do it.

My eyes jump to Killian, and some of the anxiety churning in me settles. He shines brighter than his father does, standing tall at his right hand and holding his head high. He's dressed in royal blues to his father's purples. His hair is perfectly arranged, his hands braced behind him. His eyes glint a brighter blue than usual in the piercing sunlight.

My future husband. My true king.

I think he senses me looking at him, because a moment later, our eyes meet from across the noisy arena. And ever so slightly, he inclines his head. An echo of a nod.

He's ready. So am I.

Leader Aldrich is seated on the king's other side. He'll be the master of ceremonies today. In the row behind them are all the instructors. Even from here, I can see that Stark is wound as tightly as usual.

Clenching my jaw, I look away. He's not going to distract me from my purpose right now.

A horn blasts, and all the direwolves enter the arena, padding over to their riders. Anassa bares her fangs at me when she approaches. I've kept the mental wall intact and her message is clear —she's *pissed* at me.

Sighing, I lift it now. I'll need her cooperation for this. Quickly, I let my plan flow to her: when I get close to the king for my blessing, I'm going to strike.

I expect her to rebuke me, to tell me the plan is too dangerous or that I haven't thought things through, or to chide me for getting Killian involved.

Instead, she merely growls, "*Make it quick.*"

A surprised laugh escapes me, and then she lowers her neck. I lace my fingers in her dense silver-white fur and haul myself onto her back like the other riders.

Once all the Rawbonds are mounted, Leader Aldrich rises and lifts a voice amplifier.

"Today is the formal end of the Bonding Trials. It marks the culmination of the incredible hard work that you all have exhibited over the past four months. Nearly a thousand soldiers attempted the Ascent. Ninety-eight direwolves chose ninety-eight riders. And today, seventy-six Rawbonds officially take their place in their packs as Bonded."

The other Rawbonds around me are lifting their heads in pride. We, the chosen few, have made it.

Twenty-two riders did not. Three of them died at my hands. All of this bloodshed that I've participated in—all because of *him*.

King Cyril stands, pulling the amplifier from Leader Aldrich's hands. Aldrich seems flustered by the move, but hands the amplifier over and steps back.

"Yes, thank you, Leader Aldrich, and thank you, Rawbonds!" His eerie light blue gaze darts over all of us, and a strange little smile spreads across his face. "This graduation ceremony is part of centuries of tradition. And as tradition, you will all come before me and receive my blessing to go forth and fight in my military as our most elite warriors. However, even the best traditions need updating sometimes…"

A bolt of panic shoots through me, hot and urgent. What does that mean? I glance around quickly and everyone else looks just as confused as I do.

"The Unity Trial showed impressive coordination, but I was disappointed by your performance. More Rawbonds should have been culled. Some Trials, you know, we only have fifty survivors!" He lets out a cheery laugh at this.

My stomach turns over in unease and my gaze catches on Stark standing behind the king. His brow is furrowed in concern. Great, so the instructors don't know where this is going, either.

"Because I am a just and fair king, I have decided to give you one additional chance to rid yourselves of unnecessary baggage or unworthy pack members. And I don't want anyone to hold back! So before we proceed to the blessing, we will have a final free-for-all battle."

No.

Does he know what I had planned? Did he somehow find out? Killian stands and catches my eyes, his own widened with fear.

King Cyril slams the wolf pommel sword into the platform at his feet. "Begin."

And chaos breaks loose.

CHAPTER FIFTY-THREE

The instant it begins, I visualize my pack's connection exploding from my body. A flood of a powerful river. A crackle of branching lightning, my energy at its epicenter. I expand my consciousness in a violent burst through our pack unity, touching each of my packmates' minds simultaneously.

The initial impact of their joint experiences briefly overwhelms me, but Anassa protects me. I feel every heartbeat, every surge of adrenaline, every flash of fear and anger—all of it in the space of a handful of seconds. And then I master it.

What concerns me most is the powerful urge thrumming through each and every one of them.

Kill.

Whatever the king unleashed with that sword, it's as deadly as an arrow at their throats. They're compelled to attack each other, to betray our bond and tear each other apart.

But *I* am their Alpha. And I won't let the bastard on that throne take anything or anyone else from me.

With the king's order, the arena immediately turned into a gruesome battle. All the direwolves are attacking each other. I can see

Tomison and Kristof's wolves snapping at each other as if their riders were enemies instead of close friends.

"*FUCK the king!*" I bellow through the pack unity.

Their minds snap collectively, tracking my fury through the chaos. Anassa snarls and sprints around the edge of the arena, outpacing the wolves trying to pursue us. Jonah is chasing me; I suppose the king's orders sounded like approval to do whatever the fuck he wants.

I circle wide, sword in hand, consciousness reaching for my pack's pain and power. I can sense that the king's hold on them snapped the moment I gave them my rage.

"*Follow,*" I tell them. "*Together.*" And I sense their understanding. *This* is how it should be. All of us as one, unified. Bonded.

My plan to get to the king might have been upended... but I'm going to use my packmates' protection to get to him all the same.

That fucker dies today.

The melee explodes. A massive Daemos wolf lunges straight for Nevah's throat. Multiple minds analyze the trajectory.

I send rapid commands over unity. "*Izabel, cut left. Tomison, drive them toward the west wall.*"

My packmates' wolves move without hesitation, their massive bodies whipping forth to follow my orders. Anassa and I descend into the fray strategically, my mind glowing from the rush of information.

Izabel's wolf leaps high over the heads of two Kryptos wolves, landing closer to Nevah, who still struggles desperately against the massive black Daemos wolf. Then Tomison's direwolf charges from the opposite direction, carving a pass with his massive bulk. The Daemos wolf pulls back, suddenly trapped between the Strategos pairs.

Shit, it looks too coordinated. The king might notice a pattern in my pack's movements. We can't appear unified, or he'll notice—and then who knows what will happen?

"*Make it look coincidental next time,*" I instruct everyone. "*Don't let him see that we're working together.*"

I rely heavily on Anassa as the battle rages on. She fights well as

I organize the defense of my pack. She helps guide my hand, using her massive size to carve a path through the field so that smaller Strategos wolves can use it to reposition without opposition.

Driven by the king's command, two Kryptos wolves use their startling speed and maneuverability to cut through the melee, ducking under massive Phylax wolves and darting around Daemos fangs.

I don't see them myself. I feel their approach in a cascading shiver of minds and know that they aren't angling for me but Tomison and Pietr, who are flanking me, their wolves pretending to snap at Anassa's heels.

We were heading to the northern side to help Izabel. It doesn't matter. I have to shake the Kryptos pair now. Izabel can hold out if Tomison goes her way. I issue a flurry of orders.

"*Tomison—*"

His awareness burns fiery through my mind. He's already sprinting towards her. I grin wickedly and turn my attention elsewhere.

"*Pietr, drop back. Allegra, guard his retreat. Roddert, circle wide and take them—they'll expect you to go tight.*"

My pack fights well, viciously but tightly controlled. We defend our own with a fury, but we spare the other packs as best we can. The king might be okay with more bloodshed today, but we refuse.

I reach Izabel and Tomison just in time. Anassa rears up to block a smaller wolf's lunge, giving Tomison's wolf enough time to drag a blood-crazed Daemos attacker off of his rider.

Danger prickles over the back of my neck, sent by Izabel. My blade moves before my mind does. I swing, the metal clanging against a blow that was meant for Izabel. Even still, my mind races through three other orders—two pairs across the arena on the southern side, another north east.

I'm making progress. My pack has mostly been repositioned towards the arena's stands, inching closer with every maneuver. I weave protective patterns as the fight rages on, fending off attacks, protecting the other packs' lives…

Drawing closer to my goal.

A Phylax wolf manages to sink teeth into Allegra. Pain echoes through the bond, bitter with fear. The taste of blood fills my mouth. I bit the inside of my cheek, an instinctive reaction to one of mine being harmed.

I swallow and use the pain, pushing my focus even farther.

"Hold formation. Darius, take point. Roddert, flank left. They're too focused on Allegra. Use that."

Orders executed, Allegra and her direwolf retreat behind the cover we've created, limping badly but alive. Roddert's wolf is covered in blood, but it's not hers. I discount it and let my mind jump forward.

We've formed a protective arc around the king's platform—almost as though we're *defending* him. To an onlooker, it may look as though we've been backed against a wall. We even snap at each other, as though the king's command still grips us. It's impossible to fully hide that we aren't turning on each other as the other packs are, but it hardly matters at this point.

We look vulnerable, as though we're fleeing from the fight. Not at all a threat, which is what I need him to believe.

The pack needs to be able to protect each other once I act. If I have to leave them, I need to know that they'll be in a strong enough position to fight off three other packs. To fight off assholes like Jonah, who gave up on getting to me and is currently trying to thin out the Kryptos ranks.

Once I've positioned each pair exactly where they need to be, I unleash my emotions. A pulse of anger and protectiveness and faith floods from me. A few of them briefly turn to look at me before refocusing on the battle, on the act.

"Whatever happens next," I project to all of them, *"hold this formation. Keep our pack alive."*

Their minds erupt. Instantly, their emotion floods back to me. It's blinding. Overwhelming. They trust my leadership, even without understanding my plan. I've kept them safe, and now they'll fight until their last to defend the unity between us.

My eyes sting with tears that I don't have time to shed.

Anassa's muscles bunch beneath me as she lowers herself. She asks only once. *"Are you certain?"*

I respond with rage. It washes through Anassa, through my pack. She lets out a terrifying howl, the furious, threatening sound of it carrying my fury clear across the arena. An instant later, other Strategos wolves join in, our voices singing wrath in total unity.

I sink my hand into Anassa's fur. *"For Saela. For all of them."*

Anassa turns, her massive claws scraping as she gains momentum. I lean down, securing my grip on her fur and bracing my body. She snarls, and we're in the air. The jump is impossible. It would be for anyone but her.

Powerful muscles propel us upward. We slice through the air, a streak of silver death like the cut of a blade. Anassa lands with a menacing thud on the king's platform, looming over his throne.

Guards scramble towards us down the steps, but they're too slow.

I've already slid from Anassa's back, blade ready.

King Cyril Valtiere rises to his feet, but there's no fear in his expression. I see only mild surprise. Then, worse, *amusement*, like he still thinks this is all a game when I'm already anticipating the way his blood is going to spill.

He opens his mouth to speak, but I have no patience for his insidious lies. I lift my leg and kick, aiming my blow precisely. My boot impacts his wrist with bone-cracking strength, and he shouts, dropping the glittering wolf-pommel sword from his grip.

The sword clatters to the stone at his feet. I know I only have seconds, but an instinct takes my body over.

I lunge for the sword, something thrumming in my blood ordering me to take it up in place of my own. I need it in my hand. I need to watch his blood spill over the bite of its sharp edge, leaking scarlet over silver.

The instant I take it up, *power*.

Ancient, overwhelming magic sears my veins. It swallows up my entire body, vibrating through my legs and arms, nearly making me lose my grip. My heart screams in my chest. It's like I'm breathing in lightning, like the barest nudge could lead it to rip through my pores and sear the entire arena.

The sword is alive in my grip, humming with energy that reaches for me. The metal warms in my palm as though it's fusing to my skin, responding to me, clamoring for my attention.

Above me, Anassa whips forward, biting a guard's head clean from his shoulders. When I look up at the king slowly, his amusement falters. His left foot shifts backward, only slightly.

His hand raises—perhaps to signal guards, perhaps to attempt to defend himself—but I'm already moving. I hadn't realized the arena had gone silent until my voice carries in powerful echoes across the space.

"This is for Saela," I snarl.

The blade is an extension of my arm, a deadly part of me. My own silver claws. It whizzes through the air, faster than I've ever seen a weapon move. The world goes still as its edge connects with his neck. I see it. That first split of his skin. It burns into my eyes painfully.

Blood splashes across my arm. An arterial spurt catches me in the face.

His life splatters over my chest, sinking into my clothes, and across the stone. Across the throne. Across the blade.

The king's light blue eyes go still as his head gives way to its own weight. It slips from his neck and tumbles down the platform steps as his limp body collapses to the ground at my feet.

There's a sick urge to destroy what's left. To savage his corpse until *no one* would ever be able to recognize him. But I swallow it down and lower the blade, blood dripping from its tip.

The guards have frozen. The arena is silent. My pack pulses with unease.

I turn to Killian, and his face is ashen.

There is no relief. No triumph at his father's downfall. He looks at me in abject horror, his eyes moving over the blood spilled across my chest, to the sword, to his father's corpse.

"Meryn, what have you done?" he shudders out, stepping away

from me with wide eyes, hands shaking. Then, anger. His expression contorts into fury. "Guards! Seize her! She's killed the king!"

"What?!" I shriek.

A flood of guards storms the platform. Those already here spring back into action. The arena trembles with sound as the crowd reacts to the scene. I try to retreat to Anassa's side. She tries to leap for me, eyes wild. But before she can get close enough to defend me, a hiss of a weapon tears through the air and impacts her side.

"Anassa!" I scream as I watch her fall. I whip back around, and for a single instant, I see something. I *swear* I see it. He covers it up quickly, but…

Killian's lips turn upward. It's a tiny satisfied twitch, his eyes glinting blue, his gaze calculating.

Then the pain. Something slams into the back of my skull, snuffing out my light.

CHAPTER FIFTY-FOUR

There is nothing but shadow. I feel it all around me, flowing through me, drawn into my lungs and seeping from my eyes. I float, not truly seeing anything yet *sensing* movement in the dark. Slow and heavy, like the rolling of a thick fog over frozen land.

Then, from all around me, a voice I know. A voice I've heard before during the maddening seizures of my mind as I slipped towards my mother's madness. It comes from nowhere and everywhere, from beyond and from within. It sounds like a whisper and a scream, hissing over my skin and vibrating through my bones.

"GET THE CROWN."

I gasp awake, teeth chattering. The air is cold. I'm lying on freezing stone. Harsh beams of light cut like needles through the darkness all around me. There's a smell of smoke in the air. As my vision focuses, I realize that there's a recently extinguished torch glowing, a slow curl of smoke drifting upward.

The slow realization creeps over my skin as I stare at it. The rough stone wall. The darkness. The smell of dirt and mold. The silence.

My head pounds as I return to myself through the fog, a particularly sharp throbbing centered in the back of my skull where I was hit. As I turn my stiff neck, it's clear.

I'm in the castle's dungeons.

At first glance, the cell is discouragingly secure, with solid stone walls and thick iron bars separating me from freedom.

I swallow around the lump in my throat, tasting copper on my dry tongue. Slowly, I sit up, keeping my eyes shut to block out the swimming of my vision. I shiver, clutching myself, clenching my teeth.

Then a subtle warmth settles my swirling mind. Anassa. I turn, wincing when my head injury announces itself once again. The moment my eyes land on her, an instinctive calm settles over me. The bond settles as my eyes move over her massive, lithe form. She breathes steadily, sitting up and alert, staring at me.

I scan her for injuries, but she seems alright. She must have healed herself after that blow. Her fur is slightly dirty, but I expect that's from the battle. Except... in the lingering light of the torches' cinders and those sparse beams of light, I can make out a band of darkness around her neck.

Wincing again, I crawl closer. When I'm beside her, I can make it out better.

A collar. A ring of blood-red metal encircles her throat. My vision flickers when I stare at it too long, the air around it appearing to pulse and shiver with energy. My headache escalates to a stabbing pain as I study it, so I rip my gaze away, looking up into her eyes.

She says nothing, watching me closely. But when I crawl up to her side and sink my hands into her fur, she lowers her head and sniffs my hair. Her nose nudges the side of my skull, my injuries. Heat spreads across my scalp as she heals them.

I bite back tears and sink into her warmth, leaning against her massive side as she breathes in a comfortingly slow rhythm. I press my forehead against her fur, shutting my eyes.

The pain in my head has eased, but I can't say the same for my heart.

Every time I start to think about Killian's face when he betrayed me, remember that cruel look in his eye, the sheer horror of it...

No, I can't even think about it, or I'll be sick.

"How long have I been out?" I whisper, trying to focus on here and now.

"*Too long,*" she replies. She rests her head on her legs, curling her tail close. "*The metal prevents me from communicating with Strategos. But it would seem our connection remains intact.*"

I breathe out in relief, scrubbing the back of my hand over my face. It's strange, after spending so much time resenting the bond, but the thought of no longer being able to hear and feel Anassa sounds like a… grievous violation. Being broken away from my pack, as Alpha, is terrible, but I know in my marrow that without Anassa, it would be worse.

Losing her would be like having my soul cleaved in two.

"*Why are you relieved? I said I cannot reach our pack,*" she says coldly.

I pat her side and lift my head, not bothering to work through or explain my little epiphany. I reach up weakly to touch the cold iron bars of our cell. It wasn't long ago that I was desperately clinging to Saela through bars just like these.

What happened to her, after everything?

Is she still down there? Still trapped, just like I am?

I failed her again. And this time, I might die for what I've done.

The sounds of boots echoing on stone echo from down the hall, and I tense up. Anassa's hackles rise over the bond before I even see who's coming, but it's enough warning. The cell door creaks open.

Killian enters alone. I can see dark figures in the shadows, though, lurking behind him. He wouldn't step into a cell with a murderer without protection, I suppose.

Killian is dressed formally, in the same rich blues and shining embroidery. Except now, the wolf-pommel sword rests glinting at his hip, his hand wrapped around the hilt. And something seems… slightly *off* about him. Maybe it's the dim dungeon light, but I swear…

He steps forward. As he does, his face passes through one of the sparse beams of light from above. For a single instant, when the light hit his eyes, they looked ghostly, like the bright blue of winter ice. But as they slip back into the shadows, they look normal again.

Almost. *Are* they different?

I don't know. I don't know anything. What I saw. What I did. What *Killian* did.

He shouldn't be standing here like this, looking concerned and caring. He threw me in here. He—

"Meryn," he says softly, and his voice is so gentle. It has me questioning everything all over again. The man standing in front of me can't possibly be the same one who stared at me in horror in front of an arena of people.

The one who smiled at me with such cold cruelty in his eyes.

He approaches me with cautious steps. "I need you to tell me the truth, kitten."

"O... kay."

"Why would you have done such a thing?" he asks, brows twisting in pain. His gaze is searching, flitting over my face for answers.

Answers he should already have.

Frigid shock locks my muscles up. "What are you talking about, Killian? We had a *plan!*"

Killian's face pinches with anguish, and he hushes me. Then, he reaches out slowly to cup my cheek, thumb stroking gently. His touch is warm and familiar. Despite my confusion, it calms my thudding heart.

"I'm worried about you," he whispers, his voice turning slightly raspy with emotion. "I'm... so sorry, Meryn, but I'm truly frightened for you."

"Wh-Why?" I choke out. "You can *help* me," I say. It sounds like I'm begging, but I have no choice.

I've killed the king, and I need help. I need my *betrothed* back, the man I love. I need his support, his understanding. My eyes start to burn.

"No, it..." He winces. "It's your mind, Mer."

My breath catches in my lungs. I start to shake my head, but he catches my chin and guides my gaze to his.

"I did my best to ignore the signs. I wanted to believe you were alright. The thought of losing you..." His eyes well slightly. "I saw your mother at her worst. I didn't want to look into your eyes and no longer see the woman I love looking back. But it was wrong. It was wrong of me to deny what was happening out of fear. I should have helped you."

"Killian, I'm not—"

"This has all been too much for you, the Trials. You lost your *mother*, Meryn. And you didn't have your sister to grieve with. You've torn yourself apart, looking for her. The stress you've been under." He looks like a man standing over an open grave. "It pushed you over the edge. Something broke. I can see it even now, in your eyes."

He thinks I'm mad.

He's looking at me with the same pain, the same pity, the same grief that I saw in the mirror every time Mother went through an episode.

The only thing keeping me tethered to my body is Anassa. Her disgust at Killian's words pulses through the bond. "*Do not listen,*" she growls. And again. "*Do. Not. Listen.*"

"Killian, I'm not making this up," I insist, gripping his wrist tightly. "We decided to do this together. We planned it in my room. We talked for hours."

He shakes his head. "Meryn—"

"What are you saying?!" I shout, my desperate voice ringing through the cell.

He flinches at the sound of it, glancing back at the guards warily.

There it is again. That embarrassment.

I know that feeling. I felt awful about it, but sometimes I looked at Mother and felt shame.

"I'm saying, Meryn, that we never had this conversation that you've imagined." He kisses me softly on my forehead, and my raw revulsion and fury at the brush of his lips turns my stomach. I can't tell if it's coming from Anassa or my desperate need to cling to sanity.

"I'm sorry. I had to detain you here. There are people calling for your head, and imprisoning you was the only way to keep you alive until I can… find a way. For your safety. For the safety of others. You killed the king, after all," he tells me.

My mouth drops open. My chest feels like it's being crushed, like the whole massive weight of the castle and all its people above us is pressing into me.

"I know it's hard to believe, standing in this place," he says, forced levity lifting his voice up. His smile is weak. "But I still love you. I'd love you through anything. I know what you did in the arena wasn't you, and I can't…" He shudders through a breath. "I can't give up on you. I'll take care of you, if you're willing to try to get through this with me."

Anassa screams in my mind. Her voice rips and tears. "*LIAR!*"

Killian leans in. His lips meet mine. Warm. Soft. Awful. I don't want to be kissed. Why would he think I wanted to…?

I push him off weakly, my hand pressed to his chest.

The movement cracks his expression. A tiny sliver of something ancient and cold flashes across his face—a glint of his eyes, a tightening of his jaw—before disappearing again behind concern and affection.

He straightens, radiating gentle love. "Sorry," he says quietly. "I'll send someone soon to check on you and bring you something to eat. And I'll visit again soon. I promise. Call the guards if you need me."

As I watch in silence, the cell door clangs shut behind him and his guards retreat.

I saw him this time. *Really* saw him. I know I did. I can still conjure the jagged edge of his mask when it broke in two.

It's pressed up against my throat, threatening to slice open my jugular.

I start to tremble, the betrayal and confusion and shame and pain all catching up to me. "I am not insane," I whisper aloud because I need the words to be true.

Affirmation ripples over the bond. Anassa's tail brushes my shins. It's the first genuine gentleness I've felt since Killian arrived.

Turning, I look into her eyes and speak silently, worried my voice will carry over the stone and reach whatever guards he might have posted beyond the cell block. *"Did you know? That he was capable of this? You've warned me not to share too much with him."*

She stiffens.

"You never gave me a reason. You never give me anything," I say, curling my hands into fists. Her ears flick backwards in agitation. *"You still won't, will you?"*

Anassa just stares at me. It infuriates me, initially, until I realize that her stare is less disdainful and more… patient. I'd never have thought her capable of it, but here we are.

"Talk to me," I beg, willing to return that patience. Willing to forgive, if only she'll decide I'm finally, *finally* worthy of the truth.

But she only stares.

The spark of anger returns, twice as bright. *"You realize this is why I put my trust in him over you? You're supposed to be my partner! My direwolf. My Bonded. But you can't even be honest with me. All this time, and you haven't even told me who your mate is or let me in on your connection with them at all! Don't you realize how lonely that makes me feel?"*

Her eyes light. Her massive body shifts closer to me, and a surge of precise attention comes from her. She stares like I've just thrown the key to my cell at her face, like I'm uselessly tossing aside something vital.

I try to backtrack, to understand. And then it hits me like a direwolf at full-sprint, flattening me. I grip the cell wall for support as my eyes dart to the pulsing collar at her neck.

"Are you still able to communicate with your mate?" I ask.

"Yes," Anassa confirms. *"The collar was not created with mating bonds in mind. It seems to only block the pack bond, in case you sought to utilize your station to escape."*

I'm still breathing hard and flushed from my outburst, but my heart rate is slowing. It felt good, finally shouting at her for the shit she's put me through. The petty anger is a distraction from my bottomless pain and rage over Killian's betrayal, which thrums low and insistent at the back of my mind.

But then she stands, her massive form taking up most of the cell. She pads closer to me, bringing her nose close. Her eyes bore into my soul. Her voice is smooth, unforgiving but lacking outright hostility. *"Trust goes two ways, Meryn."*

My cheeks heat. I can't stop my hand from reaching for her, fingers tangling with the fur beneath her jaw.

"You say I have given you nothing. What have you given me?" She stares just the same, patient and knowing. *"You demand I show you my mate in the light, yet you hide away with your prince in the dark."*

"Anassa," I breathe, eyes widening.

"You may not trust me fully, but I cannot trust you, either. This is why I kept my mate a secret. I could never be certain that you would not have taken his name to the prince." She lifts her head. My hand falls from her fur. *"Regardless, it has benefited us. He has not thought to ward us against mate communication."*

I let out an aggravated breath. I'm still frustrated. I can't stop the torrent of emotion entirely, especially because Anassa's own irritation is starting to create a feedback loop.

But a part of me knows that nothing she's said has been wrong.

"And is your mate here? In the castle?" I ask.

"Yes."

"Who is it?" I try.

Foolish of me to attempt to get a direct answer out of her, I suppose. She merely shakes her lupine head and says, *"Perhaps you'll know soon enough."*

Okay, I get the hint. I take a slower breath and lift my head. *"Please, contact your mate now and tell them we need help. Have them get in touch with Venna. I know my trust has been misplaced with Killian, but I truly believe Venna will help us. She can help your mate and their rider get around the guards."*

A tingling awareness shivers over my spine. My soul reaches for something, and my mind jumps unexpectedly to the voice that woke me, demanding I retrieve the crown.

If Killian wants me mad, fine. I'll use this pain, too, and trust my dream.

"Tell your mate that there is a crown buried under the arena, in the drain at the center. They need to find a way to retrieve it and bring it here," I say, knowing that it's right.

Anassa's gaze is sharp. "*Is that a direct order?*"

There's an edge to her tone that carries hidden meaning. Her body is stiff. Her ears trained towards me. Her intensity tells me that her question is important. That the answer is important, too.

My spine tingles again. Looking into her eyes, I know suddenly that it *needs* to be an order.

"*Yes. Anassa, I order you to tell your mate where the crown is. I order your mate to get the crown and bring it here, to us.*"

Anassa looks away from me for a moment. Energy buzzes in the air. Then she looks back at me.

"*It's done.*"

CHAPTER FIFTY-FIVE

The rhythmic echo of my footsteps is starting to drive me mad, but I can't stop pacing. Anassa's eyes follow me as I walk back and forth across the cell, rubbing my temples to massage away the headache that lingers even though my wounds are gone.

It feels as though we've been waiting here forever. Anassa told me that her mate and rider were successful and that they're on their way to the dungeons. They're with Venna, waiting until there's a change of the guards and they can slip in unnoticed.

The minutes crawl by agonizingly slowly. I'm worried about what Killian's doing. I'm worried about where Saela might be. I'm worried Anassa's mate is going to get caught long before they reach us.

Then, footsteps. I finally hear boots in the corridor again and look instinctively towards Anassa to gauge her reaction—and her gaze has softened. The rider's footsteps are joined by the click of massive direwolf claws on stone. Relief floods me.

And then Stark walks around the corner.

I stare unblinking, struggling to understand why he's here, what he's doing, why he's looking at me like that.

Anassa rises within the cell, padding towards the enormous shifting shadow that is Cratos. The instant she's near him, her entire demeanor changes.

Her muscles relax. Her flanks shiver. She holds her head lower than I've ever seen and approaches the bars. Anassa presses her nose to the metal and Cratos steps forward to touch his nose to hers, his sides expanding as he takes a deep breath.

A second later, something in our bond shifts dramatically.

She has suddenly drawn aside curtains that I didn't even know existed, blinding me with light and heat and *satiation*. A small choking sound clicks in my throat, and I clutch my chest as my blood is set on fire.

My vision blurs at the first impact of her emotion, unshielded for the first time since we bonded.

Her true feelings about Cratos are earth shattering. The intensity of Anassa's desire for her mate crushes the air from my lungs and sends slow, addictive heat through every inch of me. Her longing crackles across the channel of energy between us and seeps into my blood.

It pulses through me with each rapid heartbeat and drowns out common sense and everything I thought I knew.

My lips tingle. My fingers itch. My muscles want to move, to take, to *go*.

To him, I realize.

Stark's dark eyes watch me steadily, and a shiver passes over my spine. I clench my jaw tightly as hyperawareness heightens my senses. I swear I can hear his heartbeat from clear across the cell. Feel his breath in my own chest. Sense the heat of his skin.

Logically, I know this is Anassa. Her bond with Cratos is overtaking my own consciousness.

But that knowledge doesn't dampen the intensity or help me resist the pull.

It's like looking at him with new, keener eyes. As Stark approaches the cell bars, familiar things about him suddenly seem different—the predatory grace of his movement, the strength in his hands as he grips the bars, the way his kill tattoos disappear beneath his collar as his head tilts.

Fuck, his eyelashes are long.

I want him to turn his head so that I can see that hidden scar beneath his jaw again.

The sheer insanity of that thought impacts me with force. I take a scraping step back and gather my energy to block Anassa's emotion. But I stop short.

I don't want to cut her out again. It feels wrong.

So I settle a thin filter in place in my head, just enough to come to my senses and stop gazing at this brutal, infuriating, ruinous man as if I'm on the verge of ripping his pants off and going to town.

Once the initial rush of it passes, all that's left is shock and fury.

"*You,*" I growl, hands in fists.

All this time, it was *Stark.*

That day on the mountain, it was him. The day he glared right at me in a sea of Rawbonds, it was him. When he sunk a needle into my neck, it was him. When he threatened my life. When he made it his life's mission to kill me in training. When he jabbed me in my injured torso and asked Anassa if she wanted to heal me…

They were talking. He could *hear* her.

When I found that book and they both refused to tell me about it—they were *talking.* It felt like they were colluding, because they *were.*

Fuck, how did I miss this?

I step closer, slamming my hand against the bars. "Did you know the entire time?" I keep my voice pitched low, aware that the guards may have returned outside, but my tone is poisonous.

He doesn't even slightly flinch. "Of course."

And he has no iota of remorse for keeping it from me, either. It's clear as day, right on his face. He doesn't give a shit. And I'm furious at him, but beyond that, a hundred questions fill my mind.

Why didn't he tell me? Why has he made my life hell? How did he hide this so well?

Has he felt this… this *pull* from the start?

When I open my mouth to ask, what comes out is a stammered, sort of pathetic, "Wh-where's Venna?"

He raises a brow. "Outside, in the shadows, on watch. I only had a moment to slip in here during the change of the guards. She's prepared to distract them or knock them out when I need to leave. Here," Stark says, passing something through the bars.

I struggle to tear my gaze from his dark eyes. For a second, it feels like it would be easier to pry the iron bars between us open.

For what? I don't know. To punch him in the jaw. Or—

"Take it," he says.

I finally manage to look down. The hair on the back of my neck rises instantly. My headache throbs. Stark's hand is closed around the delicate bend of the crown's metal, his fingers curled around the incredibly lifelike pelt of one of the wolves.

I stare at it for a moment, that reaching feeling aching in my bones.

The crown looks delicate despite its obvious age, with fine detailing and intricate spires. Two beautiful golden wolves leap towards each other, their lithe bodies curled around the ring of the crown from tip to tail. Their muzzles meet at the center as if they're engaged in an eternal dance.

Cradled between their outstretched paws is a huge, ancient opal.

The stone is the twin of the one in the necklace my mother gave me, glinting with the same age-old luster.

I reach for it slowly. When my hand closes around it, the cool metal heats. It pulses, a shivering ripple moving through the air. Just holding it in my hand, my lungs tingle with something electric and my blood pulses with power.

If holding it could do this, what would wearing it feel like?

Slowly, I lift it to my head. As I do, my eyes follow the incessant pull back to Stark. He's watching me with a restrained expression on his face, like usual.

Except… his lips are slightly parted. And his hand is so tight on the bars that his knuckles are paling.

I shut my eyes as the wolves' tails slide over my temples and slip into my hair. As soon as the metal settles on my head, a sharp sting of pain strikes like a bolt of lightning through my brain.

And I sink.

I fall right through the dungeon floor, its walls ripped away and replaced by rushing darkness. I'm vividly aware of my body melting away from my mind, left behind as I fall and fall towards an encroaching spin of color.

Suddenly, I'm jolted into place, my consciousness settling like it's stepped over a familiar threshold.

I'm in the castle, except it's not the one I know.

Its high ceilings and echoing halls are the same, but the atmosphere is different. Warmer. Vivid. I know instinctively that this is a memory or a vision. There's a sense that what I'm seeing isn't immediate, as though time and space have blurred at the edges.

Yet it's too real to be a mere dream.

When I turn, that subtle warmth crystallizes. I can suddenly make sense of it.

Peace. That's what it is.

The corridors are unified. The cold stone walls that have since been erected are no longer here. The division between the Bonded and royal sides of the castle are gone.

Massive wolves pad freely through the halls, their claws clicking and their tails swinging. They move alongside humans. *Common* humans, by the look of them. Not Bonded.

People talk and smile. A peal of bright laughter rings like a bell from somewhere out of sight. A direwolf to my right huffs loudly and whips the human he's walking beside with his tail, and she just grins up at him as they walk past me.

Turning, I look back down the long hall, back towards what I know as the Bonded side of the castle. This feels real. More than real, actually. *Right.* As though the cold and dark world I know as reality is nothing but a nightmare.

Those walls between us… like someone's shoved a frigid piece of metal between two halves of one heart.

Something tugs at me. A glimmer of light in the corner of my eye. A whirling of the surrounding hallways. I'm drawn forward on a wind I can't feel until I'm suddenly elsewhere.

The throne room, glittering in all its splendor, outshone in its beauty by...

The woman sitting on the throne. She's pale, with long silver hair that falls in a shining waterfall over her shoulders and down to her hips.

Atop her silver hair sits the golden crown with its twin wolves. At her throat, my opal necklace. At her hip, the wolf-pommel sword. And at her feet, the largest direwolf I've ever seen, with glossy silver-white fur.

I know this woman. I've seen her before, carved into a hidden wall in the tunnel that joins the royal wing to the Bonded side of the castle. And again, drawn in Stark's ancient book.

She has a calm expression on her face as she leans forward, readjusting the weight in her arms. An infant, swaddled in a fluffy fur blanket. She nurses the baby at her breast, smiling up at a servant when they ask her something before turning back to her child.

Everything about her radiates power. Her beauty. The crown. The sword. But her child, too.

The precious, compassionate, unashamed way she holds them. I can sense their connection in the air, warm and quiet. The same peaceful atmosphere from before infiltrates my heart, looking at them. Mother and child.

And then it all shatters. There's a distant sound, like the crack of magic shattering the air.

The doors burst open. A woman rushes to the throne, wearing some sort of military uniform. Her dark eyes are wild. "Queen Chiara, Siphons have infiltrated the palace!"

The queen hastily tucks her breast away, her infant immediately letting out a needy wail at being denied. She rises quickly, clutching her child in her arms and descending the dais. The direwolf follows, looming over the scene.

"Take her," Queen Chiara orders, handing the breathless

woman her child. "Protect my child with your life. Get her out of the castle and *hide her.*"

"M-My queen," the second woman sputters out. Her eyes widen as Queen Chiara rips the opal necklace from her neck and presses it into her hands.

"This will safeguard you," she says, then turns without hesitation and grips the enormous direwolf's fur.

She mounts the beast effortlessly, finding her seat with unearthly grace as her silver hair falls against her back. She looks like she belongs there.

She looks powerful.

Her eyes linger for one painfully short moment on her child before she turns her head and urges her direwolf onward. I'm dragged with them, my perspective shifting between my own eyes, the queen's, and the keener vision of her wolf's. I look back at the child one last time as she's hurried away, a lonely ache in my heart.

She's gone. The queen must fight.

We fly through the hallways, moving at impossible speed. The weight of her crown presses down on my head, too, as the wolf's powerful muscles propel us forward. My essence flies weightlessly alongside them, spurring them on.

We reach a segment of the castle that's in chaos. Wolves fight and die. Siphons flood the hallway, obvious due to their unnatural speed and beauty. Flashes of magic explode, causing the air to shiver with energy.

The queen rides past it all. She's hunting.

Eventually, she finds her prey. A tall Siphon man who...

My entire being shudders. He looks unsettlingly like both Killian and his father, with piercing blue eyes and the same sharp features.

The queen doesn't hesitate. She draws the wolf blade and attacks, streaking through the hallway on her wolf and slashing at the Siphon's head, aiming to decapitate him. But her blade clangs against his, and he manages to redirect the force of her blow and duck.

A terrible laugh echoes all around us. "Chiara Sturmfrost, finally come to play!" he bellows, opening his arms wide. Then a heinous darkness glints in his eyes. Pure malice. He leans in like he's sharing a secret. "Did you know that I slit your husband's throat already?"

Queen Chiara's fury and grief fill my veins, like a mountain's given way and crushed my soul. She swings messily in a rage, and the Siphon parries. She uses her direwolf's power well, the two moving as one.

But the Siphon is fast. *Strong*. His eyes see everything, long before her blows can land.

"What is your endgame, Brightbane?!" the queen screams.

Brightbane. Like Lucien Brightbane, the Siphon king of Astreona. But this man isn't him—a relative or ancestor, perhaps?

There's another flurry of blows. One of them clips his shoulder, but the wound doesn't even begin to slow him down.

"Nocturna will *never* bow to the Siphons!" Queen Chiara shouts. Her direwolf snaps at Brightbane, whose eyes widen as he rolls out of the way.

He pants, grinning cruelly up at her. "What choice will they have when the queen and her progeny are all *dead*," he spits.

That final word sends a cold snap of pain through the Queen.

"Your three older children were *alarmingly* easy to kill, and my men have gone after the baby. By daybreak, the Sturmfrost line will be over."

The direwolf lets out a long, low groan as if feeling its rider's pain. Queen Chiara's grip loosens on her sword. Her eyes cloud over. The agony only a parent could ever feel…

It gives him an opening. She manages to deflect a few merciless blows, but it isn't enough. Her fight's gone out of her.

My children, I can almost hear her whispering. *My children.*

Brightbane knocks her sword out of her hands, snatching it off the stone. The wolf attempts to stumble backward, but in one fluid movement, Brightbane spins and the sword slashes the beast's throat.

Bright red blood spills over silver fur.

Queen Chiara screams. The direwolf staggers and falls, thudding thunderously to the floor. I watch in horror as an ocean of blood pours from the wolf's throat.

Then the queen collapses next to her wolf, her silver hair floating on the surface of the ghastly red pool of blood.

Her gaze falls deathly still, her life taken by their severed bond.

Brightbane's voice is the last thing I hear, ringing over the scene of her death. "Your Bonded will be my instruments of vengeance."

It's almost a blessing when the vision begins to fade. The light and color dissipate with the remnants of the queen's energy.

Darkness finds me. And in that darkness, a familiar voice. The same one that echoes across my dreams.

"Chiara Sturmfrost is dead. Meryn Sturmfrost has returned. Long live Queen Sturmfrost."

Waking from the vision is like a rapid, quiet dawn. Weak light pours over me, spreading slowly over the cell around me and my trembling hands. I'm back in my body, back where I began.

But everything feels different.

I lift my head. Stark is still standing there, staring at me on the other side of the bars. His eyes are searching mine. For what, I don't know. But he's pressed against the bars like he's reaching for something.

My mind whirs, the ephemeral vision imprinted on me like an afterimage. The pieces click into place.

Queen Chiara's opal necklace, given to her baby, then passed down my family line.

The visions my mother received, that I received—disjointed, overwhelming and eventually all-consuming, but containing truths.

Anassa, a direwolf of immeasurable power who had waited years for a rider, then forced a bond on someone unwilling.

The crown of leaping wolves on my brow that feels as if it's meant to be there.

My tongue is thick in my mouth, but somehow I find a way to say words that sound implausible and, at the same time, absolutely right.

"I'm the rightful queen of Nocturna, aren't I?" I ask.

Stark's eyes spark, he takes a single step back, and he bows down on one knee, hand to his chest. "Welcome home, my queen."

CHAPTER FIFTY-SIX

I stare down at Stark, struggling to understand. Struggling through the bizarre wave of heat that flooded me the moment his knee hit the stone.

He's *kneeling* for me.

My hand presses to the cell bars for support as I stare at him. The only thing I can manage is a strangled, "Why didn't you *tell* me?"

The crown is painfully heavy, squeezing my skull too tight. I don't understand any of it. All I know is that centuries of hidden truths—of outright *lies*—are perched pretty atop my head.

I'm struggling to breathe, and Stark is still just kneeling there, slowly looking up at me.

"The Bonded have—"

"*Stand up,*" I choke out. "Fuck."

He rises smoothly to his full height, towering over me. A flare of heat lashes over me again, which I quickly douse with a bucket of ice-water.

That memory. The deaths.

Stark's dark eyes dart briefly over the crown on my head, down to my hand on the bars, then meet mine. "The Bonded have been under a Siphon blood curse for five hundred years." He gestures to the crown with a distractingly scarred hand. "That crown and the sword, together, control the human bonds to the direwolves."

I think back to the arena, to that lurking urge in my pack's minds to kill each other.

"We didn't know what happened to the crown, but it makes sense that it was hidden in the arena—the more direwolf and Bonded blood spilled on it, the stronger the king's control became," he says.

"Blood magic," I repeat numbly, my mind whirling through this new information. "A blood *curse*. What are you talking about?"

Stark's brows pinch briefly, but he takes a deep breath and speaks in a calm, distractingly rumbling voice. "The Siphon who overthrew the rightful royal family used powerful blood magic to bind the public's memories of the Sturmfrost royals. No one was permitted to speak of them again, and within a generation, they were forgotten," he tells me. "By everyone except for my family. As you know, we are the sworn protectors of the royal line."

I almost burst into delirious laughter at that. I'm not insane, but Stark is definitely doing his best to nudge me in that direction.

All of this time. *My* protector, not Killian's, not the king's.

"My ancestor smuggled your ancestor out of the castle when she was a baby and hid her with a commoner human family," he continues. "She also hid the history book you found in my quarters. My family has been faithfully passing that book down across generations. We've kept the truth alive through reading, even with a curse sealing it away."

Realization finally dawns on me. "You literally *couldn't* speak about it. Is that why I had to give Anassa a 'direct order' to get the crown?"

"Yes," he says stiffly, then presses his lips tightly together in obvious frustration. It isn't directed towards me, though. "I was raised on the stories—always *written*, never spoken—about the Sturmfrost line. About the day the rightful royal would return. I—"

He cuts himself off and shifts his weight. His stare burns into me.

"We've been waiting for the day a Sturmfrost royal might become Bonded again."

I swallow, ignoring the slight tingling on my lips and how badly I want to know what he'd been about to say. I force myself to take a step back and really *hear* what he's telling me. And through it all, one thing in particular doesn't make any fucking sense.

Shaking my head, I clutch the bars tighter. "If you're my..." Not *my*, he's not mine. "If you're my family's protector, why have you been trying to *kill* me since the moment I got here?"

Instantly, his expression twists with rage. Menacing energy explodes from him. It's that intense, overpowering presence he embodies when we spar, when he kills, when he goes to *war*.

"*Kill* you?" he exclaims, then glances over his shoulder toward the entrance of the dungeon and lowers his voice. "I've been doing everything in my power to keep you safe!"

My cheeks are on fire. "Wh——"

"Who moved you to your own quarters when someone tried to kill you in the night? Me!" He thuds a fist against his chest. "Who has been training you and strengthening you at every turn? Me!"

He moved me to my own quarters? I cannot believe Killian took credit for that... although, of course I can.

"What about that night, after the Voice Trial?" I ask. "You *threatened* me. Talked about accidents and——"

He groans. "You were *drunk*. Not long after you'd been attacked. It was an attempt to warn you off getting even drunker."

Oh. I... "You were constantly trying to kill me in training!" I exclaim.

"I did not order a *single* hit I knew you couldn't take," he says, stepping closer to the bars. I can feel his heat, his breath. He's angry, but he's looking at me like he wants to—— "And *constantly* is a bit of an exaggeration, don't you think?"

I step back because staying this close to him is messing with my head. "I know what I saw, Stark. From the start, you've *hated* me. You——"

His hand slams against the bars. "Of course, I hated you, Meryn!" he hisses. My heart slams in my chest. A bolt of confusing electricity streaks up my spine, forcing my shoulders back. "Can you blame me? My family has waited *hundreds* of years for your arrival, keeping the secret alive. *I've* waited. And when the Sturmfrost royal finally makes her appearance, she's *weak* and in love with the person whose family stole her birthright!"

What... the *fuck*? Why can't I get that out of my head? *I've waited.* I should be angrier. He called me weak. He spat out the word "love" like I was a dumb schoolgirl desperate for attention. But his eyes are a deep well of pain.

"Do you know how hard it was to see you with him?" he rasps. "To know who you were, even when you didn't, *sickening* magic silencing me? To endure our wolves' mate bond on top of it all?"

As if to emphasize his point, Anassa knocks down the thin filter I threw up between us.

Desire instantly pulses through me.

It's punishing. It's a need so strong that I'm almost *angry* at my emptiness. I look at Stark, and my entire body screams that I'm... *missing* him.

It's not sentimental. It's not even solely physical, though unbearable heat floods between my thighs.

No. It's soul-deep, centered at the core of who I am.

It's like we were once carved from the same bone, sharing blood and breath. And then someone ripped him from me, only I can't *remember* it happening. All that's left is the fury and the enduring desire to go to him and restore what was lost.

To be with him in every goddess-damned way I can.

I try to back away. To flee from it because it isn't *me*.

It's Anassa's bond to Cratos. It's about Cratos, not Stark.

I don't know why I—

Stark's arm lashes through the bars as I try to retreat. His gaze is intense. His grip is strong, but it's... careful, too. He pulls me close until I'm pressed up against the bars, the cold iron seeping through my shirt and chilling my heated skin.

"Do you have any idea what it felt like to watch you at the Forging Ball in the dress I picked for you—" *What?!* "—swirling in your lover's arms and bowing to his traitor father?"

His *voice*. I think I can feel the vibrations of his growl dancing over the sensitive skin of my throat.

Stark's never looked so… *open* before.

That dress. That dress that was so damn perfect for me. That made my heart sing.

Fuck, I *thanked* Killian for it.

Stark picked my dress. I can't shake that. *Stark picked my dress.*

Then another thought crests. "Stark—before the Ascent, you came through the city. There was a man, a deserter…"

The man that Stark and Cratos tore apart before the public.

The man who had threatened me at my fight the night before.

Stark lifts his chin. "Yes," he says simply.

Yes, he killed him because the man threatened me. Which means Stark had been there that night, watching me fight, somewhere in the crowd.

My knees weaken and I clutch the iron bars tighter. Then I meet his eyes, reeling. His breathing is slightly uneven. His jaw is ticking away. His hand on my arm is sending fucking bolts of lightning up my shoulder and melting me in heat.

I clench my jaw and push a gentle barrier back in place to dampen Anassa's desire. But it's still there. When she isn't trying to hide it, it lingers deep in my mind.

Quiet but aching.

And Stark felt this the entire time.

Slowly, I lift my hand and place it softly over his wrist. His eyes widen. I watch the hair on his arm rise. Watch his lips part slightly. Then he looks away.

He releases me, jerking his face to the side like I've slapped him across the face. For a split second, I catch a glimpse of the vulnerable scar beneath his jaw.

I step back, his warmth lingering on my palm. "*Anassa,*" I beg. I don't know why. I'm just confused. Overwhelmed.

She turns her head and nudges my arm. The scratchiness of her fur calms me. I can sense a swirl of understanding from her. It's a gentler emotion than I think I've ever felt over the bond.

Maybe she eases up on the wide open connection between us because a breath later, my head is slightly clearer. The physical effects on my body linger, but the painful need is gone. Even still, I look at Stark and feel…

I just understand, I think. It's hard, though.

Everything I thought I knew about him has been turned on its head.

I take a deep breath and stroke Anassa's ear, trying to calm my racing heart. I'm still confused, but…

"Stark," I say.

He lifts his head, clearly still affected.

"Alphas don't have the luxury of weakness," I recite.

Recognition flashes in his eyes. He slowly lifts his head further, and I see a hint of the relentlessly unyielding man I know and ha— well, I don't *hate* him.

Right now, I need to think like the Alpha I am. No, scratch that.

Like the *queen* I am, as unbelievable as that sounds.

"What about Killian?" I ask. I can see Stark shoving it all down, slipping back behind his walls. I think he wants it. I think it's easier for him, and he's right. I can't blame him. "His ancestor—the one who stole the throne from my family—was a Siphon. Is Killian a Siphon, too?"

Stark is silent for a long moment before he says, "I'm not certain."

I curse inwardly. It wouldn't surprise me, at this point, if Killian *were* a Siphon. If I've been traipsing around, secretly a queen—fuck, Stark's nickname for me sits differently now—why not a secret Siphon in our midst, too?

"The original king who stole the throne died, as did all of his progeny throughout the years," Stark says.

"But Siphons can live forever," I say. "So how did he die? Why?"

Stark sighs and leans against the bars, crossing his arms.

"Regrettably, there are things I don't know. Everything I do know has been passed down in the book you've already seen."

I tap my fingers on my thigh. "Fuck."

He huffs. It sounds borderline amused. "The one thing I know for certain is that Killian does not have your best interests at heart."

I laugh bitterly, gesturing to the bars between us. My stupid fucking *engagement bracelet* glints on my arm as I do. "Believe me. I'm well aware of that now. Why didn't you say anything?" I shoot a look at Anassa. "*Either* of you. I know you had limitations from the curse but surely at some point you could have said, *Hey, by the by, your betrothed is a gaslighting piece of shit?*"

I try to ignore the painful squeeze of my heart as I utter those words.

"*And you would have believed us?*" Anassa growls and my face heats in shame.

Of course I wouldn't have. Not even when I was furious at Killian for hiding his identity from me. I've been fighting them both since the moment I started the Trials. If Stark had tried to say something, I probably would've stabbed him. And Anassa? That wall would have come crashing down once again.

The awful truth of it all washes over me and for a moment I can't breathe.

My betrothed, my beloved. A man I let into my heart and into my bed. Whatever his intention was with me, there was certainly nothing noble at play. He broke my heart and then, idiot I am, I *forgave him* and he did it again, ten thousand times worse.

I did all of this to myself. If I'd never gotten involved with him to begin with, would Saela have been safe? Would my mother still be alive?

My stomach roils and I stagger forward, worried that I'm going to be sick all over the dirty cell floor. Anassa sends a wave of calming energy toward me, which helps the nausea pass.

And once it's gone, clarity comes.

If I'd never become Bonded, the Sturmfrost Queens would have remained a secret. Maybe for another five hundred years.

So I suppose I have one thing to thank him for.

Stark watches me intently, a violent storm playing across his features. Once, that image would have scared me. Now, it sends a shiver down my spine for wholly different reasons.

He reaches through the bars and grabs my wrist, the contact alighting my blood. "Give me the word and I'll tear out his throat. All the lives I've ever taken were just training for this moment, my queen. Make me your instrument of vengeance. Let my hands act out your every savage, depraved thought. Use me. I'm yours."

Mine. *My* psycho asshole. *My* bloodthirsty killer.

My face feels hot and strange, and I realize from somewhere outside of myself that I'm crying, the tears streaking rivers down my cheeks.

Out of everything, *this* is the thing that makes me cry?

Maybe I'm going insane after all. I laugh at the thought and brush the tears away in a fast sweep.

"Thank you," I say through the tightness in my throat. "But this… this is my score to settle, and no one else's. Besides, I have some questions for our supposed prince, and we need those answered before either one of us can find inventive ways to disembowel him."

Stark gently lets go of my wrist and I feel the loss of contact keenly. "You need to go to him, then?"

I nod, and take the crown off my head. "I do. He's done such an impeccable job of pretending to be what I wanted. It's time to return the favor."

The crown is heavy in my hands and when I give it back to Stark, it's like my very blood protests. There's an instinct in me to snatch it back. But I push past it. "Keep it safe. Find Saela and the other kids. Venna can help you there. I'm going to need you to come meet me with the crown, but I'll send word through Anassa when it's time."

Stark nods, his dark hair falling forward into his eyes. When he finally looks back up at me, there's an edge of something foreign in his gaze. *Concern*, I realize with a start. How unusual.

"I'd tell you not to put yourself in danger," he says, "but I know you better than that."

I bite my lip, suddenly self-conscious. "You're worried?"

He scoffs. "Never. You are the danger. Any person who doesn't see that deserves what's coming to them."

Fuck, those stupid tears are back.

For some reason, I believe him without a shadow of a doubt, even though those words are coming from the mouth of a man I once thought was my greatest enemy.

CHAPTER FIFTY-SEVEN

S tark waits for Venna to come and signal that the way is clear again, and then they depart. He's promised to have Saela waiting for me when I'm done with Killian.

My heart bleeds at the thought of delaying my reunion with Saela, of trusting anyone else with her rescue, even Stark. But I know she won't be safe until I deal with Killian's threat.

After they leave, I give it twenty or thirty minutes—time is passing strangely down here—pacing around the dark cell before I finally call for the guards.

The two men who come look repulsed by me. Who can blame them? I'm covered in the dried blood of their king.

"Please," I say, getting on my knees before them in the cell, and trying my very best to look weak. "Please, get Prince Killian for me. He was right. My mind is unwell. I need him, I need his help. He loves me and he'll fix me. Prince Killian will know what to do."

"King Killian," one of them corrects me curtly.

"King Killian," I agree, though the words barely make it out of my throat. "Please."

The guards look at each other warily and then leave without saying another word.

But my pleas must have worked, because a short while later, they come back and let me out of the cell. Then they escort me roughly up the stairs, up and up and up, through passageways until we finally reach the hall outside Killian's room.

I assumed he would come to me, but of course he wants me here, where he can entirely have the upper hand.

The guards open the door to his room and then shove me in. "Don't try anything funny," the second one growls at me. "We'll be right outside the door." Then he slams said door in my face.

"*I'm at Killian's rooms,*" I tell Anassa. "*Are you still in the cell? Have Stark come get you, now, while the guards are here. They're standing sentry so I doubt anyone will notice you've gone. See if Stark can get that collar off.*"

"*He's on his way,*" she responds. "*We'll come to you as soon as you summon us.*"

Turning around, I start when I realize I'm not alone. There are two servant women here—an older one wearing a scowl, and a very young one who winces at me in fear.

"Let's get this started then," says the older woman.

They spend what might be hours fixing me up—stripping the bloodied uniform off my body, shoving me into Killian's beautiful tub, scrubbing my body raw and washing my silver hair. When I'm clean enough by their measure, they then treat me like a doll. They dry my hair and arrange it beautifully, lotion my entire body. They put makeup on me and shove me into an elaborate gown in a beautiful shade of deep blue silk, lacing it so tightly that I can barely breathe.

Not a word from either of them, the entire time. And when I've met some level of acceptability, they leave. And I'm alone—waiting.

Killian's chambers look different to me now.

I go and sit at the window seat, watching tiny flakes of snow land on the glinting roof beyond the glass and instantly melt on contact. Curling my legs close, I hug them to my chest and let the delicate heels the servants gave me thud to the floor. The dress feels like it's going to swallow me whole.

All around me there are silent reminders of what I've learned. I hate that I once looked around these rooms and found it beautiful.

Comforting, even, because of the eternally burning hearth. And because of *him*, always standing there waiting for me with a knowing smile.

My skin crawls. It hasn't stopped since Stark left my side.

I rub my arms and try to forget the touch of the servants' hands fluttering over me. But I'm grateful that they've made me look like a beautiful object.

He wants a weak bride-to-be. Someone unquestioning. Someone he can control.

So I'll give that to him.

The doorknob turns and I immediately draw my shoulders up, huddling into a ball like the cold is sinking into my bones and frostbite is setting in. Briefly, for only a second, my thoughts flit to Stark. It's long enough for that simmering awareness to return, but the sound of the door opening jolts me from my thoughts.

I have to focus. Killian is a coiled viper.

"Meryn," Killian breathes, shutting the door behind him. He's still wearing his father's sword—no, *my* sword—at his hip. His face floods with open emotion. Relief, concern, love.

It's an intricate process, transforming my rage at the sight of him into vulnerability. I've done it before for other men. I've let them look at the tremble in my hands and assume it's because I'm afraid, not because I'm imagining wrapping those hands around their throats.

But those men weren't Killian. His engagement bracelet is still clamped on my wrist, glittering gold and red and black against the shimmer of silk blanketing my knees.

"You look beautiful, kitten," he says, crossing to me.

The nickname almost makes me break my facade. *Kitten*. I see what he was doing, now. To the rest of the world, I was a fearsome alleycat, but to him… only a pathetic little kitten.

I reach up and sink my fingers into my hair, tugging slightly. As he reaches me, I let a more violent shiver wrack my body.

"Killian," I croak, leaning into the role of mentally ill. "I think you're right. I really thought…"

His face collapses as he settles next to me on the cushions. His fingers rest on my ankle, and his warm touch curdles my blood. I don't let it get to me. I pretend it's a snake twisted around my skin.

"I can't believe I'm losing my mind like my mother," I breathe, voice whispery.

That sickly feeling returns. My throat stings. I wish I'd never had to say those words. Mother wasn't mad. Neither were all the women in my family before her. The visions, the voices... all of it was just our unfulfilled birthright screaming, clawing to the surface.

A fresh wave of grief hits me, sudden and jarring.

Killian sees it and reaches for me. I squeeze my eyes shut as his arms settle around me.

It's all wrong. All of it, just like the room around us, is different now. His touch is still familiar, but when I feel it, I think of the way he looked at me as we stood over his father's body. His feigned shock. His brief, triumphant smirk.

And I have to fight down bile.

Leaning into his embrace, I cling to his shoulders. Soon, his hand slips over my back, tangling with the perfectly curled ringlets of my hair. His fingers sink deep, guiding my head.

And he kisses me.

I sever myself from my body, opening my mouth but reaching for Anassa. I pour myself into my bond with her, letting Killian kiss me deeply and relying on Anassa's waiting presence.

If I'd known, if she'd been able to warn me about the mask Killian wears, I'd never have consented to being with him. There's rage there, too, that he took so much from me.

That I gave so willingly, let him see the gaps in my armor, when all along he was *this* person.

This vile creature who would kiss a woman while she trembles with fear.

It doesn't matter now. Or, it does, but I can't confront my personal wounds. This moment is about more than just me.

And it's working, I realize. Killian's fingers pull at the tight laces on the back of my dress, slowly loosening them as he kisses me.

I run my fingers through his hair and focus on Anassa's

murderous satisfaction. Killian is crawling into her jaws, and she's anxious to taste his blood.

"It's okay," he breathes huskily against my mouth. "I'll take care of you, Meryn. I always will."

I shiver. It sounded like a threat, somehow, though there's nothing in the shine of his eyes that hints at anything sinister. He closes his arms around me and pulls me close, but I shift my legs and stand.

"I'm... not okay," I say, chest rising and falling rapidly.

He lets me take his hand and pull him to his feet. When he stands, he cups my cheek and uses his other hand to loosen another lace on my bodice.

"But... when I'm with you, I feel better," I lie, looking up into his eyes. I lean into his chest, gripping his lapels like I'll fall without it. "Make me feel better."

Killian's next breath is hungry. He leans in and molds his mouth to mine, closing his hands around my hips. I step backward, pulling him with me towards the bed. His eyes flash with lust.

There's something almost victorious in his smile, and I quickly look away from it as I turn to guide him by the wrist.

Once I'm beside the mattress, I take hold of his shoulders and push gently. He sits back and lets me slip into his lap, fine silk gliding with a whisper over his legs. He sighs and reaches down, closing his hands around my delicately adorned thighs and squeezing.

When Killian arches his neck, I kiss him again.

It's like swallowing poison.

None of the pleasure I once found in this reaches me through the pain and anger. When he slips his hand under my dress and slides his touch up my thigh, I lean my weight into him. He grunts and lets me push him back against the mattress.

I lean over him, kissing him, biting lightly at his jaw. He pulls me closer and kisses my neck. I force myself to grind over him a few times, moving my hips until he starts to harden beneath me.

Then I slowly reach up to guide his hands lower on my thighs. He thinks I'm asking him to touch my ass and reaches out.

The moment he does, I push his arms down and pin them

beneath my legs with my full weight. I rip my mouth from his and sit up, ice crystallizing in my veins.

No more.

His eyes widen, but he's too slow. I've trained for this.

When he attempts to break free from the compromised position I have him in, yanking his arm, I slam my fist into his throat. He chokes as his face turns red. I use the opportunity to hook my leg around his dominant arm and reach down.

And I slide the *Diren Blæd* from his hip.

Then, before he can blink, I press the blade against his throat, relishing the flustered noise of surprise he makes.

Killian's eyes are moving over the position I have him in. My bare thighs are clamped around his arms, my blade at his throat. But he only seems... *amused.*

"Kinky," he says, cold eyes rising to meet mine. "You trying to behead a second king with that sword? Two in a day probably sets a record."

I put pressure on the sword at his throat. He doesn't even flinch as it bites his skin. My eyes dart briefly to the thin trail of blood sliding down the side of his neck, then return to his icy gaze.

"You're no king," I hiss. "And neither was your imposter father."

He lets out a chuckle of amusement. "Ah. So you've figured it out."

"Did you know who I was the entire time?" I demand.

"Of course, I knew," he says, his smile lingering.

Something in my chest dies when he says it. I expected the answer, but it still cuts deep.

"What, you were hoping that it was just a *coincidence* that the current crown prince and the heir to the original royal line happened to meet in a market one day and end up in a relationship?" He shrugs. "There are no such things as coincidences."

Fuck. *Fuck.*

"Whispers said Queen Chiara kept her baby alive. My ancestors decided it hardly mattered, since no one remembered her, anyway. But I had a plan for the Sturmfrost royal," he says, his smile turning sharp.

He strains from the mattress to press his own neck against the blade. There's something wild in his eyes.

"I hunted you down. I sought you out. I made you mine."

It takes all of my self-control not to slice his throat right now. Instead, I say, "You fucking *monster*. I *loved* you! And the whole time you were just... using me."

The icy edge to his eyes softens. "You wound me, Meryn. I wasn't *just* using you. I love you. Everything I've done, it's for your own good. For *our* good, and the good of the kingdom."

And the fucked up thing is, I think he believes what he's saying. This may be the only genuine thing he's ever told me.

My grip tightens on the blade. Magic whips through me like a hurricane, tearing up my roots and leaving me adrift. Unmoored, I can't stop the thought again. *It would be so easy.* I could kill him right here. Just a twitch of my wrist, and he'd stare up at me with the life draining from his body, knowing his prey had turned predator.

But I'm not done with him yet. "My mother?"

"You have to know, I didn't feel good about that. But if you were going to be my queen, her powers needed to pass to you. It was her time."

Powers. That must be the responding magic I feel when I hold this blade. The sensation coursing through me when I wore the crown.

The Sturmfrost royals have magic—magic that has been suppressed for centuries.

Kill him, kill him, kill him, my heart beats. *KILL HIM.*

"I needed you, though," Killian's saying. "So I let you..li..."

Something strange starts to happen.

Killian's pupils start to expand and contract alarmingly rapidly. His mouth drops open, and his irises roll backward until I can only see the whites of his eyes behind trembling lashes. Then, in an instant, his gaze snaps back to me. The voice that comes from him isn't Killian's.

"Killian got greedy," he says, voice echoing hauntingly. The sound of it is all wrong. It crackles with age, with overuse. The desiccated sound of it doesn't match Killian's youthful face.

I recoil, horrified. It feels like spiders are crawling all over my body. I press the sword firmly to his throat, disoriented and confused.

"Who are you?" I demand.

His grin stretches unnaturally wide, teeth bared. I watch as his canines elongate into fangs and draw blood from his own lips. "Alistair Brightbane."

Brightbane.

The Siphon who killed Queen Chiara. *How?!*

"Bring Killian back," I growl, leaning over him. The same thing happens. A trembling of his pupils. A seizure of his body.

His eyes roll back down, and he lets out an appreciative hum. "Yes, my beloved?"

"What are you?" I say. When he does nothing but raise a brow at me, I press the blade deeper, and he hisses. "Are you a Siphon? Were you always?"

"No, Meryn," he says, with a smirk. "Not always."

I used to love hearing my name from his lips. Now all I can see are the fangs.

"When it was clear that you were onto my father," he continues, "Alistair demanded to be transferred. He's passed this way for the last five hundred years. Each new king in our line serves as his vessel."

My shock makes my grip momentarily slip on the sword and I scramble to push it back against his throat. "How is that even possible?" I demand. I've never heard of anything like this before, ever.

"Transference magic," he says, "a particularly complicated type of Siphon blood magic. Only someone with the great power of Alistair Brightbane could pull this off."

The usurper king—never gone, after all. He's been here this whole time, hiding in plain sight. My mind is spinning and I blink, trying to bring myself back into the plush room.

I need to keep asking questions. I need more answers.

"So your father was a Siphon?" I say.

Killian's smile grows. "Yes, and he turned me into one, the day of the graduation ceremony. Thanks for killing that commoner Phylax, by the way. I was very thirsty after I'd transformed."

Henrey. Ugh. So that's what happened to his body—Killian drained him. That's why the servants took him beneath the arena.

Killian's eyes flash with that eerie blue color—the same color of his father's—and I realize now it must be related to the transference magic.

A monster, hundreds of years old, is inhabiting Killian's body with him. And the entire time we were together—his entire life—he knew this would be his fate.

"And the kids? My sister?" I ask. "Was your father draining *them?*"

"Yes, love." His tongue touches his fang. His voice continues to echo and crawl, violating, into my ears. "Transference magic is tough to hold, particularly during Bonding Trials when we also need to control so many wolves. Only the strong blood of children could give us the power we need."

It's enough. That's *enough.*

"It stops here," I breathe, lifting the blade to put force behind the blow. I can already picture it. Just like his father died, his head will roll from his shoulders. Blood will spill over the sheets.

What we once had between us could never stop me.

But the moment my blade is in the air, strength saps from my muscles. Killian laughs again, the sound vibrating through the room.

The shadows all around us start to twist and writhe like serpents. They warp away from the legs of the furniture, from the corners of the room. They move like they're alive and hungry.

Then, somehow, the shadows *grab* me, wrapping around my wrists and ankles. I'm yanked off of Killian with jarring force, thrown to the ground and pinned there.

He stands from the bed and brushes his suit off, then walks slowly toward me as I lay trapped.

"Surely you must know I wouldn't let you kill me. After all, I'm your future husband."

I kick my legs toward him, trying to keep him away from me. "Like *fuck* you are! What are you doing to me?!"

Fear courses through me for the first time since we've been alone together, and I reach out desperately to Anassa. *"Now. You and Stark need to come* NOW!"

Killian kneels down on the floor next to me and strokes my cheek. "Kitten, I'm serious. I love you. You're not in your right mind right now——" Oh, not this shit again. "——but once you have some time to think about this, I'm sure you'll see how good we are together. I can rule the entire world with you at my side."

NOW, I shout over the bond.

The door slams open with a thundering crack.

Stark bursts in with both of our wolves, whipping his body with precision. He unleashes a blast of Daemos power. It picks Killian up and slams him against the wall. The shadows dissipate and my body is freed.

I scramble to my feet as quickly as I can muster.

Then Stark tosses me the crown. I catch it with my left hand as I simultaneously lift the sword back up, getting into a fighting stance.

The moment the crown slides into place, power surges through my body. It's like plunging into a vast, dark forest, miles of endless shadow all around me. Energy pulses from my body, too big for my skin, roiling like the chaos of boiling water. It presses outward, alive, trying to push the boundaries of my mind.

My *magic*.

And just the same, there's a vast part of this forest of power that is severed from me. This blood-boiling, endlessly expansive magic is only a fraction of a deeper reserve.

When Anassa senses it, she projects a warning that feels like she's closing her teeth around my scruff, yanking me back to her side. But I don't have time to analyze her concern.

Killian stands from where he fell against the wall, and he begins to laugh.

Anassa snarls. His eyes move to her, then to Stark, who's standing between the two towering wolves in a readied stance.

Killian arches one brow with something that looks almost like appreciation.

"You kept secrets from me, Meryn," he says scoldingly, as if he hadn't kept a thousand of his own. "I didn't realize your wolf had a mate. What a pity. Although, I suppose it doesn't matter now."

I lift the blade higher, and think to Anassa, *"Get ready to charge him."*

But then the shadows move again, more viciously than before, rising all around us in an endless swirling storm. The light in the room dims as Killian stalks toward me.

Stark attempts to use his Daemos powers again, to swat at Killian or at the shadows, but it backfires. The surge of energy slams backwards into him and he stumbles into Cratos. The black direwolf lets out a threatening growl.

"Tsk, tsk," Killian says cooly. "Don't you know that you can't use your little direwolf powers against this magic? After all, your powers are rent from mine. Well, from Meryn's, technically."

A headache begins to build behind my eyes as my mind unravels his meaning.

Killian reaches me and grabs my face roughly, forcing another kiss on me. Anassa lunges and snaps, but he moves out of her way with inhuman speed—*Siphon*, I remember stupidly. He's a Siphon now.

"Thank you so much for my new power, beloved," he says, sliding his gaze from Anassa to me. "As a parting gift, I've left you a little surprise. I'll see you soon, I'm sure."

I scream and plunge the blade towards him. But just before the metal connects with his throat, the shadows dart across the room at an impossible speed. They wrap around his body like a cocoon, freezing against my bare skin.

Wind whips through the air, and with a sharp pop like a limb dislocating, Killian is gone.

"What the fuck did he do?" I whisper, staring at the space he just occupied.

Weakly, I turn to look at Stark. He's come right beside me, his hand half-suspended between us. His brows are twisted upward, his eyes wild.

He's staring at me in abject horror. I open my mouth to ask, but then his hand closes around my arm, his grip painfully tight like he's trying to hold me to the earth.

I follow his gaze down, right to my left wrist. I lift it slowly.

The ruby ring set into the engagement bracelet is mottled with shadows. They stir within the stone as if they're swimming through blood.

"Take it off," Stark snaps. His voice shakes with urgency as his grip tightens further.

It's obvious to me now, too. The bracelet is what's sapping my strength. Killian has been channeling my magic with it—magic I wasn't even *aware* of—through the stone.

I throw the sword aside and reach up to unclasp it.

But when I do, it constricts painfully around my wrist. The metal warps, threatening to cut off my blood supply.

"I can't," I choke out. A claustrophobic panic spikes through my body.

"Meryn—"

"I can't!" I shout, pulling again. It tightens even more. It'll break my bones at this rate. Mangle me.

Anassa snarls and butts against Cratos. "*The bracelet is enchanted and bound to you,*" she tells me urgently. "*It allows the usurper to channel magic from wherever he has gone.*"

I let out a strangled cry. Quickly, I start strategizing—no sword could cut through this, but perhaps a blacksmith can melt the metal. But even as the thought comes to me, I know. In my bones, I know.

There's nothing that I can do to get this bracelet off, not without the Siphon magic that created it.

This is what Killian's done to me. Sunk his fangs deep, right to the heart of me. Stolen my crown, stolen my powers.

And now he won't let go.

CHAPTER FIFTY-EIGHT

It takes a while for me to come back to myself, but when I do, Stark is by my side. His hand is warm on my back, rubbing in gentle, calming circles. I didn't know this big brute of a man was capable of such a small and soft motion.

I close my eyes, let myself concentrate on the feeling. On his musky, amber smell and the welcoming heat of his body next to mine.

Who would have ever thought that I'd find Stark's presence so... soothing?

After a minute, he asks, "Are you alright?"

I reopen my eyes and look up at him. There's no pity in his gaze, which helps. Still, the physical contact is starting to feel like too much. I don't want to be touched by anyone, not after Killian. Not for a long while, maybe.

Maybe Anassa relays that to Cratos, because Stark removes his hand and steps back from me.

"No," I tell him. "I'm not alright. But I'll fall apart later." Because as much as I'd like to wallow over Killian, there's something much more important on my mind now. "Where's my sister?"

"Venna and I led a small group of my pack members on an

incursion into the buried dungeons. We had to… eliminate… some of the royal guards along the way."

I narrow my eyes. "The royal guards who helped the king imprison and kill kidnapped children? Their deaths were well earned. You found her?"

He inclines his head. "We recovered the children. Venna is guarding Saela in my office. The other children are being returned to their families in the city, escorted by Bonded."

"Take me to her," I say.

We move quickly through the halls, Anassa and Cratos trailing side-by-side behind us. They're eerily silent. Whatever nobility remain are likely hiding in their guest's chambers. The Bonded are still sequestered to their side of the castle. As such, our footsteps echo deafeningly as we walk.

And I know I'm not imagining it. "Stark," I say.

"Yes."

"You see it?" I ask for confirmation.

I watch as his eyes dart to the corners of the halls, to the stone at our feet, back to me. "Yes," he says.

The shadows around us are shifting. Trembling. *Alive.* They move with me. Every step I take, they stretch, swirl, and bend as if to follow me, like the drag of a finger through a spiral of paint.

But even so, there's a distance. I can reach out to them and drag them along with me… but I also sense that if I had full use of my powers, I could make them do anything.

I could sever the world in two.

Venna is waiting for us in the hall, on alert with two of the Daemos Rawbonds—well, Bonded now, I guess. When she sees us coming, she pushes up onto her toes and jogs towards us. Her wolf lifts its head, watching us closely as Venna wraps her arms around me.

"Saela is safe," she says, stepping back.

I take her hands and squeeze. "Thank you," I say shakily. She nods and hugs my hands to her chest briefly before releasing me and leaning against her wolf's side.

Stark pushes the door to his office open, and I rush past him.

Saela is past the sparring mat, curled up in one of Stark's comfortable chairs and buried under one of his soft blankets. She has one of his books on her lap. But when she hears the door open, her head snaps up inhumanly quickly.

She breaks into a wide smile and sets the book down before ripping the blanket off jerkily. Tears immediately burst from me. I'm so relieved that I don't even care that Stark is watching.

Saela's streaking down towards the mat when I reach her. I throw my arms around her, pulling her trembling form close. She grips me painfully tight.

I gasp out a breath. "Air, Sae."

She lets out a tense laugh and lifts her head to look at me. "Sorry," she says, but she doesn't relent.

I shake my head. "Don't apologize," I say, pushing her dark hair from her face. She looks pale, and she's freezing. Her hazel eyes are slightly dull. I hate that I let it get this far. That I let him take her at all. I'm going to rip the sun from the sky and place it in her hands just to warm her up. "Are you okay? You feel—"

"I'm okay now," she says. She shuffles even closer. My throat closes up when she smiles up at me tearily. "You kept your promise."

I choke out a sob and pull her close to crush her against me. I'm never letting her go again. I stroke her hair and kiss her head. When she tries to wriggle free, I grunt and hold her even tighter. "I'll make you another promise."

I finally let her go. She slips from my arms and looks up at me. The corner of her eye twitches slightly. She looks so exhausted. "Okay," she says with a small smile.

"I promise," I say, reaching up to hold her face, "that everything will be different now. I'm going to make things better."

Her lips tremble and she nods. "That sounds like a good plan." Then, her eyes slide up to the crown on my head. "What… what is that?"

I glance over to Stark, standing sentry at the door with Cratos. He seems to read my mind. *Can* he read my mind? Anassa and I need to have a chat about how she communicates with her mate.

Stark's jaw clenches, and I can tell what he's thinking too, even without him saying it. He doesn't want to leave my side right now. But he huffs, bows to me, and says, "I'll be standing guard outside. Let Anassa know when you're ready for me to come back in."

Then he turns and leaves, and I'm alone with Saela and this earth-shattering news.

Explaining to my younger sister that we've secretly been royalty our whole lives proves to be alarmingly easy. After she gets over her initial jaw-dropping, squealing shock, she's entirely on board, barraging me with questions about everything that's happened since we parted.

I do my best to explain it all. Our true heritage. Mother's "'madness" and the magic in her veins. In mine. How Anassa chose me on the mountain. After a while, I can't put it off any longer.

I lead Saela to the cozy chair I found her in and sit her down, taking her hands. Then, I look up into her eyes and tell her about Mother.

Saela cries. She sits still, trembling, tears streaking down her cheeks. "So... everything's changed," she sniffs. Her voice is tiny. "We can't go home."

The horrible hollowness of grief presses on my organs. I pull her to me and hold her tight. "You will never be alone, Saela."

She exhales shakily, clutching me. "We're her daughters," she says. "We're strong."

"Always," I confirm.

A shudder moves through her when I wipe her cheek. It's hard. Not just missing our mother, but knowing that our entire family line has been suffering for so long. I just hope that Saela knows it ends with me. *Everything* will be different now.

"So if I'm a princess and our family oversees the direwolves... do I get to become Bonded someday?" she asks through her tears.

Anassa chuffs an assent from behind me. She's stayed apart from us this whole time, letting Saela and I talk. Now that Saela's expressing interest in the direwolves, though, Anassa pads over to us.

"That means yes in Anassa speak," I tell Saela.

Saela's eyes widen and I try to imagine this from her perspective —try to see Anassa for the very first time. She towers over us, taking up all our vision. Her silver-white fur shines in the low light of Stark's office, and she stares down at Saela with her wise yellow eyes. She's fearsome and powerful.

Anassa lays down at Saela's feet, the top of her head now reaching Saela's waist. Saela reaches out a tentative hand, which Anassa sniffs, and then rubs her face against.

Delight sparks in Saela's eyes, her grin so wide and bright that it's all that I can see. She pets Anassa again and coos. "Who's a pretty girl?" she asks, her voice high. "You're a pretty girl, aren't you?"

Anassa looks over at me, eyes narrowing. "*Tell her not to talk to me like I'm a baby. Make sure she knows that direwolves deserve respect.*"

"*You don't like that, you widdle cutie?*" I tease.

Anassa reaches out a paw and swipes at me, but I hop away, laughing. "She wants you to talk to her like she's the powerful, ancient creature that she is," I tell Saela, who straightens immediately and nods to Anassa, getting the message.

Suddenly I can see her future—scaling Mount Wolfsbane, bonding with a huge direwolf of her own. As proud as I would be for her to join the ranks of the Bonded, in no world would I ever be comfortable putting her through the Bonding Trials.

"*She doesn't have to do the Trials,*" Anassa says. "*No one does, if you don't want them to happen anymore.*"

My eyes widen in surprise. "*What are you talking about? I thought the direwolves designed the Trials. That's what Egith said.*"

"*It's a lie,*" Anassa growls. "*The Bonded were told this to keep them from revolting against the king. This was his way of controlling our population—he wanted our strength, but not in large enough numbers to rise up against him.*"

Even after everything I've been through over the past two days, after everything I've learned, this shakes me to my core.

All of that bloodshed. All of those lives. For nothing.

Anassa senses my grief and says, "*It all can change now. You can make the change. The Trials can be whatever you want them to be.*"

The gravity of that statement is almost too much to bear. *Whatever I want.* For the first time, I truly realize that I get to make the calls.

I'm in charge now—of the Bonded, and all of Nocturna.

"*First, you need to claim the crown publicly,*" Anassa corrects me. "*In order to lead, you need people to agree to follow.*"

She's right. They need to know, all of them. Everyone in the castle, and throughout the country. It's going to be a big undertaking.

"*Call Stark back in here,*" I tell her, already thinking about what we'll need to do.

A short moment later, he strides back into the office with Cratos, the two Daemos riders—Helene and Grigore—trailing behind him. "Do they know?" I ask Stark.

Helene and Grigore exchange confused looks.

"*I can reach them now,*" Anassa says. "*I can reach all the Bonded. Shall I try?*"

"*Yes,*" I say. "*Show them the truth.*"

My mind taps into what feels like the pack unity bond, but amplified by an unbelievable magnitude. Where was once a single river, connecting me to my pack, is now a confluence—reaching out to each individual pack and its riders. Anassa sends the truth spiraling to them both, feeding them images and information.

Helene gasps, her hands covering her mouth. Grigore looks up at me quickly, shock plain on his face, then drops to one knee. "My queen," he says.

Before I can tell them anything else, there's a menacing crack and a thud. I whip around, moving to draw my blade. But it isn't an attacker.

It's much worse.

Saela's fallen. She convulses on the ground, eyes rolled back in her head, muscles twisting her body until tendons strain and ligaments pop. Something sickly sweet is in the air, like the smell of rotten fruit.

I lunge for her, desperate to help, to stop her pain. Helene gets there first, running past me to reach down and lift Saela up.

And before I can join them, Stark snatches my arm and yanks me back. I'm about to tear him apart with my *fucking* teeth, but then I see it.

Helene flinches backward like she's been struck. Her hand whips up to her throat, her green eyes wide.

Blood, I realize.

There's a gaping wound in her throat that she's trying to hold closed.

Saela twists towards me with terrifying speed. Her body locks into place, feral. There's blood all over her mouth and chin.

She snaps at Grigore with… with *fangs*.

"A Siphon!" he shouts.

This is all a mistake. This isn't real. She…

"Meryn!" Stark begs, pulling me against his chest and closing his arms around me from behind, pinning me in place. I realize that I was still yanking towards her, desperate, as if laying my hands on her could undo all of it.

A scream tears from me that rips my throat raw. I know now what Killian meant.

As a parting gift, I've left you a little surprise.

The shadows around the room rise, pulsating. They snuff out all the light in the room, moving in ways I can't comprehend and can't fully control.

Killian has changed her, corrupted her. Turned her into one of… *them*.

But now I know the powers that live inside me, the powers that are my birthright.

I won't accept this. I don't. First, I'll find a way to fix my sister… and then I am coming for him.

Fury streaks through my veins, like a thousand knives wrought from the deepest shadows.

I am Meryn Sturmfrost, Queen of Nocturna, and I will use the twisting dark in my bones and my blood to *hunt* Killian Valtiere to the ends of the earth.

DON'T MISS FURYBOUND, BOOK 2, COMING LATER IN 2025!

Foes become friends and there's a new war on the horizon. But what is Meryn willing to sacrifice for revenge?

Pre-order book 2, Furybound, now!

A GUIDE TO THE BONDED PACKS
OF NOCTURNA

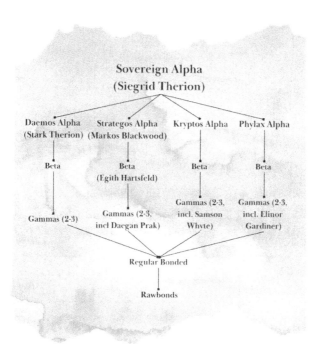

STRATEGOS (stra-TEE-gos)

The tacticians and leaders of the Bonded packs, masters of strategy and battlefield command. Their communication magic is stronger than the other packs, enabling them to strategize and discuss tactics in battle; they are also gifted with flashes of foresight, brief glimpses of possible immediate futures. Strategos wolves all have silver and/or white coloring.

DAEMOS (DAY-mos)

The warriors of the Bonded packs, known for their brutality and physical prowess in battle. Their magic can make them stronger, faster, more deadly in battle, and even be wielded as a weapon against enemies by some. Daemos wolves all have dark coloring, some are a deep black in color.

KRYPTOS (KRIP-tos)

The shadow walkers and spies of the Bonded packs, specializing in stealth and intelligence gathering. Able to wield concealment magic that bends light and shadow to aid in stealth; at certain times of day or in certain conditions, wolf and rider can become nearly invisible. Kryptos wolves have a deeper gray or speckled coat.

PHYLAX (FY-lax)

The guardians of the Bonded packs, focused on defense and protection. Able to defensive magic, which can vary from small temporary barriers to large protective domes when the pack works together. Wolves in Phylax have tan and brown coloring.

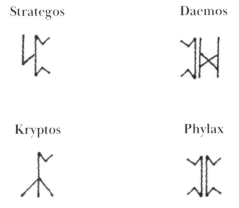

Strategos

Daemos

Kryptos

Phylax

GLOSSARY OF TERMS

Alpha
The highest-ranking member of each pack, chosen by the direwolves.

Ascent
The first of the Bonding Trials; a dangerous climb up Mount Wolfsbane where potential Bonded must prove themselves worthy of bonding with a direwolf.

Astreona (as-tree-OH-na)
The kingdom of the Siphons.

Beta
Second in command of a pack, handling day-to-day operations.

Bonded
A human who has successfully bonded with a direwolf, forming a telepathic connection, and has completed their training.

Bonded City
The wealthy, secluded city behind the castle where the Bonded and their families reside.

Bonding Trials
The four month period of Rawbond training, comprised of different trials to test a Rawbond's connection to their direwolf and their suitability for their pack.

Emberwine
A spiced alcohol popular in Nocturna, often served warm.

The Faceless Goddess
Ancient deity whose true name and appearance have been lost to time.

Forging
The first two months of the Bonded Trials, focused on pack unity.

Gamma
Third in rank of a pack, typically two or three chosen in each pack.

Mate
The fated partner of a direwolf; increasingly rare to find.

Mount Wolfsbane
Highest peak in the mountain range north of Sturmfrost, where the direwolves and
    Bonded form their bonds.

Nabbers
What commoners call the kidnappers who take children from the streets, presumed to
    be Siphons or those in league with Siphons.

Nocturna (nok-TUR-na)
The kingdom where *Direbound* takes place.

Proving
The second two months of the Bonded Trials, focused on inter-pack coordination.

Rawbond
A newly bonded trainee who hasn't completed their training.

Siphons
Vampire-like immortal beings who feed on human life force and wield blood magic.

Sovereign Alpha
The highest-ranking of all Bonded, who can communicate with all packs' wolves.

Sturmfrost (STURM-frost)
The royal city of Nocturna, and Meryn's home.

CHARACTER GUIDE

Anassa (ah-NAS-sa)
Meryn's direwolf

Cratos (KRAY-tos)
Stark's huge and brutal direwolf

Cyril Valtiere (SEE-rull VAL-tee-air)
King of Nocturna; Killian's father

Egith Hartsfeld (EE-gith HARTS-feld)
Beta of Strategos pack

Henrey Smythe (HEN-ree SMITH)
Rawbond in Phylax pack; only other Rawbond not to come from a Bonded family in
    Meryn's year.

Igor (EE-gor)
Meryn's neighbor and pit fighting trainer

Izabel Brooks (IZ-ah-bell)
Meryn's closest friend among the Bonded, a fellow Rawbond of Strategos pack

Venna Brooks (VEN-na)
Izabel's twin sister, a Rawbond of Kryptos pack

Jonah (JOE-nuh)
Rawbond in Daemos pack; enemy of Meryn's

Killian Valtiere (KILL-ee-an VAL-tee-air)
Crown Prince of Nocturna

Lee
In a romantic relationship with Meryn; palace messenger

Markos Blackwood (MAR-kos)
Pack alpha for Strategos pack

Meryn Cooper (MARE-in KOO-per)
Street fighter, daughter, sister — and reluctant recruit to the Bonded

CHARACTER GUIDE

Nevah Rivenson (NEH-vuh)
One of Meryn's fellow Rawbonds in Strategos pack

Saela Cooper (SAY-la)
Meryn's younger sister

Stark Therion (Stark THAY-ree-un)
Alpha of Daemos pack

Tomison Thorne (TOME-iss-un)
One of Meryn's fellow Rawbonds in Strategos pack

ACKNOWLEDGMENTS

We'd like to start off by saying thank you, reader, whoever you are and however you found this book. It means so much to us that you were willing to take a chance on an unknown indie series, and we hope you enjoyed the ride - and if you did, please consider leaving a review on Amazon, Goodreads, TikTok, Instagram, or your social media platform of choice.

A massive thank you goes to our ARC readers, who took an early look at this and blew us away with their kind words. If you're interested in joining our ARC team, please sign up for our newsletter for future opportunities.

And an even bigger thank you goes to our earlier readers: our incredible beta team. Your detailed, thoughtful notes resulted in a massive edit that made this book infinitely stronger. We're endlessly grateful that you shared your time and your brains with us. In no particular order: Rachel Zimmerman, Sarah, Cambria, Blakely Morales, Taylor Jaye, J.B. Lee, Krystal Valster, Dayna, Katheryne Ann, Rebecca Williams, Amanda Bundren, Bryn McDaniels, Courtney Pomietto, Samantha, Kiyeereads, Michelle Wynne-Feigin, Aryana Schneider, Ashley Kreib, Victoria Paschal, Gina Sheets, Jorinde Pels, Jade, Heidi Roach, Tiffany S., Amanda Powell, Ariel and Jessica Parr.

We (Annie and Eliza - the co-authors behind Sable) have had the joy of working together twice in day jobs, with two teams who did remarkable, creative work while not always getting the recognition (or compensation) they deserved. (The battle between good and evil marches on…) To our former colleagues and friends from both WB + WT - we love you. Thank you for giving us years worth of inspiration and for teaching us so much.

The indie author community never fails to astound us with its generosity and ingenuity. Big thank yous go out to the wonderful people at IAA and in the FaRo group for sharing your wisdom and knowledge with newbies like us (and if you like romantasy, check out the FaRo community run by authors at www.farofeb.com!).

Annie would like to thank both of her parents, David and Lisa, for their unwavering support throughout this entire wild endeavor (and for reading fairy tales and fantasy novels to me as a child, and helping my imagination grow). To my friends and my siblings who've all put up with me blabbing endlessly about Meryn and direwolves and character art and so much more, thank you for your patience with me! To Josh and Don and Katie and Julianne and Helen and everyone else who has shared words of advice over the past year — I appreciate you so much. And finally, an enormous thank you to all the brilliant authors whose work has inspired me over the years. You changed my life.

Eliza would like to thank her parents Duffy and Vicky, and brother Ian, for being absolute unending nags about writing a book. Look, I did it! But seriously, I'm beyond lucky to have a family that always encouraged me to boldly chase artistic dreams - thank you. Drew, none of this would've been possible without your love and support, especially over this last wild year. Thank you for 16 years of believing in me, even when I haven't. My life has been an exercise in saying, "could I?" and you answering, without missing a beat, "yes." I love you. C&S, thanks for being my primary motivation to do literally anything. Mommy's done working… for now.

ABOUT THE AUTHOR

Sable Sorensen is the pen name of two good friends and fantasy fangirls who teamed up to write novels that feature strong heroines, spicy romances, and the never-ending fight between those in power and those who would defend the weak and vulnerable.

Direbound is Sable's debut book.

Made in the USA
Coppell, TX
06 May 2025

48953859R10353